# Harry Potter
AND THE GOBLET OF FIRE

# J.K. ROWLING

④

英汉对照版

# Harry Potter

哈利·波特与火焰杯[下]

〔英〕J.K. 罗琳 / 著
马爱农　马爱新 / 译

WIZARDING WORLD

人民文学出版社
PEOPLE'S LITERATURE PUBLISHING HOUSE

WIZARDING WORLD

# CHAPTER TWENTY-ONE

# The House-Elf Liberation Front

Harry, Ron and Hermione went up to the Owlery that evening to find Pigwidgeon, so that Harry could send Sirius a letter, telling him that he had managed to get past his dragon unscathed. On the way, Harry filled Ron in on everything Sirius had told him about Karkaroff. Though shocked at first to hear that Karkaroff had been a Death Eater, by the time they entered the Owlery Ron was saying that they ought to have suspected it all along.

'Fits, doesn't it?' he said. 'Remember what Malfoy said on the train, about his dad being friends with Karkaroff? Now we know where they knew each other. They were probably running around in masks together at the World Cup ... I'll tell you one thing, though, Harry, if it *was* Karkaroff who put your name in the Goblet, he's going to be feeling really stupid now, isn't he? Didn't work, did it? You only got a scratch! Come here – I'll do it –'

Pigwidgeon was so over-excited at the idea of a delivery, he was flying round and round Harry's head, hooting incessantly. Ron snatched Pigwidgeon out of the air and held him still while Harry attached the letter to his leg.

'There's no way any of the other tasks are going to be that dangerous, how could they be?' Ron went on, as he carried Pigwidgeon to the window. 'You know what? I reckon you could win this Tournament, Harry, I'm serious.'

Harry knew that Ron was only saying this to make up for his behaviour of the last few weeks, but he appreciated it all the same. Hermione, however, leant against the Owlery wall, folded her arms and frowned at Ron.

'Harry's got a long way to go before he finishes this Tournament,' she said seriously. 'If that was the first task, I hate to think what's coming next.'

'Right little ray of sunshine, aren't you?' said Ron. 'You and Professor

## 第 21 章

## 家养小精灵解放阵线

那天晚上,哈利、罗恩和赫敏到猫头鹰棚屋去找小猪,哈利想给小天狼星发一封信,说一说自己安然无恙穿越火龙的经过。路上,哈利把小天狼星提醒他警惕卡卡洛夫的话全对罗恩说了。罗恩听说卡卡洛夫过去是个食死徒,起初大吃一惊,可当他们走进猫头鹰棚屋时,罗恩又说他们早就应该怀疑到这点了。

"这就对了!"罗恩说,"还记得马尔福在火车上说的话吗,说他爸爸和卡卡洛夫是朋友?现在我们知道他们是在什么地方认识的了。他们大概在世界杯赛上一起戴着面具游行来着……不过,有一点我要告诉你,哈利,如果是卡卡洛夫把你的名字放进火焰杯的,那么他现在就感到有点儿傻眼了,是不是?阴谋没有得逞。你只擦破了点儿皮!过来——让我来——"

小猪一听说要让它送信,激动得发了疯似的,在哈利头顶上飞了一圈又一圈,不停地鸣叫。罗恩一把将小猪从空中抓下来摁住,哈利把信拴在它的腿上。

"另外两个项目不可能这么危险了,绝对不可能。"罗恩抱着小猪向窗口走去,一边说道,"你知道吗?我认为这次争霸赛你能赢,真的,哈利,我说的是真话。"

哈利知道,罗恩这么说只是为了弥补自己前几个星期的行为,但他仍然觉得很感激。赫敏靠在棚屋的墙上,抱着双臂,对罗恩皱起了眉头。

"要完成这次争霸赛,哈利前面的路还长着呢。"她严肃地说,"第一个项目就这样危险,我真不愿意想象接下来会是什么。"

"你还真是乐观啊。"罗恩说,"赫敏,你和特里劳尼教授应该找个

## CHAPTER TWENTY-ONE    The House-Elf Liberation Front

Trelawney should get together some time.'

He threw Pigwidgeon out of the window. Pigwidgeon plummeted twelve feet before managing to pull himself back up again; the letter attached to his leg was much longer and heavier than usual – Harry hadn't been able to resist giving Sirius a blow-by-blow account of exactly how he had swerved, circled and dodged the Horntail.

They watched Pigwidgeon disappear into the darkness, and then Ron said, 'Well, we'd better get downstairs for your surprise party, Harry – Fred and George should have nicked enough food from the kitchens by now.'

Sure enough, when they entered the Gryffindor common room it exploded with cheers and yells again. There were mountains of cakes and flagons of pumpkin juice and Butterbeer on every surface; Lee Jordan had let off some Dr Filibuster's Fabulous No-Heat, Wet-Start Fireworks, so that the air was thick with stars and sparks; and Dean Thomas, who was very good at drawing, had put up some impressive new banners, most of which depicted Harry zooming around the Horntail's head on his Firebolt, though a couple showed Cedric with his head on fire.

Harry helped himself to food; he had almost forgotten what it was like to feel properly hungry, and sat down with Ron and Hermione. He couldn't believe how happy he felt; he had Ron back on his side, he'd got through the first task, and he wouldn't have to face the second one for three months.

'Blimey, this is heavy,' said Lee Jordan, picking up the golden egg, which Harry had left on a table, and weighing it in his hands. 'Open it, Harry, go on! Let's just see what's inside it!'

'He's supposed to work out the clue on his own,' Hermione said swiftly. 'It's in the Tournament rules ...'

'I was supposed to work out how to get past the dragon on my own, too,' Harry muttered, so only Hermione could hear him, and she grinned rather guiltily.

'Yeah, go on, Harry, open it!' several people echoed.

Lee passed Harry the egg, and Harry dug his fingernails into the groove that ran all the way around it, and prised it open.

It was hollow and completely empty – but the moment Harry opened it, the most horrible noise, a loud and screechy wailing, filled the room. The nearest thing to it Harry had ever heard was the ghost orchestra at Nearly

时间一起聊聊。"

他把小猪从窗口扔了出去。小猪向下坠落了十二英尺，才挣扎着重新飞起来。拴在它腿上的那封信比往常长得多、重得多——哈利忍不住向小天狼星一五一十地描述了他与树蜂周旋的经过，怎样辗转腾挪、左躲右闪。

他们注视着小猪消失在夜空中，然后罗恩说："好了，哈利，我们最好下楼去参加为你举办的惊喜晚会吧——弗雷德和乔治肯定已经从厨房偷来不少好吃的了。"

果然，当他们走进格兰芬多公共休息室时，里面再次爆发出一片欢呼和喧哗。桌子上和椅子上，蛋糕已经堆成了山，还有一壶壶南瓜汁和黄油啤酒。李·乔丹燃放了一些费力拔博士见水开花神奇冷烟火，空气里闪动着许多星星和火花。擅长绘画的迪安·托马斯挂起了好几条醒目的新横幅，大多数横幅上都画着哈利骑着火弩箭绕树蜂穿梭飞行的场面，但也有两幅表现了塞德里克脑袋着火的情景。

哈利吃了起来。这些日子，他几乎忘记什么是正常的饥饿感了。他和罗恩、赫敏一起坐了下来。他简直无法相信自己有多么开心：罗恩又回到了他身边，他通过了第一个项目，而第二个项目要三个月以后才去面对。

"天哪，还挺沉的，"李·乔丹拿起哈利放在桌上的金蛋，用双手掂量着说，"快把它打开，哈利！让我们看看里面是什么！"

"他应该自己解开线索，"赫敏赶忙说道，"争霸赛的章程规定了……"

"其实我也应该自己解决穿越火龙的问题的。"哈利嘀咕了一句。他的声音很低，只有赫敏能听见，赫敏心虚地咧开嘴笑了。

"好了，来吧，哈利，把它打开！"几个人响应道。

李把金蛋递给了哈利，哈利用指甲抠进金蛋上的一圈凹槽，把蛋撬开了。

里面是空的，什么也没有——但就在哈利把它打开的瞬间，一种极为恐怖、尖厉刺耳的惨叫声充满了整个房间。哈利以前只在差点没头的尼克的忌辰晚会上听到过类似的声音，那是幽灵乐队用乐锯演奏

## CHAPTER TWENTY-ONE  The House-Elf Liberation Front

Headless Nick's Deathday Party, who had all been playing the musical saw.

'Shut it!' Fred bellowed, his hands over his ears.

'What was that?' said Seamus Finnigan, staring at the egg as Harry slammed it shut again. 'Sounded like a banshee ... maybe you've got to get past one of those next, Harry!'

'It was someone being tortured!' said Neville, who had gone very white, and spilled sausage rolls over the floor. 'You're going to have to fight the Cruciatus Curse!'

'Don't be a prat, Neville, that's illegal,' said George. 'They wouldn't use the Cruciatus Curse on the champions. I thought it sounded a bit like Percy singing ... maybe you've got to attack him while he's in the shower, Harry.'

'Want a jam tart, Hermione?' said Fred.

Hermione looked doubtfully at the plate he was offering her. Fred grinned.

'It's all right,' he said. 'I haven't done anything to them. It's the custard creams you've got to watch –'

Neville, who had just bitten into a custard cream, choked and spat it out.

Fred laughed. 'Just my little joke, Neville ...'

Hermione took a jam tart.

Then she said, 'Did you get all this from the kitchens, Fred?'

'Yep,' said Fred, grinning at her. He put on a high-pitched squeak and imitated a house-elf. '"Anything we can get you, sir, anything at all!" They're dead helpful ... get me a roast ox if I said I was peckish.'

'How do you get in there?' Hermione said, in an innocently casual sort of voice.

'Easy,' said Fred, 'concealed door behind a painting of a bowl of fruit. Just tickle the pear, and it giggles and –' He stopped, and looked suspiciously at her. 'Why?'

'Nothing,' said Hermione quickly.

'Going to try and lead the house-elves out on strike now, are you?' said George. 'Going to give up all the leaflet stuff and try and stir them up into rebellion?'

Several people chortled. Hermione didn't answer.

'Don't you go upsetting them and telling them they've got to take clothes and salaries!' said Fred warningly. 'You'll put them off their cooking!'

Just then, Neville caused a slight diversion by turning into a large canary.

## 第21章　家养小精灵解放阵线

的噪音。

"快关上！"弗雷德用手捂着耳朵吼道。

哈利把金蛋猛地合上。"那是什么？"西莫·斐尼甘盯着金蛋问道，"像是女鬼的叫声……哈利，你下次可能要从一个女鬼身边通过！"

"好像是什么人在受折磨！"纳威说——他脸色惨白，把香肠卷撒了一地，"你要对付的是钻心咒！"

"别说傻话，纳威，那是不合法的，"乔治说，"他们不能在勇士身上念钻心咒。我倒觉得这声音有点像珀西在唱歌……说不定你要在他冲澡的时候去袭击他，哈利。"

"来一块果酱馅饼吗，赫敏？"

赫敏怀疑地望着他递过来的盘子。弗雷德咧开嘴笑了。

"放心，"他说，"我没对它们做什么手脚。你需要留神的是蛋奶饼干——"

纳威刚咬了一口蛋奶饼干，一听这话就噎住了，把饼干吐了出来。

弗雷德哈哈大笑。"我只是开个小玩笑，纳威……"

赫敏拿起了一块果酱馅饼。

然后她说："弗雷德，这些东西都是你们从厨房拿来的？"

"是啊。"弗雷德说，笑嘻嘻地望着赫敏。他憋出一种尖细刺耳的声音，模仿着家养小精灵："'我们可以为你准备一切，先生，什么都行！'他们真是热心啊……只要我一说有点儿饿了，他们就会给我烤一头牛。"

"你们是怎么进去的？"赫敏用一种若无其事的随便口吻问道。

"很方便，"弗雷德说，"有一扇门藏在画着一碗水果的那幅画后面。只要轻轻挠一挠那个梨子，它就会咿咿发笑，然后——"他住了嘴，警惕地打量着赫敏，"怎么啦？"

"没什么。"赫敏赶紧说道。

"又想领导家养小精灵出来罢工，是吗？"乔治问，"你准备放弃那些传单之类的玩意儿，动员他们起来造反？"

有几个人被逗得咯咯直笑。赫敏没有回答。

"你可不要把他们的思想搅乱，告诉他们必须穿衣服，拿工钱！"弗雷德警告她说，"你会弄得他们不想做饭的！"

就在这时，纳威突然变成了一只大金丝雀，暂时分散了大家的注意力。

### CHAPTER TWENTY-ONE    The House-Elf Liberation Front

'Oh – sorry, Neville!' Fred shouted, over all the laughter. 'I forgot – it *was* the custard creams we hexed –'

Within a minute, however, Neville had moulted, and once his feathers had fallen off, he reappeared looking entirely normal. He even joined in laughing.

'Canary Creams!' Fred shouted to the excitable crowd. 'George and I invented them – seven Sickles each, bargain!'

It was nearly one in the morning when Harry finally went up to the dormitory with Ron, Neville, Seamus and Dean. Before he pulled the curtains of his four-poster shut, Harry set his tiny model of the Hungarian Horntail on the table next to his bed, where it yawned, curled up and closed its eyes. Really, Harry thought, as he pulled the hangings on his four-poster closed, Hagrid had a point ... they were all right, really, dragons ...

The start of December brought wind and sleet to Hogwarts. Draughty though the castle always was in winter, Harry was glad of its fires and thick walls every time he passed the Durmstrang ship on the lake, which was pitching in the high winds, its black sails billowing against the dark skies. He thought the Beauxbatons caravan was likely to be pretty chilly, too. Hagrid, he noticed, was keeping Madame Maxime's horses well provided with their preferred drink of single-malt whisky; the fumes wafting from the trough in the corner of their paddock were enough to make the entire Care of Magical Creatures class light headed. This was unhelpful, as they were still tending the horrible Skrewts, and needed their wits about them.

'I'm not sure whether they hibernate or not,' Hagrid told the shivering class in the windy pumpkin patch next lesson. 'Thought we'd jus' try an' see if they fancied a kip ... We'll jus' settle 'em down in these boxes ...'

There were now only ten Skrewts left; apparently their desire to kill each other had not been exercised out of them. Each of them was now approaching six feet in length. Their thick grey armour, their powerful, scuttling legs, their fire-blasting ends, their stings and their suckers, combined to make the Skrewts the most repulsive things Harry had ever seen. The class looked dispiritedly at the enormous boxes Hagrid had brought out, all lined with pillows and fluffy blankets.

'We'll jus' lead 'em in here,' Hagrid said, 'an' put the lids on, and we'll see what happens.'

## 第21章 家养小精灵解放阵线

"哟——对不起,纳威!"弗雷德在大家的笑声中喊道,"我忘记了——是被我们施了魔法的蛋奶饼干——"

还好,不到一分钟,纳威就脱去了羽毛,当羽毛全部掉光后,他的样子又完全正常了。他甚至也和别人一起大笑起来。

"金丝雀饼干!"弗雷德对情绪高涨的人群喊道,"我和乔治发明的——七个银西可一块,很便宜啦!"

当哈利终于和罗恩、纳威、西莫、迪安一起回到楼上的宿舍时,已经差不多凌晨一点了。哈利在拉上四柱床的帷帐前,把那个匈牙利树蜂小模型放在了床边的桌子上。小龙打了个哈欠,蜷缩起身子,闭上了眼睛。哈利一边拉上帷帐,一边想道,海格其实是有道理的……火龙还是蛮可爱的,真的……

十二月给霍格沃茨带来了狂风和雨夹雪。城堡里冬天总是有穿堂风,但哈利每次走过停在湖面的德姆斯特朗大船时,都为城堡里热腾腾的炉火和厚实的墙壁感到庆幸。那艘大船随着狂风颠簸摇摆,黑色的船帆在黑暗的夜空中翻飞起舞。他想,布斯巴顿的马车里一定也冷得够呛。哈利还注意到,海格不断地给马克西姆女士的那些骏马提供它们最喜欢的纯麦芽威士忌。临时马厩角落里的饲料槽飘过来一阵阵酒味,熏得上保护神奇动物课的同学们都有点晕晕乎乎。这并没有什么好处,因为他们仍然在照料可怕的炸尾螺,很需要动用一些智慧呢。

"我拿不准它们是不是冬眠,"在下一节课上,海格告诉在南瓜地里瑟瑟发抖的同学们,"我们不妨试一试,看它们想不想睡觉……我们把它们安顿在这些箱子里……"

现在只剩下十条炸尾螺了。显然,它们互相残杀的欲望并没有彻底根除。如今每条炸尾螺都接近六英尺长。厚厚的灰色保护层,胡乱摆动的有力的腿,不断爆炸喷火的尾巴,还有它们的刺和吸盘,所有加在一起,使炸尾螺成为哈利见过的最令人恶心的东西。同学们无精打采地望着海格搬出来的大箱子,箱子里都铺着枕头和毛茸茸的毯子。

"我们把它们领进来,"海格说,"然后盖上盖子,看看会出现什么情况。"

## CHAPTER TWENTY-ONE  The House-Elf Liberation Front

But the Skrewts, it transpired, did *not* hibernate, and did not appreciate being forced into pillow-lined boxes and nailed in. Hagrid was soon yelling 'Don' panic, now, don' panic!' while the Skrewts rampaged around the pumpkin patch, now strewn with the smouldering wreckage of the boxes. Most of the class – Malfoy, Crabbe and Goyle in the lead – had fled into Hagrid's cabin through the back door and barricaded themselves in; Harry, Ron and Hermione, however, were among those who remained outside trying to help Hagrid. Together they managed to restrain and tie up nine of the Skrewts, though at the cost of numerous burns and cuts; finally, only one Skrewt was left.

'Don' frighten him, now!' Hagrid shouted, as Ron and Harry used their wands to shoot jets of fiery sparks at the Skrewt, which was advancing menacingly on them, its sting arched, quivering, over its back. 'Jus' try an' slip the rope round his sting, so he won' hurt any o' the others!'

'Yeah, we wouldn't want that!' Ron shouted angrily, as he and Harry backed into the wall of Hagrid's cabin, still holding the Skrewt off with their sparks.

'Well, well, well ... this *does* look like fun.'

Rita Skeeter was leaning on Hagrid's garden fence, looking in at the mayhem. She was wearing a thick magenta cloak with a furry purple collar today, and her crocodile-skin handbag was over her arm.

Hagrid launched himself forward on top of the Skrewt that was cornering Harry and Ron and flattened it; a blast of fire shot out of its end, withering the pumpkin plants nearby.

'Who're you?' Hagrid asked Rita Skeeter, as he slipped a loop of rope around the Skrewt's sting and tightened it.

'Rita Skeeter, *Daily Prophet* reporter,' Rita replied, beaming at him. Her gold teeth glinted.

'Thought Dumbledore said you weren' allowed inside the school any more?' said Hagrid, frowning slightly as he got off the slightly squashed Skrewt and started tugging it over to its fellows.

Rita acted as though she hadn't heard what Hagrid had said.

'What are these fascinating creatures called?' she asked, beaming still more widely.

'Blast-Ended Skrewts,' grunted Hagrid.

'Really?' said Rita, apparently full of lively interest. 'I've never heard of

## 第21章 家养小精灵解放阵线

结果,他们发现炸尾螺并不冬眠,而且不喜欢被人塞进铺着枕头的箱子,盖上盖子。很快,海格便喊叫起来:"别紧张,别紧张!"因为炸尾螺在南瓜地里横冲直撞,地里撒满了冒着青烟的箱子碎片。大多数同学——马尔福、克拉布和高尔打头——已经从后门逃进了海格的小屋,把自己关在里面。哈利、罗恩、赫敏则和其他一些同学留在外面帮助海格。他们齐心协力,总算制服了九条炸尾螺,把它们捆了起来,但是也付出了惨重的代价,身上被烧伤和划伤了无数处。最后,只剩下一条炸尾螺了。

"哎,别吓着它!"当哈利和罗恩用魔杖朝炸尾螺喷射火星时,海格喊道——炸尾螺恶狠狠地朝他们逼近,背上的刺拱了起来,微微颤动——"用绳子拴住它的刺,它就不会伤害别的炸尾螺了!"

"是啊,我们可不愿意发生这样的事!"罗恩生气地嚷道,这时他和哈利退到海格小屋的墙根下,仍然在用魔杖的火星阻止炸尾螺靠近。

"好啊,好啊,好啊……看起来确实很好玩。"

丽塔·斯基特靠在海格菜园子的栅栏上,看着这一幕闹剧。她今天穿着一件厚厚的洋红色长袍,紫色的领子是翻毛皮的,那只鳄鱼皮手袋挂在她的胳膊上。

炸尾螺把哈利和罗恩逼得走投无路,海格扑过来压在它身上,把它制服了。它尾巴后面喷出一团火焰,把旁边的南瓜苗都烧焦了。

"你是谁?"海格一边问丽塔·斯基特,一边把一个绳扣套在炸尾螺的刺上系紧。

"我叫丽塔·斯基特,《预言家日报》的记者。"丽塔回答,满脸带笑地望着海格,嘴里的金牙闪闪发光。

"好像邓布利多说过,不许你再进学校了。"海格微皱着眉头说,翻身从压得有点儿变形的炸尾螺上下来,用力拖着它朝它的同伴们走去。

丽塔好像根本没听见海格的话。

"这些迷人的动物叫什么?"她问,脸上笑得更灿烂了。

"炸尾螺。"海格粗声粗气地回答。

"真的吗?"丽塔说,一副兴趣盎然的样子,"我以前从没有听说

## CHAPTER TWENTY-ONE  The House-Elf Liberation Front

them before ... where do they come from?'

Harry noticed a dull red flush rising up out of Hagrid's wild black beard, and his heart sank. Where *had* Hagrid got the Skrewts from?

Hermione, who seemed to be thinking along the same lines, said quickly, 'They're very interesting, aren't they? Aren't they, Harry?'

'What? Oh, yeah ... ouch ... interesting,' said Harry, as she stepped on his foot.

'Ah, *you're* here, Harry!' said Rita Skeeter as she looked around. 'So you like Care of Magical Creatures, do you? One of your favourite lessons?'

'Yes,' said Harry stoutly. Hagrid beamed at him.

'Lovely,' said Rita. 'Really lovely. Been teaching long?' she added to Hagrid.

Harry noticed her eyes travel over Dean (who had a nasty cut across one cheek), Lavender (whose robes were badly singed), Seamus (who was nursing several burnt fingers), and then to the cabin windows, where most of the class stood, their noses pressed against the glass, waiting to see if the coast was clear.

'This is on'y me second year,' said Hagrid.

'Lovely ... I don't suppose you'd like to give an interview, would you? Share some of your experience of magical creatures? The *Prophet* does a zoological column every Wednesday, as I'm sure you know. We could feature these – er – Bang-Ended Scoots.'

'Blast-Ended Skrewts,' Hagrid said eagerly. 'Er – yeah, why not?'

Harry had a very bad feeling about this, but there was no way of communicating it to Hagrid without Rita Skeeter seeing, so he had to stand and watch in silence as Hagrid and Rita Skeeter made arrangements to meet in the Three Broomsticks for a good long interview later that week. Then the bell rang up at the castle, signalling the end of the lesson.

'Well, goodbye, Harry!' Rita Skeeter called merrily to him, as he set off with Ron and Hermione. 'Until Friday night, then, Hagrid!'

'She'll twist everything he says,' Harry said under his breath.

'Just as long as he didn't import those Skrewts illegally or anything,' said Hermione desperately. They looked at each other – it was exactly the sort of thing Hagrid might do.

'Hagrid's been in loads of trouble before, and Dumbledore's never sacked

过……它们是从哪儿弄来的？"

哈利注意到海格蓬乱的黑胡子后面的脸涨得通红，他的心往下一沉。海格是从哪儿弄到这些炸尾螺的？

赫敏似乎也想到了同样的问题，赶紧说道："它们很有趣，是不是？你说呀，哈利，是不是呀？"

"什么？噢，是啊……哎哟……很有趣。"哈利被赫敏踩了一下脚，支吾着说。

"啊，你也在这里，哈利！"丽塔·斯基特转过脸来，说道，"这么说，你喜欢保护神奇动物课，是吗？是你最爱上的一门课吗？"

"是的。"哈利毫不含糊地说。海格笑容满面地望着他。

"太好了，"丽塔说，"真的太好了。教书时间长吗？"她又问海格。

哈利发现丽塔正把目光移向迪安（半边面颊上有一道难看的伤口）、拉文德（长袍被烧焦了一大块）、西莫（正在护理几根被烧伤的手指），接着她的目光又移向小屋的窗户，大多数同学站在那里，鼻子压在窗玻璃上，看危险是不是已经过去。

"刚教第二年。"海格说。

"太好了……不知道你是不是愿意接受一次采访，嗯？把你教保护神奇动物课的经验与读者分享一下？《预言家日报》每星期三有一个动物学专栏，我想你一定知道。我们可以介绍一下这些——嗯——响尾狼。"

"炸尾螺，"海格热切地说，"呃——是啊，可以嘛。"

哈利觉得这件事有点不妙，但在丽塔·斯基特的眼皮底下，他没办法把这种想法传递给海格，只好站在一边，默默注视着海格和丽塔·斯基特安排本周晚些时候在三把扫帚见面，好好长谈一次。这时，城堡的铃声响了，这堂课结束了。

"好了，再见，哈利！"当哈利和罗恩、赫敏离开时，丽塔·斯基特愉快地喊道，"那么说定了，海格，星期五见！"

"她会任意歪曲海格说的每一句话。"哈利压低声音说。

"但愿海格没有非法进口那些炸尾螺和其他东西。"赫敏焦虑地说。他们互相对视——这正是海格可能会做的事情。

"海格以前惹过很多麻烦，邓布利多一直没有开除他，"罗恩宽慰

## CHAPTER TWENTY-ONE  The House-Elf Liberation Front

him,' said Ron consolingly. 'Worst that can happen is Hagrid'll have to get rid of the Skrewts. Sorry ... did I say worst? I meant best.'

Harry and Hermione laughed, and, feeling slightly more cheerful, went off to lunch.

Harry thoroughly enjoyed double Divination that afternoon; they were still doing star charts and predictions, but now that he and Ron were friends once more, the whole thing seemed very funny again. Professor Trelawney, who had been so pleased with the pair of them when they had been predicting their own horrific deaths, quickly became irritated as they sniggered through her explanation of the various ways in which Pluto could disrupt everyday life.

'I would *think*,' she said, in a mystical whisper that did not conceal her obvious annoyance, 'that *some* of us' – she stared very meaningfully at Harry – 'might be a little less *frivolous* had they seen what I have seen, during my crystal-gazing last night. As I sat here, absorbed in my needlework, the urge to consult the orb overpowered me. I arose, I settled myself before it, and I gazed into its crystalline depths ... and what do you think I saw gazing back at me?'

'An ugly old bat in outsize specs?' Ron muttered under his breath.

Harry fought hard to keep his face straight.

'*Death*, my dears.'

Parvati and Lavender both put their hands over their mouths, looking horrified.

'Yes,' said Professor Trelawney, nodding impressively, 'it comes, ever closer, it circles overhead like a vulture, ever lower ... ever lower over the castle ...'

She stared pointedly at Harry, who yawned very widely and obviously.

'It'd be a bit more impressive if she hadn't done it about eighty times before,' Harry said, as they finally regained the fresh air of the staircase beneath Professor Trelawney's room. 'But if I'd dropped dead every time she's told me I'm going to, I'd be a medical miracle.'

'You'd be a sort of extra-concentrated ghost,' said Ron, chortling, as they passed the Bloody Baron going in the opposite direction, his wide eyes staring sinisterly. 'At least we didn't get homework. I hope Hermione got loads off Professor Vector, I love not working when she is ...'

But Hermione wasn't at dinner, and nor was she in the library when they

## 第21章 家养小精灵解放阵线

他们道,"最坏的可能性就是海格必须丢掉炸尾螺。对不起……我说的是最坏吗?我想说的是最好。"

哈利和赫敏笑了起来,他们去吃午饭时,觉得心情轻松了一些。

那天下午,哈利觉得那两节占卜课上得愉快极了。他们仍然要画星象图,要作预测,但现在罗恩重新成了他的朋友,这一切就又显得非常滑稽可笑了。由于哈利和罗恩一直在预言自己可怕的死亡,特里劳尼教授对他们非常满意。可是今天,当她解释冥王星干扰日常生活的不同方式时,他们一直咯咯笑个不停,她很快就恼火了。

"我认为,"她说,声音低低的,充满神秘感,但并没有掩盖她显而易见的恼怒,"我们中间的一些人,"——她意味深长地盯着哈利——"如果看见我昨晚做水晶球占卜时看见的东西,恐怕就不会这样轻狂了。昨晚我坐在这里,埋头做我的针线活儿,突然产生了一种无法遏制的冲动,想请教一下我的水晶球。我站起来,坐到水晶球面前,凝视着晶体的深处……你们说,我看见了什么东西在凝望着我?"

"一只丑陋的老蝙蝠,戴着一副特大眼镜?"罗恩压低声音嘟哝着。

哈利拼命绷着脸,不让自己笑出来。

"是死亡,我亲爱的。"

帕瓦蒂和拉文德都用手捂住了嘴巴,神色惊恐。

"是的,"特里劳尼教授煞有介事地点点头,说道,"它来了,越来越近了,像一只兀鹰在头顶上盘旋,越来越低……越来越低,就在城堡上空……"

她目光犀利地盯着哈利,哈利毫不掩饰地打了个大大的哈欠。

"她这套把戏已经玩过差不多八十遍了,如果不是这样,倒确实有点儿吓人。"哈利说——这时他们终于来到特里劳尼教授房间下面的楼梯上,重新呼吸到了新鲜空气,"可是,如果每次她说我要死,我都倒地死去,我就变成一个医学上的奇迹了。"

"你会成为一种超浓缩的幽灵。"罗恩说着,咻咻地笑了,"至少我们没有家庭作业呀。我希望赫敏从维克多教授那儿领回一大堆作业,我最喜欢她做作业时我们闲着……"这时他们与血人巴罗擦肩而过,巴罗那双睁得大大的眼睛恶狠狠地瞪着。

可是赫敏不在晚饭桌上,后来他们去图书馆找她,也不见她的影

## CHAPTER TWENTY-ONE  The House-Elf Liberation Front

went to look for her afterwards. The only person in there was Viktor Krum. Ron hovered behind the bookshelves for a while, watching Krum, debating in whispers with Harry whether he should ask for an autograph – but then Ron realised that six or seven girls were lurking in the next row of books, debating exactly the same thing, and he lost his enthusiasm for the idea.

'Wonder where she's got to?' Ron said, as he and Harry went back to Gryffindor Tower.

'Dunno ... Balderdash.'

But the Fat Lady had barely begun to swing forwards, when the sound of racing feet behind them announced Hermione's arrival.

'Harry!' she panted, skidding to a halt beside him (the Fat Lady stared down at her, eyebrows raised). 'Harry, you've got to come – you've *got* to come, the most amazing thing's happened – please –'

She seized Harry's arm and started to try and drag him back along the corridor.

'What's the matter?' Harry said.

'I'll show you when we get there – oh, come on, quick –'

Harry looked around at Ron; he looked back at Harry, intrigued.

'OK,' Harry said, starting off back down the corridor with Hermione, Ron hurrying to keep up.

'Oh, don't mind me!' the Fat Lady called irritably after them. 'Don't apologise for bothering me! I'll just hang here, wide open, until you get back, shall I?'

'Yeah, thanks,' Ron shouted over his shoulder.

'Hermione, where are we going?' Harry asked, after she had led them down through six floors, and started down the marble staircase into the Entrance Hall.

'You'll see, you'll see in a minute!' said Hermione excitedly.

She turned left at the bottom of the staircase, and hurried towards the door through which Cedric Diggory had gone the night after the Goblet of Fire had regurgitated his and Harry's names. Harry had never been through here before. He and Ron followed Hermione down a flight of stone steps, but instead of ending up in a gloomy underground passage like the one which led to Snape's dungeon, they found themselves in a broad, stone corridor, brightly lit with torches, and decorated with cheerful paintings that were mainly of food.

'Oh, hang on ...' said Harry slowly, halfway down the corridor. 'Wait a

## 第21章 家养小精灵解放阵线

子。那里只有威克多尔·克鲁姆一个人。罗恩在书架后面徘徊了一会儿，望着克鲁姆，一边小声与哈利争论要不要请他签名——但后来罗恩发现六七个女生躲在旁边那排书架后，为同样的事情争论不休，便对这个想法失去了热情。

"真奇怪，她到哪儿去了呢？"在和哈利一起返回格兰芬多塔楼时，罗恩说。

"不知道……胡言乱语。"

胖夫人刚开始向前转开，他们身后就传来急促的脚步声，赫敏来了。

"哈利！"她气喘吁吁地说，在哈利身边刹住脚步（胖夫人垂眼望着她，扬起了眉毛），"哈利，你必须来一下——你必须来一下，出了一件最离奇的事——求求你，快来吧——"

她一把抓住哈利的胳膊，拉着他往走廊上走。

"出了什么事？"哈利说。

"到了那里你就会看见——哦，走吧，快点儿——"

哈利扭头看着罗恩，罗恩也看着哈利，一副迷惑不解的样子。

"好吧。"哈利说，和赫敏一起沿着走廊往回走，罗恩加快脚步跟了上来。

"喂，你们不管我啦！"胖夫人在他们身后恼火地喊道，"你们打搅了我，一声抱歉也不说！难道我要一直开在这里，等你们回来吗？"

"是啊，谢谢了！"罗恩扭头喊了一声。

"赫敏，我们去哪儿？"哈利问。这时赫敏已经领着他们下了六层楼，正顺着大理石楼梯进入下面的门厅。

"你们会看到的，很快就会看到的！"赫敏兴奋地说。

到了楼梯下面，她往左一拐，匆匆朝一扇门走去。哈利曾经看见塞德里克·迪戈里进过这扇门，那是在火焰杯喷出他和哈利名字的那个晚上。哈利以前没有到这里来过。他和罗恩跟着赫敏走下一道石阶，下面并不是一条昏暗阴森、像通往斯内普地下教室的那种地下通道。相反，他们发现自己来到了一条宽阔的石廊里，火把照得四周很明亮，到处装饰着令人愉快的图画，上面画的主要是各种食物。

"噢，慢着……"在石廊里走到一半时，哈利慢慢地说，"等一等，

## CHAPTER TWENTY-ONE    The House-Elf Liberation Front

minute, Hermione ...'

'What?' She turned around to look at him, anticipation all over her face.

'I know what this is about,' said Harry.

He nudged Ron, and pointed to the painting just behind Hermione. It showed a gigantic silver fruit-bowl.

'Hermione!' said Ron, cottoning on. 'You're trying to rope us into that spew stuff again!'

'No, no, I'm not!' she said hastily. 'And it's not *spew*, Ron –'

'Changed the name, have you?' said Ron, frowning at her. 'What are we now, then, the House-Elf Liberation Front? I'm not barging into that kitchen and trying to make them stop work, I'm not doing it –'

'I'm not asking you to!' Hermione said impatiently. 'I came down here just now, to talk to them all, and I found – oh, come *on*, Harry, I want to show you!'

She seized his arm again, pulled him in front of the picture of the giant fruit-bowl, stretched out her forefinger and tickled the huge green pear. It began to squirm, chuckling, and suddenly turned into a large green door handle. Hermione seized it, pulled the door open, and pushed Harry hard in the back, forcing him inside.

He had one brief glimpse of an enormous, high-ceilinged room, large as the Great Hall above it, with mounds of glittering brass pots and pans heaped around the stone walls, and a great brick fireplace at the other end, when something small hurtled towards him from the middle of the room, squealing, 'Harry Potter, sir! *Harry Potter!*'

Next second all the wind had been knocked out of him as the squealing elf hit him hard in the midriff, hugging him so tightly he thought his ribs would break.

'D-Dobby?' Harry gasped.

'It *is* Dobby, sir, it is!' squealed the voice from some where around his navel. 'Dobby has been hoping and hoping to see Harry Potter, sir, and Harry Potter has come to see him, sir!'

Dobby let go and stepped back a few paces, beaming up at Harry, his enormous, green, tennis-ball-shaped eyes brimming with tears of happiness. He looked almost exactly as Harry remembered him; the pencil-shaped nose, the bat-like ears, the long fingers and feet – all except the clothes, which were

## 第21章 家养小精灵解放阵线

赫敏……"

"怎么啦?"赫敏转脸望着他,期待他说出答案。

"我知道是怎么回事了。"哈利说。

他用胳膊肘捅了捅罗恩,指着赫敏身后的那幅图画,画面上是一只盛满水果的巨大银碗。

"赫敏!"罗恩明白过来了,说,"你又想说服我们参加你那套'呕吐'的把戏!"

"不是,不是,我没有!"赫敏着急地说,"而且不是呕吐,罗恩——"

"怎么,改名字了?"罗恩对她皱着眉头,说道,"那么是什么呢?家养小精灵解放阵线?我可不愿冲进厨房,动员他们停止干活,我决不会——"

"我没有要你这么做!"赫敏不耐烦地说,"我刚才来过这里,跟他们交谈过了,我发现——哦,快来,哈利,我要带你去看!"

她又抓住哈利的胳膊,把他拉到那幅大水果碗的图画跟前。她伸出食指,轻轻挠了挠那只碧绿的大梨子。梨子蠕动起来,咯咯笑着,突然变成了一个很大的绿色门把手。赫敏抓住它把门拉开,用力推了一下哈利的后背,把他推了进去。

匆匆一瞥之间,哈利只看见一个天花板很高的大房间,和上面的礼堂一样大,周围的石墙边堆着许多闪亮的铜锅和铜盆,房间另一头有个砖砌的大壁炉。还没等他看得更清楚,就有一个小东西从房间中央飞快地朝他跑来,一边尖声叫着:"哈利·波特,先生!哈利·波特!"

接着,尖叫的小精灵猛地撞在他的上腹部,把他紧紧地、紧紧地搂住了,他觉得肋骨都要被勒断了,肺里的空气全被挤了出来。

"多——多比?"哈利喘着气说。

"是多比,先生,是多比!"那个声音从他的肚脐附近尖叫着说,"多比一直盼呀盼呀,盼着见到哈利·波特,先生,结果哈利·波特亲自来看他了,先生!"

多比松开手,向后退了几步,满脸带笑地抬头望着哈利,那双网球般大小的绿眼睛里含着喜悦的泪花。他和哈利记忆中的样子分毫不差。那只像铅笔一样细长的鼻子,那对蝙蝠状的耳朵,还有那长长的

## CHAPTER TWENTY-ONE  The House-Elf Liberation Front

very different.

When Dobby had worked for the Malfoys, he had always worn the same filthy old pillowcase. Now, however, he was wearing the strangest assortment of garments Harry had ever seen; he had made an even worse job of dressing himself than the wizards at the World Cup. He was wearing a tea-cosy for a hat, on which he had pinned a number of bright badges; a tie patterned with horseshoes over a bare chest, a pair of what looked like children's football shorts, and odd socks. One of these, Harry saw, was the black one he had removed from his own foot and tricked Mr Malfoy into giving Dobby, thereby setting Dobby free. The other was covered in pink and orange stripes.

'Dobby, what're you doing here?' Harry said in amazement.

'Dobby has come to work at Hogwarts, sir!' Dobby squealed excitedly. 'Professor Dumbledore gave Dobby and Winky jobs, sir!'

'Winky?' said Harry. 'She's here, too?'

'Yes, sir, yes!' said Dobby, and he seized Harry's hand, and pulled him off into the kitchen between the four long wooden tables that stood there. Each of these tables, Harry noticed as he passed them, was positioned exactly beneath the four house tables above, in the Great Hall. At the moment, they were clear of food, dinner having finished, but he supposed that an hour ago they had been laden with dishes that were then sent up through the ceiling to their counterparts above.

At least a hundred little elves were standing around the kitchen, beaming, bowing and curtseying as Dobby led Harry past them. They were all wearing the same uniform; a tea-towel stamped with the Hogwarts crest, and tied, as Winky's had been, like a toga.

Dobby stopped in front of the brick fireplace, and pointed.

'Winky, sir!' he said.

Winky was sitting on a stool by the fire. Unlike Dobby, she had obviously not foraged for clothes. She was wearing a neat little skirt and blouse with a matching blue hat, which had holes in it for her large ears. However, while every one of Dobby's strange collection of garments was so clean and well cared for that it looked brand new, Winky was plainly not taking care of her clothes at all. There were soup stains all down her blouse and a burn in her skirt.

'Hello, Winky,' said Harry.

## 第21章 家养小精灵解放阵线

手指和双脚——什么都没有变，只是衣服与原来的大不一样了。

当年多比为马尔福家干活时，一年到头穿着那只脏兮兮的旧枕套。现在，他这一身穿戴真是哈利见过的最奇怪的组合，比世界杯赛上的那些巫师穿戴得还要糟糕。他头上顶着一只茶壶保暖套，上面别着一大堆鲜艳的徽章；赤裸的胸膛上挂着一条马蹄图案的领带，下身穿的是类似儿童足球短裤的东西，脚上是两只不配对的袜子。哈利看到，其中一只正是他从自己脚上脱下来，诱骗马尔福先生扔给多比，从而使多比获得自由的那只黑袜子。另一只袜子上印满粉红色和橘黄色的条纹。

"多比，你在这里做什么？"哈利惊奇地问。

"多比来霍格沃茨工作了，先生！"多比兴奋地尖叫道，"邓布利多教授给了多比和闪闪工作。先生！"

"闪闪？"哈利说，"她也在这里？"

"是啊，先生，是啊！"多比说着，一把抓住哈利的手，拉着他穿过四张长长的木桌子，走进里面的厨房。哈利发现这些桌子摆放的位置跟上面礼堂里四个学院的桌子一模一样。此刻晚餐已经结束，桌上没有食物，但他推测一小时前这里肯定堆满了美味佳肴，然后通过天花板送到上面对等的桌子上。

至少有一百个小精灵站在厨房里，当多比领着哈利从他们身边经过时，他们一个个满脸堆笑，鞠躬，行屈膝礼。他们都穿着同样的制服：一条印着霍格沃茨饰章的茶巾。他们像闪闪以前那样，把茶巾当袍子裹在身上。

多比在砖砌的壁炉前停住脚步，指给哈利看。

"你看，先生，闪闪在这儿！"他说。

闪闪坐在炉火旁的一张凳子上。她和多比不同，看样子不是随随便便找来衣服就穿。她穿着一套整整齐齐的小裙子和短上衣，头上还戴着一顶配套的蓝帽子，上面掏了两个洞，露出她的两只大耳朵。不过，多比那身奇怪组合的衣服保护得一尘不染，像是崭新的一样，而闪闪则显然对自己的衣服毫不在意。她的短上衣上溅满了汤渍，裙子上有一块地方烧焦了。

"你好，闪闪。"哈利说。

## CHAPTER TWENTY-ONE  The House-Elf Liberation Front

Winky's lip quivered. Then she burst into tears, which spilled out of her great brown eyes and splashed down her front, just as they had done at the Quidditch World Cup.

'Oh, dear,' said Hermione. She and Ron had followed Harry and Dobby to the end of the kitchen. 'Winky, don't cry, please don't ...'

But Winky cried harder than ever. Dobby, on the other hand, beamed up at Harry.

'Would Harry Potter like a cup of tea?' he squeaked loudly, over Winky's sobs.

'Er – yeah, OK,' said Harry.

Instantly, about six house-elves came trotting up behind him, bearing a large silver tray laden with a teapot, cups for Harry, Ron and Hermione, a milk jug and a large plate of biscuits.

'Good service!' Ron said, in an impressed voice. Hermione frowned at him, but the elves all looked delighted; they bowed very low and retreated.

'How long have you been here, Dobby?' Harry asked, as Dobby handed round the tea.

'Only a week, Harry Potter, sir!' said Dobby happily. 'Dobby came to see Professor Dumbledore, sir. You see, sir, it is very difficult for a house-elf who has been dismissed to get a new position, sir, very difficult indeed –'

At this, Winky howled even harder, her squashed tomato of a nose dribbling all down her front, though she made no effort to stem the flow.

'Dobby has travelled the country for two whole years, sir, trying to find work!' Dobby squeaked. 'But Dobby hasn't found work, sir, because Dobby wants paying now!'

The house-elves all around the kitchen, who had been listening and watching with interest, all looked away at these words, as though Dobby had said something rude and embarrassing.

Hermione, however, said, 'Good for you, Dobby!'

'Thank you, miss!' said Dobby, grinning toothily at her. 'But most wizards doesn't want a house-elf who wants paying, miss. "That's not the point of a house-elf," they says, and they slammed the door in Dobby's face! Dobby likes work, but he wants to wear clothes and he wants to be paid, Harry Potter ... Dobby likes being free!'

The Hogwarts house-elves had now started edging away from Dobby, as

## 第21章 家养小精灵解放阵线

闪闪的嘴唇发抖,接着便放声大哭,眼泪从她那对棕色的大眼睛里滚出来,洒落在胸前,和魁地奇世界杯赛上一模一样。

"哦,天哪。"赫敏说——她和罗恩也跟着哈利和多比一起来到厨房尽头,"闪闪,别哭了,求求你……"

可是闪闪哭得更凶了。多比倒是喜滋滋地抬头望着哈利。

"哈利·波特想喝一杯茶吗?"他用尖细的嗓音大声问,盖过闪闪的哭泣声。

"呃——行,好吧。"哈利说。

立刻,就有六个家养小精灵从他后面匆匆跑上来,端着一只很大的银托盘,上面放着一把茶壶,还放着哈利、罗恩和赫敏的杯子、一壶牛奶和一大盘饼干。

"服务真好!"罗恩用一种很激动的声音说。赫敏朝他皱了皱眉头,但小精灵们看上去都很高兴。他们低低地鞠躬,退了回去。

"你来这里多久了,多比?"多比递茶时,哈利问道。

"刚一个星期,哈利·波特,先生!"多比欢快地说,"多比来见邓布利多先生,先生。你知道,先生,一个被开除的家养小精灵是很难找到新工作的,先生,真的很难很难——"

听了这话,闪闪号啕得更厉害了,鼻涕从她那像个被压扁的西红柿一般的鼻子里淌出来,啪嗒啪嗒地滴在胸前,她也不想把它止住。

"多比四处游荡了两年,先生,就为了找一份工作!"多比尖声尖气地说,"可是多比没有找到工作,先生,因为多比现在要工钱了!"

厨房里的那些家养小精灵本来都很感兴趣地看着他们,听他们说话,但听到这里,一个个都把目光移开了,就好像多比说了一些粗鲁的、令人尴尬的话似的。

赫敏却说:"好样的,多比!"

"谢谢你,小姐!"多比说着,朝赫敏一笑,露出好多牙齿,"但是大多数巫师都不想要一个拿工钱的家养小精灵,小姐。'那不是一个家养小精灵的品质。'他们说,然后就对着多比把门重重关上!多比喜欢工作,但他也想穿衣服、拿工钱,哈利·波特……多比喜欢自由!"

霍格沃茨的家养小精灵开始悄悄地挪开,躲避多比,好像他身上

## CHAPTER TWENTY-ONE    The House-Elf Liberation Front

though he was carrying something contagious. Winky, however, remained where she was, though there was a definite increase in the volume of her crying.

'And then, Harry Potter, Dobby goes to visit Winky, and finds out Winky has been freed, too, sir!' said Dobby delightedly.

At this, Winky flung herself forwards off her stool, and lay, face down, on the flagged stone floor, beating her tiny fists upon it and positively screaming with misery. Hermione hastily dropped down to her knees beside her, and tried to comfort her, but nothing she said made the slightest difference.

Dobby continued with his story, shouting shrilly over Winky's screeches. 'And then Dobby had the idea, Harry Potter, sir! "Why doesn't Dobby and Winky find work together?" Dobby says. "Where is there enough work for two house-elves?" says Winky. And Dobby thinks, and it comes to him, sir! *Hogwarts!* So Dobby and Winky came to see Professor Dumbledore, sir, and Professor Dumbledore took us on!'

Dobby beamed very brightly, and happy tears welled in his eyes again.

'And Professor Dumbledore says he will pay Dobby, sir, if Dobby wants paying! And so Dobby is a free elf, sir, and Dobby gets a Galleon a week and one day off a month!'

'That's not very much!' Hermione shouted indignantly from the floor, over Winky's continued screaming and fist-beating.

'Professor Dumbledore offered Dobby ten Galleons a week, and weekends off,' said Dobby, suddenly giving a little shiver, as though the prospect of so much leisure and riches was frightening, 'but Dobby beat him down, miss ... Dobby likes freedom, miss, but he isn't wanting too much, miss, he likes work better.'

'And how much is Professor Dumbledore paying *you*, Winky?' Hermione asked kindly.

If she had thought this would cheer Winky up, she was wildly mistaken. Winky did stop crying, but when she sat up she was glaring at Hermione through her massive brown eyes, her whole face sopping wet and suddenly furious.

'Winky is a disgraced elf, but Winky is not yet getting paid!' she squeaked. 'Winky is not sunk so low as that! Winky is properly ashamed of being freed!'

'Ashamed?' said Hermione blankly. 'But – Winky, come on! It's Mr

## 第21章 家养小精灵解放阵线

带着某种传染病菌。闪闪倒是待着没动,但她哭号的音量显然又增高了。

"后来,哈利·波特,多比去拜访闪闪,发现闪闪也被释放了,先生!"多比兴高采烈地说。

闪闪听了这话,从凳子上往前一扑,脸朝下倒在石板铺的地面上,捶打着小小的拳头,痛苦地尖叫起来。赫敏赶紧蹲在她身边,试着安慰她,可是不管赫敏说什么都不起任何作用。

多比继续讲他的故事,高声叫着,盖过了闪闪的哭号。"然后多比突然有了主意,哈利·波特,先生!'多比和闪闪为什么不能一起找工作呢?'多比说。'哪里有工作够两个家养小精灵干的呢?'闪闪问。多比想啊想啊,就想起来了,先生!霍格沃茨!多比和闪闪就来找邓布利多教授了,先生!邓布利多教授就把我们俩收下了!"

多比脸上露出非常灿烂的笑容,喜悦的泪水又充盈在他眼睛里。

"邓布利多教授说,既然多比想要工钱,他可以付给多比工钱!所以啊,多比是一个自由的小精灵,先生,多比每星期得到一个加隆,每个月放一天假!"

"那不算很多!"赫敏在地板上气愤地喊道,盖过闪闪不断哭喊和捶拳头的声音。

"邓布利多教授本来要给多比一星期十个加隆,周末放假,"多比说着,突然打了个寒战,好像这么多财富和闲暇时间是非常可怕的,"可是多比跟他讨价还价,小姐……多比喜欢自由,小姐,但他不想要太多的自由,他更喜欢工作!"

"那么你呢,闪闪,邓布利多教授付你多少工钱?"赫敏好心好意地问。

她如果以为这会使闪闪高兴起来,就真是大错特错了。闪闪确实停止了哭泣,她坐了起来,但两只巨大的棕色眼睛狠狠瞪着赫敏,湿漉漉的脸上突然变得怒气冲冲。

"闪闪是一个被扫地出门的家养小精灵,但闪闪还没到拿工钱的地步!"她尖声刺耳地说,"闪闪还没有堕落到那个程度!闪闪为自由感到羞愧!"

"羞愧?"赫敏茫然地说,"可是——闪闪,听我说!感到羞愧的

## CHAPTER TWENTY-ONE  The House-Elf Liberation Front

Crouch who should be ashamed, not you! You didn't do anything wrong, he was really horrible to you –'

But at these words, Winky clapped her hands over the holes in her hat, flattening her ears so that she couldn't hear a word, and screeched, 'You is not insulting my master, miss! You is not insulting Mr Crouch! Mr Crouch is a good wizard, miss! Mr Crouch is right to sack bad Winky!'

'Winky is having trouble adjusting, Harry Potter,' squeaked Dobby confidentially. 'Winky forgets she is not bound to Mr Crouch any more; she is allowed to speak her mind now, but she won't do it.'

'Can't house-elves speak their minds about their masters, then?' Harry asked.

'Oh, no, sir, no,' said Dobby, looking suddenly serious. ''Tis part of the house-elf's enslavement, sir. We keeps their secrets and our silence, sir, we upholds the family's honour, and we never speaks ill of them – though Professor Dumbledore told Dobby he does not insist upon this. Professor Dumbledore said we is free to – to –'

Dobby looked suddenly nervous, and beckoned Harry closer. Harry bent forwards.

Dobby whispered, 'He said we is free to call him a – a barmy old codger if we likes, sir!'

Dobby gave a frightened sort of giggle.

'But Dobby is not wanting to, Harry Potter,' he said, talking normally again, and shaking his head so that his ears flapped. 'Dobby likes Professor Dumbledore very much, sir, and is proud to keep his secrets for him.'

'But you can say what you like about the Malfoys now?' Harry asked him, grinning.

A slightly fearful look came into Dobby's immense eyes.

'Dobby – Dobby could,' he said doubtfully. He squared his small shoulders. 'Dobby could tell Harry Potter that his old masters were – were – *bad Dark wizards!*'

Dobby stood for a moment, quivering all over, horror-struck by his own daring – then he rushed over to the nearest table, and began banging his head on it, very hard, squealing, '*Bad Dobby! Bad Dobby!*'

Harry seized Dobby by the back of his tie and pulled him away from the table.

## 第21章 家养小精灵解放阵线

应该是克劳奇先生,不是你!你没有做错任何事,他对你太残忍了——"

可是闪闪听了这话,赶紧把手捂在她帽子的两个洞眼上,把耳朵压扁,这样她就听不见了,然后她尖叫起来:"不许你辱骂我的主人,小姐!不许你辱骂我的克劳奇先生!克劳奇先生是一个好巫师,小姐!克劳奇先生开除了坏闪闪,他做得对!"

"闪闪还调整不过来,哈利·波特,"多比尖声尖气地悄悄告诉他们,"闪闪忘记她跟克劳奇先生已经一刀两断了。她现在可以怎么想就怎么说,可是她做不到。"

"怎么,家养小精灵评论他们的主人时,不能怎么想就怎么说吗?"哈利问。

"哦,不能,先生,绝对不能,"多比说,表情突然严肃起来,"这是家养小精灵的奴隶身份必须遵守的,先生。我们为主人保守秘密,保持沉默,先生。我们维护家族的荣誉,从不说主人的坏话——不过邓布利多教授对多比说,他并不要求我们必须做到这点。邓布利多教授说,我们可以随意……随意……"

多比突然显得局促不安起来,示意哈利靠近,哈利倾下身子。

多比小声说:"他说如果我们愿意,可以叫他傻瓜大笨蛋,先生!"

多比发出一声恐惧的干笑。

"可是多比不想这么做,哈利·波特,"他说,现在语气又正常了——他摇晃着脑袋,两只耳朵啪啪地拍打,"多比非常喜欢邓布利多教授,先生,愿意替他保守秘密,为他保持沉默,并为此自豪。"

"那么对马尔福呢,你现在是不是想怎么说就怎么说了?"哈利咧嘴笑着,追问多比。

一丝恐惧的神色掠过多比那双巨大的眼睛。

"多比……多比可以,"他不很确定地说,挺起小小的胸膛,"多比可以告诉哈利·波特,多比的旧主人是……是……很坏的黑巫师!"

多比呆立了片刻,浑身发抖,被自己的大胆行为吓傻了——然后他一头冲向最近的桌子,开始把脑袋狠狠地往上面撞,一边尖叫道:"坏多比!坏多比!"

哈利抓住多比的领带后面,把他从桌子旁拉开了。

## CHAPTER TWENTY-ONE    The House-Elf Liberation Front

'Thank you, Harry Potter, thank you,' said Dobby breathlessly, rubbing his head.

'You just need a bit of practice,' Harry said.

'Practice!' squealed Winky furiously. 'You is ought to be ashamed of yourself, Dobby, talking that way about your masters!'

'They isn't my masters any more, Winky!' said Dobby defiantly. 'Dobby doesn't care what they think any more!'

'Oh, you is a bad elf, Dobby!' moaned Winky, tears leaking down her face once more. 'My poor Mr Crouch, what is he doing without Winky? He is needing me, he is needing my help! I is looking after the Crouches all my life, and my mother is doing it before me, and my grandmother is doing it before her ... oh, what is they saying if they knew Winky was freed? Oh, the shame, the shame!' She buried her face in her skirt again and bawled.

'Winky,' said Hermione, firmly, 'I'm quite sure Mr Crouch is getting along perfectly well without you. We've seen him, you know –'

'You is seeing my master?' said Winky breathlessly, raising her tear-stained face out of her skirt once more, and goggling at Hermione. 'You is seeing him here at Hogwarts?'

'Yes,' said Hermione. 'He and Mr Bagman are judges in the Triwizard Tournament.'

'Mr Bagman comes, too?' squeaked Winky, and to Harry's great surprise (and Ron and Hermione's, too, by the looks on their faces), she looked angry again. 'Mr Bagman is a bad wizard! A very bad wizard! My master isn't liking him, oh no, not at all!'

'Bagman – bad?' said Harry.

'Oh yes,' Winky said, nodding her head furiously. 'My master is telling Winky some things! But Winky is not saying ... Winky – Winky keeps her master's secrets ...'

She dissolved yet again in tears; they could hear her sobbing into her skirt, 'Poor master, poor master, no Winky to help him no more!'

They couldn't get another sensible word out of Winky. They left her to her crying, and finished their tea, while Dobby chatted happily about his life as a free elf, and his plans for his wages.

## 第21章 家养小精灵解放阵线

"谢谢你,哈利·波特,谢谢你。"多比上气不接下气地说,用手揉着脑袋。

"你只需要多练习练习。"哈利说。

"练习!"闪闪气愤地尖声嚷道,"你应该为自己感到羞愧,多比,那样评论你的主人!"

"他们已经不是我的主人了,闪闪!"多比不服气地说,"多比再也不在乎他们怎么想了!"

"哦,你真是一个坏精灵,多比!"闪闪呜咽着说,眼泪又一次顺着面颊扑簌簌滚下来,"我可怜的克劳奇先生,他没有了闪闪该怎么办呢?他需要我,他需要我的帮助!我从一生下来就照顾克劳奇一家,在我之前,是我妈妈,在我妈妈之前,是我外婆……哦,如果她们知道闪闪被释放了,会怎么说呢?哦,耻辱啊,真是耻辱!"她又把脸埋在裙子里,放声大哭。

"闪闪,"赫敏语气坚决地说,"我可以肯定,克劳奇先生没有你照样过得很好。你知道吗,我们见过他——"

"你们见过我的主人?"闪闪喘着气问,从裙子里重新抬起泪痕斑斑的脸,瞪大眼睛望着赫敏,"你在这里,在霍格沃茨看见他的?"

"是的,"赫敏说,"他和巴格曼先生是三强争霸赛的裁判。"

"巴格曼先生也来了?"闪闪尖声问道,突然又变得怒气冲冲,令哈利大吃一惊(从罗恩和赫敏脸上的神情看,他们也吃惊不小),"巴格曼先生是一个坏巫师!一个很坏很坏的巫师!我的主人不喜欢他,哦,一点儿也不喜欢!"

"巴格曼——坏巫师?"哈利说。

"哦,是的,"闪闪说着,气愤地点着头,"主人告诉了闪闪一些事情!可是闪闪不能说……闪闪——闪闪替主人保守秘密……"

她再一次泪如雨下。他们可以听见她把脸埋在裙子里哭泣:"可怜的主人,可怜的主人,再也没有闪闪侍候他了!"

除此之外,他们从闪闪嘴里再也问不出一句明白的话。于是他们随她去哭泣,只管自己喝茶。多比在一旁兴高采烈地说个不停,讲他作为一个自由小精灵是怎么生活的,以及他打算怎么花他的工钱。

## CHAPTER TWENTY-ONE  The House-Elf Liberation Front

'Dobby is going to buy a jumper next, Harry Potter!' he said happily, pointing at his bare chest.

'Tell you what, Dobby,' said Ron, who seemed to have taken a great liking to the elf, 'I'll give you the one my mum knits me this Christmas, I always get one from her. You don't mind maroon, do you?'

Dobby was delighted.

'We might have to shrink it a bit to fit you,' Ron told him, 'but it'll go well with your tea-cosy.'

As they prepared to take their leave, many of the surrounding elves pressed in upon them, offering snacks to take back upstairs. Hermione refused, with a pained look at the way the elves kept bowing and curtseying, but Harry and Ron loaded their pockets with cream cakes and pies.

'Thanks a lot!' Harry said to the elves, who had all clustered around the door to say goodnight. 'See you, Dobby!'

'Harry Potter ... can Dobby come and see you sometimes, sir?' Dobby asked tentatively.

"Course you can,' said Harry, and Dobby beamed.

'You know what?' said Ron, once he, Hermione and Harry had left the kitchens behind, and were climbing the steps into the Entrance Hall again. 'All these years I've been really impressed with Fred and George, nicking food from the kitchens – well, it's not exactly difficult, is it? They can't wait to give it away!'

'I think this is the best thing that could have happened to those elves, you know,' said Hermione, leading the way back up the marble staircase. 'Dobby coming to work here, I mean. The other elves will see how happy he is, being free, and slowly it'll dawn on them that they want that, too!'

'Let's hope they don't look too closely at Winky,' said Harry.

'Oh, she'll cheer up,' said Hermione, though she sounded a bit doubtful. 'Once the shock's worn off, and she's got used to Hogwarts, she'll see how much better off she is without that Crouch man.'

'She seems to love him,' said Ron thickly (he had just started on a cream cake).

'Doesn't think much of Bagman, though, does she?' said Harry. 'Wonder

## 第21章 家养小精灵解放阵线

"多比下一步就买一件套头衫,哈利·波特!"他指着赤裸的胸脯,高兴地说。

"告诉你吧,多比,"罗恩似乎对这个小精灵产生了极大的好感,他说,"我要把我妈妈这个圣诞节给我织的毛衣送给你,我每年都能从她那里得到一件。你不讨厌暗紫红色吧?"

多比开心极了。

"我们必须把它缩小一些,适合你的身材,"罗恩对他说,"它跟你的茶壶保暖套倒是很配呢。"

他们准备告辞时,旁边的许多小精灵都围拢过来,向他们递来一大堆点心,让他们带上楼去。赫敏不肯拿,她望着小精灵们不停鞠躬、行屈膝礼的样子,脸上露出痛苦的神情。哈利和罗恩却往口袋里装了好多奶油蛋糕和馅饼。

"太感谢了!"哈利对小精灵们说——他们都簇拥到门边,向三人道晚安,"再见,多比!"

"哈利·波特……多比有时候可以来看你吗,先生?"多比试探地问。

"当然可以。"哈利说,多比顿时眉开眼笑。

"你们知道吗?"罗恩说道——这时他和赫敏、哈利刚离开厨房,正往通向门厅的楼梯上走,"这些年来,我一直觉得弗雷德和乔治很了不起,能从厨房里偷出吃的东西——闹了半天,实际上并不困难,是吗?小精灵们那么热情地把东西塞给你!"

"我认为,对于那些家养小精灵来说,这是最理想的事,"赫敏领头往大理石楼梯上走,一边说道,"我指的是多比来这里工作。别的小精灵会看到他获得自由是多么愉快,慢慢就会明白自己也愿意那样!"

"但愿他们不要太仔细地观察闪闪。"哈利说。

"哦,闪闪会高兴起来的。"赫敏说,不过她的口气也有些犹疑,"等这场惊吓过去,她习惯了霍格沃茨的生活,就会明白离开了那个叫克劳奇的家伙,日子要好过得多!"

"她似乎很爱那个男人。"罗恩含混不清地说(他刚咬了一口奶油蛋糕)。

"不过,她对巴格曼的评价可不高,是吗?"哈利说,"不知道克

## CHAPTER TWENTY-ONE — The House-Elf Liberation Front

what Crouch says at home about him?'

'Probably says he's not a very good Head of Department,' said Hermione, 'and let's face it ... he's got a point, hasn't he?'

'I'd still rather work for him than old Crouch,' said Ron. 'At least Bagman's got a sense of humour.'

'Don't let Percy hear you saying that,' Hermione said, smiling slightly.

'Yeah, well, Percy wouldn't want to work for anyone with a sense of humour, would he?' said Ron, now starting on a chocolate éclair. 'Percy wouldn't recognise a joke if it danced naked in front of him wearing Dobby's tea-cosy.'

劳奇在家里是怎么议论巴格曼的?"

"大概说他不是一个很称职的司长,"赫敏说,"说句实话……他这么说不无道理,是不是?"

"跟克劳奇那老家伙比起来,我还是情愿在巴格曼手下工作,"罗恩说,"至少他还有点儿幽默感。"

"可别让珀西听见你这么说。"赫敏说,淡淡地笑了笑。

"是啊,说到珀西,他可不愿在任何一个有幽默感的人手下工作,是不是?"罗恩说——他现在又开始吃一块巧克力松饼了,"一个笑话哪怕只戴着多比的茶壶保暖套,几乎是光着身子在他面前跳舞,他也认不出来。"

## CHAPTER TWENTY-TWO

# The Unexpected Task

'Potter! Weasley! *Will you pay attention?*'

Professor McGonagall's irritated voice cracked like a whip through the Transfiguration class on Thursday, and Harry and Ron both jumped and looked up.

It was the end of the lesson; they had finished their work; the guinea-fowl they had been changing into guinea-pigs had been shut away in a large cage on Professor McGonagall's desk (Neville's guinea-pig still had feathers); they had copied down their homework from the blackboard ('Describe, with examples, the ways in which Transforming Spells must be adapted when performing Cross-Species Switches'). The bell was due to ring at any moment, and Harry and Ron, who had been having a sword fight with a couple of Fred and George's fake wands at the back of the class, looked up, Ron now holding a tin parrot, and Harry, a rubber haddock.

'Now Potter and Weasley have been kind enough to act their age,' said Professor McGonagall, with an angry look at the pair of them as the head of Harry's haddock drooped and fell silently to the floor – Ron's parrot's beak had severed it moments before – 'I have something to say to you all.

'The Yule Ball is approaching – a traditional part of the Triwizard Tournament and an opportunity for us to socialise with our foreign guests. Now, the ball will be open only to fourth-years and above – although you may invite a younger student if you wish –'

Lavender Brown let out a shrill giggle. Parvati Patil nudged her hard in the ribs, her face working furiously as she, too, fought not to giggle. They both looked around at Harry. Professor McGonagall ignored them, which Harry thought was distinctly unfair, as she had just told off him and Ron.

'Dress robes will be worn,' Professor McGonagall continued, 'and the

第 22 章

意外的挑战

"波特！韦斯莱！你们能不能专心一点儿？"

麦格教授恼火的声音像鞭子一样，在星期四的变形课教室里噼啪响起，惊得哈利和罗恩都抬起头来。

这堂课快要结束了。他们完成了老师布置的工作：那些被他们变成天竺鼠的珍珠鸡，现在已关在麦格教授讲台上的一只大笼子里（纳威的那只身上还留着羽毛）；黑板上的家庭作业，他们也已经抄在了本子上（"试举例说明，进行跨物种转换时，变形咒必须做怎样的调整"）。下课铃随时都会响起，哈利和罗恩正拿着弗雷德和乔治发明的两根假魔杖，在教室后排你来我往地比剑术，两人此刻抬起头来，罗恩手里是一只镀锡的鹦鹉，哈利手里是一条橡皮的黑线鳕鱼。

"既然波特和韦斯莱终于使自己的行为与年龄相称了，"麦格教授说着，愤怒地扫了他们俩一眼，就在这时，哈利那条黑线鳕鱼的脑袋掉了下来，无声地落到地板上——是罗恩那只鹦鹉的利喙把它啄断了——"我正好有几句话要对你们大家说。

"圣诞舞会就要来临了——这是三强争霸赛的一个传统部分，也是我们与外国客人交往的一个大好机会。是这样，舞会只对四年级以上的学生开放——不过如果你们愿意，可以邀请一位低年级学生——"

拉文德·布朗发出一声刺耳的傻笑。帕瓦蒂·佩蒂尔用劲捅了捅她，自己脸上的肌肉也在使劲绷着，因为她在拼命克制着不笑出来。她们俩都转过脸来望着哈利。麦格教授没有理会她们，哈利觉得这特别不公平，刚才她还数落他和罗恩来着。

"要穿上你们的礼服长袍，"麦格教授继续说道，"舞会将于圣诞节

## CHAPTER TWENTY-TWO   The Unexpected Task

ball will start at eight o'clock on Christmas Day, finishing at midnight, in the Great Hall. Now then –'

Professor McGonagall stared deliberately around the class.

'The Yule Ball is of course a chance for us all to – er – let our hair down,' she said, in a disapproving voice.

Lavender giggled harder than ever, with her hand pressed hard against her mouth to stifle the sound. Harry could see what was funny this time: Professor McGonagall, with her hair in a tight bun, looked as though she had never let her hair down in any sense.

'But that does NOT mean,' Professor McGonagall went on, 'that we will be relaxing the standards of behaviour we expect from Hogwarts students. I will be most seriously displeased if a Gryffindor student embarrasses the school in any way.'

The bell rang, and there was the usual scuffle of activity as everyone packed their bags and swung them onto their shoulders.

Professor McGonagall called above the noise, 'Potter – a word, if you please.'

Assuming this had something to do with his headless rubber haddock, Harry proceeded gloomily to the teacher's desk.

Professor McGonagall waited until the rest of the class had gone, and then said, 'Potter, the champions and their partners –'

'What partners?' said Harry.

Professor McGonagall looked suspiciously at him, as though she thought he was trying to be funny.

'Your partners for the Yule Ball, Potter,' she said coldly. 'Your *dance partners*.'

Harry's insides seemed to curl up and shrivel. 'Dance partners?'

He felt himself going red. 'I don't dance,' he said quickly.

'Oh, yes, you do,' said Professor McGonagall irritably. 'That's what I'm telling you. Traditionally, the champions and their partners open the ball.'

Harry had a sudden mental image of himself in a top hat and tails, accompanied by a girl in the sort of frilly dress Aunt Petunia always wore to Uncle Vernon's work parties.

'I'm not dancing,' he said.

'It is traditional,' said Professor McGonagall firmly. 'You are a Hogwarts champion, and you will do what is expected of you as a representative of the

## 第22章 意外的挑战

晚上八点在礼堂举行，午夜十二点结束。听着——"

麦格教授从容不迫地打量着全班同学。

"圣诞舞会无疑会使我们有机会——嗯——散开头发，放松自己。"她以一种不以为然的口吻说。

拉文德笑得更厉害了，使劲用手捂住嘴巴，不让声音发出来。哈利知道这次的笑点在哪里：麦格教授的头发总是绾成紧紧的小圆髻，她似乎从来没有把头发散开过。

"但那并**不**意味着，"麦格教授继续说道，"我们会放松对霍格沃茨学生的行为要求。如果格兰芬多的某个学生以任何方式给学校丢脸，我将感到十分痛心。"

下课铃响了，大家和往常一样，把书本塞进书包，再把书包甩到肩头，教室里一阵忙乱。

麦格教授提高嗓门，在一片噪声中喊道："波特——请留一下，我要对你说几句话。"

哈利心想这一定是因为他那条无头的橡皮黑线鳕鱼，便无精打采地朝讲台走去。麦格教授等全班同学都走光了，才说道："波特，勇士都有自己的伴侣——"

"什么伴侣？"哈利说。

麦格教授怀疑地望着他，似乎以为他在开玩笑。

"你带去参加圣诞舞会的伴侣，波特，"麦格教授冷冷地说，"你的舞伴。"

哈利仿佛觉得自己的内脏在扭曲皱缩。"舞伴？"

他感到自己的脸红了。"我不跳舞。"他急忙说道。

"哦，你必须跳舞，"麦格教授烦躁地说，"我正要告诉你这一点。按传统惯例，舞会是由勇士和他们的舞伴开舞的。"

哈利的脑海里突然浮现出自己头戴黑色高顶大礼帽、身穿燕尾服的模样，他身边还有一个姑娘，穿着满是褶边的裙子，就是佩妮姨妈参加弗农姨父公司里的舞会时穿的那种。

"我不跳舞。"他说。

"这是传统惯例，"麦格教授坚决地说，"你是霍格沃茨的勇士，作

## CHAPTER TWENTY-TWO — The Unexpected Task

school. So make sure you get yourself a partner, Potter.'

'But – I don't –'

'You heard me, Potter,' said Professor McGonagall, in a very final sort of way.

A week ago, Harry would have said finding a partner for a dance would be a cinch compared to taking on a Hungarian Horntail. But now that he had done the latter, and was facing the prospect of asking a girl to the ball, he thought he'd rather have another round with the Horntail.

Harry had never known so many people to put their names down to stay at Hogwarts for Christmas; he always did, of course, because the alternative was usually going back to Privet Drive, but he had always been very much in the minority before now. This year, however, everyone in the fourth year and above seemed to be staying, and they all seemed to Harry to be obsessed with the coming ball – or, at least, all the girls were, and it was amazing how many girls Hogwarts suddenly seemed to hold; he had never quite noticed that before. Girls giggling and whispering in the corridors, girls shrieking with laughter as boys passed them, girls excitedly comparing notes on what they were going to wear on Christmas night ...

'Why do they have to move in packs?' Harry asked Ron, as a dozen or so girls walked past them, sniggering and staring at Harry. 'How're you supposed to get one on their own to ask them?'

'Lasso one?' Ron suggested. 'Got any idea who you're going to try?'

Harry didn't answer. He knew perfectly well whom he'd *like* to ask, but working up the nerve was something else ... Cho was a year older than he was; she was very pretty; she was a very good Quidditch player, and she was also very popular.

Ron seemed to know what was going on inside Harry's head.

'Listen, you're not going to have any trouble. You're a champion. You've just beaten a Hungarian Horntail. I bet they'll be queuing up to go with you.'

In tribute to their recently repaired friendship, Ron had kept the bitterness in his voice to a bare minimum. Moreover, to Harry's amazement, he turned out to be quite right.

A curly-haired third-year Hufflepuff girl to whom Harry had never spoken in his life asked him to go to the ball with her the very next day. Harry was

## 第22章 意外的挑战

为学校的一名代表，你必须照大家期望的那样去做。所以，你必须给自己找一个舞伴，波特。"

"可是——我不——"

"你听见我的话了，波特！"麦格教授用一种不容置疑的口吻说。

一星期前哈利会说，找一个舞伴跟对付一条匈牙利树蜂比起来，简直是小菜一碟。可是现在他战胜了树蜂，正面临着找一个姑娘跳舞的挑战。他觉得自己宁愿再与树蜂搏斗一个回合。

哈利从未见过这么多登记在霍格沃茨过圣诞节的同学。当然啦，他自己总是留校过圣诞节的，因为如果不这样，就要回女贞路去，但以前留校的人总是极小一部分。今年就不同了，四年级以上的所有同学似乎都要留下来。哈利觉得，他们都对即将到来的舞会非常痴迷——至少所有的女生都是这样，他忽然惊讶地发现霍格沃茨竟然容纳了这么多女生，他以前根本就没有留意。女生们在走廊里咭咭笑着、窃窃私语，女生们每当有男生走过时就尖声大笑，女生们兴奋地交换意见，谈论圣诞节晚上穿什么衣服……

"她们为什么都成群结队地活动呢？"哈利问罗恩——这时正有十来个女生从旁边走过，她们打量着哈利，偷偷地傻笑，"你怎么才能等到她们单独行动，抓住一个提出要求呢？"

"用绳套套住一个？"罗恩建议道，"你有没有想好请谁？"

哈利没有回答。他很清楚自己愿意请谁，但能不能鼓起勇气就是另外一回事了……秋·张比他高一年级，长得非常漂亮，还是一个非常出色的魁地奇球员，她的人缘也很好。

罗恩似乎看透了哈利的内心。

"听着，你是不会有什么麻烦的。你是勇士嘛。刚刚打败了匈牙利树蜂。我敢说她们会排着队争着跟你跳舞的。"

为了维护他们刚刚修复的友谊，罗恩把声音里的苦涩味道控制到了最低限度。而且哈利惊讶地发现，事实证明罗恩的判断非常正确。

就在第二天，一个赫奇帕奇学院三年级的鬈发女生——哈利以前从没与她说过话，主动来邀请哈利与她一起去参加舞会。哈利太吃惊了，

## CHAPTER TWENTY-TWO   The Unexpected Task

so taken aback he said 'no' before he'd even stopped to consider the matter. The girl walked off looking rather hurt, and Harry had to endure Dean's, Seamus's and Ron's taunts about her all through History of Magic. The following day, two more girls asked him, a second-year and (to his horror) a fifth-year who looked as though she might knock him out if he refused.

'She was quite good-looking,' said Ron fairly, after he'd stopped laughing.

'She was a foot taller than me,' said Harry, still unnerved. 'Imagine what I'd look like trying to dance with her.'

Hermione's words about Krum kept coming back to him. 'They only like him because he's famous!' Harry doubted very much if any of the girls who had asked to be his partner so far would have wanted to go to the ball with him if he hadn't been school champion. Then he wondered if this would bother him if Cho asked him.

On the whole, Harry had to admit that even with the embarrassing prospect of opening the ball before him, life had definitely improved since he had got through the first task. He wasn't attracting nearly as much unpleasantness in the corridors any more, which he suspected had a lot to do with Cedric – he had an idea Cedric might have told the Hufflepuffs to leave Harry alone, in gratitude for Harry's tip-off about the dragons. There seemed to be fewer *Support CEDRIC DIGGORY* badges around, too. Draco Malfoy, of course, was still quoting Rita Skeeter's article at him at every possible opportunity, but he was getting fewer and fewer laughs out of it – and just to heighten Harry's feeling of well-being, no story about Hagrid had appeared in the *Daily Prophet*.

'She didn' seem very int'rested in magical creatures, ter tell yeh the truth,' Hagrid said, when Harry, Ron and Hermione asked him how his interview with Rita Skeeter had gone during the last Care of Magical Creatures lesson of term. To their very great relief, Hagrid had given up on direct contact with the Skrewts now, and they were merely sheltering behind his cabin today, sitting at a trestle table and preparing a fresh selection of food with which to tempt the Skrewts.

'She jus' wanted me ter talk about you, Harry,' Hagrid continued in a low voice. 'Well, I told her we'd been friends since I went ter fetch yeh from the Dursleys. "Never had to tell him off in four years?" she said. "Never played you up in lessons, has he?" I told her no, an' she didn' seem happy at all.

## 第22章 意外的挑战

连想也没想就拒绝了。那女生走开时一副备受伤害的样子。在整堂魔法史课上,哈利不得不忍受迪安、西莫和罗恩拿那女生来挖苦和嘲笑他。接下来的一天,又有两个女生来邀请他,一个是二年级的,还有一个(他惊恐地发现)竟然是五年级的,看她那样子,似乎如果哈利敢拒绝,她就会把他打昏过去。

"她长得蛮漂亮的。"罗恩笑够了以后,公正地说。

"她比我高一英尺呢。"哈利说,仍然惊魂未定,"想象一下吧,我跟她一起跳舞,那还不出丑!"

哈利经常想起赫敏谈论克鲁姆的话:"她们喜欢他,只是因为他名气大!"哈利十分怀疑,如果自己不是学校的勇士,那些邀请他做舞伴的女生是否还愿意跟他一起去参加舞会。接着他又问自己,如果是秋·张主动邀请他,他还会考虑这个问题吗?

总的来说,哈利不得不承认,尽管面临着参加舞会这件令人尴尬的事,但自从他通过第一个项目之后,生活还是大有改善。他在走廊里不再遇到那么多不愉快的冲突了,他怀疑这在很大程度上是因为塞德里克——他总觉得是塞德里克叫赫奇帕奇的同学放哈利一马的,为的是感谢哈利向他通风报信,告诉他火龙的事。而且,周围支持**塞德里克·迪戈里**的徽章也少多了。当然啦,德拉科·马尔福只要一有机会,还是会引用丽塔·斯基特文章里的话来嘲笑哈利,但他得到的笑声越来越少——大概是为了给哈利愉快的心情锦上添花吧,《预言家日报》上并没有出现有关海格的报道。

"实话对你们说吧,她好像对神奇动物不怎么感兴趣。"海格说,这是在学期的最后一节保护神奇动物课上,哈利、罗恩和赫敏询问他和丽塔·斯基特面谈的情况。海格终于放弃了直接接触炸尾螺的做法,这使他们松了一口气。今天,他们只是躲在海格的小屋后面,坐在一张搁板桌旁准备一批新挑选的食物,要用它们来引诱炸尾螺。

"她只是要我谈你,哈利,"海格继续压低声音说道,"我嘛,我就告诉她,自从我把你从德思礼家接来的那天起,我们就是好朋友。'这四年里,你从来不需要训斥他吗?'她问,'他从来没有在课堂上调皮捣蛋?'我对她说没有,她就显得很不高兴。她好像希望我把你说得

## CHAPTER TWENTY-TWO   The Unexpected Task

Yeh'd think she wanted me to say yeh were horrible, Harry.'

'*Course she did,' said Harry, throwing lumps of dragon liver into a large metal bowl and picking up his knife to cut some more. 'She can't keep writing about what a tragic little hero I am, it'll get boring.'

'She wants a new angle, Hagrid,' said Ron wisely, as he shelled salamander eggs. 'You were supposed to say Harry's a mad delinquent!'

'But he's not!' said Hagrid, looking genuinely shocked.

'She should've interviewed Snape,' said Harry grimly. 'He'd give her the goods on me any day. *Potter has been crossing lines ever since he first arrived at this school ...*'

'Said that, did he?' said Hagrid, while Ron and Hermione laughed. 'Well, yeh might've bent a few rules, Harry, bu' yeh're all righ' really, aren' you?'

'Cheers, Hagrid,' said Harry, grinning.

'You coming to this ball thing on Christmas Day, Hagrid?' said Ron.

'Though' I might look in on it, yeah,' said Hagrid gruffly. 'Should be a good do, I reckon. You'll be openin' the dancin', won' yeh, Harry? Who're you takin'?'

'No one, yet,' said Harry, feeling himself going red again. Hagrid didn't pursue the subject.

The last week of term became increasingly boisterous as it progressed. Rumours about the Yule Ball were flying everywhere, though Harry didn't believe half of them – for instance, that Dumbledore had bought eight hundred barrels of mulled mead from Madam Rosmerta. It seemed to be fact, however, that he had booked the Weird Sisters. Exactly who or what the Weird Sisters were Harry didn't know, never having had access to a wizard's wireless, but he deduced from the wild excitement of those who had grown up listening to the WWN (Wizarding Wireless Network) that they were a very famous musical group.

Some of the teachers, like little Professor Flitwick, gave up trying to teach them much when their minds were so clearly elsewhere; he allowed them to play games in his lesson on Wednesday, and spent most of it talking to Harry about the perfect Summoning Charm he had used during the first task of the Triwizard Tournament. Other teachers were not so generous. Nothing would ever deflect Professor Binns, for example, from ploughing on through his notes on goblin rebellions – as Binns hadn't let his own death stand in

## 第22章 意外的挑战

很糟糕,哈利。"

"她当然是这样,"哈利说着,把一块块龙肝扔进一只大金属碗里,又拿起刀子准备再切一些,"她不能总写我是一个多么富有悲剧色彩的小英雄啊,那会使人厌烦的。"

"她需要换一个新的角度,海格,"罗恩明智地说,一边剥着火蜥蜴的蛋壳,"你应该说哈利是一个无法无天的少年犯!"

"但他不是啊!"海格说,似乎完全被惊呆了。

"她应该采访一下斯内普,"哈利气呼呼地说,"斯内普随时会在她面前告我一状。波特自打进了这个学校之后,就一直在违反校规……"

"他说过这样的话,是吗?"海格问——罗恩和赫敏都在哈哈大笑,"说起来,你大概确实违反过几条校规,哈利,但你的表现一直很不错,是不是?"

"谢谢你,海格。"哈利说着,咧开嘴笑了。

"圣诞节那天,你来参加那倒霉的舞会吗,海格?"罗恩说。

"我想顺便去看看,"海格声音粗哑地说,"我认为应该会很热闹。舞会由你开舞,是不是,哈利?你带谁去?"

"还没有人。"哈利说,觉得自己的脸又红了。海格没有追问下去。

学期的最后一星期,学校里一天比一天热闹、嘈杂。人们四处谣传关于圣诞舞会的消息,但其中大部分哈利都不相信——比如,邓布利多从三把扫帚的罗斯默塔那里买了八百桶热蜂蜜酒。不过,他预定古怪姐妹的事倒有可能是真的。至于古怪姐妹究竟是谁或什么东西,哈利并不知道,因为他从没听过巫师无线联播,但从那些从小就听WWN(巫师无线联播)的同学们的兴奋劲儿来看,古怪姐妹似乎是一个非常有名的音乐组合。

有些老师,如小个子弗立维教授,看到同学们显然都心不在焉,便索性不再讲课了。他允许他们在星期三他的课上做游戏,自己则大部分时间都在跟哈利说话,谈论哈利在三强争霸赛的第一个项目里使用的那个精彩的召唤咒。其他老师就没有这么好说话了。比如,宾斯教授的注意力是没有任何事情能够转移的,他还是继续在那堆关于妖精叛乱的笔记中艰难跋涉——同学们推测,宾斯既然没有让自己的死亡

## CHAPTER TWENTY-TWO    The Unexpected Task

the way of continuing to teach, they supposed a small thing like Christmas wasn't going to put him off. It was amazing how he could make even bloody and vicious goblin riots sound as boring as Percy's cauldron-bottom report. Professors McGonagall and Moody kept them working until the very last second of their classes, too, and Snape, of course, would no sooner let them play games in class than adopt Harry. Staring nastily around at them all, he informed them that he would be testing them on poison antidotes during the last lesson of the term.

'Evil, he is,' Ron said bitterly that night in the Gryffindor common room. 'Springing a test on us on the last day. Ruining the last bit of term with a whole load of revision.'

'Mmm ... you're not exactly straining yourself, though, are you?' said Hermione, looking at him over the top of her Potions notes. Ron was busy building a card castle out of his Exploding Snap pack – a much more interesting pastime than with Muggle cards, because of the chance that the whole thing would blow up at any second.

'It's Christmas, Hermione,' said Harry lazily; he was rereading *Flying with the Cannons* for the tenth time in an armchair near the fire.

Hermione looked severely over at him, too. 'I'd have thought you'd be doing something constructive, Harry, even if you don't want to learn your antidotes!'

'Like what?' Harry said, as he watched Joey Jenkins of the Cannons belt a Bludger towards a Ballycastle Bats Chaser.

'That egg!' Hermione hissed.

'Come on, Hermione, I've got 'til February the twenty-fourth,' Harry said.

He had put the golden egg upstairs in his trunk, and hadn't opened it since the celebration party after the first task. There were still two and a half months to go until he needed to know what all the screechy wailing meant, after all.

'But it might take weeks to work it out!' said Hermione. 'You're going to look a real idiot if everyone else knows what the next task is and you don't!'

'Leave him alone, Hermione, he's earned a bit of a break,' said Ron, and he placed the last two cards on top of the castle and the whole lot blew up, singeing his eyebrows.

'Nice look, Ron ... go well with your dress robes, that will.'

It was Fred and George. They sat down at the table with Harry, Ron and

## 第22章 意外的挑战

阻挡他继续教书的道路，像圣诞节这样的小事，就更不可能使他分心了。说来真是奇怪，他居然能把血淋淋、惊心动魄的妖精叛乱讲得像珀西的坩埚底报告那样枯燥乏味。麦格教授和穆迪教授也不让学生们闲着，直到下课前的最后一秒钟。斯内普就更不用说了，他宁愿收养哈利当干儿子，也不愿让同学们在课堂上做游戏。他目光阴沉地打量着全班同学，告诉他们说，他将在学期的最后一节课上测验他们的解毒剂。

"他真坏，"那天晚上，罗恩在格兰芬多的公共休息室里气愤地说，"在最后一天来测验我们。用一大堆功课破坏学期最后的一点儿时光。"

"嗯……实际上你并没有怎么用功，是不是？"赫敏从她的魔药课笔记上望着罗恩。罗恩正忙着用他那副噼啪爆炸牌搭城堡——这种娱乐可比麻瓜的扑克牌有趣多了，如果弄得不好，搭的东西随时都会整个爆炸。

"这是圣诞节啊，赫敏。"哈利懒洋洋地说。他坐在炉火边的一把扶手椅里，第十遍阅读《与火炮队一起飞翔》。

赫敏又用严肃的目光望着他，"哈利，我认为你即便不想学习解药，也会做一些更有意义的事情吧。"

"比如什么？"哈利一边问，一边注视着火炮队的乔艾·詹肯斯把一只游走球狠狠地击向巴里堡蝙蝠队的一名追球手。

"那只金蛋！"赫敏咬着牙小声说。

"好了，赫敏，我可以休息到二月二十四日呢。"哈利说。

哈利把那只金蛋放在楼上他的箱子里了，自从第一个项目的庆祝晚会结束后，他就再也没有打开过它。反正还有两个半月他才需要知道那一声声刺耳的惨叫意味着什么呢。

"但是解开那个谜可能要花好几个星期！"赫敏说，"如果别人都知道下一个项目是什么，就你一个人蒙在鼓里，你可就真的成为一个大傻瓜了！"

"别烦他了，赫敏，他应该休息休息了。"罗恩说着，把最后两张牌放到城堡顶上，轰隆一声，整个城堡爆炸了，烧焦了他的眉毛。

"真好看，罗恩……跟你的礼服长袍倒是很般配。"

是弗雷德和乔治。他们在哈利、罗恩和赫敏的桌旁坐下，罗恩摸

## CHAPTER TWENTY-TWO   The Unexpected Task

Hermione as Ron felt how much damage had been done.

'Ron, can we borrow Pigwidgeon?' George asked.

'No, he's off delivering a letter,' said Ron. 'Why?'

'Because George wants to invite him to the ball,' said Fred sarcastically.

'Because *we* want to send a letter, you stupid great prat,' said George.

'Who d'you two keep writing to, eh?' said Ron.

'Nose out, Ron, or I'll burn that for you, too,' said Fred, waving his wand threateningly. 'So … you lot got dates for the ball yet?'

'Nope,' said Ron.

'Well, you'd better hurry up, mate, or all the good ones will be gone,' said Fred.

'Who're you going with, then?' said Ron.

'Angelina,' said Fred promptly, without a trace of embarrassment.

'What?' said Ron, taken aback. 'You've already asked her?'

'Good point,' said Fred. He turned his head and called across the common room, 'Oi! Angelina!'

Angelina, who had been chatting to Alicia Spinnet near the fire, looked over at him.

'What?' she called back.

'Want to come to the ball with me?'

Angelina gave Fred an appraising sort of look.

'All right, then,' she said, and she turned back to Alicia and carried on chatting, with a bit of a grin on her face.

'There you go,' said Fred to Harry and Ron, 'piece of cake.'

He got to his feet, yawning, and said, 'We'd better use a school owl then, George, come on …'

They left. Ron stopped feeling his eyebrows and looked across the smouldering wreck of his card castle at Harry.

'We *should* get a move on, you know … ask someone. He's right. We don't want to end up with a pair of trolls.'

Hermione let out a splutter of indignation. 'A pair of … *what*, excuse me?'

## 第22章 意外的挑战

着眉毛，检查被烧焦了多少。

"罗恩，我们可以借小猪用一下吗？"乔治问道。

"不行，它出去送信了。"罗恩说，"做什么？"

"因为乔治想邀请它参加舞会。"弗雷德讽刺地说。

"因为我们有一封信要送，你这个愚蠢的大呆瓜。"乔治说。

"你们两个给谁写信，嗯？"罗恩说。

"别多管闲事，罗恩，不然我把你的鼻子也烧焦。"弗雷德说，一边挥舞着魔杖威胁罗恩，"怎么……你们这些家伙还没有找到舞伴？"

"没有。"罗恩说。

"我说，伙计，最好加快速度，不然好姑娘就被挑光了。"弗雷德说。

"那么你和谁一起去呢？"罗恩说。

"安吉利娜。"弗雷德不假思索地回答，没有一点儿不好意思。

"什么？"罗恩吃惊地问，"你已经邀请她了？"

"问得好。"弗雷德说。他转过头，朝公共休息室的那头喊道："喂，安吉利娜！"

安吉利娜正在炉火边与艾丽娅·斯平内特聊天，听到喊声，朝弗雷德望过来。

"怎么啦？"她大声问道。

"愿意和我一起参加舞会吗？"

安吉利娜用掂量的目光看了看弗雷德。

"好吧。"她说，然后又转过脸去跟艾丽娅继续聊天，脸上带着一丝淡淡的微笑。

"成了，"弗雷德对哈利和罗恩说，"小菜一碟。"

他站起来，打了个哈欠，说道："我们最好还是用一只学校的猫头鹰吧，乔治，快走……"

他们离去了。罗恩不再摸眉毛，而是隔着已成废墟、还在冒烟的纸牌城堡望着哈利。

"我们也应该采取行动了……邀请一个人。他说得对。我们可不想最后跟一对巨怪跳舞。"

赫敏气坏了，说话也显得有些结巴。"对不起，一对……什么？"

## CHAPTER TWENTY-TWO    The Unexpected Task

'Well – you know,' said Ron, shrugging, 'I'd rather go alone than with – with Eloise Midgen, say.'

'Her acne's loads better lately – and she's really nice!'

'Her nose is off-centre,' said Ron.

'Oh, I see,' Hermione said, bristling. 'So basically, you're going to take the best-looking girl who'll have you, even if she's completely horrible?'

'Er – yeah, that sounds about right,' said Ron.

'I'm going to bed,' Hermione snapped, and she swept off towards the girls' staircase without another word.

The Hogwarts staff, demonstrating a continued desire to impress the visitors from Beauxbatons and Durmstrang, seemed determined to show the castle at its best this Christmas. When the decorations went up, Harry noticed that they were the most stunning he had yet seen inside the school. Everlasting icicles had been attached to the banisters of the marble staircase; the usual twelve Christmas trees in the Great Hall were bedecked with everything from luminous holly berries to real, hooting, golden owls, and the suits of armour had all been bewitched to sing carols whenever anyone passed them. It was quite something to hear 'Oh Come, All Ye faithful' sung by an empty helmet that only knew half the words. Several times, Filch the caretaker had to extract Peeves from inside the armour, where he had taken to hiding, filling in the gaps in the songs with lyrics of his own invention, all of which were very rude.

And still Harry hadn't asked Cho to the ball. He and Ron were getting very nervous now, though as Harry pointed out, Ron would look much less stupid than he would without a partner; Harry was supposed to be starting the dancing with the other champions.

'I suppose there's always Moaning Myrtle,' he said gloomily, referring to the ghost who haunted the girls' toilets on the second floor.

'Harry – we've just got to grit our teeth and do it,' said Ron on Friday morning, in a tone that suggested they were planning the storming of an impregnable fortress. 'When we get back to the common room tonight, we'll both have partners – agreed?'

'Er ... OK,' said Harry.

## 第22章 意外的挑战

"唉——不说你也知道,"罗恩耸了耸肩膀,说道,"我情愿一个人去——也不愿找,比如说吧,爱洛伊丝·米德根。"

"最近她的粉刺好多了——而且她非常友善!"

"她的鼻子有点儿歪。"罗恩说。

"哦,明白了,"赫敏被激怒了,说道,"原来,从根本上,你是想邀请一个愿意接受你的最漂亮的姑娘,即便她是彻头彻尾的大坏蛋?"

"嗯——是啊,说得基本正确。"罗恩说。

"我要去睡觉了。"赫敏没好气地说,然后没再说一个字便快步朝女生宿舍的楼梯走去。

霍格沃茨的师生不断表现出想给布斯巴顿和德姆斯特朗的客人留下深刻印象的欲望,似乎决心在这个圣诞节展示出城堡的最佳风貌。学校里张灯结彩地布置起来,哈利发现他进校以来从没见过这么漂亮的装饰。大理石楼梯的扶手上挂满了永远不化的冰柱,礼堂里惯常摆放的那十二棵圣诞树上,装饰着各种各样的小玩意儿,从闪闪发亮的冬青果,到不停鸣叫的活的金色猫头鹰。那些盔甲都被施了魔法,只要有人经过,就会演唱圣诞颂歌。听一顶空头盔唱"哦,来吧,你们这些虔诚的人",真是特别滑稽。盔甲只知道一半的歌词,有好几次管理员费尔奇不得不把皮皮鬼从盔甲里拽出来,因为皮皮鬼躲在里面,盔甲唱不下去时,他就自己编一些歌词填进去,都是些非常粗野难听的话。

然而,哈利还没有邀请秋·张参加舞会。他和罗恩现在非常着急了,尽管哈利指出,罗恩即使没有舞伴,也不会像他那样出丑。哈利是要和其他勇士一起跳第一支舞的啊。

"我想哭泣的桃金娘总是跑不了的。"他愁闷地说,指的是躲在三楼女生盥洗室里的那个幽灵。

"哈利——我们必须咬咬牙豁出去了。"星期五的时候,罗恩说道,听他的口气就好像他们正在计划攻破一座固若金汤的要塞,"今晚我们回到公共休息室时,必须都找到舞伴——说定了?"

"呃……好吧。"哈利说。

## CHAPTER TWENTY-TWO  The Unexpected Task

But every time he glimpsed Cho that day – during break, and then lunchtime, and once on the way to History of Magic – she was surrounded by friends. Didn't she *ever* go anywhere alone? Could he perhaps ambush her as she was going into a bathroom? But no – she even seemed to go there with an escort of four or five girls. Yet if he didn't do it soon, she was bound to have been asked by somebody else.

He found it hard to concentrate in Snape's Antidote test, and consequently forgot to add the key ingredient – a bezoar – meaning that he received bottom marks. He didn't care though; he was too busy screwing up his courage for what he was about to do. When the bell rang, he grabbed his bag, and hurried to the dungeon door.

'I'll meet you at dinner,' he said to Ron and Hermione, and he dashed off upstairs.

He'd just have to ask Cho for a private word, that was all ... he hurried off through the packed corridors looking for her, and (rather sooner than he had expected) he found her, emerging from a Defence Against the Dark Arts lesson.

'Er – Cho? Could I have a word with you?'

Giggling should be made illegal, Harry thought furiously, as all the girls around Cho started doing it. She didn't, though. She said, 'OK', and followed him out of earshot of her classmates.

Harry turned to look at her and his stomach gave a weird lurch as though he had missed a step going downstairs.

'Er,' he said.

He couldn't ask her. He couldn't. But he had to. Cho stood there looking puzzled, watching him.

The words came out before Harry had quite got his tongue around them.

'Wangoballwime?'

'Sorry?' said Cho.

'D'you – d'you want to go to the ball with me?' said Harry. Why did he have to go red now? *Why?*

'Oh!' said Cho, and she went red, too. 'Oh, Harry, I'm really sorry,' and she looked it, too. 'I've already said I'll go with someone else.'

'Oh,' said Harry.

## 第22章 意外的挑战

可是，那天他几次看见秋·张——课间休息时，午饭时，还有一次是在去上魔法史课的路上——她身边总是围着好多朋友。难道她从不独自去什么地方吗？也许可以在她去盥洗室时打她的埋伏？不行——她即使是去盥洗室，身边也跟着四五个女生。可是如果再不采取行动，她肯定被别人邀请去了。

在斯内普魔药课上做解药测验时，哈利觉得很难集中思想，结果忘记加入一种主要成分——粪石，这就意味着他只能得最低分了。不过他不在乎。他正忙着鼓起勇气，准备采取果断行动。下课铃一响，他就抓起书包，朝地下教室的门口冲去。

"晚饭桌上见。"他对罗恩和赫敏说，一边冲上楼去。

他只要单独问秋·张一句话，就这么简单……他匆匆穿过拥挤的走廊，寻找她的身影，很快（他没想到会这么快）他就看见了她。她正从黑魔法防御术课的教室里走出来。

"呃——秋·张？我能跟你说一句话吗？"

法律应该规定不许咯咯笑，哈利气愤地想，因为秋·张周围的女生都咯咯地笑了起来。还好，秋·张没有笑。她说了声"好吧"，便跟着哈利走到她的同班同学们听不见的地方。

哈利转身望着她，内心突然出现了一阵古怪的痉挛，就好像他下楼时踏空了一级台阶。

"呃。"他支吾着。

他不能问她。他不能。但他必须问。秋·张站在那里，带着困惑的神情望着他。

那句话从哈利嘴里脱口而出，说得语无伦次，字音都没来得及咬准。

"做伴跟我行吗？"

"对不起，你说什么？"秋·张说。

"你——你愿不愿意跟我一起去参加舞会？"哈利问。他为什么要脸红呢？为什么？

"噢！"秋·张说——她的脸也红了，"唉，哈利，我真的很抱歉，"她面带歉意地说，"我已经说好要跟另外一个人去了。"

"噢。"哈利说。

## CHAPTER TWENTY-TWO    The Unexpected Task

It was odd; a moment before, his insides had been writhing like snakes, but suddenly he didn't seem to have any insides at all.

'Oh, OK,' he said, 'no problem.'

'I'm really sorry,' she said again.

'That's OK,' said Harry.

They stood there looking at each other, and then Cho said, 'Well –'

'Yeah,' said Harry.

'Well, bye,' said Cho, still very red. She walked away.

Harry called after her, before he could stop himself.

'Who're you going with?'

'Oh – Cedric,' she said. 'Cedric Diggory.'

'Oh, right,' said Harry.

His insides had come back again. It felt as though they had been filled with lead in their absence.

Completely forgetting about dinner, he walked slowly back up to Gryffindor Tower, Cho's voice echoing in his ears with every step he took. '*Cedric – Cedric Diggory.*' He had been starting to quite like Cedric – prepared to overlook the fact that he had once beaten him at Quidditch, and was handsome, and popular, and nearly everyone's favourite champion. Now he suddenly realised that Cedric was in fact a useless pretty-boy who didn't have enough brains to fill an eggcup.

'Fairy lights,' he said dully to the Fat Lady – the password had been changed the previous day.

'Yes, indeed, dear!' she trilled, straightening her new tinsel hairband as she swung forwards to admit him.

Entering the common room, Harry looked around, and to his surprise he saw Ron sitting ashen faced in a distant corner. Ginny was sitting with him, talking to him in what seemed to be a low, soothing voice.

'What's up, Ron?' said Harry, joining them.

Ron looked up at Harry, a sort of blind horror in his face.

'Why did I do it?' he said wildly. 'I don't know what made me do it!'

'What?' said Harry.

## 第22章 意外的挑战

这感觉真是古怪：一分钟前，他觉得内脏像蛇一般蠕动不停，现在突然之间，他觉得自己仿佛根本没有内脏了。

"噢，好吧，"他说，"没关系。"

"我真的很抱歉。"秋·张又说了一遍。

"没关系。"哈利说。

他们站在那里互相对视，然后秋·张说："就这样吧——"

"行。"哈利说。

"好吧，再见了。"秋·张说，脸仍然很红。她转身离开了。

哈利从后面叫住了她，他没来得及阻止自己这么做。

"你和谁一起去？"

"噢——塞德里克，"她说，"塞德里克·迪戈里。"

"噢，好吧。"哈利说。

他的内脏又回来了。他觉得它们刚才被人拿去灌满了铅。

哈利把晚饭忘得一干二净。他慢慢走回楼上的格兰芬多公共休息室，每走一步，耳边就回响起秋·张的声音："塞德里克——塞德里克·迪戈里。"他本来已经有些喜欢塞德里克了——已经准备原谅那些事情，如塞德里克曾在魁地奇比赛中打败过他。塞德里克长得英俊，人缘好，是几乎人人都喜爱的勇士。现在哈利突然意识到，塞德里克实际上是一个没用的小白脸，他那点脑子还不够装满一只鸡蛋壳呢。

"仙境之光。"他干巴巴地对胖夫人说——口令是前一天改的。

"对了，对了，亲爱的！"胖夫人带着颤音说，捋了捋她那新系上的金银丝发带，一边向前转开，让他进去。

进了公共休息室，哈利环顾四周，惊奇地看见罗恩脸色灰白地坐在远处一个角落里。金妮坐在他身边，用很低的声音跟他说话，像是在安慰他。

"怎么啦，罗恩？"哈利问道，向他们走去。

罗恩抬头望着哈利，脸上带有一种惊魂未定的神情。

"我干吗要那么做呢？"他迷乱地说，"我不知道自己怎么会做出那种事！"

"什么？"哈利说。

## CHAPTER TWENTY-TWO    The Unexpected Task

'He – er – just asked Fleur Delacour to go to the ball with him,' said Ginny. She looked as though she was fighting back a smile, but she kept patting Ron's arm sympathetically.

'You *what?*' said Harry.

'I don't know what made me do it!' Ron gasped again. 'What was I playing at? There were people – all around – I've gone mad – everyone watching! I was just walking past her in the Entrance Hall – she was standing there talking to Diggory – and it sort of came over me – and I asked her!'

Ron moaned and put his face in his hands. He kept talking, though the words were barely distinguishable. 'She looked at me like I was a sea slug or something. Didn't even answer. And then – I dunno – I just sort of came to my senses and ran for it.'

'She's part Veela,' said Harry. 'You were right – her grandmother was one. It wasn't your fault, I bet you just walked past when she was turning on the old charm for Diggory and got a blast of it – but she was wasting her time. He's going with Cho Chang.'

Ron looked up.

'I asked her to go with me just now,' Harry said dully, 'and she told me.'

Ginny had suddenly stopped smiling.

'This is mad,' said Ron, 'we're the only ones left who haven't got anyone – well, except Neville. Hey – guess who he asked? *Hermione!*'

'*What?*' said Harry, completely distracted by this startling news.

'Yeah, I know!' said Ron, some of the colour coming back into his face as he started to laugh. 'He told me after Potions! Said she's always been really nice, helping him out with work and stuff – but she told him she was already going with someone. Ha! As if! She just didn't want to go with Neville ... I mean, who would?'

'Don't!' said Ginny, annoyed. 'Don't laugh –'

Just then Hermione climbed in through the portrait hole.

'Why weren't you two at dinner?' she said, coming over to join them.

'Because – oh, shut up laughing, you two – because they've both just been turned down by girls they asked to the ball!' said Ginny.

That shut Harry and Ron up.

'Thanks a bunch, Ginny,' said Ron sourly.

## 第22章 意外的挑战

"他——呃——他刚才邀请芙蓉·德拉库尔和他一起去参加舞会。"金妮说。她似乎正拼命忍住笑,但仍然同情地拍着罗恩的胳膊。

"你做了什么?"哈利问。

"我不知道我怎么会做出这种事!"罗恩喘着粗气又说,"我在开什么玩笑呢?那里都是人——挤满了人——我真是昏了头——大家都在看着!我走过门厅时遇见了她——她站在那里正和迪戈里说话——我突然就控制不住自己——就上前问了她!"

罗恩呻吟着,用手捂住了脸。他还在不停地说,但他的话只能勉强听得清楚了。"她望着我,就好像我是一条海参什么的。根本不屑于回答。然后——我也不知道——我就突然回过神来,赶紧跑了。"

"她有部分媚娃血统,"哈利说,"你原先说得对——她奶奶就是媚娃。这不是你的错,我敢说她当时正在对迪戈里施魔法,你正巧经过,就被击中了——不过她这次是白费工夫了。迪戈里和秋·张一起去。"

罗恩抬起头来。

"我刚才请秋·张和我一起去,"哈利闷闷地说,"她就告诉了我。"

金妮突然不笑了。

"简直太荒唐了,"罗恩说,"只剩下我们俩没有舞伴——噢,除了纳威。对了——你猜他邀请谁了?赫敏!"

"什么?"哈利说,他完全被这个令人惊诧的消息吸引住了。

"是吧,想不到吧!"罗恩说着笑了起来,脸上又恢复了一些血色,"纳威在魔药课后告诉我的!他说她一直这么善良,帮他做功课什么的——但赫敏对他说,她已经答应别人了。哈!说得跟真的似的!她只是不想跟纳威去罢了……我的意思是,谁会请她?"

"不许笑!"金妮恼怒地说,"不许笑——"

就在这时,赫敏从肖像后的洞口爬了进来。

"你们俩为什么不去吃晚饭?"她说,走过来跟他们坐在一起。

"因为——你们两个别笑了——因为他们俩邀请姑娘参加舞会,都遭到了拒绝!"金妮说。

哈利和罗恩立刻不吭气了。

"多谢你了,金妮。"罗恩阴阳怪气地说。

## CHAPTER TWENTY-TWO   The Unexpected Task

'All the good-looking ones taken, Ron?' said Hermione loftily. 'Eloise Midgen starting to look quite pretty now, is she? Well, I'm sure you'll find someone *somewhere* who'll have you.'

But Ron was staring at Hermione as though suddenly seeing her in a whole new light. 'Hermione, Neville's right – you *are* a girl ...'

'Oh, well spotted,' she said acidly.

'Well – you can come with one of us!'

'No, I can't,' snapped Hermione.

'Oh, come on,' he said impatiently, 'we need partners, we're going to look really stupid if we haven't got any, everyone else has ...'

'I can't come with you,' said Hermione, now blushing, 'because I'm already going with someone.'

'No, you're not!' said Ron. 'You just said that to get rid of Neville!'

'Oh, *did* I?' said Hermione, and her eyes flashed dangerously. 'Just because it's taken *you* three years to notice, Ron, doesn't mean no one *else* has spotted I'm a girl!'

Ron stared at her. Then he grinned again.

'OK, OK, we know you're a girl,' he said. 'That do? Will you come now?'

'I've already told you!' Hermione said, very angrily. 'I'm going with someone else!'

And she stormed off towards the girls' dormitories again.

'She's lying,' said Ron flatly, watching her go.

'She's not,' said Ginny quietly.

'Who is it, then?' said Ron sharply.

'I'm not telling you, it's her business,' said Ginny.

'Right,' said Ron, who looked extremely put out, 'this is getting stupid. Ginny, *you* can go with Harry, and I'll just –'

'I can't,' said Ginny, and she went scarlet too. 'I'm going with – with Neville. He asked me when Hermione said no, and I thought ... well ... I'm not going to be able to go otherwise, I'm not in fourth year.' She looked extremely miserable. 'I think I'll go and have dinner,' she said, and she got up

## 第22章 意外的挑战

"漂亮姑娘都被人挑走了,是吗,罗恩?"赫敏高傲地说,"爱洛伊丝·米德根也开始变得很漂亮了,是吗?没关系,我相信你总会在什么地方找到一个愿意接受你的人的。"

罗恩瞪眼望着赫敏,似乎突然用全新的目光审视着她。"赫敏,纳威是对的——你是个姑娘……"

"噢,观察得很敏锐嘛。"赫敏尖刻地说。

"那么——你可以在我们俩中间挑一个!"

"不行,我不能。"赫敏断然拒绝。

"哦,快点儿吧,"罗恩不耐烦地说,"我们需要舞伴,如果别人都有,就我们没有,就显得太没面子了……"

"我不能跟你们一起去,"赫敏说,她的脸红了,"因为我已经答应别人了。"

"不会的,你没有!"罗恩说,"你那么说只是为了摆脱纳威!"

"哦,是吗?"赫敏说,眼里放出吓人的光,"你花了三年时间才发现我是个姑娘,罗恩,这并不意味着就没有别人注意到这一点!"

罗恩呆呆地望着她,接着,他又咧开嘴笑了。

"好了,好了,我们知道你是个姑娘,"他说,"行了吗?你可以答应了吧?"

"我已经告诉过你们了!"赫敏非常气愤地说,"我已经答应另外的人了!"

说完,她气冲冲地朝女生宿舍奔去。

"她在撒谎。"罗恩望着她的背影,毫无表情地说。

"她没有。"金妮小声说。

"哦,那个人是谁?"罗恩厉声问道。

"我不能告诉你,那是她的私事。"金妮说。

"好吧,"罗恩说,他显得烦躁极了,"真是越来越荒唐了。金妮,你可以跟哈利一起去,我就——"

"我不能,"金妮说,她的脸也涨得通红,"我已经答应了——答应了纳威。赫敏拒绝他以后,他就邀请了我,我想……反正……反正,如果不答应他,我也去不成,我还没上四年级呢。"她显得非常沮丧,"我

## CHAPTER TWENTY-TWO  The Unexpected Task

and walked off to the portrait hole, her head bowed.

Ron goggled at Harry.

'What's got into them?' he demanded.

But Harry had just seen Parvati and Lavender come in through the portrait hole. The time had come for drastic action.

'Wait here,' he said to Ron, and he stood up, walked straight up to Parvati and said, 'Parvati? Will you go to the ball with me?'

Parvati went into a fit of giggles. Harry waited for them to subside, his fingers crossed in the pocket of his robes.

'Yes, all right, then,' she said finally, blushing furiously.

'Thanks,' said Harry, in relief. 'Lavender – will you go with Ron?'

'She's going with Seamus,' said Parvati, and the pair of them giggled harder than ever.

Harry sighed.

'Can't you think of anyone who'd go with Ron?' he said, lowering his voice so that Ron wouldn't hear.

'What about Hermione Granger?' said Parvati.

'She's going with someone else.'

Parvati looked astonished.

'Ooooh – *who?*' she said keenly.

Harry shrugged. 'No idea,' he said. 'So what about Ron?'

'Well ...' said Parvati slowly, 'I suppose my sister might ... Padma, you know ... in Ravenclaw. I'll ask her if you like.'

'Yeah, that would be great,' said Harry. 'Let me know, will you?'

And he went back over to Ron, feeling that this ball was a lot more trouble than it was worth, and hoping very much that Padma Patil's nose was dead centre.

## 第22章 意外的挑战

想我得去吃晚饭了。"说着,她站起来,低垂着脑袋向肖像后的洞口走去。

罗恩瞪大眼睛望着哈利。

"她们都出了什么毛病?"他问。

哈利正巧看见帕瓦蒂和拉文德从肖像后的洞口进来。这次必须一不做二不休了。

"你等在这里,"他对罗恩说,然后他站起来,径直朝帕瓦蒂走去,说道,"帕瓦蒂?你愿意跟我一起去参加舞会吗?"

帕瓦蒂发出一串咯咯的笑声。哈利等着她的笑声过去,他的手指在长袍的口袋里交叉着。

"行,好吧。"帕瓦蒂终于说道,脸红得像要滴出血来。

"谢谢。"哈利说,总算松了口气,"拉文德——你愿意跟罗恩一起去吗?"

"她已经答应西莫了。"帕瓦蒂说,她们俩笑得更厉害了。

哈利叹了口气。

"你们能不能想一想,有谁能跟罗恩一起去呢?"他说,压低了声音,不让罗恩听见。

"赫敏·格兰杰怎么样?"帕瓦蒂说。

"她已经答应了别人。"

帕瓦蒂显得非常吃惊。

"哦——谁?"她急切地问。

哈利耸了耸肩膀。"不知道。"他说,"那么罗恩怎么办?"

"让我想想……"帕瓦蒂慢悠悠地说,"我妹妹大概可以……她叫帕德玛,你知道……在拉文克劳。如果你们愿意,我就去问问她。"

"行,那太好了,"哈利说,"有消息就告诉我们,行吗?"

他回到罗恩身边,觉得这场舞会实在太麻烦了,真有些划不来。他满心希望帕德玛·佩蒂尔的鼻子长得周正些。

## CHAPTER TWENTY-THREE

# The Yule Ball

Despite the very heavy load of homework that the fourth-years had been given for the holidays, Harry was in no mood to work when term ended, and spent the week leading up to Christmas enjoying himself as fully as possible along with everyone else. Gryffindor Tower was hardly less crowded now than during term-time; it seemed to have shrunk slightly, too, as its inhabitants were being so much rowdier than usual. Fred and George had had a great success with their Canary Creams, and for the first couple of days of the holidays, people kept bursting into feather all over the place. Before long, however, all the Gryffindors had learnt to treat food anybody else offered them with extreme caution, in case it had a Canary Cream concealed in the centre, and George confided to Harry that he and Fred were now working on developing something else. Harry made a mental note never to accept so much as a crisp from Fred and George in future. He still hadn't forgotten Dudley and the Ton-Tongue Toffee.

Snow was falling thickly upon the castle and its grounds now. The pale blue Beauxbatons carriage looked like a large, chilly, frosted pumpkin next to the iced gingerbread house that was Hagrid's cabin, while the Durmstrang ship's portholes were glazed with ice, the rigging white with frost. The house-elves down in the kitchen were outdoing themselves with a series of rich, warming stews and savoury puddings, and only Fleur Delacour seemed to be able to find anything to complain about.

'It is too 'eavy, all zis 'Ogwarts food,' they heard her saying grumpily, as they left the Great Hall behind her one evening (Ron skulking behind Harry, keen not to be spotted by Fleur). 'I will not fit into my dress robes!'

'Oooh, there's a tragedy,' said Hermione snappily, as Fleur went out into the Entrance Hall. 'She really thinks a lot of herself, that one, doesn't she?'

## 第23章

## 圣诞舞会

老师们给四年级学生假期里布置了一大堆家庭作业,但是学期结束后,哈利根本没有心思做功课。在圣诞节前的那个星期,他和大家一起尽情玩耍。格兰芬多塔楼里的人几乎和放假前一样多,而且塔楼似乎缩小了,因为住在里面的人都比平时吵闹多了。弗雷德和乔治的金丝雀饼干销路很好,在刚放假的一两天,动不动就有人忽的一下,全身长出了羽毛。不过很快格兰芬多的同学们就吸取了教训,对别人递过来的食物非常警惕了,以免中间藏着一块金丝雀饼干。乔治很信任地告诉哈利,他和弗雷德正在研制另一种新产品。哈利告诫自己,以后千万不能接受弗雷德和乔治递过来的任何东西,哪怕是一个土豆片。他仍然没有忘记达力和肥舌太妃糖的事。

大雪纷纷飘落在城堡和场地上。布斯巴顿那辆浅蓝色的马车看上去像冬天里一只挂霜的大南瓜,旁边那个洒了糖霜的姜饼小房子便是海格的小屋;德姆斯特朗大船的船舷上结了一层冰,变得光滑透亮,帆索上也染了一层白霜。下面厨房里的家养小精灵忙得不亦乐乎,准备了多种口味的热腾腾的炖菜和甜美的布丁,只有芙蓉·德拉库尔能找到借口抱怨几句。

"霍格沃茨的食物都太油腻了,"一天晚上,他们离开礼堂时(罗恩躲在哈利身后,生怕被芙蓉看见),听见芙蓉皱着眉头这么说,"我的礼服长袍都要穿不下了!"

"哦,那可太悲惨了。"赫敏看着芙蓉走出礼堂进入门厅,毫不客气地说,"她自我感觉真的很好,是不是?"

## CHAPTER TWENTY-THREE  The Yule Ball

'Hermione – who are you going to the ball with?' said Ron.

He kept springing this question on her, hoping to startle her into a response by asking it when she least expected it. However, Hermione merely frowned and said, 'I'm not telling you, you'll just make fun of me.'

'You're joking, Weasley?' said Malfoy, behind them. 'You're not telling me someone's asked *that* to the ball? Not the long-molared Mudblood?'

Harry and Ron both whipped around, but Hermione said loudly, waving to somebody over Malfoy's shoulder, 'Hello, Professor Moody!'

Malfoy went pale and jumped backwards, looking wildly around for Moody, but he was still up at the staff table, finishing his stew.

'Twitchy little ferret, aren't you, Malfoy?' said Hermione scathingly, and she, Harry and Ron went up the marble staircase laughing heartily.

'Hermione,' said Ron, looking sideways at her, suddenly frowning, 'your teeth ...'

'What about them?' she said.

'Well, they're different ... I've just noticed ...'

'Of course they are – did you expect me to keep those fangs Malfoy gave me?'

'No, I mean, they're different to how they were before he put that hex on you ... they're all ... straight and – and normal-sized.'

Hermione suddenly smiled very mischievously, and Harry noticed it too: it was a very different smile to the one he remembered.

'Well ... when I went up to Madam Pomfrey to get them shrunk, she held up a mirror, and told me to stop her when they were back to how they normally were,' she said. 'And I just ... let her carry on a bit.' She smiled even more widely. 'Mum and Dad won't be too pleased. I've been trying to persuade them to let me shrink them for ages, but they wanted me to carry on with my brace. You know, they're dentists, they just don't think teeth and magic should – look! Pigwidgeon's back!'

Ron's tiny owl was twittering madly on the top of the icicle-laden banisters, a scroll of parchment tied to his leg. People passing him were pointing and laughing, and a group of third-year girls paused and said, 'Oh, look at the weeny owl! Isn't he *cute*?'

## 第23章 圣诞舞会

"赫敏——你要跟谁一起去参加舞会？"罗恩问。

他总是这样出其不意地向赫敏提出这个问题，指望她在最没有防备的时候，一惊之下说出实话。可是赫敏只是皱了皱眉头，说道："我不告诉你，你会取笑我的。"

"你在开玩笑吧，韦斯莱！"他们身后突然响起马尔福的声音，"怎么，居然有人邀请那家伙去参加舞会？那个大板牙泥巴种？"

哈利和罗恩猛地转过身，赫敏却朝马尔福身后的什么人挥手致意，大声地说："你好，穆迪教授！"

马尔福的脸唰地白了，往后跳了一步，慌里慌张地四下张望，寻找穆迪，却见穆迪还坐在教工桌子旁，吃他的那一份炖菜呢。

"你是个浑身抽搐的小白鼬，是不是，马尔福？"赫敏尖刻地说完，便和哈利、罗恩走上大理石楼梯，一边开心地放声大笑。

"赫敏，"罗恩说，侧过脸望着她，突然皱起了眉头，"你的牙齿……"

"怎么啦？"赫敏说。

"我的天，它们不一样了……我刚注意到……"

"它们当然不一样了——怎么，你指望我一直留着马尔福给我的那些大长牙吗？"

"不对，我的意思是，它们跟马尔福给你施那个魔法前的样子也不一样……它们都……整整齐齐的，而且——而且大小也正常了。"

赫敏突然非常调皮地笑了，于是哈利也注意到：赫敏的笑容确实和他记忆中的大不一样。

"是这样的……我去找庞弗雷女士缩小那些中了魔法的长牙时，她举着一面镜子对我说，当牙齿恢复到以前的正常状态时就叫停。"赫敏说，"我就……让她做过头了一点儿。"她笑得更开心了，"爸爸妈妈不会高兴的。好多年来，我一直劝说他们让我把牙齿缩小，但他们希望我坚持戴那套钢丝矫齿架。你们知道，他们都是牙医，认为牙齿和魔法不应该——快看！小猪回来了！"

罗恩的小猫头鹰在挂满冰柱的栏杆顶上疯狂地扑扇翅膀，它的腿上系着一卷羊皮纸。路过的人们都指着它哈哈大笑，一群三年级女生停下脚步，说："哦，快看那只小不点儿猫头鹰！它多么可爱啊！"

## CHAPTER TWENTY-THREE    The Yule Ball

'Stupid little feathery git!' Ron hissed, hurrying up the stairs and snatching Pigwidgeon up. 'You bring letters straight to the addressee! You don't hang around showing off!'

Pigwidgeon hooted happily, his head protruding over Ron's fist. The third-year girls all looked very shocked.

'Clear off!' Ron snapped at them, waving the fist holding Pigwidgeon, who hooted more happily than ever as he soared through the air. 'Here – take it, Harry,' Ron added in an undertone, as the third-year girls scuttled away looking scandalised. He pulled Sirius' reply off Pigwidgeon's leg, Harry pocketed it, and they hurried back to Gryffindor Tower to read it.

Everyone in the common room was much too busy letting off more holiday steam to observe what anyone else was up to. Harry, Ron and Hermione sat apart from everyone else by a dark window that was gradually filling up with snow, and Harry read out:

> *Dear Harry,*
>     *Congratulations on getting past the Horntail, whoever put your name in that Goblet shouldn't be feeling too happy right now! I was going to suggest a Conjunctivitis curse, as a dragon's eyes are its weakest point –*

'That's what Krum did!' Hermione whispered.

> *– but your way was better, I'm impressed.*
>     *Don't get complacent, though, Harry. You've only done one task; whoever put you in for the Tournament's got plenty more opportunity if they're trying to hurt you. Keep your eyes open – particularly when the person we discussed is around – and concentrate on keeping yourself out of trouble.*
>     *Keep in touch, I still want to hear about anything unusual.*
>     *Sirius*

'He sounds exactly like Moody,' said Harry quietly, tucking the letter away again inside his robes, '"Constant vigilance!" You'd think I walk around with

## 第23章 圣诞舞会

"这只小笨鸟！"罗恩咬牙切齿地说，三步并作两步赶上楼去，一把抓住小猪，"你应该把信送给收件人！不能在这里炫耀！"

小猪高兴地叫着，脑袋从罗恩的拳头上伸出来。那些三年级女生似乎都吓坏了。

"快走开！"罗恩恶狠狠地对她们说，一边挥舞那只捏着小猪的拳头。小猪扑扇着翅膀，挣扎着朝空中飞去，叫得比以前更欢快了。罗恩从小猪腿上扯下小天狼星的回信。"给——拿去吧，哈利。"罗恩压低声音说，那些三年级女生正在散去，一个个都显得很气愤。哈利把信塞进口袋，然后三个人匆匆赶向格兰芬多塔楼去看信。

公共休息室里的每个人都忙着释放假期里多余的精力，根本顾不上观察别人在做什么。哈利、罗恩和赫敏避开众人，坐在一扇正被大雪慢慢覆盖的昏暗的窗户旁，哈利出声地念道：

亲爱的哈利：

　　祝贺你成功闯过了树蜂。那个把你名字投进火焰杯的人不管是谁，现在心里都会感到很不是滋味了！我本来想建议你使用一种"眼疾咒"，因为眼睛是龙最薄弱的地方——

"克鲁姆就是这样做的！"赫敏低声说。

——但你的办法更妙，我十分欣赏。

不过，千万不要沾沾自喜，哈利。你只完成了一个项目。迫使你参加三强争霸赛的人不管是谁，他要想置你于死地还有很多机会。提高警惕——特别是当我们上次谈到的那个人在场的时候——随时保持警醒，使自己避免一切麻烦。

保持联系，我仍然希望你一有异常情况就写信告诉我。

小天狼星

"他说话的口气和穆迪一模一样，"哈利小声说，一边把信重新塞进长袍里面，"'随时保持警醒！'就好像我整天闭着眼睛走路，总往

## CHAPTER TWENTY-THREE  The Yule Ball

my eyes shut, banging off the walls ...'

'But he's right, Harry,' said Hermione, 'you *have* still got two tasks to do. You really ought to have a look at that egg, you know, and start working out what it means ...'

'Hermione, he's got ages!' snapped Ron. 'Want a game of chess, Harry?'

'Yeah, OK,' said Harry. Then, spotting the look on Hermione's face, he said, 'Come on, how'm I supposed to concentrate with all this noise going on? I won't even be able to hear the egg over this lot.'

'Oh, I suppose not,' she sighed, and she sat down to watch their chess match, which culminated in an exciting checkmate of Ron's, involving a couple of recklessly brave pawns and a very violent bishop.

Harry awoke very suddenly on Christmas Day. Wondering what had caused his abrupt return to consciousness, he opened his eyes, and saw something with very large, round, green eyes staring back at him in the darkness, so close they were almost nose to nose.

'*Dobby!*' Harry yelled, scrambling away from the elf so fast he almost fell out of bed. 'Don't *do* that!'

'Dobby is sorry, sir!' squeaked Dobby anxiously, jumping backwards with his long fingers over his mouth. 'Dobby is only wanting to wish Harry Potter "Merry Christmas" and bring him a present, sir! Harry Potter did say Dobby could come and see him sometimes, sir!'

'It's OK,' said Harry, still breathing rather faster than usual, while his heart rate returned to normal. 'Just – just prod me or something in future, all right, don't bend over me like that ...'

Harry pulled back the hangings around his four-poster, took his glasses from his bedside table and put them on. His yell had awoken Ron, Seamus, Dean and Neville. All of them were peering through the gaps in their own hangings, heavy eyed and tousle haired.

'Someone attacking you, Harry?' Seamus asked sleepily.

'No, it's just Dobby,' Harry muttered. 'Go back to sleep.'

'Nah ... presents!' said Seamus, spotting the large pile at the foot of his bed. Ron, Dean and Neville decided that now they were awake they might as well get down to some present-opening, too. Harry turned back to Dobby, who was now standing nervously next to Harry's bed, still looking worried that he had upset Harry. There was a Christmas bauble tied to the loop on top of his tea-cosy.

## 第23章 圣诞舞会

墙上撞似的……"

"可是他说得对啊，哈利，"赫敏说，"你还有两个项目要完成呢。你真的应该看看那只金蛋，琢磨琢磨它到底是什么意思了……"

"赫敏，时间还早着呢！"罗恩把她驳了回去，"想下盘棋吗，哈利？"

"行，没问题。"哈利说，他转眼看见赫敏脸上的神情，赶紧又说，"好了好了，这里乱成这样，我怎么可能集中思想呢？在这些噪音中，我连金蛋的叫声都听不见。"

"唉，你说得也对。"赫敏叹了口气，坐下来看他们下棋。最后，罗恩用一对横冲直撞的兵和一个心狠手辣的主教将死了哈利，场面惊心动魄。

圣诞节那天早晨，哈利猛地惊醒。他一边睁开眼睛，一边猜想是什么使自己突然惊醒了。他看见一个长着两只绿色大圆眼睛的东西，正在黑暗中瞅着他，那东西离他很近很近，几乎鼻尖碰鼻尖。

"多比！"哈利喊道，一边急忙从小精灵面前挪开，慌乱中差点儿从床上摔下去，"不要这样！"

"多比很抱歉，先生！"多比惊慌地尖叫着，向后一跳，用细长的手指捂住嘴巴，"多比只想祝哈利·波特圣诞快乐，还给他带来一件礼物，先生！哈利·波特说过的，多比可以偶尔过来看他，先生！"

"行了，没关系。"哈利说，他呼吸仍比平时急促，心跳倒恢复了正常，"以后——以后只要捅捅我就行了，好不好，不要那样弯腰盯着我……"

哈利拉开四柱床的帷帐，从床边的桌子上拿起眼镜戴好。他的喊声把罗恩、西莫、迪安和纳威都惊醒了。他们都从自己的帷帐缝中朝外望着，一个个睡眼惺忪，头发乱蓬蓬的。

"有人偷袭你吗，哈利？"西莫睡意未消地问。

"没有，是多比，"哈利小声说，"接着睡吧。"

"不睡了……礼物！"西莫看见他床尾的一大堆东西，说道。罗恩、迪安和纳威也认为既然已经醒了，就下床把礼物拆开看看吧。哈利转过脸来望着多比，只见多比局促不安地站在他的床边，仍然为惊扰了他而诚惶诚恐。他那只茶壶保暖套顶端的环扣里系着一个圣诞装饰球。

## CHAPTER TWENTY-THREE  The Yule Ball

'Can Dobby give Harry Potter his present?' he squeaked tentatively.

''Course you can,' said Harry. 'Er ... I've got something for you, too.'

It was a lie; he hadn't bought anything for Dobby at all, but he quickly opened his trunk, and pulled out a particularly knobbly rolled-up pair of socks. They were his oldest and foulest, mustard yellow, and had once belonged to Uncle Vernon. The reason they were extra knobbly was that Harry had been using them to cushion his Sneakoscope for over a year now. He pulled out the Sneakoscope and handed the socks to Dobby, saying, 'Sorry, I forgot to wrap them ...'

But Dobby was utterly delighted.

'Socks are Dobby's favourite, favourite clothes, sir!' he said, ripping off his odd ones and pulling on Uncle Vernon's. 'I has seven now, sir ... but, sir ...' he said, his eyes widening, having pulled both socks up to their highest extent, so that they reached to the bottom of his shorts, 'they has made a mistake in the shop, Harry Potter, they is giving you two the same!'

'Ah, no, Harry, how come you didn't spot that!' said Ron, grinning over from his own bed, which was now strewn with wrapping paper. 'Tell you what, Dobby – here you go – take these two, and you can mix them up properly. And here's your jumper.'

He threw Dobby a pair of violet socks he had just unwrapped, and the hand-knitted sweater Mrs Weasley had sent.

Dobby looked quite overwhelmed. 'Sir is very kind!' he squeaked, his eyes brimming with tears again, bowing deeply to Ron. 'Dobby knew sir must be a great wizard, for he is Harry Potter's greatest friend, but Dobby did not know that he was also as generous of spirit, as noble, as selfless –'

'They're only socks,' said Ron, who had gone slightly pink around the ears, though looking rather pleased all the same. 'Wow, Harry –' he had just opened Harry's present, a Chudley Cannon hat. 'Cool!' He jammed it onto his head, where it clashed horribly with his hair.

Dobby now handed Harry a small package, which turned out to be – socks.

'Dobby is making them himself, sir!' the elf said happily. 'He is buying the wool out of his wages, sir!'

The left sock was bright red, and had a pattern of broomsticks upon it;

## 第23章 圣诞舞会

"多比可不可以把他的礼物送给哈利·波特？"多比尖声尖气地试探着问道。

"当然可以，"哈利说，"嗯……我也有东西要送给你呢。"

这是说谎，哈利并没有给多比买东西，但他迅速打开箱子，从里面抽出一双疙里疙瘩、卷成一团的袜子。这是他最旧最难看的一双袜子，暗黄色，原先是弗农姨父的。这双袜子之所以这样疙里疙瘩，是因为一年多来哈利一直用它们包裹他的窥镜。现在他掏出窥镜，把袜子递给了多比，说道："对不起，我忘记把它们包起来了……"

多比却高兴得眉飞色舞。

"袜子是多比最喜欢最喜欢的东西，先生！"他说着，脱掉脚上那双不配对的袜子，换上弗农姨父的，"我有七只了，先生……可是先生……"他把两只袜子使劲往上拉，一直拉到他短裤的裤脚，这时突然睁大眼睛，吃惊地说："店里的人弄错了，哈利·波特，他们给了你两只一样的！"

"啊，糟糕，哈利，你怎么没有注意到这一点呢？"罗恩说，他从堆满包装纸的床上朝哈利咧嘴笑着，"喂，多比——这个给你——你拿着这两只袜子，把它们搭配一下混着穿。这是你的毛衣。"

他扔给多比一双紫色的袜子，这是他刚才从礼物包里拆出来的，还有韦斯莱夫人寄来的手编毛衣。多比简直高兴坏了。

"先生太好心了！"他尖叫着说，朝罗恩深深鞠了一躬，眼睛里又充满了泪水，"多比知道先生一定会成为一个伟大的巫师，因为他是哈利·波特最伟大的朋友，但多比没想到先生竟然和哈利·波特一样慷慨，一样高贵，一样无私——"

"只是一双袜子罢了。"罗恩说，他耳朵边微微有些泛红，但还是显得非常高兴。"哇，哈利——"他打开哈利送给他的礼物，是一顶查德里火炮队的帽子，"真酷啊！"他把帽子胡乱套在头上，帽子和他的头发顿时发生了激烈的冲突。

这时，多比递给哈利一个小包裹，里面竟然也是——袜子。

"多比自己织的，先生！"小精灵开心地说，"他用自己的工钱买了毛线，先生！"

左脚的袜子是鲜红色的，上面有飞天扫帚的图案，右脚的则是绿

## CHAPTER TWENTY-THREE  The Yule Ball

the right sock was green, with a pattern of Snitches.

'They're ... they're really ... well, thanks, Dobby,' said Harry, and he pulled them on, causing Dobby's eyes to leak with happiness again.

'Dobby must go now, sir, we is already making Christmas dinner in the kitchens!' said Dobby, and he hurried out of the dormitory, waving goodbye to Ron and the others as he passed.

Harry's other presents were much more satisfactory than Dobby's odd socks – with the obvious exception of the Dursleys', which consisted of a single tissue, an all-time low – Harry supposed they, too, were remembering the Ton-Tongue Toffee. Hermione had given Harry a book called *Quidditch Teams of Britain and Ireland*; Ron, a bulging bag of Dungbombs; Sirius, a handy penknife with attachments to unlock any lock and undo any knot; and Hagrid, a vast box of sweets including all Harry's favourites – Bertie Bott's Every Flavour Beans, Chocolate Frogs, Drooble's Best Blowing Gum and Fizzing Whizzbees. There was also, of course, Mrs Weasley's usual package, including a new jumper (green, with a picture of a dragon on it – Harry supposed Charlie had told her all about the Horntail) and a large quantity of home-made mince pies.

Harry and Ron met up with Hermione in the common room, and they went down to breakfast together. They spent most of the morning in Gryffindor Tower, where everyone was enjoying their presents, then returned to the Great Hall for a magnificent lunch, which included at least a hundred turkeys and Christmas puddings, and large piles of Cribbages Wizarding Crackers.

They went out into the grounds in the afternoon; the snow was untouched except for the deep channels made by the Durmstrang and Beauxbatons students on their way up to the castle. Hermione chose to watch Harry and the Weasleys' snowball fight rather than join in, and at five o'clock said she was going back upstairs to get ready for the ball.

'What, you need three hours?' said Ron, looking at her incredulously, and paying for his lapse in concentration when a large snowball, thrown by George, hit him hard on the side of the head. 'Who're you going with?' he yelled after Hermione, but she just waved, and disappeared up the stone steps into the castle.

There was no Christmas tea today, as the ball included a feast, so at seven o'clock, when it had become hard to aim properly, the others abandoned their

# 第23章 圣诞舞会

色的,上面的图案是金色飞贼。

"真是……真是……太好了,谢谢你,多比。"哈利说着就把袜子穿上了,这使多比又一次高兴得热泪盈眶。

"多比必须走了,先生,我们已经在厨房里准备圣诞宴会了!"多比说完便匆匆离开了宿舍,临出门时朝罗恩和其他人挥手告别。

与多比那双不配对的袜子相比,哈利的另外几件礼物要称心得多——但德思礼家送的除外:只有一张纸巾,创历史最低纪录——哈利猜想他们大概还没有忘记肥舌太妃糖的事。赫敏送给哈利一本书,名叫《不列颠和爱尔兰的魁地奇球队》;罗恩送了一口袋鼓鼓囊囊的粪弹;小天狼星送的是一把轻便削笔刀,上面还附带着能开各种锁、能解各种结的小玩意儿;海格送了一大盒糖果,哈利爱吃的口味应有尽有:比比多味豆、巧克力蛙、吹宝超级泡泡糖、滋滋蜜蜂糖。当然啦,韦斯莱夫人照例每年都寄来一个包裹,里面有一件新毛衣(绿色的,上面是一条火龙——哈利猜想查理已经把树蜂的事原原本本地告诉她了),以及一大堆自制的肉馅饼。

哈利和罗恩在公共休息室里与赫敏碰头,一起下楼去吃早饭。他们几乎整个上午都待在格兰芬多塔楼里,同学们都在美滋滋地欣赏自己收到的礼物。然后他们回到礼堂里享受了一顿丰盛的午餐,包括至少一百只火鸡和一大堆圣诞布丁,还有堆积如山的克里比奇巫师小脆饼干。

下午,他们来到外面的场地上。雪地白皑皑的,几乎没有人踩过,只有德姆斯特朗和布斯巴顿的学生们走向城堡时踏出的一道深深的足迹。赫敏只愿意观看哈利和韦斯莱兄弟打雪仗,自己不肯参加,五点钟的时候,她就说要回楼上为舞会做准备了。

"什么,你需要三个小时?"罗恩不敢相信地望着她问,他这样一分神,就被乔治扔过来的一个大雪球狠狠打中了面颊,"你和谁一起去?"他冲着赫敏的背影喊道,但赫敏只是挥了挥手,就踏着石阶进了城堡。

今天没有圣诞茶点,因为舞会上有宴席。到了七点,天色昏暗下来,不太容易瞄准目标了,他们便放弃了打雪仗,一起返回公共休息室。

## CHAPTER TWENTY-THREE  The Yule Ball

snowball fight and trooped back to the common room. The Fat Lady was sitting in her frame with her friend Violet from downstairs, both of them extremely tipsy, empty boxes of chocolate liqueurs littering the bottom of her picture.

'Lairy fights, that's the one!' she giggled when they gave the password, and she swung forwards to let them inside.

Harry, Ron, Seamus, Dean and Neville changed into their dress robes up in their dormitory, all of them looking very self-conscious, but none as much as Ron, who surveyed himself in the long mirror in the corner with an appalled look on his face. There was just no getting around the fact that his robes looked more like a dress than anything else. In a desperate attempt to make them look more manly, he used a Severing Charm on the ruff and cuffs. It worked fairly well; at least he was now lace-free, although he hadn't done a very neat job, and the edges still looked depressingly frayed as they set off downstairs.

'I still can't work out how you two got the best-looking girls in the year,' muttered Dean.

'Animal magnetism,' said Ron gloomily, pulling stray threads out of his cuffs.

The common room looked strange, full of people wearing different colours instead of the usual mass of black. Parvati was waiting for Harry at the foot of the stairs. She looked very pretty indeed, in robes of shocking pink, with her long dark plait braided with gold, and gold bracelets glimmering at her wrists. Harry was relieved to see that she wasn't giggling.

'You – er – look nice,' he said awkwardly.

'Thanks,' she said. 'Padma's going to meet you in the Entrance Hall,' she added to Ron.

'Right,' said Ron, looking around. 'Where's Hermione?'

Parvati shrugged. 'Shall we go down, then, Harry?'

'OK,' said Harry, wishing he could just stay in the common room. Fred winked at Harry as he passed him on the way out of the portrait hole.

The Entrance Hall was packed with students too, all milling around waiting for eight o'clock, when the doors to the Great Hall would be thrown open. Those people who were meeting partners from different houses were edging through the crowd, trying to find each other. Parvati found her sister Padma and led her over to Harry and Ron.

## 第23章 圣诞舞会

胖夫人和她的朋友——楼下的维奥莱特一起坐在相框里，两个人都晕乎乎醉醺醺的，肖像底部扔着好几个空了的酒心巧克力盒子。

"鲜艳之光，没错，是这样！"她听了他们的口令，咯咯笑着向前转开，让他们进去了。

哈利、罗恩、西莫、迪安和纳威在楼上的宿舍里换上了各自的礼服长袍，一个个都显得局促不安，但谁也没有像罗恩那样沮丧，他在墙角的长镜子前打量着自己，脸上是一副惊恐的表情。他的礼服长袍像一条裙子，这是一个无法回避的事实。为了给礼袍增加一点男子气，他孤注一掷，给那些褶皱和花边念了一道切割咒。还算管用，至少衣服上的花边没有了，但他的活儿干得并不利索，当几个男生动身下楼时，他的领口袖口仍然泛着毛边，真令人泄气。

"我真不明白，你们俩是怎么把全年级最漂亮的姑娘弄到手的。"迪安低声嘟哝着。

"异性相吸嘛。"罗恩闷闷不乐地回答，一边把袖口的线头揪掉。

公共休息室里看上去怪怪的，里面的人们不再是清一色的黑袍，而是穿着五颜六色的礼服长袍。帕瓦蒂在楼梯下面等着哈利。她看上去确实非常漂亮，穿着扎眼的粉红色礼袍，乌黑的秀发用金丝带编成了辫子，手腕上的金手镯闪闪发亮。哈利见她没有发出咯咯的傻笑，不由得松了口气。

"你……呃……很漂亮。"他很不自然地说。

"谢谢。"帕瓦蒂说道，"帕德玛会在门厅里与你碰头。"她又对罗恩说。

"好吧。"罗恩说，一边东张西望，"赫敏在哪儿？"

帕瓦蒂耸了耸肩："我们下去吧，好吗，哈利？"

"好吧。"哈利说，他真希望能够留在公共休息室里。哈利在钻出肖像洞口时碰见了弗雷德，弗雷德冲他调皮地眨眨眼睛。

门厅里也挤满了学生，都在来回打转，等待八点钟的到来，那时礼堂的大门才会敞开。有些人要与其他学院的舞伴碰头，便侧着身子在人群里挤来挤去，寻找对方的身影。帕瓦蒂找到了她的妹妹帕德玛，领着她过来见哈利和罗恩。

## CHAPTER TWENTY-THREE   The Yule Ball

'Hi,' said Padma, who was looking just as pretty as Parvati in robes of bright turquoise. She didn't look too enthusiastic about having Ron as a partner, though; her dark eyes lingered on the frayed neck and sleeves of his dress robes as she looked him up and down.

'Hi,' said Ron, not looking at her, but staring around at the crowd. 'Oh, no ...'

He bent his knees slightly to hide behind Harry, because Fleur Delacour was passing, looking stunning in robes of silver-grey satin, and accompanied by the Ravenclaw Quidditch captain, Roger Davies. When they had disappeared, Ron stood straight again and stared over the heads of the crowd.

'Where *is* Hermione?' he said again.

A group of Slytherins came up the steps from their dungeon common room. Malfoy was in front; he was wearing dress robes of black velvet with a high collar, which in Harry's opinion made him look like a vicar. Pansy Parkinson was clutching Malfoy's arm, in very frilly robes of pale pink. Crabbe and Goyle were both wearing green; they resembled moss-coloured boulders, and neither of them, Harry was pleased to see, had managed to find a partner.

The oak front doors opened, and everyone turned to look as the Durmstrang students entered with Professor Karkaroff. Krum was at the front of the party, accompanied by a pretty girl in blue robes Harry didn't know. Over their heads he saw that an area of lawn right in front of the castle had been transformed into a sort of grotto full of fairy lights – meaning hundreds of actual living fairies were sitting in the rose bushes that had been conjured there, and fluttering over the statues of what seemed to be Father Christmas and his reindeer.

Then Professor McGonagall's voice called, 'Champions over here, please!'

Parvati readjusted her bangles, beaming; she and Harry said 'See you in a minute' to Ron and Padma, and walked forwards, the chattering crowd parting to let them through. Professor McGonagall, who was wearing dress robes of red tartan, and had arranged a rather ugly wreath of thistles around the brim of her hat, told them to wait on one side of the doors while everyone else went inside; they were to enter the Great Hall in procession when the rest of the students had sat down. Fleur Delacour and Roger

## 第23章 圣诞舞会

"你好。"帕德玛说,她长得和她姐姐一样漂亮,穿着一件艳绿色的礼袍。不过,她似乎对罗恩做她的舞伴并没有什么太高的兴致。她乌黑的眼睛上下打量着罗恩,目光停留在他礼服长袍上起毛的领子和袖口处。

"你好,"罗恩说,但眼睛并不看着她,而是在人群里东张西望,"哦,糟糕……"

他微微弯下膝盖,躲在哈利身后,因为芙蓉·德拉库尔走过来了。她穿着银灰色的缎子礼袍,真是美艳惊人,身边陪伴她的是拉文克劳学院魁地奇队的队长罗杰·戴维斯。等他们走远了,罗恩才又挺直身子,越过人群朝远处眺望。

"赫敏在哪儿?"他又问。

一群斯莱特林的学生沿着台阶从他们的地下公共休息室里上来了。走在最前面的是马尔福,他穿着一件黑天鹅绒的高领礼服长袍,哈利觉得他活像一个教区牧师。潘西·帕金森则穿着满是褶边的浅粉红色礼袍,紧紧吊着马尔福的胳膊。克拉布和高尔都是一身绿色,像两块长满青苔的大石头,哈利满意地看到他们俩都没能找到舞伴。

橡木前门被打开了,大家转过头,看见德姆斯特朗的学生和卡卡洛夫教授一起走了进来。克鲁姆走在最前面,身边是一位哈利不认识的穿蓝色礼袍的漂亮姑娘。越过他们的头顶,哈利看见城堡前面的一块草坪被变成了一个岩洞,里面闪烁着星星点点的仙子之光——意味着有几百个真正的仙子,她们或坐在魔法变出的玫瑰花丛中,或在雕像上扑扇着翅膀,那些雕像似乎是圣诞老人和他的驯鹿。

这时,麦格教授的声音响起:"请勇士们到这边来!"

帕瓦蒂调整了一下她的手镯,脸上露出灿烂的笑容。她和哈利对罗恩和帕德玛说了一句"待会儿见",就向前走去,叽叽喳喳的人群闪出一条通道,让他们经过。麦格教授穿着一件红格子呢的礼袍,帽檐上装饰着一圈很难看的蓟草花环。她叫他们站在门边等候,让其他人先进去。等同学们都坐定后,他们再排队走进礼堂。芙蓉·德拉库尔和罗杰·戴维斯站在离门最近的地方。戴维斯似乎不敢相信自己有这么好的运气,竟能得到芙蓉这样的舞伴,他简直无法把目光从她身

## CHAPTER TWENTY-THREE    The Yule Ball

Davies stationed themselves nearest the doors; Davies looked so stunned by his good fortune in having Fleur for a partner that he could hardly take his eyes off her. Cedric and Cho were close to Harry, too; he looked away from them so he wouldn't have to talk to them. His eyes fell instead on the girl next to Krum. His jaw dropped.

It was Hermione.

But she didn't look like Hermione at all. She had done something with her hair; it was no longer bushy, but sleek and shiny, and twisted up into an elegant knot at the back of her head. She was wearing robes made of a floaty, periwinkle-blue material, and she was holding herself differently, somehow – or maybe it was merely the absence of the twenty or so books she usually had slung over her back. She was also smiling – rather nervously, it was true – but the reduction in the size of her front teeth was more noticeable than ever. Harry couldn't understand how he hadn't spotted it before.

'Hi, Harry!' she said. 'Hi, Parvati!'

Parvati was gazing at Hermione in unflattering disbelief. She wasn't the only one, either; when the doors to the Great Hall opened, Krum's fan club from the library stalked past, throwing Hermione looks of deepest loathing. Pansy Parkinson gaped at her as she walked by with Malfoy, and even he didn't seem to be able to find an insult to throw at her. Ron, however, walked right past Hermione without looking at her.

Once everyone else was settled in the Hall, Professor McGonagall told the champions and their partners to get in line in pairs, and follow her. They did so, and everyone in the Great Hall applauded as they entered and started walking up towards a large round table at the top of the Hall, where the judges were sitting.

The walls of the Hall had all been covered in sparkling silver frost, with hundreds of garlands of mistletoe and ivy crossing the starry black ceiling. The house tables had vanished; instead, there were about a hundred smaller, lantern-lit ones, each seating about a dozen people.

Harry concentrated on not tripping over his feet. Parvati seemed to be enjoying herself; she was beaming around at everybody, steering Harry so forcefully that he felt as though he was a show dog she was putting through its paces. He caught sight of Ron and Padma as he neared the top table. Ron was watching Hermione pass with narrowed eyes. Padma was looking sulky.

## 第23章 圣诞舞会

上挪开。塞德里克和秋·张也站在哈利旁边。哈利移开目光，这样就不用跟他们说话了。他的目光落在了克鲁姆身边那个姑娘身上。突然，他吃惊得张大了嘴巴。

是赫敏。

但她看上去一点儿也不像赫敏了。她对自己的头发做了一些手脚，它们不再是乱蓬蓬的，而是变得柔顺而有光泽，在脑后绾成一个高雅的发髻。她穿着一件用飘逸的浅紫光蓝色的面料做成的礼袍，而且不知怎的，她的气质也不一样了——也许只是因为卸掉了她平常总挎在身上的二十多本厚书吧。她也在微笑——当然啦，有点儿紧张——但那对门牙看上去明显缩小了。哈利真不明白他以前怎么就没有注意到。

"你好，哈利！"她说，"你好，帕瓦蒂！"

帕瓦蒂用一种毫不掩饰的怀疑目光盯着赫敏。这样做的不止她一个。礼堂的门打开时，图书馆里那些克鲁姆追星俱乐部的成员大步走过，都朝赫敏投去极度憎恨的目光。潘西·帕金森挽着马尔福的胳膊走过，瞪眼望着赫敏，就连马尔福似乎也找不出一句话来侮辱她。而罗恩呢，径直从赫敏身边走过，看也没看她一眼。

大家都在礼堂里落座后，麦格教授叫勇士和他们的舞伴两个两个地排好队，跟着她进去。他们鱼贯而入，朝礼堂前面一张坐着裁判的大圆桌走去，礼堂里的人们热烈地鼓起掌来。

礼堂的墙壁上布满了闪闪发亮的银霜，天花板上是星光灿烂的夜空，还挂着好几百只槲寄生小枝和常春藤编成的花环。四张学院桌子不见了，取而代之的是一百张点着灯笼的小桌子，每张桌子旁坐着十来个人。

哈利集中思想，小心着不要绊倒。帕瓦蒂似乎很开心。她朝每个人露出灿烂的微笑，一个劲儿地领着哈利往前走。哈利觉得自己就像一条马戏团的狗，由她领着表演把戏。走近主宾席时，他看见了罗恩和帕德玛。罗恩正眯着眼睛注视赫敏走过。帕德玛绷着脸，似乎在生气。

## CHAPTER TWENTY-THREE  The Yule Ball

Dumbledore smiled happily as the champions approached the top table but Karkaroff wore an expression remarkably like Ron's as he watched Krum and Hermione draw nearer. Ludo Bagman, tonight in robes of bright purple with large yellow stars, was clapping as enthusiastically as any of the students; and Madame Maxime, who had changed her usual uniform of black satin for a flowing gown of lavender silk, was applauding them politely. But Mr Crouch, Harry suddenly realised, was not there. The fifth seat at the table was occupied by Percy Weasley.

When the champions and their partners reached the table, Percy drew out the empty chair beside him, staring pointedly at Harry. Harry took the hint and sat down next to Percy, who was wearing brand-new, navy-blue dress robes, and an expression of great smugness.

'I've been promoted,' Percy said, before Harry could even ask, and from his tone, he might have been announcing his election as Supreme Ruler of the Universe. 'I'm now Mr Crouch's personal assistant, and I'm here representing him.'

'Why didn't he come?' Harry asked. He wasn't looking forward to being lectured on cauldron bottoms all through dinner.

'I'm afraid to say Mr Crouch isn't well, not well at all. Hasn't been right since the World Cup. Hardly surprising – overwork. He's not as young as he was – though still quite brilliant, of course, the mind remains as great as it ever was. But the World Cup was a fiasco for the whole Ministry, and then Mr Crouch suffered a huge personal shock with the misbehaviour of that house-elf of his, Blinky or whatever she was called. Naturally, he dismissed her immediately afterwards, but – well, as I say, he's getting on, he needs looking after, and I think he's found a definite drop in his home comforts since she left. And then we had the Tournament to arrange, and the aftermath of the Cup to deal with – that revolting Skeeter woman buzzing around – no, poor man, he's having a well-earned, quiet Christmas. I'm just glad he knew he had someone he could rely upon to take his place.'

Harry wanted very much to ask whether Mr Crouch had stopped calling Percy 'Weatherby' yet, but resisted the temptation.

There was no food as yet on the glittering golden plates, but small menus lying in front of each of them. Harry picked his up uncertainly, and looked around – there were no waiters. Dumbledore, however, looked carefully

## 第23章 圣诞舞会

勇士们来到主宾席前面,邓布利多高兴地笑着,但卡卡洛夫看到克鲁姆和赫敏越走越近,脸上却露出和罗恩一模一样的表情。卢多·巴格曼今晚穿着艳紫色的礼袍,上面印着黄色的大星星,他和同学们一样热烈地拍着巴掌。马克西姆女士脱去了平常的黑缎子制服,穿着一件淡紫色的飘逸长裙。可是,哈利突然注意到克劳奇先生没有来。桌旁的第五个座位上坐着珀西·韦斯莱。

勇士们及其舞伴走到桌旁,珀西拉开身边的一把空椅子,目光炯炯地望着哈利。哈利明白了他的意思,就在珀西旁边坐了下来。珀西穿着一件崭新的藏青色礼服长袍,脸上一副得意扬扬、自命不凡的样子。

"我被提升了,"珀西没等哈利开口就说道——听他的口气,你还以为他刚被选为宇宙的最高统治者呢,"我现在是克劳奇先生的私人助理了,我代表他来这里。"

"他为什么不来?"哈利问。他可不愿意整个宴会都听珀西没完没了地唠叨坩埚底的厚度。

"我很遗憾,克劳奇先生情况不好,十分不好。自从世界杯赛后,他就一直不对劲儿。这并不奇怪——工作太辛苦了。他不像以前那样年轻了——尽管,当然啦,他仍然非常出色,头脑仍然和以前一样敏锐。但是世界杯赛对整个魔法部来说是一次可怕的失败,克劳奇先生因为他那个家养小精灵,叫亮亮还是什么的,行为不轨,个人的情绪受到很大刺激。自然啦,他事后立刻就把那小精灵开除了,可是——唉,正像我刚才说的,他上了年纪,需要得到照顾。我想自从那个小精灵走后,他发现家里的舒适程度一落千丈。后来我们又要筹备三强争霸赛,还要进行世界杯赛的善后工作——那个名叫斯基特的可恶女人到处散布谣言——唉,可怜的人,他正在安安静静地过一个圣诞节,他太需要休息了。我很高兴他知道有一个值得信赖的人,可以代他处理一些事情。"

哈利很想问一句,克劳奇先生是否不再管珀西叫"韦瑟比"了,但他克制住了这种冲动。

金光闪亮的盘子里还没有食物,但每个人面前都摆着一份小菜单。哈利毫无把握地拿起自己的菜单,四下里望了望——没有侍者。只见

## CHAPTER TWENTY-THREE  The Yule Ball

down his own menu, then said very clearly to his plate, 'Pork chops!'

And pork chops appeared. Getting the idea, the rest of the table placed their orders with their plates, too. Harry glanced up at Hermione to see how she felt about this new and more complicated method of dining – surely it meant plenty of extra work for the house-elves? – but, for once, Hermione didn't seem to be thinking about S.P.E.W. She was deep in talk with Viktor Krum, and hardly seemed to notice what she was eating.

It now occurred to Harry that he had never actually heard Krum speak before, but he was certainly talking now, and very enthusiastically at that.

'Vell, ve have a castle also, not as big as this, nor as comfortable, I am thinking,' he was telling Hermione. 'Ve have just four floors, and the fires are lit only for magical purposes. But ve have grounds larger even than these – though in vinter, ve have very little daylight, so ve are not enjoying them. But in summer ve are flying every day, over the lakes and the mountains –'

'Now, now, Viktor!' said Karkaroff, with a laugh that didn't reach his cold eyes. 'Don't go giving away anything else, now, or your charming friend will know exactly where to find us!'

Dumbledore smiled, his eyes twinkling. 'Igor, all this secrecy … one would almost think you didn't want visitors.'

'Well, Dumbledore,' said Karkaroff, displaying his yellowing teeth to their fullest extent, 'we are all protective of our private domains, are we not? Do we not jealously guard the halls of learning that have been entrusted to us? Are we not right to be proud that we alone know our school's secrets, and right to protect them?'

'Oh, I would never dream of assuming I know all Hogwarts' secrets, Igor,' said Dumbledore amicably. 'Only this morning, for instance, I took a wrong turning on the way to the bathroom and found myself in a beautifully proportioned room I have never seen before, containing a really rather magnificent collection of chamber-pots. When I went back to investigate more closely, I discovered that the room had vanished. But I must keep an eye out for it. Possibly it is only accessible at five thirty in the morning. Or it may only appear at the quarter moon – or when the seeker has an exceptionally full bladder.'

Harry snorted into his plate of goulash. Percy frowned, but Harry could have sworn Dumbledore had given him a very small wink.

## 第23章 圣诞舞会

邓布利多仔细看了看他那份菜单，然后对着他的盘子，非常清晰地说："猪排！"

猪排立刻就出现了。桌上的其他人恍然大悟，纷纷仿效，给盘子里点了自己喜欢的食物。哈利抬眼望了望赫敏，想看看她对这种更为复杂的新式就餐有何感受——这肯定意味着家养小精灵要付出更多的劳动，是不是？——然而，破天荒第一次，赫敏似乎把S.P.E.W.忘到了脑后。她和威克多尔·克鲁姆正谈得投机，根本没注意自己在吃什么。

哈利突然想到他以前居然从没听见过克鲁姆说话，但他现在确实在说话，而且说得兴高采烈。

"啊，我们也有一个城堡，我觉得没有这里的大，也不如这里舒服。"他对赫敏说，"我们的只有四层楼，而且只在施魔法时才能点火。但我们的场地要比这里的宽敞——不过冬天白昼很短，不能在场地上玩。到了夏天，我们每天都在外面飞来飞去，飞过湖面，飞过山脉——"

"行了，行了，威克多尔！"卡卡洛夫说着，笑了一声，但冰冷的眼睛里并无丝毫笑意，"不要再泄露更多秘密了，不然你这位迷人的朋友就会知道我们在什么地方了！"

邓布利多笑了，眼睛闪闪发光。"伊戈尔，这样严守秘密……人们会以为你不欢迎别人去参观呢。"

"哎呀，邓布利多，"卡卡洛夫说，咧开大嘴，露出一口黄牙，"我们都想保护自己的私人领地，是不是？我们难道不需要小心守护我们受托保管的学校殿堂吗？只有我们自己知道学校的秘密，难道不应该为此感到自豪吗？难道不应该保守这些秘密吗？"

"哦，我做梦也不敢断言我知道霍格沃茨的所有秘密，伊戈尔。"邓布利多友善地说，"比如说吧，就在今天早晨，我上厕所时拐错了弯，发现自己来到了一个以前从没见过的、布置得非常精美的房间，里面摆着各种各样精致豪华的便壶。等我回去仔细调查时，却发现这个房间消失了。但我必须密切注意。它大概只在清晨五点半时才能进入，或者只在弦月时出现——也可能是在找厕所的人膀胱胀得特别满的时候。"

哈利对着他那盘匈牙利红烩牛肉偷笑。珀西皱起了眉头，但哈利可以发誓邓布利多几乎不易察觉地朝自己眨了一下眼睛。

## CHAPTER TWENTY-THREE  The Yule Ball

Meanwhile Fleur Delacour was criticising the Hogwarts decorations to Roger Davies.

'Zis is nothing,' she said dismissively, looking around at the sparkling walls of the Great Hall. 'At ze Palace of Beauxbatons, we 'ave ice sculptures all around ze Dining Chamber at Chreestmas. Zey do not melt, of course ... zey are like 'uge statues of diamond, glittering around ze place. And ze food is seemply superb. And we 'ave choirs of wood-nymphs, 'oo serenade us as we eat. We 'ave none of zis ugly armour in ze 'alls, and eef a poltergeist ever entaired into Beauxbatons, 'e would be expelled like *zat*.' She slapped her hand onto the table impatiently.

Roger Davies was watching her talk with a very dazed look on his face, and he kept missing his mouth with his fork. Harry had the impression that Davies was too busy staring at Fleur to take in a word she was saying.

'Absolutely right,' he said quickly, slapping his own hand down on the table in imitation of Fleur. 'Like *that*. Yeah.'

Harry looked around the Hall. Hagrid was sitting at one of the other staff tables; he was back in his horrible hairy brown suit, and gazing up at the top table. Harry saw him give a small wave and, looking around, saw Madame Maxime return it, her opals glittering in the candlelight.

Hermione was now teaching Krum to say her name properly; he kept calling her 'Hermy-own'.

'Her – my – oh – nee,' she said, slowly and clearly.

'Herm – own – ninny.'

'Close enough,' she said, catching Harry's eye and grinning.

When all the food had been consumed, Dumbledore stood up and asked the students to do the same. Then, at a wave of his wand, the tables zoomed back along the walls, leaving the floor clear, and then he conjured a raised platform into existence along the right-hand wall. A set of drums, several guitars, a lute, a cello and some bagpipes were set upon it.

The Weird Sisters now trooped up onto the stage to wildly enthusiastic applause; they were all extremely hairy, and dressed in black robes that had been artfully ripped and torn. They picked up their instruments, and Harry, who had been so interested in watching them that he had almost forgotten what was coming, suddenly realised that the lanterns on all the other tables had gone out, and that the other champions and their partners were standing up.

## 第23章 圣诞舞会

与此同时，芙蓉·德拉库尔正在对罗杰·戴维斯批评霍格沃茨的装潢布置。

"这不算什么，"她看了看礼堂周围星光闪烁的墙壁，轻蔑地说，"在布斯巴顿城堡，我们的礼堂在圣诞节时摆满了冰雕。当然啦，它们不会融化……就像巨大的钻石雕像，在礼堂里闪闪发光。食物也是超一流的。我们还有山林仙女合唱团，我们吃饭的时候，她们就唱小夜曲给我们听。我们墙边根本没有这些丑陋的盔甲，如果哪个恶作剧精灵胆敢闯进布斯巴顿，肯定会被赶出去，就像这样。"她不耐烦地用手拍了一下桌子。

罗杰·戴维斯看着她说话，脸上带着如痴如醉的神情，好几次叉子都拿歪了，没有把食物送进嘴里。哈利觉得戴维斯只顾盯着芙蓉看，根本没有听清她在说些什么。

"对极了！"戴维斯忙不迭地响应，一边模仿芙蓉，也用手拍了一下桌子，"就像这样。没错。"

哈利环顾礼堂。海格坐在另外一张教工桌子旁。他又穿上了那件难看的毛茸茸的棕色西装，正抬眼望着主宾席呢。哈利看见海格挥了挥手，他扭过头，看见马克西姆女士也朝海格挥手致意，她的蛋白石饰品在烛光下熠熠闪亮。

这时，赫敏正在教克鲁姆把她的名字念准确。他一直叫她"赫米—翁。"

"赫—敏。"她慢慢地、一字一顿地说。

"赫—米—恩。"

"差不多了。"赫敏说。她碰到哈利的目光，笑了笑。

东西都吃完了，邓布利多站起身，叫同学们也站起来。然后他一挥魔杖，所有的桌子都嗖地飞到墙边，留出中间一片空地。他又变出一个高高的舞台，贴在右墙根边，上面放着一套架子鼓、几把吉他、一把鲁特琴、一把大提琴和几架风琴。

这时，古怪姐妹一起拥上舞台，观众们爆发出雷鸣般的热烈掌声。他们的毛发都特别浓密，穿着故意撕得破破烂烂的黑色长袍。他们拿起各自的乐器，哈利兴致盎然地注视着他们，几乎忘记了下面要做什么。他突然发现其他桌子上的灯笼熄灭了，另外几位勇士和他们的舞伴都站了起来。

## CHAPTER TWENTY-THREE    The Yule Ball

'Come on!' Parvati hissed. 'We're supposed to dance!'

Harry tripped over his dress robes as he stood up. The Weird Sisters struck up a slow, mournful tune; Harry walked onto the brightly lit dance floor, carefully avoiding catching anyone's eye (he could see Seamus and Dean waving at him and sniggering), and next moment, Parvati had seized his hands, placed one around her waist, and was holding the other tightly in hers.

It wasn't as bad as it could have been, Harry thought, revolving slowly on the spot (Parvati was steering). He kept his eyes fixed over the heads of the watching people, and very soon many of them, too, had come onto the dance floor, so that the champions were no longer the centre of attention. Neville and Ginny were dancing nearby – he could see Ginny wincing frequently as Neville trod on her feet – and Dumbledore was waltzing with Madame Maxime. He was so dwarfed by her that the top of his pointed hat barely tickled her chin; however, she moved very gracefully for a woman so large. Mad-Eye Moody was doing an extremely ungainly two-step with Professor Sinistra, who was nervously avoiding his wooden leg.

'Nice socks, Potter,' Moody growled as he passed, his magical eye staring through Harry's robes.

'Oh – yeah, Dobby the house-elf knitted them for me,' said Harry, grinning.

'He is so *creepy*!' Parvati whispered, as Moody clunked away. 'I don't think that eye should be *allowed*!'

Harry heard the final, quavering note from the bagpipe with relief. The Weird Sisters stopped playing, applause filled the Hall once more, and Harry let go of Parvati at once. 'Let's sit down, shall we?'

'Oh – but – this is a really good one!' Parvati said, as the Weird Sisters struck up a new song, which was much faster.

'No, I don't like it,' Harry lied, and he led her away from the dance floor, past Fred and Angelina, who were dancing so exuberantly that people around them were backing away for fear of injury, and over to the table where Ron and Padma were sitting.

'How's it going?' Harry asked Ron, sitting down and opening a bottle of Butterbeer.

Ron didn't answer. He was glaring at Hermione and Krum, who were dancing nearby. Padma was sitting with her arms and legs crossed, one foot

## 第23章 圣诞舞会

"快点儿！"帕瓦蒂小声说，"我们应该跳舞了！"

哈利站起来时踩在袍子上，差点儿绊了一跤。古怪姐妹奏出一支缓慢忧伤的曲子。哈利走进灯火通明的舞池，小心地避开众人的目光（他可以看见西莫和迪安在朝他招手，偷偷地取笑他），接着帕瓦蒂抓住了他的两只手，一只放在她的腰际，另一只被她紧紧捏在手里。

还好，并没有原先想象的那样糟糕，哈利想道，一边慢慢地原地转圈（帕瓦蒂操纵着他）。他的目光盯着旁观者的头顶上方，很快，许多人也进入了舞场，勇士不再是大家注意的中心。纳威和金妮在近旁跳舞——他可以看见金妮频频地皱眉、躲闪，因为纳威踩了她的脚——邓布利多正跟马克西姆女士跳华尔兹呢。和她一比，邓布利多简直成了一个小矮人，他的尖帽子顶刚刚碰到她的下巴。不过，对于这么大块头的女人来说，马克西姆女士的舞步可真够优雅的。疯眼汉穆迪正十分笨拙地和辛尼斯塔教授跳两步舞，辛尼斯塔教授紧张地躲避着他的木头假腿。

"袜子很漂亮，波特。"穆迪经过时，粗声粗气地说，他那只魔眼穿透了哈利的长袍。

"哦——是啊，家养小精灵多比给我织的。"哈利说着，露出了微笑。

"他真是太恐怖了！"帕瓦蒂看着穆迪噔噔地走开，小声说道，"我认为不应该允许那样的眼睛存在！"

哈利听见风琴奏出最后一个颤抖的音符，不由得松了口气。古怪姐妹停止了演奏，礼堂里再次爆发出热烈的掌声，哈利立刻松开了帕瓦蒂。"我们坐下吧，好吗？"

"哦——可是——这支曲子很好听呢！"帕瓦蒂说，这时古怪姐妹又开始演奏一首新曲子了，节奏比刚才的快得多。

"不好，我不喜欢。"哈利撒谎道。他领着帕瓦蒂退出了舞场，朝罗恩和帕德玛坐的桌子旁走去。路上经过弗雷德和安吉利娜身边，他们俩跳得太奔放了，周围的人们纷纷向后闪开，以免被撞伤。

"怎么样？"哈利问罗恩，一边坐下来，打开一瓶黄油啤酒。

罗恩没有回答，气呼呼地瞪着在近旁跳舞的赫敏和克鲁姆。帕德玛双臂交叉，跷着二郎腿坐着，一只脚随着音乐的节拍抖动。时不时地，

## CHAPTER TWENTY-THREE  The Yule Ball

jiggling in time to the music. Every now and then she threw a disgruntled look at Ron, who was completely ignoring her. Parvati sat down on Harry's other side, crossed her arms and legs too, and within minutes, was asked to dance by a boy from Beauxbatons.

'You don't mind, do you, Harry?' Parvati said.

'What?' said Harry, who was now watching Cho and Cedric.

'Oh, never mind,' snapped Parvati, and she went off with the boy from Beauxbatons. When the song ended, she did not return.

Hermione came over and sat down in Parvati's empty chair. She was a bit pink in the face from dancing.

'Hi,' said Harry. Ron didn't say anything.

'It's hot, isn't it?' said Hermione, fanning herself with her hand. 'Viktor's just gone to get some drinks.'

Ron gave her a withering look.

'*Viktor?*' he said. 'Hasn't he asked you to call him *Vicky* yet?'

Hermione looked at him in surprise.

'What's up with you?' she said.

'If you don't know,' said Ron scathingly, 'I'm not going to tell you.'

Hermione stared at him, then at Harry, who shrugged. 'Ron, what –?'

'He's from Durmstrang!' spat Ron. 'He's competing against Harry! Against Hogwarts! You – you're –' Ron was obviously casting around for words strong enough to describe Hermione's crime, '*fraternising with the enemy*, that's what you're doing!'

Hermione's mouth fell open.

'Don't be so stupid!' she said after a moment. 'The *enemy*! Honestly – who was the one who was all excited when they saw him arrive? Who was the one who wanted his autograph? Who's got a model of him up in their dormitory?'

Ron chose to ignore this. 'I s'pose he asked you to come with him while you were both in the library?'

'Yes, he did,' said Hermione, the pink patches on her cheeks glowing more brightly. 'So what?'

'What happened – trying to get him to join *spew*, were you?'

## 第23章 圣诞舞会

她用不满的目光朝罗恩翻个白眼,罗恩完全把她冷落在一边了。帕瓦蒂在哈利的另一侧坐下,也交叉起双臂,跷起二郎腿,几分钟后,就有一个布斯巴顿的男生过来请她跳舞。

"你不介意吧,哈利?"帕瓦蒂说。

"什么?"哈利说,他正注视着秋·张和塞德里克呢。

"噢,没什么。"帕瓦蒂干脆地说,就和布斯巴顿的男生一起离去了。曲子结束后,她也没有回来。

赫敏过来了,坐在帕瓦蒂空出来的椅子上。她跳舞跳得面颊上微微有些泛红。

"你好。"哈利说。罗恩一声不吭。

"真热,是不是?"赫敏说,用手掌给自己扇着风,"威克多尔去拿饮料了。"

罗恩酸溜溜地看了她一眼。

"威克多尔?"他说,"他没有让你叫他'威基'吗?"

赫敏吃惊地看着他。

"你怎么啦?"她问。

"要是你不知道,"罗恩刻薄地说,"那我也不想告诉你。"

赫敏吃惊地望着他,又看看哈利,哈利耸了耸肩。"罗恩,你怎么——"

"他是德姆斯特朗的人!"罗恩厉声说,"是哈利的竞争对手!是霍格沃茨的竞争对手!你——你这是——"罗恩显然在搜肠刮肚,寻找足以形容赫敏的滔天大罪的有力字眼,"你这是亲敌行为,这就是你干的好事!"

赫敏吃惊地张大了嘴巴。

"别说傻话了!"过了片刻她说道,"亲敌!谁是敌人?说实在的——看见他来了,是谁激动得控制不住自己?是谁一心想得到他的签名?是谁在宿舍里摆着他的模型?"

罗恩决定不理睬这些话:"他大概是趁你们俩都在图书馆时邀请你的吧?"

"是啊,没错。"赫敏说,面颊上的红晕更鲜艳了,"那又怎么样?"

"事情是怎么发生的——你动员他参加'呕吐'?"

## CHAPTER TWENTY-THREE  The Yule Ball

'No, I wasn't! If you *really* want to know, he — he said he'd been coming up to the library every day to try and talk to me, but he hadn't been able to pluck up the courage!'

Hermione said this very quickly, and blushed so deeply that she was the same colour as Parvati's robes.

'Yeah, well — that's his story,' said Ron nastily.

'And what's that supposed to mean?'

'Obvious, isn't it? He's Karkaroff's student, isn't he? He knows who you hang around with ... he's just trying to get closer to Harry — get inside information on him — or get near enough to jinx him —'

Hermione looked as though Ron had slapped her. When she spoke, her voice quivered. 'For your information, he hasn't asked me *one single thing* about Harry, not one —'

Ron changed tack at the speed of light. 'Then he's hoping you'll help him find out what his egg means! I suppose you've been putting your heads together during those cosy little library sessions —'

'I'd *never* help him work out that egg!' said Hermione, looking outraged. '*Never*. How could you say something like that — I want Harry to win the Tournament. Harry knows that, don't you, Harry?'

'You've got a funny way of showing it,' sneered Ron.

'This whole Tournament's supposed to be about getting to know foreign wizards and making friends with them!' said Hermione shrilly.

'No, it isn't!' shouted Ron. 'It's about winning!'

People were starting to stare at them.

'Ron,' said Harry quietly, 'I haven't got a problem with Hermione coming with Krum —'

But Ron ignored Harry too.

'Why don't you go and find Vicky, he'll be wondering where you are,' said Ron.

'*Don't call him Vicky!*' Hermione jumped to her feet, and stormed off across the dance floor, disappearing into the crowd.

Ron watched her go with a mixture of anger and satisfaction on his face.

'Are you going to ask me to dance at all?' Padma asked him.

'No,' said Ron, still glaring after Hermione.

'fine,' snapped Padma, and she got up and went to join Parvati and the

## 第23章 圣诞舞会

"没有,才不是呢!如果你真想知道,我告诉你吧,他——他说他每天都上图书馆来,就是为了能跟我搭上话,但他一直鼓不起勇气!"

赫敏说得很快,脸红得更厉害了,几乎和帕瓦蒂的长袍一个颜色。

"是吗,哼——那是他自己这么说。"罗恩尖酸地说。

"那么他是什么意思呢?"

"那还不明显?他是卡卡洛夫的学生,是不是?他知道你整天跟谁泡在一起……他只是想接近哈利——窃取他的情报——或者靠近哈利身边,给他施一个恶咒——"

赫敏气坏了,好像罗恩扇了她一记耳光。她说话时声音微微发颤。"告诉你一个情报吧,他从来没问过哈利一个字,从来没有——"

罗恩以光的速度改变战术。"那么,他希望你帮助他搞清那只金蛋是什么意思!我猜,你们在温暖舒适的图书馆里会面,两颗脑袋紧紧挨着——"

"我从来没有帮助他研究那只金蛋!"赫敏简直怒不可遏了,"从来没有。你怎么能说出这样的话来——我希望哈利在比赛中取胜,哈利知道这一点,是不是,哈利?"

"你的表现方式可有些古怪。"罗恩讥讽道。

"整个这次争霸赛就是让大家结交外国巫师,并和他们建立友谊!"赫敏激动地说。

"不,才不是呢!"罗恩大喊,"是为了赢得比赛!"

人们转过脸来瞪着他们。

"罗恩,"哈利小声说,"我认为赫敏和克鲁姆在一起没什么要紧——"

可是罗恩对哈利的话也不予理睬。

"你为什么不去找威基,他找不到你会发愁的。"罗恩说。

"不许叫他威基!"赫敏一跃而起,怒气冲冲地穿过舞场,消失在人群中。罗恩望着她的背影,脸上带着一种愤怒和解恨交织的神情。

"你还准备请我跳舞吗?"帕德玛问他。

"不。"罗恩说,仍然瞪着赫敏的背影。

"很好。"帕德玛没好气地说,然后便站起来去找帕瓦蒂和那个布

## CHAPTER TWENTY-THREE   The Yule Ball

Beauxbatons boy, who conjured up one of his friends to join them so fast that Harry could have sworn he had zoomed him there by a Summoning Charm.

'Vare is Herm-own-ninny?' said a voice.

Krum had just arrived at their table clutching two Butterbeers.

'No idea,' said Ron mulishly, looking up at him. 'Lost her, have you?'

Krum was looking surly again.

'Vell, if you see her, tell her I haff drinks,' he said, and he slouched off.

'Made friends with Viktor Krum, have you, Ron?'

Percy had bustled over, rubbing his hands together and looking extremely pompous. 'Excellent! That's the whole point, you know – international magical co-operation!'

To Harry's annoyance, Percy promptly took Padma's vacated seat. The top table was now empty; Professor Dumbledore was dancing with Professor Sprout; Ludo Bagman, with Professor McGonagall; Madame Maxime and Hagrid were cutting a wide path around the dance floor as they waltzed through the students and Karkaroff was nowhere to be seen. When the next song ended, everybody applauded once more, and Harry saw Ludo Bagman kiss Professor McGonagall's hand and make his way back through the crowds, at which point Fred and George accosted him.

'What do they think they're doing, annoying senior Ministry members?' Percy hissed, watching Fred and George suspiciously. '*No* respect ...'

Ludo Bagman shook off Fred and George fairly quickly, however, and, spotting Harry, waved and came over to their table.

'I hope my brothers weren't bothering you, Mr Bagman?' said Percy at once.

'What? Oh, not at all, not at all!' said Bagman. 'No, they were just telling me a bit more about those fake wands of theirs. Wondering if I could advise them on the marketing. I've promised to put them in touch with a couple of contacts of mine at Zonko's Joke Shop ...'

Percy didn't look happy about this at all, and Harry was prepared to bet he would be rushing to tell Mrs Weasley about it the moment he got home. Apparently Fred and George's plans had grown even more ambitious lately, if they were hoping to sell to the public.

Bagman opened his mouth to ask Harry something, but Percy diverted him. 'How do you feel the Tournament's going, Mr Bagman? *Our*

## 第23章 圣诞舞会

斯巴顿男生了。那个男生立刻招来他的一个朋友,加入他们一伙。那动作之快,哈利简直敢说他是念了召唤咒,让那个人嗖地飞过来的。

"赫—米—恩在哪里?"一个声音问。

克鲁姆来到他们桌旁,手里攥着两杯黄油啤酒。

"不知道。"罗恩倔头倔脑地说,抬头望着他,"你把她丢了,是吗?"

克鲁姆的脸又阴沉下来。

"好吧,如果你看见她,就说我拿了饮料。"他说完就没精打采地走了。

"你和威克多尔·克鲁姆交上朋友啦,罗恩?"

珀西匆匆赶过来,搓着两只手,一副自以为了不起的派头。"太好了!这才是最关键的,你知道——为了国际魔法界的合作!"

珀西坐在了帕德玛空出来的座位上,这使哈利有些心烦。主宾席上现在没有人了:邓布利多教授正和斯普劳特教授跳舞;卢多·巴格曼和麦格教授跳舞;马克西姆女士和海格跳着华尔兹在学生中间穿梭,在舞场上划出一道很宽的轨迹;卡卡洛夫不知上哪儿去了。又一支曲子结束了,大家再次鼓掌,哈利看见,卢多·巴格曼吻了一下麦格教授的手,便穿过人群出去了,弗雷德和乔治追上去跟他说话。

"你说,他们在做什么呢,干扰魔法部的高级官员?"珀西警惕地望着弗雷德和乔治,小声地说,"一点儿也不尊重……"

卢多·巴格曼很快就摆脱了弗雷德和乔治,他看见了哈利,挥了挥手,朝他们的桌子走来。

"我的两个弟弟没有打扰你吧,巴格曼先生?"珀西立刻说道。

"什么?没有,没有!"巴格曼说道,"没有,他们只是又告诉我一些他们那些假魔杖的事,问我能不能在销路方面给他们一些提示。我答应帮他们和佐科笑话店的两个联络人联系一下……"

珀西听了这话很不高兴,哈利可以打赌,珀西一回家就会迫不及待地把这一切告诉韦斯莱夫人。弗雷德和乔治希望向大众推销他们的产品,如此看来,他们最近又有了一些更雄心勃勃的计划。

巴格曼张了张嘴,想问哈利几句话,但珀西转移了他的注意力。"你觉得争霸赛的情况怎么样,巴格曼先生?我们司感到非常满意——火

## CHAPTER TWENTY-THREE  The Yule Ball

department's quite satisfied – the hitch with the Goblet of Fire' – he glanced at Harry – 'was a little unfortunate, of course, but it seems to have gone very smoothly since, don't you think?'

'Oh, yes,' Bagman said cheerfully, 'it's all been enormous fun. How's old Barty doing? Shame he couldn't come.'

'Oh, I'm sure Mr Crouch will be up and about in no time,' said Percy importantly, 'but in the meantime, I'm more than willing to take up the slack. Of course, it's not all attending balls –' he laughed airily – 'oh, no, I've had to deal with all sorts of things that have cropped up in his absence – you heard Ali Bashir was caught smuggling a consignment of flying carpets into the country? And then we've been trying to persuade the Transylvanians to sign the International Ban on Duelling, I've got a meeting with their Head of Magical Co-operation in the new year –'

'Let's go for a walk,' Ron muttered to Harry, 'get away from Percy ...'

Pretending they wanted more drinks, Harry and Ron left the table, edged around the dance floor and slipped out into the Entrance Hall. The front doors stood open, and the fluttering fairy lights in the rose garden winked and twinkled as they went down the front steps, where they found themselves surrounded by bushes, winding ornamental paths, and large stone statues. Harry could hear splashing water, which sounded like a fountain. Here and there, people were sitting on carved benches. He and Ron set off along one of the winding paths through the rose bushes, but they had gone only a short way when they heard an unpleasantly familiar voice.

'... don't see what there is to fuss about, Igor.'

'Severus, you cannot pretend this isn't happening!' Karkaroff's voice sounded anxious and hushed, as though keen not to be overheard. 'It's been getting clearer and clearer for months, I am becoming seriously concerned, I can't deny it –'

'Then flee,' said Snape's voice curtly. 'Flee, I will make your excuses. I, however, am remaining at Hogwarts.'

Snape and Karkaroff came around the corner. Snape had his wand out, and was blasting rose bushes apart, his expression most ill-natured. Squeals issued from many of the bushes, and dark shapes emerged from them.

'Ten points from Hufflepuff, Fawcett!' Snape snarled, as a girl ran past him. 'And ten points from Ravenclaw, too, Stebbins!' as a boy went

焰杯出了点儿故障,"他扫了哈利一眼,"令人感到遗憾,这个自不必说,但从那以后,似乎一切都很顺利,你认为呢?"

"啊,是啊,"巴格曼愉快地说,"真是太好玩了。老巴蒂在做什么?他不能来,实在是遗憾。"

"哦,我相信克劳奇先生很快就会恢复健康,"珀西煞有介事地说,"在此之前,我非常愿意把无人管理的工作抓起来。当然啦,并不都是参加舞会什么的。"他傲慢地笑了笑,"唉,他不在期间出现的各种事情,我都不得不替他处理——你听说了阿里·巴什尔在向国内走私飞毯时被抓获的事吗?此外,我们还一直在说服特兰西瓦尼亚人在《国际禁止决斗法》上签字。我在新年和他们的魔法合作司司长有一个约会——"

"我们去散散步吧,"罗恩低声对哈利说,"离开珀西……"

于是,哈利和罗恩假装去拿饮料,离开了桌子,侧身绕过舞场,悄悄溜出了门,来到门厅。前门敞开着,他们走下台阶时,玫瑰花园里的仙子之光闪闪烁烁。他们发现周围都是低矮的灌木丛、装饰华丽的曲折小径和巨大的石雕像。哈利可以听见哗啦哗啦的溅水声,像是一个喷泉,间或可以看见人们坐在镂花的板凳上。他和罗恩顺着一条曲折的小径,在玫瑰花丛中穿行,但没走几步,就听见了一个令人不快的熟悉声音。

"……不明白为什么要这样大惊小怪,伊戈尔。"

"西弗勒斯,你不能假装这一切没有发生!"卡卡洛夫的声音听上去惶恐而沙哑,好像生怕被人听见似的,"几个月来,它变得越来越明显了。我现在非常担心,我不能否认——"

"那就逃跑吧,"斯内普的声音不耐烦地说,"逃跑吧——我会为你开脱的。但是我想留在霍格沃茨。"

斯内普和卡卡洛夫转过一个弯。斯内普手里拿着魔杖,把玫瑰花丛向两边轰开。他板着脸,表情很难看。花丛里传出尖叫声,几个黑乎乎的身影从里面蹿了出来。

"拉文克劳扣十分,福西特!"斯内普凶狠地说——一个女生从他身边跑过,"赫奇帕奇也扣十分,斯特宾斯!"一个男生追着那女生而

## CHAPTER TWENTY-THREE  The Yule Ball

rushing after her. 'And what are you two doing?' he added, catching sight of Harry and Ron on the path ahead. Karkaroff, Harry saw, looked slightly discomposed to see them standing there. His hand went nervously to his goatee, and he began winding it around his finger again.

'We're walking,' Ron told Snape shortly. 'Not against the law, is it?'

'Keep walking, then!' Snape snarled, and he brushed past them, his long black cloak billowing out behind him. Karkaroff hurried away after Snape. Harry and Ron continued down the path.

'What's got Karkaroff all worried?' Ron muttered.

'And since when have he and Snape been on first-name terms?' said Harry slowly.

They had reached a large stone reindeer now, over which they could see the sparkling jets of a tall fountain. The shadowy outlines of two enormous people were visible on a stone bench, watching the water in the moonlight. And then Harry heard Hagrid speak.

'Momen' I saw yeh, I knew,' he was saying, in an oddly husky voice.

Harry and Ron froze. This didn't sound like the sort of scene they ought to walk in on, somehow ... Harry looked around, back up the path, and saw Fleur Delacour and Roger Davies standing half concealed in a rose bush nearby. He tapped Ron on the shoulder and jerked his head towards them, meaning that they could easily sneak off that way without being noticed (Fleur and Davies looked very busy to Harry) but Ron, eyes widening in horror at the sight of Fleur, shook his head vigorously, and pulled Harry deeper into the shadows behind the reindeer.

'What did you know, 'Agrid?' said Madame Maxime, a distinct purr in her low voice.

Harry definitely didn't want to listen to this; he knew Hagrid would hate to be overheard in a situation like this (he certainly would have done) – if it had been possible he would have put his fingers in his ears and hummed loudly, but that wasn't really an option. Instead he tried to interest himself in a beetle crawling along the stone reindeer's back, but the beetle just wasn't interesting enough to block out Hagrid's next words.

'I jus' knew ... knew you were like me ... was it yer mother or yer father?'

'I – I don't know what you mean, 'Agrid ...'

'It was my mother,' said Hagrid quietly. 'She was one o' the las' ones in Britain. 'Course, I can' remember her too well ... she left, see. When I

## 第23章 圣诞舞会

去。"还有，你们俩在做什么？"他一眼瞥见哈利和罗恩在前面的小径上，问道。哈利发现卡卡洛夫看见他们站在这里，显得有些惊慌。他不安地伸手去摸他的山羊胡子，然后又把胡须缠在手指上。

"我们在散步。"罗恩不客气地对斯内普说，"这并不犯法吧？"

"那就接着散步吧！"斯内普气呼呼地嚷道，然后大步流星地从他们身边走过，长长的黑袍在身后飘荡。卡卡洛夫也跟着斯内普匆匆走开了。哈利和罗恩继续沿着小径漫步。

"卡卡洛夫干吗那样忧心忡忡的？"罗恩小声问。

"他和斯内普什么时候开始互相用教名称呼了？"哈利慢慢地说。

这时，他们来到一个很大的石雕驯鹿旁边，越过石鹿看见一个高高的喷泉，水花迸溅，闪闪发光。两个模模糊糊的巨大人影坐在一张石凳上，望着月光下的泉水。接着，哈利听见海格在说话。

"我一看见你，心里就明白了。"他用一种很异样的嘶哑声音说。

哈利和罗恩呆住了。看来，这一幕似乎是他们不应该惊扰的……哈利环顾四周，又回头望望小径，看见芙蓉·德拉库尔和罗杰·戴维斯隐藏在近旁的一片玫瑰丛里。他拍了拍罗恩的肩膀，朝那两个人扭了扭头，意思是他们可以从那条路溜走，不会引起别人的注意（在哈利看来，芙蓉和戴维斯正忙得很呢）。可是罗恩一看见芙蓉就惊恐地睁大眼睛，拼命摇头，拉着哈利躲进了驯鹿后面更幽深的阴影中。

"你明白了什么，海格？"马克西姆女士问，她低沉的嗓音里带着一种喵喵的声音。

哈利真的不想再听下去了。他知道在此情此景中，海格肯定讨厌别人偷听（哈利自己肯定讨厌）——如果可能的话，他会用手堵住耳朵，嘴里大声地嗡嗡叫，但是那样做也不合适。于是他强迫自己对一只在驯鹿背上爬行的甲虫发生兴趣，可是，甲虫并没有那么好玩，海格下面的话还是钻进了他的耳朵。

"我明白了……明白了你和我一样……是你母亲还是父亲？"

"我——我不懂你是什么意思，海格……"

"是我母亲，"海格轻声地说，"她是英国仅存的几个之一。当然啦，我对她已经记不太清了……她离开了，知道吧。大概在我三岁的时候，

## CHAPTER TWENTY-THREE  The Yule Ball

was abou' three. She wasn' really the maternal sort. Well … it's not in their natures, is it? Dunno what happened to her … might be dead fer all I know …'

Madame Maxime didn't say anything. And Harry, in spite of himself, took his eyes off the beetle, and looked over the top of the reindeer's antlers, listening … he had never heard Hagrid talk about his childhood before.

'Me dad was broken-hearted when she wen'. Tiny little bloke, my dad was. By the time I was six I could lift him up an' put him on top o' the dresser if he annoyed me. Used ter make him laugh …' Hagrid's deep voice broke. Madame Maxime was listening, motionless, apparently staring at the silvery fountain. 'Dad raised me … but he died, o' course, jus' after I started school. Sorta had ter make me own way after that. Dumbledore was a real help, mind. Very kind ter me, he was …'

Hagrid pulled out a large, spotted silk handkerchief and blew his nose heavily. 'So … anyway … enough abou' me. What about you? Which side you got it on?'

But Madame Maxime had suddenly got to her feet.

'It is chilly,' she said – but whatever the weather was doing, it was nowhere near as cold as her voice. 'I think I will go in now.'

'Eh?' said Hagrid blankly. 'No, don' go! I've – I've never met another one before!'

'Anuzzer *what*, precisely?' said Madame Maxime, her tone icy.

Harry could have told Hagrid it was best not to answer; he stood there in the shadows, gritting his teeth, hoping against hope he wouldn't – but it was no good.

'Another half-giant, o' course!' said Hagrid.

''Ow dare you!' shrieked Madame Maxime. Her voice exploded through the peaceful night air like a foghorn; behind him, Harry heard Fleur and Roger fall out of their rose bush. 'I 'ave nevair been more insulted in my life! 'Alf-giant? Moi? I 'ave – I 'ave big bones!'

She stormed away; great multi-coloured swarms of fairies rose into the air as she passed, angrily pushing aside bushes. Hagrid was still sitting on the bench, staring after her. It was much too dark to make out his expression. Then, after about a minute, he stood up and strode away, not back to the castle, but off out into the dark grounds in the direction of his cabin.

说实在的，她不太像一个母亲。唉……她们天性里没有母性，是不是？不知道她后来怎么样了……据我所知，大概已经死了……"

马克西姆女士一声不吭。哈利不由自主地把目光从甲虫上挪开，越过驯鹿的茸角尖眺望着，倾听着……他从没听海格谈起自己的童年。

"她离开后，爸爸伤心极了。我爸爸是一个小矮个儿。我六岁时，如果他把我惹恼了，我就把他举起来放在衣柜顶上，总是把他逗得哈哈大笑……"海格低沉的声音哽咽了。马克西姆女士听着，一动不动，似乎在凝望银色的喷泉。"爸爸把我带大……可是，唉，他死了，就在我上学之后。打那以后，我就靠自己闯荡了。邓布利多给了我很大帮助，说真的。他对我非常好……"

海格掏出一块印着圆点点的丝绸大手帕，响亮地擤着鼻子。"就是这样……行了……我的情况说完了。你呢？你是从哪边得到的遗传？"

不料马克西姆女士突然站了起来。

"太冷了。"她说——其实，不管气温多低，都不会像她的声音这样寒冷刺骨，"我想进去了。"

"呃？"海格困惑地说，"不，你别走！我——我以前从没碰见过另一个同类！"

"另一个什么？你说清楚！"马克西姆女士说，语气冷冰冰的。

哈利真想告诉海格最好别回答。他站在阴影里咬紧牙关，心里存有一线希望，但愿海格别说傻话——然而无济于事。

"另一个混血统巨人啊，那还用说！"海格说。

"你好大的胆子！"马克西姆女士尖叫起来，"我这辈子从没有受过这种侮辱！混血统巨人？我？我只是——我只是骨架子大！"她的声音像雾角一样划破了宁静的夜空。哈利听见芙蓉和罗杰从他身后的玫瑰花丛里蹿了出来。

马克西姆女士气冲冲地走开了，一路愤怒地拨开花丛，惊得一群群五颜六色的小仙子飞向空中。海格仍然坐在长凳上，望着她的背影。天太黑了，看不清他脸上的表情。然后，过了一分钟左右，他站起来，大踏步地走了。他没有返回城堡，而是朝着他小屋的方向，走向外面漆黑的场地。

## CHAPTER TWENTY-THREE  The Yule Ball

'C'mon,' Harry said, very quietly to Ron. 'Let's go …'

But Ron didn't move.

'What's up?' said Harry, looking at him.

Ron looked around at Harry, his expression very serious indeed.

'Did you know?' he whispered. 'About Hagrid being half-giant?'

'No,' Harry said, shrugging. 'So what?'

He knew immediately from the look Ron was giving him, that he was once again revealing his ignorance of the wizarding world. Brought up by the Dursleys, there were many things that wizards took for granted that were revelations to Harry, but these surprises had become fewer as he had moved up the school. Now, however, he could tell that most wizards would not have said 'So what?' upon finding out that one of their friends had a giantess for a mother.

'I'll explain inside,' said Ron quietly. 'C'mon …'

Fleur and Roger Davies had disappeared, probably into a more private clump of bushes. Harry and Ron returned to the Great Hall.

Parvati and Padma were now sitting at a distant table with a whole crowd of Beauxbatons boys, and Hermione was once more dancing with Krum. Harry and Ron sat down at a table far removed from the dance floor.

'So?' Harry prompted Ron. 'What's the problem with giants?'

'Well, they're … they're …' Ron struggled for words, 'not very nice,' he finished lamely.

'Who cares?' Harry said. 'There's nothing wrong with Hagrid!'

'I know there isn't, but … blimey, no wonder he keeps it quiet,' Ron said, shaking his head. 'I always thought he'd got in the way of a bad Engorgement Charm when he was a kid or something. Didn't like to mention it …'

'But what's it matter if his mother was a giantess?' said Harry.

'Well … no one who knows him will care, 'cos they'll know he's not dangerous,' said Ron, slowly. 'But … Harry, they're just vicious, giants. It's like Hagrid said, it's in their natures, they're like trolls … they just like killing, everyone knows that. There aren't any left in Britain now, though.'

'What happened to them?'

## 第23章 圣诞舞会

"快点儿，"哈利声音很低地对罗恩说，"我们走吧……"

可是罗恩没有动弹。

"怎么啦？"哈利望着他，问道。

罗恩转过脸看着哈利，脸上的表情非常严肃。

"你原先知道吗？"他小声问，"海格是个混血统巨人？"

"不知道。"哈利说，耸了耸肩，"那又怎么样？"

从罗恩看他的目光中，哈利立刻明白了：他又一次暴露了自己对魔法世界的无知。他在德思礼家里长大，巫师们认为理所当然的许多事情，对他来说都是新奇的发现，但随着时间一年年过去，这种大惊小怪的情况越来越少了。此刻他突然醒悟：大多数巫师发现某个朋友的母亲是个巨人时，都不会问"那又怎么样？"的。

"进去我再跟你解释。"罗恩轻声说，"走吧……"

芙蓉和罗杰·戴维斯不见了，大概是钻进了更隐秘的树丛里。哈利和罗恩回到了礼堂。

帕瓦蒂和帕德玛和一大群布斯巴顿的男生一起，坐在远处的一张桌子旁，赫敏又和克鲁姆一起跳舞了。哈利和罗恩在一张远离舞池的桌子旁坐下。

"说吧。"哈利催促罗恩，"巨人有什么问题？"

"是这样，他们都……他们都……"罗恩搜索枯肠，找不到一句合适的话，"……都不太好。"他有气无力地说。

"谁在乎呢？"哈利说，"海格没有哪里不好！"

"我知道是这样，但是……天哪，怪不得他始终不说。"罗恩说着，摇了摇头，"我一直以为他是小时候不小心中了歹毒的膨胀咒什么的，不愿意谈起……"

"即便他母亲是个巨人，又有什么要紧呢？"哈利说。

"嗯……认识他的人都觉得没关系，因为知道他没有危险性。"罗恩慢慢地说，"但是……哈利，巨人是很凶狠的。就像海格说的，这是他们的天性，巨人就像巨怪一样……生来就喜欢杀人，这点大家都知道。不过，现在英国已经没有巨人了。"

"他们上哪儿去了？"

## CHAPTER TWENTY-THREE   The Yule Ball

'Well, they were dying out anyway, and then loads got themselves killed by Aurors. There're supposed to be giants abroad, though ... they hide out in mountains mostly ...'

'I don't know who Maxime thinks she's kidding,' Harry said, watching Madame Maxime sitting alone at the judges' table, looking very sombre. 'If Hagrid's half-giant, she definitely is. Big bones ... the only thing that's got bigger bones than her is a dinosaur.'

Harry and Ron spent the rest of the ball discussing giants in their corner, neither of them having any inclination to dance. Harry tried not to watch Cho and Cedric; it gave him a strong desire to kick something.

When the Weird Sisters finished playing at midnight, everyone gave them a last, loud round of applause, and started to wend their way into the Entrance Hall. Many people were expressing the wish that the ball could have gone on longer, but Harry was perfectly happy to be going to bed; as far as he was concerned, the evening hadn't been much fun.

Out in the Entrance Hall, Harry and Ron saw Hermione saying goodnight to Krum before he went back to the Durmstrang ship. She gave Ron a very cold look, and swept past him up the marble staircase without speaking. Harry and Ron followed her, but halfway up the marble staircase, Harry heard someone calling him.

'Hey – Harry!'

It was Cedric Diggory. Harry could see Cho waiting for him in the Entrance Hall below.

'Yeah?' said Harry coldly, as Cedric ran up the stairs towards him.

Cedric looked as though he didn't want to say whatever it was in front of Ron, who shrugged, looking bad-tempered, and continued to climb the stairs.

'Listen ...' Cedric lowered his voice as Ron disappeared. 'I owe you one for telling me about the dragons. You know that golden egg? Does yours wail when you open it?'

'Yeah,' said Harry.

'Well ... take a bath, OK?'

'What?'

'Take a bath, and – er – take the egg with you, and – er – just mull things over in the hot water. It'll help you think ... trust me.'

Harry stared at him.

## 第23章 圣诞舞会

"噢,慢慢地灭绝了,还有一大批被傲罗杀死了。不过,国外应该还有巨人……他们多半都躲在大山里……"

"我不知道马克西姆想骗谁。"哈利说,一边注视着马克西姆女士独自坐在裁判桌旁,一副闷闷不乐的样子,"如果海格是混血统巨人,那她肯定也是。骨架子大……比她骨架子更大的只有恐龙了。"

在舞会剩下来的时间里,哈利和罗恩一直坐在角落里谈论巨人,谁也没有心思跳舞。哈利克制着自己不去注视秋·张和塞德里克,那会使他产生踢东西的强烈冲动。

午夜十二点,古怪姐妹停止了演奏,大家最后一次对他们报以热烈掌声,然后开始朝门厅走去。许多人都希望舞会能延长一些时候,可是哈利巴不得回去睡觉。在他看来,这个晚上过得并不开心。

出门来到门厅里,哈利和罗恩看见赫敏正在跟克鲁姆告别,然后克鲁姆就返回德姆斯特朗的船上去了。赫敏冷冷地扫了罗恩一眼,一句话没说,就与他们擦身而过,上了大理石台阶。哈利和罗恩跟在她后面,但刚上了一半楼梯,哈利就听见有人喊他。

"喂——哈利!"

是塞德里克·迪戈里。哈利可以看见秋·张在下面的门厅里等他。

"怎么?"哈利冷淡地问,塞德里克上楼朝他跑来。

塞德里克似乎有话不便当着罗恩的面说,罗恩耸了耸肩,显得很不高兴,继续朝楼上走去。

"听着……"塞德里克等罗恩走远了,压低声音说道,"你告诉我火龙的事,我欠你一份人情。你知道那只金蛋吗?你打开你的金蛋时,它发出惨叫吗?"

"是啊。"哈利说。

"那好……去洗个澡,明白吗?"

"什么?"

"洗个澡,然后……呃……带着金蛋,然后……呃……在热水里仔细琢磨。热水会帮助你思考……相信我的话吧。"

哈利不解地望着他。

## CHAPTER TWENTY-THREE    The Yule Ball

'Tell you what,' Cedric said, 'use the Prefects' bathroom. Fourth door to the left of that statue of Boris the Bewildered on the fifth floor. Password's *Pine-fresh*. Gotta go ... want to say goodnight –'

He grinned at Harry again and hurried back down the stairs to Cho.

Harry walked back to Gryffindor Tower alone. That had been extremely strange advice. Why would a bath help him to work out what the wailing egg meant? Was Cedric pulling his leg? Was he trying to make Harry look a fool, so Cho would like Cedric even more by comparison?

The fat Lady and her friend Vi were snoozing in the picture over the portrait hole. Harry had to yell 'Fairy lights!' before he woke them up, and when he did, they were extremely irritated. He climbed into the common room, and found Ron and Hermione having a blazing row. Standing ten feet apart, they were bellowing at each other, each scarlet in the face.

'Well, if you don't like it, you know what the solution is, don't you?' yelled Hermione; her hair was coming down out of its elegant bun now, and her face was screwed up in anger.

'Oh yeah?' Ron yelled back. 'What's that?'

'Next time there's a ball, ask me before someone else does, and not as a last resort!'

Ron mouthed soundlessly like a goldfish out of water as Hermione turned on her heel and stormed up the girls' staircase to bed. Ron turned to look at Harry.

'Well,' he spluttered, looking thunderstruck, 'well – that just proves – completely missed the point –'

Harry didn't say anything. He liked being back on speaking terms with Ron too much to speak his mind right now – but he somehow thought that Hermione had got the point much better than Ron had.

## 第23章 圣诞舞会

"你听我说,"塞德里克说,"用级长的盥洗室。在六楼糊涂蛋波里斯雕像左边的第四个门。口令是新鲜凤梨。我得走了……想跟她说晚安——"

他又咧嘴对哈利笑了一下,然后匆匆下楼,找秋·张去了。

哈利独自回到格兰芬多塔楼。这真是一个古怪透顶的忠告。凭什么洗个澡就能弄清那只惨叫的金蛋是什么意思?难道塞德里克在捉弄他?他想让哈利出丑,这样对比之下,秋·张就会更喜欢他了?

胖夫人和她的朋友维奥莱特在肖像洞口的相框里呼呼大睡。哈利不得不大喊"仙境之光!"才把她们唤醒。她们被吵醒后非常恼火。哈利钻进公共休息室,看见罗恩和赫敏正吵得不可开交。他们面对面站着,隔着十英尺远,朝对方大喊大叫,两个人都面红耳赤。

"好吧,如果你不愿意这样,你知道该怎样解决,不是吗?"赫敏嚷道,她的头发已从高雅的发髻里散开,脸庞因为愤怒而扭曲。

"哦,是吗?"罗恩也朝她嚷道,"怎样解决?"

"下次再有舞会,你就赶在别人之前邀请我,别等到没办法了才想到我!"

罗恩嘴巴嚅动着,却发不出声音,像一条出水的金鱼。这时赫敏猛地转身,气呼呼地登上女生宿舍楼梯,回去睡觉了。罗恩转过头来望着哈利。

"你看看,"他结结巴巴地说,似乎完全被惊呆了,"你看看——这叫什么事儿——完全没抓住问题的实质——"

哈利没有吭声。他很珍惜现在和罗恩又说话了,因此谨慎地保持沉默,没有说出自己的观点——实际上,他认为跟罗恩比起来,赫敏才更准确地抓住了问题的实质。

## CHAPTER TWENTY-FOUR

# Rita Skeeter's Scoop

Everybody got up late on Boxing Day. The Gryffindor common room was much quieter than it had been lately, many yawns punctuating the lazy conversations. Hermione's hair was bushy again; she confessed to Harry that she had used liberal amounts of Sleekeazy's Hair Potion on it for the ball, 'but it's way too much bother to do every day,' she said matter-of-factly, scratching a purring Crookshanks behind the ears.

Ron and Hermione seemed to have reached an unspoken agreement not to discuss their argument. They were being quite friendly to each other, though oddly formal. Ron and Harry wasted no time in telling Hermione about the conversation they had overheard between Madame Maxime and Hagrid, but Hermione didn't seem to find the news that Hagrid was a half-giant nearly as shocking as Ron did.

'Well, I thought he must be,' she said, shrugging. 'I knew he couldn't be pure giant, because they're about twenty feet tall. But honestly, all this hysteria about giants. They can't *all* be horrible ... it's the same sort of prejudice that people have towards werewolves ... it's just bigotry, isn't it?'

Ron looked as though he would have liked to reply scathingly, but perhaps he didn't want another row, because he contented himself with shaking his head disbelievingly while Hermione wasn't looking.

It was time now to think of the homework they had neglected during the first week of the holidays. Everybody seemed to be feeling rather flat, now that Christmas was over – everybody except Harry, that is, who was starting (once again) to feel slightly nervous.

The trouble was that February the twenty-fourth looked a lot closer from this side of Christmas, and he still hadn't done anything about working out the clue inside the golden egg. He therefore started taking the egg out of his

# 第24章

## 丽塔·斯基特的独家新闻

圣诞节的第二天，大家都起得很晚。格兰芬多的公共休息室里比前些日子安静了许多，人们有一搭没一搭地交谈着，不时被哈欠打断。赫敏的头发又变得乱蓬蓬了。她对哈利坦白说，为了参加舞会，她在头发上喷了大量的速顺滑发剂。"但是每天都这么做就太麻烦了。"她很实际地说，一边抓挠着克鲁克山的耳根，猫舒服得直哼哼。

罗恩和赫敏似乎达成了一种默契，都闭口不提他们吵架的事。现在他们互相都很友好，但是客客气气的，显得有些不自然。罗恩和哈利马上就把他们偷听到的马克西姆女士和海格之间的谈话告诉了赫敏，但赫敏不像罗恩那样，认为海格是个混血统巨人这个消息有多么吓人。

"其实，我早就认为他肯定有巨人血统。"赫敏说着，耸了耸肩膀，"我知道他不可能是纯血统巨人，因为他们都高达二十英尺左右呢。但说实在的，我们犯不着为巨人这么神经过敏。他们不可能都那么可怕……那是一种偏见，就像人们对狼人的态度一样……只是一种先入之见，不是吗？"

罗恩似乎很想用几句刻薄的话回敬赫敏，但也许是不想再吵架吧，他只是趁赫敏没注意的时候，不以为然地摇了摇头。

放假的第一个星期，他们只顾玩耍，现在应该考虑一下家庭作业了。圣诞节过去了，大家似乎感到兴味索然起来——只有哈利不同，他（又一次）开始感到有点儿紧张了。

麻烦在于，圣诞节一过，二月二十四日一下子就显得近了许多，而他还根本没有好好考虑藏在金蛋里的线索到底是什么。因此，他现在一回到宿舍，就从箱子里拿出金蛋，打开来仔细倾听，希望能弄清

## CHAPTER TWENTY-FOUR    Rita Skeeter's Scoop

trunk every time he went up to the dormitory, opening it and listening intently, hoping that this time it would make some sense. He strained to think what the sound reminded him of, apart from thirty musical saws, but he had never heard anything else like it. He closed the egg, shook it vigorously, and opened it again to see if the sound had changed, but it hadn't. He tried asking the egg questions, shouting over all the wailing, but nothing happened. He even threw the egg across the room – though he hadn't really expected that to help.

Harry had not forgotten the hint that Cedric had given him, but his less-than-friendly feelings towards Cedric just now meant that he was keen not to accept his help if he could avoid it. In any case, it seemed to him that if Cedric had really wanted to give Harry a hand, he would have been a lot more explicit. He, Harry, had told Cedric exactly what was coming in the first task – and Cedric's idea of a fair exchange had been to tell Harry to take a bath. Well, he didn't need that sort of rubbishy help – not from someone who kept walking down corridors hand in hand with Cho, anyway. And so the first day of the new term arrived, and Harry set off to lessons, weighed down with books, parchment and quills as usual, but also with the lurking worry of the egg heavy in his stomach, as though he was carrying that around with him too.

Snow was still thick upon the grounds, and the greenhouse windows were covered in condensation so thick that they couldn't see out of them in Herbology. Nobody was looking forward to Care of Magical Creatures much in this weather, though, as Ron said, the Skrewts would probably warm them up nicely, either by chasing them or by blasting off so forcefully that Hagrid's cabin caught fire.

When they arrived at Hagrid's cabin, however, they found an elderly witch with closely cropped grey hair and a very prominent chin standing before his front door.

'Hurry up, now, the bell rang five minutes ago,' she barked at them, as they struggled towards her through the snow.

'Who're you?' said Ron, staring at her. 'Where's Hagrid?'

'My name is Professor Grubbly-Plank,' she said briskly, 'I am your temporary Care of Magical Creatures teacher.'

'Where's Hagrid?' Harry repeated loudly.

'He is indisposed,' said Professor Grubbly-Plank shortly.

## 第24章 丽塔·斯基特的独家新闻

其中的奥秘。他强迫自己思索这声音除了使他想到三十把乐锯外，还能使他想到别的什么，然而想不起来，他以前从没听见过这样的声音。他合上金蛋，使劲地摇晃着，然后又把它打开，看声音有没有什么变化。没有，还是那样。他还试着向金蛋提问题，在它的惨叫声中扯着嗓门叫喊，但是一无所获。他甚至把金蛋扔到房间那头——不过他自己也不指望这样做会有什么用。

哈利没有忘记塞德里克告诉他的那个办法，但他目前对塞德里克没有什么好感，所以但凡有一点儿办法，就希望自己不要接受塞德里克的帮助。而且在哈利看来，如果塞德里克真的想给哈利一点儿帮助，就应该说得更明确一些。自己当时就明明白白地告诉了塞德里克第一个项目是什么——而塞德里克作为公平交换的，却是叫哈利去洗一个澡。哼，哈利可不需要那一类毫无价值的帮助——况且，向他提供这种帮助的人还整天和秋·张手拉手在走廊里来来去去。因此，新学期第一天哈利去上课时，不仅像往常一样背着书本、羊皮纸和羽毛笔，同时内心还压着金蛋这个沉重的负担，就像他把金蛋也随身带着似的。

场地上仍然覆盖着厚厚的积雪，温室的窗户上凝结着细密的水珠，他们上草药课时看不见窗外的情景。在这样的天气里，谁也不想去上保护神奇动物课，尽管罗恩说炸尾螺大概会使他们暖和起来，它们或者会追着同学们到处跑，或者会炸出大量火花，使海格的小屋着起火来。

然而，当他们来到海格的小屋时，却看到门口站着一个上了年纪的女巫。她灰白的头发剪得很短，下巴非常突出。

"快点儿，快点儿，上课铃已经响了五分钟了。"她厉声对他们说。他们深一脚浅一脚地在雪地里穿行，朝她走去。

"你是谁？"罗恩瞪着她，问道，"海格呢？"

"我是格拉普兰教授。"女巫干脆利落地说，"是你们保护神奇动物课的临时代课教师。"

"海格上哪儿去了？"哈利又大声问了一遍。

"他不舒服。"格拉普兰教授不愿多说。

## CHAPTER TWENTY-FOUR    Rita Skeeter's Scoop

Soft and unpleasant laughter reached Harry's ears. He turned; Draco Malfoy and the rest of the Slytherins were joining the class. All of them looked gleeful, and none of them looked surprised to see Professor Grubbly-Plank.

'This way, please,' said Professor Grubbly-Plank, and she strode off around the paddock where the huge Beauxbatons horses were shivering. Harry, Ron and Hermione followed her, looking back over their shoulders at Hagrid's cabin. All the curtains were closed. Was Hagrid in there, alone and ill?

'What's wrong with Hagrid?' Harry said, hurrying to catch up with Professor Grubbly-Plank.

'Never you mind,' she said, as though she thought he was being nosy.

'I do mind, though,' said Harry hotly. 'What's up with him?'

Professor Grubbly-Plank acted as though she couldn't hear him. She led them past the paddock where the Beauxbatons horses were standing, huddled against the cold, and towards a tree on the edge of the Forest, where a large and beautiful unicorn was tethered.

Many of the girls 'Ooooohed!' at the sight of the unicorn.

'Oh, it's so beautiful!' whispered Lavender Brown. 'How did she get it? They're supposed to be really hard to catch!'

The unicorn was so brightly white that it made the snow all around look grey. It was pawing the ground nervously with its golden hooves, and throwing back its horned head.

'Boys keep back!' barked Professor Grubbly-Plank, throwing out an arm and catching Harry hard in the chest. 'They prefer the woman's touch, unicorns. Girls to the front, and approach with care. Come on, easy does it ...'

She and the girls walked slowly forwards towards the unicorn, leaving the boys standing near the paddock fence, watching.

The moment Professor Grubbly-Plank was out of earshot, Harry turned to Ron. 'What d'you reckon's wrong with him? You don't think a Skrewt –?'

'Oh, he hasn't been attacked, Potter, if that's what you're thinking,' said Malfoy softly. 'No, he's just too ashamed to show his big ugly face.'

'What d'you mean?' said Harry sharply.

Malfoy put his hand inside the pocket of his robes, and pulled out a folded page of newsprint.

'There you go,' he said. 'Hate to break it to you, Potter ...'

## 第24章 丽塔·斯基特的独家新闻

哈利耳边突然传来不怀好意的轻笑声。他回头一看，德拉科·马尔福和斯莱特林的其他同学走了过来。他们一个个兴高采烈，看见格拉普兰教授时，谁也没有露出吃惊的样子。

"请大家这边走。"格拉普兰教授说着，绕过临时马厩朝远处走去，马厩里那些布斯巴顿的骏马在瑟瑟发抖。哈利、罗恩和赫敏跟在她后面，一边走，一边回头望着海格的小屋。所有的窗帘都拉上了。海格在里面吗？生着病，孤苦伶仃？

"海格出什么事啦？"哈利紧走几步，追上格拉普兰教授，问道。

"你就别管了。"她说，似乎以为哈利是多管闲事。

"我就要管。"哈利激动地说，"他到底怎么啦？"

格拉普兰教授好像没听见他的话。她领着他们走过马厩，那些庞大的布斯巴顿骏马站在那里，互相偎依着抵御严寒。他们朝禁林边缘的一棵大树走去，树下拴着一头漂亮的大独角兽。

许多女生一看见独角兽，都发出啧啧赞叹。

"哦，真是太漂亮了！"拉文德·布朗轻声说，"她怎么弄到它的？据说独角兽很难捕获呢！"

这头独角兽白得耀眼，相比之下，周围的白雪都显得有些灰暗了。它不安地用金色的蹄子刨着泥土，扬起带角的脑袋。

"男生们退后！"格拉普兰教授厉声喊道，一边甩起一只胳膊，重重地打在哈利胸口，"独角兽喜欢女性的抚摸。女生们站在前面，小心地接近它，过来，放松点儿……"

她和女生们慢慢地朝独角兽走去，男生们则留在马厩栅栏旁，站在那里注视着她们。

哈利看到格拉普兰教授走得听不见他说话了，就转身对罗恩说："你认为他出了什么事？不会是一条炸尾螺——"

"哦，波特，如果你是担心这一点，我可以告诉你，他没有受到攻击，"马尔福轻声说，"没有，他只是太害臊了，不敢露出他那张丑陋的大脸。"

"你这是什么意思？"哈利厉声问道。

马尔福把手伸进长袍的口袋，掏出一张折起来的报纸。

"你自己看吧。"他说，"真不愿向你透露这个消息，波特……"

## CHAPTER TWENTY-FOUR — Rita Skeeter's Scoop

He smirked as Harry snatched the page, unfolded it, and read it, with Ron, Seamus, Dean and Neville looking over his shoulder. It was an article topped with a picture of Hagrid looking extremely shifty.

### DUMBLEDORE'S GIANT MISTAKE

Albus Dumbledore, eccentric headmaster of Hogwarts School of Witchcraft and Wizardry, has never been afraid to make controversial staff appointments, *writes Rita Skeeter, Special Correspondent.* In September of this year, he hired Alastor 'Mad-Eye' Moody, the notoriously jinx-happy ex-Auror, to teach Defence Against the Dark Arts, a decision that caused many raised eyebrows at the Ministry of Magic, given Moody's well-known habit of attacking anybody who makes a sudden movement in his presence. Mad-Eye Moody, however, looks responsible and kindly, when set beside the part-human Dumbledore employs to teach Care of Magical Creatures.

Rubeus Hagrid, who admits to being expelled from Hogwarts in his third year, has enjoyed the position of gamekeeper at the school ever since, a job secured for him by Dumbledore. Last year, however, Hagrid used his mysterious influence over the Headmaster to secure the additional post of Care of Magical Creatures teacher, over the heads of many better-qualified candidates.

An alarmingly large and ferocious-looking man, Hagrid has been using his new-found authority to terrify the students in his care with a succession of horrific creatures. While Dumbledore turns a blind eye, Hagrid has maimed several pupils during a series of lessons which many admit to be 'very frightening'.

'I was attacked by a Hippogriff, and my friend Vincent Crabbe got a bad bite off a Flobberworm,' says Draco Malfoy, a fourth-year student. 'We all hate Hagrid, but we're just too scared to say anything.'

Hagrid has no intention of ceasing his campaign of intimidation, however. In conversation with a *Daily Prophet* reporter last month, he admitted breeding creatures he has dubbed 'Blast-Ended Skrewts', highly dangerous crosses between manticores and fire crabs. The creation of new breeds of magical creature is, of course, an activity usually closely observed by the Department for the Regulation and Control of Magical Creatures. Hagrid, it seems, considers himself to be above such petty restrictions.

'I was just having some fun,' he says, before hastily changing the subject.

他得意地笑着,哈利一把抓过报纸展开来,罗恩、西莫、迪安和纳威也围拢过来和他一起看。是一篇文章,上面登着海格的照片,他脸上的神情显得鬼鬼祟祟。

## 邓布利多的重大失误

本报特约记者丽塔·斯基特报道,霍格沃茨魔法学校校长、古怪的阿不思·邓布利多一向敢于聘用有争议的教员。今年九月,他聘用了"疯眼汉"阿拉斯托·穆迪担任黑魔法防御术课的老师,这项决定令魔法部的许多人大跌眼镜。穆迪以喜欢使用恶咒闻名,以前当过傲罗。众所周知,只要有人在他面前突然移动,他就会发起攻击。不过,与邓布利多雇来教授保护神奇动物课的半人类相比,疯眼汉就算是认真负责、和蔼亲切的了。

鲁伯·海格承认,他在三年级时被霍格沃茨开除,从那以后一直担任学校的猎场看守,这是邓布利多为他找的一份工作。去年,海格竟然对校长运用了神秘影响,从许多更有资格的竞选者中胜出,又为自己谋到了保护神奇动物课老师这个职位。

海格是一个体格庞大、相貌凶狠的男人,他滥用自己新得手的权力,弄来一连串可怕的动物吓唬他负责照管的学生。在一系列被许多人称为"非常恐怖"的课上,海格已导致几名学生受伤致残,而邓布利多对此视而不见。

"我受到了一头鹰头马身有翼兽的攻击,我的朋友文森特·克拉布被一只弗洛伯毛虫狠狠咬了一口。"一位名叫德拉科·马尔福的四年级学生说,"我们都讨厌海格,但是敢怒不敢言。"

然而海格无意停止他的恐吓行为。上个月在与《预言家日报》记者的谈话中,他承认自己正在饲养一种他命名为"炸尾螺"的动物,这种动物介于人头狮身蝎尾兽和火螃蟹之间,具有很大的危险性。培育新的魔法动物种类的行为,通常受到魔法部神奇动物管理控制司的密切监视。但海格认为他可以超越这类烦琐的条条框框。

"我只是觉得怪好玩的。"他说,然后便匆忙改变了话题。

## CHAPTER TWENTY-FOUR    Rita Skeeter's Scoop

As if this were not enough, the *Daily Prophet* has now unearthed evidence that Hagrid is not – as he has always pre-tended – a pure-blood wizard. He is not, in fact, even pure human. His mother, we can exclusively reveal, is none other than the giantess Fridwulfa, whose whereabouts are currently unknown.

Bloodthirsty and brutal, the giants brought themselves to the point of extinction by warring among themselves during the last century. The handful that remained joined the ranks of He Who Must Not Be Named, and were responsible for some of the worst mass Muggle-killings of his reign of terror.

While many of the giants who served He Who Must Not Be Named were killed by Aurors working against the Dark side, Fridwulfa was not among them. It is possible she escaped to one of the giant communities still existing in foreign mountain ranges. If his antics during Care of Magical Creatures lessons are any guide, however, Fridwulfa's son appears to have inherited her brutal nature.

In a bizarre twist, Hagrid is reputed to have developed a close friendship with the boy who brought about You-Know-Who's fall from power – thereby driving Hagrid's own mother, like the rest of You-Know-Who's supporters, into hiding. Perhaps Harry Potter is unaware of the unpleasant truth about his large friend – but Albus Dumbledore surely has a duty to ensure that Harry Potter, along with his fellow students, is warned about the dangers of associating with part-giants.

Harry finished reading and looked up at Ron, whose mouth was hanging open.

'How did she find out?' he whispered.

But that wasn't what was bothering Harry.

'What d'you mean, "We all hate Hagrid"?' Harry spat at Malfoy. 'What's this rubbish about *him*' – he pointed at Crabbe – 'getting a bad bite off a flobberworm? They haven't even got teeth!'

Crabbe was sniggering, apparently very pleased with himself.

'Well, I think this should put an end to the oaf's teaching career,' said Malfoy, his eyes glinting. 'Half-giant ... and there was me thinking he'd just swallowed a bottle of Skele-Gro when he was young ... none of the mummies and daddies are going to like this at all ... they'll be worried he'll eat their kids, ha, ha ...'

## 第24章 丽塔·斯基特的独家新闻

似乎这还不够,《预言家日报》最近又发现证据,海格不像他自己一贯伪装的那样是一位纯血统的巫师。实际上他甚至不是一个纯血统的人。我们可以独家透露,他的母亲正是巨人弗里德瓦法,目前下落不明。

巨人生性残暴、嗜血,上个世纪因自相残杀而濒临灭绝。仅存的十几个加入了神秘人的麾下,在神秘人统治的恐怖时期,他们制造了几起最残酷的麻瓜屠杀案。

许多为神秘人效力的巨人都死在了与黑魔势力斗争的傲罗手下,但弗里德瓦法并不在其列。她很可能已经逃至某个仍存在于国外山区的巨人村落。不过,如果我们就海格在保护神奇动物课上的古怪行为加以分析,弗里德瓦法的儿子似乎继承了其母亲残酷的天性。

令人意想不到的是,据说海格与一个男孩建立了亲密的友谊,而正是这个男孩使神秘人痛失权势——从而使海格的亲生母亲像神秘人的其他追随者一样,隐姓埋名,东躲西藏。也许哈利·波特尚不了解他这位体格庞大的朋友这些令人不快的事情——但阿不思·邓布利多无疑有责任确保哈利·波特及其同学们清醒地认识到与混血统巨人交往的危险性。

哈利看完了,抬头望着罗恩。罗恩呆呆地张大了嘴巴。

"她是怎么发现的?"他小声问。

但哈利心里想的不是这个。

"你是什么意思?'我们都讨厌海格'?"哈利厉声责问马尔福,"这说的是什么混账话,"——他指着克拉布——"他被一只弗洛伯毛虫狠狠咬了一口?它们根本连牙齿都没有!"

克拉布咯咯地傻笑着,显然感到非常得意。

"行了,我认为这个蠢货的教学生涯应该结束了。"马尔福说,一双眼睛闪闪发光,"混血统巨人……我原来以为他只是小时候喝了一瓶生骨灵呢……学生家长都不会答应的……担心他会吃掉他们的孩子,哈哈……"

## CHAPTER TWENTY-FOUR    Rita Skeeter's Scoop

'You –'

'Are you paying attention over there?'

Professor Grubbly-Plank's voice carried over to the boys; the girls were all clustered around the unicorn now, stroking it. Harry was so angry that the *Daily Prophet* article shook in his hands as he turned to stare unseeingly at the unicorn, whose many magical properties Professor Grubbly-Plank was now enumerating in a loud voice, so that the boys could hear too.

'I hope she stays, that woman!' said Parvati Patil, when the lesson had ended, and they were all heading back to the castle for lunch. 'That's more what I thought Care of Magical Creatures would be like … proper creatures like unicorns, not monsters …'

'What about Hagrid?' Harry said angrily, as they went up the steps.

'What about him?' said Parvati, in a hard voice. 'He can still be gamekeeper, can't he?'

Parvati had been very cool towards Harry since the ball. He supposed that he ought to have paid her a bit more attention, but she seemed to have had a good time all the same. She was certainly telling anybody who would listen that she had made arrangements to meet the boy from Beauxbatons in Hogsmeade on the next weekend trip.

'That was a really good lesson,' said Hermione, as they entered the Great Hall. 'I didn't know half the things Professor Grubbly-Plank told us about uni–'

'Look at this!' Harry snarled, and he shoved the *Daily Prophet* article under Hermione's nose.

Hermione's mouth fell open as she read. Her reaction was exactly the same as Ron's. 'How did that horrible Skeeter woman find out? You don't think Hagrid *told* her?'

'No,' said Harry, leading the way over to the Gryffindor table and throwing himself into a chair, furious. 'He never even told us, did he? I reckon she was so mad he wouldn't give her loads of horrible stuff about me, she went ferreting around to get back at him.'

'Maybe she heard him telling Madame Maxime at the ball,' said Hermione quietly.

'We'd have seen her in the garden!' said Ron. 'Anyway, she's not supposed to come into school any more, Hagrid said Dumbledore banned her …'

## 第24章 丽塔·斯基特的独家新闻

"你——"

"你们在专心听讲吗?"

格拉普兰教授的声音远远地传到了男生这里。这时女生们都围拢在独角兽身边,抚摸着它。哈利气极了,他用失神的目光瞪着独角兽,那篇《预言家日报》的文章在他手里瑟瑟发抖。格拉普兰教授正在列举独角兽的许多神奇属性,她把声音放得很大,好让男生们也能听见。

"我真希望她能留下来,这位女老师!"帕瓦蒂·佩蒂尔说——这时已经下课,大家正返回城堡去吃午饭,"这才是我心目中的保护神奇动物课……像独角兽这样体面的动物,而不是怪兽……"

"海格怎么办?"他们登上台阶时,哈利气愤地问。

"他怎么办?"帕瓦蒂冷冰冰地说,"他照样可以当他的猎场看守,不是吗?"

自从舞会之后,帕瓦蒂就一直对哈利很冷淡。哈利猜想他在舞会上应该更多地关心她,可是她看上去照样玩得很痛快呀。她现在逢人就说,她已经约好下个周末和那个布斯巴顿的男生在霍格莫德村见面。

"这堂课上得真好。"他们走进礼堂时,赫敏说道,"格拉普兰教授告诉我们的关于独角兽的知识,我一半都不知道——"

"看看这个吧!"哈利气呼呼地吼道,把《预言家日报》的文章塞到赫敏的鼻子底下。

赫敏读着文章,吃惊地张大了嘴巴。她的反应和罗恩一模一样。

"那个讨厌的女人斯基特是怎么打听到的?不会是海格告诉她的吧?"

"不会。"哈利说着,领头朝格兰芬多的桌子走去,然后一屁股坐在椅子上,气得要命,"他连我们都一直瞒着,是不是?我认为,上次海格不肯对那女人说我的坏话,把她气疯了,就四处搜寻海格的情况,对他进行报复。"

"也许她在舞会上听见了海格告诉马克西姆女士的话。"赫敏小声说。

"要是那样的话,我们会在花园里看见她的!"罗恩说,"而且,她不应该再进学校来,海格说邓布利多禁止她……"

## CHAPTER TWENTY-FOUR    Rita Skeeter's Scoop

'Maybe she's got an Invisibility Cloak,' said Harry, ladling chicken casserole onto his plate and splashing it everywhere in his anger. 'Sort of thing she'd do, isn't it, hide in bushes listening to people.'

'Like you and Ron did, you mean,' said Hermione.

'We weren't trying to hear him!' said Ron indignantly. 'We didn't have any choice! The stupid git, talking about his giantess mother where anyone could have heard him!'

'We've got to go and see him,' said Harry. 'This evening, after Divination. Tell him we want him back ... You *do* want him back?' he shot at Hermione.

'I – well, I'm not going to pretend it didn't make a nice change, having a proper Care of Magical Creatures lesson for once – but I do want Hagrid back, of course I do!' Hermione added hastily, quailing under Harry's furious stare.

So that evening after dinner, the three of them left the castle once more, and went down through the frozen grounds to Hagrid's cabin. They knocked, and Fang's booming barks answered.

'Hagrid, it's us!' Harry shouted, pounding on the door. 'Open up!'

He didn't answer. They could hear Fang scratching at the door, whining, but it didn't open. They hammered on it for ten more minutes; Ron even went and banged on one of the windows, but there was no response.

'What's he avoiding *us* for?' Hermione said, when they had finally given up, and were walking back to the school. 'He surely doesn't think we'd care about him being half-giant?'

But it seemed that Hagrid did care. They didn't see a sign of him all week. He didn't appear at the staff table at meal-times, they didn't see him going about his gamekeeper duties in the grounds, and Professor Grubbly-Plank continued to take the Care of Magical Creatures classes. Malfoy was gloating at every possible opportunity.

'Missing your half-breed pal?' he kept whispering to Harry, whenever there was a teacher around, so that he was safe from Harry's retaliation. 'Missing the elephant man?'

There was a Hogsmeade visit halfway through January. Hermione was very surprised that Harry was planning to go.

'I just thought you'd want to take advantage of the common room being quiet,' she said. 'Really get to work on that egg.'

## 第24章 丽塔·斯基特的独家新闻

"也许她有一件隐形衣。"哈利说,一边用长柄勺把炖鸡汤舀进自己的盘子——他太气愤了,把汤洒得到处都是,"这种事情她做得出来的,是不是?躲在灌木丛里偷听别人说话。"

"你的意思是,就像你和罗恩?"赫敏说。

"我们没有刻意偷听!"罗恩愤怒地说,"当时我们没有别的选择!那个傻瓜居然在一个任何人都有可能听到的地方大谈他的母亲是个巨人!"

"我们必须去看看他。"哈利说,"就在今天傍晚,上完占卜课以后,告诉他我们想要他回来……你想要他回来吗?"他冷不防地问赫敏。

"我——唉,我不想说假话,偶尔上一次像样的保护神奇动物课,换换口味,倒也不错——但我确实希望海格回来,我当然希望!"赫敏被哈利愤怒的目光吓坏了,急忙补充道。

于是,那天吃过晚饭,他们三个再次离开城堡,穿过覆盖着冰雪的场地,朝海格的小屋走去。他们敲了敲门,听见了牙牙低沉的吠叫声。

"海格,是我们!"哈利喊道,使劲捶打着门,"快开门!"

海格没有回答。可以听见牙牙在抓门,呜呜地低声叫着,但是门没有开。他们又重重地敲了十多分钟。罗恩甚至过去敲了敲一扇窗户,还是没有回音。

"他为什么躲着我们?"赫敏说——这时他们终于作罢,向学校走去,"他总不会以为我们在乎他是个混血统巨人吧?"

然而,看来海格确实很在乎。整整一个星期他们都没有看见他的身影。吃饭的时候,他没有在教工桌子旁露面,他们也没有看见他在场地上履行他猎场看守的职责。格拉普兰教授继续担任保护神奇动物课的代课教师。马尔福一有机会就说些幸灾乐祸的话。

"想念你的那个杂种伙伴了?"每当有老师在旁边,马尔福确信哈利不敢报复时,总是小声对哈利说,"想念那个大象般的家伙了?"

一月中旬,同学们都到霍格莫德村去游玩。赫敏听说哈利也去,非常吃惊。

"我还以为你会趁公共休息室没有人,比较安静,利用一下那里呢。"她说,"你真的得好好研究一下那只金蛋了。"

## CHAPTER TWENTY-FOUR    Rita Skeeter's Scoop

'Oh, I – I reckon I've got a pretty good idea what it's about now,' Harry lied.

'Have you really?' said Hermione, looking impressed. 'Well done!'

Harry's insides gave a guilty squirm, but he ignored them. He still had five weeks to work out that egg clue, after all, and that was ages ... and if he went into Hogsmeade, he might run into Hagrid, and get a chance to persuade him to come back.

He, Ron and Hermione left the castle together on Saturday, and set off through the cold, wet grounds towards the gates. As they passed the Durmstrang ship moored in the lake, they saw Viktor Krum emerge onto the deck, dressed in nothing but swimming trunks. He was very skinny, but apparently a lot tougher than he looked, because he climbed up onto the side of the ship, stretched out his arms and dived, right into the lake.

'He's mad!' said Harry, staring at Krum's dark head, as it bobbed out into the middle of the lake. 'It must be freezing, it's January!'

'It's a lot colder where he comes from,' said Hermione. 'I suppose it feels quite warm to him.'

'Yeah, but there's still the giant squid,' said Ron. He didn't sound anxious – if anything, he sounded hopeful. Hermione noticed his tone of voice, and frowned.

'He's really nice, you know,' she said. 'He's not at all like you'd think, coming from Durmstrang. He likes it much better here, he told me.'

Ron said nothing. He hadn't mentioned Viktor Krum since the ball, but Harry had found a miniature arm under his bed on Boxing Day, which had looked very much as though it had been snapped off a small model figure wearing Bulgaria Quidditch robes.

Harry kept his eyes skinned for a sign of Hagrid all the way down the slushy High Street, and suggested a visit to the Three Broomsticks once he had ascertained that Hagrid was not in any of the shops.

The pub was as crowded as ever, but one quick look around at all the tables told Harry that Hagrid wasn't there. Heart sinking, he went up to the bar with Ron and Hermione, ordered three Butterbeers from Madam Rosmerta, and thought gloomily that he might just as well have stayed behind and listened to the egg wailing after all.

'Doesn't he *ever* go into the office?' Hermione whispered suddenly. 'Look!'

"噢,我——我觉得我已经差不多琢磨出它是什么意思了。"哈利撒了个谎。

"真的吗?"赫敏说,显得非常高兴,"太好了!"

哈利觉得内疚,心中惶惶不安,但他无视了这种感觉。毕竟,他还有五个星期可以研究金蛋的线索,时间还长着呢……而且如果去了霍格莫德,说不定会碰到海格,有机会劝说他回来呢。

星期六,他和罗恩、赫敏一起离开城堡,穿过阴冷、潮湿的场地,向学校大门走去。当他们经过停泊在湖面上的德姆斯特朗大船时,看见威克多尔·克鲁姆从船舱里走到甲板上,身上只穿着一条游泳裤。他确实瘦极了,但他的身体比看上去要强健得多,只见他敏捷地爬到船舷上,伸开双臂,扑通一声钻进了水里。

"他疯了!"哈利望着克鲁姆乌黑的脑袋在湖中央浮动,说道,"现在是一月,肯定冷得要命!"

"他来的地方比这里冷得多。"赫敏说,"我想,对他来说这里还相当暖和呢。"

"是啊,可是湖里有巨乌贼啊。"罗恩说,但口气里并没有担忧的成分——仔细听来,他似乎希望发生点什么呢。赫敏注意到了罗恩的这种口气,皱起了眉头。

"他真的不错,你们知道的。"赫敏说,"虽然他是德姆斯特朗的,但根本不像你们所想的那样。他告诉我,他更喜欢我们这儿。"

罗恩没有说话。自从舞会以后,他就只字不提威克多尔·克鲁姆了。圣诞节的第二天,哈利在他床底下看见了一只小胳膊,很像是从那个穿着保加利亚魁地奇队服的小模型上掰下来的。

在覆满融雪的大街上溜达时,哈利一直在留心寻找海格。当确信一家家商店里都没有海格的身影时,他又提出到三把扫帚去坐坐。

小酒馆和往常一样拥挤,哈利的目光迅速将所有的桌子都扫视了一遍,没有发现海格。他心情沉重地和罗恩、赫敏一起走向吧台,从罗斯默塔女士那里买了三杯黄油啤酒。他闷闷不乐地想,早知如此,还不如留在学校里听听金蛋的惨叫声呢。

"他难道从来不去办公室吗?"赫敏突然悄声说,"看!"

## CHAPTER TWENTY-FOUR    Rita Skeeter's Scoop

She pointed into the mirror behind the bar, and Harry saw Ludo Bagman reflected there, sitting in a shadowy corner with a bunch of goblins. Bagman was talking very fast in a low voice to the goblins, all of whom had their arms crossed, and were looking rather menacing.

It was indeed odd, Harry thought, that Bagman was here at the Three Broomsticks on a weekend when there was no Triwizard event, and therefore no judging to be done. He watched Bagman in the mirror. He was looking strained again, quite as strained as he had done that night in the forest before the Dark Mark had appeared. But just then Bagman glanced over at the bar, saw Harry, and stood up.

'In a moment, in a moment!' Harry heard him say brusquely to the goblins, and Bagman hurried through the pub towards Harry, his boyish grin back in place.

'Harry!' he said. 'How are you? Been hoping to run into you! Everything going all right?'

'Fine, thanks,' said Harry.

'Wonder if I could have a quick, private word, Harry?' said Bagman eagerly. 'You couldn't give us a moment, you two, could you?'

'Er – OK,' said Ron, and he and Hermione went off to find a table.

Bagman led Harry along the bar to the end furthest from Madam Rosmerta.

'Well, I just thought I'd congratulate you again on your splendid performance against that Horntail, Harry,' said Bagman. 'Really superb.'

'Thanks,' said Harry, but he knew this couldn't be all that Bagman wanted to say, because he could have congratulated Harry in front of Ron and Hermione. Bagman didn't seem in any particular rush to spill the beans, though. Harry saw him glance into the mirror over the bar at the goblins, who were all watching him and Harry in silence through their dark, slanting eyes.

'Absolute nightmare,' said Bagman to Harry in an undertone, noticing Harry watching the goblins, too. 'Their English isn't too good ... it's like being back with all the Bulgarians at the Quidditch World Cup ... but at least *they* used sign language another human could recognise. This lot keep gabbling in Gobbledegook ... and I only know one word of Gobbledegook. *Bladvak*. It means 'pickaxe'. I don't like to use it in case they think I'm threatening them.' He gave a short, booming laugh.

## 第24章 丽塔·斯基特的独家新闻

她指着吧台后面的那面镜子,哈利看见镜子里映出卢多·巴格曼的身影,他和一伙妖精一起坐在昏暗的角落里。巴格曼正压低声音,飞快地对妖精们说着什么,妖精们都交叉着手臂,一副气势汹汹的样子。

这确实有些奇怪,哈利想,今天是周末,没有三强争霸赛的活动,用不着裁判,巴格曼怎么会出现在三把扫帚里呢?他注视着镜子里的巴格曼。只见他神情又显得很紧张,就像那天夜里黑魔标记出现之前在树林里一样。就在这时,巴格曼向吧台扫了一眼,看见哈利,便站了起来。

"等一会儿,等一会儿!"哈利听见巴格曼生硬地对妖精们说,然后匆匆朝哈利走来,那张娃娃脸上又露出了笑容。

"哈利!"他说,"你怎么样?我就希望碰到你!一切都好吧?"

"很好,谢谢。"哈利说。

"不知我能不能跟你单独说几句话,哈利?"巴格曼热切地说,"你们俩能不能给我们一个方便?"

"呃——好吧。"罗恩说完,便和赫敏去找位子了。

巴格曼领着哈利来到远离罗斯默塔女士的吧台尽头。

"哈利,我想再次祝贺你在对付那条树蜂时的出色表现。"巴格曼说,"真是太棒了!"

"谢谢。"哈利说,但他知道巴格曼想说的不止这些,因为他完全可以当着罗恩和赫敏的面祝贺哈利。不过,巴格曼似乎并不急于揭开谜底。哈利看见他朝镜子里吧台那边的妖精们扫了一眼,他们都斜着黑眼睛,默默地望着巴格曼和哈利。

"绝对是一场噩梦。"巴格曼发现哈利也望着妖精们,便压低声音说道,"他们英语说得不好……这就像又回到了魁地奇世界杯赛上,和那些保加利亚人纠缠不清……但至少保加利亚人还能比比画画,使人能够明白。这帮家伙一个劲儿地咕噜咕噜,说他们的妖精话……而我对妖精话只知道一个单词。布拉德瓦,意思是'刀、剑'。我不愿意使用这个词,生怕他们以为我在威胁他们。"他低沉而短促地笑了一声。

## CHAPTER TWENTY-FOUR  Rita Skeeter's Scoop

'What do they want?' Harry said, noticing how the goblins were still watching Bagman very closely.

'Er – well ...' said Bagman, looking suddenly nervous. 'They ... er ... they're looking for Barty Crouch.'

'Why are they looking for him here?' said Harry. 'He's at the Ministry in London, isn't he?'

'Er ... as a matter of fact, I've no idea where he is,' said Bagman. 'He's sort of ... stopped coming to work. Been absent for a couple of weeks now. Young Percy, his assistant, says he's ill. Apparently he's just been sending instructions in by owl. But would you mind not mentioning that to anyone, Harry? Because Rita Skeeter's still poking around everywhere she can, and I'm willing to bet she'd work Barty's illness up into something sinister. Probably say he's gone missing like Bertha Jorkins.'

'Have you heard anything about Bertha Jorkins?' Harry asked.

'No,' said Bagman, looking strained again. 'I've got people looking, of course ...' (About time, thought Harry) 'and it's all very strange. She definitely *arrived* in Albania, because she met her second cousin there. And then she left the cousin's house to go south and see an aunt ... and she seems to have vanished without trace, en route. Blowed if I can see where she's got to ... she doesn't seem the type to elope, for instance ... but still ... what are we doing, talking about goblins and Bertha Jorkins? I really wanted to ask you,' he lowered his voice, 'how are you getting on with your golden egg?'

'Er ... not bad,' Harry said untruthfully.

Bagman seemed to know he wasn't being honest.

'Listen, Harry,' he said (still in a very low voice), 'I feel very bad about all this ... you were thrown into this Tournament, you didn't volunteer for it ... and if' (his voice was so quiet now, Harry had to lean closer to listen) '... if I can help at all ... a prod in the right direction ... I've taken a liking to you ... the way you got past that dragon! ... Well, just say the word.'

Harry looked up into Bagman's round, rosy face, and wide, baby-blue eyes.

'We're supposed to work out the clues alone, aren't we?' he said, careful to keep his voice casual, and not sound as though he was accusing the Head of the Department of Magical games and Sports of breaking the rules.

## 第24章 丽塔·斯基特的独家新闻

"他们想要什么?"哈利说,注意到妖精们仍然在死死地盯着巴格曼。

"呃——是这样……"巴格曼说,突然显得紧张起来,"他们……呃……他们在寻找巴蒂·克劳奇。"

"为什么到这里来找他?"哈利说,"他在伦敦的魔法部里,不是吗?"

"呃……说句实话,我也不知道他在哪里。"巴格曼说,"他……他突然就不来上班了。到现在已经有两个星期了。他的助手,年轻的珀西说他病了。看样子他不断地派猫头鹰发来指示。不过,这件事你可千万别对任何人说,好吗,哈利?因为丽塔·斯基特还在无孔不入地到处打听,我敢说她准会给巴蒂的病添油加醋,把它渲染成一个灾难事件。她大概会说巴蒂也像伯莎·乔金斯一样失踪了。"

"伯莎·乔金斯有消息了吗?"哈利问道。

"没有。"巴格曼说,神情又紧张起来,"当然啦,我已经派人去寻找了……(早该这么做了,哈利想)事情非常奇怪。她肯定到了阿尔巴尼亚,因为她在那里见到了她的二表姐。然后她离开二表姐家,到南部去看望一个姨妈……从此便消失得无影无踪。真该死,我就是不明白她上哪儿去了……她又不像是那种私奔、潜逃的人……不过谁知道呢……咳,我们在这里只顾谈论妖精和伯莎·乔金斯干吗?我实际上是想问你,"——他放低声音——"你对那只金蛋研究得怎么样了?"

"嗯……还行。"哈利不诚实地说。

巴格曼似乎知道他没有说实话。

"听着,哈利,"他说(声音仍然很低),"我对这一切感到很难过……你被强行拉进了这场争霸赛,不是自愿参加的……如果……(他的声音低极了,哈利不得不靠近了才能听清)如果我能帮得上忙……给你一个恰当的提醒……我对你产生了好感……你对付那条巨龙时真是勇敢!……没关系,你只要说一句话。"

哈利抬头望着巴格曼红扑扑的圆脸,以及那双睁得大大的、浅蓝色的眼睛。

"我们应该独自解开谜团,不是吗?"哈利说,尽量使自己的语气听上去很随意,不要显得像是在指责魔法体育运动司的司长擅自违反章程。

## CHAPTER TWENTY-FOUR    Rita Skeeter's Scoop

'Well ... well, yes,' said Bagman impatiently, 'but – come on, Harry – we all want a Hogwarts victory, don't we?'

'Have you offered Cedric help?' Harry said.

The smallest of frowns creased Bagman's smooth face.

'No, I haven't,' he said. 'I – well, like I say, I've taken a liking to you. Just thought I'd offer ...'

'Well, thanks,' said Harry, 'but I think I'm nearly there with the egg ... couple more days should crack it.'

He wasn't entirely sure why he was refusing Bagman's help, except that Bagman was almost a stranger to him, and accepting his assistance would feel somehow much more like cheating than asking advice from Ron, Hermione or Sirius.

Bagman looked almost affronted, but couldn't say much more as Fred and George turned up at that point.

'Hello, Mr Bagman,' said Fred brightly. 'Can we buy you a drink?'

'Er ... no,' said Bagman, with a last disappointed glance at Harry, 'no thank you, boys ...'

Fred and George looked quite as disappointed as Bagman, who was surveying Harry as though he had let him down badly.

'Well, I must dash,' he said. 'Nice seeing you all. Good luck, Harry.'

He hurried out of the pub. The goblins all slid off their chairs and exited after him. Harry went to rejoin Ron and Hermione.

'What did he want?' Ron said, the moment Harry had sat down.

'He offered to help me with the golden egg,' said Harry.

'He shouldn't be doing that!' said Hermione, looking very shocked. 'He's one of the judges! And anyway, you've already worked it out – haven't you?'

'Er ... nearly,' said Harry.

'Well, I don't think Dumbledore would like it if he knew Bagman was trying to persuade you to cheat!' said Hermione, still looking deeply disapproving. 'I hope he's trying to help Cedric as much!'

'He's not. I asked,' said Harry.

'Who cares if Diggory's getting help?' said Ron. Harry privately agreed.

## 第24章　丽塔·斯基特的独家新闻

"哦……是啊，是啊，"巴格曼不耐烦地说，"可是——别傻了，哈利——我们都希望霍格沃茨一举夺魁，是不是？"

"你给塞德里克也提供过帮助吗？"哈利问。

巴格曼光滑的脸上微微皱起了眉头。"没有。"他说，"我——唉，就像我刚才说的，对你产生了好感。我就想给你……"

"那就谢谢你了。"哈利说，"但是，我想我对金蛋已经钻研得差不多了……再有一两天就可以水落石出了。"

他并不完全明白自己为什么要拒绝巴格曼的帮助，大概因为巴格曼在他眼里几乎是个陌生人，向罗恩、赫敏和小天狼星请教不算什么，而接受巴格曼的帮助就使人感觉更像是作弊。

巴格曼看上去简直有点恼火了，但他没来得及说出什么，因为弗雷德和乔治正好在这个时候出现了。

"你好，巴格曼先生，"弗雷德愉快地说，"我们可以请你喝一杯吗？"

"嗯……不用了。"巴格曼说着，又失望地看了哈利最后一眼，"不用了，谢谢你们，孩子……"

弗雷德和乔治似乎和巴格曼同样失望。巴格曼打量着哈利，就好像哈利不知好歹地拂了他的美意。

"好了，我得赶紧走了。"他说，"很高兴看见你们大家。祝你好运，哈利。"

他匆匆走出小酒馆。妖精们都从椅子上站起来，跟在他后面走了出去。哈利回到罗恩和赫敏身边。

"他想要什么？"哈利刚坐下来，罗恩就问道。

"他提出要帮助我解开金蛋的秘密。"哈利说。

"他不应该这么做！"赫敏显得十分震惊，说道，"他是裁判之一啊！而且，你已经自己琢磨出来了——是不是？"

"呃……差不多吧。"哈利说。

"哼，我想，如果邓布利多知道巴格曼在劝你作弊，肯定会很不高兴的！"赫敏说，仍然是一副不以为然的神情，"我希望他也向塞德里克提供同样的帮助！"

"他没有，我问过了。"哈利说。

"我们才不关心迪戈里是不是得到帮助呢。"罗恩说，哈利暗自赞同。

## CHAPTER TWENTY-FOUR    Rita Skeeter's Scoop

'Those goblins didn't look very friendly,' said Hermione, sipping her Butterbeer. 'What were they doing here?'

'Looking for Crouch, according to Bagman,' said Harry. 'He's still ill. Hasn't been into work.'

'Maybe Percy's poisoning him,' said Ron. 'Probably thinks if Crouch snuffs it he'll be made Head of the Department of International Magical Co-operation.'

Hermione gave Ron a don't-joke-about-things-like-that look, and said, 'Funny, goblins looking for Mr. Crouch ... they'd normally deal with the Department for the Regulation and Control of Magical Creatures.'

'Crouch can speak loads of different languages, though,' said Harry. 'Maybe they need an interpreter.'

'Worrying about poor 'ickle goblins, now, are you?' Ron asked Hermione. 'Thinking of starting up S.P.U.G. or something? Society for the Protection of Ugly Goblins?'

'Ha, ha, ha,' said Hermione sarcastically. 'Goblins don't need protection. Haven't you been listening to what Professor Binns has been telling us about goblin rebellions?'

'No,' said Harry and Ron together.

'Well, they're quite capable of dealing with wizards,' said Hermione, sipping more of her Butterbeer. 'They're very clever. They're not like house-elves, who never stick up for themselves.'

'Uh oh,' said Ron, staring at the door.

Rita Skeeter had just entered. She was wearing banana-yellow robes today; her long nails were painted shocking pink, and she was accompanied by her paunchy photographer. She bought drinks, and she and the photographer made their way through the crowds to a table nearby, Harry, Ron and Hermione glaring at her as she approached. She was talking fast and looking very satisfied about something.

'... didn't seem very keen to talk to us, did he, Bozo? Now, why would that be, do you think? And what's he doing with a pack of goblins in tow anyway? Showing them the sights ... what nonsense ... he was always a bad liar. Reckon something's up? Think we should do a bit of digging? *Disgraced Ex-Head of Magical Sports, Ludo Bagman* ... snappy start to a sentence, Bozo – we just need to find a story to fit it –'

## 第24章 丽塔·斯基特的独家新闻

"那些妖精看上去不太友好，"赫敏一边小口喝着黄油啤酒，一边说道，"他们在这儿干什么？"

"据巴格曼说，是在寻找克劳奇。"哈利说，"克劳奇的病还没好，一直没有上班。"

"可能是珀西给他下了毒吧。"罗恩说，"他大概以为，如果克劳奇断了气儿，他就会成为国际魔法合作司的司长了。"

赫敏瞪了罗恩一眼，意思是别拿这样的事情开玩笑，然后她说："真滑稽，妖精居然寻找克劳奇先生……一般来说，他们是跟神奇动物管理控制司打交道的呀。"

"不过，克劳奇会说许多种语言，"哈利说，"妖精们大概需要一个翻译。"

"怎么，你又开始为讨厌的小妖精们操心了？"罗恩问赫敏，"又想成立一个 S.P.U.G. 什么的？丑陋妖精保护协会？"

"哈，哈，哈，"赫敏讽刺地说，"妖精才不需要保护呢。你没有听见宾斯教授讲妖精叛乱时是怎么说的吗？"

"没有。"哈利和罗恩同时说道。

"听着，妖精们可非常擅长对付巫师，"赫敏说着，又喝了一口黄油啤酒，"他们非常聪明。他们才不像家养小精灵那样不会维护自己的权益呢。"

"哎哟！"罗恩盯着门口，叫道。

丽塔·斯基特走了进来。她今天穿着一件香蕉黄的长袍，长长的指甲涂成耀眼的粉红色，身边跟着她那个大腹便便的摄影师。她买了饮料，和摄影师一起穿过人群，朝近旁的一张桌子走来。哈利、罗恩和赫敏都瞪眼望着她。她正在飞快地说着什么，似乎对什么事感到非常满意。

"……他似乎不太愿意跟我们说话，是不是，博佐？你说，为什么会这样呢？他在做什么，后面跟着一大群妖精？还说是带他们逛风景……完全是胡说八道……他从来都不会撒谎。是不是出什么事了？我们要不要再挖掘一下？魔法体育运动司前司长卢多·巴格曼名誉扫地……这个开头真够劲儿，博佐——我们只需要给它找一个合适的故事——"

## CHAPTER TWENTY-FOUR    Rita Skeeter's Scoop

'Trying to ruin someone else's life?' said Harry loudly.

A few people looked around. Rita Skeeter's eyes widened behind her jewelled spectacles as she saw who had spoken.

'Harry!' she said, beaming. 'How lovely! Why don't you come and join –?'

'I wouldn't come near you with a ten-foot broomstick,' said Harry furiously. 'What did you do that to Hagrid for, eh?'

Rita Skeeter raised her heavily pencilled eyebrows.

'Our readers have the right to know the truth, Harry, I am merely doing my –'

'Who cares if he's half-giant?' Harry shouted. 'There's nothing wrong with him!'

The whole pub had gone very quiet. Madam Rosmerta was staring over from behind the bar, apparently oblivious of the fact that the flagon she was filling with mead was overflowing.

Rita Skeeter's smile flickered very slightly, but she hitched it back almost at once; she snapped open her crocodileskin handbag, pulled out her Quick-Quotes Quill and said, 'How about giving me an interview about the Hagrid *you* know, Harry? The man behind the muscles? Your unlikely friendship and the reasons behind it. Would you call him a father substitute?'

Hermione stood up very abruptly, her Butterbeer clutched in her hand as though it was a grenade.

'You horrible woman,' she said, through gritted teeth, 'you don't care, do you, anything for a story, and anyone will do, won't they? Even Ludo Bagman –'

'Sit down, you silly little girl, and don't talk about things you don't understand,' said Rita Skeeter coldly, her eyes hardening as they fell on Hermione. 'I know things about Ludo Bagman that would make your hair curl ... Not that it needs it –' she added, eyeing Hermione's bushy hair.

'Let's go,' said Hermione. 'C'mon, Harry – Ron ...'

They left; many people were staring at them as they went. Harry glanced back as they reached the door. Rita Skeeter's Quick-Quotes Quill was out; it was zooming backwards and forwards over a piece of parchment on the table.

'She'll be after you next, Hermione,' said Ron, in a low and worried voice as they walked quickly back up the street.

## 第24章 丽塔·斯基特的独家新闻

"又想毁掉一个人的生活?"哈利大声说。

几个人转过脸来。丽塔·斯基特看清了说话的是谁,镶着珠宝的眼镜后面的眼睛一下子睁大了。

"哈利!"她说,顿时笑容满面,"太好了!你们为什么不过来一起——"

"即使骑着一把十英尺长的飞天扫帚,我也不愿接近你!"哈利气愤地说,"你为什么要那样对待海格,嗯?"

丽塔·斯基特扬起描得很浓的眉毛。

"我们的读者有权知道真相,哈利。我只是履行我的——"

"谁在乎他是不是混血统巨人呢?"哈利喊道,"他没有一点儿不正常的地方!"

整个小酒馆一下子变得鸦雀无声。罗斯默塔女士从吧台后面朝这边望——她正在往大酒壶里倒蜂蜜酒,大酒壶都满得溢出来了,她也没有觉察。

丽塔·斯基特的笑容微微闪动了一下,但她马上又把它重新固定好了。她打开鳄鱼皮手袋,掏出她的速记笔,说道:"愿意跟我谈谈你所了解的海格吗,哈利?一身腱子肉后面的人性?你们令人费解的友谊,以及友谊后面的缘由。你是不是把他看作父亲?"

赫敏猛地站了起来,手里紧紧攥着那杯黄油啤酒,就好像那是一颗手榴弹。

"你这个讨厌的女人,"她咬牙切齿地说,"真是不择手段,只要能捞到故事,不管是谁都不放过,是不是?就连卢多·巴格曼——"

"坐下,你这个傻乎乎的小丫头,对自己不明白的事不要乱说。"丽塔·斯基特冷冷地说,目光落到赫敏身上时变得冷漠而凶狠,"我知道卢多·巴格曼的一些事情,它们会吓得你头发都竖起来……不过也用不着……"她说,打量着赫敏乱蓬蓬的头发。

"我们走吧,"赫敏说,"快点儿,哈利——罗恩……"

他们离开了,许多人都望着他们。走到门边时,哈利回头看了一眼,丽塔·斯基特的速记笔拿出来了,在桌上一张羊皮纸上嗖嗖地来回划动着。

"她接下来就要对付你了,赫敏。"他们快步来到大街上时,罗恩压低声音担忧地说。

'Let her try!' said Hermione shrilly; she was shaking with rage. 'I'll show her! Silly little girl, am I? Oh, I'll get her back for this, first Harry, then Hagrid ...'

'You don't want to go upsetting Rita Skeeter,' said Ron nervously. 'I'm serious, Hermione, she'll dig something up on you –'

'My parents don't read the *Daily Prophet*, she can't scare me into hiding!' said Hermione, now striding along so fast that it was all Harry and Ron could do to keep up with her. The last time Harry had seen Hermione in a rage like this, she had hit Draco Malfoy around the face. 'And Hagrid isn't going to hide any more! He should *never* have let that excuse for a human being upset him! Come *on*!'

Breaking into a run, she led them all the way back up the road, through the gates flanked by winged boars, and up through the grounds to Hagrid's cabin.

The curtains were still drawn, and they could hear Fang barking as they approached.

'Hagrid!' Hermione shouted, pounding on his front door. 'Hagrid, that's enough! We know you're in there! Nobody cares if your mum was a giantess, Hagrid! You can't let that foul Skeeter woman do this to you! Hagrid, get out here, you're just being –'

The door opened. Hermione said 'About t–!' and then stopped, very suddenly, because she had found herself face to face, not with Hagrid, but with Albus Dumbledore.

'Good afternoon,' he said pleasantly, smiling down at them.

'We – er – we wanted to see Hagrid,' said Hermione in a rather small voice.

'Yes, I surmised as much,' said Dumbledore, his eyes twinkling. 'Why don't you come in?'

'Oh ... um ... OK,' said Hermione.

She, Ron and Harry went into the cabin; Fang launched himself upon Harry the moment he entered, barking madly and trying to lick his ears. Harry fended Fang off, and looked around.

Hagrid was sitting at his table, where there were two large mugs of tea. He looked a real mess. His face was blotchy, his eyes swollen, and he had gone to the other extreme where his hair was concerned; far from trying to make it behave, it now looked like a wig of tangled wire.

'Hi, Hagrid,' said Harry.

Hagrid looked up.

"让她试试吧!"赫敏满不在乎地说,但气得浑身发抖,"我会给她点厉害尝尝!我是傻乎乎的小丫头?哼,我会让她付出代价的。先是为哈利,然后是为海格……"

"你可别去招惹丽塔·斯基特。"罗恩紧张地说,"我说正经的,赫敏,她会挖掘你的一些情况——"

"我爸爸妈妈不看《预言家日报》。她不会把我吓得东躲西藏的!"赫敏说,"而且海格不能再躲藏了!他不应该被这个败类搅得心烦意乱!快走!"赫敏迈着大步,走得飞快,哈利和罗恩铆足了劲儿才赶上她。上次哈利看见赫敏气成这样,是她打了德拉科·马尔福一记耳光的时候。

她撒腿跑了起来,领着他们一路飞奔,穿过那道两边被带翅野猪护着的大门,跑过场地,来到海格的小屋旁。

窗帘仍然拉得严严实实,他们走近时可以听见牙牙的叫声。

"海格!"赫敏喊道,一边敲打着房门,"海格,够了!我们知道你在里面!没有人在乎你妈妈是个巨人,海格!斯基特那个讨厌的女人,你不能让她得逞!海格,快出来吧,你不过是在——"

门开了。赫敏刚说了句"你早该——",又猛地住了口,因为她发现与她面对面的不是海格,而是阿不思·邓布利多。

"下午好。"邓布利多愉快地说,笑眯眯地低头望着他们。

"我们……嗯……我们想看看海格。"赫敏声音很轻地说。

"啊,我已经猜到了。"邓布利多说,眼睛里闪着诙谐的光,"为什么不进来呢?"

"噢……呃……好吧。"赫敏说。

她和罗恩、哈利走进了小屋。哈利刚进门,牙牙就忽地朝他扑来,猖猖狂吠着,想要舔他的耳朵。哈利躲开牙牙,四下张望着。

海格坐在桌旁,面前放着两只大茶杯。他的模样十分狼狈,脸上斑斑点点,眼睛又红又肿,在头发的问题上又走向了另一个极端:他不再想办法把头发弄整洁了,现在它们变成了一堆缠在一起的电线。

"你好,海格。"哈利说。

海格抬起头来。

## CHAPTER TWENTY-FOUR  Rita Skeeter's Scoop

''Lo,' he said, in a very hoarse voice.

'More tea, I think,' said Dumbledore, closing the door behind Harry, Ron and Hermione, drawing out his wand and twiddling it; a revolving tea-tray appeared in mid-air, along with a plate of cakes. Dumbledore magicked the tray onto the table, and everybody sat down. There was a slight pause, and then Dumbledore said, 'Did you by any chance hear what Miss Granger was shouting, Hagrid?'

Hermione went slightly pink, but Dumbledore smiled at her, and continued, 'Hermione, Harry and Ron still seem to want to know you, judging by the way they were attempting to break down the door.'

'Of course we still want to know you!' Harry said, staring at Hagrid. 'You don't think anything that Skeeter cow – sorry, Professor,' he added quickly, looking at Dumbledore.

'I have gone temporarily deaf and haven't any idea what you said, Harry,' said Dumbledore, twiddling his thumbs and staring at the ceiling.

'Er – right,' said Harry sheepishly. 'I just meant – Hagrid, how could you think we'd care what that – woman – wrote about you?'

Two fat tears leaked out of Hagrid's beetle-black eyes and fell slowly into his tangled beard.

'Living proof of what I've been telling you, Hagrid,' said Dumbledore, still looking carefully up at the ceiling. 'I have shown you the letters from the countless parents who remember you from their own days here, telling me in no uncertain terms that, if I sacked you, they would have something to say about it –'

'Not all of 'em,' said Hagrid hoarsely. 'Not all of 'em wan' me ter stay.'

'Really, Hagrid, if you are holding out for universal popularity, I'm afraid you will be in this cabin for a very long time,' said Dumbledore, now peering sternly over his half-moon spectacles. 'Not a week has passed, since I became Headmaster of this school, when I haven't had at least one owl complaining about the way I run it. But what should I do? Barricade myself in my study and refuse to talk to anybody?'

'Yeh – yeh're not half-giant!' said Hagrid croakily.

'Hagrid, look what I've got for relatives!' Harry said furiously. 'Look at the Dursleys!'

'An excellent point,' said Professor Dumbledore. 'My own brother,

## 第24章 丽塔·斯基特的独家新闻

"好。"他用非常沙哑的声音说。

"再喝点茶吧。"邓布利多说,在哈利、罗恩和赫敏身后关上房门,掏出魔杖,轻轻摆弄着,空中立刻出现了一只旋转的茶盘和一盘蛋糕。邓布利多用魔法使茶盘落在桌上,大家都坐了下来。静默了片刻,邓布利多说道:"海格,你有没有听见格兰杰小姐喊的那些话?"

赫敏的脸微微有些红,邓布利多朝她笑了笑,继续说道:"从他们刚才想破门而入的架势看,赫敏、哈利和罗恩似乎还愿意交你这个朋友。"

"我们当然还愿意同你交朋友!"哈利望着海格,说,"你难道认为斯基特那头母牛——对不起,教授。"他赶紧说道,转眼望着邓布利多。

"我一时耳聋,没听见你在说什么,哈利。"邓布利多说。他玩弄着两个大拇指,眼睛瞪着天花板。

"呃——好吧,"哈利局促不安地说,"我的意思是——海格,你怎么以为我们会在乎那个——女人——写的东西呢?"

两颗滚圆的泪珠从海格甲虫般黑亮的眼睛里流出来,慢慢渗进了他纠结的胡子里。

"海格,这恰好证明了我刚才的话。"邓布利多说,仍然专心地打量着天花板,"我给你看了无数个家长写来的信,他们自己当年在这里上过学,对你印象很深。他们十分坚决地对我说,如果我把你开除,他们决不会善罢甘休——"

"并不是每个人,"海格沙哑地说,"并不是每个人都愿意我留下。"

"说实在的,海格,你如果想等到全世界人的支持,恐怕就要在这个小屋里待很长时间了。"邓布利多说,目光从半月形镜片后面严厉地射过来,"自从我担任这个学校的校长以来,每星期至少有一只猫头鹰送信来,对我管理学校的方式提出批评。你说我应该怎么办呢?把自己关在书房里,拒绝跟任何人说话?"

"可是——你不是混血统巨人啊!"海格声音嘶哑地说。

"海格,你看看我有什么样的亲戚吧!"哈利生气地说,"看看德思礼一家!"

"绝妙的观点!"邓布利多教授说,"我的亲弟弟阿不福思,因为对

## CHAPTER TWENTY-FOUR    Rita Skeeter's Scoop

Aberforth, was prosecuted for practising inappropriate charms on a goat. It was all over the papers, but did Aberforth hide? No, he did not! He held his head high and went about his business as usual! Of course, I'm not entirely sure he can read, so that may not have been bravery ...'

'Come back and teach, Hagrid,' said Hermione quietly, 'please come back, we really miss you.'

Hagrid gulped. More tears leaked out down his cheeks and into his tangled beard. Dumbledore stood up.

'I refuse to accept your resignation, Hagrid, and I expect you back at work on Monday,' he said. 'You will join me for breakfast at eight thirty in the Great Hall. No excuses. Good afternoon to you all.'

Dumbledore left the cabin, pausing only to scratch Fang's ears. When the door had shut behind him, Hagrid began to sob into his dustbin-lid-sized hands. Hermione kept patting his arm, and at last Hagrid looked up, his eyes very red indeed, and said, 'Great man, Dumbledore ... great man ...'

'Yeah, he is,' said Ron. 'Can I have one of these cakes, Hagrid?'

'Help yourself,' said Hagrid, wiping his eyes on the back of his hand. 'Ar, he's righ', o' course – yeh're all righ' ... I bin stupid ... my ol' dad woulda bin ashamed o' the way I've bin behavin' ...' More tears leaked out, but he wiped them away more forcefully, and said, 'Never shown you a picture of my old dad, have I? Here ...'

Hagrid got up, went over to his dresser, opened a drawer and pulled out a picture of a short wizard with Hagrid's crinkled black eyes, beaming as he sat on top of Hagrid's shoulder. Hagrid was a good seven or eight feet tall, judging by the apple tree beside him, but his face was beardless, young, round and smooth – he looked hardly older than eleven.

'Tha' was taken jus' after I got inter Hogwarts,' said Hagrid, croakily. 'Dad was dead chuffed ... thought I migh' not be a wizard, see, 'cos me mum ... well, anyway. 'Course, I never was great shakes at magic, really ... but at least he never saw me expelled. Died, see, in me second year ...

'Dumbledore was the one who stuck up for me after Dad went. Got me the gamekeeper job ... trusts people, he does. Gives 'em second chances ... tha's what sets him apar' from other Heads, see. He'll accept anyone at Hogwarts, s'long as they've got the talent. Knows people can turn out OK even if their

## 第24章 丽塔·斯基特的独家新闻

一只山羊滥施魔法而被起诉。这件事在报纸上登得铺天盖地,可是阿不福思躲起来没有呢?没有,根本没有!他把头抬得高高的,照样我行我素!当然啦,我不能肯定他认识字,所以他也许并不是胆子大……"

"回来教课吧,海格。"赫敏轻声说,"求求你回来吧,我们真的很想念你。"

海格深吸了一口气。又有许多眼泪顺着他的面颊滚落下来,渗进乱蓬蓬的胡子里。邓布利多站了起来。

"我不接受你的辞职报告,海格,我希望你下星期一就回来上课。"他说,"你八点半到礼堂和我一起吃早饭。不许找理由推托。祝你们大家下午好。"

邓布利多向门口走去,只停下来弯腰挠了挠牙牙的耳朵,就离开了小屋。当房门在他身后关上后,海格便把脸埋在垃圾箱盖一般大的手掌里,伤心地哭泣起来。赫敏不停地拍着他的胳膊,最后,海格终于抬起了头,两只眼睛通红,他说:"真是了不起的人啊,邓布利多……了不起的人……"

"是啊,他很了不起。"罗恩说,"我可以吃一块蛋糕吗,海格?"

"尽管吃吧,"海格说着,用手背擦了擦眼睛,"唉,当然,他说得对——你们说得都对……我太傻了……我这么做,我的老爸爸一定会为我感到脸红……"眼泪又流出来了,他用力把它们擦去,又说道,"我还没有给你们看过我老爸爸的照片呢,是不是?在这里……"

海格站起来走到衣柜前,拉开一个抽屉,取出一张照片,上面有一个小矮个儿的巫师,眼睛和海格的一样,也是乌溜溜的,眯成一道缝,他坐在海格的肩膀上笑得很欢。参照旁边的一棵苹果树看,海格足有七八英尺高,但他的脸年轻、饱满、光滑,没有胡子——看上去最多十一岁。

"这是我进霍格沃茨后不久照的,"海格声音嘶哑地说,"爸爸高兴坏了……他还以为我成不了一名巫师呢,你们知道,因为我妈妈……唉,不提也罢。当然,我在魔法方面一直不大开窍……但爸爸至少没有看见我被开除。他死了,明白吗,就在我上二年级的时候……

"爸爸死后,是邓布利多一直护着我。给我找了份猎场看守的工作……他很信任别人。总是给人第二次机会……这正是他和其他校长不同的地方,明白吗?一个人只要有天分,邓布利多就会接受他到霍

## CHAPTER TWENTY-FOUR  Rita Skeeter's Scoop

families weren' ... well ... all tha' respectable. But some don' understand that. There's some who'd always hold it against yeh ... there's some who'd even pretend they just had big bones rather than stand up an' say – I am what I am, an' I'm not ashamed. "Never be ashamed," my ol' dad used ter say, "there's some who'll hold it against you, but they're not worth botherin' with." An' he was right. I've bin an idiot. I'm not botherin' with *her* no more, I promise yeh that. Big bones ... I'll give her big bones.'

Harry, Ron and Hermione looked at each other nervously; Harry would rather have taken fifty Blast-Ended Skrewts for a walk than admit to Hagrid that he had overheard him talking to Madame Maxime, but Hagrid was still talking, apparently unaware that he had said anything odd.

'Yeh know wha', Harry?' he said, looking up from the photograph of his father, his eyes very bright. 'When I firs' met you, you reminded me o' me a bit. Mum an' dad gone, an' you was feelin' like yeh wouldn' fit in at Hogwarts, remember? Not sure yeh were really up to it ... an' now look at yeh, Harry! School champion!'

He looked at Harry for a moment and then said, very seriously, 'Yeh know what I'd love, Harry? I'd love yeh ter win, I really would. It'd show 'em all ... yeh don' have ter be pure-blood ter do it. Yeh don' have ter be ashamed of what yeh are. It'd show 'em Dumbledore's the one who's got it righ', lettin' anyone in as long as they can do magic. How you doin' with that egg, Harry?'

'Great,' said Harry. 'Really great.'

Hagrid's miserable face broke into a wide, watery smile. 'Tha's my boy ... You show 'em, Harry, you show 'em. Beat 'em all.'

Lying to Hagrid wasn't quite like lying to anyone else. Harry went back to the castle later that afternoon with Ron and Hermione, unable to banish the image of the happy expression on Hagrid's whiskery face as he had imagined Harry winning the Tournament. The incomprehensible egg weighed more heavily than ever on Harry's conscience that evening, and by the time he had got into bed, he had made up his mind – it was time to shelve his pride, and see if Cedric's hint was worth anything.

格沃茨来。他知道一个人即使出身不好,也是会有出息的……唉……这种做法很值得尊敬。但有些人不理解这一点。有些人总是因为你的出身而歧视你……有些人甚至假装说自己是骨架子大,而不敢大胆地说真话——我就是我,没什么可羞愧的。'永远别感到羞愧,'我的老爸爸过去常说,'有人会因为这个而歧视你,但他们不值得你烦恼。'他是对的。我太傻了。我再也不会为那女人而烦恼了,我向你们保证。大骨架子……我要让她尝尝我的大骨架子!"

哈利、罗恩和赫敏不安地互相望了望。哈利宁愿领五十条炸尾螺去散步,也不愿向海格承认他偷听了他和马克西姆女士的对话。但海格还在说个不停,显然并没有意识到自己说了一些莫名其妙的话。

"你知道吗,哈利?"他说,从他父亲的照片上抬起头,眼睛非常明亮,"我第一次见到你时,你使我想到了我自己。你父母双亡,担心自己在霍格沃茨不适应,记得吗?你不相信自己真的有能力……可是现在再看看你,哈利!学校的勇士!"

他朝哈利望了片刻,然后非常严肃地说:"你知道我希望什么,是不是,哈利?我希望你赢,真的希望。这会使他们都看到……并不是只有纯血统巫师才能做到。用不着为自己的出身而羞愧。这会使他们都看到邓布利多的观点才是正确的,一个人只要有魔法才能,就应该允许他入校。你那只金蛋钻研得怎么样了,哈利?"

"很好,"哈利说,"真的很好。"

海格愁苦的脸上绽开了湿漉漉的灿烂笑容:"真是我的好孩子……让他们看看,哈利,让他们看看。把他们都打败。"

对海格撒谎和对别人撒谎的感觉不一样。那天傍晚,哈利和罗恩、赫敏一起返回城堡时,他眼前一直浮现着海格幻想哈利赢得争霸赛冠军时,那胡子拉碴的脸上的喜悦表情,这形象在他脑海里挥之不去。那天晚上,那只琢磨不透的金蛋比以往任何时候都更沉重地压在哈利心头。上床睡觉时,他终于决定——应该放下自己的傲气,考虑一下塞德里克的提示是否管用。

## CHAPTER TWENTY-FIVE

# The Egg and the Eye

As Harry had no idea how long a bath he would need to work out the secret of the golden egg, he decided to do it at night, when he would be able to take as much time as he wanted. Reluctant though he was to accept more favours from Cedric, he also decided to use the Prefects' bathroom; far fewer people were allowed in there, so it was much less likely that he would be disturbed.

Harry planned his excursion carefully, because he had been caught out of bed and out of bounds by Filch the caretaker in the middle of the night once before, and had no desire to repeat the experience. The Invisibility Cloak would, of course, be essential, and as an added precaution, Harry thought he would take the Marauder's Map, which, next to the Cloak, was the most useful aid to rule-breaking Harry owned. The map showed the whole of Hogwarts, including its many shortcuts and secret passageways and, most importantly of all, it revealed the people inside the castle as minuscule, labelled dots, moving around the corridors, so that Harry would be forewarned if somebody was approaching the bathroom.

On Thursday night, Harry sneaked up to bed, put on the Cloak, crept back downstairs and, just as he had done on the night when Hagrid had shown him the dragons, waited for the portrait hole to open. This time it was Ron who waited outside to give the Fat Lady the password ('Banana fritters'). 'Good luck,' Ron muttered, climbing into the common room as Harry crept out past him.

It was awkward moving under the Cloak tonight, because Harry had the heavy egg under one arm, and the map held in front of his nose with the other. However, the moonlit corridors were empty and silent, and by checking the map at strategic intervals, Harry was able to ensure that he wouldn't run into anyone he wanted to avoid. When he reached the statue

# 第 25 章

# 金蛋和魔眼

哈利不知道这个澡要洗多长时间，才能解开金蛋的奥秘，因此决定夜里行动，这样就能想洗多长时间就洗多长时间了。尽管他很不愿意接受塞德里克更多的恩惠，但还是决定使用级长的洗澡间。很少有人能够进入级长的洗澡间，所以他受到打扰的可能性也就小得多。

哈利仔细筹划着他的这次行动，以前他因为半夜起床到处乱逛被管理员费尔奇抓住过一回，他不希望这种经历重演。隐形衣自然是不可缺少的，但为了保险起见，哈利还想带上活点地图。活点地图的重要性仅次于隐形衣，是哈利违反校规时最有用的辅助工具。地图上显示出霍格沃茨的全景，包括许多错综复杂的捷径和秘密通道。最重要的一点，它还用标着名字的小点显示城堡里的人在走廊里走动的情形，这样，如果有人走近洗澡间，哈利就会预先得到警告。

星期四夜里，哈利偷偷从床上起来，穿上隐形衣，蹑手蹑脚地溜下楼梯，然后就像海格带他去看火龙的那天夜里一样，等着肖像洞口打开。这次等在外面的是罗恩，他对胖夫人说了口令（"香蕉炸面团"）。"祝你好运。"罗恩低声说，一边钻进公共休息室，哈利与他擦身而过。

今天夜里，哈利穿着隐形衣行动非常别扭，因为一只胳膊下夹着沉重的金蛋，另一只胳膊还要举着地图凑到鼻子底下。还好，月光映照的走廊里空荡荡的，非常安静，哈利在几个关键的地方都查看了地图，确保自己不会撞见任何人。他来到糊涂蛋波里斯的雕像前——这是一个表情茫然的巫师，两只手上的手套戴反了。哈利像塞德里克告诉他

## CHAPTER TWENTY-FIVE    The Egg and the Eye

of Boris the Bewildered, a lost-looking wizard with his gloves on the wrong hands, he located the right door, leant close to it, and muttered the password, '*Pine-fresh*', just as Cedric had told him.

The door creaked open. Harry slipped inside, bolted the door behind him, and pulled off the Invisibility Cloak, looking around.

His immediate reaction was that it would be worth becoming a Prefect just to be able to use this bathroom. It was softly lit by a splendid candle-filled chandelier, and everything was made of white marble, including what looked like an empty, rectangular swimming pool sunk into the middle of the floor. About a hundred golden taps stood all around the pool's edges, each with a different-coloured jewel set into its handle. There was also a diving board. Long white linen curtains hung at the windows; a large pile of fluffy white towels sat in a corner, and there was a single golden-framed painting on the wall. It featured a blonde mermaid, who was fast asleep on a rock, her long hair fluttering over her face every time she snored.

Harry put down his Cloak, the egg and the map, and moved forwards, looking around, his footsteps echoing off the walls. Magnificent though the bathroom was – and quite keen though he was to try out a few of those taps – now he was here he couldn't quite suppress the feeling that Cedric might have been having him on. How on earth was this supposed to help solve the mystery of the egg? Nevertheless, he put one of the fluffy towels, the Cloak, the map and the egg at the side of the swimming-pool-sized bath, then knelt down and turned on a few of the taps.

He could tell at once that they carried different sorts of bubble bath mixed with the water, though it wasn't bubble bath as Harry had ever experienced it. One tap gushed pink and blue bubbles the size of footballs, another poured ice-white foam so thick that Harry thought it would have supported his weight if he'd cared to test it; a third sent heavily perfumed purple clouds hovering over the surface of the water. Harry amused himself for a while turning the taps on and off, particularly enjoying the effect of one whose jet bounced off the surface of the water in large arcs. Then, when the deep pool was full of hot water, foam and bubbles (which took a very short time considering its size), Harry turned off all the taps, pulled off his pyjamas, slippers and dressing-gown, and slid into the water.

It was so deep that his feet barely touched the bottom, and he actually did a couple of lengths before swimming back to the side and treading water,

## 第 25 章 金蛋和魔眼

的那样,找到雕像旁边的那扇门,靠上去低声说出了那个口令:"新鲜凤梨。"

门吱呀一声开了。哈利闪了进去,回身把门插好,脱掉隐形衣,四下张望。

他的第一反应是,当一个级长真不赖,单是能够使用这个洗澡间就值了。一个点着蜡烛的豪华枝形吊灯给房间里投下温馨的柔光,每件东西都是用雪白的大理石做成的,包括中间那个陷入地面的浴池,它就像一个长方形的游泳池。浴池边上大约有一百个金色的龙头,每个龙头的把手上都镶着一块不同颜色的宝石。此外还有一块跳水板。窗户上挂着长长的雪白亚麻窗帘;一大堆松软的白毛巾放在一个墙角,墙上只挂着一幅画,镶在镀金的相框里。画上是一个金发的美人鱼,躺在岩石上睡得正香,长长的秀发拂在脸上,随着她的每一次呼吸声微微颤抖着。

哈利放下他的隐形衣、金蛋和地图,走上前去,左右张望,他的脚步声在四壁间回响。这个洗澡间确实豪华漂亮——他也确实渴望试一试其中的几个龙头——但此刻站在这里,却忍不住感到塞德里克是在捉弄他。这个洗澡间对他解开金蛋的奥秘会有什么帮助呢?他尽管这么想着,还是把一条松软的毛巾、隐形衣、活点地图和金蛋放在泳池一般大的浴池边,然后跪下去,拧开了几个龙头。

哈利立刻发现,这些龙头喷出的是各种各样混着热水的泡泡浴液,但它们又和哈利以前接触过的泡泡浴完全不同。其中一个龙头喷出足球那么大的粉红色和蓝色的泡泡;另一个喷出晶莹剔透、又密又厚的泡沫——哈利觉得如果他愿意试一下,这些泡沫准会把他托在水面,沉不下去;第三个龙头喷出香味浓郁的紫色雾气,在水面上弥漫。哈利玩弄着这些龙头,一会儿开,一会儿关,他特别欣赏一个龙头喷出弧形水柱、从水面划过的奇妙景象。一转眼间,深深的浴池就放满了热水、泡沫和泡泡,偌大的浴池这么快就满了,真是神速。哈利关掉所有的龙头,脱去睡衣、拖鞋和浴袍,钻进了水里。

水真深啊,他的脚勉强能够到池底,他在水里游了两个来回,才回到池边,一边踩着水,一边仔细端详金蛋。在热腾腾的、浮着

## CHAPTER TWENTY-FIVE   The Egg and the Eye

staring at the egg. Highly enjoyable though it was to swim in hot and foamy water with clouds of different-coloured steam wafting all around him, no stroke of brilliance came to him, no sudden burst of understanding.

Harry stretched out his arms, lifted the egg in his wet hands and opened it. The wailing, screeching sound filled the bathroom, echoing and reverberating off the marble walls, but it sounded just as incomprehensible as ever, if not more so with all the echoes. He snapped it shut again, worried that the sound would attract Filch, wondering whether that hadn't been Cedric's plan – and then, making him jump so badly that he dropped the egg, which clattered away across the bathroom floor, someone spoke.

'I'd try putting it *in* the water, if I were you.'

Harry had swallowed a considerable amount of bubbles in shock. He stood up, spluttering, and saw the ghost of a very glum-looking girl sitting cross-legged on top of one of the taps. It was Moaning Myrtle, who was usually to be heard sobbing in the S-bend of a toilet three floors below.

'Myrtle!' Harry said in outrage. 'I'm – I'm not wearing anything!'

The foam was so dense that this hardly mattered, but he had a nasty feeling that Myrtle had been spying on him from out of one of the taps ever since he had arrived.

'I closed my eyes when you got in,' she said, blinking at him through her thick spectacles. 'You haven't been to see me for *ages*.'

'Yeah ... well ...' said Harry, bending his knees slightly, just to make absolutely sure Myrtle couldn't see anything but his head, 'I'm not supposed to come into your bathroom, am I? It's a girls' one.'

'You didn't used to care,' said Myrtle miserably. 'You used to be in there all the time.'

This was true, though only because Harry, Ron and Hermione had found Myrtle's out-of-order toilets a convenient place to brew Polyjuice Potion in secret – a forbidden potion which had turned Harry and Ron into living replicas of Crabbe and Goyle for an hour, so that they could sneak into the Slytherin common room.

'I got told off for going in there,' said Harry, which was half-true; Percy had once caught him coming out of Myrtle's bathroom. 'I thought I'd better not come back after that.'

'Oh ... I see ...' said Myrtle, picking at a spot on her chin in a morose sort

## 第25章 金蛋和魔眼

泡沫的水里游泳，周围漂浮着一团团五颜六色的雾气，这滋味真是妙不可言，但是他并没有因此而产生灵感，脑子里也没有灵光一现，豁然开窍。

哈利伸出手臂，用湿漉漉的双手托起金蛋，把它打开。顿时，刺耳的惨叫声充斥了洗澡间，在大理石的墙壁间回响、震荡，但这声音还是那样莫名其妙，而且和所有的回音混在一起，更加令人费解。他啪的一下把金蛋合上，担心这声音会把费尔奇招引过来。他甚至怀疑这就是塞德里克的阴谋——就在这时，突然有人说起话来，吓得他灵魂出窍，金蛋从手里掉落，在洗澡间的地上当啷啷地滚远了。

"如果我是你，就把它放在水里试试。"

哈利一惊之下，吞下了几大口泡泡。他站起来呸呸地吐着，才看见一个愁眉苦脸的女幽灵跷着二郎腿，坐在一个龙头上。是哭泣的桃金娘，人们常常听见她在三层楼下的一个马桶的下水管道里伤心地哭泣。

"桃金娘！"哈利恼火地说，"我——我什么都没穿！"

其实这没有关系，因为水里的泡沫很厚，但哈利有一种很不舒服的感觉。他怀疑自从他进门，桃金娘就一直躲在一个龙头里窥视着他。

"你进去时，我闭上眼睛来着，"桃金娘说，从厚厚的镜片后面朝他眨了眨眼睛，"你好长时间没来看我了。"

"是啊……嗯……"哈利说，一边微微弯曲膝盖，确保桃金娘除了他的脑袋以外，什么也看不见，"我不应该进你那个盥洗室，是不是？那是女生盥洗室啊。"

"你原先并不在乎呀，"桃金娘悲凄凄地说，"你以前整天待在那里。"

这倒是事实，不过那是因为哈利、罗恩和赫敏发现桃金娘那个失修的盥洗室非常安全，他们可以在里面偷偷熬制复方汤剂——那是一种禁止使用的魔药，曾把他和罗恩变成了克拉布和高尔的活生生的复制品，持续了一个小时，使他们能够混进斯莱特林的公共休息室。

"我因为到那儿去挨了批评，"哈利说，这话有一半是事实，珀西有一次碰巧看见他从桃金娘的盥洗室里出来，"后来，我想最好还是别去了。"

"噢……明白了……"桃金娘说，一边忧郁地捏着自己的下巴，"好

## CHAPTER TWENTY-FIVE  The Egg and the Eye

of way. 'Well ... anyway ... I'd try the egg in the water. That's what Cedric Diggory did.'

'Have you been spying on him, too?' said Harry indignantly. 'What d'you do, sneak up here in the evenings to watch the Prefects take baths?'

'Sometimes,' said Myrtle, rather slyly, 'but I've never come out to speak to anyone before.'

'I'm honoured,' said Harry darkly. 'You keep your eyes shut!'

He made sure Myrtle had her glasses well covered before hoisting himself out of the bath, wrapping the towel firmly around himself and going to get the egg.

Once he was back in the water, Myrtle peered through her fingers and said, 'Go on, then ... open it under the water!'

Harry lowered the egg beneath the foamy surface, and opened it ... and, this time, it did not wail. A gurgling song was coming out of it, a song whose words he couldn't distinguish through the water.

'You need to put your head under, too,' said Myrtle, who seemed to be thoroughly enjoying bossing him around. 'Go on!'

Harry took a great breath, and slid under the surface – and now, sitting on the marble bottom of the bubble-filled bath, he heard a chorus of eerie voices singing to him from the open egg in his hands:

> '*Come seek us where our voices sound,*
> *We cannot sing above the ground,*
> *And while you're searching, ponder this:*
> *We've taken what you'll sorely miss,*
> *An hour long you'll have to look,*
> *And to recover what we took,*
> *But past an hour – the prospect's black*
> *Too late, it's gone, it won't come back.*'

Harry let himself float back upwards and broke the bubbly surface, shaking his hair out of his eyes.

'Hear it?' said Myrtle.

'Yeah ... "Come seek us where our voices sound ..." and if I need

## 第25章 金蛋和魔眼

吧……不说了……我会把金蛋放在水里试试的。塞德里克·迪戈里就是这么做的。"

"你也偷看他来着？"哈利气愤地问，"你这是干什么？夜里溜到这里，偷看级长们洗澡？"

"有时候吧，"桃金娘十分诡秘地说，"但我以前从没有出来跟人说过话。"

"我很荣幸，"哈利闷闷不乐地说，"你把眼睛闭上！"

他看到桃金娘确实把镜片捂得严严的了，才从浴池里站起来，用毛巾紧紧裹住腰部，过去把金蛋捡了起来。

他刚钻进水里，桃金娘就从指缝里看着他，说："行了，快点儿吧……在水下把它打开！"

哈利把金蛋放在布满泡沫的水面下，打开……这次金蛋没有惨叫。它发出汩汩的歌声，这歌声从水底下传来，他听不清唱的是什么。

"你需要把你的脑袋也钻进水里，"桃金娘说，似乎很高兴能对哈利指手画脚，"钻进去吧。"

哈利深深吸了口气，钻到了水下——现在，他坐在泡泡浴水底的大理石上，听见手上被打开的金蛋里有一些古怪的声音在齐声合唱：

> 寻找我们吧，在我们声音响起的地方，
> 我们在地面上无法歌唱。
> 当你搜寻时，请仔细思量：
> 我们抢走了你最不舍的宝贝。
> 你只有一个钟头的时间，
> 要寻找和夺回我们拿走的物件，
> 过了一小时便希望全无，
> 它已彻底消逝，永不出现。

哈利浮上去，钻出漂满泡泡的水面。他甩了甩头，把头发从眼睛上甩掉。

"听见了吗？"桃金娘问。

"听见了……'寻找我们吧，在我们声音响起的地方……'而我这

## CHAPTER TWENTY-FIVE  The Egg and the Eye

persuading ... hang on, I need to listen again ...' He sank back beneath the water.

It took three more underwater renditions of the egg's song before Harry had it memorised; then he trod water for a while, thinking hard, while Myrtle sat and watched him.

'I've got to go and look for people who can't use their voices above the ground ...' he said slowly. 'Er ... who could that be?'

'Slow, aren't you?'

He had never seen Moaning Myrtle so cheerful, apart from the day when Hermione's dose of Polyjuice Potion had given her the hairy face and tail of a cat.

Harry stared around the bathroom, thinking ... if the voices could only be heard underwater, then it made sense for them to belong to underwater creatures. He ran this theory past Myrtle, who smirked at him.

'Well, that's what Diggory thought,' she said. 'He lay there talking to himself for ages about it. Ages and ages ... nearly all the bubbles had gone ...'

'Underwater ...' Harry said slowly. 'Myrtle ... what lives in the lake, apart from the giant squid?'

'Oh, all sorts,' she said. 'I sometimes go down there ... sometimes don't have any choice, if someone flushes my toilet when I'm not expecting it ...'

Trying not to think about Moaning Myrtle zooming down a pipe to the lake with the contents of a toilet, Harry said, 'Well, does anything in there have human voices? Hang on –'

Harry's eyes had fallen on the picture of the snoozing mermaid on the wall. 'Myrtle, there aren't *merpeople* in there, are there?'

'Oooh, very good,' she said, her thick glasses twinkling. 'It took Diggory much longer than that! And that was with *her* awake, too – Myrtle jerked her head towards the mermaid with an expression of great dislike on her glum face – 'giggling and showing off and flashing her fins ...'

'That's it, isn't it?' said Harry excitedly. 'The second task's to go and find the merpeople in the lake and ... and ...'

But he suddenly realised what he was saying, and he felt the excitement drain out of him as though someone had just pulled a plug in his stomach. He wasn't a very good swimmer; he'd never had much practice. Dudley

## 第25章 金蛋和魔眼

么做是为了要……等一等,我需要再听一遍……"他再次钻进水里。

金蛋的歌声在水下唱了三遍,哈利才把它牢记在心。然后他一边踩水,一边使劲地思索,桃金娘就坐在那里望着他。

"我必须去寻找那些不能在地面上发出声音的人……"他慢慢地说,"嗯……那可能是谁呢?"

"你真笨,不是吗?"

哈利从没见过桃金娘这么开心过,除了那天赫敏服了复方汤剂后,脸上变得毛茸茸的,还长出了一条猫尾巴时。当时桃金娘也高兴得心花怒放。

哈利望着洗澡间,思索着……如果声音只在水下才能听见,那么一定是属于某种水下动物。他把这个想法告诉了桃金娘,桃金娘给了他一顿奚落。

"啊,迪戈里也是这么想的。"她说,"他躺在那里,自言自语,琢磨着这个问题,琢磨了好长时间。好长好长时间……几乎所有的泡泡都消失了……"

"水下……"哈利慢慢地说,"桃金娘……湖里除了巨乌贼外,还生活着什么动物?"

"噢,种类多着呢。"她说,"我有时也到湖里去……有时别无选择,有人在我没防备的时候冲了我的马桶……"

哈利克制着不去想桃金娘随着马桶的秽物冲进下水道、流到湖里的情景。他说:"那么,那里的什么东西能发出人的声音呢?慢着——"

哈利的目光落到墙上那幅酣睡的美人鱼图画上:"桃金娘,那里没有人鱼吧,有吗?"

"噢,很好,"她说——厚厚的镜片闪闪发亮,"迪戈里花的时间要长得多!而且当时她还是醒着的,"——桃金娘用脑袋指了指美人鱼,愁苦的脸上带着非常反感的表情——"咯咯笑着,搔首弄姿,炫耀她的鳍……"

"这就对了,是吗?"哈利兴奋地说,"第二个项目是到湖里去找人鱼,然后……然后……"

他突然反应过来自己在说什么,兴奋的情绪陡然从心里溜走,就好像心一下子被人掏去了似的。他不太擅长游泳,一直很少训练。达

## CHAPTER TWENTY-FIVE   The Egg and the Eye

had had lessons in their youth, but Aunt Petunia and Uncle Vernon, no doubt hoping that Harry would drown one day, hadn't bothered to give him any. A couple of lengths of this bath was all very well, but that lake was very large, and very deep ... and merpeople would surely live right at the bottom ...

'Myrtle,' Harry said slowly, 'how am I supposed to *breathe*?'

At this, Myrtle's eyes filled with sudden tears again.

'Tactless!' she muttered, groping in her robes for a handkerchief.

'What's tactless?' said Harry, bewildered.

'Talking about breathing in front of *me*!' she said shrilly, and her voice echoed loudly around the bathroom. 'When I can't ... when I haven't ... not for ages ...' She buried her face in her handkerchief and sniffed loudly.

Harry remembered how touchy Myrtle had always been about being dead, but none of the other ghosts he knew made such a fuss about it. 'Sorry,' he said impatiently. 'I didn't mean – I just forgot ...'

'Oh, yes, very easy to forget Myrtle's dead,' said Myrtle, gulping, looking at him out of swollen eyes. 'Nobody missed me, even when I was alive. Took them hours and hours to find my body – I know, I was sitting there waiting for them. Olive Hornby came into the bathroom – "Are you in here again, sulking, Myrtle?" she said. "Because Professor Dippet asked me to look for you –" And then she saw my body ... ooooh, she didn't forget it until her dying day, I made sure of that ... followed her around and reminded her, I did, I remember at her brother's wedding –'

But Harry wasn't listening; he was thinking about the merpeople's song again. '*We've taken what you'll sorely miss.*' That sounded as though they were going to steal something of his, something he had to get back. What were they going to take?

'– and then, of course, she went to the Ministry of Magic to stop me stalking her, so I had to come back here and live in my toilet.'

'Good,' said Harry vaguely. 'Well, I'm a lot further on than I was ... shut your eyes again, will you, I'm getting out.'

He retrieved the egg from the bottom of the bath, climbed out, dried himself and pulled on his pyjamas and dressing-gown again.

'Will you come and visit me in my bathroom again sometime?' Moaning Myrtle asked mournfully, as Harry picked up the Invisibility Cloak.

## 第 25 章 金蛋和魔眼

力小时候上过游泳课，但佩妮姨妈和弗农姨父无疑是希望哈利有朝一日被淹死，从来没让他学过游泳。在这个浴池里游一两个来回还行，可那个湖非常宽非常深……人鱼肯定生活在水底最深处……

"桃金娘，"哈利慢慢地说，"我该怎么呼吸呢？"

听了这话，桃金娘眼里突然又冒出了泪水。

"缺心眼！"她嘟哝着，在长袍里摸索着寻找手帕。

"什么缺心眼？"哈利问，觉得摸不着头脑。

"竟然在我面前讨论呼吸！"桃金娘尖声说道，声音在洗澡间里发出响亮的回音，"明明知道我不能……明明知道我……好长好长时间都没有……"她把脸埋在手帕里，大声地擤着鼻子。

哈利想起桃金娘一直对自己已经死了这件事非常敏感，而他认识的其他幽灵都没有这样大惊小怪。"对不起，"他不耐烦地说，"我不是故意的——我只是忘记了……"

"噢，是啊，很容易忘记桃金娘已经死了，"桃金娘说，一边哽咽着，用红肿的眼睛望着他，"即使在我活着的时候，也没有一个人牵挂我。他们花了好长好长时间才发现我的尸体——我知道，我就坐在那里等着他们。奥利芙·洪贝走进盥洗室——'你又在这里生闷气吗，桃金娘？'她说，'迪佩特教授叫我来找你——'这时她突然看见了我的尸体……哦，她直到临死都忘不了那一幕，我可以保证……我到处跟踪她，提醒她。我记得，在她哥哥的婚礼上——"

然而哈利没有听，他又在思索人鱼的那首歌了。"我们抢走了你最不舍的宝贝"，这似乎是说它们要偷走他的什么东西，他必须夺回来。它们要拿走的是什么呢？

"——后来，当然啦，她找到魔法部，阻止我再跟踪她，我就只好回到这儿，住在我的盥洗室里。"

"不错，"哈利淡淡地说，"好吧，我总算取得了很大的进展……再把眼睛闭上，好吗？我要出来了。"

他从浴池底捡起金蛋，爬了上来，擦干身子，重新穿上睡衣和浴袍。

"你还会到我的盥洗室来看我吗？"哭泣的桃金娘看到哈利拿起隐形衣，忧伤地问。

## CHAPTER TWENTY-FIVE   The Egg and the Eye

'Er ... I'll try,' Harry said, though privately thinking the only way he'd be visiting Myrtle's bathroom again was if every other toilet in the castle got blocked. 'See you, Myrtle ... thanks for your help.'

'Bye, bye,' she said gloomily, and as Harry put on the Invisibility Cloak, he saw her zoom back up the tap.

Out in the dark corridor, Harry examined the Marauder's Map to check that the coast was still clear. Yes, the dots belonging to Filch and Mrs. Norris were safely in their office ... nothing else seemed to be moving apart from Peeves, who was bouncing around the trophy room on the floor above ... Harry had taken his first step back towards Gryffindor Tower, when something else on the map caught his eye ... something distinctly odd.

Peeves was *not* the only thing that was moving. A single dot was flitting around a room in the bottom left-hand corner – Snape's office. But the dot wasn't labelled *Severus Snape* ... it was Bartemius Crouch.

Harry stared at the dot. Mr. Crouch was supposed to be too ill to go to work or to come to the Yule Ball – so what was he doing, sneaking into Hogwarts at one o'clock in the morning? Harry watched closely as the dot moved round and round the room, pausing here and there ...

Harry hesitated, thinking ... and then his curiosity got the better of him. He turned, and set off in the opposite direction, towards the nearest staircase. He was going to see what Crouch was up to.

Harry walked down the stairs as quietly as possible, though the faces in some of the portraits still turned curiously at the squeak of a floorboard, the rustle of his pyjamas. He crept along the corridor below, pushed aside a tapestry about halfway along and proceeded down a narrower staircase, a shortcut which would take him down two floors. He kept glancing down at the map, wondering ... it just didn't seem in character, somehow, for correct, law-abiding Mr. Crouch to be sneaking around somebody else's office this late at night ...

And then, halfway down the staircase, not thinking about what he was doing, not concentrating on anything but the peculiar behaviour of Mr. Crouch, Harry's leg suddenly sank right through the trick step Neville always forgot to jump. He gave an ungainly wobble, and the golden egg, still damp from the bath, slipped from under his arm – he lurched forwards to try and catch it, but too late; the egg fell down the long staircase with a bang as loud

## 第25章 金蛋和魔眼

"嗯……我争取吧。"哈利说，但他暗想，只有当城堡里所有的盥洗室都被封死了，他才可能再去光顾桃金娘的盥洗室，"再见，桃金娘……谢谢你给我的帮助。"

"再会了。"桃金娘惆怅地说。哈利穿上隐形衣时，看见她哧溜一下又钻回水龙头里去了。

来到外面漆黑的走廊上，哈利又检查了一下活点地图，看看有什么风吹草动。还好，图上费尔奇和他的猫洛丽丝夫人的那两个小点，还安安稳稳地待在他们的办公室里呢……城堡里一片寂静，只有皮皮鬼在活动，但他是在楼上的奖品陈列室里大闹……哈利刚要迈步返回格兰芬多塔楼，突然地图上有个什么东西吸引了他的视线……这实在太蹊跷了。

活动的不止皮皮鬼一个。还有一个小点在底层左手拐角的那个房间里动来动去——那是斯内普的办公室。但小点旁标的名字却不是西弗勒斯·斯内普……而是巴蒂·克劳奇。

哈利盯着那个小点。克劳奇先生据说是生了重病，不能上班，也不能来参加圣诞舞会——可是，他凌晨一点偷偷溜进霍格沃茨来做什么呢？哈利仔细注视着那个小点在房间里移来移去，这里停停，那里站站……

哈利迟疑着，思索着……然后，他的好奇心占了上风。他转了个身，朝相反的方向走去，爬上最近的楼梯。他要看看克劳奇在做什么。

哈利蹑手蹑脚地往楼下走，尽量不发出声音，但肖像里的几个人还是听见了地板的吱呀声和他睡衣的窸窣声，都好奇地转过脸来。到了楼下，他悄悄顺着走廊走到一半，然后撩开墙上的一幅挂毯，沿着一道更狭窄的楼梯往下走。这是一条近路，可以通到两层楼以下。他不停地扫一眼地图，一边暗自纳闷……向来严谨自律、遵纪守法的克劳奇先生怎么会在半夜三更溜进别人的办公室？这不符合他的性格呀……

哈利只顾琢磨克劳奇先生的古怪行为，没有集中思想走路，结果，在楼梯上走到一半时，他的一条腿突然陷进一个捉弄人的台阶，那是纳威经常忘记跳过的。哈利笨手笨脚地晃动一下，那只金蛋，仍然湿漉漉地沾着洗澡水，突然从他胳膊下滑落了。他赶紧探身去抓，来不及了，金蛋顺着长长的楼梯滚了下去，每下一级台阶，都发出当啷一声巨响，像敲响了一只大鼓——隐形衣也滑脱了——哈利赶紧一把抓

## CHAPTER TWENTY-FIVE  The Egg and the Eye

as a bass drum on every step – the Invisibility Cloak slipped – Harry snatched at it, and the Marauder's Map fluttered out of his hand, and slid down six stairs, where, sunk in the step to above his knee, he couldn't reach it.

The golden egg fell through the tapestry at the bottom of the staircase, burst open and began wailing loudly in the corridor below. Harry pulled out his wand and struggled to touch the Marauder's Map, to wipe it blank, but it was too far away to reach –

Pulling the Cloak back over himself Harry straightened up, listening hard, his eyes screwed up with fear ... and, almost immediately –

'PEEVES!'

It was the unmistakeable hunting cry of Filch the caretaker. Harry could hear his rapid, shuffling footsteps coming nearer and nearer, his wheezy voice raised in fury.

'What's this racket? Wake up the whole castle, will you? I'll have you, Peeves, I'll have you, you'll ... and what is this?'

Filch's footsteps stopped; there was a clink of metal on metal, and the wailing stopped – Filch had picked up the egg and closed it. Harry stood very still, one leg still jammed tightly in the magical step, listening. Any moment now, Filch was going to pull aside the tapestry, expecting to see Peeves ... and there would be no Peeves ... but if he came up the stairs, he would spot the Marauder's Map ... and, Invisibility Cloak or not, the map would show 'Harry Potter' standing exactly where he was.

'Egg?' Filch said quietly at the foot of the stairs. 'My sweet!' – Mrs. Norris was obviously with him – 'This is a Triwizard clue! This belongs to a school champion!'

Harry felt sick; his heart was hammering very fast –

'PEEVES!' Filch roared gleefully. 'You've been stealing!'

He ripped back the tapestry below, and Harry saw his horrible pouchy face, and bulging, pale eyes staring up the dark and (to Filch) deserted staircase.

'Hiding, are you?' he said softly. 'I'm coming to get you, Peeves ... you've gone and stolen a Triwizard clue, Peeves ... Dumbledore'll have you out of here for this, you filthy pilfering poltergeist ...'

Filch started to climb the stairs, his scrawny, dust-coloured cat at his heels. Mrs. Norris's lamp-like eyes, so very like her master's, were fixed

## 第 25 章  金蛋和魔眼

住,结果活点地图从他手里飘出去,落到了六级台阶以下。哈利陷在齐膝深的恶作剧台阶里,够不到它。

金蛋滚到楼梯底部,从挂毯下钻了出去,弹开了,开始在下面的走廊里尖声惨叫。哈利掏出魔杖,挣扎着去触碰活点地图,想让它变成一张白纸,可是它太远了,他够不着——

哈利用隐形衣重新裹住自己,直起身子,紧紧地闭上眼睛,心惊胆战地倾听着……几乎是一眨眼的工夫,就听——

"皮皮鬼!"

毫无疑问,这是管理员费尔奇警惕的叫声。哈利可以听见他急速的、踢踢踏踏的脚步声越来越近,那气喘吁吁的声音因为愤怒而提高了。

"这里吵吵嚷嚷的在做什么?想把城堡里的人都吵醒吗?我一定要抓住你,皮皮鬼,我要抓住你,你……咦,这是什么?"

费尔奇的脚步声停住了。只听咔嗒一声,是金属互相碰撞的声音,惨叫声停止了——费尔奇捡起金蛋,把它合上了。哈利一动不动地站着、倾听着,一条腿仍然死死地卡在带魔法的台阶里。现在,费尔奇随时都会掀开挂毯,以为会看见皮皮鬼……其实根本没有什么皮皮鬼……但如果他往楼梯上走,就会看见活点地图……不管有没有隐形衣,地图上都会显示哈利·波特就站在他现在的位置上。

"金蛋?"费尔奇在楼梯下面轻声说道,"我的宝贝猫儿!"——看来洛丽丝夫人也和他在一起——"这是三强争霸赛的线索啊!属于学校的一位勇士!"

哈利觉得脑袋发晕,心跳得跟打鼓一样——

"皮皮鬼!"费尔奇喜悦地大叫,"你偷东西了!"

他在下面一把扯开挂毯,哈利看见了他那可怕的、皮肉松垂的脸和那双暴突的浅色眼睛,正朝上瞪着漆黑的、(对他来说)空无一人的楼梯。

"躲起来了,是吗?"他小声说,"我要来抓你,皮皮鬼……你居然偷了三强争霸赛的线索,皮皮鬼……邓布利多这次决不会轻饶你,你这个肮脏的、偷鸡摸狗的恶作剧精灵……"

费尔奇开始往楼梯上爬,后面跟着他那只骨瘦如柴、毛色暗灰的猫。洛丽丝夫人那双灯泡般的大眼睛和它主人的一模一样,此刻正死死盯

## CHAPTER TWENTY-FIVE  The Egg and the Eye

directly upon Harry. He had had occasion before now to wonder whether the Invisibility Cloak worked on cats ... sick with apprehension, he watched Filch drawing nearer and nearer in his old flannel dressing-gown – he tried desperately to pull his trapped leg free, but it merely sank a few more inches – any second now, Filch was going to spot the map or walk right into him –

'Filch? What's going on?'

Filch stopped a few steps below Harry, and turned. At the foot of the stairs stood the only person who could make Harry's situation worse – Snape. He was wearing a long grey nightshirt and he looked livid.

'It's Peeves, Professor,' Filch whispered malevolently. 'He threw this egg down the stairs.'

Snape climbed up the stairs quickly and stopped beside Filch. Harry gritted his teeth, convinced his loudly thumping heart would give him away at any second ...

'Peeves?' said Snape softly, staring at the egg in Filch's hands. 'But Peeves couldn't get into my office ...'

'This egg was in your office, Professor?'

'Of course not,' Snape snapped, 'I heard banging and wailing –'

'Yes, Professor, that was the egg –'

'– I was coming to investigate –'

'– Peeves threw it, Professor –'

'– And when I passed my office, I saw that the torches were lit and a cupboard door was ajar! Somebody has been searching it!'

'But Peeves couldn't –'

'I know he couldn't, Filch!' Snape snapped. 'I seal my office with a spell none but a wizard could break!' Snape looked up the stairs, straight through Harry, and then down into the corridor below. 'I want you to come and help me search for the intruder, Filch.'

'I – yes, Professor – but –'

Filch looked yearningly up the stairs, right through Harry, who could see that he was very reluctant to forgo the chance of cornering Peeves. *Go*, Harry pleaded with him silently, *go with Snape* ... *go* ... Mrs. Norris was peering around Filch's legs ... Harry had the distinct impression that she could smell

## 第25章 金蛋和魔眼

着哈利。哈利以前就曾怀疑隐形衣对猫类不起作用……他恐惧得简直要晕倒了，注视着身穿旧天鹅绒晨衣的费尔奇一步步逼近——他拼命挣扎，想把被卡住的脚拔出来，结果反而越陷越深——现在，费尔奇随时都会看见地图，或者走过来撞在他身上——

"费尔奇？出了什么事？"

费尔奇停下脚步，转过身，这时他和哈利只差几级台阶了。楼梯底下站着一个人，如果有谁能使哈利的处境更加险恶，就只有这个人了：斯内普。他穿着一件灰色的衬衫式长睡衣，脸色铁青。

"是皮皮鬼，教授，"费尔奇恶狠狠地小声说，"他把这只蛋从楼梯上扔了下来。"

斯内普快步上楼，停在费尔奇身边。哈利咬紧牙关，相信他怦怦的心跳声随时都会暴露他的存在……

"皮皮鬼？"斯内普轻声说，眼睛盯着费尔奇手中的金蛋，"可是皮皮鬼不可能闯进我的办公室……"

"这只金蛋原先在你的办公室里吗，教授？"

"当然不是，"斯内普厉声说，"我听见了一阵砰砰乱响，还有惨叫声——"

"没错，教授，那正是金蛋——"

"——我就过来调查一下——"

"——是皮皮鬼扔的，教授——"

"——经过我的办公室时，我看见火把亮着，一个柜门开着一道缝！有人在里面找东西！"

"可是皮皮鬼不可能——"

"我知道他不可能，费尔奇！"斯内普的声音又严厉起来，"我用咒语把我的办公室封死了，只有巫师才能闯进去！"斯内普抬头望望楼梯上，目光径直穿过哈利的身体，然后他又低头望着下面的走廊，"我要你过来帮我搜查那个闯进来的人，费尔奇。"

"我——好的，教授——可是——"

费尔奇眼巴巴地望着楼梯上面，目光直接穿透了哈利。哈利看得出来，他很不甘心放弃这个堵截皮皮鬼的好机会。快走吧，哈利不出声地祈求道，跟斯内普一起走吧……走吧……洛丽丝夫人在费尔奇的

## CHAPTER TWENTY-FIVE  The Egg and the Eye

him ... why had he filled that bath with so much perfumed foam?

'The thing is, Professor,' said Filch plaintively, 'the Headmaster will have to listen to me this time, Peeves has been stealing from a student, it might be my chance to get him thrown out of the castle once and for all –'

'Filch, I don't give a damn about that wretched poltergeist, it's my office that's –'

*Clunk. Clunk. Clunk.*

Snape stopped talking very abruptly. He and Filch both looked down at the foot of the stairs. Harry saw Mad-Eye Moody limp into sight through the narrow gap between their heads. Moody was wearing his old travelling cloak over his nightshirt, and leaning on his staff as usual.

'Pyjama party, is it?' he growled up the stairs.

'Professor Snape and I heard noises, Professor,' said Filch at once. 'Peeves the poltergeist, throwing things around as usual – and then Professor Snape discovered that someone had broken into his off–'

'Shut up!' Snape hissed to Filch.

Moody took a step closer to the foot of the stairs. Harry saw Moody's magical eye travel over Snape, and then, unmistakeably, onto himself.

Harry's heart gave a horrible jolt. *Moody could see through Invisibility Cloaks ...* he alone could see the full strangeness of the scene ... Snape in his nightshirt, Filch clutching the egg, and he, Harry, trapped in the stairs behind them. Moody's lop-sided gash of a mouth opened in surprise. For a few seconds, he and Harry stared straight into each other's eyes. Then Moody closed his mouth and turned his blue eye upon Snape again.

'Did I hear that correctly, Snape?' he asked slowly. 'Someone broke into your office?'

'It is unimportant,' said Snape coldly.

'On the contrary,' growled Moody, 'it is very important. Who'd want to break into your office?'

'A student, I daresay,' said Snape. Harry could see a vein flickering horribly on Snape's greasy temple. 'It has happened before. Potion ingredients have gone missing from my private store cupboard ... students attempting illicit mixtures, no doubt ...'

'Reckon they were after potion ingredients, eh?' said Moody. 'Not hiding anything else in your office, are you?'

Harry saw the edge of Snape's sallow face turn a nasty brick colour, the

## 第25章 金蛋和魔眼

腿边探头探脑……哈利明显感觉到它能闻出他身上的气味……唉，他为什么要往浴池里放那么多带香味的泡沫呢？

"是这样的，教授，"费尔奇垂头丧气地说，"校长这次恐怕得听我的了。皮皮鬼偷了一个学生的东西，我这次可能有机会把他永远赶出城堡——"

"费尔奇，我不管那个讨厌的恶作剧精灵，是我的办公室遭到了——"

噔。噔。噔。

斯内普猛地停住话头。他和费尔奇都低头望着楼梯下面。透过他们俩脑袋之间的缝隙，哈利看见疯眼汉穆迪一瘸一拐地出现了。穆迪在衬衫式长睡衣外披着他那件旧旅行斗篷，像往常一样拄着拐杖。

"睡衣派对，嗯？"他粗声粗气地朝楼梯上说。

"斯内普教授和我听见了一些声音，教授，"费尔奇立刻说道，"是专爱搞恶作剧的皮皮鬼，像往常一样乱扔东西——后来斯内普教授发现有人闯进了他的办公——"

"闭嘴！"斯内普压低声音对费尔奇说。

穆迪朝楼梯前又移动了一步。哈利看见穆迪那只魔眼扫过斯内普，然后，毫无疑问地落到了自己身上。

哈利的心剧烈地狂跳了一下。穆迪的目光能穿透隐形衣……只有他才能把这奇怪的一幕尽收眼底：斯内普穿着衬衫式长睡衣，费尔奇手里紧紧搂着金蛋，他——哈利，在他们后面，陷在楼梯里出不来。穆迪的嘴巴——那道歪斜的大口子吃惊地张大了。一时间，他和哈利径直瞪着对方的眼睛。然后穆迪闭上嘴巴，又将他的蓝眼睛转到了斯内普身上。

"我没有听错吧，斯内普？"他慢慢地问，"有人闯进了你的办公室？"

"那无关紧要。"斯内普冷冷地说。

"恰恰相反，"穆迪粗声吼道，"那非常重要。谁会闯进你的办公室呢？"

"大概是一个学生吧，"斯内普说，哈利可以看见一根血管在斯内普油亮亮的太阳穴上可怕地跳动着，"这种事情以前就发生过。我私人储藏室里的魔药配料不见了……毫无疑问，学生想制作违禁魔药……"

"你认为他们在寻找魔药配料，嗯？"穆迪问，"你办公室里没有藏着别的东西吧？"

哈利看见斯内普土灰色的面孔变成了一种难看的砖红色，太阳穴

## CHAPTER TWENTY-FIVE   The Egg and the Eye

vein in his temple pulsing more rapidly.

'You know I'm hiding nothing, Moody,' he said, in a soft and dangerous voice, 'as you've searched my office pretty thoroughly yourself.'

Moody's face twisted into a smile. 'Auror's privilege, Snape. Dumbledore told me to keep an eye –'

'Dumbledore happens to trust me,' said Snape, through clenched teeth. 'I refuse to believe that he gave you orders to search my office!'

'Course Dumbledore trusts you,' growled Moody. 'He's a trusting man, isn't he? Believes in second chances. But me – I say there are spots that don't come off, Snape. Spots that never come off, d'you know what I mean?'

Snape suddenly did something very strange. He seized his left forearm convulsively with his right hand, as though something on it had hurt him.

Moody laughed. 'Get back to bed, Snape.'

'You don't have the authority to send me anywhere!' Snape hissed, letting go of his arm as though angry with himself. 'I have as much right to prowl this school after dark as you do!'

'Prowl away,' said Moody, but his voice was full of menace. 'I look forward to meeting you in a dark corridor some time ... you've dropped something, by the way ...'

With a stab of horror, Harry saw Moody point at the Marauder's Map, still lying on the staircase six steps below him. As Snape and Filch both turned to look at it, Harry threw caution to the winds; he raised his arms under the Cloak and waved furiously at Moody to attract his attention, mouthing, 'It's mine! *Mine!*'

Snape had reached out for it, a horrible expression of dawning comprehension on his face –

'*Accio* parchment!'

The map flew up into the air, slipped through Snape's outstretched fingers, and soared down the stairs into Moody's hand.

'My mistake,' Moody said calmly. 'It's mine – must've dropped it earlier –'

But Snape's black eyes were darting from the egg in Filch's arms to the map in Moody's hand, and Harry could tell he was putting two and two together, as only Snape could ...

## 第25章 金蛋和魔眼

上的那根血管跳得更快了。

"你知道我什么也没藏，穆迪，"他用一种低沉而阴险的声音说，"你不是亲自把我的办公室搜了个底朝天吗？"

穆迪的脸扭曲着，挤出一个笑容："这是傲罗的特权，斯内普。邓布利多叫我密切监视——"

"邓布利多恰好很信任我，"斯内普咬牙切齿地说，"我不相信是他吩咐你搜查我办公室的！"

"邓布利多当然信任你，"穆迪吼道，"他是个很轻信的人，是不是？总认为应该给人第二次机会。可是我——我认为有些污点是洗不掉的，斯内普。有些污点是永远也洗不掉的，你明白我的意思吧？"

斯内普突然做了一件非常奇怪的事。他猛地用右手抓住左胳膊，就好像胳膊上有什么东西疼了起来。

穆迪大笑起来："回去睡觉吧，斯内普。"

"你没有权力支使我去任何地方！"斯内普嘶嘶地说，松开胳膊，似乎对自己感到很恼火，"我和你一样有权利在夜里巡视这所学校！"

"那你就尽管巡视吧，"穆迪说，声音里充满威胁，"我盼着下回再在某个漆黑的走廊里碰到你……随便说一句，你的东西丢了……"

哈利恐惧地看见，穆迪指着还躺在六级台阶下的活点地图。趁斯内普和费尔奇都低头看着它时，哈利把谨慎抛到了九霄云外。他在隐形衣下面举起两只手臂，拼命朝穆迪挥动，想引起他的注意，一边用口型夸张地说："是我的！我的！"

斯内普伸手去捡地图，他的脸上慢慢出现了一种可怕的、若有所悟的表情——

"羊皮纸飞来！"

地图嗖地蹿到空中，从斯内普张开的手指间滑过，飞下楼梯，落在穆迪手里。

"我弄错了，"穆迪不动声色地说，"这是我的——一定是我早些时候丢的——"

可是斯内普的黑眼睛看看费尔奇怀里的金蛋，又看看穆迪手里的地图，哈利知道，他把这两件事联系起来了，只有斯内普能做到这点……

## CHAPTER TWENTY-FIVE  The Egg and the Eye

'Potter,' he said quietly.

'What's that?' said Moody calmly, folding up the map and pocketing it.

'Potter!' Snape snarled, and he actually turned his head and stared right at the place where Harry was, as though he could suddenly see him. 'That egg is Potter's egg. That piece of parchment belongs to Potter. I have seen it before, I recognise it! Potter is here! Potter, in his Invisibility Cloak!'

Snape stretched out his hands like a blind man, and began to move up the stairs; Harry could have sworn his overlarge nostrils were dilating, trying to sniff Harry out – trapped, Harry leant backwards, trying to avoid Snape's fingertips, but any moment now –

'There's nothing there, Snape!' barked Moody. 'But I'll be happy to tell the Headmaster how quickly your mind jumped to Harry Potter!'

'Meaning what?' snarled Snape, turning again to look at Moody, his hands still outstretched, inches from Harry's chest.

'Meaning that Dumbledore's very interested to know who's got it in for that boy!' said Moody, limping nearer still to the foot of the stairs. 'And so am I, Snape ... very interested ...' The torchlight flickered across his mangled face, so that the scars, and the chunk missing from his nose, looked deeper and darker than ever.

Snape was looking down at Moody, and Harry couldn't see the expression on his face. For a moment, nobody moved or said anything. Then Snape slowly lowered his hands.

'I merely thought,' said Snape, in a voice of forced calm, 'that if Potter was wandering around after hours again ... it's an unfortunate habit of his ... he should be stopped. For – for his own safety.'

'Ah, I see,' said Moody softly. 'Got Potter's best interests at heart, have you?'

There was a pause. Snape and Moody were still staring at each other. Mrs. Norris gave a loud miaow, still peering around Filch's legs, looking for the source of Harry's bubble-bath smell.

'I think I will go back to bed,' Snape said curtly.

'Best idea you've had all night,' said Moody. 'Now, Filch, if you'll just give me that egg –'

'No!' said Filch, clutching the egg as though it was his first-born son.

## 第25章 金蛋和魔眼

"波特。"他轻声说。

"什么意思？"穆迪平静地问，一边把地图折起来放进口袋。

"波特！"斯内普怒气冲冲地说，而且他居然转过头，直直地望着哈利所在的地方，仿佛突然能看见他了，"那只金蛋是波特的，那张羊皮纸也是波特的，我以前看见过，我认出来了！波特在这里！波特，穿着他的隐形衣！"

斯内普像瞎子一样张开双手，朝楼梯上走来。哈利相信自己看到斯内普已经很大的鼻孔张得更大了，想嗅出哈利所在的位置——哈利陷在楼梯里动弹不得，只好把身体拼命往后仰，不让斯内普的指尖碰到他，可是随时都——

"那里什么也没有，斯内普！"穆迪吼道，"不过我倒很乐意告诉校长，你是怎样动不动就怀疑哈利·波特的！"

"什么意思？"斯内普又转头望着穆迪，双手仍然张开着，离哈利的胸脯只差几寸。

"我的意思是，邓布利多很有兴趣知道谁对那个男孩不怀好意！"穆迪说，又一瘸一拐地朝楼梯前挪动了几步，"而且，斯内普，我也……很有兴趣……"火把的光掠过他扭曲破损的脸，使那些伤疤和鼻子上的大洞显得比以往更深，更阴森可怖。

斯内普低头望着穆迪，哈利看不见他脸上的表情。一时间，谁也不动，谁也不说话了。然后，斯内普慢慢放下双手。

"我只是觉得，"斯内普说，竭力使自己的语气显得平静，"如果波特又在半夜里闲逛……这是他的一个令人遗憾的坏习惯……应该阻止他。为了——为了他自身的安全。"

"啊，我明白了，"穆迪轻声说，"你把波特的利益放在心头，是吗？"

片刻的静默。斯内普和穆迪仍然凝视着对方。洛丽丝夫人喵地大叫一声，仍然在费尔奇的腿边探头探脑，寻找哈利身上泡泡浴香味的来源。

"我想回去睡觉了。"斯内普突然说道。

"你今晚只有这个想法最合理。"穆迪说，"好了，费尔奇，你能不能把那只金蛋给我——"

"不行！"费尔奇说，一边牢牢地搂着金蛋，就像搂着他的头生儿子，

## CHAPTER TWENTY-FIVE    The Egg and the Eye

'Professor Moody, this is evidence of Peeves's treachery!'

'It's the property of the champion he stole it from,' said Moody. 'Hand it over, now.'

Snape swept downstairs and passed Moody without another word. Filch made a chirruping noise to Mrs. Norris, who stared blankly at Harry for a few more seconds before turning and following her master. Still breathing very fast, Harry heard Snape walking away down the corridor; Filch handed Moody the egg, and disappeared from view too, muttering to Mrs. Norris, 'Never mind, my sweet … we'll see Dumbledore in the morning … tell him what Peeves was up to …'

A door slammed. Harry was left staring down at Moody, who placed his staff on the bottom-most stair, and started to climb laboriously towards him, a dull *clunk* on every other step.

'Close shave, Potter,' he muttered.

'Yeah … I – er … thanks,' said Harry weakly.

'What is this thing?' said Moody, drawing the Marauder's Map out of his pocket and unfolding it.

'Map of Hogwarts,' said Harry, hoping Moody was going to pull him out of the staircase soon; his leg was really hurting him.

'Merlin's beard,' Moody whispered, staring at the map, his magical eye going haywire. 'This … this is some map, Potter!'

'Yeah, it's … quite useful,' Harry said. His eyes were starting to water from the pain. 'Er – Professor Moody, d'you think you could help me –?'

'What? Oh! Yes … yes, of course …'

Moody took hold of Harry's arms and pulled; Harry's leg came free of the trick step, and he climbed onto the one above it.

Moody was still gazing at the map. 'Potter …' he said slowly, 'you didn't happen, by any chance, to see who broke into Snape's office, did you? On this map, I mean?'

'Er … yeah, I did …' Harry admitted. 'It was Mr. Crouch.'

Moody's magical eye whizzed over the entire surface of the map. He looked suddenly alarmed.

'Crouch?' he said. 'You're – you're sure, Potter?'

'Positive,' said Harry.

'Well, he's not here any more,' said Moody, his eye still whizzing over the

## 第 25 章 金蛋和魔眼

"穆迪教授，这是皮皮鬼偷东西的证据！"

"这是他从一位勇士那里偷的，是那位勇士的东西。"穆迪说，"拿过来吧。"

斯内普一言不发地快步下楼，从穆迪身边走过。费尔奇对洛丽丝夫人发出咂嘴的声音，猫茫然地又注视了哈利几秒钟，才转身跟着主人走了。哈利仍然急促地呼吸着，听见斯内普顺着走廊远去。费尔奇把金蛋递给穆迪，也走开了，一边还低声对洛丽丝夫人嘀咕："没关系，亲爱的……我们一早就去找邓布利多……告诉他皮皮鬼干的好事……"

一扇门砰地响了一声。现在只剩下哈利和穆迪面面相觑。穆迪把拐杖拄在楼梯的最底层，费力地往楼梯上爬，朝哈利走来，每走一步，都发出一个空洞的声音：噔。

"真够危险的，波特。"他低声说。

"是啊……我……呃……谢谢你。"哈利有气无力地说。

"这是什么东西？"穆迪说着，从口袋里掏出活点地图展开来。

"霍格沃茨的地图。"哈利说。他希望穆迪赶紧把他从楼梯里拉出来，他的腿疼得要命。

"梅林的胡子啊，"穆迪瞪着地图，低声说道，那只魔眼疯狂地乱转，"这……这张地图可不同一般，波特！"

"是啊，它……很管用。"哈利说，他已经疼得眼泪直流了，"呃——穆迪教授，你能不能帮我一把——？"

"什么？噢，好的……好的，没问题……"

穆迪抓住哈利的双臂，用力一拉。哈利的腿从那捉弄人的台阶里解脱了出来，他爬到上面一级台阶上。

穆迪仍然盯着地图。"波特……"他慢吞吞地说，"你有没有碰巧看见是谁闯进了斯内普的办公室？我的意思是，在这张地图上？"

"呃……我看见了……"哈利承认道，"是克劳奇先生。"

穆迪那只魔眼嗖嗖地在地图上来回扫动。他突然显得很警觉。

"克劳奇？"他说，"你——你能肯定吗，波特？"

"绝对肯定。"哈利说。

"哦，他已经不在了，"穆迪说，眼睛仍然在地图上扫来扫去，"克

## CHAPTER TWENTY-FIVE  The Egg and the Eye

map. 'Crouch ... that's very – very interesting ...'

He said nothing for almost a minute, still staring at the map. Harry could tell that this news meant something to Moody, and very much wanted to know what it was. He wondered whether he dared ask. Moody scared him slightly ... yet Moody had just helped him avoid an awful lot of trouble ...

'Er ... Professor Moody ... why d'you reckon Mr. Crouch wanted to look around Snape's office?'

Moody's magical eye left the map and fixed, quivering, upon Harry. It was a penetrating glare, and Harry had the impression that Moody was sizing him up, wondering whether to answer or not, or how much to tell him.

'Put it this way, Potter,' Moody muttered finally, 'they say old Mad-Eye's obsessed with catching Dark wizards ... but Mad-Eye's nothing – *nothing* – compared to Barty Crouch.'

He continued to stare at the map. Harry was burning to know more.

'Professor Moody?' he said again. 'D'you think ... could this have anything to do with ... maybe Mr. Crouch thinks there's something going on ...'

'Like what?' said Moody sharply.

Harry wondered how much he dare say. He didn't want Moody to guess that he had a source of information outside Hogwarts; that might lead to tricky questions about Sirius.

'I don't know,' Harry muttered, 'odd stuff's been happening lately, hasn't it? It's been in the *Daily Prophet* ... the Dark Mark at the World Cup, and the Death Eaters and everything ...'

Both of Moody's mismatched eyes widened.

'You're a sharp boy, Potter,' he said. His magical eye roved back to the Marauder's Map. 'Crouch could be thinking along those lines,' he said slowly. 'Very possible ... there have been some funny rumours flying around lately – helped along by Rita Skeeter, of course. It's making a lot of people nervous, I reckon.' A grim smile twisted his lop-sided mouth. 'Oh, if there's one thing I hate,' he muttered, more to himself than Harry, and his magical eye was fixed on the bottom left-hand corner of the map, 'it's a Death Eater who walked free ...'

Harry stared at him. Could Moody possibly mean what Harry thought he meant?

## 第25章 金蛋和魔眼

劳奇……真是非常——非常有意思……"

有那么一分钟的时间,他什么也没说,只是盯着地图。哈利看得出来,这个消息对穆迪来说意味着一些什么,他很想知道到底是怎么回事。他不知道自己敢不敢问穆迪。他有点害怕穆迪……不过穆迪刚才帮助他躲过了一大堆麻烦……

"呃……穆迪教授……你认为克劳奇先生为什么要搜查斯内普的办公室呢?"

穆迪那只魔眼从地图上抬起来,牢牢地、微微颤抖地盯着哈利。这是一种具有穿透力的凝视,哈利感到穆迪在审视他,在考虑要不要回答他,在考虑告诉他多少。

"这么说吧,波特,"穆迪最后小声说,"他们说疯眼汉这老家伙一心痴迷于抓黑巫师……但是我跟巴蒂·克劳奇相比,简直不算什么——不算什么。"

他继续盯着地图。哈利急不可耐地想了解更多的情况。

"穆迪教授?"他又问,"你认为……这件事会不会和……也许克劳奇先生认为,有一些异常的……"

"比如什么?"穆迪尖锐地问。

哈利不知道自己敢坦白多少。他不想让穆迪猜到,在霍格沃茨以外还有人向他提供情报,那会使穆迪提出一些牵扯到小天狼星的问题,很难回答。

"我不知道,"哈利含糊地说,"最近总发生一些怪事儿,是不是?《预言家日报》上写着呢……世界杯赛上的黑魔标记,还有食死徒什么的……"

穆迪那两只不对称的眼睛都睁大了。

"你是个目光很敏锐的孩子,波特。"他说。那只魔眼又转了回去,盯着活点地图。"克劳奇大概也是这样的思路,"他慢悠悠地说,"很有可能……最近风言风语的,有一些古怪的谣传——当然啦,丽塔·斯基特又起了推波助澜的作用。我想,这使许多人惶惶不安。"一丝阴森的笑容使他歪斜的嘴变得扭曲了。"要说我对什么事情恨之入骨的话,"他低声道,不像是对哈利说话,更像是在自言自语,那只魔眼盯着地图左边的一角,"那就是让一个食死徒逍遥在外……"

哈利愣愣地望着他。穆迪的意思难道真的是哈利所想的那样吗?

## CHAPTER TWENTY-FIVE  The Egg and the Eye

'And now I want to ask *you* a question, Potter,' said Moody, in a more businesslike tone.

Harry's heart sank; he had thought this was coming. Moody was going to ask where he had got this map, which was a very dubious magical object – and the story of how it had fallen into his hands incriminated not only him, but his own father, Fred and George Weasley, and Professor Lupin, their last Defence Against the Dark Arts teacher. Moody waved the map in front of Harry, who braced himself –

'Can I borrow this?'

'Oh!' said Harry. He was very fond of his map, but on the other hand, he was extremely relieved that Moody wasn't asking where he'd got it, and there was no doubt that he owed Moody a favour. 'Yeah, OK.'

'Good boy,' growled Moody. 'I can make good use of this ... this might be *exactly* what I've been looking for ... right, bed, Potter, come on, now ...'

They climbed to the top of the stairs together, Moody still examining the map as though it was a treasure the like of which he had never seen before. They walked in silence to the door of Moody's office, where he stopped, and looked up at Harry. 'You ever thought of a career as an Auror, Potter?'

'No,' said Harry, taken aback.

'You want to consider it,' said Moody, nodding, and looking at Harry thoughtfully. 'Yes, indeed ... and incidentally ... I'm guessing you weren't just taking that egg for a walk tonight?'

'Er – no,' said Harry, grinning. 'I've been working out the clue.'

Moody winked at him, his magical eye going haywire again. 'Nothing like a night-time stroll to give you ideas, Potter ... see you in the morning ...' He went back into his office, staring down at the Marauder's Map again, and closed the door behind him.

Harry walked slowly back to Gryffindor Tower, lost in thought about Snape, and Crouch, and what it all meant ... Why was Crouch pretending to be ill, if he could manage to get to Hogwarts when he wanted to? What did he think Snape was concealing in his office?

And Moody thought he, Harry, ought to be an Auror! Interesting idea ... but as Harry got quietly into his four-poster ten minutes later, the egg and the Cloak now safely back in his trunk, he somehow thought he'd like to check how scarred the rest of them were, before he chose it as a career.

## 第25章 金蛋和魔眼

"那么,我想问你一个问题,波特。"穆迪以一本正经的口吻说。

哈利的心往下一沉。他早就知道是逃不过去的。穆迪肯定要问他这张地图是从哪儿弄来的,因为这是一件令人起疑的魔法物品——如果老实交代地图是怎么落到他手里的,不仅会给他自己带来麻烦,还会牵连他的父亲、弗雷德和乔治·韦斯莱,以及卢平教授——他们上学期的黑魔法防御术课老师。穆迪在哈利面前挥动着地图,哈利鼓足勇气,做好了准备——

"这个能借我用一用吗?"

"噢!"哈利说。他非常喜欢这张地图,但另一方面,看到穆迪没有追问地图是从哪里弄来的,他又感到松了口气,而且毫无疑问,他还欠着穆迪一份人情呢。"行,没问题。"

"好孩子,"穆迪粗声粗气地说,"我可以拿它派大用场……这大概正是我想找的东西……好了,上床睡觉去吧,波特,快点儿,走吧……"

两人一起走到楼梯上面,穆迪仍然在仔细研究地图,似乎这是一个他以前从没见过的宝物。他们默默地走向穆迪办公室的门口,然后穆迪停住脚步,抬头望着哈利。"你有没有想过以后当一名傲罗,波特?"

"没有。"哈利说,感到很吃惊。

"你需要考虑一下了,"穆迪说,他点着头,若有所思地看着哈利,"真的……噢,顺便说一句……我猜你今晚不会只是拿着金蛋散步吧?"

"嗯——不是,"哈利咧嘴笑着说,"我在琢磨线索呢。"

穆迪朝他眨眨眼睛,那只魔眼又疯狂地转个不停。"半夜溜达是不会给你什么灵感的,波特……明天早晨见……"他转身进了办公室,一边低头钻研活点地图,一边回手把门关上了。

哈利慢慢地走回格兰芬多塔楼,一路沉思:斯内普、克劳奇,这一切都意味着什么呢……克劳奇既然能够随心所欲地溜进霍格沃茨,为什么又要装病呢?他认为斯内普在办公室里藏了什么呢?

还有,穆迪认为他——哈利应该成为一名傲罗!这个想法真有趣……然而……十分钟后,当哈利把金蛋和隐形衣放回箱子里,自己悄悄钻进四柱床时,又想,他还要检查一下其他傲罗身上有多少伤疤,再决定以后当不当傲罗。

# CHAPTER TWENTY-SIX

# The Second Task

'You said you'd already worked out that egg clue!' said Hermione indignantly.

'Keep your voice down!' said Harry crossly. 'I just need to – sort of finetune it, all right?'

He, Ron and Hermione were sitting at the very back of the Charms class with a table to themselves. They were supposed to be practising the opposite of the Summoning Charm today – the Banishing Charm. Owing to the potential for nasty accidents when objects kept flying across the room, Professor Flitwick had given each student a stack of cushions on which to practise, the theory being that these wouldn't hurt anyone if they went off target. It was a good theory, but it wasn't working very well. Neville's aim was so poor that he kept accidentally sending much heavier things flying across the room – Professor Flitwick, for instance.

'Just forget the egg for a minute, all right?' Harry hissed, as Professor Flitwick went whizzing resignedly past them, landing on top of a large cabinet. 'I'm trying to tell you about Snape and Moody ...'

This class was ideal cover for a private conversation, as everyone was having far too much fun to pay them any attention. Harry had been recounting his adventures of the previous night in whispered instalments for the last half an hour.

'Snape said Moody's searched his office as well?' Ron whispered, his eyes alight with interest as he Banished a cushion with a sweep of his wand (it soared into the air and knocked Parvati's hat off). 'What ... d'you reckon Moody's here to keep an eye on Snape as well as Karkaroff?'

'Well, I dunno if that's what Dumbledore asked him to do, but he's definitely doing it,' said Harry, waving his wand without paying much

# 第 26 章

## 第二个项目

"你明明说已经解开金蛋的线索了!"赫敏气愤地说。

"你小声点儿!"哈利恼火地说,"我只是需要——弄得更清楚些,不行吗?"

在魔咒课上,他和罗恩、赫敏单独坐在教室后面的一张桌子旁。今天要练习的咒语和召唤咒正好相反——驱逐咒。因为东西在教室里飞来飞去容易造成不幸事故,弗立维教授给了每个学生一大堆软垫做练习,这样,即使走偏了,也不会把人砸伤。这个想法倒不错,但执行起来并不顺利。纳威念咒时太没有准头了,总是不小心把一些很重的东西弄得满屋乱飞——比如弗立维教授。

"暂时忘掉金蛋吧,行吗?"哈利压低声音说,这时弗立维教授无奈地从他们身边飞过,落在一个大柜子上,"我要告诉你们斯内普和穆迪的事……"

这堂课是进行密谈的理想的保护伞,因为同学们都玩得很开心,根本顾不上注意他们。在刚才半小时里,哈利分几次小声地讲述了他昨天夜里的遭遇。

"斯内普说穆迪也搜查了他的办公室?"罗恩小声说,兴奋得两眼放光,一挥魔杖,对一个软垫念了驱逐咒(软垫飞到空中,撞掉了帕瓦蒂的帽子),"啊……穆迪在这里不光留意卡卡洛夫,还在监视斯内普,你说是吗?"

"我也不知道是不是邓布利多叫他这么做的,但他肯定去搜查了。"哈利说,一边漫不经心地挥了挥魔杖,他的软垫怪模怪样地贴着桌子滑了下去,"穆迪说邓布利多之所以让斯内普留在这里,是为了给他第

## CHAPTER TWENTY-SIX    The Second Task

attention, so that his cushion did an odd sort of belly flop off the desk. 'Moody said Dumbledore only lets Snape stay here because he's giving him a second chance or something ...'

'What?' said Ron, his eyes widening, his next cushion spinning high into the air, ricocheting off the chandelier and dropping heavily onto Flitwick's desk. 'Harry ... maybe Moody thinks *Snape* put your name in the Goblet of Fire!'

'Oh, Ron,' said Hermione, shaking her head sceptically, 'we thought Snape was trying to kill Harry before, and it turned out he was saving Harry's life, remember?'

She Banished a cushion and it flew across the room and landed in the box they were all supposed to be aiming at. Harry looked at Hermione, thinking ... it was true that Snape had saved his life once, but the odd thing was, Snape definitely loathed him, just as he'd loathed Harry's father when they had been at school together. Snape loved taking points from Harry, and had certainly never missed an opportunity to give him punishments, or even to suggest that he should be suspended from the school.

'I don't care what Moody says,' Hermione went on, 'Dumbledore's not stupid. He was right to trust Hagrid and Professor Lupin, even though loads of people wouldn't have given them jobs, so why shouldn't he be right about Snape, even if Snape is a bit –'

'– evil,' said Ron promptly. 'Come on, Hermione, why are all these Dark-wizard-catchers searching his office, then?'

'Why has Mr. Crouch been pretending to be ill?' said Hermione, ignoring Ron. 'It's a bit funny, isn't it, that he can't manage to come to the Yule Ball, but he can get up here in the middle of the night when he wants to?'

'You just don't like Crouch because of that elf, Winky,' said Ron, sending a cushion soaring into the window.

'*You* just want to think Snape's up to something,' said Hermione, sending her cushion zooming neatly into the box.

'I just want to know what Snape did with his first chance, if he's on his second one,' said Harry grimly, and his cushion, to his very great surprise, flew straight across the room, and landed neatly on top of Hermione's.

Obedient to Sirius' wish of hearing about anything odd at Hogwarts, Harry sent him a letter by brown owl that night, explaining all about Mr. Crouch

## 第26章 第二个项目

二次机会……"

"什么?"罗恩说,眼睛睁得大大的,他的第二个软垫旋转着飞到高空,把枝形吊灯撞得飞了起来,然后重重地落在弗立维的讲台上,"哈利……也许穆迪认为是斯内普把你的名字投进火焰杯的!"

"哦,罗恩,"赫敏怀疑地摇了摇头,说道,"上次我们以为斯内普想害死哈利,结果没想到他却是在救哈利,你还记得吗?"

她给一个软垫念了驱逐咒,软垫从教室上空飞过,落在他们应该瞄准的箱子里。哈利望着赫敏,沉思着……不错,斯内普以前确实救过他的命,但奇怪的是,斯内普同时又对他恨之入骨,就像当年一起上学时他仇恨哈利的父亲一样。斯内普喜欢给哈利扣分,而且决不错过任何机会惩罚哈利,甚至提出要把哈利从学校开除。

"我可不在乎穆迪说什么,"赫敏继续说道,"邓布利多并不傻。拿海格和卢平教授来说吧,许多人都不肯给他们工作,邓布利多却相信他们。他做得对,所以他对斯内普的看法也很可能是正确的,尽管斯内普有点儿——"

"——坏。"罗恩迅速接口,"那么,赫敏,那些专抓黑巫师的猎手为什么都要搜查他的办公室呢?"

"克劳奇先生为什么要装病呢?"赫敏不理罗恩,自顾自地说,"他不能来参加圣诞舞会,却能在半夜三更随心所欲地溜到这里来,这真有些蹊跷,不是吗?"

"你就是因为那个小精灵闪闪才不喜欢克劳奇的。"罗恩说,一边给软垫念了个咒,软垫朝窗户飞去。

"你就是总以为斯内普想干坏事。"赫敏说,也给软垫念了个咒,她的软垫干净利落地飞进了箱子。

"我只想知道,如果这是斯内普的第二次机会,那么他原先究竟做了什么。"哈利板着脸说。他的软垫竟然径直飞过教室上空,稳稳地落在赫敏的那个软垫上面,这使他大为惊讶。

小天狼星希望了解霍格沃茨的每一个异常情况,因此,那天晚上,哈利派一只棕褐色猫头鹰给他送了封信,把克劳奇先生闯进斯内普办

## CHAPTER TWENTY-SIX    The Second Task

breaking into Snape's office, and Moody and Snape's conversation. Then Harry turned his attention in earnest to the most urgent problem facing him: how to survive underwater for an hour on the twenty-fourth of February.

Ron quite liked the idea of using the Summoning Charm again – Harry had explained about aqualungs, and Ron couldn't see why Harry shouldn't Summon one from the nearest Muggle town. Hermione squashed this plan by pointing out that, in the unlikely event that Harry managed to learn how to operate an aqualung within the set limit of an hour, he was sure to be disqualified for breaking the International Code of Wizarding Secrecy – it was too much to hope that no Muggles would spot an aqualung zooming across the countryside to Hogwarts.

'Of course, the ideal solution would be for you to Transfigure yourself into a submarine or something,' she said. 'If only we'd done human Transfiguration already! But I don't think we start that until sixth year, and it can go badly wrong if you don't know what you're doing ...'

'Yeah, I don't fancy walking around with a periscope sticking out of my head,' said Harry. 'I s'pose I could always attack someone in front of Moody, he might do it for me ...'

'I don't think he'd let you choose what you wanted to be turned into, though,' said Hermione seriously. 'No, I think your best chance is some sort of charm.'

So Harry, thinking that he would soon have had enough of the library to last him a lifetime, buried himself once more among the dusty volumes, looking for any spell that might enable a human to survive without oxygen. However, though he, Ron and Hermione searched through their lunchtimes, evenings and whole weekends – though Harry asked Professor McGonagall for a note of permission to use the Restricted Section, and even asked the irritable, vulture-like librarian, Madam Pince, for help – they found nothing whatsoever that would enable Harry to spend an hour underwater and live to tell the tale.

Familiar flutterings of panic were starting to disturb Harry now, and he was finding it difficult to concentrate in lessons again. The lake, which Harry had always taken for granted as just another feature of the grounds, drew his eyes whenever he was near a classroom window, a great, iron-grey mass of chilly water, whose dark and icy depths were starting to seem as distant as the moon.

Just as it had done before he had faced the Horntail, time was slipping

## 第26章 第二个项目

公室,以及穆迪和斯内普之间的对话,原原本本地告诉了他。然后,哈利把全部注意力都转向了眼下这个迫在眉睫的问题:二月二十四日那天,他怎样才能在水下存活一小时。

罗恩倾向于再一次使用召唤咒——哈利跟他们说过水肺的作用,罗恩认为哈利完全可以从附近的麻瓜城镇弄一套水肺过来。赫敏断然否定了这个建议,指出,即便哈利在规定的一小时内学会了怎样操作水肺(这是不可能的),他也肯定会被取消参赛资格,因为他违反了《国际魔法保密准则》——一套水肺嗖嗖地穿过乡村朝霍格沃茨飞来,要想不被麻瓜看见简直是白日做梦。

"当然啦,最理想的办法是让你自己变形,变成一艘潜水艇什么的。"赫敏说,"要是我们已经练习过人类变形就好了!可是六年级才讲到这个内容呢,而如果你没有完全掌握就擅自给自己变形,后果不堪设想……"

"是啊,我可不愿意脑袋上支棱着一个潜水望远镜走来走去。"哈利说,"我想我可以在穆迪面前进攻别人,这样他就会给我变形了……"

"不过,我认为他可不会让你想变成什么就变成什么。"赫敏严肃地说,"不行,我认为你最好还是用个咒语。"

就这样,哈利又一次埋头钻研那些布满灰尘的大部头书,寻找一个能使人在没有氧气的情况下存活的咒语,他想他很快就会厌烦图书馆,一辈子都不愿再进去了。在午饭时间、晚上和整个周末,他和罗恩、赫敏都泡在那里,苦苦搜寻——哈利还请麦格教授给他写了一张纸条,批准他使用禁书区的藏书,甚至还向那个长得像兀鹫的图书馆管理员平斯女士请求过帮助——然而,他们没有找到任何办法,可以使哈利在水下待一小时还能活着讲述自己的故事。

现在,哈利心头又笼罩着以前有过的那种紧张感了,又觉得上课很难集中思想了。那个大湖,哈利以前总拿它不当回事,把它看成是场地的一部分。现在每当他靠近教室的窗户,大湖就会吸引住他的视线,那一大片铁灰色的阴冷的湖面,它那黢黑而寒冷的水底像月亮一样遥不可及。

就像上次面对树蜂之前一样,时间又在哗哗地溜走,仿佛有人给

## CHAPTER TWENTY-SIX  The Second Task

away as though somebody had bewitched the clocks to go extra fast. There was a week to go before February the twenty-fourth (there was still time) ... there were five days to go (he was bound to find something soon) ... three days to go (please let me find something ... *please* ...).

With two days left, Harry started to go off food again. The only good thing about breakfast on Monday was the return of the brown owl he had sent to Sirius. He pulled off the parchment, unrolled it, and saw the shortest letter Sirius had ever written to him.

*Send date of next Hogsmeade weekend by return owl.*

Harry turned the parchment over and looked at the back, hoping to see something else, but it was blank.

'Weekend after next,' whispered Hermione, who had read the note over Harry's shoulder. 'Here – take my quill and send this owl back straight away.'

Harry scribbled the dates down on the back of Sirius' letter, tied it back onto the brown owl's leg, and watched it take flight again. What had he expected? Advice on how to survive underwater? He had been so intent on telling Sirius all about Snape and Moody, he had completely forgotten to mention the egg's clue.

'What's he want to know about the next Hogsmeade weekend for?' said Ron.

'Dunno,' said Harry dully. The momentary happiness that had flared inside him at the sight of the owl had died. 'Come on ... Care of Magical Creatures.'

Whether Hagrid was trying to make up for the Blast-Ended Skrewts, or because there were now only two Skrewts left, or because he was trying to prove he could do anything that Professor Grubbly-Plank could, Harry didn't know, but he had been continuing her lessons on unicorns ever since he'd returned to work. It turned out that Hagrid knew quite as much about unicorns as he did about monsters, though it was clear that he found their lack of poisonous fangs disappointing.

Today he had managed to capture two unicorn foals. Unlike full-grown unicorns, they were pure gold. Parvati and Lavender went into transports of delight at the sight of them, and even Pansy Parkinson had to work hard to conceal how much she liked them.

## 第26章 第二个项目

钟表施了魔法，让它们转得飞快。离二月二十四日只有一个星期了（还有时间）……只有五天了（他肯定很快就会想出办法）……只有三天了（快让我想出办法吧……求求你了）……

只剩两天了，哈利又开始吃不下饭。星期一的早饭桌上，唯一令人宽慰的是他派去给小天狼星送信的棕褐色猫头鹰回来了。哈利抽出那张羊皮纸展开，看见的是小天狼星跟他通信以来写得最短的一封信。

> 派送回信的猫头鹰告知你们下次到霍格莫德过周末的日期。

哈利把羊皮纸翻过来看了看背面，希望能看到些别的，但背面什么也没有。

"下下个周末，"赫敏在哈利身后看了短信的内容，小声说道，"拿着——用我的羽毛笔，马上就派这只猫头鹰送回信。"

哈利把日期草草写在小天狼星回信的背面，把信系在棕褐色猫头鹰的腿上，看着它又飞走了。他原先指望得到什么呢？指望小天狼星告诉他如何在水下存活？他写信时只顾告诉小天狼星关于斯内普和穆迪的事了，把金蛋忘得一干二净，只字未提。

"他为什么想知道我们下次到霍格莫德过周末的具体日期呢？"罗恩问。

"不知道。"哈利干巴巴地说，他看见猫头鹰时内心闪过的短暂喜悦消失了，"走吧……去上保护神奇动物课。"

哈利不知道海格是为了弥补在炸尾螺上的过错，还是因为炸尾螺只剩了最后两条，或者是因为他想证明格拉普兰教授能做到的，他海格也照样能做到。反正，海格回来上课后，就把格拉普兰教授关于独角兽的课继续上了下去。结果证明，海格对独角兽的了解并不比他对巨怪的了解少，不过，他显然觉得独角兽没有獠牙是一件令人失望的事。

今天，他居然抓到了两只独角兽小崽。小崽与成年的独角兽不同，它们是纯金色的。帕瓦蒂和拉文德一看见它们，就高兴得发了狂似的，就连潘西·帕金森也不得不拼命掩饰，以免暴露自己是多么喜欢它们。

## CHAPTER TWENTY-SIX  The Second Task

'Easier ter spot than the adults,' Hagrid told the class. 'They turn silver when they're abou' two years old, an' they grow horns at aroun' four. Don' go pure white 'til they're full-grown, round about seven. They're a bit more trustin' when they're babies ... don' mind boys so much ... c'mon, move in a bit, yeh can pat 'em if yeh want ... give 'em a few o' these sugar lumps ...

'You OK, Harry?' Hagrid muttered, moving aside slightly, while most of the others swarmed around the baby unicorns.

'Yeah,' said Harry.

'Jus' nervous, eh?' said Hagrid.

'Bit,' said Harry.

'Harry,' said Hagrid, clapping a massive hand on his shoulder, so that Harry's knees buckled under its weight, 'I'd've bin worried before I saw yeh take on tha' Horntail, but I know now yeh can do anythin' yeh set yer mind ter. I'm not worried at all. Yeh're goin' ter be fine. Got yer clue worked out, haven' yeh?'

Harry nodded, but even as he did so, an insane urge to confess that he didn't have any idea how to survive at the bottom of the lake for an hour came over him. He looked up at Hagrid – perhaps he had to go into the lake sometimes, to deal with the creatures in it? He looked after everything else in the grounds, after all –

'Yeh're goin' ter win,' Hagrid growled, patting Harry's shoulder again, so that Harry actually felt himself sink a couple of inches into the muddy ground. 'I know it. I can feel it. *Yeh're goin' ter win, Harry.*'

Harry just couldn't bring himself to wipe the happy, confident smile off Hagrid's face. Pretending he was interested in the young unicorns, he forced a smile in return, and moved forwards to pat them with the others.

By the evening before the second task, Harry felt as though he was trapped in a nightmare. He was fully aware that even if, by some miracle, he managed to find a suitable spell, he'd have a real job mastering it overnight. How could he have let this happen? Why hadn't he got to work on the egg's clue sooner? Why had he ever let his mind wander in class – what if a teacher had once mentioned how to breathe underwater?

He, Ron and Hermione sat in the library as the sun set outside, tearing

## 第26章 第二个项目

"小崽比成年的容易发现。"海格对全班同学说,"它们两岁左右变成银色,大约四岁的时候出角。直到成年后才会变成纯白色,那大约是在七岁左右。它们小的时候比较轻信……对男孩子不怎么反感……过来,靠近一点,你们如果愿意,可以拍拍它们……把这些方糖给它们吃几块……"

"你没事吧,哈利?"海格趁大家都聚拢在独角兽小崽周围时,踱到一边,低声问道。

"没事。"哈利说。

"有点儿紧张,是吗?"海格说。

"有点儿吧。"哈利说。

"哈利,"海格说着,用粗重的手拍拍他的肩膀,压得哈利的膝盖直打弯,"在你对付那条树蜂前,我确实替你担心过,但我现在知道了,只要是你想做的事,没有做不成的。我一点也不担心了。你肯定会成功的。线索解出来了吗,嗯?"

哈利点了点头,但他尽管在点头,内心却产生了一种荒唐的冲动,想坦白承认自己不知道怎样在湖底下存活一小时。他抬头望着海格——也许海格有时候必须钻进水底,去对付湖里的动物?因为场地上的其他东西都是他负责照料的——

"你会赢的,"海格嗓音粗粗地说,又拍了拍哈利的肩膀——哈利觉得自己往松软的泥地里陷了两英寸,"我知道。我能够感觉到。你一定会赢的,哈利!"

哈利不忍心抹去海格脸上喜悦的充满信心的笑容。他假装对小独角兽很感兴趣,勉强对海格笑了笑,就走上前,和同学们一起去抚摸两个小崽了。

到了第二个项目的前一天傍晚,哈利觉得自己仿佛陷入了一场噩梦。他十分清楚,即使奇迹出现,他发现了一个合适的咒语,也很难在一夜之间掌握它。他怎么会让事情落到这步田地呢?他为什么不早点开始钻研金蛋提供的线索呢?他为什么在课堂上开小差——也许某个老师曾经提到过怎样在水下呼吸呢?

窗外的太阳渐渐西沉,他和赫敏、罗恩坐在图书馆里,心急火燎地

## CHAPTER TWENTY-SIX   The Second Task

feverishly through page after page of spells, hidden from each other by the massive piles of books on the desk in front of each of them. Harry's heart gave a huge leap every time he saw the word 'water' on a page, but more often than not it was merely 'Take two pints of water, half a pound of shredded mandrake leaves and a newt ...'.

'I don't reckon it can be done,' said Ron's voice flatly from the other side of the table. 'There's nothing. *Nothing.* Closest was that thing to dry up puddles and ponds, that Drought Charm, but that was nowhere near powerful enough to drain the lake.'

'There must be something,' Hermione muttered, moving a candle closer to her. Her eyes were so tired she was poring over the tiny print of *Olde and Forgotten Bewitchments and Charmes* with her nose about an inch from the page. 'They'd never have set a task that was undoable.'

'They have,' said Ron. 'Harry, just go down to the lake tomorrow, right, stick your head in, yell at the merpeople to give back whatever they've nicked and see if they chuck it out. Best you can do, mate.'

'There's a way of doing it!' Hermione said crossly. 'There just has to be!'

She seemed to be taking the library's lack of useful information on the subject as a personal insult; it had never failed her before.

'I know what I should have done,' said Harry, resting, face down, on *Saucy Tricks for Tricky Sorts*. 'I should've learnt to be an Animagus like Sirius.'

'Yeah, you could've turned into a goldfish any time you wanted!' said Ron.

'Or a frog,' yawned Harry. He was exhausted.

'It takes years to become an Animagus, and then you have to register yourself and everything,' said Hermione vaguely, now squinting down the index of *Weird Wizarding Dilemmas and Their Solutions*. 'Professor McGonagall told us, remember ... you've got to register yourself with the Improper Use of Magic Office ... what animal you become, and your markings, so you can't abuse it ...'

'Hermione, I was joking,' said Harry, wearily. 'I know I haven't got a chance of turning into a frog by tomorrow morning ...'

'Oh, this is no use,' Hermione said, snapping *Weird Wizarding Dilemmas* shut. 'Who on earth wants to make their nose hair grow into ringlets?'

'I wouldn't mind,' said Fred Weasley's voice. 'Be a talking point, wouldn't it?'

## 第 26 章 第二个项目

翻阅一本本咒语书,每个人面前的桌上都堆着好几摞书,互相都看不见对方。每当哈利在书上看见"水"这个词,心都要狂跳一下,但再仔细一看,那上面经常是取两品脱水、半磅切碎的曼德拉草,再加一条水螈……

"我觉得这样行不通,"罗恩的声音干巴巴地从桌子那头传来,"什么都找不到。什么都没有。也许淘干咒还比较接近,把池塘、水坑的水淘干,但是你不可能有那么大力量,把整个湖里的水都淘干。"

"肯定有办法的。"赫敏低声嘟哝道,把一支蜡烛挪得更近了些。她的眼睛太疲劳了,不得不凑得很近,鼻子离书页只有一英寸,才能看清《被遗忘的古老魔法和咒语》上细密的小字。"他们不可能设计一个无法完成的项目。"

"他们会的。"罗恩说,"哈利,你明天就直接走到湖边,把脑袋扎进去,大声喊话,叫人鱼把偷的东西还给你,看他们会不会把它扔出来。这是你最好的办法了,伙计。"

"办法肯定有的!"赫敏急躁地说,"肯定有的!"

她似乎把图书馆缺乏有用资料看成是对她自己的侮辱,以前她的问题总能在书本里找到答案。

"我知道应该怎么做了。"哈利说,他脸朝下趴在《对付恶作剧的锦囊妙计》上,"我应该学会做一个阿尼马格斯,就像小天狼星那样。"

"对啊,你可以随心所欲地把自己变成一条金鱼!"罗恩说。

"或者一只青蛙。"哈利打了个哈欠。他太累了。

"成为阿尼马格斯要花好几年时间呢,然后你还要去登记,麻烦多着呢。"赫敏含混地说,她正眯着眼睛查找《古怪的魔法难题及其解答》的索引,"麦格教授告诉过我们,记得吗……你必须到禁止滥用魔法办公室登记……你要变成什么动物,有什么标记,这样才能防止滥用……"

"赫敏,我不过是开个玩笑,"哈利有气无力地说,"我知道我绝对不可能明天一早就变成一只青蛙……"

"哦,根本没有用,"赫敏说着,啪地合上《古怪的魔法难题及其解答》,"谁想使自己的鼻毛长成小卷卷呢?"

"我倒不反对,"弗雷德·韦斯莱的声音突然传来,"这可就成为别人的话题了,是不是?"

## CHAPTER TWENTY-SIX    The Second Task

Harry, Ron and Hermione looked up. Fred and George had just emerged from behind some bookshelves.

'What're you two doing here?' Ron asked.

'Looking for you,' said George. 'McGonagall wants you, Ron. And you, Hermione.'

'Why?' said Hermione, looking surprised.

'Dunno ... she was looking a bit grim, though,' said Fred.

'We're supposed to take you down to her office,' said George.

Ron and Hermione stared at Harry, who felt his stomach drop. Was Professor McGonagall about to tell Ron and Hermione off? Perhaps she'd noticed how much they were helping him, when he ought to be working out how to do the task alone?

'We'll meet you back in the common room,' Hermione told Harry, as she got up to go with Ron – both of them looked very anxious. 'Bring as many of these books as you can, OK?'

'Right,' said Harry uneasily.

By eight o'clock, Madam Pince had extinguished all the lamps and came to chivvy Harry out of the library. Staggering under the weight of as many books as he could carry, Harry returned to the Gryffindor common room, pulled a table into a corner and continued to search. There was nothing in *Madcap Magic for Wacky Warlocks* ... nothing in *A Guide to Medieval Sorcery* ... not one mention of underwater exploits in *An Anthology of Eighteenth-Century Charms*, or in *Dreadful Denizens of the Deep*, or *Powers You Never Knew You Had* and *What to Do With Them Now You've Wised Up*.

Crookshanks crawled into Harry's lap and curled up, purring deeply. The common room emptied slowly around Harry. People kept wishing him luck for the next morning in cheery, confident voices like Hagrid's, all of them apparently convinced that he was about to pull off another stunning performance like the one he had managed in the first task. Harry couldn't answer them, he just nodded, feeling as though there was a golf-ball stuck in his throat. By ten to midnight, he was alone in the room with Crookshanks. He had searched all the remaining books, and Ron and Hermione had not come back.

It's over, he told himself. You can't do it. You'll just have to go down to the lake in the morning and tell the judges ...

He imagined himself explaining that he couldn't do the task. He pictured

## 第 26 章 第二个项目

哈利、罗恩和赫敏抬起头。弗雷德和乔治刚从书架后面走出来。

"你们俩在这里做什么？"罗恩问。

"找你呀，"乔治说，"麦格叫你去，罗恩。还有你，赫敏。"

"干什么？"赫敏问，显得很吃惊。

"不知道……不过，她的样子怪严肃的。"弗雷德说。

"我们要把你们带到她的办公室去。"乔治说。

罗恩和赫敏望着哈利，哈利觉得心头一沉。麦格教授是不是要训斥罗恩和赫敏呢？也许她已经注意到他们在帮助他？他应该自己琢磨怎样完成比赛项目的呀！

"我们在公共休息室和你见面，哈利，"赫敏对哈利说，一边起身和罗恩一同离开——两人都显得非常紧张，"这些书，你能带回去多少就带回去多少，好吗？"

"好吧。"哈利说，心中惴惴不安。

八点钟的时候，平斯女士关掉所有的灯，过来把哈利赶出了图书馆。哈利抱着一大堆书，跟跟跄跄地回到格兰芬多公共休息室，走到墙角的一张桌子旁，又开始继续搜寻。《怪男巫的疯狂魔法》里什么也没有……《中世纪巫术指南》里什么也没有……在《十八世纪魔咒选》《地底深处的可怕动物》《你不知道自己所拥有的能力，以及你一旦明白后怎样运用它们》里，也没有一个字提到水下生存的办法。

克鲁克山爬到哈利的膝头，蜷缩着身体，香甜地打起了呼噜。公共休息室里的人渐渐走光了。同学们临走时都祝他明天好运，口气和海格一样愉快而充满信心。显然，他们都相信他又要完成一个精彩绝伦的表演，就像在第一个项目中那样。哈利无法回答他们，只好点点头，觉得嗓子眼里仿佛塞了一个高尔夫球。十二点差十分的时候，休息室里只剩下他和克鲁克山了。他把所有的书都找了个遍，罗恩和赫敏还没有回来。

完了，他对自己说。你做不到了。你明天只好走到湖边，告诉裁判……

他幻想着自己在向裁判解释他无法完成这个项目。他想象着巴格曼睁圆了眼睛，一脸的惊讶；卡卡洛夫露出黄牙，幸灾乐祸地笑着。

## CHAPTER TWENTY-SIX   The Second Task

Bagman's look of round-eyed surprise, Karkaroff's satisfied, yellow-toothed smile. He could almost hear Fleur Delacour saying, '*I knew it ... 'e is too young, 'e is only a little boy.*' He saw Malfoy flashing his POTTER STINKS badge at the front of the crowd, saw Hagrid's crest-fallen, disbelieving face ...

Forgetting that Crookshanks was on his lap, Harry stood up very suddenly; Crookshanks hissed angrily as he landed on the floor, gave Harry a disgusted look and stalked away with his bottle-brush tail in the air, but Harry was already hurrying up the spiral staircase to his dormitory ... he would grab the Invisibility Cloak and go back to the library, he'd stay there all night if he had to ...

'*Lumos*,' Harry whispered fifteen minutes later, as he opened the library door.

Wand tip alight, he crept along the bookshelves, pulling down more books – books of hexes and charms, books on merpeople and water monsters, books on famous witches and wizards, on magical inventions, on anything at all that might include one passing reference to underwater survival. He carried them over to a table, then set to work, searching them by the narrow beam of his wand, occasionally checking his watch ...

One in the morning ... two in the morning ... the only way he could keep going was to tell himself, over and over again, *Next book ... in the next one ... the next one ...*

The mermaid in the painting in the Prefects' bathroom was laughing. Harry was bobbing like a cork in bubbly water next to her rock, while she held his Firebolt over his head.

'Come and get it!' she giggled maliciously. 'Come on, jump!'

'I can't,' Harry panted, snatching at the Firebolt, and struggling not to sink. 'Give it to me!'

But she just poked him painfully in the side with the end of the broom, laughing at him.

'That hurts – get off – ouch –'

'Harry Potter must wake up, sir!'

'Stop poking me –'

'Dobby must poke Harry Potter, sir, he must wake up!'

Harry opened his eyes. He was still in the library; the Invisibility Cloak had slipped off his head as he'd slept, and the side of his face was stuck to the pages of *Where There's a Wand, There's a Way.* He sat up, straightening his

## 第26章 第二个项目

他几乎能听见芙蓉·德拉库尔的声音:"我早就知道……他年纪太小了,还是个小男孩呢。"他看见马尔福在人群前面闪动着**波特臭大粪**的徽章,看见海格沮丧的难以置信的脸……

哈利忘记了腿上的克鲁克山,猛地站了起来。克鲁克山掉到地板上,气呼呼地嘶嘶叫着,厌恶地白了哈利一眼,迈着大步走开了,那条瓶刷子般的尾巴翘得高高的。但哈利已经匆匆登上旋转楼梯,回宿舍去了……他去拿隐形衣,然后再溜回图书馆,如果必要的话,他要在那里熬一个通宵……

"荧光闪烁。"十五分钟后,他打开图书馆大门时低声说道。

就着魔杖顶上发出的一点微光,他溜进书架间,抽下一本又一本书——关于魔法和咒语的书,关于人鱼和水下怪物的书,关于著名巫师的书,关于魔法发明的书,等等,只要可能有片言只语提及水下生存的书,他都抽出来了。他把这些书搬到一张桌子上,埋头啃读起来,靠着魔杖的那点微光,苦苦搜寻,偶尔看看手表……

凌晨一点……凌晨两点……唯一能使他坚持下去的,是他一遍又一遍地告诉自己:下一本书……在下一本书里……下一本……

级长洗澡间那幅画里的美人鱼在大笑。哈利像个软木塞一样,在靠近她躺着的那块岩石的泡泡浴液里一沉一浮,美人鱼把他的火弩箭高高举在他头顶上。

"过来拿呀!"她调皮地咯咯笑着,"过来,跳起来!"

"我过不去,"哈利喘着气说,他试着去抓火弩箭,并挣扎着不要沉下去,"还给我!"

可美人鱼只是一边大声嘲笑他,一边用扫帚尖戳他的身体,弄得他疼痛难忍。

"疼死了——别戳我——哎哟——"

"哈利·波特必须醒一醒了,先生!"

"别戳我——"

"多比必须戳哈利·波特,先生,他必须醒一醒了!"

哈利睁开眼睛。他仍然在图书馆里,在他睡着时隐形衣已经从他头上滑落到地板上,他的面颊贴在《只要有魔杖,就有办法》的书页上。

## CHAPTER TWENTY-SIX    The Second Task

glasses, blinking in the bright daylight.

'Harry Potter needs to hurry!' squeaked Dobby. 'The second task starts in ten minutes, and Harry Potter –'

'Ten minutes?' Harry croaked. 'Ten – *ten minutes?*'

He looked down at his watch. Dobby was right. It was twenty past nine. A large, dead weight seemed to fall through Harry's chest into his stomach.

'Hurry, Harry Potter!' squeaked Dobby, plucking at Harry's sleeve. 'You is supposed to be down by the lake with the other champions, sir!'

'It's too late, Dobby,' Harry said hopelessly. 'I'm not doing the task, I don't know how –'

'Harry Potter *will* do the task!' squeaked the elf. 'Dobby knew Harry had not found the right book, so Dobby did it for him!'

'What?' said Harry. 'But *you* don't know what the second task is –'

'Dobby knows, sir! Harry Potter has to go into the lake and find his Wheezy –'

'Find my what?'

'– and take his Wheezy back from the merpeople!'

'What's a Wheezy?'

'Your Wheezy, sir, your Wheezy – Wheezy who is giving Dobby his jumper!'

Dobby plucked at the shrunken maroon sweater he was now wearing over his shorts.

'*What?*' Harry gasped. 'They've got ... they've got *Ron?*'

'The thing Harry Potter will miss most, sir!' squeaked Dobby. 'And past an hour–'

'– "*the prospect's black*",' Harry recited, staring, horror-struck, at the elf, '"*Too late, it's gone, it won't come back* ..." Dobby – what've I got to do?'

'You has to eat this, sir!' squeaked the elf, and he put his hand in the pocket of his shorts and drew out a ball of what looked like slimy, greyish green rat tails. 'Right before you go into the lake, sir – Gillyweed!'

'What's it do?' said Harry, staring at the Gillyweed.

'It will make Harry Potter breathe underwater, sir!'

## 第26章 第二个项目

他坐起来，整了整眼镜，明亮的日光刺得他直眨眼睛。

"哈利·波特必须赶快了！"多比尖声尖气地说，"第二个项目还有十分钟就要开始了，哈利·波特——"

"十分钟？"哈利声音嘶哑地说，"十——十分钟？"

他低头一看表。多比没有说错。现在已经九点二十了。顿时，似乎有一块沉重的大石头从哈利的胸腔落进了胃里。

"快点儿，哈利·波特！"多比尖着嗓子说，一边拉着哈利的袖子，"你应该和其他勇士一起，到下面的湖边去，先生！"

"太晚了，多比，"哈利绝望地说，"我不做这个项目了，我不知道怎样——"

"哈利·波特会做这个项目的！"小精灵尖声说，"多比知道哈利没有找到合适的书，所以多比就替他找到了！"

"什么？"哈利说，"但你不知道第二个项目是什么——"

"多比知道，先生！哈利·波特必须到湖里去，找到他的韦崽——"

"找到我的什么？"

"——把他的韦崽从人鱼手里夺回来！"

"韦崽是什么？"

"你的韦崽，先生，你的韦崽——就是把自己的毛衣送给多比的那个韦崽！"

多比拉了拉他穿在短裤上面的那件缩小了的暗紫红色毛衣。

"什么？"哈利喘着气说，"他们抓走了……他们抓走了罗恩？"

"那是哈利·波特最舍不得的东西，先生！"多比尖声说，"过了一小时——"

"——便希望全无，"哈利背诵道，一边惊恐地瞪着小精灵，"它已彻底消逝，永不出现。多比——我怎么办呢？"

"你必须把这个吃下去，先生！"小精灵尖声说着，把手伸进短裤口袋，掏出一团东西，像是无数根滑溜溜的灰绿色老鼠尾巴，"就在你下水前吃，先生——鳃囊草！"

"做什么用的？"哈利盯着鳃囊草，问道。

"它可以使哈利·波特在水下呼吸，先生！"

## CHAPTER TWENTY-SIX    The Second Task

'Dobby,' said Harry frantically, 'listen – are you sure about this?'

He couldn't quite forget that the last time Dobby had tried to 'help' him, he had ended up with no bones in his right arm.

'Dobby is quite sure, sir!' said the elf earnestly. 'Dobby hears things, sir, he is a house-elf, he goes all over the castle as he lights the fires and mops the floors, Dobby heard Professor McGonagall and Professor Moody in the staff room, talking about the next task ... Dobby cannot let Harry Potter lose his Wheezy!'

Harry's doubts vanished. Jumping to his feet he pulled off the Invisibility Cloak, stuffed it into his bag, grabbed the Gillyweed and put it into his pocket, then tore out of the library with Dobby at his heels.

'Dobby is supposed to be in the kitchens, sir!' Dobby squealed as they burst into the corridor. 'Dobby will be missed – good luck, Harry Potter, sir, good luck!'

'See you later, Dobby!' Harry shouted, and he sprinted along the corridor and down the stairs, three at a time.

The Entrance Hall contained a few last-minute stragglers, all leaving the Great Hall after breakfast and heading through the double oak doors to watch the second task. They stared as Harry flashed past, sending Colin and Dennis Creevey flying as he leapt down the stone steps and out into the bright, chilly grounds.

As he pounded down the lawn he saw that the seats that had encircled the dragons' enclosure in November were now ranged along the opposite bank, rising in stands that were packed to bursting point and reflected in the lake below; the excited babble of the crowd echoed strangely across the water as Harry ran, flat out, around the other side of the lake towards the judges, who were sitting at another gold-draped table at the water's edge. Cedric, Fleur and Krum were beside the judges' table, watching Harry sprint towards them.

'I'm ... here ...' Harry panted, skidding to a halt in the mud and accidentally splattering Fleur's robes.

'Where have you been?' said a bossy, disapproving voice. 'The task's about to start!'

Harry looked around. Percy Weasley was sitting at the judges' table – Mr. Crouch had failed to turn up again.

'Now, now, Percy!' said Ludo Bagman, who was looking intensely relieved to see Harry. 'Let him catch his breath!'

Dumbledore smiled at Harry, but Karkaroff and Madame Maxime didn't

## 第 26 章 第二个项目

"多比,"哈利欣喜若狂地说,"听着——你真的有把握吗?"

他无法彻底忘记多比上次对他的"帮助",当时害得他右胳膊里的骨头全失去了。

"多比绝对有把握,先生!"小精灵认真地说,"多比能听见一些事情,先生,多比是个家养小精灵,他生火和拖地板时,走遍了城堡的每个角落。多比听见麦格教授和穆迪教授在教工休息室里谈论下一个项目……多比不能让哈利·波特失去他的韦恩!"

哈利的疑虑一扫而光。他一跃而起,脱掉隐形衣,胡乱地塞进书包,又抓过鳃囊草装进口袋,然后大步走出图书馆,多比紧紧跟在后面。

"多比应该到厨房去了,先生!"他们匆匆来到走廊上时,多比尖声说道,"他们会找多比的——祝你好运,哈利·波特。先生,祝你好运!"

"再见,多比!"哈利喊道,然后飞快地冲过走廊,一步三级地奔下楼梯。

门厅里还剩下最后几个拖拉的人,他们都已吃过早饭,正穿过两扇橡木大门,出去观看第二个项目。他们吃惊地望着哈利闪电般地跑过,他跳下石阶时,把科林和丹尼斯·克里维兄弟俩撞得飞了起来。他终于来到了外面阳光明媚却寒冷的场地上。

哈利顺着草坪往下跑时,看见去年十一月火龙围场四周的那些座位,现在一层层地排在了湖对岸,已经是座无虚席,在下面的湖里映出倒影,人群的喧闹声虚幻地在湖面上回荡着。哈利拼命绕过湖,朝裁判们跑去,他们坐在水边另一张铺着金黄色桌布的桌子旁。塞德里克、芙蓉和克鲁姆站在裁判桌旁,望着哈利全速向他们奔来。

"我……我来了……"哈利上气不接下气地说,在泥地里一滑,停住了脚步,不小心把芙蓉的长袍溅脏了。

"你上哪儿去了?"一个盛气凌人的声音不满地说,"比赛马上就要开始了!"

哈利转过头。珀西·韦斯莱坐在裁判桌旁——克劳奇先生又没能来。

"好了,好了,珀西!"卢多·巴格曼说,他看到哈利,似乎心中的一块石头落了地,"让他喘口气吧!"

邓布利多朝哈利微笑,但卡卡洛夫和马克西姆女士却似乎很不高

## CHAPTER TWENTY-SIX    The Second Task

look at all pleased to see him ... it was obvious from the looks on their faces that they had thought he wasn't going to turn up.

Harry bent over, hands on his knees, gasping for breath; he had a stitch in his side that felt as though he had a knife between his ribs, but there was no time to get rid of it; Ludo Bagman was now moving among the champions, spacing them along the bank at intervals of ten feet. Harry was on the very end of the line, next to Krum, who was wearing swimming trunks, and was holding his wand ready.

'All right, Harry?' Bagman whispered, as he moved Harry a few feet further away from Krum. 'Know what you're going to do?'

'Yeah,' Harry panted, massaging his ribs.

Bagman gave his shoulder a quick squeeze, and returned to the judges' table; he pointed his wand at his throat as he had done at the World Cup, said '*Sonorus!*' and his voice boomed out across the dark water towards the stands.

'Well, all our champions are ready for the second task, which will start on my whistle. They have precisely an hour to recover what has been taken from them. On the count of three, then. One ... two ... *three*!'

The whistle echoed shrilly in the cold, still air; the stands erupted with cheers and applause; without looking to see what the other champions were doing, Harry pulled off his shoes and socks, pulled the handful of Gillyweed out of his pocket, stuffed it into his mouth, and waded out into the lake.

The lake was so cold he felt the skin on his legs searing as though this was fire, not icy water. His sodden robes weighed him down as he walked in deeper; now the water was over his knees, and his rapidly numbing feet were slipping over silt and flat, slimy stones. He was chewing the Gillyweed as hard and fast as he could; it felt unpleasantly slimy and rubbery, like octopus tentacles. Waist-deep in the freezing water he stopped, swallowed, and waited for something to happen.

He could hear laughter in the crowd, and knew he must look stupid, walking into the lake without showing any sign of magical power. The part of him that was still dry was covered in goose-pimples; half immersed in the icy water, a cruel breeze lifting his hair, Harry started to shiver violently. He avoided looking at the stands; the laughter was becoming louder, and there were catcalls and jeering from the Slytherins ...

Then, quite suddenly, Harry felt as though an invisible pillow had been

## 第 26 章 第二个项目

兴看见他……从他们脸上的表情看，他们显然以为哈利不会露面了。

哈利弯下腰，用手扶着膝盖，大口地喘着气。他胸腹一侧突然剧痛难忍，好像一把刀子插进了他的肋骨间，可是来不及缓解这种疼痛了。卢多·巴格曼已经来到勇士们中间，吩咐他们在岸边一字排开，每人间隔十英尺。哈利排在最后一个，紧挨着克鲁姆。克鲁姆穿着游泳裤，已经拿出魔杖，做好了准备。

"怎么样，哈利？"巴格曼领着哈利又往前走了几步，避开克鲁姆，小声问道，"知道自己要做什么吗？"

"知道。"哈利喘着气说，一边按摩着肋骨。

巴格曼用力捏了一下哈利的肩膀，反身回到了裁判桌旁。他用魔杖指着自己的喉咙，就像在世界杯赛上那样，说了句："声音洪亮！"于是他的声音就像雷鸣一样，掠过暗黑色的湖面传到看台上。

"大家听好，我们的勇士已经各就各位。我一吹口哨，第二个项目就开始。他们有整整一小时的时间，夺回他们被抢走的东西。我数到三。一……二……三！"

尖厉的口哨声在寒冷静止的空气中回响。看台上爆发出一阵欢呼和掌声。哈利没有观望其他勇士在做什么，他只顾三下两下脱掉鞋袜，从口袋里掏出那一把鳃囊草，塞进嘴里，然后蹚水走进湖中。

真冷啊，他觉得双腿的皮肤火辣辣地疼，好像他蹚着的是火，而不是冰冷的水。越往前走，湖水越深，湿透的长袍重重地往下坠着。现在湖水已经没过膝盖，两只迅速麻木的脚踩在泥沙和光溜溜黏糊糊的石子上，不停地打滑。他飞快地使劲嚼着鳃囊草，那感觉不太好，韧韧的、滑腻腻的，像章鱼的触手。他在齐腰深的水里停住脚步，把鳃囊草咽了下去，等待奇迹的发生。

他听见观众席上传来笑声，知道自己的样子一定很蠢，就这样走进湖里，没有表现出任何魔法本领。下半身已经浸在寒冷刺骨的湖水中，凛冽的寒风毫不留情地吹动着他的头发，他剧烈地颤抖起来。他身体没有沾水的部分起满了鸡皮疙瘩，他故意不去看观众。笑声更响了，其中还夹杂着斯莱特林们的嘘声尖叫和嘲笑……

接着，突如其来地，哈利觉得似乎有一个看不见的枕头压住了他

# CHAPTER TWENTY-SIX  The Second Task

clapped over his mouth and nose. He tried to draw breath, but it made his head spin; his lungs were empty, and he suddenly felt a piercing pain on either side of his neck –

Harry clapped his hands around his throat, and felt two large slits just below his ears, flapping in the cold air ... *he had gills.* Without pausing to think, he did the only thing that made sense – he flung himself forwards into the water.

The first gulp of icy lake water felt like the breath of life. His head had stopped spinning; he took another great gulp of water and felt it pass smoothly through his gills, sending oxygen back to his brain. He stretched out his hands in front of him and stared at them. They looked green and ghostly under the water, and they had become webbed. He twisted around and looked at his bare feet – they had become elongated and his toes were webbed, too; it looked as though he had sprouted flippers.

The water didn't feel icy any more, either ... on the contrary, he felt pleasantly cool, and very light ... Harry struck out once more, marvelling at how far and fast his flipper-like feet propelled him through the water, and noticing how clearly he could see, and how he no longer needed to blink. He had soon swum so far into the lake that he could no longer see the bottom. He flipped over, and dived into its depths.

Silence pressed upon his ears as he soared over a strange, dark, foggy landscape. He could only see ten feet around him, so that as he sped through the water new scenes seemed to loom suddenly out of the oncoming darkness: forests of rippling, tangled black weed, wide plains of mud littered with dull, glimmering stones. He swam deeper and deeper, out towards the middle of the lake, his eyes wide, staring through the eerily grey-lit water around him to the shadows beyond, where the water became opaque.

Small fish flickered past him like silver darts. Once or twice he thought he saw something larger moving ahead of him, but when he got nearer, he discovered it to be nothing but a large, blackened log, or a dense clump of weed. There was no sign of any of the other champions, merpeople, Ron – nor, thankfully, the giant squid.

Light-green weed stretched ahead of him as far as he could see, two feet deep, like a meadow of very overgrown grass. Harry was staring unblinkingly ahead of him, trying to discern shapes through the gloom ... and then, without warning, something grabbed hold of his ankle.

## CHAPTER TWENTY-SIX    The Second Task

Harry twisted his body around and saw a Grindylow, a small, horned water demon, poking out of the weeds, its long fingers clutched tightly around Harry's leg, its pointed fangs bared – Harry stuck his webbed hand quickly inside his robes and fumbled for his wand – by the time he had grasped it, two more Grindylows had risen out of the weed, had seized handfuls of Harry's robes, and were attempting to drag him down.

'*Relashio!*' Harry shouted, except that no sound came out ... a large bubble issued from his mouth, and his wand, instead of sending sparks at the Grindylows, pelted them with what seemed to be a jet of boiling water, for where it struck them, angry red patches appeared on their green skin. Harry pulled his ankle out of the Grindylows' grip and swam as fast as he could, occasionally sending more jets of hot water over his shoulder at random; every now and then he felt one of the Grindylows snatch at his foot again, and kicked out, hard; finally, he felt his foot connect with a horned skull, and looking back, saw the dazed Grindylow floating away, cross-eyed, while its fellows shook their fists at Harry, and sank back into the weed.

Harry slowed down a little, slipped his wand back inside his robes and looked around, listening again. He turned full circle in the water, the silence pressing harder than ever against his eardrums. He knew he must be even deeper in the lake now, but nothing was moving except the rippling weed.

'How are you getting on?'

Harry thought he was having a heart attack. He whipped around, and saw Moaning Myrtle floating hazily in front of him, gazing at him through her thick pearly glasses.

'Myrtle!' Harry tried to shout – but, once again, nothing came out of his mouth but a very large bubble. Moaning Myrtle actually giggled.

'You want to try over there!' she said, pointing. 'I won't come with you ... I don't like them much, they always chase me when I get too close ...'

Harry gave her the thumbs-up to show his thanks, and set off once more, careful to swim a bit higher over the weed, to avoid any more Grindylows that might be lurking there.

He swam on for what felt like at least twenty minutes. He was passing over vast expanses of black mud now, which swirled murkily as he disturbed the water. Then, at long last, he heard a snatch of haunting mer-song.

## 第 26 章 第二个项目

的嘴和鼻子。一吸气，只觉得脑子里天旋地转。他肺里空空的，脖子两侧突然一阵刀割般的剧痛——

哈利赶紧用两手抓住喉咙，摸到耳朵下有两道狭长的裂缝，在寒冷的空气里一开一合……他有鳃了！他没有犹豫，采取了唯一合理的举动——一头钻进了水里。

吸进第一口冰冷的湖水，就像获得了生命所需的氧气。他的脑袋不再天旋地转。他又使劲吸了一口湖水，感觉水从他的鳃里顺畅地流过，把氧气输送进大脑。他把双手伸到面前，仔细打量。它们在水下显得有些发绿，样子怪可怕的，而且手指间有蹼连着。他转过头去看自己光裸的脚——脚变长了，脚趾间也有蹼连着，就好像他的脚突然变成了鸭蹼。

湖水不再冰冷刺骨……相反，他觉得很凉爽，很舒服，身体也变得非常轻盈……哈利继续向前划水，惊喜地发现两只带蹼的脚能使他在水中前进得这么远，这么快。他还发现，似乎根本不需要眨眼睛就可以看得清清楚楚了。很快，他就游出很远，再也看不见湖底。他翻了一个身，朝湖的深处扎下去。

他在一片黑乎乎、朦朦胧胧的奇异景色中游来游去，耳边一片寂静。他只能看见方圆十英尺内的情景，因此，他在水里每划行一下，就有崭新的景色从前面的黑暗中突然浮现：波动、缠结的黑色水草构成的丛林，散落着亮晶晶的小石子的宽阔平整的泥沙。他越游越深，朝着湖中央前进。他的眼睛睁得大大的，目光穿透灰亮、诡谲的湖水，望着远处的黑影，那里的湖水是阴暗朦胧的。

小鱼儿轻捷地游过他身边，像一支支银色的飞镖。有一两次，他仿佛看见了一个大家伙正在前面移动，但等游近了一看，才发现不过是一根黑乎乎的大木头，或是一团茂密纠结的水草。看不见其他勇士、人鱼和罗恩——谢天谢地，也没有看见巨乌贼。

他使劲往远处看，前面是一片碧绿的水草，有两英尺深，真像一片过于茂密的草坪。哈利两眼一眨不眨地望着前面，竭力辨认阴影中的形体……就在这时，没有一点儿防备地，他的脚脖子突然被什么东西抓住了。

## 第26章 第二个项目

哈利扭动着转过身体，看见了一个格林迪洛——一个头上长角的水怪，从水草中探出身体，长长的指甲紧紧抓住哈利的腿，嘴里露出尖尖的长牙——哈利赶紧把带蹼的手伸进长袍，摸他的魔杖。他刚抓到魔杖，又有两个格林迪洛从水草里钻了出来，抓住哈利的长袍，拼命把他往下拉。

"力松劲泄！"哈利喊道，可是并没有发出声音……一个大水泡从嘴里冒了出来，他的魔杖没有朝格林迪洛喷出火花，而似乎用一道沸腾的水柱射向了它们，只见它们身上被水柱击中的地方，绿色的皮肤顿时变得通红。哈利把脚从格林迪洛的纠缠中挣脱出来，奋力向前游去，不时地又朝身后放出一些滚热的水柱。偶尔，他感到一个格林迪洛又抓住了他的脚，便用力把它踢走。最后他觉得自己的脚碰到了一个带角的脑袋，低头一看，一个被踢昏了的格林迪洛两眼发直，顺水漂去，它的同伴朝哈利挥了挥拳头，隐到水草中去了。

哈利放慢速度，把魔杖塞回长袍里，环顾四周，仔细倾听。他在水里转了个三百六十度，只感到寂静压迫着他的耳膜。他知道自己一定在很深的湖底了，但是周围除了随着水流起伏的水草，没有任何活动的东西。

"你进展如何啊？"

哈利以为自己犯了心脏病。他猛地转过身，模模糊糊地看见哭泣的桃金娘在他前面漂动，透过厚厚的珍珠色镜片望着他。

"桃金娘！"哈利想喊——但是仍然发不出声音，嘴里只冒出一个很大的水泡。哭泣的桃金娘居然咯咯地笑出了声。

"你应该到那边去试试！"她指了指，说道，"我不陪你去了……我不大喜欢他们，每次我一靠近，他们就过来追我……"

哈利朝她竖起两个大拇指表示感谢，然后又出发了，这次他注意游得高一些，远离那些水草，以免遭到格林迪洛的暗算。

他又游了至少二十分钟。现在水底是大片大片的黑色淤泥，湖水因为他的搅动泛起黑乎乎的水涡。过了好久，他终于听见了人鱼那令人难忘的歌声。

## CHAPTER TWENTY-SIX    The Second Task

> *'An hour long you'll have to look,*
> *And to recover what we took ...'*

Harry swam faster, and soon saw a large rock emerge out of the muddy water ahead. It had paintings of merpeople on it; they were carrying spears, and chasing what looked like the giant squid. Harry swam on past the rock, following the mer-song.

> *'... your time's half gone, so tarry not*
> *Lest what you seek stays here to rot ...'*

A cluster of crude stone dwellings stained with algae loomed suddenly out of the gloom on all sides. Here and there at the dark windows, Harry saw faces ... faces that bore no resemblance at all to the painting of the mermaid in the Prefects' bathroom ...

The merpeople had greyish skins and long, wild, dark green hair. Their eyes were yellow, as were their broken teeth, and they wore thick ropes of pebbles around their necks. They leered at Harry as he swam past; one or two of them emerged from their caves to watch him better, their powerful, silver fishtails beating the water, spears clutched in their hands.

Harry sped on, staring around, and soon the dwellings became more numerous; there were gardens of weed around some of them, and he even saw a pet Grindylow tied to a stake outside one door. Merpeople were emerging on all sides now, watching him eagerly, pointing at his webbed hands and gills, talking behind their hands to each other. Harry sped around a corner, and a very strange sight met his eyes.

A whole crowd of merpeople were floating in front of the houses that lined what looked like a mer-version of a village square. A choir of merpeople were singing in the middle, calling the champions towards them, and behind them rose a crude sort of statue; a gigantic merperson hewn from a boulder. Four people were bound tightly to the tail of the stone merperson.

Ron was tied between Hermione and Cho Chang. There was also a girl who looked no older than eight, whose clouds of silvery hair made Harry feel sure that she was Fleur Delacour's sister. All four of them appeared to be in a very deep sleep. Their heads were lolling onto their shoulders, and fine

## 第26章 第二个项目

只有一个钟头的时间，
要寻找和夺回我们拿走的物件……

哈利游得更快了，不一会儿，他就看见前面浑浊的湖水里出现了一块大岩石，上面绘着许多人鱼，他们手里拿着长矛，正在追逐着一些看上去像是巨乌贼的东西。哈利从岩石旁游过，追寻着人鱼的歌声。

……别再拖延，时间已过去一半，
以免你寻找的东西在这里腐烂……

突然，四下里赫然出现许多粗糙的石头蜗居，上面斑斑点点地沾着水藻。哈利看见那些黑乎乎的窗户里有一些面孔……这些面孔与级长洗澡间里那幅画上的人鱼完全不一样……

这些人鱼的皮肤呈铁灰色，墨绿色的头发长长的，蓬蓬乱乱。他们的眼睛是黄色的，残缺不全的牙齿也是黄色，脖子上戴着用粗绳子串起的卵石。哈利游过时，他们不怀好意地朝他笑着。有一两个为了看得更清楚些，还从洞穴里跑出来，手里拿着长矛，用粗壮有力的银色鱼尾拍击着湖水。

哈利飞快地向前游去，一边环顾四周。很快，石头蜗居越来越多，有些蜗居周围还带有水草花园。他甚至还看见一扇门前拴着一个小格林迪洛。人鱼从四面八方涌现，都好奇地望着他，冲着他长蹼的手和鳃囊指指点点，并用手掩着嘴窃窃私语。哈利迅速转了个弯，眼前出现了一片十分奇特的景象。

这地方似乎是人鱼小村庄的广场，四周坐落着一些房子，房子前面漂浮着一大群人鱼。中间有一些人鱼在齐声歌唱，呼唤勇士过去。他们身后耸立着一座粗糙的雕像：一个用巨石雕刻成的大人鱼。在人鱼石像的尾巴上，牢牢地捆绑着四个人。

罗恩被拴在赫敏和秋·张之间。另外还有一个最多八岁的小姑娘，那一头云雾般的银发使哈利确信她是芙蓉·德拉库尔的妹妹。他们四个看上去都睡得很沉，脑袋无力地耷拉在肩膀上，嘴里不停地冒出一

## CHAPTER TWENTY-SIX  The Second Task

streams of bubbles kept issuing from their mouths.

Harry sped towards the hostages, half expecting the merpeople to lower their spears and charge at him, but they did nothing. The ropes of weed tying the hostages to the statue were thick, slimy and very strong. For a fleeting second he thought of the knife Sirius had brought him for Christmas – locked in his trunk in the castle a quarter of a mile away, no use to him whatsoever.

He looked around. Many of the merpeople surrounding them were carrying spears. He swam swiftly towards a seven-foot-tall merman with a long green beard and a choker of shark fangs, and tried to mime a request to borrow the spear. The merman laughed and shook his head.

'We do not help,' he said in a harsh, croaky voice.

'Come ON!' Harry said fiercely (but only bubbles issued from his mouth), and he tried to pull the spear away from the merman, but the merman yanked it back, still shaking his head and laughing.

Harry swirled around, staring about. Something sharp ... anything ...

There were rocks littering the lake bottom. He dived and snatched up a particularly jagged one, and returned to the statue. He began to hack at the ropes binding Ron, and after several minutes' hard work, they broke apart. Ron floated, unconscious, a few inches above the lake bottom, drifting a little in the ebb of the water.

Harry looked around. There was no sign of any of the other champions. What were they playing at? Why didn't they hurry up? He turned back to Hermione, raised the jagged rock and began to hack at her bindings, too –

At once, several pairs of strong grey hands seized him. Half a dozen mermen were pulling him away from Hermione, shaking their green-haired heads and laughing.

'You take your own hostage,' one of them said to him. 'Leave the others ...'

'No way!' said Harry furiously – but only two large bubbles came out.

'Your task is to retrieve your own friend ... leave the others ...'

'*She's* my friend, too!' Harry yelled, gesturing towards Hermione, an enormous silver bubble emerging soundlessly from his lips. 'And I don't want *them* to die, either!'

Cho's head was on Hermione's shoulder; the small silver-haired girl was ghostly green and pale. Harry struggled to fight off the mermen, but they

## 第26章 第二个项目

串细细的水泡。

哈利奋力朝人质游去。他以为人鱼会把长矛横过来朝他进攻，但他们并没有这样做。把人质拴在雕像上的绳子是水草编的，又粗又滑，非常结实。哈利脑海里闪过一个念头，想起了小天狼星圣诞节给他买的那把小刀——锁在四分之一英里外城堡中他的箱子里呢，完全派不上用场。

他看了看旁边。人质周围的许多人鱼手里都拿着长矛。他飞快地朝一个长着绿色长胡子、戴着鲨鱼牙齿做的短项链的七英尺高的人鱼游去，比比画画地要求借它的长矛一用。人鱼哈哈大笑，摇了摇头。

"我们不能帮忙。"人鱼用沙哑低沉的声音说。

"**拿过来！**"哈利恶狠狠地说（但嘴里只冒出一些水泡），他使劲想从人鱼手里夺过长矛，但人鱼把长矛拽了回去，仍然摇着头，哈哈大笑。

哈利在水里转了个身，朝四下张望着。需要一个锋利的东西……什么都行……

湖底散落着一些岩石。他俯冲下去，抓起一块特别尖的，回到雕像旁边。他用石头拼命砍砸捆绑罗恩的绳子，几分钟后，绳子被砸断了。罗恩神志不清地浮在湖底上方几英寸的地方，随着水波漂来荡去。

哈利看看四周。不见其他勇士的影子。他们在磨蹭什么呢？为什么不抓紧一些？他回到赫敏身边，又举起尖石头，开始砍砸赫敏身上的绳子——

立刻，好几双粗壮的灰色大手抓住了他。六七个人鱼把他从赫敏身边拽开，他们摇着绿头发的脑袋，哈哈大笑。

"你只能带走你自己的人质，"其中一个对他说，"别管其他人……"

"不行！"哈利气愤地说——但嘴里只冒出两个大气泡。

"你的项目是救出你自己的朋友……别管其他人……"

"她也是我的朋友！"哈利指着赫敏嚷道，一个银色的大气泡无声地从他嘴唇间冒出来，"而且我也不希望她们死掉！"

秋·张的脑袋靠在赫敏肩上，那个银色头发的小姑娘脸色发青，看上去毫无生气。哈利挣扎着想摆脱人鱼，但他们笑得更厉害了，

## CHAPTER TWENTY-SIX — The Second Task

laughed harder than ever, holding him back. Harry looked wildly around. Where were the other champions? Would he have time to take Ron to the surface, and come back down for Hermione and the others? Would he be able to find them again? He looked down at his watch to see how much time was left – it had stopped working.

But then the merpeople around him started pointing excitedly over his head. Harry looked up and saw Cedric swimming towards them. There was an enormous bubble around his head, which made his features look oddly wide and stretched.

'Got lost!' he mouthed, looking panic-stricken. 'Fleur and Krum're coming now!'

Feeling enormously relieved, Harry watched Cedric pull a knife out of his pocket and cut Cho free. He pulled her upwards and out of sight.

Harry looked around, waiting. Where were Fleur and Krum? Time was getting short and, according to the song, the hostages would be lost after an hour ...

The merpeople started screeching excitedly. Those holding Harry loosened their grip, staring behind them. Harry turned, and saw something monstrous cutting through the water towards them: a human body in swimming trunks with the head of a shark ... it was Krum. He appeared to have Transfigured himself – but badly.

The shark-man swam straight to Hermione and began snapping and biting at her ropes: the trouble was that Krum's new teeth were positioned very awkwardly for biting anything smaller than a dolphin, and Harry was quite sure that if Krum wasn't careful, he was going to rip Hermione in half. Darting forwards, Harry hit Krum hard on the shoulder, and held up the jagged stone. Krum seized it, and began to cut Hermione free. Within seconds, he had done it; he grabbed Hermione around the waist and, without a backward glance, began to rise rapidly with her towards the surface.

Now what? Harry thought desperately. If he could be sure that Fleur was coming ... But still no sign. There was nothing for it ...

He snatched up the stone, which Krum had dropped, but the mermen now closed in around Ron and the little girl, shaking their heads at him.

Harry pulled out his wand. 'Get out of the way!'

Only bubbles flew out of his mouth, but he had the distinct impression

## 第26章 第二个项目

又把他拉了回去。哈利绝望地看着四周。其他勇士都上哪儿去了？如果他把罗恩送到水面，再回来解救赫敏和其他人，还来得及吗？他还能找到她们吗？他低头看了看表，想知道还剩多少时间——表停了。

就在这时，周围的人鱼突然兴奋地指着他的脑袋上方。哈利一抬头，看见塞德里克正朝他们游来。他脑袋周围有一个巨大的气泡，使他的五官看上去都被拉长加宽了，显得非常滑稽。

"迷路了！"他用口型说，神情十分慌张，"芙蓉和克鲁姆也快过来了！"

哈利觉得一块石头落了地，他看着塞德里克从口袋里掏出一把小刀，割断绳子，救出了秋·张。他拉着秋·张往上游去，很快就不见了。

哈利环顾四周，等待着。怎么不见芙蓉和克鲁姆呢？时间不多了，根据那首歌里唱的，过了一小时，人质就永远找不回来了……

人鱼突然欢快地尖叫起来。那些抓住哈利的人鱼松开了手，扭头向后张望。哈利转过身，看见一个庞然大物正朝他们游来，下面是人的身体，穿着游泳裤，上面是鲨鱼的脑袋……是克鲁姆。看来他想给自己变形来着——可是不太成功。

半人半鲨鱼的克鲁姆径直游向赫敏，对着她身上的绳子又扯又咬，问题是克鲁姆的新牙齿结构古怪，凡是比海豚小的东西，他咬起来都很别扭，而且哈利可以断定克鲁姆的动作要是有个不小心，就要把赫敏撕成两半了。哈利冲上前去，重重地拍了一下克鲁姆的肩膀，举起那块尖石头。克鲁姆一把抓过去，开始砍砸赫敏身上的绳子。几秒钟后，他成功了。他抓住赫敏的腰，没有再回头望一眼，就带着她迅速升向水面。

现在怎么办呢？哈利焦急地想。只要能确信芙蓉正在赶来……怎么还不见她的影子啊。没有别的办法，只有……

他抓起克鲁姆扔下的那块石头，但是人鱼纷纷围拢在罗恩和小姑娘身边，对哈利拼命摇头。

哈利拔出魔杖。"闪开！"

他嘴里只冒出一串气泡，但他清楚地意识到人鱼们明白了他的意

## CHAPTER TWENTY-SIX — The Second Task

that the mermen had understood him, because they suddenly stopped laughing. Their yellowish eyes were fixed upon Harry's wand, and they looked scared. There might be a lot more of them than there were of him, but Harry could tell, by the looks on their faces, that they knew no more magic than the giant squid did.

'You've got until three!' Harry shouted; a great stream of bubbles burst from him, but he held up three fingers to make sure they got the message. 'One ...' (he put down a finger) – 'two ...' (he put down a second) –

They scattered. Harry darted forwards and began to hack at the robes binding the small girl to the statue; and at last she was free. He seized the little girl around the waist, grabbed the neck of Ron's robes, and kicked off from the bottom.

It was very slow work. He could no longer use his webbed hands to propel himself forwards; he worked his flippers furiously, but Ron and Fleur's sister were like potato-filled sacks dragging him back down ... he fixed his eyes skywards, though he knew he must still be very deep, the water above him was so dark ...

Merpeople were rising with him. He could see them swirling around him with ease, watching him struggle through the water ... would they pull him back down to the depths when the time was up? Did they perhaps eat humans? Harry's legs were seizing up with the effort to keep swimming; his shoulders were aching horribly with the effort of dragging Ron and the girl ...

He was drawing breath with extreme difficulty. He could feel pain on the sides of his neck again ... he was becoming very aware of how wet the water was in his mouth ... yet the darkness was definitely thinning now ... he could see daylight above him ...

He kicked hard with his flippers and discovered that they were nothing more than feet ... water was flooding through his mouth into his lungs ... he was starting to feel dizzy, but he knew light and air were only ten feet above him ... he had to get there ... he had to ...

Harry kicked his legs so hard and fast it felt as though his muscles were screaming in protest; his very brain felt waterlogged, he couldn't breathe, he needed oxygen, he had to keep going, he could not stop –

And then he felt his head break the surface of the lake; wonderful, cold, clear air was making his wet face sting; he gulped it down, feeling as though he had never breathed properly before, and, panting, pulled Ron and the little girl up with him. All around him, wild, green-haired heads were

## 第26章 第二个项目

思,因为他们突然都不笑了,一双双黄眼睛盯着哈利的魔杖,显出很害怕的样子。他们人多势众,他孤身一人,但哈利从他们脸上的神情看出,他们和巨乌贼一样,对魔法一窍不通。

"我数到三!"哈利喊道,一大串气泡从嘴里喷出,他竖起三根手指,确保他们明白他的意思,"一……"(他放下一根手指)"二……"(他又放下一根手指)——

人鱼散开了。哈利冲上前,开始砍砸把小姑娘捆在雕像上的绳子,终于,她也自由了。哈利拦腰抱起小姑娘,抓住罗恩长袍的领子,两腿一蹬,离开了水底。

他前进得真慢啊。他没法再用带蹼的双手来推动身体向前;他拼命拍打带蹼的双脚,但罗恩和芙蓉的妹妹像两只装满土豆的口袋,拖着他往下沉……他眼睛望着上空,知道自己一定还在很深的水下,水面望上去还是漆黑一片……

人鱼和他一起游了上来。他看见他们轻快自如地在周围游来游去,望着他在水里挣扎……是不是时间一到,他们就会把他拉回到水底?他们会不会吃人?哈利使出吃奶的力气游着,最后两条腿都发僵了,肩膀也因为罗恩和小姑娘的拖累而痛得要命……

他越来越喘不上气。脖子两侧又感到疼痛难忍……他开始非常清楚地意识到,他嘴里的湖水是多么潮湿……不过沉甸甸的黑色已经越来越淡……他可以看见上面的天光了……

他用带蹼的双脚奋力踢蹬,却发现它们又变成了普通的脚……水从他的嘴里涌进肺中……他开始感到晕晕乎乎,但知道日光和空气就在十英尺的上方……他一定要到达那里……一定……

哈利踢蹬着双腿,速度那么快,用了那么大的力气,肌肉似乎都在尖叫着发出抗议了;他的脑袋里仿佛也浸满了水,他喘不上气来,他需要氧气,他必须前进,不能停止——

突然,他感到自己的头猛地露出了水面;美妙、清新、凉爽的空气拂过他潮湿的脸庞,他感到隐隐作痛;他大口地吞咽着空气,觉得自己一辈子都没有好好呼吸过,他一边喘着气,一边拉着罗恩和小姑娘继续向前。在他周围,许多绿发蓬乱的脑袋和他一起冒出水面,但

## CHAPTER TWENTY-SIX    The Second Task

emerging out of the water with him, but they were smiling at him.

The crowd in the stands was making a great deal of noise; shouting and screaming, everybody seemed to be on their feet; Harry had the impression they thought that Ron and the little girl might be dead, but they were wrong ... both of them had opened their eyes; the girl looked scared and confused, but Ron merely expelled a great spout of water, blinked in the bright light, turned to Harry and said, 'Wet, this, isn't it?' Then he spotted Fleur's sister. 'What did you bring her for?'

'Fleur didn't turn up. I couldn't leave her,' Harry panted.

'Harry, you prat,' said Ron, 'you didn't take that song thing seriously, did you? Dumbledore wouldn't have let any of us drown!'

'But the song said –'

'Only to make sure you got back inside the time limit!' said Ron. 'I hope you didn't waste time down there acting the hero!'

Harry felt both stupid and annoyed. It was all very well for Ron; *he'd* been asleep, he hadn't felt how eerie it was down in the lake, surrounded by spear-carrying merpeople who'd looked more than capable of murder.

'C'mon,' Harry said shortly, 'help me with her, I don't think she can swim very well.'

They pulled Fleur's sister through the water, back towards the bank where the judges stood watching, twenty merpeople accompanying them like a guard of honour, singing their horrible screechy songs.

Harry could see Madam Pomfrey fussing over Hermione, Krum, Cedric and Cho, all of whom were wrapped in thick blankets. Dumbledore and Ludo Bagman stood beaming at Harry and Ron from the bank as they swam nearer, but Percy, who looked very white and somehow much younger than usual, came splashing out to meet them. Meanwhile Madame Maxime was trying to restrain Fleur Delacour, who was quite hysterical, fighting tooth and nail to return to the water.

'Gabrielle! *Gabrielle! Is she alive? Is she 'urt?*'

'She's fine!' Harry tried to tell her, but he was so exhausted he could hardly talk, let alone shout.

Percy seized Ron and was dragging him back to the bank ('Gerroff, Percy, I'm all right!'); Dumbledore and Bagman were pulling Harry upright; Fleur had broken free of Madame Maxime and was hugging her sister.

## 第26章 第二个项目

他们都对他善意地微笑着。

看台上人声鼎沸,又叫又嚷,似乎一个个全都站了起来。哈利猜想他们大概以为罗恩和小姑娘都死了,但他们错了……罗恩和小姑娘双双睁开了眼睛。小姑娘看上去惊恐而迷茫,罗恩只是吐出一大口湖水,在明亮的光线下眨了几下眼睛,便转向哈利说:"全湿透了,是不是?"接着他看见了芙蓉的妹妹,"你把她也弄上来干什么?"

"芙蓉没有出现,我不能把她撇在下面。"哈利喘着气回答。

"哈利,你这个傻瓜,"罗恩说,"你该不会把那首歌当真了吧?邓布利多不会让我们哪一个人淹死的!"

"那首歌里说——"

"那只是为了让你们在规定时间里回来!"罗恩说,"但愿你在下面没有因为逞英雄而耽误时间!"

哈利觉得又泄气又恼火。对罗恩来说这一切都没什么,他睡着了,他感觉不到湖底下多么阴森恐怖,周围都是拿着长矛的人鱼,一个个都像是杀人的老手。

"好了,"哈利没好气地说,"帮我拉她一把,她可能不大会游泳。"

他们拖着芙蓉的妹妹,蹚水走向岸边。裁判们都站在那里望着,二十个人鱼像仪仗队一样陪伴着他们,嘴里尖声尖气地唱着难听的歌。

哈利可以看见庞弗雷女士大惊小怪地围着赫敏、克鲁姆、塞德里克和秋·张团团转,他们都裹着厚厚的毯子。哈利和罗恩游近岸边时,邓布利多和卢多·巴格曼微笑地望着他们,珀西脸色煞白,看上去年龄比平常小了好几岁,急不可耐地冲过来迎接他们。与此同时,马克西姆女士正在使劲拉住芙蓉·德拉库尔。芙蓉完全歇斯底里了,拼命挣扎着要往水里扑。

"加布丽!加布丽!她还活着吗?她受伤了吗?"

"她很好!"哈利想告诉芙蓉,但他太疲劳了,连话都说不出,更别说大声喊叫了。

珀西抓住罗恩,把他拽到岸上("放开,珀西,我没事!");邓布利多和巴格曼把哈利拉了起来;芙蓉挣脱了马克西姆女士的阻拦,一把搂住了妹妹。

## CHAPTER TWENTY-SIX   The Second Task

'It was ze Grindylows ... zey attacked me ... oh, Gabrielle, I thought ... I thought ...'

'Come here, you,' said Madam Pomfrey's voice; she seized Harry and pulled him over to Hermione and the others, wrapped him so tightly in a blanket that he felt as though he was in a straitjacket, and forced a measure of very hot potion down his throat. Steam gushed out of his ears.

'Harry, well done!' Hermione cried. 'You did it, you found out how, all by yourself!'

'Well –' said Harry. He would have told her about Dobby, but he had just noticed Karkaroff watching him. He was the only judge who had not left the table; the only judge not showing signs of pleasure and relief that Harry, Ron and Fleur's sister had got back safely. 'Yeah, that's right,' said Harry, raising his voice slightly so that Karkaroff could hear him.

'You haff a water-beetle in your hair, Herm-own-ninny,' said Krum.

Harry had the impression that Krum was drawing her attention back onto himself; perhaps to remind her that he had just rescued her from the lake, but Hermione brushed the beetle away impatiently and said, 'You're well outside the time limit, though, Harry ... Did it take you ages to find us?'

'No ... I found you OK ...'

Harry's feeling of stupidity was growing. Now he was out of the water, it seemed perfectly clear that Dumbledore's safety precautions wouldn't have permitted the death of a hostage just because their champion hadn't turned up. Why hadn't he just grabbed Ron and gone? He would have been first back ... Cedric and Krum hadn't wasted time worrying about anyone else; they hadn't taken the mer-song seriously ...

Dumbledore was crouching at the water's edge, deep in conversation with what seemed to be the chief merperson, a particularly wild- and ferocious-looking female. He was making the same sort of screechy noises that the merpeople made when they were above water; clearly, Dumbledore could speak Mermish. Finally he straightened up, turned to his fellow judges and said, 'A conference before we give the marks, I think.'

The judges went into a huddle. Madam Pomfrey had gone to rescue Ron from Percy's clutches; she led him over to Harry and the others, gave him a blanket and some Pepper-Up Potion, then went to fetch Fleur and her sister. Fleur had many cuts on her face and arms, and her robes were torn, but she didn't seem to care, nor would she allow Madam Pomfrey to clean them.

## 第26章 第二个项目

"是格林迪洛……那些格林迪洛朝我进攻……哦,加布丽,我以为……我以为……"

"你们都到这儿来。"庞弗雷女士说。她抓住哈利,把他拉到赫敏和其他人身边,用一条毯子严严实实地裹住他,哈利觉得自己仿佛穿上了束缚犯人和疯子的约束衣。庞弗雷女士还把一种火辣辣的药剂强行灌进他嘴里,顿时就有热气从他耳朵里冒了出来。

"哈利,干得好!"赫敏喊道,"你成功了,完全是自己解决的!"

"其实——"哈利说。他刚想跟赫敏说说多比的事,但一转眼看见卡卡洛夫正盯着自己。几个裁判中,唯有他没有离开桌子,也唯有他看见哈利、罗恩和芙蓉的妹妹平安回来后,没有露出喜悦和宽慰的表情。"是啊,没错。"哈利改口说,并故意提高一点声音,好让卡卡洛夫听见。

"你头发里有一只水甲虫,赫—米—恩。"克鲁姆说。

哈利感到克鲁姆是想把赫敏的注意力吸引到自己身上,也许是为了提醒赫敏刚才是他把她从湖底救上来的。但是赫敏不耐烦地拂去水甲虫,说道:"可是,哈利,你超过时间了……你花了很长时间才找到我们吗?"

"没有……我找到你们并不算晚……"

哈利越来越觉得自己真是傻透了。现在他离开了水面,便完全清楚邓布利多肯定布置了有效的安全防御措施,不会允许人质因为勇士没有露面而丧生的,这是明摆着的呀。他为什么不能抓起罗恩就走呢?他完全可以第一个回来的……塞德里克和克鲁姆就没有浪费时间替别人操心,他们没有把人鱼的歌当真……

邓布利多蹲在水边,正在和那个首领模样的特别粗野凶狠的女人鱼密切交谈。邓布利多发出了人鱼在水面上发出的那种尖厉刺耳的声音,显然,他也会说人鱼的话。最后,他站直身子转向其他裁判,说道:"先开个碰头会再打分吧。"

几个裁判聚在一起。庞弗雷女士从珀西紧紧拽着的手里抢出罗恩,把他领到哈利和其他人身边,给了他一条毯子和一些提神剂,然后又过去领来芙蓉和她的妹妹。芙蓉的脸上和胳膊上左一道右一道都是伤痕,袍子也撕破了,但她似乎毫不介意,也不让庞弗雷女士替她清理。

## CHAPTER TWENTY-SIX  The Second Task

'Look after Gabrielle,' she told her, and then she turned to Harry. 'You saved 'er,' she said breathlessly. 'Even though she was not your 'ostage.'

'Yeah,' said Harry, who was now heartily wishing he'd left all three girls tied to the statue.

Fleur bent down, kissed Harry twice on each cheek (he felt his face burn and wouldn't have been surprised if steam was coming out of his ears again), then said to Ron, 'And you, too – you 'elped –'

'Yeah,' said Ron, looking extremely hopeful, 'yeah, a bit –'

Fleur swooped down on him, too, and kissed him. Hermione looked simply furious, but just then, Ludo Bagman's magically magnified voice boomed out beside them, making them all jump, and causing the crowd in the stands to go very quiet.

'Ladies and gentlemen, we have reached our decision. Merchieftainess Murcus has told us exactly what happened at the bottom of the lake, and we have therefore decided to award marks out of fifty for each of the champions, as follows …

'Miss Fleur Delacour, though she demonstrated excellent use of the Bubble-Head Charm, was attacked by Grindylows as she approached her goal, and failed to retrieve her hostage. We award her twenty-five points.'

Applause from the stands.

'I deserved zero,' said Fleur throatily, shaking her magnificent head.

'Mr. Cedric Diggory, who also used the Bubble-Head Charm, was first to return with his hostage, though he returned one minute outside the time limit of an hour.' Enormous cheers from the Hufflepuffs in the crowd; Harry saw Cho give Cedric a glowing look. 'We therefore award him forty-seven points.'

Harry's heart sank. If Cedric had been outside the time limit, he most certainly had been.

'Mr. Viktor Krum used an incomplete form of Transfiguration, which was nevertheless effective, and was second to return with his hostage. We award him forty points.'

Karkaroff clapped particularly hard, looking very superior.

'Mr. Harry Potter used Gillyweed to great effect,' Bagman continued. 'He returned last, and well outside the time limit of an hour. However, the Merchieftainess informs us that Mr. Potter was first to reach the hostages, and that the delay in his return was due to his determination to return all

## 第 26 章 第二个项目

"去照料加布丽吧,"她对庞弗雷女士说,接着又转向哈利,"你救了她,"她激动得几乎喘不上气,"尽管她不是你的人质。"

"是啊。"哈利说。他现在真希望自己当时别管那三个姑娘,就让她们拴在石雕像上好了。

芙蓉低下头,在哈利的每边面颊上各亲了两口(哈利觉得脸上像着了火似的,如果他耳朵里再冒出热气,他一点也不会感到奇怪),然后又对罗恩说:"还有你——你也帮了忙——"

"是啊。"罗恩说,一副满怀期望的样子,"是啊,帮了一点儿忙——"

芙蓉扑过来,也亲了罗恩几口。赫敏看上去气得要命,但就在这时,卢多·巴格曼那被魔法放大的声音在他们耳边突然响起,把他们吓了一跳,也使看台上的观众顿时安静下来。

"女士们,先生们,我们终于做出了决定。人鱼女首领默库斯把湖底下发生的一切原原本本告诉了我们,我们决定在满分为五十分的基础上,给各位勇士打分如下……

"芙蓉·德拉库尔尽管表现出对泡头咒的出色运用,但在接近目标时遭到格林迪洛的攻击,未能成功解救人质。我们给她二十五分。"

看台上传来一片掌声。

"我应该得零分的。"芙蓉摇了摇她优美的头,声音沙哑地说。

"塞德里克·迪戈里也采用了泡头咒,他是第一个带着人质返回的,但是在规定的一小时外超出了一分钟。"人群中赫奇帕奇的学生们热烈欢呼,声音震耳欲聋。哈利看见秋·张用欣喜的目光望了塞德里克一眼。"因此,我们给他四十七分。"

哈利的心往下一沉。如果塞德里克都超过了规定时间,他肯定也超时了。

"威克多尔·克鲁姆运用了变形术,虽不完整,但仍然很有效,他是第二个带着人质返回的。我们给他四十分。"

卡卡洛夫巴掌拍得格外起劲,一副得意扬扬的样子。

"哈利·波特服用了鳃囊草,取得了惊人的效果。"巴格曼继续说道,"他最后一个返回,远远超过了一小时的规定时间。然而,人鱼女首领告诉我们,波特先生是第一个找到人质的,他没能及时返回,是因为

## CHAPTER TWENTY-SIX — The Second Task

hostages to safety, not merely his own.'

Ron and Hermione both gave Harry half-exasperated, half-commiserating looks.

'Most of the judges' – and here, Bagman gave Karkaroff a very nasty look – 'feel that this shows moral fibre and merits full marks. However ... Mr. Potter's score is forty-five points.'

Harry's stomach leapt – he was now tying for first place with Cedric. Ron and Hermione, caught by surprise, stared at Harry, then laughed and started applauding hard with the rest of the crowd.

'There you go, Harry!' Ron shouted over the noise. 'You weren't being thick after all – you were showing moral fibre!'

Fleur was clapping very hard, too, but Krum didn't look very happy at all. He attempted to engage Hermione in conversation again, but she was too busy cheering Harry to listen.

'The third and final task will take place at dusk on the twenty-fourth of June,' continued Bagman. 'The champions will be notified of what is coming, precisely one month beforehand. Thank you all for your support of the champions.'

It was over, Harry thought dazedly, as Madam Pomfrey began herding the champions and hostages back to the castle to get into dry clothes ... it was over, he had got through ... he didn't have to worry about anything now until June the twenty-fourth ...

Next time he was in Hogsmeade, he decided, as he walked back up the stone steps into the castle, he was going to buy Dobby a pair of socks for every day of the year.

## 第26章 第二个项目

他要确保所有的人质都平安回来,而不是只关心他自己的人质。"

罗恩和赫敏都半是气恼半是同情地望了哈利一眼。

"大多数裁判,"说到这里,巴格曼非常不满地扫了卡卡洛夫一眼,"觉得这充分体现了高尚的道德风范,值得满分。然而……波特先生的分数是四十五分。"

哈利的心欢跳起来——他现在与塞德里克并列第一位。罗恩和赫敏惊讶极了,呆呆地望着哈利,随即开心地哈哈大笑,和其他观众一起拼命鼓起掌来。

"真有你的,哈利!"罗恩在喧哗声中扯着嗓子喊道,"原来你不是犯傻啊——你是在表现道德风范!"

芙蓉也用力拍着巴掌,但是克鲁姆显得很不高兴。他又想跟赫敏搭话,但赫敏只顾为哈利欢呼喝彩,根本不理睬他。

"第三个,也是最后一个项目将在六月二十四日傍晚进行,"巴格曼继续说道,"勇士们将提前一个月得知项目的具体内容。感谢大家对勇士们的支持。"

结束了,哈利迷迷糊糊地想,这时庞弗雷女士开始护送勇士和人质们返回城堡,去换干爽的衣服……结束了,他通过了……什么也不用操心了,直到六月二十四日……

哈利踏上进入城堡的石阶时,心里想道,下次再去霍格莫德村,一定要给多比买一大堆袜子,让他一年到头每天都能穿上新袜子。

## CHAPTER TWENTY-SEVEN

# Padfoot Returns

One of the best things about the aftermath of the second task was that everybody was very keen to hear details of what had happened down in the lake, which meant that for once Ron was getting to share Harry's limelight. Harry noticed that Ron's version of events changed subtly with every retelling. At first, he gave what seemed to be the truth; it tallied with Hermione's story, anyway – Dumbledore had put all the hostages into a bewitched sleep in Professor McGonagall's office, first assuring them that they would be quite safe, and would awake when they were back above the water. One week later, however, Ron was telling a thrilling tale of kidnap in which he struggled single-handedly against fifty heavily armed merpeople who had to beat him into submission before tying him up.

'But I had my wand hidden up my sleeve,' he assured Padma Patil, who seemed to be a lot keener on Ron now that he was getting so much attention, and was making a point of talking to him every time they passed in the corridors. 'I could've taken those mer-idiots any time I wanted.'

'What were you going to do, snore at them?' said Hermione waspishly. People had been teasing her so much about being the thing that Viktor Krum would most miss that she was in a rather tetchy mood.

Ron's ears went red, and he reverted thereafter to the bewitched-sleep version of events.

As they entered March the weather became drier, but cruel winds skinned their hands and faces every time they went out into the grounds. There were delays in the post because the owls kept being blown off course. The brown owl that Harry had sent to Sirius with the dates of the Hogsmeade weekend turned up at breakfast on Friday morning with half its feathers sticking up the wrong way; Harry had no sooner torn off Sirius' reply than it took flight,

## 第 27 章

## 大脚板回来了

第二个项目结束后,最美妙的一件事就是大家都急于知道湖底下到底发生了什么事,这也就意味着罗恩平生第一次和哈利一样,成了人们关注的中心。哈利注意到,罗恩把故事讲了一遍又一遍,每次都略有不同。起初,他说的还算符合事实,跟赫敏的说法大致相同——在麦格教授的办公室里,邓布利多用魔法给人质催眠,并首先向他们保证,说绝对没有危险,而且一出水面就会醒来。然而一星期后,罗恩却讲起了一个惊心动魄的绑架故事,说他怎样赤手空拳地跟五十个全副武装的人鱼搏斗,他们要先迫使他就范,然后才把他捆绑起来。

现在罗恩变得这样引人注目,帕德玛对他热情多了,每次在走廊上遇见,她总是主动找罗恩说话。"没关系,我把魔杖藏在袖子里呢,"他向帕德玛·佩蒂尔保证道,"只要我愿意,我就能把那些人鱼傻瓜制服。"

"你想怎么做呢?冲他们打呼噜吗?"赫敏尖刻地说。她成了威克多尔·克鲁姆最心爱的宝贝,大家整天拿这件事来取笑她,所以她现在脾气非常暴躁。

罗恩的耳朵红了,从这以后,他的故事又回到了被魔法催眠的那个版本。

进入三月后,天气变得干燥了一些,但每次来到外面的场地上,凛冽的寒风仍然吹得他们的手和脸生疼。猫头鹰们不能及时把信送来,因为狂风总是把它们吹得偏离目标。哈利之前派出一只棕褐色猫头鹰去给小天狼星送信,把周末去霍格莫德村的日期告诉了他。那只猫头鹰在星期五的早饭时间出现了,身上一半的羽毛都被风吹得东倒西歪。哈利刚把小天狼星的信扯下来,猫头鹰就急忙飞走了,显然是害怕再

## CHAPTER TWENTY-SEVEN  Padfoot Returns

clearly afraid it was going to be sent outside again.

Sirius' letter was almost as short as the previous one.

> *Be at stile at end of road out of Hogsmeade (past Dervish & Banges) at two o'clock on Saturday afternoon. Bring as much food as you can.*

'He hasn't come back to Hogsmeade?' said Ron incredulously.

'It looks like it, doesn't it?' said Hermione.

'I can't believe him,' said Harry tensely. 'If he's caught …'

'Made it so far, though, hasn't he?' said Ron. 'And it's not like the place is swarming with Dementors any more.'

Harry folded up the letter, thinking. If he was honest with himself, he really wanted to see Sirius again. He therefore approached the final lesson of the afternoon – double Potions – feeling considerably more cheerful than he usually did when descending the steps to the dungeons.

Malfoy, Crabbe and Goyle were standing in a huddle outside the classroom door with Pansy Parkinson's gang of Slytherin girls. All of them were looking at something Harry couldn't see and sniggering heartily. Pansy's pug-like face peered excitedly around Goyle's broad back as Harry, Ron and Hermione approached.

'There they are, there they are!' she giggled, and the knot of Slytherins broke apart. Harry saw that Pansy had a magazine in her hands – *Witch Weekly*. The moving picture on the front showed a curly-haired witch who was smiling toothily and pointing at a large sponge cake with her wand.

'You might find something to interest you in there, Granger!' Pansy said loudly, and she threw the magazine at Hermione, who caught it, looking startled. At that moment, the dungeon door opened, and Snape beckoned them all inside.

Hermione, Harry and Ron headed for a table at the back of the dungeon as usual. Once Snape had turned his back on them to write up the ingredients of today's potion on the blackboard, Hermione hastily riffled through the magazine under the desk. At last, in the centre pages, Hermione found what they were looking for. Harry and Ron leant in closer. A colour photograph of Harry headed a short piece entitled:

## 第27章 大脚板回来了

被派出去送信。

小天狼星的信几乎和上一封一样短。

> 星期六下午两点在霍格莫德村外（经过德维斯-班斯店）道路尽头的栅栏旁。尽量多带些吃的。

"他难道去了霍格莫德？"罗恩难以置信地说。

"看来是这样，不是吗？"赫敏说。

"真不敢相信，"哈利紧张地说，"如果他被抓住……"

"到目前为止他还是安全的，对吧？"罗恩说，"而且现在不像过去那样，到处都挤满摄魂怪了。"

哈利折起信，沉思着。说句老实话，他真的很渴望再见到小天狼星。下午，他去上最后一堂课——两节连在一起的魔药课。当他顺着台阶走向地下教室时，感觉心情比平时愉快多了。

马尔福、克拉布和高尔站在教室外，和那帮以潘西·帕金森为首的斯莱特林女生们聚在一起。他们都在看什么东西（哈利看不见那是什么），一个个咯咯地笑得开心极了。哈利、罗恩和赫敏走近时，潘西兴奋地把她那张狮子狗似的脸从高尔肥阔的后背旁探了出来。

"他们来了，他们来了！"她咯咯笑着说，聚成一堆的斯莱特林们散开了。哈利看见潘西手里拿着一份杂志——《女巫周刊》。封面上的活动照片是一个鬈发女巫，她咧嘴笑着，露出满口的牙齿，用魔杖指着一块大大的海绵状蛋糕。

"你在里面会找到你感兴趣的东西，格兰杰！"潘西大声说，把杂志扔给了赫敏。赫敏伸手接过，显得有些惊慌。就在这时，地下教室的门开了，斯内普招呼大家进去。

赫敏、哈利和罗恩像往常一样走向教室后面的一张桌子。斯内普刚转身在黑板上写出今天要制作的魔药的配料，赫敏就急忙在桌子底下翻开那本杂志。终于，赫敏在杂志中间发现了要找的东西。哈利和罗恩也凑了过去。在哈利的一张彩色照片下面，是这样一篇短文：

CHAPTER TWENTY-SEVEN   Padfoot Returns

## Harry Potter's Secret Headache

A BOY LIKE NO OTHER, perhaps – yet a boy suffering all the usual pangs of adolescence, *writes Rita Skeeter*. Deprived of love since the tragic demise of his parents, fourteen-year-old Harry Potter thought he had found solace in his steady girlfriend at Hogwarts, Muggle-born Hermione Granger. Little did he know that he would shortly be suffering yet another emotional blow in a life already littered with personal loss.

Miss Granger, a plain but ambitious girl, seems to have a taste for famous wizards that Harry alone cannot satisfy. Since the arrival at Hogwarts of Viktor Krum, Bulgaria Seeker and hero of the last World Quidditch Cup, Miss Granger has been toying with both boys' affections. Krum, who is openly smitten with the devious Miss Granger, has already invited her to visit him in Bulgaria over the summer holidays, and insists that he has 'never felt this way about any other girl'.

However, it might not be Miss Granger's doubtful natural charms which have captured these unfortunate boys' interest.

'She's really ugly,' says Pansy Parkinson, a pretty and vivacious fourth-year student, 'but she'd be well up to making a Love Potion, she's quite brainy. I think that's how she's doing it.'

Love Potions are of course banned at Hogwarts, and no doubt Albus Dumbledore will want to investigate these claims. In the meantime, Harry Potter's well-wishers must hope that, next time, he bestows his heart upon a worthier candidate.

'I told you!' Ron hissed at Hermione, as she stared down at the article. 'I *told* you not to annoy Rita Skeeter! She's made you out to be some sort of – of scarlet woman!'

Hermione stopped looking astonished and snorted with laughter.

'*Scarlet woman?*' she repeated, shaking with suppressed giggles as she looked round at Ron.

'It's what my mum calls them,' Ron muttered, his ears going red again.

'If that's the best Rita can do, she's losing her touch,' said Hermione, still

## 第27章 大脚板回来了

### 哈利·波特的秘密伤心史

　　他或许是一个与众不同的男孩——但他同样经历着青春期男孩常有的痛苦，丽塔·斯基特报道。在痛失双亲之后，十四岁的哈利·波特以为他终于在霍格沃茨，在那个与他形影相伴的女朋友——麻瓜家庭出身的赫敏·格兰杰身上，找到了感情的慰藉，但他哪里想到，在他已然历经很多伤痛的生命里，很快又要遭受另一次感情创伤。

　　格兰杰小姐是一个长相平平但野心勃勃的姑娘，似乎对大名鼎鼎的巫师情有独钟，但哈利一个人满足不了她的胃口。自从保加利亚队找球手、上届世界杯赛的英雄威克多尔·克鲁姆来到霍格沃茨后，格兰杰小姐就一直在玩弄两个男孩的感情。克鲁姆显然已被狡猾的格兰杰小姐弄得神魂颠倒，他已邀请她暑假去保加利亚，并坚持说他"从没对其他女孩有过这种感觉"。

　　不过，使这些不幸的男孩如此痴迷的恐怕并不是格兰杰小姐的天生丽质。

　　"她真的很丑，"潘西·帕金森说，她是一个漂亮活泼的四年级女生，"她很可能制作了一种迷情剂，她脑子挺机灵的。没错，我认为她就是这么做的。"

　　在霍格沃茨，迷情剂自然属于被禁止之列，阿不思·邓布利多无疑需要认真调查此事。与此同时，对哈利·波特存有良好愿望的人们希望，下次他再奉献真情时，一定要挑选一个更有价值的候选人。


　　"我告诉过你！"罗恩小声对低头看文章的赫敏说，"我告诉过你，别去招惹丽塔·斯基特！她把你丑化成了那种——那种荡妇！"

　　赫敏脸上惊讶的表情不见了，她嘲讽地大笑起来。

　　"荡妇？"她重复了一遍，一边扭头望着罗恩，拼命忍住笑，浑身直颤。

　　"我妈妈就是这样称呼她们的。"罗恩喃喃地说，耳朵红了。

　　"如果丽塔充其量就会玩这一手，那她可没有显出多少本事，"赫

giggling, as she threw *Witch Weekly* onto the empty chair beside her. 'What a pile of old rubbish.'

She looked over at the Slytherins, who were all watching her and Harry closely across the room to see if they had been upset by the article. Hermione gave them a sarcastic smile and a wave, and she, Harry and Ron started unpacking the ingredients they would need for their Wit-Sharpening Potion.

'There's something funny, though,' said Hermione ten minutes later, holding her pestle suspended over a bowl of scarab beetles. 'How could Rita Skeeter have known ...?'

'Known what?' said Ron quickly. 'You *haven't* been mixing up Love Potions, have you?'

'Don't be stupid,' Hermione snapped, starting to pound up her beetles again. 'No, it's just ... how did she know Viktor asked me to visit him over the summer?'

Hermione blushed scarlet as she said this, and determinedly avoided Ron's eyes.

'What?' said Ron, dropping his pestle with a loud clunk.

'He asked me right after he'd pulled me out of the lake,' Hermione muttered. 'After he'd got rid of his shark's head. Madam Pomfrey gave us both blankets and then he sort of pulled me away from the judges so they wouldn't hear, and he said, if I wasn't doing anything over the summer, would I like to –'

'And what did you say?' said Ron, who had picked up his pestle and was grinding it on the desk, a good six inches from his bowl, because he was looking at Hermione.

'And he *did* say he'd never felt the same way about anyone else,' Hermione went on, going so red now that Harry could almost feel the heat coming from her, 'but how could Rita Skeeter have heard him? She wasn't there ... or was she? Maybe she *has* got an Invisibility Cloak, maybe she sneaked into the grounds to watch the second task ...'

'And what did you *say*?' Ron repeated, pounding his pestle down so hard that it dented the desk.

'Well, I was too busy seeing whether you and Harry were OK to –'

'Fascinating though your social life undoubtedly is, Miss Granger,' said an icy voice right behind them, 'I must ask you not to discuss it in my class. Ten points from Gryffindor.'

Snape had glided over to their desk while they had been talking. The

## 第27章 大脚板回来了

敏说,仍然咯咯笑着,随手把那本《女巫周刊》扔到旁边的空椅子上,"整个儿一堆破烂。"

她抬头望着那些斯莱特林的学生,他们都远远地注视着她和哈利,看他们读了文章是不是很恼火。赫敏对他们露出讽刺的笑容,还朝他们挥了挥手,接着,她和哈利、罗恩开始取出制作增智剂所需要的配料。

"不过,事情有些古怪,"十分钟后,赫敏举着捣槌,停在一碗圣甲虫上,说道,"丽塔·斯基特怎么会知道……?"

"知道什么?"罗恩迅速问道,"莫非你真的在炮制迷情剂?"

"别说傻话,"赫敏不耐烦地说,又开始捣她的甲虫,"不对,真奇怪……她怎么会知道威克多尔邀请我暑假去拜访他呢?"

赫敏说这话时,满脸羞得通红,而且打定主意避开罗恩的目光。

"什么?"罗恩说,当啷一声,他的捣槌重重地掉在桌上。

"他把我从湖里一拉上来,就对我发出了邀请,"赫敏低声道,"那时他刚刚除掉了他的鲨鱼头。庞弗雷女士把毯子发给我们俩,这时克鲁姆就把我拉到一边,不让裁判们听见,他说,如果我暑假没有别的事情,是不是愿意——"

"你是怎么说的?"罗恩问。他已经捡起捣槌,在桌子上胡乱地捣着,离他的碗还差着六七寸呢,因为他心不在焉,眼睛一直望着赫敏。

"而且,他确实说过他从没对别人有过这种感觉,"赫敏继续说道——脸红得像着了火似的,哈利简直能感觉到她身上散出的热气,"可是丽塔·斯基特怎么会听见他说的话呢?她当时并不在场……难道她在场?也许她也有一件隐形衣,也许她偷偷溜到了场地上,观看第二个项目……"

"你是怎么说的?"罗恩追问道,把捣锤重重地砸下去,把桌面砸出了一个小坑。

"噢,我当时只顾看你和哈利是不是平安——"

"格兰杰小姐,尽管你的社交生活丰富多彩,"后面突然传来一个冷冰冰的声音,把他们三人都吓了一跳,"但我必须警告你,不许在我的课堂上交头接耳。格兰芬多扣掉十分。"

斯内普趁他们谈话的当儿,悄没声儿地走到他们的桌子旁。全班

## CHAPTER TWENTY-SEVEN    Padfoot Returns

whole class was now looking around at them; Malfoy took the opportunity to flash *POTTER STINKS* across the dungeon at Harry.

'Ah ... reading magazines under the table as well?' Snape added, snatching up the copy of *Witch Weekly*. 'A further ten points from Gryffindor ... oh, but of course ...' Snape's black eyes glittered as they fell on Rita Skeeter's article. 'Potter has to keep up with his press cuttings ...'

The dungeon rang with the Slytherins' laughter, and an unpleasant smile curled Snape's thin mouth. To Harry's fury, he began to read the article aloud.

'*Harry Potter's Secret Heartache* ... dear, dear, Potter, what's ailing you now? *A boy like no other, perhaps* ...'

Harry could feel his face burning now. Snape was pausing at the end of every sentence to allow the Slytherins a hearty laugh. The article sounded ten times worse when read by Snape.

'... *Harry Potter's well-wishers must hope that, next time, he bestows his heart upon a worthier candidate*. How very touching,' sneered Snape, rolling up the magazine to continued gales of laughter from the Slytherins. 'Well, I think I had better separate the three of you, so you can keep your minds on your potions rather than your tangled love lives. Weasley, you stay here. Miss granger, over there, beside Miss Parkinson. Potter – that table in front of my desk. Move. Now.'

Furious, Harry threw his ingredients and his bag into his cauldron, and dragged it up to the front of the dungeon to the empty table. Snape followed, sat down at his desk and watched Harry unload his cauldron. Determined not to look at Snape, Harry resumed the mashing of his scarab beetles, imagining each one to have Snape's face.

'All this press attention seems to have inflated your already overlarge head, Potter,' said Snape quietly, once the rest of the class had settled down again.

Harry didn't answer. He knew Snape was trying to provoke him; he had done this before. No doubt he was hoping for an excuse to take a round fifty points from Gryffindor before the end of the class.

'You might be labouring under the delusion that the entire wizarding world is impressed with you,' Snape went on, so quietly that no one else

## 第27章　大脚板回来了

同学都回过头来望着他们。马尔福抓住这个机会,从教室那头把**波特臭大粪**的徽章对准了哈利,一闪一闪的。

"呵……还躲在桌子底下看杂志?"斯内普又说道,一把抓过那本《女巫周刊》,"格兰芬多再扣掉十分……不过,当然啦……"斯内普的目光落到丽塔·斯基特的那篇文章上,黑眼睛顿时冒出光来,"波特需要收集剪报嘛……"

地下教室里哄响着斯莱特林们的笑声,斯内普的薄嘴唇也扭动着,露出一个不怀好意的笑容。令哈利大为恼火的是,斯内普居然大声念起了那篇文章。

"哈利·波特的秘密伤心史……天哪,天哪,波特,你又犯了什么毛病?他或许是一个与众不同的男孩……"

哈利觉得脸在发烧。斯内普每念完一句都停顿一下,让斯莱特林们笑个够。这篇文章经斯内普的嘴一念,效果更糟糕十倍。

"……对哈利·波特存有良好愿望的人们希望,下次他再奉献真情时,一定要挑选一个更有价值的候选人。多么动人啊,"斯内普讥讽地说,一边在斯莱特林们的阵阵狂笑声中把杂志卷了起来,"哼,我认为最好把你们三个分开,这样你们就能集中思想配制药剂,而不是光想着这些乱七八糟的风流韵事了。韦斯莱,你坐在这里不动。格兰杰小姐,你上那儿去,坐在帕金森小姐旁边。波特——到我讲台前的那张桌子去。好了,快行动吧。"

哈利气得要命,把配料和书包扔进坩埚,然后端着坩埚走向教室前面的那张空桌子。斯内普也跟了过去,坐在讲台边,注视着哈利把坩埚里的东西一样样拿出来。哈利打定主意不去看斯内普,开始捣他的圣甲虫,幻想着每只甲虫都长着一张斯内普的脸。

"你成了媒体关注的中心,这似乎使你本来就不小的脑袋更加膨胀了,波特。"班上其他同学都安静下来后,斯内普轻声说道。

哈利没有回答。他知道斯内普是想挑逗他、激怒他,斯内普以前就这么做过。不用说,他是想找借口赶在下课前扣掉格兰芬多五十分。

"你大概想当然地以为,整个魔法界都在为你惊叹,"斯内普继续说道,声音很轻,其他同学都听不见(哈利只管捣他的圣甲虫,尽管

## CHAPTER TWENTY-SEVEN   Padfoot Returns

could hear him (Harry continued to pound his scarab beetles, even though he had already reduced them to a very fine powder), 'but I don't care how many times your picture appears in the papers. To me, Potter, you are nothing but a nasty little boy who considers rules to be beneath him.'

Harry tipped the powdered beetles into his cauldron and started cutting up his ginger roots. His hands were shaking slightly out of anger, but he kept his eyes down, as though he couldn't hear what Snape was saying to him.

'So I give you fair warning, Potter,' Snape continued, in a softer and more dangerous voice, 'pint-sized celebrity or not – if I catch you breaking into my office one more time –'

'I haven't been anywhere near your office!' said Harry angrily, forgetting his feigned deafness.

'Don't lie to me,' Snape hissed, his fathomless black eyes boring into Harry's. 'Boomslang skin. Gillyweed. Both come from my private stores, and I know who stole them.'

Harry stared back at Snape, determined not to blink, or to look guilty. In truth, he hadn't stolen either of these things from Snape. Hermione had taken the Boomslang skin back in their second year – they had needed it for the Polyjuice Potion – and while Snape had suspected Harry at the time, he had never been able to prove it. Dobby, of course, had stolen the Gillyweed.

'I don't know what you're talking about,' Harry lied coldly.

'You were out of bed on the night my office was broken into!' Snape hissed. 'I know it, Potter! Now, Mad-Eye Moody might have joined your fan club, but I will not tolerate your behaviour! One more night-time stroll into my office, Potter, and you will pay!'

'Right,' said Harry coolly, turning back to his ginger roots, 'I'll bear that in mind if I ever get the urge to go in there.'

Snape's eyes flashed. He plunged a hand into the inside of his black robes. For one wild moment, Harry thought Snape was about to pull out his wand and curse him – then he saw that Snape had drawn out a small crystal bottle of a completely clear potion. Harry stared at it.

'Do you know what this is, Potter?' Snape said, his eyes glittering dangerously again.

'No,' said Harry, completely honestly this time.

'It is Veritaserum – a Truth Potion so powerful that three drops would

它们已被碾成细细的粉末），"但是我才不关心你的照片在报纸上出现多少次呢。在我眼里，波特，你不过是一个讨厌的小男孩，但你却觉得自己可以无视所有的规章制度。"

哈利把甲虫粉末倒进坩埚，开始切割姜根。他气得双手微微发抖，但始终低垂着眼睛，好像根本听不见斯内普对他说的话。

"因此，我要给你一个善意的警告，波特，"斯内普用更轻柔也更阴险的声音说，"尽管你小有名气——如果我再发现你闯进我的办公室——"

"我从来没有靠近过你的办公室！"哈利气愤地说，把刚才的装聋作哑抛到了一边。

"别对我撒谎，"斯内普压低声音说，那双深不可测的黑眼睛狠狠地瞪着哈利的眼睛，"非洲树蛇皮、鳃囊草，这两样都是我的私人储藏品，我知道是谁偷的。"

哈利毫不示弱地瞪着斯内普，坚决不眨眼睛，也不显出心虚的样子。说实话，他并没有从斯内普那里偷这两样东西。赫敏二年级的时候拿了非洲树蛇皮——他们需要用它配制复方汤剂——当时斯内普怀疑了哈利，但一直没有证据。那鳃囊草呢，不用说，是多比偷的。

"我不知道你在说些什么。"哈利冷冷地撒谎道。

"有人闯进我办公室的那天夜里，你不在自己的床上！"斯内普嘶嘶地说，"这瞒不过我，波特！不错，疯眼汉穆迪大概也加入了你的追星俱乐部，但我再也不会容忍你的行为了！如果你再半夜三更溜进我的办公室，波特，你就等着瞧吧！"

"好吧，"哈利冷静地说，又低头切他的姜根，"我会记住这一点的，以免我什么时候心血来潮想去那儿。"

斯内普的眼睛闪了闪。他把一只手伸进黑袍子里面。一时间，哈利以为斯内普要抽出魔杖，给他念咒——接着他看见斯内普掏出了一个小小的水晶瓶，里面是一种清澈透明的药剂。哈利仔细地望着。

"你知道这是什么吗，波特？"斯内普说，那双眼睛里又闪着恶意的光芒。

"不知道。"哈利说，这次他说的完全是实话。

"这是吐真剂——一种教你说实话的药剂，效果奇强，只要三滴，

have you spilling your innermost secrets for this entire class to hear,' said Snape viciously. 'Now, the use of this Potion is controlled by very strict Ministry guidelines. But unless you watch your step, you might just find that my hand *slips* –' he shook the crystal bottle slightly '– right over your evening pumpkin juice. And then, Potter ... then we'll find out whether you've been in my office or not.'

Harry said nothing. He turned back to his ginger roots once more, picked up his knife and started slicing them again. He didn't like the sound of that Truth Potion at all, and nor would he put it past Snape to slip him some. He repressed a shudder at the thought of what might come spilling out of his mouth if Snape did ... quite apart from landing a whole lot of people in trouble – Hermione and Dobby, for a start – there were all the other things he was concealing ... like the fact that he was in contact with Sirius ... and – his insides squirmed at the thought – how he felt about Cho ... He tipped his ginger roots into the cauldron too, and wondered whether he ought to take a leaf out of Moody's book and start drinking only from a private hip-flask.

There was a knock on the dungeon door.

'Enter,' said Snape, in his usual voice.

The class looked around as the door opened. Professor Karkaroff came in. Everyone watched him as he walked up towards Snape's desk. He was twisting his finger around his goatee again, and looking agitated.

'We need to talk,' said Karkaroff abruptly, when he had reached Snape. He seemed so determined that nobody should hear what he was saying that he was barely opening his lips; it was as though he was a rather poor ventriloquist. Harry kept his eyes on his ginger roots, listening hard.

'I'll talk to you after my lesson, Karkaroff –' Snape muttered, but Karkaroff interrupted him.

'I want to talk now, while you can't slip off, Severus. You've been avoiding me.'

'After the lesson,' Snape snapped.

Under the pretext of holding up a measuring cup to see if he'd poured out enough armadillo bile, Harry sneaked a sidelong glance at the pair of them. Karkaroff looked extremely worried, and Snape looked angry.

Karkaroff hovered behind Snape's desk for the rest of the double period. He seemed intent on preventing Snape slipping away at the end of class.

## 第27章　大脚板回来了

就能使你透露出内心深处的秘密，让全体同学洗耳恭听。"斯内普恶狠狠地说，"当然，对这种药剂的使用，魔法部有十分严格的规定加以控制。但是你必须格外留神，不然我就会失手，"——他微微摇晃着水晶瓶——"倒在你晚餐的南瓜汁里。然后，波特……然后我们就会弄清你究竟去没去过我的办公室。"

哈利没有说话。他又一次转向他的姜根，拿起小刀，开始把它们切成碎片。他十分厌恶斯内普谈到的那种吐真剂，而且认为斯内普很有可能偷偷给他洒上几滴。他不知道如果斯内普真的这么做了，自己嘴里会吐露些什么，一想到这点，他就忍不住打了个寒战……他不仅会使许多人陷入麻烦——首先是赫敏和多比——更要命的是，他心里还藏着许多其他秘密呢……比如他一直在跟小天狼星保持联系……还有——他一想起来就觉得心里翻江倒海——他对秋的感情……他把姜根也倒进了坩埚，一边暗想，不知是否应该学学穆迪的样子，也在屁股后面挂一个酒瓶，从此只喝那里面的东西。

这时，教室外有人敲门。

"进来。"斯内普用他惯常的声音说。

门开了，全班同学都扭头看去。卡卡洛夫教授走了进来，大家望着他走向斯内普的讲台。他用手指卷着他的山羊胡须，显得焦躁不安。

"我们需要谈谈。"卡卡洛夫刚走到斯内普身边，就唐突地说。他似乎打定主意不让任何人听见他说的话，所以嘴唇几乎没有动，就好像他是一个很蹩脚的腹语专家。哈利眼睛盯着姜根，侧耳细听。

"我下课以后再跟你谈，卡卡洛夫。"斯内普小声说，但卡卡洛夫打断了他。

"我想现在就谈，趁你还没办法溜走，西弗勒斯。你一直在躲着我。"

"下课再说。"斯内普严厉地说。

哈利假装举起一只量杯，看倒出来的犰狳胆汁是不是够了，一边偷偷用眼角扫了那两人一眼。卡卡洛夫一副惊慌失措的样子，斯内普显得很生气。

在那两节课剩下来的时间里，卡卡洛夫一直在斯内普的讲台后面徘徊。他似乎决意不让斯内普下课后溜走。哈利很想听听卡卡洛夫要

## CHAPTER TWENTY-SEVEN — Padfoot Returns

Keen to hear what Karkaroff wanted to say, Harry deliberately knocked over his bottle of armadillo bile with two minutes to go to the bell, which gave him an excuse to duck down behind his cauldron and mop up while the rest of the class moved noisily towards the door.

'What's so urgent?' he heard Snape hiss at Karkaroff.

'*This*,' said Karkaroff, and Harry, peering around the edge of his cauldron, saw Karkaroff pull up the left-hand sleeve of his robe, and show Snape something on his inner forearm.

'Well?' said Karkaroff, still making every effort not to move his lips. 'Do you see? It's never been this clear, never since –'

'Put it away!' snarled Snape, his black eyes sweeping the classroom.

'But you must have noticed –' Karkaroff began in an agitated voice.

'We can talk later, Karkaroff!' spat Snape. 'Potter! What are you doing?'

'Clearing up my armadillo bile, Professor,' said Harry innocently, straightening up and showing Snape the sodden rag he was holding.

Karkaroff turned on his heel and strode out of the dungeon. He looked both worried and angry. Not wanting to remain alone with an exceptionally angry Snape, Harry threw his books and ingredients back into his bag, and left at top speed to tell Ron and Hermione what he had just witnessed.

They left the castle at noon the next day to find a weak silver sun shining down upon the grounds. The weather was milder than it had been all year, and by the time they arrived in Hogsmeade, all three of them had taken off their cloaks and thrown them over their shoulders. The food Sirius had told them to bring was in Harry's bag; they had sneaked a dozen chicken legs, a loaf of bread and a flask of pumpkin juice from the lunch table.

They went into Gladrags Wizardwear to buy a present for Dobby, where they had fun selecting all the most lurid socks they could find, including a pair patterned with flashing gold and silver stars, and another that screamed loudly when they became too smelly. Then, at half past one, they made their way up the High Street, past Dervish and Banges, and out towards the edge of the village.

Harry had never been in this direction before. The winding lane was leading them out into the wild countryside around Hogsmeade. The cottages were fewer here, and their gardens larger; they were walking towards the foot of the mountain in whose shadow Hogsmeade lay. Then they turned a

## 第27章 大脚板回来了

说什么，便故意在还有两分钟就打下课铃的时候，把装犰狳胆汁的瓶子打翻了，这样，当其他同学都闹哄哄地朝门口走去时，他就有借口蹲在坩埚后面，用抹布擦地了。

"什么事这么紧急？"他听见斯内普压低声音问卡卡洛夫。

"你看。"卡卡洛夫说，哈利从坩埚边缘偷偷望去，看见卡卡洛夫撩起长袍的左边袖子，给斯内普看他小臂上的什么东西。

"怎么样？"卡卡洛夫说，仍然很费劲地不让自己的嘴唇移动，"看见了吗？从来没有这样明显，自从——"

"快藏起来！"斯内普恶狠狠地说，那双黑眼睛扫视着教室。

"可是你一定注意到了——"卡卡洛夫语气焦虑地说。

"我们以后再谈，卡卡洛夫！"斯内普厉声说，"波特！你在干什么？"

"把我洒的犰狳胆汁擦干净，教授。"哈利假装无辜地说，一边直起身子，举起手里的湿抹布给斯内普看。

卡卡洛夫转了个身，大步走出了教室。他看上去既担忧又恼火。哈利不想单独和怒气冲天的斯内普待在一起，便赶紧把书本和配料扔进书包，飞快地走了出去，他要把刚才看见的事情告诉罗恩和赫敏。

第二天中午他们离开城堡时，看见微弱的银白色太阳照耀着场地。天气是一年来最暖和的，当他们到达霍格莫德村时，三个人都把斗篷脱了下来，搭在肩膀上。小天狼星叫他们带的食物就放在哈利的书包里。他们从午饭桌上偷了十来个鸡腿、一个长面包，还有一瓶南瓜汁。

他们走进风雅牌巫师服装店，给多比买礼物。他们把能够找到的最鲜艳、最夸张的袜子都挑选出来，有一双上面是闪耀的金星银星，还有一双一旦太臭就会大声尖叫。他们挑来挑去，觉得非常开心。一点半钟的时候，他们沿着马路经过德维斯－班斯，朝村外走去。

哈利从没有往这个方向来过。曲折的小路把他们带到了霍格莫德村周围荒野的田间。这里只有很少几座小木屋，但它们附带的园地却很大。他们朝山脚走去，霍格莫德村就坐落在这座大山的阴影里。随后，他们拐过一个弯，看见小路尽头有一道栅栏。在那里等着他们的是一

## CHAPTER TWENTY-SEVEN    Padfoot Returns

corner, and saw a stile at the end of the lane. Waiting for them, its front paws on the topmost bar, was a very large, shaggy black dog, which was carrying some newspapers in its mouth, and looked very familiar …

'Hello, Sirius,' said Harry, when they had reached him.

The black dog sniffed Harry's bag eagerly, wagged its tail once, then turned, and began to trot away from them across the scrubby patch of ground which rose to meet the rocky foot of the mountain. Harry, Ron and Hermione climbed over the stile and followed.

Sirius led them to the very foot of the mountain, where the ground was covered with boulders and rocks. It was easy for him, with his four paws, but Harry, Ron and Hermione were soon out of breath. They followed Sirius higher, up onto the mountain itself. For nearly half an hour they climbed a steep, winding and stony path, following Sirius' wagging tail, sweating in the sun, the shoulder straps of Harry's bag cutting into his shoulders.

Then, at last, Sirius slipped out of sight, and when they reached the place where he had vanished, they saw a narrow fissure in the rock. They squeezed into it, and found themselves in a cool, dimly lit cave. Tethered at the end of it, one end of his rope around a large rock, was Buckbeak the Hippogriff. Half grey horse, half giant eagle, Buckbeak's fierce orange eye flashed at the sight of them. All three of them bowed low to him, and after regarding them imperiously for a moment, Buckbeak bent his scaly front knees, and allowed Hermione to rush forward and stroke his feathery neck. Harry, however, was looking at the black dog, which had just turned into his godfather.

Sirius was wearing ragged grey robes; the same ones he had been wearing when he had left Azkaban. His black hair was longer than it had been when he had appeared in the fire, and it was untidy and matted once more. He looked very thin.

'Chicken!' he said hoarsely, after removing the old *Daily Prophets* from his mouth and throwing them down onto the cave floor.

Harry pulled open his bag and handed over the bundle of chicken legs and bread.

'Thanks,' said Sirius, opening it, grabbing a drumstick, sitting down on the cave floor and tearing off a large chunk with his teeth. 'I've been living off rats mostly. Can't steal too much food from Hogsmeade; I'd draw attention to myself.'

He grinned up at Harry, but Harry returned the grin only reluctantly.

## 第27章 大脚板回来了

条邋里邋遢的大黑狗，前爪搭在最高的那根栅栏上，嘴里叼着几张报纸，这条狗看上去很眼熟……

"你好，小天狼星。"他们走过去时，哈利说道。

黑狗急切地嗅着哈利的书包，摇了一下尾巴，然后一转身，在一片灌木丛生的场地上小跑起来，这片场地通向布满岩石的山脚。哈利、罗恩和赫敏赶紧爬过栅栏，跟了上去。

小天狼星领着他们一直来到山脚下，这里的地面上布满大大小小的石头。他因为有四个爪子，走起来轻松自如，可是哈利、罗恩和赫敏很快就累得气喘吁吁了。他们跟着小天狼星越走越高，开始往山上爬。三个人追随着小天狼星摇摆的尾巴，在蜿蜒陡峭、怪石嶙峋的小径上攀登了将近半小时，烈日烤得他们汗流浃背，哈利的书包带勒得他肩膀生疼。

终于，小天狼星一闪身不见了。他们来到他消失的地方，看见岩石上有一道狭窄的裂口。他们挤进去，发现来到了一个凉爽的、光线昏暗的岩洞里。巴克比克，那头鹰头马身有翼兽，就拴在岩洞尽头，绳子绕在一块大岩石上。巴克比克一半的身子是匹灰马，另一半则像是只巨大的鹰。它看到他们，锐利的橘黄色眼睛闪了闪。他们三个都对它深深地鞠躬，巴克比克傲慢地打量了他们片刻，然后弯下多鳞的前腿，让赫敏上前抚摸它长着羽毛的脖子。哈利却望着那条黑狗，就在这时，黑狗摇身一变，成了他的教父。

小天狼星穿着破破烂烂的灰袍子，就是他离开阿兹卡班时穿的那件。他的黑头发比上次在炉火里出现时长得多，而且又变得蓬乱纠结了。他看上去很消瘦。

"鸡肉！"他刚把嘴里破旧的《预言家日报》扔在岩洞的地上，就沙哑着嗓子说。

哈利扯开书包，把那包鸡腿和面包递了过去。

"谢谢，"小天狼星说了一句，便急切地打开包裹，抓起一个鸡腿，一屁股坐在地上，用牙齿撕下一大块鸡肉，"我几乎是靠吃老鼠过日子的，没法从霍格莫德偷到多少吃的东西，否则会引起别人注意。"

他抬头看着哈利笑了，但哈利只是很勉强地笑了一下。

## CHAPTER TWENTY-SEVEN  Padfoot Returns

'What're you doing here, Sirius?' he said.

'Fulfilling my duty as godfather,' said Sirius, gnawing on the chicken bone in a very dog-like way. 'Don't worry about me, I'm pretending to be a loveable stray.'

He was still grinning, but seeing the anxiety in Harry's face, said more seriously, 'I want to be on the spot. Your last letter ... well, let's just say things are getting fishier. I've been stealing the paper every time someone throws one out, and by the looks of things, I'm not the only one who's getting worried.'

He nodded at the yellowing *Daily Prophets* on the cave floor, and Ron picked them up and unfolded them.

Harry, however, continued to stare at Sirius. 'What if they catch you? What if you're seen?'

'You three and Dumbledore are the only ones round here who know I'm an Animagus,' said Sirius, shrugging, and continuing to devour the chicken leg.

Ron nudged Harry, and passed him the *Daily Prophets*. There were two; the first bore the headline *Mystery Illness of Bartemius Crouch*, the second, *Ministry Witch Still Missing – Minister for Magic Now Personally Involved*.

Harry looked down the story about Crouch. Phrases jumped out at him: *hasn't been seen in public since November ... house appears deserted ... St Mungo's Hospital for Magical Maladies decline comment ... Ministry refuses to confirm rumours of critical illness ...*

'They're making it sound like he's dying,' said Harry slowly. 'But he can't be that ill if he managed to get up here ...'

'My brother's Crouch's personal assistant,' Ron informed Sirius. 'He says Crouch is suffering from overwork.'

'Mind you, he *did* look ill, last time I saw him up close,' said Harry slowly, still reading the story. 'The night my name came out of the Goblet ...'

'Getting his comeuppance for sacking Winky, isn't he?' said Hermione coldly. She was stroking Buckbeak, who was crunching up Sirius' chicken bones. 'I bet he wishes he hadn't done it now – bet he feels the difference now she's not there to look after him.'

## 第27章 大脚板回来了

"你在这里干什么,小天狼星?"他问。

"履行我作为教父的义务。"小天狼星说,一边啃咬着鸡骨头,那动作活像一条狗,"别为这个操心了,我假装自己是一条从别人家走失的可爱的狗。"

他仍然那样笑着,不过看到哈利脸上焦虑的神情,他便正色说道:"我必须亲临现场。你最后那封信……至少,我们可以说事情变得越来越可疑了。每次人们扔掉报纸,我都把它们偷捡回来,从现在的事态看,忧心忡忡的可不止我一个人。"

他冲着地上那几份发黄的《预言家日报》点点头,罗恩把报纸捡起来打开。但哈利仍然盯着小天狼星。

"如果他们抓住你怎么办?如果你被人发现了怎么办?"

"在这附近,只有你们三个和邓布利多知道我是一个阿尼马格斯。"小天狼星说着耸了耸肩,继续大口啃着鸡腿。

罗恩用胳膊肘捅了捅哈利,把《预言家日报》递给了他。报纸共有两份,其中一份印着这样的标题:巴蒂·克劳奇病得蹊跷;另一份上印着:魔法部女巫仍然下落不明——目前部长本人也卷入此事。

哈利迅速浏览了一下关于克劳奇的那篇报道。一些只言片语映入他的眼帘:自十一月起便没有露面……家中似乎无人居住……圣芒戈魔法伤病医院拒绝发表评论……魔法部不肯证实他病入膏肓的传言……

"听他们的口气,就好像他快要死了。"哈利慢慢地说,"既然他有力气闯到这里来,就不可能病得那么重……"

"我哥哥是克劳奇的私人助理,"罗恩告诉小天狼星说,"他说克劳奇是因为工作太累,积劳成疾了。"

"但别忘了,上次我靠近了打量他,发现他确实像有病的样子,"哈利慢慢地说,一边仍然浏览着那篇报道,"就是我的名字从火焰杯里喷出来的那天晚上……"

"这是他开除闪闪而得到的报应,不是吗?"赫敏说,语气有些尖刻,巴克比克嘎吱嘎吱地嚼着小天狼星吃剩的鸡骨头,赫敏温柔地抚摸着它,"我敢说他现在后悔自己不该那么做了——我敢说没有闪闪在身边照料,他觉得生活大不如以前了。"

## CHAPTER TWENTY-SEVEN  Padfoot Returns

'Hermione's obsessed with house-elves,' Ron muttered to Sirius, casting Hermione a dark look.

Sirius, however, looked interested. 'Crouch sacked his house-elf?'

'Yeah, at the Quidditch World Cup,' said Harry, and he launched into the story of the Dark Mark's appearance, and Winky being found with Harry's wand clutched in her hand, and Mr. Crouch's fury.

When Harry had finished, Sirius was on his feet again, and had started pacing up and down the cave. 'Let me get this straight,' he said after a while, brandishing a fresh chicken leg. 'You first saw the elf in the Top Box. She was saving Crouch a seat, right?'

'Right,' said Harry, Ron and Hermione together.

'But Crouch didn't turn up for the match?'

'No,' said Harry. 'I think he said he'd been too busy.'

Sirius paced all around the cave in silence. Then he said, 'Harry, did you check your pockets for your wand after you'd left the Top Box?'

'Erm ...' Harry thought hard. 'No,' he said finally. 'I didn't need to use it before we got in the forest. And then I put my hand in my pocket, and all that was in there were my Omnioculars.' He stared at Sirius. 'Are you saying whoever conjured the Mark stole my wand in the Top Box?'

'It's possible,' said Sirius.

'Winky didn't steal that wand!' said Hermione shrilly.

'The elf wasn't the only one in that box,' said Sirius, his brow furrowed as he continued to pace. 'Who else was sitting behind you?'

'Loads of people,' said Harry. 'Some Bulgarian ministers ... Cornelius Fudge ... the Malfoys ...'

'The Malfoys!' said Ron suddenly, so loudly that his voice echoed all around the cave, and Buckbeak tossed his head nervously. 'I bet it was Lucius Malfoy!'

'Anyone else?' said Sirius.

'No one,' said Harry.

'Yes, there was, there was Ludo Bagman,' Hermione reminded him.

'Oh, yeah ...'

## 第27章 大脚板回来了

"赫敏对家养小精灵着了迷。"罗恩小声对小天狼星说,一边朝赫敏翻了个白眼。

但小天狼星却显得很感兴趣:"克劳奇开除了他的家养小精灵?"

"是啊,在魁地奇世界杯赛上。"哈利说,接着便一五一十地讲了黑魔标记怎样出现,闪闪怎样被发现手里抓着哈利的魔杖,克劳奇先生怎样大发雷霆。

哈利讲完了,小天狼星又站了起来,开始在岩洞里踱来踱去。"我来把这件事搞清楚。"过了一会儿他说,手里挥动着一个刚拿出来的鸡腿,"你先是在顶层包厢看见了那个小精灵,她在替克劳奇占位子,对吗?"

"没错。"哈利、罗恩和赫敏异口同声地说。

"但是克劳奇并没有来观看比赛?"

"没有,"哈利说,"我记得他说自己太忙了。"

小天狼星默默地在岩洞里来回踱步。接着他说:"哈利,你离开顶层包厢后有没有摸摸口袋,看你的魔杖还在不在?"

"嗯……"哈利努力回忆,"没有,"他最后说,"在进入树林前,我不需要使用魔杖。一进林子,我把手伸进口袋,里面就只有我的那架全景望远镜了。"他望着小天狼星,"你是说,变出黑魔标记的那个人在顶层包厢偷走了我的魔杖?"

"很有可能。"小天狼星说。

"闪闪没有偷那根魔杖!"赫敏坚决地说。

"包厢里除了小精灵还有别人呢。"小天狼星说。他蹙起眉头,又开始踱步:"坐在你后面的还有谁?"

"好多人呢,"哈利说,"保加利亚的几位部长……康奈利·福吉……还有马尔福一家……"

"马尔福!"罗恩突然喊道,声音很大,在岩洞里嗡嗡回响,巴克比克不安地抖动着脑袋,"我敢说就是卢修斯·马尔福干的!"

"还有别人吗?"小天狼星问。

"没有了。"哈利说。

"有,还有卢多·巴格曼呢。"赫敏提醒道。

"噢,对了……"

'I don't know anything about Bagman, except that he used to be Beater for the Wimbourne Wasps,' said Sirius, still pacing. 'What's he like?'

'He's OK,' said Harry. 'He keeps offering to help me with the Triwizard Tournament.'

'Does he, now?' said Sirius, frowning more deeply. 'I wonder why he'd do that?'

'Says he's taken a liking to me,' said Harry.

'Hmm,' said Sirius, looking thoughtful.

'We saw him in the forest just before the Dark Mark appeared,' Hermione told Sirius. 'Remember?' she said to Harry and Ron.

'Yeah, but he didn't stay in the forest, did he?' said Ron. 'The moment we told him about the riot, he went off to the campsite.'

'How d'you know?' Hermione shot back. 'How d'you know where he Disapparated to?'

'Come off it,' said Ron incredulously, 'are you saying you reckon Ludo Bagman conjured the Dark Mark?'

'It's more likely he did it than Winky,' said Hermione stubbornly.

'Told you,' said Ron, looking meaningfully at Sirius, 'told you she's obsessed with house–'

But Sirius held up a hand to silence Ron. 'When the Dark Mark had been conjured, and the elf had been discovered holding Harry's wand, what did Crouch do?'

'Went to look in the bushes,' said Harry, 'but there wasn't anyone else there.'

'Of course,' Sirius muttered, pacing up and down, 'of course, he'd want to pin it on anyone but his own elf ... and then he sacked her?'

'Yes,' said Hermione in a heated voice, 'he sacked her, just because she hadn't stayed in her tent and let herself get trampled –'

'Hermione, *will* you give it a rest with the elf!' said Ron.

But Sirius shook his head and said, 'She's got the measure of Crouch better than you have, Ron. If you want to know what a man's like, take a good look at how he treats his inferiors, not his equals.'

## 第27章 大脚板回来了

"我对巴格曼不太了解,只知道他曾经是温布恩黄蜂队的击球手。"小天狼星仍然踱着步说,"他怎么样?"

"挺好的,"哈利说,"好几次都提出要在三强争霸赛中帮助我。"

"哦,是吗?"小天狼星说,眉头皱得更紧了,"真奇怪,他为什么要这样做呢?"

"他说对我产生了好感。"哈利说。

"唔。"小天狼星显然若有所思。

"就在黑魔标记出现之前,我们在树林里看见了他。"赫敏对小天狼星说。"记得吗?"她问哈利和罗恩。

"是的,但他并没有留在树林里,对不对?"罗恩说,"我们一告诉他发生了暴乱,他就赶到营地去了。"

"你怎么知道?"赫敏立刻反问,"你怎么知道他幻影移形,移到什么地方去了?"

"别胡扯了,"罗恩不敢相信地说,"难道你认为是卢多·巴格曼变出了黑魔标记?"

"他比闪闪更有可能。"赫敏固执地说。

"我告诉过你,"罗恩意味深长地望着小天狼星,说,"我告诉过你,赫敏对家养——"

但是小天狼星举起一只手,止住了罗恩的话头。

"当黑魔标记被变出来,那个小精灵握着哈利的魔杖被人发现时,克劳奇是怎么做的?"

"他钻进灌木丛看了看,"哈利说,"但那里什么人也没有。"

"当然,"小天狼星一边踱步,一边轻声嘀咕,"当然,他想把事情归罪于别人,而不是他自己的小精灵……然后他就开除了她?"

"是的,"赫敏用十分气愤的口气说,"他开除了她,就因为她没有待在帐篷里,由着别人践踏——"

"赫敏,你能不能不要揪住小精灵不放!"罗恩说。

小天狼星摇了摇头,说:"赫敏比你更了解克劳奇的本性,罗恩。如果你想了解一个人的为人,就要留意他是如何对待他的下级的,而不能光看他如何对待与他地位相等的人。"

He ran a hand over his unshaven face, evidently thinking hard. 'All these absences of Barty Crouch's ... he goes to the trouble of making sure his house-elf saves him a seat at the Quidditch World Cup, but doesn't bother to turn up and watch. He works very hard to reinstate the Triwizard Tournament, and then stops coming to that, too ... it's not like Crouch. If he's ever taken a day off work because of illness before this, I'll eat Buckbeak.'

'D'you know Crouch, then?' said Harry.

Sirius' face darkened. He suddenly looked as menacing as the night when Harry had first met him, the night when Harry had still believed Sirius to be a murderer.

'Oh, I know Crouch all right,' he said quietly. 'He was the one who gave the order for me to be sent to Azkaban – without a trial.'

'*What?*' said Ron and Hermione together.

'You're kidding!' said Harry.

'No, I'm not,' said Sirius, taking another great bite of chicken. 'Crouch used to be Head of the Department of Magical Law Enforcement, didn't you know?'

Harry, Ron and Hermione shook their heads.

'He was tipped as the next Minister for Magic,' said Sirius. 'He's a great wizard, Barty Crouch, powerfully magical – and power-hungry. Oh, never a Voldemort supporter,' he said, reading the look on Harry's face. 'No, Barty Crouch was always very outspoken against the Dark side. But then a lot of people who were against the Dark side ... well, you wouldn't understand ... you're too young ...'

'That's what my dad said at the World Cup,' said Ron, with a trace of irritation in his voice. 'Try us, why don't you?'

A grin flashed across Sirius' thin face. 'All right, I'll try you ...'

He walked once up the cave, back again, and then said, 'Imagine that Voldemort's powerful now. You don't know who his supporters are, you don't know who's working for him and who isn't; you know he can control people so that they do terrible things without being able to stop themselves. You're scared for yourself, and your family, and your friends. Every week, news comes of more deaths, more disappearances, more torturing ... the Ministry of Magic's in disarray, they don't know what to do, they're trying to keep everything hidden from the Muggles, but meanwhile, Muggles are dying too.

## 第27章 大脚板回来了

他用手抚摸着胡子拉碴的面颊，显然在苦苦思索什么。"巴蒂·克劳奇这么多次缺席……在魁地奇世界杯赛上，他花了功夫让家养小精灵给他占座位，自己却没有去观看比赛。他加班加点地工作，恢复了三强争霸赛，自己却不去参加……这不符合克劳奇的性格。如果他以前因为生病请过一天假，我就把巴克比克生吞活吃了。"

"怎么，你认识克劳奇？"哈利说。

小天狼星的表情暗淡了。他突然变得挺吓人的，就像哈利第一次见到他的那天夜里一样，当时哈利还相信小天狼星是个杀人魔王呢。

"哦，我当然认识克劳奇，"他轻声说，"就是他下令把我送到阿兹卡班的——连审判也免了。"

"什么？"罗恩和赫敏同时说。

"你在开玩笑吧！"哈利说。

"没有，不是玩笑。"小天狼星说着，又咬了一大口鸡肉，"克劳奇曾是魔法法律执行司的司长，你们不知道吧？"

哈利、罗恩和赫敏摇了摇头。

"有人预测他有可能当选下一届魔法部部长。"小天狼星说，"他是个了不起的巫师，巴蒂·克劳奇，法力高强——权力欲望也很强。哦，绝不会是伏地魔的支持者。"他看到哈利脸上的表情，说道："不，巴蒂·克劳奇总是公开声明他是反对黑魔法的。可是许多反对黑魔法的人都……唉，你们不会明白……你们年纪太小了……"

"我爸爸在世界杯赛上就是这么说的。"罗恩说，语气里带着一点儿恼火，"你就试试嘛，看我们能不能明白。"

小天狼星消瘦的脸上闪过一丝笑容。"好吧，我就试试……"

他走到岩洞那头，又折回来，说道，"现在想象一下，在伏地魔势力强大的时候，你不知道谁是他的支持者，谁不是，不知道谁在为他效命，谁不是。你知道他能把人牢牢控制，使他们不由自主地做一些可怕的事。你为自己、你的家人和你的朋友感到害怕。每个星期都有噩耗传来，又有人死亡，又有人失踪，又有人在遭受折磨……魔法部一片混乱，他们不知道该怎么办，还要千方百计地瞒着麻瓜，而与此同时，麻瓜们也在死亡。到处都是一片恐怖……紧张……混乱……当时就是这

## CHAPTER TWENTY-SEVEN    Padfoot Returns

Terror everywhere ... panic ... confusion ... that's how it used to be.

'Well, times like that bring out the best in some people, and the worst in others. Crouch's principles might've been good in the beginning – I wouldn't know. He rose quickly through the Ministry, and he started ordering very harsh measures against Voldemort's supporters. The Aurors were given new powers – powers to kill rather than capture, for instance. And I wasn't the only one who was handed straight to the Dementors without trial. Crouch fought violence with violence, and authorised the use of the Unforgivable Curses against suspects. I would say he became as ruthless and cruel as many on the Dark side. He had his supporters, mind you – plenty of people thought he was going about things the right way, and there were a lot of witches and wizards clamouring for him to take over as Minister for Magic. When Voldemort disappeared, it looked like only a matter of time until Crouch got the top job. But then something rather unfortunate happened ...' Sirius smiled grimly. 'Crouch's own son was caught with a group of Death Eaters who'd managed to talk their way out of Azkaban. Apparently they were trying to find Voldemort and return him to power.'

'Crouch's *son* was caught?' gasped Hermione.

'Yep,' said Sirius, throwing his chicken bone to Buckbeak, and flinging himself back down on the ground beside the loaf of bread, and tearing it in half. 'Nasty little shock for old Barty, I'd imagine. Should have spent a bit more time at home with his family, shouldn't he? Ought to have left the office early once in a while ... got to know his own son.'

He began to wolf down large pieces of bread.

'*Was* his son a Death Eater?' said Harry.

'No idea,' said Sirius, still stuffing down bread. 'I was in Azkaban myself when he was brought in. This is mostly stuff I've found out since I got out. The boy was definitely caught in the company of people I'd bet my life were Death Eaters – but he might have been in the wrong place at the wrong time, just like the house-elf.'

'Did Crouch try and get his son off?' Hermione whispered.

Sirius let out a laugh that was much more like a bark. 'Crouch let his son off? I thought you had the measure of him, Hermione? Anything that threatened to tarnish his reputation had to go, he had dedicated his whole life to becoming Minister for Magic. You saw him dismiss a devoted house-

## 第27章 大脚板回来了

样的状况。

"唉,像这样的时候,总能使好人体现出最高尚的品德,使坏人暴露出最恶劣的本质。一开始,克劳奇的原则大概还不错——我不太清楚。他在部里很快步步高升,开始采取一些非常强硬的措施,对付伏地魔的支持者们。傲罗们获得了一些新的权力——比如,他们有权杀人,而不仅仅是抓捕。未经审判就被直接移交摄魂怪的不止我一个人。克劳奇用暴力对付暴力,允许对嫌疑者采用不可饶恕咒。在我看来,他变得像黑魔势力那边的许多人一样心狠手辣、冷酷无情。你们知道吗,他也有自己的支持者——许多人认为他这样处理事情是对的,许多巫师大声疾呼,要求他担任魔法部部长。伏地魔失踪后,克劳奇出任第一把手似乎只是一个时间问题。然而就在这时,发生了一件十分不幸的事……"小天狼星露出冷酷的笑容,"克劳奇的亲生儿子被抓住了,他和一群凭着花言巧语没有被关进阿兹卡班的食死徒在一起。看样子他们在寻找伏地魔,想使他卷土重来。"

"克劳奇的儿子被抓住了?"赫敏吃惊地问。

"是啊。"小天狼星说,把鸡骨头扔给巴克比克,又一屁股坐在地上,拿起身边的那个面包撕成两半,"可以想象,这对巴蒂那老家伙来说真是一个不小的打击。他应该多花点时间和家人待在一起,是不是?应该时不时地早点下班……多了解了解自己的儿子。"

他狼吞虎咽地吃起了面包。

"他儿子是一个食死徒吗?"哈利说。

"不清楚。"小天狼星说,继续往嘴里塞着面包,"他被关进阿兹卡班时,我也在那里。这些都是我出来后才打听到的。那个男孩被捕的时候,和他在一起的人都是食死徒,这点我可以用性命打赌——但他也许只是不该在那个时候出现在那个地点,就像那个家养小精灵一样。"

"克劳奇有没有替他的儿子开脱?"赫敏小声问道。

小天狼星发出一声怪笑,很像是犬吠。"克劳奇替他的儿子开脱?赫敏,我刚才还以为你挺了解他的本性呢!一切威胁到他名誉的事物,都必然被抛到一边。他的全部生命都献给了要成为魔法部部长这项事业。你们看见他开除了一个忠心耿耿的家养小精灵,就因为这个小精灵

## CHAPTER TWENTY-SEVEN  Padfoot Returns

elf because she associated him with the Dark Mark again – doesn't that tell you what he's like? Crouch's fatherly affection stretched just far enough to give his son a trial and, by all accounts, it wasn't much more than an excuse for Crouch to show how much he hated the boy ... then he sent him straight to Azkaban.'

'He gave his own son to the Dementors?' asked Harry quietly.

'That's right,' said Sirius, and he didn't look remotely amused now. 'I saw the Dementors bringing him in, watched them through the bars in my cell door. He can't have been more than nineteen. They took him into a cell near mine. He was screaming for his mother by nightfall. He went quiet after a few days, though ... they all went quiet in the end ... except when they shrieked in their sleep ...'

For a moment, the deadened look in Sirius' eyes became more pronounced than ever, as though shutters had closed behind them.

'So he's still in Azkaban?' Harry said.

'No,' said Sirius dully. 'No, he's not in there any more. He died about a year after they brought him in.'

'He *died?*'

'He wasn't the only one,' said Sirius bitterly. 'Most go mad in there, and plenty stop eating in the end. They lose the will to live. You could always tell when a death was coming, because the Dementors could sense it, they got excited. That boy looked pretty sickly when he arrived. Crouch being an important Ministry member, he and his wife were allowed a deathbed visit. That was the last time I saw Barty Crouch, half carrying his wife past my cell. She died herself, apparently, shortly afterwards. Grief. Wasted away just like the boy. Crouch never came for his son's body. The Dementors buried him outside the fortress, I watched them do it.'

Sirius threw aside the bread he had just lifted to his mouth, and instead picked up the flask of pumpkin juice and drained it.

'So old Crouch lost it all, just when he thought he had it made,' he continued, wiping his mouth with the back of his hand. 'One moment, a hero, poised to become Minister for Magic ... next, his son dead, his wife dead, the family name dishonoured, and, so I've heard since I escaped, a big drop in popularity. Once the boy had died, people started feeling a bit more sympathetic towards him, and started asking how a nice young lad from a

## 第27章 大脚板回来了

又把他和黑魔标记联系在了一起——你们还看不出他是个什么样的人吗？克劳奇的父爱充其量只表现在他让儿子受审上，根据各种流传的说法，这实际上是给了克劳奇一个借口，可以展示一下他是多么仇恨那个男孩……然后他就把儿子送进了阿兹卡班。"

"他把自己的儿子交给了摄魂怪？"哈利轻声问。

"正是这样，"小天狼星说，现在他脸上完全不是觉得好笑的神情了，"我看见摄魂怪把他带了进来，我隔着牢门的铁栏杆注视着他们。他最多也就十九岁。他们把他投进了我旁边的一间牢房。傍晚的时候，他尖声呼喊着妈妈。不过几天之后，他就无声无息了……他们最后都无声无息了……只偶尔在睡梦中发出尖叫……"

一时间，小天狼星眼睛里郁闷的神情变得格外凝重，就好像眼睛后面的百叶窗突然关闭了。

"这么说，他还在阿兹卡班？"哈利问。

"不在了，"小天狼星淡淡地说，"他已经不在那里了。在他们把他带进来一年之后，他就死了。"

"死了？"

"死了的不止他一个，"小天狼星痛苦地说，"在那里，大多数人都发了疯，许多人最后都绝食了。他们丧失了生活下去的愿望。一个人什么时候死是可以知道的，因为摄魂怪能够感觉到，每到这时他们就兴奋不已。那个男孩来的时候就病歪歪的。克劳奇是魔法部的重要官员，他和妻子获准看望临终前的儿子。那是我最后一次看见巴蒂·克劳奇，他半搂半扶着妻子，从我的牢房前走过。显然，他妻子很快就死了。悲伤过度。像那个男孩一样憔悴而死。克劳奇没有来领取儿子的尸体。摄魂怪把他埋在了堡垒外面。我亲眼看着他们这么做的。"

小天狼星把举到嘴边的面包扔到一旁，抓起那瓶南瓜汁一口气喝干。

"因此，就在可怜的克劳奇以为大功告成的时候，他失去了一切。"小天狼星用手背擦擦嘴唇，继续说道，"刚才还是一个英雄，信心十足地要成为魔法部部长……转眼间，儿子死了，妻子也死了，家庭的名誉被玷污了，而且，我逃跑出来后听说，他在公众心目中的威信急剧下降。男孩死去后，人们开始更多地同情他儿子，并且提出疑问：为

## CHAPTER TWENTY-SEVEN    Padfoot Returns

good family had gone so badly astray. The conclusion was that his father never cared much for him. So Cornelius Fudge got the top job, and Crouch was shunted sideways into the Department of International Magical Co-operation.'

There was a long silence. Harry was thinking of the way Crouch's eyes had bulged as he'd looked down at his disobedient house-elf back in the wood at the Quidditch World Cup. This, then, must have been why Crouch had overreacted to Winky being found beneath the Dark Mark. It had brought back memories of his son, and the old scandal, and his fall from grace at the Ministry.

'Moody says Crouch is obsessed with catching Dark wizards,' Harry told Sirius.

'Yeah, I've heard it's become a bit of a mania with him,' said Sirius, nodding. 'If you ask me, he still thinks he can bring back the old popularity by catching one more Death Eater.'

'And he sneaked up here to search Snape's office!' said Ron triumphantly, looking at Hermione.

'Yes, and that doesn't make sense at all,' said Sirius.

'Yeah, it does!' said Ron excitedly.

But Sirius shook his head. 'Listen, if Crouch wants to investigate Snape, why hasn't he been coming to judge the Tournament? It would be an ideal excuse to make regular visits to Hogwarts and keep an eye on him.'

'So you think Snape could be up to something, then?' asked Harry, but Hermione broke in.

'Look, I don't care what you say, Dumbledore trusts Snape –'

'Oh, come off it, Hermione,' said Ron impatiently, 'I know Dumbledore's brilliant and everything, but that doesn't mean a really clever Dark wizard couldn't fool him –'

'Why did Snape save Harry's life in the first year, then? Why didn't he just let him die?'

'I dunno – maybe he thought Dumbledore would kick him out –'

'What d'you think, Sirius?' Harry said loudly, and Ron and Hermione stopped bickering to listen.

'I think they've both got a point,' said Sirius, looking thoughtfully at

## 第27章 大脚板回来了

什么一个来自良好家庭的孩子会走上这样的邪路？得出的结论是他父亲从来都不怎么关心他。就这样，康奈利·福吉坐上了第一把交椅，克劳奇被平调到了国际魔法合作司。"

接着便是良久的沉默。哈利想起魁地奇世界杯赛那天在树林里，克劳奇低头望着他那不听话的家养小精灵时，眼珠向外突起的样子。怪不得闪闪在黑魔标记下被人抓住时，克劳奇会有那样过激的反应呢。那一定使他想起了自己的儿子，想起了过去那段丑闻，以及他在魔法部名誉扫地的惨痛经历。

"穆迪说克劳奇整天痴迷于抓黑巫师。"哈利告诉小天狼星。

"是啊，我听说这成了他的一种嗜好。"小天狼星点了点头，说道，"我的看法是，他仍然以为只要他多抓住一个食死徒，就可以重新赢得公众的支持。"

"他还偷偷溜到这里，搜查斯内普的办公室！"罗恩得意地说，眼睛望着赫敏。

"是啊，但那说明不了任何问题。"小天狼星说。

"哎呀，很能说明问题！"罗恩激动地说。

但小天狼星摇了摇头："听着，如果克劳奇想调查斯内普，为什么不来担任争霸赛的裁判呢？那样他可以堂而皇之地定期拜访霍格沃茨，监视斯内普的行为。"

"那么，你认为斯内普可能有什么不轨行为吗？"哈利问，但是赫敏插了进来。

"喂，不管你们怎么说，反正邓布利多是相信斯内普的——"

"哦，你就消停一会儿吧，赫敏。"罗恩不耐烦地说，"我知道邓布利多很出色，很了不起，但那并不说明一个非常狡猾的黑巫师就骗不了他——"

"那么，一年级的时候，斯内普为什么要救哈利的命呢？他为什么不让哈利死了拉倒呢？"

"我不知道——也许他以为邓布利多会把他赶出去——"

"你认为呢，小天狼星？"哈利大声地问，罗恩和赫敏停止了争吵，准备听他说话。

"我认为你们俩说的都有道理。"小天狼星若有所思地望着罗恩和

## CHAPTER TWENTY-SEVEN — Padfoot Returns

Ron and Hermione. 'Ever since I found out Snape was teaching here, I've wondered why Dumbledore hired him. Snape's always been fascinated by the Dark arts, he was famous for it at school. Slimy, oily, greasy-haired kid, he was,' Sirius added, and Harry and Ron grinned at each other. 'Snape knew more curses when he arrived at school than half the kids in seventh year and he was part of a gang of Slytherins who nearly all turned out to be Death Eaters.'

Sirius held up his fingers, and began ticking off names. 'Rosier and Wilkes – they were both killed by Aurors the year before Voldemort fell. The Lestranges – they're a married couple – they're in Azkaban. Avery – from what I've heard he wormed his way out of trouble by saying he'd been acting under the Imperius Curse – he's still at large. But as far as I know, Snape was never even accused of being a Death Eater – not that that means much. Plenty of them were never caught. And Snape's certainly clever and cunning enough to keep himself out of trouble.'

'Snape knows Karkaroff pretty well, but he wants to keep that quiet,' said Ron.

'Yeah, you should've seen Snape's face when Karkaroff turned up in Potions yesterday!' said Harry quickly. 'Karkaroff wanted to talk to Snape, he says Snape's been avoiding him. Karkaroff looked really worried. He showed Snape something on his arm, but I couldn't see what it was.'

'He showed Snape something on his arm?' said Sirius, looking frankly bewildered. He ran his fingers distractedly through his filthy hair, then shrugged again. 'Well, I've no idea what that's about … but if Karkaroff's genuinely worried, and he's going to Snape for answers …'

Sirius stared at the cave wall, then made a grimace of frustration. 'There's still the fact that Dumbledore trusts Snape, and I know Dumbledore trusts where a lot of other people wouldn't, but I just can't see him letting Snape teach at Hogwarts if he'd ever worked for Voldemort.'

'Why are Moody and Crouch so keen to get into Snape's office, then?' said Ron stubbornly.

'Well,' said Sirius slowly, 'I wouldn't put it past Mad-Eye to have searched every single teacher's office when he got to Hogwarts. He takes his Defence Against the Dark Arts seriously, Moody. I'm not sure *he* trusts anyone at all, and after the things he's seen, it's not surprising. I'll say this for Moody,

赫敏说，"自从我听说斯内普在这里教书后，就一直纳闷邓布利多为什么要聘用他。斯内普一向对黑魔法非常着迷，上学时就因此而出名。他当时是个身上和头发上都黏糊糊、油腻腻的小男孩。"小天狼星补充说，哈利和罗恩笑着对视了一下，"斯内普刚进校时，他知道的咒语就比七年级的半数学生都多，他还是一个斯莱特林团伙的成员，后来那个团伙里的人几乎都变成了食死徒。"

小天狼星举起手，开始扳着手指报出一个个人名："罗齐尔和威尔克斯——在伏地魔倒台前一年都被傲罗杀死了。莱斯特兰奇夫妇，被关在阿兹卡班。埃弗里——据我了解，他用欺骗的办法使自己摆脱了干系，说他是中了夺魂咒，行为不由自主——至今仍逍遥在外。不过据我所知，斯内普从来没有被指控为食死徒——这也不能说明多少问题。他们许多人都没被抓住。斯内普无疑是狡猾机灵的，完全可以把自己洗刷得干干净净。"

"斯内普和卡卡洛夫非常熟悉，但他不想让别人知道这点。"罗恩说。

"是啊，你真应该看到卡卡洛夫昨天闯进魔药课教室时，斯内普脸上的那副表情！"哈利很快地说，"卡卡洛夫想跟斯内普谈谈，他说斯内普一直在躲着他。卡卡洛夫显得非常焦虑。他给斯内普看他胳膊上的什么东西，我没看清那到底是什么。"

"他给斯内普看他胳膊上的什么东西？"小天狼星说，显得十分困惑。他漫不经心地用手指梳理脏兮兮的头发，然后又耸了耸肩膀："唉，我也不知道那是怎么回事……但如果卡卡洛夫万分焦虑，并且找斯内普拿主意的话……"

小天狼星盯着岩壁，然后泄气地做了个鬼脸。"不错，邓布利多相信斯内普，有时候邓布利多相信的人，其他许多人都不相信，但是我想，如果斯内普曾经为伏地魔效过力，邓布利多是决不会让他在霍格沃茨教书的。"

"那么，为什么穆迪和克劳奇这样急切地闯进斯内普的办公室呢？"罗恩固执地问。

"我想，"小天狼星慢吞吞地说，"疯眼汉进入霍格沃茨后，很可能把每个教师的办公室都搜了个遍。穆迪这个人，把他的黑魔法防御术课很当回事呢。他大概谁都不相信，在目睹了这么多事情之后，他这

though, he never killed if he could help it. Always brought people in alive where possible. He was tough, but he never descended to the level of the Death Eaters. Crouch, though ... he's a different matter ... is he really ill? If he is, why did he make the effort to drag himself up to Snape's office? And if he's not ... what's he up to? What was he doing at the World Cup that was so important he didn't turn up in the Top Box? What's he been doing while he should have been judging the Tournament?'

Sirius lapsed into silence, still staring at the cave wall. Buckbeak was ferreting around on the rocky floor, searching for bones he might have overlooked.

Finally, Sirius looked up at Ron. 'You say your brother's Crouch's personal assistant? Any chance you could ask him if he's seen Crouch lately?'

'I can try,' said Ron doubtfully. 'Better not make it sound like I reckon Crouch is up to anything dodgy, though. Percy loves Crouch.'

'And you might try and find out whether they've got any leads on Bertha Jorkins while you're at it,' said Sirius, gesturing at the second copy of the *Daily Prophet*.

'Bagman told me they hadn't,' said Harry.

'Yes, he's quoted in the article in there,' said Sirius, nodding at the paper. 'Blustering on about how bad Bertha's memory is. Well, maybe she's changed since I knew her, but the Bertha I knew wasn't forgetful at all – quite the reverse. She was a bit dim, but she had an excellent memory for gossip. It used to get her into a lot of trouble, she never knew when to keep her mouth shut. I can see her being a bit of a liability at the Ministry of Magic ... maybe that's why Bagman didn't bother to look for her for so long ...'

Sirius heaved an enormous sigh and rubbed his shadowed eyes. 'What's the time?'

Harry checked his watch, then remembered it hadn't been working since it had spent an hour in the lake.

'It's half past three,' said Hermione.

'You'd better get back to school,' Sirius said, getting to his feet. 'Now, listen ...' he looked particularly hard at Harry – 'I don't want you lot sneaking out of school to see me, all right? Just send notes to me here. I still want to hear about anything odd. But you're not to go leaving Hogwarts without

## 第27章 大脚板回来了

么做并不奇怪。不过,我要为穆迪说一句公道话,只要能够避免,他从不滥杀无辜。他总是尽可能地把人活捉回来。他很粗暴,但从不把自己降低到食死徒的档次上。而克劳奇……他就完全不同了……他真的病了吗?如果有病,为什么还挣扎着闯进斯内普的办公室?如果没病……他到底想干什么?在世界杯赛上,他到底在处理什么大不了的事情,竟然没到顶层包厢去观看比赛?当他应该为争霸赛做裁判时,他又在做什么呢?"

小天狼星陷入了沉思,眼睛仍然盯着岩壁。巴克比克在布满岩石的地上寻寻觅觅,看有没有漏掉的鸡骨头。

最后,小天狼星抬头望着罗恩。"你说你哥哥是克劳奇的私人助理?你能不能问问他最近有没有看见克劳奇?"

"可以试试,"罗恩迟疑地说,"不过,最好别让他听出我认为克劳奇在做一些见不得人的事。珀西爱上了克劳奇。"

"你还可以顺便打听一下,他们有没有查到伯莎·乔金斯的下落。"小天狼星说,指了指第二份《预言家日报》。

"巴格曼告诉我说还没有。"哈利说。

"是啊,文章里引了他的话,"小天狼星说着,冲报纸点点头,"他激动地说伯莎的记性多么糟糕。我以前认识伯莎,除非她后来完全变了。但在我的印象里,伯莎一点儿也不健忘——而是正好相反。她有点儿笨,但在聊八卦方面的记性堪称一流。这经常使她陷入一大堆麻烦;从来不知道什么时候应该闭嘴。我可以想象,她在魔法部里肯定是个讨厌的累赘……也许正因为这个,巴格曼才迟迟没有着手去找她……"

小天狼星长长地叹了口气,用手揉了揉带黑圈的眼睛。"什么时间了?"

哈利看了看表,随即想起那次他在湖里待了一小时后,他的表就不走了。

"三点半。"赫敏说。

"你们最好回学校去吧。"小天狼星说着站了起来,"现在听我说……"他特别认真地望着哈利,"我不要你们几个从学校里溜出来看我,懂吗?往这里给我送信就行了。我仍然想知道有没有什么异常情况。但你决不能未经允许就离开霍格沃茨。如果有人想对你下手,那可是

## CHAPTER TWENTY-SEVEN — Padfoot Returns

permission, it would be an ideal opportunity for someone to attack you.'

'No one's tried to attack me so far, except a dragon and a couple of Grindylows,' Harry said.

But Sirius scowled at him. 'I don't care … I'll breathe freely again when this Tournament's over, and that's not until June. And don't forget, if you're talking about me among yourselves, call me Snuffles, OK?'

He handed Harry the empty napkin and flask, and went to pat Buckbeak goodbye. 'I'll walk to the edge of the village with you,' said Sirius, 'see if I can scrounge another paper.'

He transformed into the great black dog before they left the cave, and they walked back down the mountainside with him, across the boulder-strewn ground, and back to the stile. Here he allowed each of them to pat him on the head, before turning and setting off at a run around the outskirts of the village.

Harry, Ron and Hermione made their way back into Hogsmeade, and up towards Hogwarts.

'Wonder if Percy knows all that stuff about Crouch?' Ron said, as they walked up the drive to the castle. 'But maybe he doesn't care … it'd probably just make him admire Crouch even more. Yeah, Percy loves rules. He'd just say Crouch was refusing to break them for his own son.'

'Percy would never throw any of his family to the Dementors,' said Hermione severely.

'I don't know,' said Ron. 'If he thought we were standing in the way of his career … Percy's really ambitious, you know …'

They walked up the stone steps into the Entrance Hall, where the delicious smells of dinner wafted towards them from the Great Hall.

'Poor old Snuffles,' said Ron, breathing deeply. 'He must really like you, Harry … imagine having to live off rats.'

## 第27章 大脚板回来了

个绝好的机会。"

"到现在为止还没有人想对我下手，除了一条火龙和几个格林迪洛。"哈利说。

但小天狼星不满地瞪着他："我不管你怎么说……等这场争霸赛结束，我才能完全放心，那要到六月份呢。别忘了，如果你们几个人谈起我，就叫我'伤风'，好吗？"

他把餐巾纸和空瓶子递给哈利，又过去拍拍巴克比克，同它告别。"我和你们一起走到村边，"小天狼星说，"看能不能再偷到一两份报纸。"

他摇身一变，又变成了那条大黑狗，然后大家一起离开了岩洞。他们和小天狼星一起下山，走过布满碎石的场地，回到了栅栏边。在这里，他让他们每个人都拍了拍他的脑袋，然后一转身，沿着村子外围跑走了。

哈利、罗恩和赫敏顺原路返回霍格莫德村，又朝霍格沃茨走去。

"不知道珀西是否了解克劳奇的那些事情，"他们走在通往城堡的车道上时，罗恩说道，"不过也许他并不在乎……这大概会使他更崇拜克劳奇的。没错，珀西酷爱规章制度。他会说克劳奇只是大义灭亲，不愿为儿子破坏章程。"

"珀西决不会把他的家人甩给摄魂怪。"赫敏严厉地说。

"这我可说不准。"罗恩说，"如果他认为我们妨碍了他的事业……珀西真是很有野心的，你们知道……"

他们走上石阶，进入门厅，迎面闻到礼堂里飘出晚餐诱人的香味。

"可怜的'伤风'，"罗恩深深地吸着气说，"他一定非常爱你，哈利……想象一下吧，靠吃老鼠过日子。"

## CHAPTER TWENTY-EIGHT

# The Madness of Mr Crouch

Harry, Ron and Hermione went up to the Owlery after breakfast on Sunday to send a letter to Percy, asking, as Sirius had suggested, whether he had seen Mr. Crouch lately. They used Hedwig, because it had been so long since she'd had a job. When they had watched her fly out of sight through the Owlery window, they proceeded down to the kitchen to give Dobby his new socks.

The house-elves gave them a very cheery welcome, bowing and curtseying and bustling around making tea again. Dobby was ecstatic about his present.

'Harry Potter is too good to Dobby!' he squeaked, wiping large tears out of his enormous eyes.

'You saved my life with that Gillyweed, Dobby, you really did,' said Harry.

'No chance of more of those éclairs, is there?' said Ron, who was looking around at the beaming and bowing house-elves.

'You've just had breakfast!' said Hermione irritably, but a great silver platter of éclairs was already zooming towards them, supported by four elves.

'We should get some stuff to send up to Snuffles,' Harry muttered.

'Good idea,' said Ron. 'Give Pig something to do. You couldn't give us a bit of extra food, could you?' he said to the surrounding elves, and they bowed delightedly and hurried off to get some more.

'Dobby, where's Winky?' said Hermione, who was looking around.

'Winky is over there by the fire, miss,' said Dobby quietly, his ears drooping slightly.

'Oh dear,' said Hermione, as she spotted Winky.

Harry looked over at the fireplace, too. Winky was sitting on the same stool as last time, but she had allowed herself to become so filthy that she was not immediately distinguishable from the smoke-blackened brick behind

# 第 28 章

# 克劳奇先生疯了

　　星期天吃过早饭，哈利、罗恩和赫敏来到猫头鹰棚屋。他们要按小天狼星的建议给珀西送一封信，问他最近有没有看见克劳奇先生。他们选用了海德薇，因为它已经失业了很长时间。他们透过棚屋的窗户望着它渐渐远去，下楼来到厨房，把新买的袜子送给多比。

　　家养小精灵们兴高采烈地欢迎了他们，又是鞠躬，又是行屈膝礼，还手忙脚乱地为他们准备茶点。多比看到礼物欣喜若狂。

　　"哈利·波特对多比太好了！"他尖声说，擦去大眼睛里冒出的大滴泪珠。

　　"你用鳃囊草救了我的命，多比，真的。"哈利说。

　　"还有那种手指饼吗？"罗恩看着周围笑容满面、连连鞠躬的家养小精灵们，问道。

　　"你刚吃过早饭！"赫敏恼火地说。然而一只装满手指饼的大银盘，已经由四个小精灵托着，旋风般送到了他们面前。

　　"我们多要一些吃的，拿去送给'伤风'。"哈利小声说道。

　　"好主意。"罗恩说，"让小猪有点事情做做。你们能不能再给我们一些吃的东西？"他问周围的小精灵。他们高兴地鞠着躬，马不停蹄地去取食物了。

　　"多比，闪闪呢？"赫敏看看四周，问道。

　　"闪闪在炉火边呢，小姐。"多比轻声说，耳朵微微耷拉着。

　　"哦，天哪。"赫敏看见闪闪，不由得惊叹道。

　　哈利也朝壁炉那边望去。闪闪还是坐在上次那张小凳子上，但她把自己弄得肮脏不堪，几乎跟她身后被烟熏黑的砖墙混为一体，很难

## CHAPTER TWENTY-EIGHT — The Madness of Mr Crouch

her. Her clothes were ragged and unwashed. She was clutching a bottle of Butterbeer and swaying slightly on her stool, staring into the fire. As they watched her, she gave an enormous hiccough.

'Winky is getting through six bottles a day now,' Dobby whispered to Harry.

'Well, it's not strong, that stuff,' Harry said.

But Dobby shook his head. "Tis strong for a house-elf, sir,' he said.

Winky hiccoughed again. The elves who had brought the éclairs gave her disapproving looks as they returned to work.

'Winky is pining, Harry Potter,' Dobby whispered sadly. 'Winky wants to go home. Winky still thinks Mr Crouch is her master, sir, and nothing Dobby says will persuade her that Professor Dumbledore is her master now.'

'Hey, Winky,' said Harry, struck by a sudden inspiration, walking over and bending down to speak to her, 'you don't know what Mr Crouch might be up to, do you? Because he's stopped turning up to judge the Triwizard Tournament.'

Winky's eyes flickered. Her enormous pupils focused on Harry. She swayed slightly again and then said, 'M-master is stopped – *hic* – coming?'

'Yeah,' said Harry, 'we haven't seen him since the first task. The *Daily Prophet's* saying he's ill.'

Winky swayed some more, staring blurrily at Harry. 'Master – *hic* – ill?'

Her bottom lip began to tremble.

'But we're not sure if that's true,' said Hermione quickly.

'Master is needing his – *hic* – Winky!' whimpered the elf. 'Master cannot – *hic* – manage – *hic* – all by himself ...'

'Other people manage to do their own housework, you know, Winky,' said Hermione severely.

'Winky – *hic* – is not only – *hic* – doing housework for Mr Crouch!' Winky squeaked indignantly, swaying worse than ever and slopping Butterbeer down her already heavily stained blouse. 'Master is – *hic* – trusting Winky with – *hic* – the most important – *hic* – the most secret –'

'What?' said Harry.

But Winky shook her head very hard, spilling more Butterbeer down herself.

'Winky keeps – *hic* – her master's secrets,' she said mutinously, swaying

## 第28章 克劳奇先生疯了

分辨出来。她的衣服没有洗过，又脏又破。她手里抓着一瓶黄油啤酒，身体在凳子上微微摇晃，眼睛直勾勾地望着炉火。就在他们注视着她时，她重重地打了个酒嗝。

"闪闪现在每天要灌下去六瓶。"多比小声告诉哈利。

"噢，这种啤酒劲儿不大。"哈利说。

多比却摇了摇头。"对家养小精灵来说相当厉害呢，先生。"他说。

闪闪又打了个嗝。端手指饼来的那几个小精灵不满地白了她一眼，又回去干活了。

"闪闪现在很憔悴，哈利·波特，"多比忧伤地小声说，"闪闪想回家。闪闪仍然认为克劳奇先生是她的主人，先生，多比反复跟她说，她现在的主人是邓布利多，可她就是听不进去。"

"嘿，闪闪，"哈利突然有了一个主意，走到她身边，弯下身子，"你知不知道克劳奇先生可能在做什么？他不来给三强争霸赛做裁判了。"

闪闪的眼睛闪动着，两只巨大的瞳孔盯住了哈利，身体又微微摇晃起来，她说："主——主人不——呃——不来了？"

"是啊，"哈利说，"从第一个项目结束后，我们就没有看见他。《预言家日报》上说他病了。"

闪闪又摇晃了几下，视线模糊地瞪着哈利。"主人——呃——病了？"她的下嘴唇哆嗦起来。

"我们还不能肯定这是不是真的。"赫敏赶紧说道。

"主人现在需要他的——呃——闪闪！"小精灵抽抽搭搭地说，"主人一个人——呃——可怎么——呃——怎么对付得了……"

"他们的家务事他们自己也能做的，闪闪。"赫敏严肃地说。

"闪闪——呃——不单单——呃——为克劳奇先生做家务事！"闪闪气愤地尖声说，身体摇晃得更厉害了，还把黄油啤酒洒在她本来就污渍斑斑的衬衫上，"主人——呃——相信闪闪，把最重要——呃——最秘密的事——都告诉了闪闪——"

"什么事？"哈利说。

但闪闪使劲摇了摇头，又把一些啤酒洒在身上。

"闪闪不能——呃——泄露主人的秘密。"她抗拒地说道，身子剧

## CHAPTER TWENTY-EIGHT    The Madness of Mr Crouch

very heavily now, frowning up at Harry with her eyes crossed. 'You is – *hic* – nosing, you is.'

'Winky must not talk like that to Harry Potter!' said Dobby angrily. 'Harry Potter is brave and noble and Harry Potter is not nosy!'

'He is nosing – *hic* – into my master's – *hic* – private and secret – *hic* – Winky is a good house-elf – *hic* – Winky keeps her silence – *hic* – people trying to – *hic* – pry and poke – *hic* –' Winky's eyelids drooped and suddenly, without warning, she slid off her stool onto the hearth, snoring loudly. The empty bottle of Butterbeer rolled away across the stone-flagged floor.

Half a dozen house-elves came hurrying forward, looking disgusted. One of them picked up the bottle, the others covered Winky with a large checked tablecloth and tucked the ends in neatly, hiding her from view.

'We is sorry you had to see that, sirs and miss!' squeaked a nearby elf, shaking his head and looking very ashamed. 'We is hoping you will not judge us all by Winky, sirs and miss!'

'She's unhappy!' said Hermione, exasperated. 'Why don't you try and cheer her up instead of covering her up?'

'Begging your pardon, miss,' said the house-elf, bowing deeply again, 'but house-elves has no right to be unhappy when there is work to be done and masters to be served.'

'Oh, for heaven's sake!' said Hermione angrily. 'Listen to me, all of you! You've got just as much right as wizards to be unhappy! You've got the right to wages and holidays and proper clothes, you don't have to do everything you're told – look at Dobby!'

'Miss will please keep Dobby out of this,' Dobby mumbled, looking scared. The cheery smiles had vanished from the faces of the house-elves around the kitchen. They were suddenly looking at Hermione as though she was mad and dangerous.

'We has your extra food!' squeaked an elf at Harry's elbow, and he shoved a large ham, a dozen cakes and some fruit into Harry's arms. 'Goodbye!'

The house-elves crowded around Harry, Ron and Hermione, and began shunting them out of the kitchen, many little hands pushing in the smalls of their backs.

'Thank you for the socks, Harry Potter!' Dobby called miserably from the

## 第28章 克劳奇先生疯了

烈地摇晃，皱着眉头，两眼失神地瞪着哈利，"你——呃——你在多管闲事。"

"闪闪不许这样跟哈利·波特说话！"多比生气地说，"哈利·波特勇敢而高尚，哈利·波特从不多管闲事！"

"他在探听——呃——我主人的——呃——秘密的私事——呃——闪闪是个好家养小精灵——呃——闪闪知道保持沉默——呃——人们千方百计地——呃——打听刺探——呃——"闪闪的眼皮耷拉下来，她突然从凳子上滑到壁炉前的地毯上，响亮地打起呼噜来。喝空的黄油啤酒瓶骨碌碌滚过石块铺的地面。

六七个家养小精灵匆匆赶过来，脸上是一副厌恶的表情。其中一个捡起酒瓶，其他人用一块方格子的大桌布盖住闪闪，并仔细掖好四角，不让别人看见她。

"让你们看到这个，真是对不起，先生小姐！"近旁的一个小精灵尖声说，一边摇着头，显得十分羞愧，"真希望你们不要根据闪闪来评判我们大家，先生小姐！"

"她不快活！"赫敏焦虑地说，"你们为什么不想办法让她快活起来，却反而把她盖住呢？"

"对不起，小姐，"那个家养小精灵说，又深深鞠了一躬，"可是当有活儿要干、有主人要伺候时，家养小精灵是没有权利不快活的。"

"哦，天哪！"赫敏生气地喊道，"你们都听我说吧！你们和巫师一样，完全有权利不快活！你们有权利拿工钱、休假、穿体面的衣服，用不着事事都听别人使唤——看看多比吧！"

"请小姐不要把多比牵扯进去。"多比含糊地说，看上去非常害怕。厨房里那些家养小精灵脸上欢快的笑容消失了。他们突然用异样的眼神望着赫敏，似乎觉得她是疯狂而危险的。

"吃的东西给你们拿来了！"哈利胳膊肘边的一个小精灵尖声说，然后把一大块火腿、十几块蛋糕和几样水果塞进哈利怀里，"再见！"

家养小精灵们围在哈利、罗恩和赫敏周围，许多只小手推着他们的腰背部，要把他们赶出厨房。

"谢谢你送我的袜子，哈利·波特！"多比在壁炉地毯上可怜巴巴

## CHAPTER TWENTY-EIGHT — The Madness of Mr Crouch

hearth, where he was standing next to the lumpy tablecloth that was Winky.

'You couldn't keep your mouth shut, could you, Hermione?' said Ron angrily, as the kitchen door slammed shut behind them. 'They won't want us visiting them now! We could've tried to get more stuff out of Winky about Crouch!'

'Oh, as if you care about that!' scoffed Hermione. 'You only like coming down here for the food!'

It was an irritable sort of day after that. Harry got so tired of Ron and Hermione sniping at each other over their homework in the common room that he took Sirius' food up to the Owlery that evening on his own.

Pigwidgeon was much too small to carry an entire ham up to the mountain by himself, so Harry enlisted the help of two school screech owls as well. When they had set off into the dusk, looking extremely odd carrying the large package between them, Harry leaned on the window-sill, looking out at the grounds, at the dark, rustling treetops of the Forbidden Forest, and the rippling sails of the Durmstrang ship. An eagle owl flew through the coil of smoke rising from Hagrid's chimney; it soared towards the castle, around the Owlery and out of sight. Looking down, Harry saw Hagrid digging energetically in front of his cabin. Harry wondered what he was doing; it looked as though he was making a new vegetable patch. As he watched, Madame Maxime emerged from the Beauxbatons carriage and walked over to Hagrid. She appeared to be trying to engage him in conversation. Hagrid leant upon his spade, but did not seem keen to prolong their talk, because Madame Maxime returned to the carriage shortly afterwards.

Unwilling to go back to Gryffindor Tower and listen to Ron and Hermione snarling at each other, Harry watched Hagrid digging until the darkness swallowed him, and the owls around Harry began to awake, swooshing past him, into the night.

By breakfast next day, Ron and Hermione's bad moods had burnt out, and to Harry's relief, Ron's dark predictions that the house-elves would send substandard food up to the Gryffindor table because Hermione had insulted them proved false; the bacon, eggs and kippers were quite as good as usual.

When the post owls arrived, Hermione looked up eagerly; she seemed to be expecting something.

'Percy won't've had time to answer yet,' said Ron. 'We only sent Hedwig yesterday.'

## 第28章　克劳奇先生疯了

地叫道，他站在被桌布盖着的闪闪旁边。

"你就不能把嘴巴闭上吗，赫敏？"厨房的门重重地在他们身后关上后，罗恩气冲冲地说，"现在他们再也不愿意我们到这儿来了！我们没法从闪闪嘴里套出克劳奇的更多情况了！"

"得了吧，你才不关心这个呢！"赫敏讥笑道，"你只是想下来捞点儿吃的！"

从这时起，那天就一直令人烦躁。晚上，罗恩和赫敏在公共休息室做家庭作业时唇枪舌剑地吵个不停，哈利厌烦透了，便一个人带着给小天狼星的食物来到猫头鹰棚屋。

小猪个头太小了，没法独自驮着一整块火腿到山里，哈利就又选了两只学校的长耳猫头鹰来帮忙。它们在暮色中飞远，中间抬着那个大包裹，显得怪模怪样的。哈利靠在窗台上，望着外面的场地，望着禁林里黑乎乎的、沙沙作响的树梢，和德姆斯特朗大船那随风飘动的船帆。一只雕枭飞过从海格小屋烟囱冒出的袅袅青烟，朝城堡飞来，然后绕过猫头鹰棚屋消失了。哈利一低头，看见海格在他的小屋前劲头十足地挖土。哈利不明白他在做什么，看上去是在开垦一片地来种菜。就在这时，马克西姆女士从布斯巴顿的马车里出来，朝海格走去。看样子她想跟海格搭话。海格挂着铲子，似乎不愿意多谈，因为马克西姆女士很快就回马车去了。

哈利不想回格兰芬多塔楼去听罗恩和赫敏互相叫骂，便默默地望着海格挖土，直到夜色吞没了海格的身影。哈利周围的猫头鹰一只只地醒来，嗖嗖地从他耳边飞向夜空。

第二天吃早饭时，罗恩和赫敏的心情终于多云转晴。罗恩曾悲观地预言，由于赫敏侮辱了家养小精灵，他们给格兰芬多桌子送的食物会大打折扣，现在证明他的预言落空了。这使哈利松了口气。那些熏咸肉、鸡蛋和腌鲱鱼和往常一样丰盛鲜美。

送信的猫头鹰飞来了，赫敏急切地抬起头。她似乎有所期待。

"珀西还来不及回信呢，"罗恩说，"我们昨天刚派海德薇给他送的信。"

## CHAPTER TWENTY-EIGHT    The Madness of Mr Crouch

'No, it's not that,' said Hermione. 'I've taken out a new subscription to the *Daily Prophet*, I'm getting sick of finding everything out from the Slytherins.'

'Good thinking!' said Harry, also looking up at the owls. 'Hey, Hermione, I think you're in luck –'

A grey owl was soaring down towards Hermione.

'It hasn't got a newspaper, though,' she said, looking disappointed. 'It's –'

But to her bewilderment, the grey owl landed in front of her plate, closely followed by four barn owls, a brown owl and a tawny.

'How many subscriptions did you take out?' said Harry, seizing Hermione's goblet before it was knocked over by the cluster of owls, all of whom were jostling close to her, trying to deliver their own letter first.

'What on earth –?' Hermione said, taking the letter from the grey owl, opening it and starting to read. 'Oh, really!' she spluttered, going rather red.

'What's up?' said Ron.

'It's – oh, how ridiculous –' She thrust the letter at Harry, who saw that it was not handwritten, but composed from pasted letters that seemed to have been cut out of the *Daily Prophet*.

> YoU are a WickEd giRL.
> HaRRy PottEr deSErveS BetteR.
> gO Back wherE yoU
> CaME from mUggle.

'They're all like it!' said Hermione desperately, opening one letter after another. '"*Harry Potter can do much better than the likes of you …*" "*You deserve to be boiled in frog-spawn …*" Ouch!'

She had opened the last envelope, and yellowish green liquid smelling strongly of petrol gushed over her hands, which began to erupt in large yellow boils.

'Undiluted Bubotuber pus!' said Ron, picking up the envelope gingerly and sniffing it.

'Ow!' said Hermione, tears starting in her eyes as she tried to rub it off her hands with a napkin, but her fingers were now so thickly covered in painful sores that it looked as though she was wearing a pair of thick, knobbly gloves.

'You'd better get up to the hospital wing,' said Harry, as the owls around

## 第28章　克劳奇先生疯了

"不，不是那个，"赫敏说，"我订了一份《预言家日报》。现在什么事情都从斯莱特林们那里知道，我烦透了。"

"好主意！"哈利说，也抬头望着那些猫头鹰，"嘿，赫敏，我觉得你运气不错——"

一只灰色猫头鹰朝赫敏飞来。

"可它并没有捎来报纸呀。"赫敏说，显得有些失望，"它——"

没想到灰色猫头鹰在她面前的盘子上落定后，紧接着又飞来四只谷仓猫头鹰、一只棕褐色猫头鹰和一只灰林猫头鹰。

"你究竟发出了多少张订单？"哈利说，一把抓过赫敏的高脚杯，免得被这一大群猫头鹰打翻。它们都争先恐后地往前挤，想第一个把信送到她手里。

"见鬼，到底怎么——"赫敏说着，接过灰色猫头鹰送来的信，打开后看了起来，"哎呀，哎呀！"她气急败坏地说，脸色变得通红。

"怎么回事？"罗恩说。

"这——这简直太荒唐了——"她把信塞给哈利，哈利看到那不是手写的笔迹，而仿佛是用《预言家日报》上剪下来的字母拼成的。

**你**是个**坏女孩**。哈利·波特**应该**得到更好的姑娘。滚回你的**麻瓜**老家去吧。

"都是这类的信！"赫敏把信一封封拆开，绝望地说，"哈利·波特应该得到比你这种货色强百倍的女孩……应该把你放在蛙卵里煮一煮……哎哟！"

她刚打开最后一个信封，一股黄绿色的液体喷到她的双手上，发出刺鼻的汽油味，她手上立刻冒出黄黄的大水泡。

"没经稀释的巴波块茎脓液！"罗恩说。他小心地拿起信封，闻了闻。

"哎哟！"赫敏叫道，她拿起一块餐巾擦去手上的脓液时，眼泪就已经流了出来。但手指上已布满厚厚的、疼痛难忍的疮疤，看上去就像戴着一双疙里疙瘩的厚手套。

"你最好赶紧去校医院，"哈利说，这时赫敏周围的猫头鹰一只只

## CHAPTER TWENTY-EIGHT    The Madness of Mr Crouch

Hermione took flight, 'we'll tell Professor Sprout where you've gone ...'

'I warned her!' said Ron, as Hermione hurried out of the Great Hall, cradling her hands. 'I warned her not to annoy Rita Skeeter! Look at this one ...' He read out one of the letters Hermione had left behind, '"*I read in* Witch Weekly *about how you are playing Harry Potter false and that boy has had enough hardship and I will be sending you a curse by next post as soon as I can find a big enough envelope.*" Blimey, she'd better watch out for herself.'

Hermione didn't turn up for Herbology. As Harry and Ron left the greenhouse for their Care of Magical Creatures class, they saw Malfoy, Crabbe and Goyle descending the stone steps from the castle. Pansy Parkinson was whispering and giggling behind them with her gang of Slytherin girls. Catching sight of Harry, Pansy called, 'Potter, have you split up with your girlfriend? Why was she so upset at breakfast?'

Harry ignored her; he didn't want to give her the satisfaction of knowing how much trouble the *Witch Weekly* article had caused.

Hagrid, who had told them last lesson that they had finished with unicorns, was waiting for them outside his cabin with a fresh supply of open crates at his feet. Harry's heart sank at the sight of the crates – surely not another Skrewt hatching? – but when he got near enough to see inside, he found himself looking at a number of fluffy black creatures with long snouts. Their front paws were curiously flat, like spades, and they were blinking up at the class, looking politely puzzled at all the attention.

'These're Nifflers,' said Hagrid, when the class had gathered around. 'Yeh find 'em down mines mostly. They like sparkly stuff ... there yeh go, look.'

One of the Nifflers had suddenly leapt up and attempted to bite Pansy Parkinson's watch off her wrist. She shrieked and jumped backwards.

'Useful little treasure detectors,' said Hagrid happily. 'Thought we'd have some fun with 'em today. See over there?' He pointed at the large patch of freshly turned earth Harry had watched him digging from the Owlery window. 'I've buried some gold coins. I've got a prize fer whoever picks the Niffler that digs up most. Jus' take off all yer valuables, an' choose a Niffler an' get ready ter set 'em loose.'

Harry took off his watch, which he was only wearing out of habit, as it didn't work any more, and stuffed it in his pocket. Then he picked up a Niffler. It put its long snout in Harry's ear and sniffed enthusiastically. It was

## 第28章 克劳奇先生疯了

地飞走了,"我们会跟斯普劳特教授说明情况的……"

"我警告过她!"赫敏捂住双手匆匆离开礼堂后,罗恩说道,"我警告过她,不要招惹丽塔·斯基特!看看这封吧……"他大声念着赫敏留下的一封信,"我在《女巫周刊》上读到你在玩弄哈利·波特的感情,那个男孩已经受了那么多苦,等着吧,我只要找到一个大信封,下次就给你寄一个咒语去。天哪,她可真得当心点儿。"

赫敏没有来上草药课。当哈利、罗恩离开温室,去上保护神奇动物课时,看见马尔福、克拉布和高尔正走下城堡的石阶。潘西·帕金森跟在他们后面,和那帮斯莱特林女生交头接耳、咯咯窃笑。潘西一看见哈利,就大声问道:"波特,你和女朋友闹翻了吗?早饭时她为什么气成那样?"

哈利没有理她。他不想让潘西知道《女巫周刊》的那篇文章引起了多大麻烦,免得她幸灾乐祸,得意忘形。

海格上节课就告诉他们,独角兽的知识已经讲完,此刻他站在小屋外面等候同学们,脚边放着一些他们以前没见过的敞开的纸板箱。哈利一看见纸板箱,心就往下一沉——该不是又孵出了一窝炸尾螺吧?——不过当他走近了往箱子里一看,才发现里面是许多毛茸茸的黑家伙,生着长长的鼻子,前爪平平的,像铲子一样,十分奇特。它们抬头朝全班同学眨着眼睛,面对这么多人的注意,似乎感到有些困惑。

"这些是嗅嗅,"海格等同学们都聚拢了,说道,"一般在矿井下可以见到。它们喜欢闪闪发亮的东西……喏,快看。"

一只嗅嗅突然一跃而起,想咬掉潘西·帕金森手腕上的手表。潘西尖叫着后退。

"很有用的小探宝器,"海格高兴地说,"今天我们可以跟它们玩个痛快了。看见那儿了吗?"他指着那一大片新翻开的土地,就是哈利在猫头鹰棚屋窗口看见他挖掘的地方,"我埋了些金币。谁挑的嗅嗅挖出金币最多,我就给谁发奖。你们把身上值钱的东西都拿掉,然后挑选一只嗅嗅,做好准备,把它们放开。"

哈利把手表摘下,塞进口袋里,手表已经停了,他只是出于习惯才戴着。然后他挑了一只嗅嗅。它把长鼻子伸进哈利的耳朵,起劲地

## CHAPTER TWENTY-EIGHT    The Madness of Mr Crouch

really quite cuddly.'

'Hang on,' said Hagrid, looking down into the crate, 'there's a spare Niffler here ... who's missin'? Where's Hermione?'

'She had to go to the hospital wing,' said Ron.

'We'll explain later,' Harry muttered; Pansy Parkinson was listening.

It was easily the most fun they had ever had in Care of Magical Creatures. The Nifflers dived in and out of the patch of earth as though it was water, each scurrying back to the student who had released it and spitting gold into their hands. Ron's was particularly efficient; it had soon filled his lap with coins.

'Can you buy these as pets, Hagrid?' he asked excitedly, as his Niffler dived back into the soil, splattering his robes.

'Yer mum wouldn' be happy, Ron,' said Hagrid, grinning, 'they wreck houses, Nifflers. I reckon they've nearly got the lot now,' he added, pacing around the patch of earth, while the Nifflers continued to dive. 'I on'y buried a hundred coins. Oh, there y'are, Hermione!'

Hermione was walking towards them across the lawn. Her hands were very heavily bandaged and she looked miserable. Pansy Parkinson was watching her beadily.

'Well, let's check how yeh've done!' said Hagrid. 'Count yer coins! An' there's no point tryin' ter steal any, Goyle,' he added, his beetle-black eyes narrowed. 'It's leprechaun gold. Vanishes after a few hours.'

Goyle emptied his pockets, looking extremely sulky. It turned out that Ron's Niffler had been most successful, so Hagrid gave him an enormous slab of Honeydukes chocolate for a prize. The bell rang across the grounds for lunch; the rest of the class set off back to the castle, but Harry, Ron and Hermione stayed behind to help Hagrid put the Nifflers back in their boxes. Harry noticed Madame Maxime watching them out of her carriage window.

'What yeh done ter your hands, Hermione?' said Hagrid, looking concerned.

Hermione told him about the hate mail she had received that morning, and the envelope full of Bubotuber pus.

'Aaah, don' worry,' said Hagrid gently, looking down at her. 'I got some o' those letters an' all, after Rita Skeeter wrote abou' me mum. "Yeh're a monster an' yeh should be put down." "Yer mother killed innocent people

嗅着。这小东西，跟人倒挺亲热的。

"慢着，"海格说，低头望着箱子里面，"这里还剩下一只嗅嗅……谁没有来？怎么不见赫敏？"

"她不得不去医院了。"罗恩说。

"我们回头再跟你解释。"哈利低声说。潘西·帕金森正竖着耳朵听呢。

这真是他们上过的最好玩的一节保护神奇动物课。嗅嗅在那片地里钻进钻出，就像在水里一样，每一只都急匆匆地赶到放开它的那个同学身边，把金币吐进他手里。罗恩的收获特别多，大腿上很快就堆满了金币。

"能把它们买下来作为宠物吗，海格？"罗恩兴奋地问，这时他的嗅嗅又一头扎进土里，把他的袍子都溅脏了。

"你妈妈不会高兴的，罗恩。"海格微笑着说，"嗅嗅这种动物会把房子毁坏的。好了，我看它们干得差不多了。"他补充道，在那片地上走来走去，嗅嗅们还在土里钻出钻进，"我只埋了一百块金币。哦，你来了，赫敏！"

赫敏穿过草坪朝他们走来。她两只手上都包着厚厚的绷带，显得怪可怜的。潘西·帕金森目光很锐利地望着她。

"好了，我来看看你们干得怎么样！"海格说，"数数你们的金币！想偷走是没有用的，高尔，"他说着，眯起亮晶晶的黑眼睛，"这是爱尔兰小矮妖的金币，几个小时之后就消失了。"

高尔掏出口袋里的金币，一副闷闷不乐的样子。最后的结果是罗恩的嗅嗅一举夺魁，海格给了罗恩一大块蜂蜜公爵的巧克力作为奖励。午饭的铃声从场地那头传来，其他同学都动身返回城堡了，哈利、罗恩和赫敏留在后面，帮海格把嗅嗅装回纸板箱里。哈利发现马克西姆女士正从马车的窗口注视着他们。

"你的两只手怎么啦，赫敏？"海格非常关心地问。

赫敏跟他说了早上收到恶意信件的事，还有那个装满巴波块茎脓液的信封。

"啊，不要担心。"海格低头望着她，温和地说，"自从丽塔·斯基特在文章里写到我妈妈后，我也收到过几封这样的信。你是个怪物，

## CHAPTER TWENTY-EIGHT    The Madness of Mr Crouch

an' if you had any decency you'd jump in a lake."'

'No!' said Hermione, looking shocked.

'Yeah,' said Hagrid, heaving the Niffler crates over by his cabin wall. 'They're jus' nutters, Hermione. Don' open 'em if yeh get any more. Chuck 'em straigh' in the fire.'

'You missed a really good lesson,' Harry told Hermione, as they headed back towards the castle. 'They're good, Nifflers, aren't they, Ron?'

Ron, however, was frowning at the chocolate Hagrid had given him. He looked thoroughly put out about something.

'What's the matter?' said Harry. 'Wrong flavour?'

'No,' said Ron shortly. 'Why didn't you tell me about the gold?'

'What gold?' said Harry.

'The gold I gave you at the Quidditch World Cup,' said Ron. 'The leprechaun gold I gave you for my Omnioculars. In the Top Box. Why didn't you tell me it disappeared?'

Harry had to think for a moment before he realised what Ron was talking about.

'Oh ...' he said, the memory coming back to him at last. 'I dunno ... I never noticed it had gone. I was more worried about my wand, wasn't I?'

They climbed the steps into the Entrance Hall and went into the Great Hall for lunch.

'Must be nice,' Ron said abruptly, when they had sat down and started serving themselves roast beef and Yorkshire puddings. 'To have so much money you don't notice if a pocketful of Galleons goes missing.'

'Listen, I had other stuff on my mind that night!' said Harry impatiently. 'We all did, remember?'

'I didn't know leprechaun gold vanishes,' Ron muttered. 'I thought I was paying you back. You shouldn't've given me that Chudley Cannon hat for Christmas.'

'Forget it, all right?' said Harry.

Ron speared a roast potato on the end of his fork, glaring at it. Then he said, 'I hate being poor.'

Harry and Hermione looked at each other. Neither of them really knew what to say.

'It's rubbish,' said Ron, still glaring down at his potato. 'I don't blame Fred

## 第28章 克劳奇先生疯了

应该把你开除。你母亲滥杀无辜，如果你还知道廉耻，就应该跳湖自杀。"

"哦，天哪！"赫敏显得很震惊。

"是啊，"海格说，一边把装嗅嗅的纸板箱搬到小屋的墙根边，"他们都是些疯子，赫敏。以后再收到这样的信，不要打开。把它们直接扔进火里。"

"你错过了一堂特别有趣的课，"他们返回城堡时，哈利对赫敏说，"这些嗅嗅可好玩了，是不是，罗恩？"

可是罗恩皱着眉头，瞪着海格给他的巧克力。他好像为什么事感到心烦意乱。

"怎么回事？"哈利问，"味道不对？"

"不是，"罗恩不耐烦地说，"你为什么不把金币的事告诉我？"

"什么金币？"哈利问。

"我在世界杯赛上给你的金币，"罗恩说，"那些爱尔兰小矮妖的金币，我用来换我的全景望远镜的。在顶层包厢上。它们后来消失了，你为什么不告诉我？"

哈利想了一会儿，才明白罗恩在说什么。

"哦……"他说，终于想起了那段往事，"我不知道……我压根儿就没注意到它们不见了。我一心只挂念着我的魔杖，不是吗？"

他们走上通往门厅的台阶，走进礼堂去吃午饭。

"这感觉一定很妙，"就在他们坐下，开始盛烤牛肉和约克郡布丁时，罗恩突然冒出一句，"钱多得数不清，连一口袋加隆不见了都没有察觉。"

"听着，那天晚上我想着别的事情！"哈利不耐烦地说，"当时我们脑子都很乱，记得吗？"

"我不知道爱尔兰小矮妖的金币会消失，"罗恩喃喃地说，"我以为已经把钱还清了。你圣诞节不应该送给我那顶查德里火炮队的帽子。"

"忘了这件事吧，好吗？"哈利说。

罗恩用叉子尖戳起一个烤土豆，愁闷地瞪着它，然后说道："我真讨厌贫穷的滋味。"

哈利和赫敏对视了一下，都不知道该说什么好。

"这感觉糟透了，"罗恩说，仍然瞪着那个土豆，"弗雷德和乔治想

## CHAPTER TWENTY-EIGHT — The Madness of Mr Crouch

and George for trying to make some extra money. Wish I could. Wish I had a Niffler.'

'Well, we know what to get you next Christmas,' said Hermione brightly. Then, when Ron continued to look gloomy, she said, 'Come on, Ron, it could be worse. At least your fingers aren't full of pus.' Hermione was having a lot of difficulty managing her knife and fork, her fingers were so stiff and swollen. 'I *hate* that Skeeter woman!' she burst out savagely. 'I'll get her back for this if it's the last thing I do!'

Hate mail continued to arrive for Hermione over the following week, and although she followed Hagrid's advice and stopped opening it, several of her ill-wishers sent Howlers, which exploded at the Gryffindor table and shrieked insults at her for the whole Hall to hear. Even those people who didn't read *Witch Weekly* knew all about the supposed Harry–Krum–Hermione triangle now. Harry was getting sick of telling people that Hermione wasn't his girlfriend.

'It'll die down, though,' he told Hermione, 'if we just ignore it ... people got bored with that stuff she wrote about me last time –'

'I want to know how she's listening into private conversations when she's supposed to be banned from the grounds!' said Hermione angrily.

Hermione hung back in their next Defence Against the Dark Arts lesson to ask Professor Moody something. The rest of the class were very eager to leave; Moody had given them such a rigorous test of hex-deflection that many of them were nursing small injuries. Harry had such a bad case of Twitchy Ears, he had to hold his hands clamped over them as he walked away from the class.

'Well, Rita's definitely not using an Invisibility Cloak!' Hermione panted five minutes later, catching up with Harry and Ron in the Entrance Hall and pulling Harry's hand away from one of his wiggling ears so that he could hear. 'Moody says he didn't see her anywhere near the judges' table at the second task, or anywhere near the lake!'

'Hermione, is there any point telling you to drop this?' said Ron.

'No!' said Hermione stubbornly. 'I want to know how she heard me talking to Viktor! *And* how she found out about Hagrid's mum!'

'Maybe she had you bugged,' said Harry.

## 第28章 克劳奇先生疯了

多赚几个钱,我觉得这没什么错。真希望我也能那样。真希望我有一只嗅嗅。"

"好了,我们知道明年圣诞节送你什么了。"赫敏愉快地说,她看见罗恩还是闷闷不乐,又说道,"行了,罗恩,这不是最糟糕的。至少你的手指上没有沾满脓液。"赫敏用起刀叉来十分费劲,她的手指全肿了,僵僵的不听使唤,"我真恨斯基特那个女人!"她突然恶狠狠地大声说,"即使我只剩最后一口气,也要让她付出代价!"

在接下来的一个星期,赫敏仍然不断收到恶意信件,尽管她听从了海格的忠告,不再打开它们,但有些对她心存恶意的人寄来了吼叫信,这些信在格兰芬多的桌子上炸开,尖声吼出侮辱她的话,全礼堂的人都能听见。就连那些不看《女巫周刊》的人,也都知道哈利、克鲁姆、赫敏的所谓三角恋关系了。哈利反复跟人解释赫敏不是他的女朋友,他觉得厌烦透了。

"慢慢会平息的,"他对赫敏说,"只要我们不理它……上次她写的那篇关于我的文章,人们就慢慢腻烦了——"

"我想知道,她本来是被禁止进入场地的,却怎么能偷听到别人私下里的谈话!"赫敏气愤地说。

在他们的下一节黑魔法防御术课上,赫敏留下来向穆迪教授请教几个问题。班上其他同学都迫不及待地离开了。穆迪在课上毫不留情地测试同学们使咒语转向的本领,许多人都受了轻伤。哈利中了很厉害的耳朵抽筋咒,离开教室时不得不用双手捂住耳朵。

"看来,丽塔肯定没有使用隐形衣!"五分钟后,赫敏在门厅里追上哈利和罗恩,气喘吁吁地说,她还把哈利的手从一只抽动的耳朵上拉开,好让哈利能听见她说话,"穆迪说,在进行第二个项目时,他没有在裁判桌或湖边什么地方看见丽塔!"

"赫敏,我叫你别想这件事了,你怎么就是不听呢?"罗恩说。

"就不听!"赫敏固执地说,"我想知道她怎么能听见我跟威克多尔的谈话!还有她怎么会打听到海格母亲的事!"

"也许她在你身上装了窃听器。"哈利说。

## CHAPTER TWENTY-EIGHT  The Madness of Mr Crouch

'Bugged?' said Ron blankly. 'What ... put fleas on her or something?'

Harry started explaining about hidden microphones and recording equipment.

Ron was fascinated, but Hermione interrupted them. 'Aren't you two ever going to read *Hogwarts: A History*?'

'What's the point?' said Ron. 'You know it off by heart, we can just ask you.'

'All those substitutes for magic Muggles use – electricity, and computers and radar, and all those things – they all go haywire around Hogwarts, there's too much magic in the air. No, Rita's using magic to eavesdrop, she must be ... if I could just find out what it is ... ooh, if it's illegal, I'll have her ...'

'Haven't we got enough to worry about?' Ron asked her. 'Do we have to start a vendetta against Rita Skeeter as well?'

'I'm not asking you to help!' Hermione snapped. 'I'll do it on my own!'

She marched back up the marble staircase without a backward glance. Harry was quite sure she was going to the library.

'What's the betting she comes back with a box of *I Hate Rita Skeeter* badges?' said Ron.

Hermione, however, did not ask Harry and Ron to help her pursue vengeance against Rita Skeeter, for which they were both grateful, because their workload was mounting ever higher in the run-up to the Easter holidays. Harry frankly marvelled at the fact that Hermione could research magical methods of eavesdropping as well as everything else they had to do. He was working flat out just to get through all their homework, though he made a point of sending regular food packages up to the cave in the mountain for Sirius; after last summer, he had not forgotten what it felt like to be continually hungry. He enclosed notes to Sirius, telling him that nothing out of the ordinary had happened, and that they were still waiting for an answer from Percy.

Hedwig didn't return until the end of the Easter holidays. Percy's letter was enclosed in a package of Easter eggs that Mrs. Weasley had sent. Both Harry's and Ron's were the size of dragon eggs, and full of homemade toffee. Hermione's, however, was smaller than a chicken's egg. Her face fell when she saw it.

'Your mum doesn't read *Witch Weekly*, by any chance, does she, Ron?' she asked quietly.

## 第28章 克劳奇先生疯了

"装窃听器？"罗恩不解地说，"什么东西……是把臭虫放在了她身上吗？"

哈利便向他解释什么是暗藏的麦克风和录音装置。

罗恩听得很入迷，可是赫敏打断了他们："你们俩没有读过《霍格沃茨：一段校史》吗？"

"有必要吗？"罗恩说，"反正你已经记得滚瓜烂熟，我们问问你就可以了。"

"麻瓜使用的魔法替代品——电啦，计算机啦，雷达啦，所有这类东西——一到霍格沃茨周围就会出故障，因为这个环境里的魔法磁场太强了。不对，丽塔是靠魔法偷听别人说话的，肯定是这样……但愿我能弄清是什么魔法……噢，如果是非法的，她可就逃不掉了……"

"我们要操心的事还不够多吗？"罗恩问她，"非要跟丽塔·斯基特闹得你死我活吗？"

"我没有请你帮忙！"赫敏没好气地说，"我自己处理这件事！"

她三步并作两步地踏上大理石楼梯，甚至没有回头望一眼。哈利相信她一定是去图书馆了。

"我敢说她会抱着一盒我恨丽塔·斯基特的徽章回来，你信不信？"罗恩说。

然而，赫敏并没有叫哈利和罗恩帮她一起找丽塔·斯基特算账，这使他俩都松了口气，因为复活节就快到了，功课越来越多。哈利坦白地承认，赫敏既要跟他们一样完成作业，又要研究偷听魔法术，真是很了不起。哈利光是对付那些家庭作业就忙得焦头烂额，但他坚持定期给山洞里的小天狼星寄去一包包食物。自从去年夏天以来，哈利就一直没有忘记天天挨饿的滋味。他还顺便给小天狼星寄信，告诉他没有任何异常情况，他们仍然在等待珀西的回信。

直到复活节快要结束时，海德薇才回来。珀西的回信附在一包复活节彩蛋里，是韦斯莱夫人寄来的。哈利和罗恩得到的彩蛋都有火龙蛋那么大，里面装满了自制的太妃糖。赫敏的彩蛋却比鸡蛋还小。她一见就拉长了脸。

"你妈妈不会碰巧也看《女巫周刊》吧，罗恩？"她轻声地问。

# CHAPTER TWENTY-EIGHT    The Madness of Mr Crouch

'Yeah,' said Ron, whose mouth was full of toffee. 'Gets it for the recipes.'
Hermione looked sadly at her tiny egg.
'Don't you want to see what Percy's written?' Harry asked her hastily.
Percy's letter was short and irritable.

> As I am constantly telling the Daily Prophet, Mr. Crouch is taking a well-deserved break. He is sending in regular owls with instructions. No, I haven't actually seen him, but I think I can be trusted to know my own superior's handwriting. I have quite enough to do at the moment without trying to quash these ridiculous rumours. Please don't bother me again unless it's something important. Happy Easter.

The start of the summer term would normally have meant that Harry was training hard for the last Quidditch match of the season. This year, however, it was the third and final task in the Triwizard Tournament for which he needed to prepare, but he still didn't know what he would have to do. Finally, in the last week of May, Professor McGonagall held him back in Transfiguration.

'You are to go down to the Quidditch pitch tonight at nine o'clock, Potter,' she told him. 'Mr. Bagman will be there to tell the champions about the third task.'

So at half past eight that night, Harry left Ron and Hermione in Gryffindor Tower, and went downstairs. As he crossed the Entrance Hall, Cedric came up from the Hufflepuff common room.

'What d'you reckon it's going to be?' he asked Harry, as they went together down the stone steps, out into the cloudy night. 'Fleur keeps going on about underground tunnels, she reckons we've got to find treasure.'

'That wouldn't be too bad,' said Harry, thinking that he would simply ask Hagrid for a Niffler to do the job for him.

They walked down the dark lawn to the Quidditch stadium, turned through a gap in the stands, and walked out onto the pitch.

'What've they done to it?' Cedric said indignantly, stopping dead.

The Quidditch pitch was no longer smooth and flat. It looked as though somebody had been building long, low walls all over it, twisting and criss-crossing in every direction.

## 第28章 克劳奇先生疯了

"没错,"罗恩说,嘴里塞满了太妃糖,"她要看上面的菜谱。"
赫敏悲哀地望着她的小彩蛋。
"你想看看珀西写了什么吗?"哈利赶紧问她。
珀西的信很短,而且口气很不耐烦。

> 正如我不断告诉《预言家日报》的,克劳奇先生工作太辛苦了,目前正在休整。他定期派猫头鹰送来指示。没有,我没有见到他本人,但我认为你们应该相信,我绝对不会认错我上司的笔迹。目前我已经忙得不可开交,却还要澄清这些无聊的谣言。请不要再打扰我了,除非有什么要紧的事。祝复活节愉快。

往常,夏季学期一开始,就意味着哈利要加紧训练,准备这个赛季的最后一场魁地奇比赛。可是今年,他要准备的是三强争霸赛的第三个也是最后一个项目,但是他仍然不知道自己需要做些什么。终于,到了五月的最后一个星期,麦格教授在上完变形课后把他留了下来。

"波特,你今晚九点到下面的魁地奇球场去,"麦格教授对他说,"巴格曼先生要在那里告诉勇士们第三个项目是什么。"

于是,那天晚上八点半,哈利在格兰芬多塔楼与罗恩和赫敏分手,来到楼下。正当他穿过门厅时,塞德里克正从赫奇帕奇公共休息室里出来。

"你认为会是什么呢?"两人一起走下石阶,融进阴云密布的夜色中时,塞德里克问哈利,"芙蓉不停地唠叨着地下隧道,她认为我们要寻找财宝。"

"那倒不坏。"哈利说,心想他只要向海格借一只嗅嗅,把事情交给它去干就行了。

他们顺着漆黑的草坪朝魁地奇球场走去,然后穿过看台间的一条窄道进入了球场。

"他们在这里搞了些什么?"塞德里克猛地停下脚步,气愤地问。

魁地奇球场不再平整光滑。看上去,似乎有人在这里砌起了无数道长长的矮墙,这些矮墙错综复杂,蜿蜒曲折地伸向四面八方。

## CHAPTER TWENTY-EIGHT    The Madness of Mr Crouch

'They're hedges!' said Harry, bending to examine the nearest one.

'Hello there!' called a cheery voice.

Ludo Bagman was standing in the middle of the pitch with Krum and Fleur. Harry and Cedric made their way towards them, climbing over the hedges. Fleur beamed at Harry as he came nearer. Her attitude to him had changed completely since he had pulled her sister out of the lake.

'Well, what d'you think?' said Bagman happily, as Harry and Cedric climbed over the last hedge. 'Growing nicely, aren't they? Give them a month and Hagrid'll have them twenty foot high. Don't worry,' he added grinning, spotting the less-than-happy expressions on Harry and Cedric's faces, 'you'll have your Quidditch pitch back to normal once the task is over! Now, I imagine you can guess what we're making here?'

No one spoke for a moment. Then –

'Maze,' grunted Krum.

'That's right!' said Bagman. 'A maze. The third task's really very straightforward. The Triwizard Cup will be placed in the centre of the maze. The first champion to touch it will receive full marks.'

'We seemply 'ave to get through the maze?' said Fleur.

'There will be obstacles,' said Bagman happily, bouncing on the balls of his feet. 'Hagrid is providing a number of creatures ... then there will be spells that must be broken ... all that sort of thing, you know. Now, the champions who are leading on points will get a head start into the maze.' Bagman grinned at Harry and Cedric. 'Then Mr. Krum will enter ... then Miss Delacour. But you'll all be in with a fighting chance, depending on how well you get past the obstacles. Should be fun, eh?'

Harry, who knew only too well the kind of creatures that Hagrid was likely to provide for an event like this, thought it was unlikely to be any fun at all. However, he nodded politely like the other champions.

'Very well ... if you haven't got any questions, we'll go back up to the castle, shall we, it's a bit chilly ...'

Bagman hurried alongside Harry as they began to wend their way out of the growing maze. Harry had the feeling that Bagman was going to start offering to help him again, but just then, Krum tapped Harry on the shoulder.

'Could I haff a vord?'

## 第28章 克劳奇先生疯了

"是树篱!"哈利说着,低头仔细观察离他最近的那道矮墙。

"你们好!"一个愉快的声音喊道。

卢多·巴格曼站在球场中央,旁边是克鲁姆和芙蓉。哈利和塞德里克跨过一道道矮墙,朝他们走去。哈利走近时,芙蓉朝他露出灿烂的微笑。自从哈利把芙蓉的妹妹从湖里救出来以后,她对他的态度有了一百八十度的转变。

"怎么样,你们觉得?"哈利和塞德里克翻过最后一道矮墙时,巴格曼愉快地问,"进展不错,是不是?再有一个月,海格就会把它们变成二十英尺高。不要担心,"他看见哈利和塞德里克脸上不快的表情,笑着说道,"争霸赛项目一结束,你们的魁地奇球场就会恢复原样!好了,我想你们大概猜得出我们在这里要做什么吧?"

一时间没有人说话,然后——

"迷宫。"克鲁姆粗声粗气地说。

"对了!"巴格曼说,"是一个迷宫。第三个项目非常简单明确。三强杯就放在迷宫中央,哪位勇士第一个碰到它,就能获得满分。"

"我们只要通过迷宫就行了?"芙蓉问。

"会有许多障碍,"巴格曼欢快地说,一边踮着脚跳来跳去,"海格提供了一大堆动物……还有一些必须解除的咒语……诸如此类的东西,你们知道。记住,得分领先的勇士首先进入迷宫。"巴格曼对哈利和塞德里克微笑着,"接着克鲁姆先生进去……最后是德拉库尔小姐。但你们都必须拼搏才会成功,就看你们穿越障碍的能力了。应该很好玩的,是吧?"

海格在这种场合会提供什么样的动物,哈利真是再清楚不过了,那可是一点也不好玩。不过,他还是像其他勇士一样礼貌地点了点头。

"很好……如果你们没有问题,我们就回城堡去吧,好吗?这里有点冷……"

大家一起跨过不断增长的矮墙时,巴格曼匆匆走在哈利身边。哈利感到巴格曼又要提出帮助他了,可就在这时,克鲁姆拍了拍哈利的肩膀。

"可以跟你说句话吗?"

## CHAPTER TWENTY-EIGHT    The Madness of Mr Crouch

'Yeah, all right,' said Harry, slightly surprised.

'Vill you valk vith me?'

'OK,' said Harry curiously.

Bagman looked slightly perturbed. 'I'll wait for you, Harry, shall I?'

'No, it's OK, Mr. Bagman,' said Harry, suppressing a smile, 'I think I can find the castle on my own, thanks.'

Harry and Krum left the stadium together, but Krum did not set a course for the Durmstrang ship. Instead, he walked towards the Forest.

'What're we going this way for?' said Harry, as they passed Hagrid's cabin, and the illuminated Beauxbatons carriage.

'Don't vant to be overheard,' said Krum shortly.

When at last they had reached a quiet stretch of ground, a short way from the Beauxbatons' horses' paddock, Krum stopped in the shade of the trees and turned to face Harry.

'I vant to know,' he said, glowering, 'vot there is between you and Hermy-own-ninny.'

Harry, who from Krum's secretive manner had expected something much more serious than this, stared up at Krum in amazement.

'Nothing,' he said. But Krum glowered at him, and Harry, somehow struck anew by how tall Krum was, elaborated. 'We're friends. She's not my girlfriend and she never has been. It's just that Skeeter woman making things up.'

'Hermy-own-ninny talks about you very often,' said Krum, looking suspiciously at Harry.

'Yeah,' said Harry, 'because we're *friends*.'

He couldn't quite believe he was having this conversation with Viktor Krum, the famous international Quidditch player. It was as though the eighteen-year-old Krum thought he, Harry, was an equal – a real rival –

'You haff never ... you haff not ...'

'No,' said Harry, very firmly.

Krum looked slightly happier. He stared at Harry for a few seconds, then said, 'You fly very well. I vos votching at the first task.'

'Thanks,' said Harry, grinning broadly, and suddenly feeling much taller himself. 'I saw you at the Quidditch World Cup. The Wronski feint, you really –'

## 第28章 克劳奇先生疯了

"可以，没问题。"哈利说，微微有些吃惊。

"你跟我走走，好吗？"

"行。"哈利好奇地说。

巴格曼显得有点儿心烦意乱。"我在这里等你，哈利，行吗？"

"噢，不用了，巴格曼先生，"哈利忍住笑，说道，"我想我自己能找到城堡，谢谢了。"

哈利和克鲁姆一起离开了球场，但克鲁姆并没有朝德姆斯特朗大船的那个方向去，而是走向了禁林。

"为什么走这条路？"哈利问，这时他们经过了海格的小屋和灯火闪亮的布斯巴顿马车。

"不想被人听见。"克鲁姆简短地说。

他们终于来到一片幽静的空地上，离布斯巴顿骏马的马厩还有一段距离，克鲁姆在树下停住脚步，转身望着哈利。

"我想知道，"他沉着脸，说，"你和赫—米—恩是怎么回事。"

哈利刚才看到克鲁姆那副讳莫如深的样子，还以为他要说什么非常严肃的事情呢。他惊愕地望着克鲁姆。

"没有什么。"他说。但克鲁姆仍然虎视眈眈地瞪着他。哈利又觉得克鲁姆的个头真高啊，便赶紧把话说得更明白些："我们是朋友。她不是我的女朋友，从来不是。都是斯基特那个女人胡乱造谣的。"

"赫—米—恩经常谈起你。"克鲁姆说，将信将疑地看着哈利。

"是啊，"哈利说，"我们是朋友嘛。"

他真不敢相信自己竟与威克多尔·克鲁姆谈论这个话题，克鲁姆可是大名鼎鼎的国际魁地奇球员啊。十八岁的克鲁姆似乎把他，哈利，看成了一个旗鼓相当的人——一个真正的对手——

"你们从来没有……你们没有……"

"没有。"哈利非常肯定地说。

克鲁姆显得开心一些了。他瞪着哈利看了几秒钟，说："你飞得很棒。我看了第一个项目。"

"谢谢。"哈利说，他轻松地笑着，一下子觉得自己高了许多，"我在魁地奇世界杯赛上看见你了。朗斯基假动作，你真——"

## CHAPTER TWENTY-EIGHT    The Madness of Mr Crouch

But something moved behind Krum in the trees, and Harry, who had some experience of the sort of thing that lurked in the Forest, instinctively grabbed Krum's arm and pulled him around.

'Vot is it?'

Harry shook his head, staring at the place where he'd seen movement. He slipped his hand inside his robes, reaching for his wand.

Next moment a man had staggered out from behind a tall oak. For a moment, Harry didn't recognise him ... then he realised it was Mr. Crouch.

He looked as though he had been travelling for days. The knees of his robes were ripped and bloody; his face scratched; he was unshaven and grey with exhaustion. His neat hair and moustache were both in need of a wash and a trim. His strange appearance, however, was nothing to the way he was behaving. Muttering and gesticulating, Mr. Crouch appeared to be talking to someone that he alone could see. He reminded Harry vividly of an old tramp he had seen once when out shopping with the Dursleys. That man, too, had been conversing wildly with thin air; Aunt Petunia had seized Dudley's hand and pulled him across the road to avoid him; Uncle Vernon had then treated the family to a long rant about what he would like to do with beggars and vagrants.

'Vosn't he a judge?' said Krum, staring at Mr. Crouch. 'Isn't he vith your Ministry?'

Harry nodded, hesitated for a moment, then walked slowly towards Mr. Crouch, who did not look at him, but continued to talk to a nearby tree: '... and when you've done that, Weatherby, send an owl to Dumbledore confirming the number of Durmstrang students who will be attending the Tournament, Karkaroff has just sent word there will be twelve ...'

'Mr. Crouch?' said Harry cautiously.

'... and then send another owl to Madame Maxime, because she might want to up the number of students she's bringing, now Karkaroff's made it a round dozen ... do that, Weatherby, will you? Will you? Will ...' Mr. Crouch's eyes were bulging. He stood staring at the tree, muttering soundlessly at it. Then he staggered sideways, and fell to his knees.

'Mr. Crouch?' Harry said loudly. 'Are you all right?'

Crouch's eyes were rolling in his head. Harry looked around at Krum, who had followed him into the trees, and was looking down at Crouch in alarm.

## 第28章 克劳奇先生疯了

突然，克鲁姆身后的树丛中出现了一些异常动静。哈利对隐藏在禁林里的东西有过一些经验，他本能地抓住克鲁姆的胳膊，把他拉了过来。

"是什么？"

哈利摇了摇头，盯着刚才有动静的地方。他把手伸进长袍，摸索魔杖。

这时，一个男人突然跌跌撞撞地从一棵高高的橡树后走了出来。哈利一时没有认出来……然后，他反应过来了，是克劳奇先生。

他看上去在外面漂泊了许多日子，长袍的膝部被撕破了，血迹斑斑，脸上也布满伤痕，胡子拉碴，面容灰白而憔悴。他原本整洁的头发和胡子都需要清洗和修剪了。克劳奇先生模样固然奇特，但更古怪的是他的行为。他嘴里不停地嘀嘀咕咕，还打着手势。他似乎在跟什么人说话，而这个人只有他自己才能看见。哈利一看见他，就想起有一次和德思礼一家出去买东西时碰到的一个老流浪汉。那人也是这样疯疯癫癫地对着空气说个不停。佩妮姨妈抓住达力的手，把他拉到马路对面，躲开那个疯子。弗农姨父则借题发挥，向全家人没完没了地唠叨他准备怎样对待乞丐和流浪汉。

"他不是个裁判吗？"克鲁姆盯着克劳奇先生问道，"他不是你们魔法部的人吗？"

哈利点了点头。他迟疑了片刻，然后慢慢朝克劳奇先生走去。克劳奇先生没有看他，只管对旁边的一棵树说个不停。"……韦瑟比，你办完这件事之后，就派一只猫头鹰给邓布利多送信，确认一下德姆斯特朗参加争霸赛的学生人数，卡卡洛夫捎信说有十二个……"

"克劳奇先生？"哈利小心地说。

"……然后再派一只猫头鹰给马克西姆女士送信，她可能也要增加学生人数，因为卡卡洛夫的人数增加到了十二个……就这么办吧，韦瑟比，行吗？行吗？行……"克劳奇先生眼珠突出。他站在那里，眼睛直勾勾地瞪着那棵树，嘴里无声地念叨着。然后，他朝旁边踉跄几步，扑通跪倒在地。

"克劳奇先生？"哈利大声叫道，"你没事吧？"

克劳奇的眼珠向上翻着。哈利扭头望望克鲁姆。克鲁姆也进了树丛，警惕地低头看着克劳奇。

## CHAPTER TWENTY-EIGHT    The Madness of Mr Crouch

'Vot is wrong with him?'

'No idea,' Harry muttered. 'Listen, you'd better go and get someone –'

'Dumbledore!' gasped Mr Crouch. He reached out and seized a handful of Harry's robes, dragging him closer, though his eyes were staring over Harry's head. 'I need ... see ... Dumbledore ...'

'OK,' said Harry, 'if you get up, Mr Crouch, we can go up to the –'

'I've done ... stupid ... thing ...' Mr Crouch breathed. He looked utterly mad. His eyes were rolling and bulging, and a trickle of spittle was sliding down his chin. Every word he spoke seemed to cost him a terrible effort. 'Must ... tell ... Dumbledore ...'

'Get up, Mr Crouch,' said Harry loudly and clearly. 'Get up, I'll take you to Dumbledore!'

Mr Crouch's eyes rolled forwards onto Harry.

'Who ... you?' he whispered.

'I'm a student at the school,' said Harry, looking around at Krum for some help, but Krum was hanging back, looking extremely nervous.

'You're not ... *his*?' whispered Crouch, his mouth sagging.

'No,' said Harry, without the faintest idea what Crouch was talking about.

'Dumbledore's?'

'That's right,' said Harry.

Crouch was pulling him closer; Harry tried to loosen Crouch's grip on his robes, but it was too powerful.

'Warn ... Dumbledore ...'

'I'll get Dumbledore if you let go of me,' said Harry. 'Just let go, Mr Crouch, and I'll get him ...'

'Thank you, Weatherby, and when you have done that, I would like a cup of tea. My wife and son will be arriving shortly, we are attending a concert tonight with Mr and Mrs Fudge.' Crouch was now talking fluently to a tree again, and seemed completely unaware that Harry was there, which surprised Harry so much he didn't notice that Crouch had released him. 'Yes, my son has recently gained twelve O.W.L.s, most satisfactory, yes, thank you, yes, very proud indeed. Now, if you could bring me that memo from the Andorran Minister for Magic, I think I will have time to draft a

## 第28章 克劳奇先生疯了

"他怎么啦？"

"不知道，"哈利低声说，"听着，你最好赶快去叫人——"

"邓布利多！"克劳奇先生大口喘着气说，他扑过来，一把抓住哈利的长袍，把哈利拉到自己身边，但眼睛却直直地盯着哈利头顶上方。"我要……见……邓布利多……"

"好的，"哈利说，"只要你起来，克劳奇先生，我们就去找——"

"我做了……一件……蠢事……"克劳奇喘着气说，看上去完全疯了，眼珠向外突出，滴溜溜地乱转，口水顺着下巴滴落，说的每个字似乎都费尽了全力，"一定要……告诉……邓布利多……"

"起来，克劳奇先生，"哈利声音很响很清楚地说，"快起来，我带你去见邓布利多！"

克劳奇先生的眼珠转了过来，瞪着哈利。

"你……是谁？"他小声地问。

"我是学校的一名学生。"哈利说，一边扭头望着克鲁姆，希望他能过来帮一把，但克鲁姆缩在后面，神情非常紧张。

"你不是……他的人？"克劳奇轻声问，嘴巴往下耷拉着。

"不是。"哈利说，一点儿也不明白克劳奇在说什么。

"是邓布利多的人？"

"对。"哈利说。

克劳奇把他拉得更近一些。哈利想松开克劳奇抓住他长袍的手，但克劳奇抓得太紧了。

"给邓布利多……提个醒……"

"如果你放开我，我就去找邓布利多。"哈利说，"放开我，克劳奇先生，我去找他……"

"谢谢你，韦瑟比，你办完那件事后，我想喝杯茶。我妻子和儿子很快就要来了，我们今晚要和福吉夫妇一起去听音乐会。"克劳奇又对着一棵树滔滔不绝地说开了，似乎一下子就把哈利忘到了脑后。哈利惊讶极了，竟没有注意到克劳奇已经松开了他。"是的，我儿子最近通过了十二项 O.W.L. 考试，成绩很令人满意，谢谢你，是的，确实很为他骄傲。好了，如果你能把安道尔魔法部长的那份备忘录拿给我，我

## CHAPTER TWENTY-EIGHT    The Madness of Mr Crouch

response ...'

'You stay here with him!' Harry said to Krum. 'I'll get Dumbledore, I'll be quicker, I know where his office is –'

'He is mad,' said Krum doubtfully, staring down at Crouch, who was still gabbling to the tree, apparently convinced it was Percy.

'Just stay with him,' said Harry, starting to get up, but his movement seemed to trigger another abrupt change in Mr. Crouch, who seized him hard around the knees and pulled Harry back to the ground.

'Don't ... leave ... me!' he whispered, his eyes bulging again. 'I ... escaped ... must warn ... must tell ... see Dumbledore ... my fault ... all my fault ... Bertha ... dead ... all my fault ... my son ... my fault ... tell Dumbledore ... Harry Potter ... the Dark Lord ... stronger ... Harry Potter ...'

'I'll get Dumbledore if you let me go, Mr. Crouch!' said Harry. He looked furiously around at Krum. 'Help me, will you?'

Looking extremely apprehensive, Krum moved forward and squatted down next to Mr. Crouch.

'Just keep him here,' said Harry, pulling himself free of Mr. Crouch. 'I'll be back with Dumbledore.'

'Hurry, von't you?' Krum called after him, as Harry sprinted away from the Forest, and up through the dark grounds. They were deserted; Bagman, Cedric and Fleur had disappeared. Harry tore up the stone steps, through the oak front doors and off up the marble staircase, towards the second floor.

Five minutes later he was hurtling towards a stone gargoyle standing halfway along an empty corridor.

'Sher-sherbet lemon!' he panted at it.

This was the password to the hidden staircase to Dumbledore's office – or, at least, it had been two years ago. The password had evidently changed, however, for the stone gargoyle did not spring to life and jump aside, but stood frozen, glaring at Harry malevolently.

'Move!' Harry shouted at it. 'C'mon!'

But nothing at Hogwarts had ever moved just because he shouted at it; he knew it was no good. He looked up and down the dark corridor. Perhaps Dumbledore was in the staff room? He started running as fast as he could towards the staircase –

## 第28章 克劳奇先生疯了

大概会有时间起草一封回信……"

"你在这里陪他！"哈利对克鲁姆说，"我去叫邓布利多，我知道他的办公室在哪儿，可以快一些——"

"他疯了。"克鲁姆迟疑地说，低头望着克劳奇。克劳奇仍然对着那棵树喋喋不休，似乎认定那就是珀西。

"你在这陪着他。"哈利说完，准备起身离开，但他的动作似乎刺激了克劳奇先生，他又猛地改变姿态，一把抱住哈利的膝盖，再一次把他拖倒在地。

"不要……离开……我！"他小声说，眼球又突了出来，"我……逃出来了……必须提醒……必须告诉……我要见邓布利多……都怪我……都怪我……伯莎……死了……都怪我……我儿子……都怪我……告诉邓布利多……哈利·波特……黑魔头……强壮起来了……哈利·波特……"

"只要你放开我，我就去找邓布利多，克劳奇先生！"哈利说，他恼怒地扭头看着克鲁姆，"你能不能帮帮我？"

克鲁姆一副忧心忡忡的样子，他走上前，蹲在克劳奇先生身边。

"你把他稳在这里，"哈利说，一边从克劳奇先生手里挣脱出来，"我领邓布利多回来。"

"快点，好吗？"克鲁姆在哈利身后喊道。哈利飞奔出禁林，奔过漆黑的场地。场地上空无一人。巴格曼、塞德里克和芙蓉都不见了。哈利三步并作两步登上石阶，穿过橡木大门，蹿上大理石楼梯，朝三楼跑去。

五分钟后，他飞速奔向空空的走廊中央立着的一只滴水嘴石兽。

"柠—柠檬雪宝糖！"他气喘吁吁地对怪兽说。

这是通往邓布利多办公室的秘密楼梯的口令——至少两年以前是这样。然而，显然口令已经变了，石兽并没有活动起来跳到一边，而是一动不动地站着，恶狠狠地瞪着哈利。

"闪开！"哈利冲它大喊，"快点儿！"

可是，霍格沃茨从来没有哪样东西是你冲它嚷嚷就会闪开的。哈利知道这不管用。他在漆黑的走廊里东张西望。也许邓布利多在教工休息室里？他又开始拼命朝楼梯奔去——

815

## CHAPTER TWENTY-EIGHT    The Madness of Mr Crouch

'POTTER!'

Harry skidded to a halt and looked around.

Snape had just emerged from the hidden staircase behind the stone gargoyle. The wall was sliding shut behind him even as he beckoned Harry back towards him. 'What are you doing here, Potter?'

'I need to see Professor Dumbledore!' said Harry, running back up the corridor and skidding to a standstill in front of Snape instead. 'It's Mr. Crouch ... he's just turned up ... he's in the Forest ... he's asking –'

'What is this rubbish?' said Snape, his black eyes glittering. 'What are you talking about?'

'Mr. Crouch!' Harry shouted. 'From the Ministry! He's ill or something – he's in the Forest, he wants to see Dumbledore! Just give me the password up to –'

'The Headmaster is busy, Potter,' said Snape, his thin mouth curling into an unpleasant smile.

'I've got to tell Dumbledore!' Harry yelled.

'Didn't you hear me, Potter?'

Harry could tell Snape was thoroughly enjoying himself, denying Harry the thing he wanted when he was so panicky.

'Look,' said Harry angrily, 'Crouch isn't right – he's – he's out of his mind – he says he wants to warn –'

The stone wall behind Snape slid open. Dumbledore was standing there, wearing long green robes, and a mildly curious expression.

'Is there a problem?' he said, looking between Harry and Snape.

'Professor!' Harry said, side-stepping Snape before Snape could speak. 'Mr. Crouch is here – he's down in the Forest, he wants to speak to you!'

Harry expected Dumbledore to ask questions but, to his relief, Dumbledore did nothing of the sort. 'Lead the way,' he said promptly, and he swept off along the corridor behind Harry, leaving Snape standing next to the gargoyle and looking twice as ugly.

'What did Mr. Crouch say, Harry?' said Dumbledore, as they walked swiftly down the marble staircase.

'Said he wants to warn you ... said he's done something terrible ... he mentioned his son ... and Bertha Jorkins ... and – and Voldemort ... something about Voldemort getting stronger ...'

## 第28章 克劳奇先生疯了

"波特!"

哈利猛地刹车,停住了。他回过头。

斯内普刚从滴水嘴石兽后面的秘密楼梯里出来。就在他招手让哈利回去时,他身后的墙壁才慢慢合上。"你在这儿干什么,波特?"

"我要见邓布利多教授!"哈利说,顺着走廊跑回去,然后哧溜一下停在斯内普面前,"是克劳奇先生……他出现了……在禁林……他要——"

"什么胡话?"斯内普说,两只黑眼睛闪闪发亮,"你在说些什么?"

"克劳奇先生!"哈利喊道,"部里的官员!他不知是病了还是怎么着——在禁林里,他想见邓布利多!快把口令告诉我——"

"校长很忙,波特。"斯内普说,薄薄的嘴唇扭曲成一个难看的笑容。

"我要去告诉邓布利多!"哈利嚷道。

"你没有听见我的话吗,波特?"

哈利看得出来,斯内普在他这样惊慌失措时不让他得到想要的东西,心里正感到快意得很呢。

"是这样,"哈利气愤地说,"克劳奇不大对头——他——他脑子不正常了——他说他想提醒——"

斯内普身后的石墙滑动着打开了,邓布利多站在那里,穿着长长的绿袍子,脸上带着略感惊奇的表情。

"出问题了?"他问,看看哈利,又看看斯内普。

"教授!"哈利不等斯内普说话,就横跨一步说道,"克劳奇先生在这里——就在禁林里,他想跟你说话!"

哈利以为邓布利多会提一些问题,但邓布利多什么也没问,这使他松了口气。"在前面领路。"邓布利多毫不迟疑地说,跟着哈利沿走廊匆匆离去,留下斯内普独自站在滴水嘴石兽旁边发呆,脸上的表情更难看了。

"克劳奇先生说了什么,哈利?"他们飞快地跑下大理石楼梯时,邓布利多问。

"说他想提醒你……说他做了件可怕的事……还提到他的儿子……和伯莎·乔金斯……还有——还有伏地魔……好像是说伏地魔变得强壮了……"

## CHAPTER TWENTY-EIGHT    The Madness of Mr Crouch

'Indeed,' said Dumbledore, and he quickened his pace as they hurried out into the pitch-darkness.

'He's not acting normally,' Harry said, hurrying along beside Dumbledore. 'He doesn't seem to know where he is. He keeps talking like he thinks Percy Weasley's there, and then he changes, and says he needs to see you ... I left him with Viktor Krum.'

'You did?' said Dumbledore sharply, and he began to take longer strides still, so that Harry was running to keep up. 'Do you know if anybody else saw Mr. Crouch?'

'No,' said Harry. 'Krum and I were talking, Mr. Bagman had just finished telling us about the third task, we stayed behind, and then we saw Mr. Crouch coming out of the Forest –'

'Where are they?' said Dumbledore, as the Beauxbatons carriage emerged from the darkness.

'Over here,' said Harry, moving in front of Dumbledore, leading the way through the trees. He couldn't hear Crouch's voice any more, but he knew where he was going; it hadn't been much past the Beauxbatons carriage ... somewhere around here ...

'Viktor?' Harry shouted.

No one answered.

'They were here,' Harry said to Dumbledore. 'They were definitely somewhere around here ...'

'*Lumos*,' Dumbledore said, lighting his wand and holding it up.

Its narrow beam travelled from black trunk to black trunk, illuminating the ground. And then it fell upon a pair of feet.

Harry and Dumbledore hurried forwards. Krum was sprawled on the Forest floor. He seemed to be unconscious. There was no sign at all of Mr. Crouch. Dumbledore bent over Krum and gently lifted one of his eyelids.

'Stunned,' he said softly. His half-moon glasses glittered in the wandlight as he peered around at the surrounding trees.

'Should I go and get someone?' said Harry. 'Madam Pomfrey?'

'No,' said Dumbledore swiftly. 'Stay here.'

He raised his wand into the air and pointed it in the direction of Hagrid's cabin. Harry saw something silvery dart out of it and streak away through the trees like a ghostly bird. Then Dumbledore bent over Krum again, pointed his wand at him, and muttered, '*Rennervate.*'

## 第28章 克劳奇先生疯了

"真的？"邓布利多说，一边加快步伐，匆匆走到外面漆黑的夜色中。

"他的行为很不正常，"哈利在邓布利多身边快步走着，说道，"他好像不知道自己在什么地方。他不停地说话，似乎以为珀西·韦斯莱在那里，然后突然就变了，说是要见你……我让威克多尔·克鲁姆看住他。"

"是吗？"邓布利多警觉地问，脚步迈得更大了，哈利必须跑步才能跟上，"你知道还有谁看见了克劳奇先生吗？"

"没有了。"哈利说，"当时克鲁姆和我在谈话，巴格曼先生刚跟我们讲完第三个项目的内容，我们俩留在后面，后来就看见克劳奇先生从禁林里出来了——"

"他们在哪儿？"邓布利多问，布斯巴顿的马车在黑暗中隐约可见。

"那边。"哈利说着，赶到邓布利多前面，领着他穿过树丛。他听不见克劳奇的声音，但知道他没有走错，那地方就在布斯巴顿马车再过去一点儿……差不多就在这里……

"威克多尔？"哈利喊道。

没有人回答。

"刚才他们在这里的，"哈利对邓布利多说，"肯定就在这附近……"

"荧光闪烁。"邓布利多说，把魔杖点亮举了起来。

这道窄窄的光柱在漆黑的树干间来回移动，照亮了下面的土地，然后落在一双脚上。

哈利和邓布利多赶紧上前。克鲁姆蜷缩着躺在禁林的地上，看上去神志不清。周围没有克劳奇先生的影子。邓布利多弯下腰，轻轻翻开克鲁姆的一只眼皮。

"中了昏迷咒。"他轻声说。他朝周围的树丛张望，半月形的镜片在魔杖的微光中闪烁。

"要不要我去叫人？"哈利说，"庞弗雷女士？"

"不要，"邓布利多很快地说，"待在这儿别动。"

他高高举起魔杖，指着海格小屋的方向。哈利看见一个银色的东西从魔杖里喷出，像一只苍白的鸟，在树丛间一闪而过。然后邓布利多又朝克鲁姆俯下身子，用魔杖指着他，低声念道："快快复苏。"

## CHAPTER TWENTY-EIGHT    The Madness of Mr Crouch

Krum opened his eyes. He looked dazed. When he saw Dumbledore, he tried to sit up, but Dumbledore put a hand on his shoulder and made him lie still.

'He attacked me!' Krum muttered, putting a hand up to his head. 'The old madman attacked me! I vos looking around to see vare Potter had gone and he attacked from behind!'

'Lie still for a moment,' Dumbledore said.

The sound of thunderous footfalls reached them, and Hagrid came panting into sight with Fang at his heels. He was carrying his crossbow.

'Professor Dumbledore!' he said, his eyes widening. 'Harry – what the –?'

'Hagrid, I need you to fetch Professor Karkaroff,' said Dumbledore. 'His student has been attacked. When you've done that, kindly alert Professor Moody –'

'No need, Dumbledore,' said a wheezy growl, 'I'm here.' Moody was limping towards them, leaning on his staff, his wand lit.

'Damn leg,' he said furiously. 'Would've been here quicker ... what's happened? Snape said something about Crouch –'

'Crouch?' said Hagrid blankly.

'Karkaroff, please, Hagrid!' said Dumbledore sharply.

'Oh yeah ... right y'are, Professor ...' said Hagrid, and he turned and disappeared into the dark trees, Fang trotting after him.

'I don't know where Barty Crouch is,' Dumbledore told Moody, 'but it is essential that we find him.'

'I'm onto it,' growled Moody, and he raised his wand, and limped off into the Forest.

Neither Dumbledore nor Harry spoke again until they heard the unmistakeable sounds of Hagrid and Fang returning. Karkaroff was hurrying along behind them. He was wearing his sleek silver furs, and he looked pale and agitated.

'What is this?' he cried, when he saw Krum on the ground, and Dumbledore and Harry beside him. 'What's going on?'

'I vos attacked!' said Krum, sitting up now, and rubbing his head. 'Mr. Crouch or votever his name –'

'Crouch attacked you? *Crouch* attacked you? The Triwizard judge?'

## 第28章 克劳奇先生疯了

克鲁姆睁开眼睛,脸上一片茫然。他一看见邓布利多就挣扎着想坐起来,但邓布利多把一只手放在他肩膀上,让他躺着别动。

"他袭击了我!"克鲁姆伸手捂着脑袋,喃喃地说,"那个老疯子袭击了我!我正在张望波特去了哪里,他就从后面对我下手了!"

"静静地躺一会儿。"邓布利多说。

一阵打雷般的脚步声传入他们耳中,海格气喘吁吁地出现了,身后跟着牙牙。海格手里拿着他的弩。

"邓布利多教授!"他说,眼睛睁得溜圆,"哈利——你怎么——?"

"海格,你赶紧去把卡卡洛夫教授叫来,"邓布利多说,"他的学生被人袭击了。然后,麻烦你再通知一下穆迪教授——"

"没有必要了,邓布利多,"一个低沉的声音呼哧呼哧地说,"我在这儿呢。"穆迪拄着拐杖,一瘸一拐地向他们走来,他的魔杖也亮着。

"该死的腿,"他气恼地说,"应该快点赶来的……出了什么事?斯内普好像说克劳奇——"

"克劳奇?"海格不解地问。

"海格,快去叫卡卡洛夫!"邓布利多严厉地说。

"噢,好的……没问题,教授……"海格说完就转身消失在漆黑的树丛中,牙牙小跑着跟在后面。

"我不知道巴蒂·克劳奇在哪里,"邓布利多对穆迪说,"但我们必须找到他。"

"我这就去找。"穆迪粗声粗气地说,随即举起魔杖,瘸着腿钻进了禁林。

邓布利多和哈利都没有说话,后来他们听见了动静,毫无疑问是海格和牙牙回来了。卡卡洛夫匆匆跟在后面,穿着那件又光又滑的银白色毛皮长袍,脸色苍白,神色焦虑。

"这是怎么回事?"他看见克鲁姆躺在地上,邓布利多和哈利守在旁边,便惊呼道,"出了什么事?"

"我被人袭击了!"克鲁姆说,他慢慢坐了起来,用手揉着脑袋,"听说那个人叫什么克劳奇先生——"

"克劳奇袭击了你?克劳奇袭击了你?三强争霸赛的裁判?"

## CHAPTER TWENTY-EIGHT  The Madness of Mr Crouch

'Igor,' Dumbledore began, but Karkaroff had drawn himself up, clutching his furs around him, looking livid.

'Treachery!' he bellowed, pointing at Dumbledore. 'It is a plot! You and your Ministry of Magic have lured me here under false pretences, Dumbledore! This is not an equal competition! First you sneak Potter into the Tournament, though he is underage! Now one of your Ministry friends attempts to put *my* champion out of action! I smell double-dealing and corruption in this whole affair, and you, Dumbledore, you, with your talk of closer international wizarding links, of rebuilding old ties, of forgetting old differences – here's what I think of *you*!'

Karkaroff spat onto the ground at Dumbledore's feet. In one swift movement, Hagrid seized the front of Karkaroff's furs, lifted him into the air, and slammed him against a nearby tree.

'Apologise!' Hagrid snarled, as Karkaroff gasped for breath, Hagrid's massive fist at his throat, his feet dangling in mid-air.

'Hagrid, *no*!' Dumbledore shouted, his eyes flashing.

Hagrid removed the hand pinning Karkaroff to the tree, and Karkaroff slid all the way down the trunk and slumped in a huddle at its roots; a few twigs and leaves showered down upon his head.

'Kindly escort Harry back up to the castle, Hagrid,' said Dumbledore sharply.

Breathing heavily, Hagrid gave Karkaroff a glowering look. 'Maybe I'd better stay here, Headmaster ...'

'You will take Harry back to school, Hagrid,' Dumbledore repeated firmly. 'Take him right up to Gryffindor Tower. And Harry – I want you to stay there. Anything you might want to do – any owls you might want to send – they can wait until morning, do you understand me?'

'Er – yes,' said Harry, staring at him. How had Dumbledore known that, at that very moment, he had been thinking about sending Pigwidgeon straight to Sirius, to tell him what had happened?

'I'll leave Fang with yeh, Headmaster,' Hagrid said, still staring menacingly at Karkaroff, who was still sprawled at the foot of the tree, tangled in furs and tree-roots. 'Stay, Fang. C'mon, Harry.'

They marched in silence past the Beauxbatons carriage and up towards the castle.

## 第28章 克劳奇先生疯了

"伊戈尔——"邓布利多想说话,但卡卡洛夫挺直身体,拽紧裹在身上的毛皮长袍,脸色铁青。

"骗局!"他指着邓布利多吼道,"这是一个阴谋!你和你们魔法部用虚假的借口把我诱骗到这里,邓布利多!这不是一场公平的竞争!首先,你们偷偷地把波特塞进来比赛,尽管他年龄不够!现在,你们魔法部的一位朋友又想使我的勇士失去战斗力!在整个事件中,我嗅出了欺骗和腐败,还有你,邓布利多,你口口声声谈什么增进国际巫师界的联系,什么恢复过去良好的关系,什么忘记昔日的分歧——我现在才明白你是个什么样的人!"

卡卡洛夫往邓布利多脚下吐了口痰。说时迟那时快,海格一把抓住卡卡洛夫毛皮长袍的前襟,把他举了起来,狠狠抵在旁边的一棵树上。

"快道歉!"海格吼道,卡卡洛夫呼哧呼哧地喘气,海格粗大的拳头抵着他的喉咙,他的双脚悬在了半空。

"海格,住手!"邓布利多喊道,眼睛锐利地闪烁着。

海格松开了把卡卡洛夫钉在树上的手,卡卡洛夫顺着树干滑下来,在树根旁瘫作一团。一些树枝和树叶下雨般地落在他头上。

"麻烦你护送哈利返回城堡,海格。"邓布利多厉声说道。

海格沉重地喘着气,狠狠地瞪了卡卡洛夫一眼。"也许我最好留在这里,校长……"

"你陪哈利回学校,海格。"邓布利多又说了一遍,口气十分坚决,"把他直接送到格兰芬多塔楼。哈利——我希望你待在那里别动。不管你想做什么——比如说想派几只猫头鹰出去送信什么的——都可以等到明天早晨,你明白我的意思吗?"

"呃——明白。"哈利望着他回答。此时此刻,他确实想派小猪赶紧送一封信给小天狼星,把所发生的事情告诉他,可是邓布利多怎么会知道呢?

"我把牙牙留给你吧,校长。"海格说,一边气势汹汹地瞪着卡卡洛夫。卡卡洛夫仍然蜷缩在树下,纠缠在乱糟糟的长袍和树根中。"别动,牙牙。走吧,哈利。"

他们默默地经过布斯巴顿的马车,朝城堡走去。

## CHAPTER TWENTY-EIGHT  The Madness of Mr Crouch

'How dare he,' Hagrid growled, as they strode past the lake. 'How dare he accuse Dumbledore. Like Dumbledore'd do anythin' like that. Like Dumbledore wanted *you* in the Tournament in the firs' place. Worried! I dunno when I seen Dumbledore more worried than he's bin lately. An' you!' Hagrid suddenly said angrily to Harry, who looked up at him, taken aback. 'What were yeh doin', wanderin' off with ruddy Krum? He's from Durmstrang, Harry! Coulda jinxed yeh right there, couldn' he? Hasn' Moody taught yeh nothin'? 'Magine lettin' him lure yeh off on yer own –'

'Krum's all right!' said Harry, as they climbed the steps into the Entrance Hall. 'He wasn't trying to jinx me, he just wanted to talk about Hermione –'

'I'll be havin' a few words with her, an' all,' said Hagrid grimly, stomping up the stairs. 'The less you lot 'ave ter do with these foreigners, the happier yeh'll be. Yeh can' trust any of 'em.'

'You were getting on all right with Madame Maxime,' Harry said, annoyed.

'Don' you talk ter me abou' her!' said Hagrid, and he looked quite frightening for a moment. 'I've got her number now! Tryin' ter get back in me good books, tryin' ter get me ter tell her what's comin' in the third task. Ha! You can' trust any of 'em!'

Hagrid was in such a bad mood, Harry was quite glad to say goodbye to him in front of the Fat Lady. He clambered through the portrait hole into the common room, and hurried straight for the corner where Ron and Hermione were sitting, to tell them what had happened.

## 第28章　克劳奇先生疯了

"他好大的胆子,"他们大步走过小湖时,海格气呼呼地说,"他怎么敢指责邓布利多,就好像邓布利多做了那种事情似的,就好像邓布利多故意让你参加比赛似的。他可真操心哪!我还没见过邓布利多像最近这样操心呢。还有你!"海格突然怒气冲冲地对哈利说,哈利大吃一惊,抬头望着他,"你和那个克鲁姆一起散什么步?他是德姆斯特朗的,哈利!他很可能在这里对你下毒手,不是吗?难道穆迪什么都没有教你吗?想象一下吧,你被他骗得不知不觉——"

"克鲁姆挺好的!"哈利说,这时他们正登上通往门厅的石阶,"他没想对我下毒手,他只想跟我谈谈赫敏——"

"我也要给赫敏提个醒,"海格噔噔噔地走上台阶,严肃地说,"你们这帮人少跟那些外国人打交道,越少越好。他们谁都不可信。"

"你原先和马克西姆女士相处得还不错呢。"哈利恼火地说。

"不许跟我提她!"海格说,神情一时间有些吓人,"我现在把她看透了!又想来讨我的好,想让我告诉她第三个项目是什么!哈哈!他们一个也不能相信!"

海格的情绪糟透了,哈利在胖夫人面前跟他告别时,感到总算松了口气。哈利从肖像洞口爬进公共休息室,快步走向罗恩和赫敏坐的那个墙角,把刚才发生的事全都告诉了他们。

## CHAPTER TWENTY-NINE

# The Dream

'It comes down to this,' said Hermione, rubbing her forehead. 'Either Mr. Crouch attacked Viktor, or somebody else attacked both of them when Viktor wasn't looking.'

'It must've been Crouch,' said Ron at once. 'That's why he was gone when Harry and Dumbledore got there. He'd done a runner.'

'I don't think so,' said Harry, shaking his head. 'He seemed really weak – I don't reckon he was up to Disapparating or anything.'

'You *can't* Disapparate in the Hogwarts grounds, haven't I told you enough times?' said Hermione.

'OK ... how's this for a theory,' said Ron excitedly, 'Krum attacked Crouch – no, wait for it – and then Stunned himself!'

'And Mr. Crouch evaporated, did he?' said Hermione coldly.

'Oh, yeah ...'

It was daybreak. Harry, Ron and Hermione had crept out of their dormitories very early, and hurried up to the Owlery together to send a note to Sirius. Now they were standing looking out at the misty grounds. All three of them were puffy-eyed and pale, because they had been talking late into the night about Mr. Crouch.

'Just go through it again, Harry,' said Hermione. 'What did Mr. Crouch actually say?'

'I've told you, he wasn't making much sense,' said Harry. 'He said he wanted to warn Dumbledore about something. He definitely mentioned Bertha Jorkins, and he seemed to think she was dead. He kept saying stuff was his fault ... he mentioned his son.'

'Well, that *was* his fault,' said Hermione testily.

'He was out of his mind,' said Harry. 'Half the time he seemed to think

# 第 29 章

# 噩 梦

"**照**这样说,"赫敏揉着额头说,"不是克劳奇袭击了威克多尔,就是什么人趁威克多尔不注意时袭击了他们俩。"

"肯定是克劳奇,"罗恩马上说,"所以哈利和邓布利多赶到那儿时他已经不见了。溜得够快的。"

"我认为不会,"哈利摇了摇头说,"他看上去很虚弱——我想他不会幻影移形什么的。"

"你不可能在霍格沃茨的场地上幻影移形,我跟你们讲过多少遍了?"赫敏说。

"哎……会不会是这样,"罗恩兴奋地说,"克鲁姆袭击了克劳奇——我还没说完——然后给他自己施了个昏迷咒!"

"然后克劳奇先生变成蒸气挥发了,是不是?"赫敏冷冷地说。

"啊,这个……"

天刚放亮,哈利、罗恩和赫敏就早早溜出宿舍,一起赶到猫头鹰棚屋给小天狼星发信。现在他们站在那里眺望雾蒙蒙的场地,三个人都眼皮浮肿,脸色苍白,因为他们昨天夜里为克劳奇先生的事讨论到很晚。

"再讲一遍吧,哈利,"赫敏说,"克劳奇先生到底说了什么?"

"我告诉过你了,他当时语无伦次,"哈利说,"说要给邓布利多提个醒。他肯定提到了伯莎·乔金斯,好像认为伯莎已经死了,还一个劲儿地说都是他的错……他还提到了他的儿子。"

"对,那当然是他的错。"赫敏恼火地说。

"他精神错乱了,"哈利说,"有一半时间好像以为他妻子和儿子还

## CHAPTER TWENTY-NINE  The Dream

his wife and son were still alive, and he kept talking to Percy about work and giving him instructions.'

'And ... remind me what he said about You-Know-Who?' said Ron tentatively.

'I've told you,' Harry repeated dully. 'He said he's getting stronger.'

There was a pause.

Then Ron said in a falsely confident voice, 'But he was out of his mind, like you said, so half of it was probably just raving ...'

'He was sanest when he was trying to talk about Voldemort,' said Harry, ignoring Ron's wince. 'He was having real trouble stringing two words together, but that was when he seemed to know where he was, and know what he wanted to do. He just kept saying he had to see Dumbledore.'

Harry turned away from the window and stared up into the rafters. Half the many perches were empty; every now and then, another owl would swoop in through one of the windows, returning from its night's hunting with a mouse in its beak.

'If Snape hadn't held me up,' Harry said bitterly, 'we might've got there in time. "The Headmaster is busy, Potter ... what's this rubbish, Potter?" Why couldn't he have just got out of the way?'

'Maybe he didn't want you to get there!' said Ron quickly. 'Maybe – hang on – how fast d'you reckon he could've got down to the Forest? D'you reckon he could've beaten you and Dumbledore there?'

'Not unless he can turn himself into a bat or something,' said Harry.

'Wouldn't put it past him,' Ron muttered.

'We need to see Professor Moody,' said Hermione. 'We need to find out whether he found Mr. Crouch.'

'If he had the Marauder's Map on him, it would've been easy,' said Harry.

'Unless Crouch was already outside the grounds,' said Ron, 'because it only shows up to the boundaries, doesn't –'

'Shh!' said Hermione suddenly.

Somebody was climbing the steps up to the Owlery. Harry could hear two voices arguing, coming closer and closer.

'– that's blackmail, that is, we could get into a lot of trouble for that –'

'– we've tried being polite, it's time to play dirty, like him. He wouldn't like the Ministry of Magic knowing what he did –'

## 第29章 噩梦

活着,他老是跟珀西讲工作上的事,给珀西下指示。"

"哎……他说神秘人什么来着?"罗恩试探地问。

"我说过了,"哈利闷闷地说,"他说那人在强壮起来。"

一阵沉默。

罗恩假装很肯定地说:"可你说他精神错乱了,所以他的话大概有一半是疯话……"

"提到伏地魔的那会儿是他最清醒的时候,"哈利说,那个名字把罗恩吓得畏缩了一下,"他话都说得不连贯,但那时似乎知道自己在哪里,知道他想干什么。他不停地说要见邓布利多。"

哈利从窗口走开,抬头望着房顶上的椽子。那些栖木有一半空着,不时有一只猫头鹰从窗口扑进来,嘴里叼着夜里捕到的田鼠。

"要不是斯内普拦住我,我们也许是能及时赶到的。"哈利愤愤地说,"'校长很忙,波特……真是一派胡言,波特。'他为什么就不能让开呢?"

"也许他根本就不希望你们赶过去!"罗恩马上说道,"也许——对了——你认为他到禁林要多长时间?他会不会抢在了你和邓布利多前面?"

"除非他把自己变成一只蝙蝠什么的。"哈利说。

"也不是不可能。"罗恩嘟哝道。

"我们需要去见穆迪教授,"赫敏说,"我们要看他找到克劳奇先生没有。"

"如果他带着活点地图,找起来应该不难。"哈利说。

"除非克劳奇已经出了这片场地,"罗恩说,"因为地图只画到校园边界,对不——"

"嘘!"赫敏突然说。

有人在楼梯上朝猫头鹰棚屋走来。哈利听到两个声音在争吵,越来越近。

"——那是敲诈,我们会惹出一大堆麻烦的——"

"——客气的办法我们已经试过,现在该做一回小人了,就像他一样。他肯定不想让魔法部知道他干的勾当——"

## CHAPTER TWENTY-NINE    The Dream

'I'm telling you, if you put that in writing, it's blackmail!'

'Yeah, and you won't be complaining if we get a nice fat payoff, will you?'

The Owlery door banged open. Fred and George came over the threshold, then froze at the sight of Harry, Ron and Hermione.

'What're you doing here?' Ron and Fred said at the same time.

'Sending a letter,' said Harry and George in unison.

'What, at this time?' said Hermione and Fred.

Fred grinned. 'Fine – we won't ask you what you're doing, if you don't ask us,' he said.

He was holding a sealed envelope in his hands. Harry glanced at it, but Fred, whether accidentally or on purpose, shifted his hand so that the name on it was covered.

'Well, don't let us hold you up,' he said, making a mock bow, and pointing at the door.

Ron didn't move. 'Who're you blackmailing?' he said.

The grin vanished from Fred's face. Harry saw George half glance at Fred, before smiling at Ron.

'Don't be stupid, I was only joking,' he said easily.

'Didn't sound like that,' said Ron.

Fred and George looked at each other.

Then Fred said abruptly, 'I've told you before, Ron, keep your nose out if you like it the shape it is. Can't see why you would, but –'

'It's my business if you're blackmailing someone,' said Ron. 'George's right, you could end up in serious trouble for that.'

'Told you, I was joking,' said George. He walked over to Fred, pulled the letter out of his hands, and began attaching it to the leg of the nearest barn owl. 'You're starting to sound a bit like our dear older brother, you are, Ron. Carry on like this and you'll be made a Prefect.'

'No, I won't!' said Ron hotly.

George carried the barn owl over to the window and it took off.

He turned round and grinned at Ron. 'Well, stop telling people what to do then. See you later.'

He and Fred left the Owlery. Harry, Ron and Hermione stared at each other.

'You don't think they know something about all this, do you?' Hermione

## 第29章 噩　梦

"我告诉你，如果你把这写下来，就是敲诈！"

"是啊，如果我们能大赚一笔，你就不会抱怨了，对吧？"

猫头鹰棚屋的门砰的一下被推开了。弗雷德和乔治跨进门槛，看见哈利、罗恩和赫敏，他们俩顿时呆住了。

"你们来这儿干什么？"罗恩和弗雷德同时问道。

"发信。"哈利和乔治异口同声地回答。

"什么，在这个时候？"赫敏和弗雷德一起说。

弗雷德咧嘴一笑。"好吧——我们不问你们在干吗，只要你们别问我们。"

他手里捏着一个封好的信封。哈利瞟了一眼，可是弗雷德的手不知是无心还是有意地动了一下，盖住了信封上的名字。

"行啦，不挡你们的路。"弗雷德装模作样地鞠了一躬，指向门口。

罗恩没有动。"你们要敲诈谁？"他问。

弗雷德脸上的笑容消失了。哈利看到乔治瞟了一下弗雷德，然后对罗恩笑了起来。

"别傻了，我是开玩笑的。"他大大咧咧地说。

"听口气不像。"罗恩说。

弗雷德和乔治对视了一下。

弗雷德突然说："我告诉过你，罗恩，要是你喜欢你鼻子现在的形状，就少管闲事。不明白你来搅和什么，不过——"

"要是你们在敲诈什么人，那就不是闲事。"罗恩说，"乔治说得对，你们会惹出大麻烦的。"

"跟你说了我是开玩笑嘛。"乔治说，他走到弗雷德身边，抽出他手里的信，绑到离他最近的一只谷仓猫头鹰的腿上，"你说话的口气有点像我们亲爱的哥哥了，罗恩。再这样下去你也会当上级长的。"

"不，我不会！"罗恩激烈地说。

乔治把谷仓猫头鹰抱到窗口，把它放走了。

他回身朝罗恩笑着。"好吧，那就别管这管那的了，再见。"

他和弗雷德离开了猫头鹰棚屋。哈利、罗恩和赫敏面面相觑。

"你认为他们会知道什么情况吗？"赫敏小声问，"关于克劳奇这

## CHAPTER TWENTY-NINE  The Dream

whispered. 'About Crouch and everything?'

'No,' said Harry. 'If it was something that serious, they'd tell someone. They'd tell Dumbledore.'

Ron, however, was looking uncomfortable.

'What's the matter?' Hermione asked him.

'Well ...' said Ron slowly, 'I dunno if they would. They're ... they're obsessed with making money lately, I noticed it when I was hanging around with them – when – you know –'

'We weren't talking,' Harry finished the sentence for him. 'Yeah, but blackmail ...'

'It's this joke-shop idea they've got,' said Ron. 'I thought they were only saying it to annoy Mum, but they really mean it, they want to start one. They've only got a year left at Hogwarts, they keep going on about how it's time to think about their future, and Dad can't help them, and they need gold to get started.'

Hermione was looking uncomfortable now. 'Yes, but ... they wouldn't do anything against the law to get gold. Would they?'

'Wouldn't they?' said Ron, looking sceptical. 'I dunno ... they don't exactly mind breaking rules, do they?'

'Yes, but this is the *law*,' said Hermione, looking scared. 'This isn't some silly school rule ... they'll get a lot more than detention for blackmail! Ron ... maybe you'd better tell Percy ...'

'Are you mad?' said Ron. 'Tell Percy? He'd probably do a Crouch and turn them in.' He stared at the window through which Fred and George's owl had departed, then said, 'Come on, let's get some breakfast.'

'D'you think it's too early to go and see Professor Moody?' Hermione said, as they went down the spiral staircase.

'Yes,' said Harry. 'He'd probably blast us through the door if we wake him at the crack of dawn, he'll think we're trying to attack him while he's asleep. Let's give it 'til break.'

History of Magic had rarely gone so slowly. Harry kept checking Ron's watch, having finally discarded his own, but Ron's was moving so slowly he could have sworn it had stopped working too. All three of them were so tired they could happily have put their heads down on the desks and slept; even

## 第29章 噩 梦

件事?"

"不会,"哈利说,"如果是那么严重的事,他们会跟别人说的,会告诉邓布利多的。"

但罗恩显得有点儿不安。

"怎么啦?"赫敏问他。

"嗯……"罗恩慢吞吞地说,"我不知道他们会不会。他们……他们最近一门心思想着赚钱。我是跟他们在一起的时候发现的——就是在——你知道——"

"我们俩闹别扭不说话那会儿。"哈利替他说道,"我知道,可是敲诈……"

"他们想开一个笑话商店,"罗恩说,"我原以为他们那么说只是为了惹妈妈生气,没想到他们真打算开一个。他们在霍格沃茨只剩下一年了,总是说是时候为将来筹划筹划了。爸爸帮不了他们,他们开店需要钱。"

现在赫敏显得不安起来。"是啊,可是……他们不会为了赚钱去干违法的事吧?"

"会不会呢?"罗恩怀疑地说,"我不知道……他们对违反不违反纪律并不在乎,是吧?"

"不错,可这是法律啊,"赫敏惊恐地说,"不是什么愚蠢的学校纪律……敲诈的后果可比关禁闭严重得多,罗恩,你最好告诉珀西……"

"你疯了吗?"罗恩说,"告诉珀西?他会像克劳奇那样告发他们的。"他凝视着弗雷德和乔治的猫头鹰飞出去的那扇窗户,然后说,"走吧,我们去吃早饭。"

"你们觉得现在去看穆迪教授是不是太早了?"走下螺旋形楼梯时赫敏问道。

"是啊,"哈利说,"要是我们天刚亮就把他吵醒,他会把我们轰出来的。他会以为我们想趁他睡着时偷袭他。还是等到下课吧。"

魔法史课从来没有像今天这样缓慢、难熬。哈利不停地看罗恩的手表,因为他终于把自己那块表扔掉了。可是罗恩的表走得那么慢,哈利简直断定它也坏了。三个人都疲倦不堪,真想伏在课桌上睡一觉。

## CHAPTER TWENTY-NINE  The Dream

Hermione wasn't taking her usual notes, but was sitting with her head on her hand, gazing at Professor Binns with her eyes out of focus.

When the bell finally rang, they hurried out into the corridors towards the Dark Arts classroom, and found Professor Moody leaving it. He looked as tired as they felt. The eyelid of his normal eye was drooping, giving his face an even more lop-sided appearance than usual.

'Professor Moody?' Harry called, as they made their way towards him through the crowd.

'Hello, Potter,' growled Moody. His magical eye followed a couple of passing first-years, who sped up, looking nervous; it rolled into the back of Moody's head and watched them around the corner before he spoke again. 'Come in here.'

He stood back to let them into his empty classroom, limped in after them and closed the door.

'Did you find him?' Harry asked, without preamble. 'Mr. Crouch?'

'No,' said Moody. He moved over to his desk, sat down, stretched out his wooden leg with a slight groan and pulled out his hip-flask.

'Did you use the map?' Harry said.

'Of course,' said Moody, taking a swig from his flask. 'Took a leaf out of your book, Potter. Summoned it from my office into the Forest. He wasn't anywhere on there.'

'So he *did* Disapparate?' said Ron.

'*You can't Disapparate in the grounds, Ron!*' said Hermione. 'There are other ways he could have disappeared, aren't there, Professor?'

Moody's magical eye quivered as it rested on Hermione.

'You're another one who might think about a career as an Auror,' he told her. 'Mind works the right way, Granger.'

Hermione flushed pink with pleasure.

'Well, he wasn't invisible,' said Harry, 'the map shows invisible people. He must've left the grounds, then.'

'But under his own steam?' said Hermione eagerly. 'Or because someone made him?'

'Yeah, someone could've – could've pulled him onto a broom and flown off with him, couldn't they?' said Ron quickly, looking hopefully at Moody, as if he, too, wanted to be told he had the makings of an Auror.

## 第29章 噩 梦

就连赫敏也没有像平常一样做笔记，只是用手支着脑袋，两眼无神地瞪着宾斯教授。

下课铃终于响了，他们匆匆跑进走廊，朝黑魔法防御术课的教室跑去，穆迪教授正好从教室里出来。他看上去和他们一样疲惫。那只正常眼睛的眼皮耷拉着，使他的脸看上去比平常更加歪斜。

"穆迪教授！"哈利喊道，他们正挤过人群走向他。

"你好，波特。"穆迪瓮声瓮气地说。他那只魔眼盯着两个一年级学生，他们赶紧加快脚步，显得有些紧张。然后那只眼睛翻向他的脑后，看着那两个学生转过了拐角，他才开始说话。"进来吧。"

他退后一步，让他们走进空荡荡的教室，自己也拖着瘸腿跟进来，关上了门。

"你找到克劳奇先生了吗？"哈利开门见山地问。

"没有。"穆迪走到讲台前坐下来，伸直他的木腿，轻轻呻吟了一声，从裤兜里掏出了酒瓶。

"你用地图了吗？"哈利问。

"当然用了，"穆迪对着瓶嘴痛饮了一口，"我也学你的样子，波特，把地图用召唤咒从我的办公室召到了禁林里，可是上面哪儿都找不到他。"

"那他真的幻影移形了？"罗恩说。

"在学校场地上你不可能幻影移形，罗恩！"赫敏说，"他要消失还有其他办法呢，是不是，教授？"

穆迪的那只魔眼微微颤动地看着赫敏。

"你也可以考虑以后当一名傲罗。"他对她说，"思路很正确，格兰杰。"

赫敏高兴得涨红了脸。

"嗯，他没有隐形，"哈利说，"地图上能显示隐形的人。他一定是离开场地了。"

"靠他自己的力量？"赫敏急切地问，"还是被别人弄走的？"

"对，可能是被人弄走的——可能被人拖到飞天扫帚上，带着飞走了，是吧？"罗恩迅速地说，一边期待地看着穆迪，好像也希望穆迪夸他具有傲罗的素质。

## CHAPTER TWENTY-NINE   The Dream

'We can't rule out kidnap,' growled Moody.

'So,' said Ron, 'd'you reckon he's somewhere in Hogsmeade?'

'Could be anywhere,' said Moody, shaking his head. 'Only thing we know for sure is that he's not here.'

He yawned widely, so that his scars stretched, and his lopsided mouth revealed a number of missing teeth.

Then he said, 'Now, Dumbledore's told me you three fancy yourselves as investigators, but there's nothing you can do for Crouch. The Ministry'll be looking for him now, Dumbledore's notified them. Potter, you just keep your mind on the third task.'

'What?' said Harry. 'Oh, yeah …'

He hadn't given the maze a single thought since he'd left it with Krum the previous night.

'Should be right up your street, this one,' said Moody, looking up at Harry and scratching his scarred and stubbly chin. 'From what Dumbledore's said, you've managed to get through stuff like this plenty of times. Broke your way through a series of obstacles guarding the Philosopher's Stone in your first year, didn't you?'

'We helped,' Ron said quickly. 'Me and Hermione helped.'

Moody grinned. 'Well, help him practise for this one, and I'll be very surprised if he doesn't win,' he said. 'In the meantime … constant vigilance, Potter. Constant vigilance.' He took another long draught from his hip-flask, and his magical eye swivelled onto the window. The topmost sail of the Durmstrang ship was visible through it.

'You two' – his normal eye was on Ron and Hermione – 'you stick close to Potter, all right? I'm keeping an eye on things, but all the same … you can never have too many eyes out.'

Sirius sent their owl back the very next morning. It fluttered down beside Harry at the same moment that a tawny owl landed in front of Hermione, clutching a copy of the *Daily Prophet* in its beak. She took the newspaper, scanned the first few pages, said 'Ha! She hasn't got wind of Crouch!', then joined Ron and Harry in reading what Sirius had to say on the mysterious events of the night before last.

## 第29章 噩 梦

"不能排除绑架。"穆迪粗声说。

"那么,你认为他在霍格莫德村吗?"罗恩问。

"在任何地方都可能,"穆迪摇头说,"我们只能肯定他不在这里。"

他大大地打了个哈欠,脸上的伤疤都绷紧了,歪斜的嘴里缺了几颗牙齿都能看见。

然后他说:"对了,邓布利多告诉我,你们三个想当侦探,可是在克劳奇这件事上你们帮不了忙。邓布利多已经通知了魔法部,部里正在派人寻找。波特,你就专心准备第三个项目吧。"

"什么?"哈利说,"噢,好吧……"

自从他和克鲁姆昨晚离开迷宫之后,他已经把它忘得一干二净。

"这次你应该是熟门熟路了,"穆迪说,抬眼看着哈利,一边挠着他那胡子拉碴、满是伤疤的下巴,"听邓布利多说,这种玩意儿你挑战成功过很多次。一年级的时候你曾经闯过一系列保护魔法石的机关,是不是?"

"我们也帮了忙,"罗恩忙不迭地说,"我和赫敏。"

穆迪笑了。"好,再帮他准备这一次吧。如果他赢不了,我会感到非常惊讶的。"穆迪说,"同时……时刻保持警惕,波特。时刻保持警惕。"他又对着酒瓶长饮一口,那只魔眼转向窗外。从那里可以看见德姆斯特朗大船上最高的一片船帆。

"你们俩,"穆迪用那只正常的眼睛看着罗恩和赫敏说道,"要紧紧跟着波特,好吗?我也在密切注意事态的发展,不过……多几双眼睛总是好的。"

第二天早上,小天狼星就把他们的猫头鹰派了回来。它拍着翅膀落在哈利身边,与此同时,一只黄褐色的猫头鹰落在赫敏面前,嘴里叼着一份《预言家日报》。赫敏拿起报纸,翻了翻前几版,说:"哈!那女人还不知道克劳奇的事!"然后她和罗恩、哈利一起读小天狼星的信,看他对前天晚上的神秘事件有什么说法。

## CHAPTER TWENTY-NINE   The Dream

*Harry – what do you think you are playing at, walking off into the Forest with Viktor Krum? I want you to swear, by return owl, that you are not going to go walking with anyone else at night. There is somebody highly dangerous at Hogwarts. It is clear to me that they wanted to stop Crouch seeing Dumbledore and you were probably feet away from them in the dark. You could have been killed.*

*Your name didn't get into the Goblet of Fire by accident. If someone's trying to attack you, they're on their last chance. Stay close to Ron and Hermione, do not leave Gryffindor Tower after hours, and arm yourself for the third task. Practise Stunning and Disarming. A few hexes wouldn't go amiss either. There's nothing you can do about Crouch. Keep your head down and look after yourself. I'm waiting for your letter giving me your word you won't stray out of bounds again.*

*Sirius*

'Who's he, to lecture me about being out of bounds?' said Harry in mild indignation, as he folded up Sirius' letter and put it inside his robes. 'After all the stuff he did at school!'

'He's worried about you!' said Hermione sharply. 'Just like Moody and Hagrid! So listen to them!'

'No one's tried to attack me all year,' said Harry. 'No one's done anything to me at all –'

'Except put your name in the Goblet of Fire,' said Hermione. 'And they must've done that for a reason, Harry. Snuffles is right. Maybe they've been biding their time. Maybe this is the task they're going to get you.'

'Look,' said Harry impatiently, 'let's say Snuffles is right, and someone Stunned Krum to kidnap Crouch. Well, they *would've* been in the trees near us, wouldn't they? But they waited 'til I was out of the way until they acted, didn't they? So it doesn't look like I'm their target, does it?'

'They couldn't have made it look like an accident if they'd murdered you in the Forest!' said Hermione. 'But if you die during a task –'

'They didn't care about attacking Krum, did they?' said Harry. 'Why didn't they just polish me off at the same time? They could've made it look like Krum and I had a duel or something.'

## 第29章 噩 梦

哈利——你以为这是好玩的吗?和威克多尔·克鲁姆走到禁林里去!我要你在回信里发誓,再也不半夜跟别人出去瞎逛了。霍格沃茨有一些非常危险的人物。我认为他们显然是想阻止克劳奇去见邓布利多,在黑暗中你也许离他们只有几步之遥。你本可能送命的。

你的名字出现在火焰杯里绝非偶然。如果有人要袭击你,这是他们最后的机会。同罗恩和赫敏待在一起,放学后不要离开格兰芬多塔楼。好好准备第三个项目,练习昏迷咒和缴械咒,学一两个恶咒也没有坏处。克劳奇的事你管不了,还是埋头照顾好你自己吧。我等你回信,你要向我保证不再有越轨行为。

小天狼星

"他是谁呀,来教训我不要有越轨行为?"哈利把小天狼星的信折了起来,放到长袍内侧的口袋里,有些生气地说,"他自己在学校里还干了那么多荒唐事呢!"

"他是为你担心!"赫敏尖锐地说,"就像穆迪和海格一样。你必须听他们的!"

"整整一年都没有人对我下手,"哈利说,"没有人敢对我做任何事情——"

"但是有人把你的名字放进了火焰杯,"赫敏说,"他们那样做一定是有原因的,哈利。'伤风'说得对,也许他们在等待时机。也许他们想在比赛时对你下手。"

"好吧,"哈利不耐烦地说,"就算'伤风'是对的,而且有人把克鲁姆击昏后绑架了克劳奇。那他们准是躲在我们附近的树丛里,对不对?可他们是等我走开之后才下手的,对不对?这么看来,我不是他们攻击的目标,对不对?"

"要是他们在禁林中杀害你,就不可能弄得像一次意外事故。"赫敏说,"可是如果你在比赛中遇难——"

"可他们对克鲁姆下手倒无所顾忌,是吧?"哈利问,"为什么不同时把我干掉呢?他们可以假装克鲁姆和我决斗嘛。"

## CHAPTER TWENTY-NINE · The Dream

'Harry, I don't understand it either,' said Hermione desperately. 'I just know there are a lot of odd things going on, and I don't like it ... Moody's right – Snuffles is right – you've got to get in training for the third task, straight away. And you make sure you write back to Snuffles and promise him you're not going to go sneaking off alone again.'

The Hogwarts grounds never looked more inviting than when Harry had to stay indoors. For the next few days he spent all of his free time either in the library with Hermione and Ron, looking up hexes, or else in empty classrooms, which they sneaked into to practise. Harry was concentrating on the Stunning Spell, which he had never used before. The trouble was that practising it involved certain sacrifices on Ron and Hermione's part.

'Can't we kidnap Mrs. Norris?' Ron suggested during Monday lunchtime, as he lay flat on his back in the middle of their Charms classroom, having just been Stunned and reawoken by Harry for the fifth time in a row. 'Let's Stun her for a bit. Or you could use Dobby, Harry, I bet he'd do anything to help you. I'm not complaining or anything' – he got gingerly to his feet, rubbing his backside – 'but I'm aching all over ...'

'Well, you keep missing the cushions, don't you!' said Hermione impatiently, rearranging the pile of cushions they had used for the Banishing Spell, which Flitwick had left in a cabinet. 'Just try and fall backwards!'

'Once you're Stunned, you can't aim too well, Hermione!' said Ron angrily. 'Why don't you take a turn?'

'Well, I think Harry's got it now, anyway,' said Hermione hastily. 'And we don't have to worry about Disarming, because he's been able to do that for ages ... I think we ought to start on some of these hexes this evening.'

She looked down the list they had made in the library.

'I like the look of this one,' she said, 'this Impediment Jinx. Should slow down anything that's trying to attack you, Harry. We'll start with that one.'

The bell rang. They hastily shoved the cushions back into Flitwick's cupboard, and slipped out of the classroom.

'See you at dinner!' said Hermione, and she set off for Arithmancy, while Harry and Ron headed towards North Tower, and Divination. Broad strips of dazzling gold sunlight fell across the corridor from the high windows. The sky outside was so brightly blue it looked as though it had been enamelled.

## 第29章 噩 梦

"哈利,我也不明白,"赫敏一筹莫展地说,"我只知道正在发生许多蹊跷的事情,我不喜欢……穆迪说得对——'伤风'说得也对——你应该好好准备第三个项目的比赛了,立即开始。你还要给'伤风'回信,保证不再一个人溜出去。"

哈利被迫待在房间里之后,觉得霍格沃茨的场地从来没有这样诱人。后来几天的空闲时间里,他不是跟赫敏和罗恩在图书馆查找恶咒,就是和他们偷偷溜进没人的空教室里练习。哈利专心练习昏迷咒,他以前从来没有使用过这种咒语。只是罗恩和赫敏要做出一些牺牲了。

"我们能不能绑架洛丽丝夫人?"星期一中午罗恩提议道,他仰面朝天躺在魔咒课教室的地板上,刚才连续五次被哈利击昏又弄醒,"用它来练习练习。或者用多比,哈利,我打赌他为了你什么都肯做的。我不是抱怨,"——他小心翼翼地站起来,揉着后背——"可我浑身都疼……"

"你老是不摔在垫子上!"赫敏不耐烦地说,一边整理着他们之前练驱逐咒时用过的那堆垫子,弗立维把它们留在了柜子里,"你要往后摔!"

"被击昏后不可能瞄得那么准,赫敏!"罗恩生气地说,"你为什么自己不试试?"

"哦,我想哈利已经掌握了,"赫敏忙说,"缴械咒用不着担心,他早就会用了……我想今晚我们应该练几个恶咒。"

她低头看着他们在图书馆开的单子。

"我觉得这个不错,"她说,"障碍咒,可以截住任何企图袭击你的东西。哈利,我们就从这个开始吧。"

铃声响了,他们匆匆把垫子塞回弗立维的柜子,溜出了教室。

"晚饭见!"赫敏说。她去上算术占卜课,哈利和罗恩去北楼上占卜课。耀眼的金色阳光透过走廊的高窗投下宽宽的光带,窗外的蓝天明亮得如同刚上过一层釉。

## CHAPTER TWENTY-NINE    The Dream

'It's going to be boiling in Trelawney's room, she never puts out that fire,' said Ron, as they started up the staircase towards the silver ladder and the trapdoor.

He was quite right. The dimly lit room was swelteringly hot. The fumes from the perfumed fire were heavier than ever. Harry's head swam as he made his way over to one of the curtained windows. While Professor Trelawney was looking the other way, disentangling her shawl from a lamp, he opened it an inch or so and settled back in his chintz armchair, so that a soft breeze played across his face. It was extremely comfortable.

'My dears,' said Professor Trelawney, sitting down in her winged armchair in front of the class and peering around at them all with her strangely enlarged eyes, 'we have almost finished our work on planetary divination. Today, however, will be an excellent opportunity to examine the effects of Mars, for he is placed most interestingly at the present time. If you will all look this way, I will dim the lights ...'

She waved her wand and the lamps went out. The fire was the only source of light now. Professor Trelawney bent down, and lifted, from under her chair, a miniature model of the solar system, contained within a glass dome. It was a beautiful thing; each of the moons glimmered in place around the nine planets and the fiery sun, all of them hanging in thin air beneath the glass. Harry watched lazily as Professor Trelawney began to point out the fascinating angle Mars was making with Neptune. The heavily perfumed fumes washed over him, and the breeze from the window played across his face. He could hear an insect humming gently somewhere behind the curtain. His eyelids began to droop ...

He was riding on the back of an eagle owl, soaring through the clear blue sky towards an old, ivy-covered house set high on a hillside. Lower and lower they flew, the wind blowing pleasantly in Harry's face, until they reached a dark and broken window in the upper storey of the house, and entered. Now they were flying along a gloomy passageway, to a room at the very end ... through the door they went, into a dark room whose windows were boarded up ...

Harry had left the owl's back ... he was watching, now, as it fluttered across the room, into a chair with its back to him ... there were two dark shapes on the floor beside the chair ... both of them were stirring ...

One was a huge snake ... the other was a man ... a short, balding man, a man with watery eyes and a pointed nose ... he was wheezing and sobbing on the hearth-rug ...

# 第29章 噩 梦

"特里劳尼的教室准热得像蒸笼一样，她从来不把火炉熄掉。"他们走上通向银色梯子和活板门的楼梯时，罗恩说道。

给他说中了，那间昏暗的教室里热得让人喘不过气来。熏香的味道比往常更加浓郁。哈利走到一扇拉着窗帘的窗户前，感到脑袋发昏。他趁特里劳尼教授看着另一边，解去挂在灯上的披巾时，偷偷把窗户打开了一条缝，然后靠在套着印度印花布的扶手椅上，一股轻风吹着他的脸，惬意极了。

"亲爱的，"特里劳尼教授坐到带翅的扶手椅上，用她那双大得出奇的眼睛扫视他们，"我们差不多已经讲完了行星占卜。但今天是研究火星作用的一个大好时机，因为它目前正处在非常有趣的位置上。请你们往这边看，我把灯关掉……"

她一挥魔杖，所有的灯都灭了。炉火成了唯一的光源。特里劳尼教授弯下腰，从椅子底下拿出一个装在圆玻璃罩里的小型太阳系模型。这个模型非常美丽，燃烧的太阳、九大行星及它们的卫星悬浮在玻璃罩中，在各自的位置上熠熠闪烁。哈利懒洋洋地看着，特里劳尼教授开始讲解火星与海王星形成的奇妙夹角。浓郁的熏香朝哈利袭来，窗口透进来的轻风抚弄着他的面颊，可以听见窗帘后一只昆虫细细的嗡鸣，他的眼皮耷拉了下来……

他骑在一只雕枭的背上，在蔚蓝明亮的天空中飞翔，一直飞到山坡上一座爬满常春藤的老房子跟前。清风吹拂着哈利的脸庞，他们越飞越低，最后从顶楼一扇黑洞洞的破窗户里飞了进去。现在他们飞过一道阴暗的走廊，走廊尽头有一扇门……他们飞进门里，这是一间黑屋子，窗户都封上了……

哈利已经不在猫头鹰背上了……他看着猫头鹰穿过房间飞到一把背对着他的椅子上……椅子旁边的地上有两个黑色的影子……它们在动……

一个是一条大蛇……另一个是人……一个秃顶的小矮个儿男人，这人长着尖鼻子，眼睛泪汪汪的……他在炉边的地毯上喘气、抽泣……

843

## CHAPTER TWENTY-NINE   The Dream

'You are in luck, Wormtail,' said a cold, high-pitched voice from the depths of the chair in which the owl had landed. 'You are very fortunate indeed. Your blunder has not ruined everything. He is dead.'

'My Lord!' gasped the man on the floor. 'My Lord, I am ... I am so pleased ... and so sorry ...'

'Nagini,' said the cold voice, 'you are out of luck. I will not be feeding Wormtail to you, after all ... but never mind, never mind ... there is still Harry Potter ...'

The snake hissed. Harry could see its tongue fluttering.

'Now, Wormtail,' said the cold voice, 'perhaps one more little reminder why I will not tolerate another blunder from you ...'

'My Lord ... no ... I beg you ...'

The tip of a wand emerged from the depths of the chair. It was pointing at Wormtail. '*Crucio*,' said the cold voice.

Wormtail screamed, screamed as though every nerve in his body was on fire, the screaming filled Harry's ears as the scar on his forehead seared with pain; he was yelling, too ... Voldemort would hear him, would know he was there ...

'Harry! *Harry!*'

Harry opened his eyes. He was lying on the floor of Professor Trelawney's room with his hands over his face. His scar was still burning so badly that his eyes were watering. The pain had been real. The whole class was standing around him, and Ron was kneeling next to him, looking terrified.

'You all right?' he said.

'Of course he isn't!' said Professor Trelawney, looking thoroughly excited. Her great eyes loomed over Harry, gazing at him. 'What was it, Potter? A premonition? An apparition? What did you see?'

'Nothing,' Harry lied. He sat up. He could feel himself shaking. He couldn't stop himself looking around, into the shadows behind him; Voldemort's voice had sounded so close ...

'You were clutching your scar!' said Professor Trelawney. 'You were rolling on the floor, clutching your scar! Come now, Potter, I have experience in these matters!'

Harry looked up at her.

'I need to go to the hospital wing, I think,' he said. 'Bad headache.'

'My dear, you were undoubtedly stimulated by the extraordinary

## 第29章 噩 梦

"算你运气,虫尾巴,"一个冷酷而尖厉刺耳的声音从猫头鹰降落的椅子后传出,"你真是非常走运。你的失误没有把事情搞糟。他已经死了。"

"主人!"地上的男人叫道,"主人,我……我太高兴了……我非常抱歉……"

"纳吉尼,"那个冷酷的声音说,"你运气不好。我不打算用虫尾巴喂你了……不过没关系……还有哈利·波特……"

大蛇发出咝咝的声音。哈利看见它在吐芯子。

"现在,虫尾巴,"那冷酷的声音又说,"也许应该提醒你一下,我不能容忍你再犯错误……"

"主人……不要……求求你……"

椅子边露出了一根魔杖的尖梢,指着虫尾巴。"钻心剜骨!"那冷酷的声音说道。

虫尾巴痛苦地尖叫起来,好像他的每根神经都着了火似的。尖叫声灌进哈利的耳朵,他额头的伤疤火烧火燎般地疼起来,他也喊出了声……伏地魔会听见的,会发现他在那里……

"哈利!哈利!"

哈利睁开眼睛。他躺在特里劳尼教授的教室的地板上,双手捂着脸,伤疤依然火烧火燎地疼,把他的眼泪都疼出来了。这疼痛是真的。全班同学都站在周围,罗恩跪在他身边,看上去吓坏了。

"你没事吧?"罗恩说。

"他当然有事!"特里劳尼教授显得兴奋极了,她的大眼睛凝视着哈利,阴森森地朝他逼近,"怎么回事,波特?一个预兆?一个幻影?你看见了什么?"

"没什么。"哈利撒了个谎。他坐起来,感到自己在发抖。他忍不住四处张望,朝身后的阴影里仔细窥视,伏地魔的声音听上去近在咫尺……

"刚才你捂着伤疤!"特里劳尼教授说,"你捂着伤疤在地上打滚!说吧,波特,这些事我有经验!"

哈利抬头看着她。

"我想我需要去医院,"他说,"头疼得厉害。"

"亲爱的,你显然是受了我教室里的超视感应的影响!"特里劳

## CHAPTER TWENTY-NINE    The Dream

clairvoyant vibrations of my room!' said Professor Trelawney. 'If you leave now, you may lose the opportunity to see further than you have ever –'

'I don't want to see anything except a headache cure,' said Harry.

He stood up. The class backed away. They all looked unnerved.

'See you later,' Harry muttered to Ron, and he picked up his bag and headed for the trapdoor, ignoring Professor Trelawney, who was wearing an expression of great frustration, as though she had just been denied a real treat.

When Harry reached the bottom of her stepladder, however, he did not set off for the hospital wing. He had no intention whatsoever of going there. Sirius had told him what to do if his scar hurt him again, and Harry was going to follow his advice: he was going straight to Dumbledore's office. He marched down the corridors, thinking about what he had seen in the dream ... it had been as vivid as the one which had awoken him in Privet Drive ... he ran over the details in his mind, trying to make sure he could remember them ... he had heard Voldemort accusing Wormtail of making a blunder ... but the owl had brought good news, the blunder had been repaired, somebody was dead ... so Wormtail was not going to be fed to the snake ... he, Harry, was going to be fed to it instead ...

Harry had walked right past the stone gargoyle guarding the entrance to Dumbledore's office without noticing. He blinked, looked around, realised what he had done and retraced his steps, stopping in front of it. Then he remembered that he didn't know the password.

'Sherbet lemon?' he tried tentatively.

The gargoyle did not move.

'OK,' said Harry, staring at it. 'Pear drop. Er – Liquorice wand. Fizzing Whizzbee. Drooble's Best Blowing Gum. Bertie Bott's Every Flavour Beans ... oh no, he doesn't like them, does he? ... Oh, just open, can't you?' he said angrily. 'I really need to see him, it's urgent!'

The gargoyle remained immovable.

Harry kicked it, achieving nothing but an excruciating pain in his big toe.

'Chocolate Frog!' he yelled angrily, standing on one leg. 'Sugar quill! Cockroach cluster!'

The gargoyle sprang to life, and jumped aside. Harry blinked.

'Cockroach cluster?' he said, amazed. 'I was only joking ...'

He hurried through the gap in the walls, and stepped onto the foot of

## 第29章 噩 梦

尼教授说,"如果你现在走开,就没有机会看到你从来没有见过的未来——"

"我只想看到治头疼的办法。"哈利说。

他站了起来,全班同学纷纷退去,脸上都带着不安的神情。

"一会儿见。"哈利小声对罗恩说。他拎起书包朝活板门走去,没有理会特里劳尼教授。她一脸沮丧,仿佛刚刚被剥夺了一顿丰盛的宴席。

但是,哈利下了活梯之后并没有往校医院去。他根本没打算去那儿。小天狼星告诉过他如果伤疤再疼应该怎么办。哈利决定照他说的去做,现在就去邓布利多的办公室。他穿过走廊,一边想着梦里的情景……它和女贞路的那个惊醒他的梦一样真切……他回忆所有的细节,努力使自己不要忘记……他听见伏地魔责备虫尾巴犯了错误……可是猫头鹰带来了好消息,过错得到了弥补,什么人死了……虫尾巴不会被喂给蛇吃了……而他哈利将被用来喂蛇……

哈利只顾沉思,从邓布利多办公室入口处的滴水嘴石兽旁走过都没有注意。他愣了一下,回头一望,才发现走过了,便又返回来,停在石兽前。这时他才想起他不知道口令。

"柠檬雪宝糖?"他试探地问道。

石兽一动不动。

"好吧,"哈利瞪着它说,"梨子硬糖。呃——甘草魔杖。滋滋蜜蜂糖。吹宝超级泡泡糖。比比多味豆……噢,不对,邓布利多教授不喜欢这个,对吧?……你开开门行不行?"他恼火地说,"我真的要见他,有要紧的事!"

石兽还是纹丝不动。

哈利踢了它一脚,除了大脚趾钻心地疼之外,没起到任何效果。

"巧克力蛙!"他跳着脚气急败坏地嚷道,"糖棒羽毛笔!蟑螂串!"

石兽一下子活了,跳到一边。哈利愣住了。

"蟑螂串?"他吃惊地说,"我只是说着玩儿的……"

他急忙穿过墙上的缺口,踏上螺旋形的石头楼梯,大门在他身后

## CHAPTER TWENTY-NINE    The Dream

a spiral stone staircase, which moved slowly upwards as the doors closed behind him, taking him up to a polished oak door with a brass door-knocker.

He could hear voices from inside the office. He stepped off the moving staircase and hesitated, listening.

'Dumbledore, I'm afraid I don't see the connection, don't see it at all!' It was the voice of the Minister for Magic, Cornelius Fudge. 'Ludo says Bertha's perfectly capable of getting herself lost. I agree we would have expected to have found her by now, but all the same, we've no evidence of foul play, Dumbledore, none at all. As for her disappearance being linked with Barty Crouch's!'

'And what do you think's happened to Barty Crouch, Minister?' said Moody's growling voice.

'I see two possibilities, Alastor,' said Fudge. 'Either Crouch has finally cracked – more than likely, I'm sure you'll agree, given his personal history – lost his mind, and gone wandering off somewhere –'

'He wandered extremely quickly, if that is the case, Cornelius,' said Dumbledore calmly.

'Or else – well ...' Fudge sounded embarrassed. 'Well, I'll reserve judgement until after I've seen the place where he was found, but you say it was just past the Beauxbatons carriage? Dumbledore, you know what that woman *is*?'

'I consider her to be a very able Headmistress – and an excellent dancer,' said Dumbledore quietly.

'Dumbledore, come!' said Fudge angrily. 'Don't you think you might be prejudiced in her favour because of Hagrid? They don't all turn out harmless – if, indeed, you can call Hagrid harmless, with that monster fixation he's got –'

'I no more suspect Madame Maxime than Hagrid,' said Dumbledore, just as calmly. 'I think it possible that it is you who are prejudiced, Cornelius.'

'Can we wrap up this discussion?' growled Moody.

'Yes, yes, let's go down into the grounds, then,' said Cornelius impatiently.

'No, it's not that,' said Moody, 'it's just that Potter wants a word with you, Dumbledore. He's just outside the door.'

## 第29章 噩 梦

关上了。楼梯缓缓地自动上升，把他送到了一扇闪闪发亮的橡木门前，门上带有黄铜门环。

办公室里有人说话。哈利走下自动楼梯，犹豫着停下脚步，侧耳倾听。

"邓布利多，我看不出有什么联系，一点也看不出！"是魔法部部长康奈利·福吉的声音，"卢多说伯莎很可能是迷路了。我也认为现在应该找到她了，但不管怎么说，我们没有发现任何行凶的迹象，邓布利多，一点也没有。至于把伯莎的失踪和巴蒂·克劳奇的失踪扯到一起，纯属乱弹琴！"

"部长，你认为巴蒂·克劳奇怎么样了？"穆迪的粗嗓门说道。

"我认为有两种可能，阿拉斯托，"福吉说，"克劳奇要么是彻底疯了——从他个人的经历来看，这是很可能的，我想你们也同意——他发了疯，迷迷糊糊，不知道走到什么地方去了——"

"如果是这样的话，他走得也太快了，康奈利。"邓布利多平静地说。

"要么……也许……"福吉的声音有些发窘，"也许，还是等我看过他被发现的地点之后再做判断吧。不过，你说他是在布斯巴顿的马车旁被发现的？邓布利多，你知道那个女人的底细吧？"

"我认为她是一位非常能干的女校长——而且舞跳得很好。"邓布利多平静地说。

"行了，邓布利多！"福吉生气地说，"你不认为你是为了海格的缘故而偏袒她吗？他们并不都是无害的——如果你能说海格没有危险，那他对巨大怪兽的那种痴迷——"

"我对马克西姆女士像对海格一样信任，"邓布利多仍是那样安详地回答，"我倒认为可能是你怀有偏见，康奈利。"

"我们能不能打住？"穆迪咆哮道。

"好，好，我们这就到场地上去。"福吉不耐烦地说。

"不，我不是这个意思。"穆迪说，"邓布利多，波特有话要对你说。他就在门外。"

# CHAPTER THIRTY

# The Pensieve

The door of the office opened.

'Hello, Potter,' said Moody. 'Come in, then.'

Harry walked inside. He had been inside Dumbledore's office once before; it was a very beautiful, circular room, lined with pictures of previous Headmasters and mistresses of Hogwarts, all of whom were fast asleep, their chests rising and falling gently.

Cornelius Fudge was standing beside Dumbledore's desk, wearing his usual pinstriped cloak and holding his lime-green bowler hat.

'Harry!' said Fudge jovially, moving forwards. 'How are you?'

'Fine,' Harry lied.

'We were just talking about the night when Mr. Crouch turned up in the grounds,' said Fudge. 'It was you who found him, was it not?'

'Yes,' said Harry. Then, feeling it was pointless to pretend that he hadn't overheard what they had been saying, he added, 'I didn't see Madame Maxime anywhere, though, and she'd have a job hiding, wouldn't she?'

Dumbledore smiled at Harry behind Fudge's back, his eyes twinkling.

'Yes, well,' said Fudge, looking embarrassed, 'we're about to go for a short walk in the grounds, Harry, if you'll excuse us ... perhaps if you just go back to your class —'

'I wanted to talk to you, Professor,' Harry said quickly, looking at Dumbledore, who gave him a swift, searching look.

'Wait here for me, Harry,' he said. 'Our examination of the grounds will not take long.'

They trooped out in silence past him, and closed the door. After a minute or so, Harry heard the clunks of Moody's wooden leg growing fainter in the corridor below. He looked around.

# 第 30 章

# 冥 想 盆

办公室的门开了。

"你好,波特,"穆迪说,"进来吧。"

哈利走进屋内。他以前来过邓布利多的办公室,这是一个非常美丽的圆形房间,墙上挂着霍格沃茨历届校长的肖像画。他们都在沉睡,胸脯轻轻起伏着。

康奈利·福吉站在邓布利多的桌旁,穿着他平常穿的那件细条纹斗篷,手里拿着他的黄绿色礼帽。

"哈利!"福吉愉快地走过来说,"你好吗?"

"挺好的。"哈利没说实话。

"我们正在讲那天夜里克劳奇先生出现在场地上的事,"福吉说,"是你发现他的,对吗?"

"是的。"哈利说,他觉得假装没有听到他们的谈话是没有用的,就补充说,"不过我没有看见马克西姆女士,她要藏得那么好可不容易,是吧?"

邓布利多在福吉身后朝哈利微笑,眼睛闪闪发亮。

"哦,哦,"福吉显得有点尴尬,"我们打算去场地上走走,哈利,如果你不介意的话……你可以回到课堂上去了——"

"教授,我想跟你谈谈。"哈利看着邓布利多急促地说,邓布利多敏锐地而探寻地看了他一眼。

"你在这里等我吧,我们查看场地用不了多长时间。"他说。

三个人默默地从哈利身边走出去,关上了房门。一分钟后,哈利听到穆迪的木头假腿在楼下走廊里渐渐远去。他开始环顾四周。

## CHAPTER THIRTY    The Pensieve

'Hello, Fawkes,' he said.

Fawkes, Professor Dumbledore's phoenix, was standing on his golden perch beside the door. The size of a swan, with magnificent scarlet and gold plumage, he swished his long tail and blinked benignly at Harry.

Harry sat down in a chair in front of Dumbledore's desk. For several minutes, he sat and watched the old Headmasters and mistresses snoozing in their frames, thinking about what he had just heard, and running his fingers over his scar. It had stopped hurting now.

He felt much calmer, somehow, now he was in Dumbledore's office, knowing he would shortly be telling him about the dream. Harry looked up at the walls behind the desk. The patched and ragged Sorting Hat was standing on a shelf. A glass case next to it held a magnificent silver sword, with large rubies set into the hilt, which Harry recognised as the one he himself had pulled out of the Sorting Hat in his second year. The sword had once belonged to Godric Gryffindor, founder of Harry's house. He was gazing at it, remembering how it had come to his aid when he had thought all hope was lost, when he noticed a patch of silvery light, dancing and shimmering on the glass case. He looked around for the source of the light, and saw a sliver of silver white shining brightly from within a black cabinet behind him, whose door had not been closed properly. Harry hesitated, glanced at Fawkes, then got up, walked across the office, and pulled the cabinet door open.

A shallow stone basin lay there, with odd carvings around the edge; runes and symbols that Harry did not recognise. The silvery light was coming from the basin's contents, which were like nothing Harry had ever seen before. He could not tell whether the substance was liquid or gas. It was a bright, whitish silver, and it was moving ceaselessly; the surface of it became ruffled like water beneath wind, and then, like clouds, separated and swirled smoothly. It looked like light made liquid – or like wind made solid – Harry couldn't make up his mind.

He wanted to touch it, to find out what it felt like, but nearly four years' experience of the magical world told him that sticking his hand into a bowl full of some unknown substance was a very stupid thing to do. He therefore pulled his wand out of the inside of his robes, cast a nervous look around the office, looked back at the contents of the basin, and prodded them. The surface of the silvery stuff inside the basin began to swirl very fast.

Harry bent closer, his head right inside the cabinet. The silvery

# 第30章 冥想盆

"你好，福克斯。"哈利说。

邓布利多教授的凤凰福克斯栖在门边的金色栖枝上，个头有天鹅那么大，鲜红色和金色的羽毛光彩夺目。它摇动着长长的尾羽，友善地朝哈利眨着眼睛。

哈利在邓布利多书桌前的一把椅子里坐下。有那么几分钟，他坐在那儿望着那些在相框里打盹的老校长们，想着刚才听到的话，一边用手抚摸着自己的伤疤，伤疤现在已经不疼了。

置身于邓布利多的办公室，而且知道马上就可以把那个梦告诉校长，哈利感觉平静多了。他朝桌子后面的墙上看去，那顶破旧的、打着补丁的分院帽搁在架子上。旁边的一个玻璃匣子里放着一把银光闪闪的宝剑，剑柄上镶有大颗的红宝石。哈利认出这正是他二年级时从分院帽里抽出的那把宝剑。它曾经属于哈利他们学院的创始人戈德里克·格兰芬多。哈利凝视着它，想起当他感到一切都完了的时候，是这把剑救了他。忽然，他发现玻璃匣上有一片银光在跳动闪烁。他环顾四周寻找亮光的来源，发现身后一个黑柜子的门没有关好，里面透出了一束明亮的银光。哈利迟疑了一下，看了看福克斯，然后起身穿过办公室走过去，拉开了柜门。

柜子里有一个浅浅的石盆，盆口有奇形怪状的雕刻：有如尼文，还有哈利认不出来的符号。银光就是由盆里的东西发出来的，哈利从没见过这样的物质，搞不清它是液体还是气体。它像一块明亮的白银，但在不停地流动，像水面在微风中泛起涟漪，又像云朵那样飘逸地散开、柔和地旋转。它像是化为液体的光——又像是凝成固体的风——哈利无法做出判断。

他想碰碰它，看是什么感觉。但在魔法世界将近四年的经验告诉他，把手伸进盛满未知物体的盆里是非常愚蠢的。于是他从袍子里抽出魔杖，紧张地看了看四周，又回来看着盆里的东西，然后对着盆里的物体戳了戳。银色物体的表面开始快速旋转。

哈利俯下身，脑袋完全伸进了柜子里。银色物体变得透明了，看

## CHAPTER THIRTY    The Pensieve

substance had become transparent; it looked like glass. He looked down into it, expecting to see the stone bottom of the basin – and saw instead an enormous room below the surface of the mysterious substance, a room into which he seemed to be looking through a circular window in the ceiling.

The room was dimly lit; he thought it might even be underground, for there were no windows, merely torches in brackets such as the ones that illuminated the walls of Hogwarts. Lowering his face so that his nose was a mere inch away from the glassy substance, Harry saw that rows and rows of witches and wizards were sat around every wall on what seemed to be benches rising in levels. An empty chair stood in the very centre of the room. There was something about the chair that gave Harry an ominous feeling. Chains encircled the arms of it, as though its occupants were usually tied to it.

Where was this place? It surely wasn't Hogwarts; he had never seen a room like that here in the castle. Moreover, the crowd in the mysterious room at the bottom of the basin was composed of adults, and Harry knew there were not nearly that many teachers at Hogwarts. They seemed, he thought, to be waiting for something; even though he could only see the tops of their pointed hats, they all seemed to be facing in one direction, and nobody was talking to anybody else.

The basin being circular, and the room he was observing square, Harry could not make out what was going on in the corners of it. He leant even closer, tilting his head, trying to see …

The tip of his nose touched the strange substance into which he was staring.

Dumbledore's office gave an almighty lurch – Harry was thrown forwards and pitched head first into the substance inside the basin –

But his head did not hit the stone bottom. He was falling through something icy cold and black; it was like being sucked into a dark whirlpool –

And suddenly, he found himself sitting on a bench at the end of the room inside the basin, a bench raised high above the others. He looked up at the high stone ceiling, expecting to see the circular window through which he had just been staring, but there was nothing there but dark, solid stone.

Breathing hard and fast, Harry looked around him. Not one of the witches and wizards in the room (and there were at least two hundred of them) was looking at him. Not one of them seemed to have noticed that a fourteen-year-old boy had just dropped from the ceiling into their midst. Harry turned to the wizard next to him on the bench, and uttered a loud cry of surprise that reverberated around the silent room.

## 第30章 冥想盆

上去像玻璃一样。他使劲往里面看,以为会看见石盆的底——可那神秘物质的表面下却是一间很大的屋子,他好像正通过一个圆形天窗朝屋子里看。

屋里光线昏暗,他猜想甚至可能是在地下,因为四周没有窗户,只有像霍格沃茨那样的插在支架上的火把照亮了墙壁。哈利把脸凑近一些,鼻子离玻璃状物质只有一英寸了。他看到一排排巫师坐在四周阶梯式的长凳上,屋子正中央摆着一把空椅子。这椅子使哈利有一种不祥的感觉,因为它的扶手上缠着锁链,好像坐在上面的人常被绑起来。

这是什么地方?肯定不是霍格沃茨,哈利在城堡中没见过这样的房间。此外,盆底的神秘房间中的那些人都是成年人,哈利知道霍格沃茨绝没有那么多教师。他想这些人似乎是在等待着什么,尽管他只能看见他们的帽顶,但所有人的脸似乎都朝着一个方向,而且没有人说话。

盆是圆形的,而那间屋子是方形的,哈利看不到角落里的情况。他凑得更近一些,歪着脑袋,努力想看清楚……

他的鼻尖碰到了那种奇异物质的表面。

邓布利多的办公室突然剧烈倾侧过来——哈利的身体朝前一冲,头朝下栽进了盆里——

但他的头没有撞到盆底。他在一片冰冷漆黑的物质中坠落,仿佛被吸进了一个黑色的漩涡——

突然,哈利发现自己坐在盆底那间屋子尽头的一条长凳上,它比别的凳子都高。他抬头仰望高高的石头天花板,想找到刚刚那个圆形天窗,可是看到的只有暗黑坚固的石块。

哈利的呼吸紧张而急促。他扫视四周,没有一个巫师在看他(屋里至少有两百个巫师),似乎谁也没有注意到一个十四岁男孩刚刚从天花板上掉到了他们中间。哈利朝长凳上旁边的那位巫师一望,不禁惊叫起来,叫声在肃静的屋子里回响。

## CHAPTER THIRTY  The Pensieve

He was sitting right next to Albus Dumbledore.

'Professor!' Harry said, in a kind of strangled whisper. 'I'm sorry – I didn't mean to – I was just looking at that basin in your cabinet – I – where are we?'

But Dumbledore didn't move or speak. He ignored Harry completely. Like every other wizard on the benches, he was staring into the far corner of the room, where there was a door.

Harry gazed, nonplussed, at Dumbledore, then around at the silently watchful crowd, then back at Dumbledore. And then it dawned on him ...

Once before, Harry had found himself a place where nobody could see or hear him. That time, he had fallen through a page in an enchanted diary, right into somebody else's memory ... and unless he was very much mistaken, something of the sort had happened again ...

Harry raised his right hand, hesitated, and then waved it energetically in front of Dumbledore's face. Dumbledore did not blink, look around at Harry, or indeed move at all. And that, in Harry's opinion, settled the matter. Dumbledore wouldn't ignore him like that. He was inside a memory, and this was not the present-day Dumbledore. Yet it couldn't be that long ago ... the Dumbledore sitting next to him now was silver-haired, just like the present-day Dumbledore. But what was this place? What were all these wizards waiting for?

Harry looked around more carefully. The room, as he had suspected when observing it from above, was almost certainly underground – more of a dungeon than a room, he thought. There was a bleak and forbidding air about the place; there were no pictures on the walls, no decorations at all; just these serried rows of benches, rising in levels all around the room, all positioned so that they had a clear view of that chair with the chains on its arms.

Before Harry could reach any conclusions about the place in which they were, he heard footsteps. The door in the corner of the dungeon opened, and three people entered – or at least, one man, flanked by two Dementors.

Harry's insides went cold. The Dementors, tall, hooded creatures whose faces were concealed, were gliding slowly towards the chair in the centre of the room, each grasping one of the man's arms with their dead and rotten-looking hands. The man between them looked as though he was about to faint, and Harry couldn't blame him ... he knew the Dementors could not touch him inside a memory, but Harry remembered their power only too well. The watching crowd recoiled slightly as the Dementors placed the man

## 第30章 冥想盆

他旁边的那人正是阿不思·邓布利多。

"教授！"哈利几乎喘不过气来地小声说，"对不起——我不是有意的——我刚才只是看着你柜里的那只石盆——我——我们在哪儿？"

可是邓布利多没有动也没有说话，他根本就没有理睬哈利。他像长凳上的其他巫师一样盯着远处的屋角，那里有一扇门。

哈利迷惑地望着邓布利多，又望望那些沉默等候的众人，然后再转脸望望邓布利多。他突然想起来了……

以前，哈利也曾到过一个地方，那里的人都看不见他，也听不见他说话。那次，他是通过一本施了魔法的日记本里的某一页掉进了另一个人的记忆中……如果他没有搞错的话，现在这种事再次发生了……

哈利举起右手，犹豫了一下，然后在邓布利多面前用力挥了挥。邓布利多没有眨眼，也没有扭头看哈利，他一动也没动。哈利认为这充分证明了自己的想法是对的。邓布利多绝不会对他这样视而不见。他此刻是在记忆里，这不是现在的邓布利多。但过去的时间不可能太久……身边的邓布利多和现在一样满头银发。可这是什么地方呢？这些巫师在等什么呢？

哈利仔细地打量四周。正如他从上面望下来时猜测的那样，这间屋子几乎可以肯定是在地下——他觉得它更像一个地牢。屋里有一种惨淡阴森的气氛，墙上没有画像，没有任何装饰，只有四周那一排排密密的长凳，阶梯式地排上去，从每一个座位都能清楚地看到那把带锁链的椅子。

哈利还没有想出这是什么地方，便听到一阵脚步声。地牢角落的门开了，走进来三个人——至少其中一个是人，正被两个摄魂怪押送着。

哈利的五脏六腑顿时变得冰凉。那两个摄魂怪——那两个脸被兜帽遮着的高大怪物——缓缓地朝屋子中央的扶手椅滑去，各自用死人般腐烂的双手紧抓着中间那人的胳膊。夹在中间的那人看上去快要晕倒了，哈利觉得这不能怪他……虽然哈利知道在记忆中摄魂怪伤害不到他，但他对它们的威力印象太深了，至今心有余悸。周围的人都显

## CHAPTER THIRTY   The Pensieve

in the chained chair and glided back out of the room. The door swung shut behind them.

Harry looked down at the man now sitting in the chair, and saw that it was Karkaroff.

Unlike Dumbledore, Karkaroff looked much younger; his hair and goatee were black. He was not dressed in sleek furs, but in thin and ragged robes. He was shaking. Even as Harry watched, the chains on the arms of the chair glowed suddenly gold, and snaked their way up his arms, binding him there.

'Igor Karkaroff,' said a curt voice to Harry's left. Harry looked around, and saw Mr. Crouch standing up in the middle of the bench beside him. Crouch's hair was dark, his face was much less lined, he looked fit and alert. 'You have been brought from Azkaban to give evidence to the Ministry of Magic. You have given us to understand that you have important information for us.'

Karkaroff straightened himself as best he could, tightly bound to the chair.

'I have, sir,' he said, and although his voice was very scared, Harry could still hear the familiar unctuous note in it. 'I wish to be of use to the Ministry. I wish to help. I – I know that the Ministry is trying to – to round up the last of the Dark Lord's supporters. I am eager to assist in any way I can …'

There was a murmur around the benches. Some of the wizards and witches were surveying Karkaroff with interest, others with pronounced mistrust. Then Harry heard, quite distinctly, from Dumbledore's other side, a familiar, growling voice saying, 'Filth.'

Harry leant forwards so that he could see past Dumbledore. Mad-Eye Moody was sitting there – though there was a very noticeable difference in his appearance. He did not have his magical eye, but two normal ones. Both were looking down upon Karkaroff, and both were narrowed in intense dislike.

'Crouch is going to let him out,' Moody breathed quietly to Dumbledore. 'He's done a deal with him. Took me six months to track him down, and Crouch is going to let him go if he's got enough new names. Let's hear his information, I say, and throw him straight back to the Dementors.'

Dumbledore made a small noise of dissent through his long, crooked nose.

'Ah, I was forgetting … you don't like the Dementors, do you, Albus?' said Moody, with a sardonic smile.

'No,' said Dumbledore calmly, 'I'm afraid I don't. I have long felt the

## 第30章 冥想盆

得有点胆怯，摄魂怪把那人放在带锁链的椅子上，缓步滑出房间，房门关上了。

哈利朝椅子上的男子看去，原来是卡卡洛夫。

与邓布利多不同，卡卡洛夫看上去比现在年轻多了，头发和胡须还是黑的。他穿的不是光滑的毛皮大衣，而是又薄又破的长袍。他在发抖。就在哈利注视的当儿，椅子扶手上的锁链突然发出金光，然后像蛇一样缠到卡卡洛夫的胳膊上，把他绑在了那里。

"伊戈尔·卡卡洛夫。"哈利左边一个声音很唐突地说。哈利转过头，看见克劳奇先生在旁边那条长凳中间站了起来。克劳奇的头发是黑的，脸上的皱纹比现在少得多。他看上去精神抖擞："你被从阿兹卡班带出来向魔法部提交证据。你告诉我们，你有重要的情报要向我们汇报。"

卡卡洛夫尽可能挺直身体，他被紧紧绑在椅子上。

"是的，先生，"他的话音中充满恐惧，但哈利仍能听出那熟悉的油滑腔调，"我愿意为魔法部效劳。我愿意提供帮助——我知道魔法部正在——搜捕黑魔头的余党。我愿意竭尽全力协助你们……"

屋子里一阵窃窃私语。一些巫师感兴趣地打量着卡卡洛夫，另一些则带着明显的不信任。哈利清楚地听到邓布利多的另一侧有个熟悉的声音粗哑地说："渣滓。"

哈利越过邓布利多探头一看，是疯眼汉穆迪坐在那里——但他的外貌有明显的不同。他还没有魔眼，只有一双普通的眼睛，这双眼睛正盯着卡卡洛夫。穆迪两眼眯缝起来，带着强烈的厌恶。

"克劳奇要把他放了，"穆迪低声对邓布利多说，"他跟他达成了一笔交易。我花了六个月才抓到他，可现在只要他能供出很多我们不知道的人的名字，克劳奇就会放掉他。要我说，不妨先听听他的情报，然后再把他扔回给摄魂怪。"

邓布利多从歪扭的长鼻子里发出了一点不以为然的声音。

"啊，我忘了……你不喜欢摄魂怪，是吗？阿不思？"穆迪带着讥讽的微笑问道。

"是的，"邓布利多平静地说，"我不喜欢。我一直觉得魔法部和这

## CHAPTER THIRTY  The Pensieve

Ministry is wrong to ally itself with such creatures.'

'But for filth like this ...' Moody said softly.

'You say you have names for us, Karkaroff,' said Mr. Crouch. 'Let us hear them, please.'

'You must understand,' said Karkaroff hurriedly, 'that He Who Must Not Be Named operated always in the greatest secrecy ... he preferred that we – I mean to say, his supporters – and I regret now, very deeply, that I ever counted myself among them –'

'Get on with it,' sneered Moody.

'– we never knew the names of every one of our fellows – he alone knew exactly who we all were –'

'Which was a wise move, wasn't it, as it prevented someone like you, Karkaroff, turning all of them in,' muttered Moody.

'Yet you say you have *some* names for us?' said Mr. Crouch.

'I – I do,' said Karkaroff breathlessly. 'And these were important supporters, mark you. People I saw with my own eyes doing his bidding. I give this information as a sign that I fully and totally renounce him, and am filled with a remorse so deep I can barely –'

'These names are?' said Mr. Crouch sharply.

Karkaroff drew a deep breath.

'There was Antonin Dolohov,' he said. 'I – I saw him torture countless Muggles and – and non-supporters of the Dark Lord.'

'And helped him do it,' murmured Moody.

'We have already apprehended Dolohov,' said Crouch. 'He was caught shortly after yourself.'

'Indeed?' said Karkaroff, his eyes widening. 'I – I am delighted to hear it!'

But he didn't look it. Harry could tell that this news had come as a real blow to him. One of his names was worthless.

'Any others?' said Crouch coldly.

'Why, yes ... there was Rosier,' said Karkaroff hurriedly. 'Evan Rosier.'

'Rosier is dead,' said Crouch. 'He was caught shortly after you were, too. He preferred to fight rather than coming quietly, and was killed in the struggle.'

'Took a bit of me with him, though,' whispered Moody to Harry's right. Harry looked around at him once more, and saw him indicating the large

## 第30章 冥想盆

些怪物搞在一起是错误的。"

"可是像这种渣滓……"穆迪轻声说。

"卡卡洛夫，你说你要告诉我们一些人的名字，"克劳奇说，"请说给我们听听。"

"你要知道，"卡卡洛夫急促地说，"神秘人行事一向非常诡秘……他希望我们——我是说他的党羽——我深深悔恨自己曾经与他们为伍——"

"少说废话。"穆迪嘲讽地说。

"——我们从来不知道所有同伙的名字——只有他清楚我们都有哪些人——"

"这一着很高明，对不对，卡卡洛夫，可以防止你这种人把他们全出卖了。"穆迪嘟哝道。

"你不是说知道一些人的名字吗？"克劳奇先生说。

"我——是的，"卡卡洛夫透不过气地说，"要知道，他们都是很重要的追随者。我亲眼看见他们按他的命令办事。我提供这些情报，以证明我彻底与他一刀两断，并且忏悔得不能再——"

"名字呢？"克劳奇先生厉声说。

卡卡洛夫深深吸了口气。

"有安东宁·多洛霍夫。"他说，"我——我看见他折磨过数不清的麻瓜和——和不支持黑魔头的人。"

"你也帮他一起干了。"穆迪嘀咕道。

"我们已经逮捕了多洛霍夫，"克劳奇说，"就在逮捕你之后不久。"

"是吗？"卡卡洛夫瞪大了眼睛，"我——我很高兴！"

但是他看上去并不高兴。哈利看出这个消息对他是个沉重的打击。他手里的一个名字已经没有用了。

"还有吗？"克劳奇冷冷地问。

"啊，有……还有罗齐尔，"卡卡洛夫急忙说，"埃文·罗齐尔。"

"罗齐尔已经死了，"克劳奇说，"也是在你之后不久被抓的。他不愿束手就擒，在搏斗中被打死了。"

"还带走了我的一点东西。"穆迪在哈利右边小声说。哈利再次扭

## CHAPTER THIRTY  The Pensieve

chunk out of his nose to Dumbledore.

'No – no more than Rosier deserved!' said Karkaroff, a real note of panic in his voice now. Harry could see that he was starting to worry that none of his information would be any use to the Ministry. Karkaroff's eyes darted towards the door in the corner, behind which the Dementors undoubtedly still stood, waiting.

'Any more?' said Crouch.

'Yes!' said Karkaroff. 'There was Travers – he helped murder the McKinnons! Mulciber – he specialised in the Imperius Curse, forced countless people to do horrific things! Rookwood, who was a spy, and passed He Who Must Not Be Named useful information from inside the Ministry itself!'

Harry could tell that, this time, Karkaroff had struck gold. The watching crowd were all murmuring together.

'Rookwood?' said Mr. Crouch, nodding to a witch sitting in front of him, who began scribbling upon her piece of parchment. 'Augustus Rookwood of the Department of Mysteries?'

'The very same,' said Karkaroff eagerly. 'I believe he used a network of well-placed wizards, both inside the Ministry and out, to collect information –'

'But Travers and Mulciber, we have,' said Mr. Crouch. 'Very well, Karkaroff, if that is all, you will be returned to Azkaban while we decide –'

'Not yet!' cried Karkaroff, looking quite desperate. 'Wait, I have more!'

Harry could see him sweating in the torchlight, his white skin contrasting strongly with the black of his hair and beard.

'Snape!' he shouted. 'Severus Snape!'

'Snape has been cleared by this council,' said Crouch coldly. 'He has been vouched for by Albus Dumbledore.'

'No!' shouted Karkaroff, straining at the chains which bound him to the chair. 'I assure you! Severus Snape is a Death Eater!'

Dumbledore had got to his feet. 'I have given evidence already on this matter,' he said calmly. 'Severus Snape was indeed a Death Eater. However, he rejoined our side before Lord Voldemort's downfall and turned spy for us, at great personal risk. He is now no more a Death Eater than I am.'

Harry turned to look at Mad-Eye Moody. He was wearing a look of deep scepticism behind Dumbledore's back.

'Very well, Karkaroff,' Crouch said coldly, 'you have been of assistance. I

## 第30章 冥想盆

头看他,他正指着鼻子上缺损的那一块给邓布利多看呢。

"这——罗齐尔是罪有应得!"卡卡洛夫的语调真的有点发慌了。哈利看出他开始担心他的情报对魔法部毫无用处。卡卡洛夫瞥了一眼屋角的那扇门,两个摄魂怪无疑还站在门后等着。

"还有吗?"克劳奇问。

"有!"卡卡洛夫说,"特拉弗斯——他协助谋杀了麦金农夫妇!还有穆尔塞伯——他专搞夺魂咒,强迫许多人做一些可怕的事情!卢克伍德,他是个奸细,从魔法部内部向那个连名字都不能提的人提供有用的情报!"

哈利看出这一次卡卡洛夫掘到了金矿。四周一片窃窃私语。

"卢克伍德!"克劳奇先生朝坐在面前的一位女巫点了点头,她便在羊皮纸上写了起来,"神秘事务司的奥古斯特·卢克伍德?"

"就是他,"卡卡洛夫急切地说,"我相信他利用一批安插在魔法部内外的巫师为他搜集情报——"

"可是特拉弗斯和穆尔塞伯是我们已经知道的。"克劳奇说,"很好,卡卡洛夫,如果只有这些,你将被送回阿兹卡班,等我们决定——"

"不要!"卡卡洛夫绝望地叫起来,"等一下,我还有!"

在火把的亮光中,哈利看到他在冒汗,苍白的皮肤与乌黑的须发形成鲜明的对比。

"斯内普!"他大声说,"西弗勒斯·斯内普!"

"斯内普已经被本委员会开释了,"克劳奇冷冷地说,"阿不思·邓布利多为他作了担保。"

"不!"卡卡洛夫喊了起来,用力想挣脱把他绑在椅子上的锁链,"我向你保证!西弗勒斯·斯内普是个食死徒!"

邓布利多已站了起来。"我已经就此事作证,"他平静地说,"西弗勒斯·斯内普确实曾经是食死徒。可他在伏地魔垮台之前就投向了我们一边,冒着很大的危险为我们做间谍。他现在和我一样,不是食死徒。"

哈利看看邓布利多身后的疯眼汉穆迪。穆迪脸上带着深深的怀疑。

"很好,卡卡洛夫,"克劳奇冷冷地说,"你协助了我们的工作。我

## CHAPTER THIRTY  The Pensieve

shall review your case. You will return to Azkaban in the meantime ...'

Mr. Crouch's voice faded. Harry looked around; the dungeon was dissolving as though it was made of smoke; everything was fading, he could see only his own body, all else was swirling darkness ...

And then, the dungeon returned. Harry was sitting in a different seat; still on the highest bench, but now to the left side of Mr. Crouch. The atmosphere seemed quite different; relaxed, even cheerful. The witches and wizards all around the walls were talking to each other, almost as though they were at some sort of sporting event. A witch halfway up the rows of benches opposite caught Harry's eye. She had short blonde hair, was wearing magenta robes, and was sucking the end of an acid-green quill. It was, unmistakeably, a younger Rita Skeeter. Harry looked around; Dumbledore was sitting beside him again, wearing different robes. Mr. Crouch looked tireder and somehow fiercer, gaunter ... Harry understood. It was a different memory, a different day ... a different trial.

The door in the corner opened, and Ludo Bagman walked into the room.

This was not, however, a Ludo Bagman gone to seed, but a Ludo Bagman who was clearly at the height of his Quidditch-playing fitness. His nose wasn't broken now; he was tall and lean and muscly. Bagman looked nervous as he sat down in the chained chair, but it did not bind him there, as it had bound Karkaroff, and Bagman, perhaps taking heart from this, glanced around at the watching crowd, waved at a couple of them, and managed a small smile.

'Ludo Bagman, you have been brought here in front of the Council of Magical Law to answer charges relating to the activities of the Death Eaters,' said Mr. Crouch. 'We have heard the evidence against you, and are about to reach our verdict. Do you have anything to add to your testimony before we pronounce judgement?'

Harry couldn't believe his ears. *Ludo Bagman, a Death Eater?*

'Only,' said Bagman, smiling awkwardly, 'well – I know I've been a bit of an idiot –'

One or two wizards and witches in the surrounding seats smiled indulgently. Mr. Crouch did not appear to share their feelings. He was staring down at Ludo Bagman with an expression of the utmost severity and dislike.

'You never spoke a truer word, boy,' someone muttered drily to Dumbledore behind Harry. He looked around, and saw Moody sitting there again. 'If I didn't know he'd always been dim, I'd have said some of those

# 第30章 冥想盆

将重审你的案子,你先回阿兹卡班……"

克劳奇的声音远去了。哈利环顾左右,地牢正在像烟雾一样消散,所有的东西渐渐隐去,他只能看见自己的身体——其他一切都变成了旋转的黑暗……

然后,地牢又出现了。哈利坐在了另一个位子上,仍然是最高的那排长凳,但现在他是在克劳奇先生的左边。气氛似乎与刚才大不相同:十分轻松,甚至很愉快。四周的巫师都在相互交谈,好像是在观看体育比赛。哈利注意到了对面中排的一个女巫,金色的短发,穿着一件洋红色长袍,吮着一支刺眼的绿色羽毛笔的笔尖。毫无疑问,这是年轻一点的丽塔·斯基特。哈利朝两边望望,邓布利多还是坐在他身旁,换了一件长袍。克劳奇先生看上去比刚才疲倦,还显得有些凶狠,有些憔悴……哈利明白了。这是另一段记忆,另一个日子……另一次审讯。

屋角的门开了,卢多·巴格曼走了进来。

但这不是衰老的卢多·巴格曼,而是鼎盛时期的魁地奇球星卢多·巴格曼。他的鼻梁还没有断,身材瘦高,体格强壮。巴格曼坐到带锁链的椅子上时显得有些紧张,但那些锁链并没有像绑卡卡洛夫一样绑他。巴格曼似乎因此精神一振,扫视了一下四座的观众,朝几个人挥了挥手,脸上还露出了一丝微笑。

"卢多·巴格曼,你被带到魔法法律委员会面前,回答对你食死徒活动的指控。"克劳奇先生说,"我们听了检举你的证词,现在将要做出判决。在宣判之前你还有什么话要说?"

哈利不敢相信自己的耳朵。卢多·巴格曼,食死徒?

"只有一句,"卢多·巴格曼不自然地微笑道,"嗯——我知道我是个傻瓜——"

周围的席位上有一两个巫师宽容地笑了。克劳奇先生却不为所动。他居高临下地审视着卢多·巴格曼,一脸的严肃和厌憎。

"这话说得再对不过了,老兄。"有人在哈利身后干巴巴地对邓布利多小声说,哈利一回头,看见又是穆迪坐在那里,"要不是我知道他一向都不机灵,我会说是那些游走球对他的大脑造成了永久性

## CHAPTER THIRTY    The Pensieve

Bludgers had permanently affected his brain ...'

'Ludovic Bagman, you were caught passing information to Lord Voldemort's supporters,' said Mr. Crouch. 'For this, I suggest a term of imprisonment in Azkaban lasting no less than –'

But there was an angry outcry from the surrounding benches. Several of the witches and wizards around the walls stood up, shaking their heads, and even their fists, at Mr. Crouch.

'But I've told you, I had no idea!' Bagman called earnestly over the crowd's babble, his round blue eyes widening. 'None at all! Old Rookwood was a friend of my dad's ... never crossed my mind he was in with You-Know-Who! I thought I was collecting information for our side! And Rookwood kept talking about getting me a job in the Ministry later on ... once my Quidditch days are over, you know ... I mean, I can't keep getting hit by Bludgers for the rest of my life, can I?'

There were titters from the crowd.

'It will be put to the vote,' said Mr. Crouch coldly. He turned to the right-hand side of the dungeon. 'The jury will please raise their hands ... those in favour of imprisonment ...'

Harry looked towards the right-hand side of the dungeon. Not one person raised their hand. Many of the witches and wizards around the walls began to clap. One of the witches on the jury stood up.

'Yes?' barked Crouch.

'We'd just like to congratulate Mr. Bagman on his splendid performance for England in the Quidditch match against Turkey last Saturday,' the witch said breathlessly.

Mr. Crouch looked furious. The dungeon was ringing with applause now. Bagman got to his feet and bowed, beaming.

'Despicable,' Mr. Crouch spat at Dumbledore, sitting down as Bagman walked out of the dungeon. 'Rookwood get him a job indeed ... the day Ludo Bagman joins us will be a very sad day for the Ministry ...'

And the dungeon dissolved again. When it had returned, Harry looked around. He and Dumbledore were still sitting beside Mr. Crouch, but the atmosphere could not have been more different. There was total silence, broken only by the dry sobs of a frail, wispy-looking witch in the seat next to Mr. Crouch. She was clutching a handkerchief to her mouth with trembling hands. Harry looked up at Crouch, and saw that he looked gaunter, and

## 第30章 冥想盆

的影响……"

"卢多·巴格曼，你在向伏地魔的党羽传递情报时被抓获，"克劳奇先生说，"为此，我建议判处你在阿兹卡班监禁至少——"

但是四座一片愤怒的喊声。有几个靠墙的巫师站起来朝克劳奇先生摇头，甚至挥舞拳头。

"可我说过，我根本不知道！"巴格曼瞪大了圆圆的蓝眼睛，在起哄声中急切地喊道，"根本不知道！老卢克伍德是我父亲的朋友……我从没想到他会是神秘人的手下！我以为我是在为我们的人收集情报呢！卢克伍德一直说以后会为我在魔法部找一份工作……等我从魁地奇球队退役之后，你知道……我是说，我不能一辈子被游走球追着打，是不是？"

观众席上发出了哧哧的笑声。

"那就表决吧。"克劳奇先生冷冷地说，他转向地牢的右侧，"请陪审团注意……同意判处监禁的举手……"

哈利朝地牢右侧望去，没有一个人举手。许多巫师开始鼓掌。陪审团中有位女巫站了起来。

"怎么？"克劳奇吼道。

"我们想祝贺巴格曼先生上星期六在对土耳其的魁地奇比赛中表现出色，为英格兰队争了光。"女巫激动地说。

克劳奇先生看上去怒不可遏。地牢里掌声雷动，巴格曼站起来鞠躬微笑。

"混账，"巴格曼走出地牢时，克劳奇先生坐了下来，气呼呼地对邓布利多说，"卢克伍德真的给他找了一份工作……卢多·巴格曼来上班的那天将是魔法部不幸的日子……"

地牢又消失了。等它再次出现时，哈利环顾四周，他和邓布利多仍然坐在克劳奇先生旁边，可是气氛却截然不同。屋子里静悄悄的，只听到克劳奇先生旁边一个弱不禁风的女巫的抽噎声。她用颤抖的双手攥着一块手帕捂在嘴上。哈利仰头看看克劳奇，发现他的面色比以

## CHAPTER THIRTY   The Pensieve

greyer than ever before. A nerve was twitching in his temple.

'Bring them in,' he said, and his voice echoed through the silent dungeon.

The door in the corner opened yet again. Six Dementors entered this time, flanking a group of four people. Harry saw the people in the crowd turn to look up at Mr. Crouch. A few of them whispered to each other.

The Dementors placed each of the four people in the four chairs with chained arms which now stood on the dungeon floor. There was a thickset man who stared blankly up at Crouch, a thinner and more nervous-looking man, whose eyes were darting around the crowd, a woman, with thick, shining dark hair, and heavily hooded eyes, who was sitting in the chained chair as though it were a throne, and a boy in his late teens, who looked nothing short of petrified. He was shivering, his straw-coloured hair all over his face, his freckled skin milk-white. The wispy little witch beside Crouch began to rock backwards and forwards in her seat, whimpering into her handkerchief.

Crouch stood up. He looked down upon the four in front of him, and there was pure hatred in his face.

'You have been brought here before the Council of Magical Law,' he said clearly, 'so that we may pass judgement on you, for a crime so heinous —'

'Father,' said the boy with the straw-coloured hair. 'Father ... please ...'

'— that we have rarely heard the like of it within this court,' said Crouch, speaking more loudly, drowning out his son's voice. 'We have heard the evidence against you. The four of you stand accused of capturing an Auror — Frank Longbottom — and subjecting him to the Cruciatus Curse, believing him to have knowledge of the present whereabouts of your exiled master, He Who Must Not Be Named —'

'Father, I didn't!' shrieked the boy in chains below. 'I didn't, I swear it, Father, don't send me back to the Dementors —'

'You are further accused,' bellowed Mr. Crouch, 'of using the Cruciatus Curse on Frank Longbottom's wife, when he would not give you information. You planned to restore He Who Must Not Be Named to power, and to resume the lives of violence you presumably led while he was strong. I now ask the jury —'

'Mother!' screamed the boy below, and the wispy little witch beside Crouch began to sob, rocking backwards and forwards. 'Mother, stop him, Mother, I didn't do it, it wasn't me!'

'I now ask the jury,' shouted Mr. Crouch, 'to raise their hands if they believe, as I do, that these crimes deserve a life sentence in Azkaban.'

## 第30章 冥想盆

前更加憔悴、灰暗，太阳穴上一根青筋在抽动。

"带进来。"克劳奇的声音在寂静的地牢中回响。

屋角的门再次打开，六个摄魂怪押着四个人走了进来。哈利看到许多人转身望着克劳奇先生，有几个在交头接耳。

摄魂怪把四个人放在地牢中央的四把带锁链的椅子上。其中一个矮胖的男子茫然地望着克劳奇；另一个较瘦的男子显得更紧张一些，眼睛往观众席上四处瞟；一个女人头发浓密乌黑、眼皮下垂，瞧她那神气倒像坐在宝座上似的；还有一个十七八岁的男孩，看上去完全吓呆了，浑身发抖，稻草色的头发披散在脸上，生有雀斑的皮肤苍白如纸。克劳奇旁边那个纤弱的女巫开始在座位上前后摇晃，用手帕捂着嘴呜咽啜泣。

克劳奇站了起来，俯视着这四个人，脸上带着极端的憎恨。

"你们被带到魔法法律委员会面前听候宣判，"他吐字清晰地说，"你们的罪行如此恶劣——"

"父亲，"稻草色头发的男孩说，"父亲……求求你……"

"——在本法庭审理的案件中是少有的。"克劳奇先生提高嗓门，盖过了他儿子的声音，"我们听了对你们的指控，你们四人绑架了一名傲罗——弗兰克·隆巴顿，对他使用了钻心咒，想从他口里打探出你们流亡的主人，那个连名字都不能提的人的下落——"

"父亲，我没有！"被绑在椅子上的男孩尖叫道，"我没有，我发誓，父亲，不要把我送回摄魂怪那里——"

"指控还说，"克劳奇先生吼道，"弗兰克·隆巴顿不肯提供情报，你们就对他的妻子使用钻心咒。你们阴谋使那个连名字都不能提的人卷土重来，以恢复他强大时期你们过的那种暴力生活。现在我请陪审团——"

"母亲！"下面那个男孩高叫道，克劳奇旁边那个瘦小的女巫抽泣起来，身体前后摇晃，"母亲，阻止他，母亲，我没做那些事，不是我！"

"现在我请陪审团表决，"克劳奇先生大声说，"和我一样认为这些罪行应当被判处在阿兹卡班终身监禁的，请举手！"

## CHAPTER THIRTY

### The Pensieve

In unison, the witches and wizards along the right-hand side of the dungeon raised their hands. The crowd around the walls began to clap as it had for Bagman, their faces full of savage triumph. The boy began to scream.

'No! Mother, no! I didn't do it, I didn't do it, I didn't know! Don't send me there, don't let him!'

The Dementors were gliding back into the room. The boy's three companions rose quietly from their seats; the woman with the heavy-lidded eyes looked up at Crouch and called, 'The Dark Lord will rise again, Crouch! Throw us into Azkaban, we will wait! He will rise again and will come for us, he will reward us beyond any of his other supporters! We alone were faithful! We alone tried to find him!'

But the boy was trying to fight the Dementors off, even though Harry could see their cold, draining power starting to affect him. The crowd were jeering, some of them on their feet, as the woman swept out of the dungeon, and the boy continued to struggle.

'I'm your son!' he screamed up at Crouch. 'I'm your son!'

'You are no son of mine!' bellowed Mr. Crouch, his eyes bulging suddenly. 'I have no son!'

The wispy witch beside him gave a great gasp, and slumped in her seat. She had fainted. Crouch appeared not to have noticed.

'Take them away!' Crouch roared at the Dementors, spit flying from his mouth. 'Take them away, and may they rot there!'

'Father! Father, I wasn't involved! No! No! Father, please!'

'I think, Harry, it is time to return to my office,' said a quiet voice in Harry's ear.

Harry started. He looked around. Then he looked on his other side.

There was an Albus Dumbledore sitting on his right, watching Crouch's son being dragged away by the Dementors – and there was an Albus Dumbledore on his left, looking right at him.

'Come,' said the Dumbledore on his left, and he put his hand under Harry's elbow. Harry felt himself rising into the air; the dungeon dissolved around him; for a moment, all was blackness, and then he felt as though he had done a slow-motion somersault, suddenly landing flat on his feet, in what seemed like the dazzling light of Dumbledore's sunlit office. The stone basin was shimmering in the cabinet in front of him, and Albus Dumbledore was standing beside him.

## 第30章 冥想盆

地牢右侧的巫师齐刷刷地举起了手。四周的观众像审判巴格曼时那样鼓起掌来，脸上带着残酷的胜利表情。男孩开始尖声惨叫。

"不！母亲，不！不是我干的，不是我，我不知道！不要把我送到那里去，阻止他！"

摄魂怪又缓缓地滑进来。男孩的三个同伴默默地从椅子上站起，眼皮下垂的女人抬头对克劳奇喊道："黑魔王还会回来的，克劳奇！把我们扔进阿兹卡班吧，我们等着！他会回来救我们。他会特别奖赏我们！只有我们是忠诚的！只有我们在设法寻找他！"

男孩竭力想摆脱摄魂怪，尽管哈利看出摄魂怪冰冷的吸力已开始对他产生作用。观众们在嘲笑，有些人站了起来。那个女人傲然走出了地牢，男孩还在反抗。

"我是你的儿子！"他向克劳奇高喊，"我是你的儿子！"

"你不是我的儿子！"克劳奇吼道，眼珠突然向外突起，"我没有儿子！"

瘦小的女巫倒吸一口气，瘫倒在凳子上。她晕过去了。克劳奇好像没看到似的。

"把他们带走！"他向摄魂怪咆哮，唾沫星子四溅，"带走，让他们在那里烂掉吧！"

"父亲！父亲，我没有参加！不要！不要！父亲，求求你！"

"哈利，我想我们该回我的办公室了。"一个声音在哈利耳边轻轻地说。

哈利吓了一跳。他回过头，然后又转脸看向另一边。

他的右边坐着一位阿不思·邓布利多，看着克劳奇的儿子被摄魂怪拽走——而他的左边还有一位阿不思·邓布利多，正在注视着他。

"来吧。"左边的邓布利多说着，伸手托住哈利的胳膊肘。哈利感到自己缓缓升到空中，地牢在消散，一时间只剩下漆黑一片。然后他觉得自己好像翻了一个慢动作的跟头，两脚突然落到地上，周围的光线令人目眩，他已经在邓布利多那间阳光明媚的办公室里了。那个石盆在他面前的柜子里闪闪发光，阿不思·邓布利多站在他身旁。

## CHAPTER THIRTY   The Pensieve

'Professor,' Harry gasped, 'I know I shouldn't've – I didn't mean – the cabinet door was sort of open and –'

'I quite understand,' said Dumbledore. He lifted the basin, carried it over to his desk, placed it upon the polished top, and sat down in the chair behind it. He motioned Harry to sit down opposite him.

Harry did so, staring at the stone basin. The contents had returned to their original, silvery white state, swirling and rippling beneath his gaze.

'What is it?' Harry asked shakily.

'This? It is called a Pensieve,' said Dumbledore. 'I sometimes find, and I am sure you know the feeling, that I simply have too many thoughts and memories crammed into my mind.'

'Er,' said Harry, who couldn't truthfully say that he had ever felt anything of the sort.

'At these times,' said Dumbledore, indicating the stone basin, 'I use the Pensieve. One simply siphons the excess thoughts from one's mind, pours them into the basin, and examines them at one's leisure. It becomes easier to spot patterns and links, you understand, when they are in this form.'

'You mean ... that stuff's your *thoughts*?' Harry said, staring at the swirling white substance in the basin.

'Certainly,' said Dumbledore. 'Let me show you.'

Dumbledore drew his wand out of the inside of his robes, and placed the tip into his own silvery hair, near his temple. When he took the wand away, hair seemed to be clinging to it – but then Harry saw that it was in fact a glistening strand of the same strange, silvery white substance that filled the Pensieve. Dumbledore added this fresh thought to the basin, and Harry, astonished, saw his own face swimming around the surface of the bowl.

Dumbledore placed his long hands on either side of the Pensieve and swirled it, rather as a gold prospector would swirl for fragments of gold ... and Harry saw his own face change smoothly into Snape's, who opened his mouth, and spoke to the ceiling, his voice echoing slightly. 'It's coming back ... Karkaroff's too ... stronger and clearer than ever ...'

'A connection I could have made without assistance,' Dumbledore sighed, 'but never mind.' He peered over the top of his half-moon spectacles at Harry, who was gaping at Snape's face, which was continuing to swirl around the bowl. 'I was using the Pensieve when Mr. Fudge arrived for our meeting, and put it away rather hastily. Undoubtedly I did not fasten the cabinet door properly. Naturally, it would have attracted your attention.'

## 第30章 冥想盆

"教授，"哈利慌乱地说，"我知道我不应该——我不是有意的——柜门开着——"

"我非常理解。"邓布利多说。他端起石盆走到书桌前，把它放在光滑的桌面上，然后在桌后的椅子上坐下，招手让哈利坐在他对面。

哈利坐下来，眼睛盯着石盆。盆里的东西又变回了银白色的状态，在他眼前打着旋，泛着涟漪。

"这是什么？"哈利声音颤抖地问。

"这个吗？它叫冥想盆，"邓布利多说，"有时候我觉得脑子里塞了太多的思想和记忆，我相信你了解这种感觉。"

"呃。"哈利不能发自内心地说自己有过这样的感觉。

"这时我就使用冥想盆，"邓布利多指着石盆说，"把过量的思想从脑子里吸出来，倒进这个盆里，有空的时候再好好看看。你知道，在这种状态下更容易看出它们的模式和彼此之间的联系。"

"你是说……这东西是你的思想？"哈利瞪着盆里旋转的银色物质说。

"正是，"邓布利多说，"我让你看看。"

邓布利多从袍子里抽出魔杖，把杖尖插进他的银发，靠近太阳穴。当他拔出魔杖时，杖尖上好像粘了一些发丝——但哈利随即发现那其实是一小缕和盆中一样的闪光的银白色物质。邓布利多把这一点新思想加到盆里，哈利吃惊地看到自己的面孔在盆里浮动。

邓布利多用修长的双手捧住冥想盆，转动着它，像淘金者转动沙盘一样……哈利看到自己的脸渐渐化成了斯内普的脸。斯内普张开嘴，朝天花板说起话来，还带着一点儿回声："它又出现了……卡卡洛夫的也是……比以前任何时候更明显、更清楚……"

"我无须帮助也能发现这之间的联系，"邓布利多叹道，"不过没关系。"他从半月形的镜片上方凝视哈利。哈利正目瞪口呆地望着斯内普的脸在盆里继续旋转。"福吉先生来时我正在使用冥想盆，我匆匆忙忙把它收了起来，想必柜门没有关严，它自然会引起你的注意。"

## CHAPTER THIRTY  The Pensieve

'I'm sorry,' Harry mumbled.

Dumbledore shook his head.

'Curiosity is not a sin,' he said. 'But we should exercise caution with our curiosity ... yes, indeed ...'

Frowning slightly, he prodded the thoughts within the basin with the tip of his wand. Instantly, a figure rose out of it, a plump, scowling girl of around sixteen, who began to revolve slowly, with her feet still in the basin. She took no notice whatsoever of Harry or Professor Dumbledore. When she spoke, her voice echoed as Snape's had done, as though it was coming from the depths of the stone basin: 'He put a hex on me, Professor Dumbledore, and I was only teasing him, sir, I only said I'd seen him kissing Florence behind the greenhouses last Thursday ...'

'But why, Bertha,' said Dumbledore sadly, looking up at the now silently revolving girl, 'why did you have to follow him in the first place?'

'Bertha?' Harry whispered, looking up at her. 'Is that – was that Bertha Jorkins?'

'Yes,' said Dumbledore, prodding the thoughts in the basin again; Bertha sank back into them, and they became silvery and opaque once more. 'That was Bertha as I remember her at school.'

The silvery light from the Pensieve illuminated Dumbledore's face, and it struck Harry suddenly how very old he was looking. He knew, of course, that Dumbledore was getting on in years, but somehow he never really thought of Dumbledore as an old man.

'So, Harry,' said Dumbledore quietly. 'Before you got lost in my thoughts, you wanted to tell me something.'

'Yes,' said Harry. 'Professor – I was in Divination just now, and – er – I fell asleep.'

He hesitated here, wondering if a reprimand was coming, but Dumbledore merely said, 'Quite understandable. Continue.'

'Well, I had a dream,' said Harry. 'A dream about Lord Voldemort. He was torturing Wormtail ... you know who Wormtail –'

'I do know,' said Dumbledore, promptly. 'Please continue.'

'Voldemort got a letter from an owl. He said something like, Wormtail's blunder had been repaired. He said someone was dead. Then he said, Wormtail wouldn't be fed to the snake – there was a snake beside his chair.

## 第30章 冥想盆

"对不起。"哈利嗫嚅地说。

邓布利多摇了摇头。

"好奇心不是罪过,"他说,"但我们在好奇的时候应当小心……的确如此……"

他微微皱起眉头,用杖尖捣了捣盆里的思想。盆中立刻升起一个人形,是个十五六岁的姑娘,胖乎乎的,一脸不高兴。她开始慢慢地旋转,双脚还站在盆里。姑娘看也不看哈利和邓布利多教授。她开口说话时,也像斯内普那样带着回声,好像是从石盆深处传出来的一样。"他对我使用了魔法,邓布利多教授,我只不过逗了逗他。我只是说我上星期四看见他在温室后面和弗洛伦斯接吻……"

"可是,伯莎,"邓布利多抬头看着此刻默默旋转的女孩,悲哀地说,"你一开始为什么要跟着他呢?"

"伯莎!"哈利抬头看着那女孩,小声说,"她是——伯莎·乔金斯?"

"是的,"邓布利多又捣了捣盆里的思想,伯莎沉了下去,盆中再次变成了不透明的银白色,"那是我记忆里学生时代的伯莎。"

冥想盆中的银光照亮了邓布利多的面庞。哈利突然发觉他是那样苍老。他当然知道邓布利多已经上了年纪,但不知为什么,以前从没觉得他是个老人。

"哈利,"邓布利多和缓地说,"在你掉进我的思想里之前,你是有一些事要告诉我的。"

"是的,"哈利说,"教授——我刚才正在上占卜课,可是,呃——我睡着了。"

他迟疑了一下,以为要挨批评了,但邓布利多却说:"可以理解,讲下去。"

"嗯,我做了个梦,"哈利说,"梦见了伏地魔,他在折磨虫尾巴……你知道虫尾巴——"

"我知道,"邓布利多马上说,"往下讲。"

"伏地魔接到了猫头鹰送去的信。他好像是说虫尾巴的错误被纠正了。他说有人死了,接着说他不打算拿虫尾巴去喂蛇了——他的椅子旁

## CHAPTER THIRTY  The Pensieve

He said – he said he'd be feeding me to it, instead. Then he did the Cruciatus Curse on Wormtail – and my scar hurt,' Harry said. 'It woke me up, it hurt so badly.'

Dumbledore merely looked at him.

'Er – that's all,' said Harry.

'I see,' said Dumbledore quietly. 'I see. Now, has your scar hurt at any other time this year, excepting the time it woke you up over the summer?'

'No, I – how did you know it woke me up over the summer?' said Harry, astonished.

'You are not Sirius' only correspondent,' said Dumbledore. 'I have also been in contact with him ever since he left Hogwarts last year. It was I who suggested the mountainside cave as the safest place for him to stay.'

Dumbledore got up, and began walking up and down behind his desk. Every now and then, he placed his wand tip to his temple, removed another shining silver thought, and added it to the Pensieve. The thoughts inside began to swirl so fast that Harry couldn't make out anything clearly; it was merely a blur of colour.

'Professor?' he said quietly, after a couple of minutes.

Dumbledore stopped pacing, and looked at Harry.

'My apologies,' he said quietly. He sat back down at his desk.

'D'you – d'you know why my scar's hurting me?'

Dumbledore looked very intently at Harry for a moment, and then said, 'I have a theory, no more than that … It is my belief that your scar hurts both when Lord Voldemort is near you, and when he is feeling a particularly strong surge of hatred.'

'But … why?'

'Because you and he are connected by the curse that failed,' said Dumbledore. 'That is no ordinary scar.'

'So you think … that dream … did it really happen?'

'It is possible,' said Dumbledore. 'I would say – probable. Harry – did you see Voldemort?'

'No,' said Harry. 'Just the back of his chair. But – there wouldn't have been anything to see, would there? I mean, he hasn't got a body, has he? But … but then how could he have held the wand?' Harry said slowly.

## 第30章 冥想盆

边有一条蛇。他又说——又说要拿我去喂蛇。然后他对虫尾巴念了钻心咒——我的伤疤就疼起来了,"哈利说,"疼得特别厉害,把我给疼醒了。"

邓布利多只是看着他。

"呃——就这些。"哈利说。

"噢,"邓布利多平静地说,"是这样,那么,你的伤疤今年还疼过吗?除了暑假里把你疼醒的那一次?"

"没有,我——你怎么知道它在暑假里把我疼醒过?"哈利惊讶地问。

"给小天狼星写信的不止你一个人。"邓布利多说,"他去年离开霍格沃茨后,我也和他保持着联系呢。是我建议他躲在山洞里的,那是最安全的地方。"

邓布利多站起来,在桌子后面来回踱步,时而把魔杖尖抵到太阳穴上,抽出一条银光闪闪的思想,加到冥想盆里。盆里的思想急速旋转起来,哈利什么也看不清了,只见一片模糊的银白色。

"教授?"几分钟后哈利轻轻叫道。

邓布利多停止了踱步,看着哈利。

"对不起。"邓布利多轻声说,重新在书桌前坐下。

"你——你知道我的伤疤为什么疼吗?"

邓布利多仔细地看了哈利一会儿,然后说:"我只有一个推测,仅仅是推测……我想,当伏地魔靠近你时,或是当他产生一种特别强烈的复仇意愿时,你的伤疤就会疼。"

"可是……为什么呢?"

"因为那个不成功的咒语把你和他连在了一起,"邓布利多说,"这不是一道普通的伤疤。"

"那你认为……那个梦……是真的吗?"

"有可能,"邓布利多说,"我要说——很有可能。哈利——你看见伏地魔了吗?"

"没有,"哈利说,"只看见了他的椅背。不过——本来也看不到什么,是吧?我是说,他没有身体,对不对?可是……那他怎么可能拿魔杖呢?"哈利慢慢地说。

## CHAPTER THIRTY · The Pensieve

'How indeed?' muttered Dumbledore. 'How indeed ...'

Neither Dumbledore nor Harry spoke for a while. Dumbledore was gazing across the room, every now and then placing his wand tip to his temple, and adding another shining, silver thought to the seething mass within the Pensieve.

'Professor,' Harry said at last, 'do you think he's getting stronger?'

'Voldemort?' said Dumbledore, looking at Harry over the Pensieve. It was the characteristic, piercing look Dumbledore had given him on other occasions, and always made Harry feel as though Dumbledore was seeing right through him, in a way that even Moody's magical eye could not. 'Once again, Harry, I can only give you my suspicions.'

Dumbledore sighed again, and he looked older, and wearier, than ever.

'The years of Voldemort's ascent to power,' he said, 'were marked with disappearances. Bertha Jorkins has vanished without trace in the place where Voldemort was certainly known to be last. Mr. Crouch, too, has disappeared ... within these very grounds. And there was a third disappearance, one which the Ministry, I regret to say, does not consider of any importance, for it concerns a Muggle. His name was Frank Bryce, he lived in the village where Voldemort's father grew up, and he has not been seen since last August. You see, I read the Muggle newspapers, unlike most of my Ministry friends.'

Dumbledore looked very seriously at Harry. 'These disappearances seem to me to be linked. The Ministry disagrees – as you may have heard, while waiting outside my office.'

Harry nodded. Silence fell between them again, Dumbledore extracting thoughts every now and then. Harry felt as though he ought to go, but his curiosity held him in his chair.

'Professor?' he said again.

'Yes, Harry?' said Dumbledore.

'Er ... could I ask you about ... that court thing I was in ... in the Pensieve?'

'You could,' said Dumbledore heavily. 'I attended it many times, but some trials come back to me more clearly than others ... particularly now ...'

'You know – you know the trial you found me in? The one with Crouch's son? Well ... were they talking about Neville's parents?'

Dumbledore gave Harry a very sharp look.

'Has Neville never told you why he has been brought up by his grandmother?' he said.

## 第30章 冥想盆

"是啊,"邓布利多喃喃道,"怎么可能呢……"

一时间两人谁也没有说话。邓布利多凝视着前方,不时用魔杖尖从太阳穴那儿取出一条银亮的思想,放进翻腾涌动的冥想盆里。

"教授,"哈利终于说,"你认为他正在强壮起来吗?"

"伏地魔吗?"邓布利多隔着冥想盆望着哈利说,又是那种特有的具有穿透力的目光,哈利在其他场合也见到过。哈利总觉得邓布利多能够完全看穿他,这是连穆迪的魔眼也做不到的。"我还是只能给你一些猜测,哈利。"

邓布利多又叹息了一声,他从未显得这么苍老疲惫过。

"伏地魔力量增强的这几年发生了好几桩失踪事件。"他说,"伯莎·乔金斯在伏地魔最后的藏身之地消失得无影无踪,克劳奇先生也失踪了……就在我们的这片场地上。还有第三起失踪事件,遗憾的是魔法部认为它无足轻重,因为失踪的是个麻瓜。他的名字叫弗兰克·布莱斯,住在伏地魔的父亲出生的村子里。他从去年八月就不见了。你知道,我是看麻瓜报纸的,这一点我和大多数部里的朋友不一样。"

邓布利多非常严肃地看着哈利。"我觉得这些失踪事件是有联系的,但部里不这样认为——你刚才在办公室外面可能也听到了。"

哈利点点头。两人又沉默了,邓布利多不时取出一些思想。哈利觉得他该走了,但好奇心使他坐着没动。

"教授?"他又叫了一声。

"怎么了,哈利?"邓布利多说。

"呃……我能不能问一下我……在冥想盆里看到的……审讯的事?"

"可以,"邓布利多沉重地说,"我参加过许多次审讯,但对其中的几次审讯记得格外清楚……尤其是现在……"

"请问——你刚才发现我在听的那次审讯,审问克劳奇儿子的那一次,嗯……他们说的是不是纳威的父母?"

邓布利多目光犀利地看了哈利一眼。

"纳威没有对你说过他为什么是由奶奶带大的吗?"

## CHAPTER THIRTY   The Pensieve

Harry shook his head, wondering, as he did so, how he could have failed to ask Neville this, in almost four years of knowing him.

'Yes, they were talking about Neville's parents,' said Dumbledore. 'His father, Frank, was an Auror just like Professor Moody. He and his wife were tortured for information about Voldemort's whereabouts after he lost his powers, as you heard.'

'So they're dead?' said Harry quietly.

'No,' said Dumbledore, his voice full of a bitterness Harry had never heard there before, 'they are insane. They are both in St Mungo's Hospital for Magical Maladies and Injuries. I believe Neville visits them, with his grandmother, during the holidays. They do not recognise him.'

Harry sat there, horror-struck. He had never known ... never, in four years, bothered to find out ...

'The Longbottoms were very popular,' said Dumbledore. 'The attacks on them came after Voldemort's fall from power, just when everyone thought they were safe. Those attacks caused a wave of fury such as I have never known. The Ministry was under great pressure to catch those who had done it. Unfortunately, the Longbottoms' evidence was – given their condition – none too reliable.'

'Then Mr. Crouch's son might not have been involved?' said Harry slowly.

Dumbledore shook his head. 'As to that, I have no idea.'

Harry sat in silence once more, watching the contents of the Pensieve swirl. There were two more questions he was burning to ask ... but they concerned the guilt of living people ...

'Er,' he said, 'Mr. Bagman ...'

'... has never been accused of any Dark activity since,' said Dumbledore calmly.

'Right,' said Harry hastily, staring at the contents of the Pensieve again, which were swirling more slowly now that Dumbledore had stopped adding thoughts. 'And ... er ...'

But the Pensieve seemed to be asking his question for him. Snape's face was swimming on the surface again. Dumbledore glanced down into it, and then up at Harry.

'No more has Professor Snape,' he said.

Harry looked into Dumbledore's light-blue eyes, and the thing he really wanted to know spilled out of his mouth before he could stop it. 'What made

## 第30章 冥想盆

哈利摇了摇头，心中纳闷他认识纳威将近四年，怎么就没想到问问这件事。

"是的，他们说的正是纳威的父母，"邓布利多说，"他父亲弗兰克和穆迪教授一样是个傲罗。你听到了，那些人残酷折磨弗兰克和他的妻子，逼他们说出伏地魔失去力量之后的下落。"

"他们死了吗？"哈利轻声问道。

"没有，"邓布利多说，声音中充满哈利从没听到过的悲痛，"他们疯了。两人都住在圣芒戈魔法伤病医院。我想纳威每到假期都和奶奶一起去探望他们。他们不认识纳威了。"

哈利恐惧地坐在那里。他一直不知道……四年了，从来没有想到问一问……

"隆巴顿夫妇人缘很好，"邓布利多说，"他们是在伏地魔垮台之后遭到袭击的，那时候大家都以为安全了。这种毒手激起了前所未有的公愤。魔法部受到很大的压力，必须捉拿凶手。不幸的是，以隆巴顿夫妇当时的状况，他们的证词不是很可靠。"

"那么，克劳奇先生的儿子有可能是无辜的吗？"哈利缓缓地问。

邓布利多摇了摇头："这一点我就不知道了。"

哈利又沉默了，看着冥想盆里的物质在那里旋转。他还有两个问题忍不住要问……可是它们涉及活着的人的罪责……

"呃，"他说，"巴格曼先生……"

"……后来再也没有被指控参与任何黑魔法活动。"邓布利多平静地说。

"噢，"哈利急促地说，再次注视着冥想盆，邓布利多不再往里面添加思想，盆中物质旋转得慢了下来，"还有……呃……"

但冥想盆似乎替他问了，斯内普的脸重新浮了上来。邓布利多看了它一眼，然后抬头望着哈利。

"斯内普教授也没有。"他说。

哈利凝视着邓布利多那双浅蓝色的眼睛，心中真正想问的话一下子脱口而出："你为什么认为他真的不再支持伏地魔了呢，教授？"

## CHAPTER THIRTY — The Pensieve

you think he'd really stopped supporting Voldemort, Professor?'

Dumbledore held Harry's gaze for a few seconds, and then said, 'That, Harry, is a matter between Professor Snape and myself.'

Harry knew that the interview was over; Dumbledore did not look angry, yet there was a finality in his tone that told Harry it was time to go. He stood up, and so did Dumbledore.

'Harry,' he said, as Harry reached the door. 'Please do not speak about Neville's parents to anybody else. He has the right to let people know, when he is ready.'

'Yes, Professor,' said Harry, turning to go.

'And –'

Harry looked back.

Dumbledore was standing over the Pensieve, his face lit from beneath by its silvery spots of light, looking older than ever. He stared at Harry for a moment, and then said, 'Good luck with the third task.'

## 第30章　冥想盆

邓布利多和哈利对视了几秒钟，然后说："这是我和斯内普教授两个人之间的事情，哈利。"

哈利知道面谈结束了。邓布利多看上去并没有生气，但语调中有一种到此为止的意思，哈利听出他该走了。他站起身，邓布利多也站了起来。

"哈利，"哈利走到门口时，邓布利多说，"请不要把纳威父母的事告诉其他人。应当由他自己来告诉大家，等他愿意说的时候。"

"好的，教授。"哈利说着，转身要走。

"还有——"

哈利回过头。

邓布利多站在冥想盆后面，盆中闪烁的银光照亮了他的面庞，他看上去比以前更加苍老。他凝视了哈利片刻，说道："第三个项目中祝你好运。"

## CHAPTER THIRTY-ONE

# The Third Task

'Dumbledore reckons You-Know-Who's getting stronger again as well?' Ron whispered.

Everything Harry had seen in the Pensieve, nearly everything Dumbledore had told and shown him afterwards, he had now shared with Ron and Hermione – and, of course, with Sirius, to whom Harry had sent an owl the moment he had left Dumbledore's office. Harry, Ron and Hermione sat up late in the common room once again that night, talking it all over until Harry's mind was reeling, until he understood what Dumbledore had meant about a head becoming so full of thoughts that it would have been a relief to siphon them off.

Ron stared into the common-room fire. Harry thought he saw Ron shiver slightly, even though the evening was warm.

'And he trusts Snape?' Ron said. 'He really trusts Snape, even though he knows he was a Death Eater?'

'Yes,' said Harry.

Hermione had not spoken for ten minutes. She was sitting with her forehead in her hands, staring at her knees. Harry thought she, too, looked as though she could have done with a Pensieve.

'Rita Skeeter,' she muttered finally.

'How can you be worrying about her now?' said Ron, in disbelief.

'I'm not worrying about her,' Hermione said to her knees. 'I'm just thinking … remember what she said to me in the Three Broomsticks? "I know things about Ludo Bagman that would make your hair curl." This is what she meant, isn't it? She reported his trial, she knew he'd passed information to the Death Eaters. And Winky, too, remember … "Mr. Bagman is a bad wizard." Mr. Crouch would have been furious he got off, he would have talked about it at home.'

# 第 31 章

## 第三个项目

"邓布利多也认为神秘人在强壮起来？"罗恩悄声问道。

哈利已经把他在冥想盆里看到的一切，以及后来他从邓布利多那里听到和看到的几乎所有东西，全都告诉了罗恩和赫敏——当然也告诉了小天狼星，哈利一离开邓布利多的办公室就给小天狼星派去了一只猫头鹰。哈利、罗恩和赫敏那天夜里又在公共休息室里待到很晚，反复讨论这些事情，说到最后哈利脑袋都晕了。他终于体会到邓布利多说的脑子里思想塞得太满，要能抽出一些才好是什么意思了。

罗恩凝视着公共休息室里的炉火。哈利似乎看到罗恩在微微发抖，尽管这个夜晚并不冷。

"他相信斯内普？"罗恩问，"他知道斯内普曾经是个食死徒，但还是真的信任他？"

"是的。"哈利说。

赫敏有十分钟没有说话。她手捧额头坐在那里，眼睛望着膝盖。哈利觉得她似乎也需要一个冥想盆。

"丽塔·斯基特。"她喃喃地说。

"你怎么现在操心起她来了？"罗恩不相信地问。

"我没有操心她，"赫敏对着膝盖说，"我只是想到……还记得她在三把扫帚对我说的话吗？'我知道卢多·巴格曼的一些事情，它们会吓得你们的头发竖起来。'她指的就是这个，是吧？她报道了当时对巴格曼的审判，知道他为食死徒传递了情报。还有闪闪，记得吗……'卢多·巴格曼是个坏巫师。'克劳奇先生可能对巴格曼没受处罚感到很恼火，他可能回家说了这件事。"

## CHAPTER THIRTY-ONE  The Third Task

'Yeah, but Bagman didn't pass information on purpose, did he?'

Hermione shrugged.

'And Fudge reckons *Madame Maxime* attacked Crouch?' Ron said, turning back to Harry.

'Yeah,' said Harry, 'but he's only saying that because Crouch disappeared near the Beauxbatons carriage.'

'We never thought of her, did we?' said Ron, slowly. 'Mind you, she's definitely got giant blood, and she doesn't want to admit it –'

'Of course she doesn't,' said Hermione sharply, looking up. 'Look what happened to Hagrid when Rita found out about his mother. Look at Fudge, jumping to conclusions about her, just because she's part giant. Who needs that sort of prejudice? I'd probably say I had big bones if I knew that's what I'd get for telling the truth.'

Hermione looked at her watch.

'We haven't done any practising!' she said, looking shocked. 'We were going to do the Impediment Jinx! We'll have to really get down to it tomorrow! Come on, Harry, you need to get some sleep.'

Harry and Ron went slowly upstairs to their dormitory. As Harry pulled on his pyjamas, he looked over at Neville's bed. True to his word to Dumbledore, he had not told Ron and Hermione about Neville's parents. As Harry took off his glasses and climbed into his four-poster, he imagined how it must feel to have parents still living, but unable to recognise you. He often got sympathy from strangers for being an orphan, but as he listened to Neville's snores, he thought that Neville deserved it more than he did. Lying in the darkness, Harry felt a rush of anger and hate towards the people who had tortured Mr. and Mrs. Longbottom ... he remembered the jeers of the crowd as Crouch's son and his companions had been dragged from the court by the Dementors ... he understood how they had felt ... then he remembered the milk-white face of the screaming boy, and realised with a jolt that he had died a year later ...

It was Voldemort, Harry thought, staring up at the canopy of his bed in the darkness, it all came back to Voldemort ... he was the one who had torn these families apart, who had ruined all these lives ...

Ron and Hermione were supposed to be revising for their exams, which would finish on the day of the third task, but they were putting most of their efforts into helping Harry prepare.

## 第31章 第三个项目

"有道理,可巴格曼不是有意传递情报的,对不对?"

赫敏耸耸肩。

"福吉认为是马克西姆女士袭击了克劳奇?"罗恩转向哈利问道。

"是啊,"哈利说,"可他那么说只是因为克劳奇是在布斯巴顿的马车附近失踪的。"

"我们从来没有想到马克西姆女士,是不是?"罗恩慢吞吞地说,"想想吧,她肯定有巨人血统,可她不愿承认——"

"她当然不愿承认,"赫敏抬起头来尖锐地说,"看看丽塔发现海格母亲的底细之后发生了什么吧。再看看福吉,就因为马克西姆女士有巨人血统,就武断地认为她是凶手。谁愿意受那样的歧视?换了我,要知道说真话的结果是这样,我大概也会说我是骨架子大。"

赫敏看了看表。

"我们一点都没有练习呢!"她惊叫起来,"我们本来应该练障碍咒的!明天必须要认真地练一练了!走吧,哈利,你需要睡会儿觉。"

哈利和罗恩慢慢上楼回到宿舍。哈利穿睡衣时朝纳威床上看了一眼。他信守了对邓布利多的承诺,没有把纳威父母的事告诉罗恩和赫敏。哈利摘下眼镜,爬到四柱床上,想象着父母虽然活着但不认识自己的滋味。他经常因为是孤儿而受到陌生人的同情,但听着纳威的鼾声,他觉得纳威比自己更值得怜悯。哈利躺在黑暗中,对折磨隆巴顿夫妇的人产生了一种强烈的愤怒和仇恨……他想起克劳奇的儿子和那几个人被摄魂怪拉出法庭时众人的嘲笑……他理解了他们的感情……接着他想起尖叫的男孩那张煞白的脸,又突然震惊地意识到他一年之后就死了……

是伏地魔,哈利在黑暗中瞪着床顶想,都是伏地魔引起的……是他拆散了这些家庭,毁掉了这么多生命……

罗恩和赫敏将在第三个项目那天结束考试,他们本来应该抓紧时间复习的,但却花了大量精力帮助哈利做准备。

## CHAPTER THIRTY-ONE    The Third Task

'Don't worry about it,' Hermione said shortly, when Harry pointed this out to them, and said he didn't mind practising on his own for a while. 'At least we'll get top marks in Defence Against the Dark Arts, we'd never have found out about all these hexes in class.'

'Good training for when we're all Aurors,' said Ron excitedly, attempting the Impediment Jinx on a wasp that had buzzed into the room, and making it stop dead in mid-air.

The mood in the castle as they entered June became excited and tense again. Everyone was looking forward to the third task, which would take place a week before the end of term. Harry was practising hexes in every available moment. He felt more confident about this task than either of the others. Difficult and dangerous though it would undoubtedly be, Moody was right: Harry had managed to find his way past monstrous creatures and enchanted barriers before now, and this time he had some notice, some chance to prepare himself for what lay ahead.

Tired of walking in on them all over the school, Professor McGonagall had given Harry permission to use the empty Transfiguration classroom at lunchtimes. He had soon mastered the Impediment Jinx, a spell to slow down and obstruct attackers, the Reductor curse, which would enable him to blast solid objects out of his way, and the Four-Point Spell, a useful discovery of Hermione's which would make his wand point due north, therefore enabling him to check whether he was going in the right direction within the maze. He was still having trouble with the Shield Charm, though. This was supposed to cast a temporary, invisible wall around himself that deflected minor curses; Hermione managed to shatter it with a well-placed Jelly-Legs Jinx. Harry wobbled around the room for ten minutes afterwards before she had looked up the counter-jinx.

'You're still doing really well, though,' Hermione said encouragingly, looking down her list, and crossing off those spells they had already learnt. 'Some of these are bound to come in handy.'

'Come and look at this,' said Ron, who was standing by the window. He was staring down into the grounds. 'What's Malfoy doing?'

Harry and Hermione went to see. Malfoy, Crabbe and Goyle were standing in the shadow of a tree below. Crabbe and Goyle seemed to be keeping a look out; both were smirking. Malfoy was holding his hand up to his mouth, and speaking into it.

'He looks like he's using a walkie-talkie,' said Harry curiously.

'He can't be,' said Hermione, 'I've told you, those sort of things don't work around

## 第31章 第三个项目

"别担心,"当哈利向他们指出这点,并说他可以自己练习一会儿时,赫敏毫不介意地说,"至少我们可以在黑魔法防御术这门课中拿高分。课堂上不可能发现这么多的咒语。"

"对我们以后当傲罗是很好的训练。"罗恩兴奋地说着,对嗡嗡飞进屋里的一只黄蜂试了试障碍咒,使它突然停在了半空中。

进入六月,城堡中的气氛又变得紧张兴奋起来。大家都期待着将于放假前一星期举行的第三项比赛。哈利一有空就练习咒语。他对于这次的任务比前两次更有信心。尽管这场比赛肯定充满艰险,但穆迪说得对:之前哈利已经找到办法顺利通过了庞大动物和魔法障碍的考验,而且这次他预先得到了通知,有机会为即将出现的东西做一些准备。

麦格教授厌烦了总是撞见哈利、赫敏和罗恩在学校各处练习,因此,她允许他们在午饭时间使用变形课教室。哈利很快掌握了障碍咒,它可以拖延和阻碍袭击者;粉碎咒,可以炸毁固体障碍物;还有赫敏发现的定向咒,能使他的魔杖指向正北,这样他在迷宫中就可以判断方向走得是否正确。但他还没有完全掌握铁甲咒,这种咒语可以在他周身暂时形成一道无形的坚壁,可以使小的咒语打偏,可惜赫敏巧妙地施了一个软腿咒把它给破了。哈利瘸着腿在屋里走了十分钟,赫敏才找到了破解咒。

"你练得不错,"赫敏鼓励地说,一边看着她的单子,勾掉他们已经学会的咒语,"肯定有一些会派上用场的。"

"快来看,"罗恩站在窗前望着下面的场地,说道,"马尔福在干什么?"

哈利和赫敏赶忙走过去看,只见马尔福、克拉布和高尔站在树荫下。克拉布和高尔好像在放哨,两个人都傻笑着。马尔福把手捂在嘴上说话。

"他好像在用对讲机。"哈利好奇地说。

"不可能,"赫敏说,"我告诉过你们,那种东西在霍格沃茨不起作用。

## CHAPTER THIRTY-ONE — The Third Task

Hogwarts. Come on, Harry,' she added briskly, turning away from the window and moving back into the middle of the room, 'let's try that Shield Charm again.'

Sirius was sending daily owls now. Like Hermione, he seemed to want to concentrate on getting Harry through the last task, before they concerned themselves with anything else. He reminded Harry in every letter that whatever might be going on outside the walls of Hogwarts was not Harry's responsibility, nor was it within his power to influence it.

> *If Voldemort is really getting stronger again* [he wrote], *my priority is to ensure your safety. He cannot hope to lay hands on you while you are under Dumbledore's protection, but all the same, take no risks: concentrate on getting through that maze safely, and then we can turn our attention to other matters.*

Harry's nerves mounted as June the twenty-fourth drew closer, but they were not as bad as those he had had before the first and second tasks. For one thing, he was confident that, this time, he had done everything in his power to prepare for the task. For another, this was the final hurdle, and however well or badly he did, the Tournament would at last be over, which would be an enormous relief.

Breakfast was a very noisy affair at the Gryffindor table on the morning of the third task. The post owls appeared, bringing Harry a good-luck card from Sirius. It was only a piece of parchment, folded over and bearing a muddy paw print on its front, but Harry appreciated it all the same. A screech owl arrived for Hermione, carrying her morning copy of the *Daily Prophet* as usual. She unfolded the paper, glanced at the front page, and spat out a mouthful of pumpkin juice all over it.

'What?' said Harry and Ron together, staring at her.

'Nothing,' said Hermione quickly, trying to shove the paper out of sight, but Ron grabbed it.

He stared at the headline, and said, 'No way. Not today. That old *cow*.'

'What?' said Harry. 'Rita Skeeter again?'

'No,' said Ron, and just like Hermione, he attempted to push the paper out of sight.

## 第31章 第三个项目

来吧,哈利。"她轻快地说,转身离开窗口走到屋子中间,"我们再来练练铁甲咒。"

小天狼星现在每天都派猫头鹰送信来。他和赫敏一样,似乎一心要帮助哈利通过第三个项目,然后才会考虑其他事情。他在每封信中都提醒哈利,霍格沃茨围墙以外的事你没有责任去管,你也没有能力对它们施加影响。

> 如果伏地魔真的在强壮起来(他写道),我首先考虑的事是要保证你的安全。有邓布利多的保护,他不可能对你下手,但你还得多加小心,不要冒险:现在你要想的是怎样安全走出迷宫,其他问题以后再说。

哈利的神经随着六月二十四日的临近而紧张起来,但比第一个和第二个项目前要好一些。首先,他相信自己这次是尽力做了准备的。而且,这是最后一个障碍,不管成绩是好是坏,争霸赛即将结束,这个大包袱终于可以卸掉了。

比赛那天,格兰芬多的早餐桌上热闹非常。送信的猫头鹰到了,给哈利捎来了小天狼星送的幸运卡。只是一张羊皮纸,一折两开,上面有一只泥乎乎的爪印,但哈利很喜欢。一只尖叫猫头鹰像往常一样给赫敏送来了早晨的《预言家日报》。赫敏打开报纸,扫了一眼头版,登时把一口南瓜汁全喷在了报纸上。

"怎么啦?"哈利和罗恩一齐盯着她问道。

"没什么。"赫敏很快地说,慌忙想把报纸藏起来,却被罗恩一把抢了过去。

他瞪着标题说:"不可能,偏偏是今天,这个老母牛。"

"怎么?"哈利问,"又是丽塔·斯基特?"

"不是。"罗恩也跟赫敏一样想把报纸藏起来。

## CHAPTER THIRTY-ONE    The Third Task

'It's about me, isn't it?' said Harry.

'No,' said Ron, in an entirely unconvincing tone.

But before Harry could demand to see the paper, Draco Malfoy shouted across the Great Hall from the Slytherin table.

'Hey, Potter! *Potter*! How's your head? You feeling all right? Sure you're not going to go berserk on us?'

Malfoy was holding a copy of the *Daily Prophet*, too. Slytherins up and down the table were sniggering, twisting in their seats to see Harry's reaction.

'Let me see it,' Harry said to Ron. 'Give it here.'

Very reluctantly, Ron handed over the newspaper. Harry turned it over, and found himself staring at his own picture, beneath a banner headline:

### HARRY POTTER 'DISTURBED AND DANGEROUS'

The boy who defeated He Who Must Not Be Named is unstable and possibly dangerous, *writes Rita Skeeter, Special Correspondent*. Alarming evidence has recently come to light about Harry Potter's strange behaviour, which casts doubts upon his suitability to compete in a demanding competition like the Triwizard Tournament, or even to attend Hogwarts school.

Potter, the *Daily Prophet* can exclusively reveal, regularly collapses at school, and is often heard to complain of pain in the scar on his forehead (relic of the curse with which You-Know-Who attempted to kill him). On Monday last, mid-way through a Divination lesson, your *Daily Prophet* reporter witnessed Potter storming from the class, claiming that his scar was hurting too badly to continue studying.

It is possible, say top experts at St Mungo's Hospital for Magical Maladies and Injuries, that Potter's brain was affected by the attack inflicted upon him by You-Know-Who, and that his insistence that the scar is still hurting is an expression of his deep-seated confusion.

'He might even be pretending,' said one specialist. 'This could be a plea for attention.'

The *Daily Prophet*, however, has unearthed worrying facts about Harry Potter that Albus Dumbledore, Headmaster of Hogwarts, has carefully concealed from the wizarding public.

'Potter can speak Parseltongue,' reveals Draco Malfoy, a Hogwarts

## 第31章 第三个项目

"写到我了是不是?"哈利问。

"不是。"罗恩以完全不可信的语调说。

但是,没等哈利提出要看那份报纸,礼堂那头斯莱特林桌子上的德拉科·马尔福就叫了起来。

"嘿,波特!波特!你的脑袋怎么样?你没事儿吧?不会朝我们发疯吧?"

马尔福手里也举着一份《预言家日报》。斯莱特林的学生们都在窃笑,在座位上扭过身看哈利的反应。

"给我看看,"哈利对罗恩说,"给我。"

罗恩极不情愿地交出报纸,哈利一翻开就看到了自己的照片,上面是文章标题:

### 哈利·波特
#### ——心烦意乱,情绪危险

打败了神秘人的男孩情绪很不稳定,而且可能相当危险,特邀记者丽塔·斯基特报道。最近有惊人的证据披露了哈利·波特的奇怪行为,使人怀疑他是否适合参加三强争霸赛这样高难度的竞赛,甚至是否适合在霍格沃茨上学。

《预言家日报》独家披露,波特在学校经常发病,对人说他额头的伤疤作痛(该伤疤是神秘人企图杀死他时念的恶咒留下的印记)。上星期一的占卜课上,《预言家日报》记者目睹了波特冲出教室,声称伤疤疼得他无法继续上课的情形。

圣芒戈魔法伤病医院的高级专家说,波特的大脑可能受到了神秘人魔法的影响,波特坚持说伤疤仍然疼痛,正表明他的精神有着根本上的混乱。

"他也可能是装的,"一位专家说,"也许想引起注意。"

但《预言家日报》还发现了哈利·波特一些令人不安的状况,霍格沃茨的校长阿不思·邓布利多一直在为其小心遮掩。

"波特会说蛇佬腔,"霍格沃茨四年级学生德拉科·马尔福透

## CHAPTER THIRTY-ONE — The Third Task

fourth-year. 'There were a lot of attacks on students a couple of years ago, and most people thought Potter was behind them after they saw him lose his temper at a Duelling Club and set a snake on another boy. It was all hushed up, though. But he's made friends with werewolves and giants too. We think he'd do anything for a bit of power.'

Parseltongue, the ability to converse with snakes, has long been considered a Dark Art. Indeed, the most famous Parselmouth of our times is none other than You-Know-Who himself. A member of the Dark Force Defence League, who wished to remain unnamed, stated that he would regard any wizard who could speak Parseltongue 'as worthy of investigation. Personally, I would be highly suspicious of anybody who could converse with snakes, as serpents are often used in the worst kinds of Dark Magic, and are historically associated with evil-doers.' Similarly, 'anyone who seeks out the company of such vicious creatures as werewolves and giants would appear to have a fondness for violence'.

Albus Dumbledore should surely consider whether a boy such as this should be allowed to compete in the Triwizard Tournament. Some fear that Potter might resort to the Dark Arts in his desperation to win the Tournament, the third task of which takes place this evening.

'Gone off me a bit, hasn't she?' said Harry lightly, folding up the paper.

Over on the Slytherin table, Malfoy, Crabbe and Goyle were laughing at him, tapping their heads with their fingers, pulling grotesquely mad faces and waggling their tongues like snakes.

'How did she know your scar hurt in Divination?' Ron said. 'There's no way she was there, there's no way she could've heard –'

'The window was open,' said Harry. 'I opened it to breathe.'

'You were at the top of North Tower!' Hermione said. 'Your voice couldn't have carried all the way down to the grounds!'

'Well, you're the one who's supposed to be researching magical methods of bugging!' said Harry. 'You tell me how she did it!'

'I've been trying!' said Hermione. 'But I ... but ...'

An odd, dreamy expression suddenly came over Hermione's face. She slowly raised a hand, and ran her fingers through her hair.

'Are you all right?' said Ron, frowning at her.

## 第31章 第三个项目

露说,"两年前许多学生受到袭击,大多数人都认为波特是幕后指使人,因为大家亲眼见到他在决斗俱乐部里发脾气放蛇去咬一个男孩。但这些都被掩盖了起来。波特还与狼人和巨人交朋友。我们认为他为了获得力量什么都干得出来。"

蛇佬腔(即与蛇对话的能力)一向被视为黑魔法。事实上,当代最著名的蛇佬腔正是神秘人本人。黑魔法防御联盟的一位不愿透露姓名的成员说,他认为任何会说蛇佬腔的巫师"都值得调查,我个人对能与蛇对话的人十分怀疑,因为蛇经常被用在最恶毒的黑魔法中,而且历史上也和坏人联系在一起"。同样,"与狼人和巨人等邪物为伍的人通常是爱好暴力的"。

阿不思·邓布利多应当考虑允许这样一个男孩参加三强争霸赛是否合适。有人担心波特会因求胜心切而使用黑魔法。第三个比赛项目将于今晚举行。

"对我不那么青睐了,是不是?"哈利折起报纸,轻松地说。

斯莱特林那边,马尔福、克拉布和高尔都在讥笑他。他们用手指敲着脑门,做出疯子的怪相,还像蛇一样吐着舌头。

"她怎么知道占卜课上你伤疤疼了?"罗恩说,"她不可能在场,也不可能听到——"

"窗户开着,"哈利说,"我开了窗想透透气。"

"你是在北塔楼的顶层!"赫敏说,"你的声音传不到下面的场地上!"

"哎,研究魔法窃听方法的应该是你啊!"哈利说,"你告诉我,她怎么知道的!"

"我正在想呢!"赫敏说,"可是……可是……"

赫敏脸上突然现出一种做梦般的奇怪表情,她慢慢地抬起一只手,捋着自己的头发。

"你没事吧?"罗恩皱着眉头问她。

## CHAPTER THIRTY-ONE  The Third Task

'Yes,' said Hermione breathlessly. She ran her fingers through her hair again, and then held her hand up to her mouth, as though speaking into an invisible walkie-talkie. Harry and Ron stared at each other.

'I've had an idea,' Hermione said, gazing into space. 'I think I know ... because then no one would be able to see ... even Moody ... and she'd have been able to get onto the window-ledge ... but she's not allowed ... she's *definitely* not allowed ... I think we've got her! Just give me two seconds in the library – just to make sure!'

With that, Hermione seized her schoolbag, and dashed out of the Great Hall.

'Oi!' Ron called after her. 'We've got our History of Magic exam in ten minutes! Blimey,' he said, turning back to Harry, 'she must really hate that Skeeter woman to risk missing the start of an exam. What're you going to do in Binns's class – read again?'

Exempt from the end-of-term tests as a Triwizard champion, Harry had been sitting at the back of every exam class so far, looking up fresh hexes for the third task.

'S'pose so,' Harry said to Ron; but just then, Professor McGonagall came walking along the Gryffindor table towards him.

'Potter, the champions are congregating in the chamber off the Hall after breakfast,' she said.

'But the task's not 'til tonight!' said Harry, accidentally spilling scrambled eggs down his front, afraid he had mistaken the time.

'I'm aware of that, Potter,' she said. 'The champions' families are invited to watch the final task, you know. This is simply a chance for you to greet them.'

She moved away. Harry gaped after her.

'She doesn't expect the Dursleys to turn up, does she?' he asked Ron blankly.

'Dunno,' said Ron. 'Harry, I'd better hurry, I'm going to be late for Binns. See you later.'

Harry finished his breakfast in the emptying Great Hall. He saw Fleur Delacour get up from the Ravenclaw table and join Cedric as he crossed to the side chamber and entered. Krum slouched off to join them shortly afterwards. Harry stayed where he was. He really didn't want to go into the chamber. He had no family – no family who would turn up to see him risk his life, anyway. But just as he was getting up, thinking that he might as well go up to the library and do a spot more hex revision, the door of the side chamber opened, and Cedric stuck his head out.

## 第31章 第三个项目

"没事。"赫敏屏住呼吸说。她又捋了捋头发,然后把手举到嘴边,像握着对讲机似的。哈利和罗恩面面相觑。

"我有了一个想法,"赫敏两眼空洞地望着前面说,"我想我知道了……因为那样谁也看不见……连穆迪都看不见……她能够爬到窗台上……但这是不允许的……这绝对是不允许的……我想我们抓住她了!给我两秒钟——去图书馆核实一下!"

话音刚落,赫敏就抓起书包奔出了礼堂。

"喂!"罗恩在后面喊道,"魔法史考试还有十分钟就开始了!天哪,"他转身向哈利说,"她一定是恨透了斯基特那个老妖婆,连考试有可能迟到都不在乎了。你在宾斯的教室里准备干什么——还是看书吗?"

哈利作为三强争霸赛的勇士,可以不参加期末考试。他每场考试都坐在教室后面,为第三个项目寻找有用的咒语。

"可能吧。"哈利对罗恩说。但麦格教授沿着格兰芬多的桌子向他走来了。

"波特,勇士们吃完早饭在礼堂旁边的会议室集合。"她说。

"可是比赛晚上才开始呀!"哈利不小心把炒鸡蛋撒到了身上,他以为自己记错了时间。

"我知道,波特,"麦格教授说,"勇士的亲属被请来观看决赛,你们可以趁现在见见面。"

她走开了。哈利望着她的背影发呆。

"她难道认为德思礼一家会来?"他茫然地问罗恩。

"不知道,"罗恩说,"哈利,我得赶紧走,考试要迟到了。一会儿见。"

哈利在渐渐冷清下来的礼堂里吃完早饭。他看到芙蓉·德拉库尔从拉文克劳桌子旁站起来,和塞德里克一起走进了会议室。不一会儿克鲁姆也懒洋洋地去了。哈利坐着没动,他实在不想去会议室。他没有亲属——反正没有愿意来看他冒生命危险的亲属。可是正当他站起身,打算还是去图书馆研究一点咒语时,会议室的门开了,塞德里克探出头来。

## CHAPTER THIRTY-ONE   The Third Task

'Harry, come on, they're waiting for you!'

Utterly perplexed, Harry got up. The Dursleys couldn't possibly be here, could they? He walked across the Hall and opened the door into the chamber.

Cedric and his parents were just inside the door. Viktor Krum was over in a corner, conversing with his dark-haired mother and father in rapid Bulgarian. He had inherited his father's hooked nose. On the other side of the room, Fleur was jabbering away in French to her mother. Fleur's little sister, Gabrielle, was holding her mother's hand. She waved at Harry, who waved back. Then he saw Mrs. Weasley and Bill standing in front of the fireplace, beaming at him.

'Surprise!' Mrs. Weasley said excitedly, as Harry smiled broadly, and walked over to them. 'Thought we'd come and watch you, Harry!' She bent down and kissed him on the cheek.

'You all right?' said Bill, grinning at Harry and shaking his hand. 'Charlie wanted to come, but he couldn't get time off. He said you were incredible against the Horntail.'

Fleur Delacour, Harry noticed, was eyeing Bill with great interest over her mother's shoulder. Harry could tell she had no objection whatsoever to long hair or earrings with fangs on them.

'This is really nice of you,' Harry muttered to Mrs. Weasley. 'I thought for a moment – the Dursleys –'

'Hmm,' said Mrs. Weasley, pursing her lips. She had always refrained from criticising the Dursleys in front of Harry, but her eyes flashed every time they were mentioned.

'It's great being back here,' said Bill, looking around the chamber (Violet, the Fat Lady's friend, winked at him from her frame). 'Haven't seen this place for five years. Is that picture of the mad knight still around? Sir Cadogan?'

'Oh, yeah,' said Harry, who had met Sir Cadogan the previous year.

'And the Fat Lady?' said Bill.

'She was here in my time,' said Mrs. Weasley. 'She gave me such a telling-off one night when I got back to the dormitory at four in the morning –'

'What were you doing out of your dormitory at four in the morning?' said Bill, surveying Mrs. Weasley with amazement.

Mrs. Weasley grinned, her eyes twinkling.

'Your father and I had been for a night-time stroll,' she said. 'He got caught by Apollyon Pringle – he was the caretaker in those days – your

## 第31章 第三个项目

"哈利,快来吧,他们在等你呢!"

哈利满心困惑地站起身。德思礼一家是不可能来的呀。他穿过大厅,推门走进了会议室。

塞德里克和他的父母站在门边。威克多尔·克鲁姆在屋子一角和他黑头发的父母说着快速的保加利亚语,他继承了父亲的鹰钩鼻。房间的另一边,芙蓉在用法语和她母亲叽叽呱呱地说个不停。芙蓉的小妹妹加布丽牵着她母亲的手。加布丽朝哈利挥了挥手,哈利也挥挥手,咧嘴一笑。然后他看见韦斯莱夫人和比尔站在壁炉前,笑盈盈地望着他。

"没想到吧!"韦斯莱夫人热情地说,哈利眉开眼笑地迎上前去,"我们想过来看你比赛,哈利!"她俯身亲了亲哈利的面颊。

"你好吗?"比尔笑着同哈利握手,"查理也想来,可是走不开。他说你大战树蜂的那一场太精彩了,简直不可思议。"

哈利注意到芙蓉·德拉库尔越过母亲的肩膀很感兴趣地打量着比尔。看得出来,她对长头发和带尖牙的耳环一点也不反感。

"你们真好,"哈利轻轻对韦斯莱夫人说,"我还想呢——德思礼——"

"唔。"韦斯莱夫人努起了嘴。她一向避免在哈利面前批评德思礼夫妇,但每次听到他们的名字,她的眼里就会冒火。

"回来真好,"比尔打量着会议室说(胖夫人的女友维奥莱特在相框里对他眨巴眼睛),"这地方我有五年没见了。那个疯骑士的肖像还在吗?卡多根爵士?"

"噢,还在呢。"哈利说。他去年碰到过卡多根爵士。

"胖夫人呢?"比尔问。

"我上学那会儿她就在了。"韦斯莱夫人说,"有一天我凌晨四点才回宿舍,她狠狠地训了我一通——"

"你凌晨四点在宿舍外面干什么?"比尔惊诧地望着母亲问。

韦斯莱夫人笑了,眼睛亮晶晶的。

"我和你爸爸散步来着。他被当时的管理员阿波里昂·普林格抓住

## CHAPTER THIRTY-ONE — The Third Task

father's still got the marks.'

'Fancy giving us a tour, Harry?' said Bill.

'Yeah, OK,' said Harry, and they made their way back towards the door into the Great Hall.

As they passed Amos Diggory, he looked around. 'There you are, are you?' he said, looking Harry up and down. 'Bet you're not feeling quite as full of yourself now Cedric's caught you up on points, are you?'

'What?' said Harry.

'Ignore him,' said Cedric in a low voice to Harry, frowning after his father. 'He's been angry ever since Rita Skeeter's article about the Triwizard Tournament – you know, when she made out you were the only Hogwarts champion.'

'Didn't bother to correct her, though, did he?' said Amos Diggory, loudly enough for Harry to hear as he made to walk out of the door with Mrs. Weasley and Bill. 'Still ... you'll show him, Ced. Beaten him once before, haven't you?'

'Rita Skeeter goes out of her way to cause trouble, Amos!' Mrs. Weasley said angrily. 'I would have thought you'd know that, working at the Ministry!'

Mr. Diggory looked as though he was going to say something angry, but his wife laid a hand on his arm, and he merely shrugged and turned away.

Harry had a very enjoyable morning walking over the sunny grounds with Bill and Mrs. Weasley, showing them the Beauxbatons carriage and the Durmstrang ship. Mrs. Weasley was intrigued by the Whomping Willow, which had been planted after she had left school, and reminisced at length about the gamekeeper before Hagrid, a man called Ogg.

'How's Percy?' Harry asked, as they walked around the greenhouses.

'Not good,' said Bill.

'He's very upset,' said Mrs. Weasley, lowering her voice and glancing around. 'The Ministry want to keep Mr. Crouch's disappearance quiet, but Percy's been hauled in for questioning about the instructions Mr. Crouch has been sending in. They seem to think there's a chance they weren't genuinely written by him. Percy's been under a lot of strain. They're not letting him fill in for Mr. Crouch as the fifth judge tonight. Cornelius Fudge is going to be doing it.'

They returned to the castle for lunch.

## 第31章 第三个项目

了——你爸爸身上现在还带着印记呢。"

"带我们转转吧,哈利?"比尔说。

"好啊。"哈利说。他们朝通向礼堂的门口走去。经过阿莫斯·迪戈里身边时,他回过头来。

"是你?"他上下打量着哈利说,"塞德里克的分数追上来了,你不那么趾高气扬了吧?"

"什么?"哈利问。

"别理他。"塞德里克在他父亲背后皱起眉头,低声对哈利说,"他看了丽塔·斯基特写的那篇三强争霸赛的文章之后一直很生气——你知道,那女人把你说成了是霍格沃茨唯一的参赛勇士。"

"他也没有去纠正她,不是吗?"哈利同韦斯莱夫人和比尔一起走出门时,听见阿莫斯·迪戈里说,"不过……你会让他看到的,塞德。你赢过他一次,不是吗?"

"丽塔·斯基特专门无事生非,阿莫斯!"韦斯莱夫人气愤地说,"你在部里工作,我以为你是知道的!"

迪戈里先生似乎想发火,但他的妻子把一只手搭在了他胳膊上,因此他只是耸了耸肩,就转过身去了。

哈利陪着比尔和韦斯莱夫人在洒满阳光的场地上散步,一上午过得非常愉快。他带他们看了布斯巴顿的马车和德姆斯特朗的大船。韦斯莱夫人对打人柳很感兴趣,那是在她离校后栽下的。她费了半天工夫,终于记起海格之前的猎场看守,他叫奥格。

"珀西好吗?"他们参观温室时哈利问道。

"不大好。"比尔说。

"他很烦,"韦斯莱夫人看了看四周,压低声音说,"部里不想把克劳奇先生失踪的事张扬出去,但是他们把珀西叫去了,盘问他克劳奇先生发来的指示。他们好像认为这些指示可能不是克劳奇亲笔写的。珀西压力很大。他们不让他代替克劳奇先生当第五名裁判,改让康奈利·福吉当了。"

三人回城堡吃午饭。

## CHAPTER THIRTY-ONE   The Third Task

'Mum – Bill!' said Ron, looking stunned, as he joined the Gryffindor table. 'What're you doing here?'

'Come to watch Harry in the last task!' said Mrs. Weasley brightly. 'I must say, it makes a lovely change, not having to cook. How was your exam?'

'Oh ... OK,' said Ron. 'Couldn't remember all the goblin rebels' names, so I invented a few. It's all right,' he said, helping himself to a Cornish pasty, while Mrs. Weasley looked stern, 'they're all called stuff like Bodrod the Bearded and Urg the Unclean, it wasn't hard.'

Fred, George and Ginny came to sit next to them, too, and Harry was having such a good time he felt almost as though he was back at The Burrow; he had forgotten to worry about that evening's task, and not until Hermione turned up, halfway through lunch, did he remember that she had had a brainwave about Rita Skeeter.

'Are you going to tell us –?'

Hermione shook her head warningly, and glanced at Mrs. Weasley.

'Hello, Hermione,' said Mrs. Weasley, much more stiffly than usual.

'Hello,' said Hermione, her smile faltering at the cold expression on Mrs. Weasley's face.

Harry looked between them, then said, 'Mrs. Weasley, you didn't believe that rubbish Rita Skeeter wrote in *Witch Weekly*, did you? Because Hermione's not my girlfriend.'

'Oh!' said Mrs. Weasley. 'No – of course I didn't!'

But she became considerably warmer towards Hermione after that.

Harry, Bill and Mrs. Weasley whiled away the afternoon with a long walk around the castle, and then returned to the Great Hall for the evening feast. Ludo Bagman and Cornelius Fudge had joined the staff table now. Bagman looked quite cheerful, but Cornelius Fudge, who was sitting next to Madame Maxime, looked stern and was not talking. Madame Maxime was concentrating on her plate, and Harry thought her eyes looked red. Hagrid kept glancing along the table at her.

There were more courses than usual, but Harry, who was starting to feel really nervous now, didn't eat much. As the enchanted ceiling overhead began to fade from blue to a dusky purple, Dumbledore rose to his feet at the staff table, and silence fell.

'Ladies and gentlemen, in five minutes' time, I will be asking you to make your way down to the Quidditch pitch for the third and last task of the

## 第31章 第三个项目

"妈妈——比尔！"罗恩坐到格兰芬多桌子旁时大吃一惊,"你们在这儿干吗？"

"来看哈利的决赛！"韦斯莱夫人兴高采烈地说,"我得说,这是个很好的调剂,不用做饭了。你考得怎么样？"

"噢……还行,"罗恩说,"我想不起所有那些叛乱妖精的名字,就胡编了几个,挺好的。"罗恩一边拿菜肉烘饼吃一边说道。一旁的韦斯莱夫人板起了面孔,罗恩说:"没关系,他们都叫长胡子长长、邋遢鬼拉拉这样的名字,编起来不难。"

弗雷德、乔治和金妮也坐过来了,哈利开心极了,好像又回到了陋居一样。他忘记了晚上的比赛,午饭吃到一半时赫敏来了,他才想起赫敏早上好像突然悟到了丽塔·斯基特的什么事情。

"你是不是要告诉我们——？"

赫敏摇摇头,像在警告他,同时瞟了韦斯莱夫人一眼。

"你好,赫敏。"韦斯莱夫人态度比往常生硬得多。

"你好。"看着韦斯莱夫人冷淡的脸色,赫敏的微笑有点发窘。

哈利朝她们俩看看,然后说道:"韦斯莱夫人,你不会相信丽塔·斯基特在《女巫周刊》上的那篇垃圾文章吧？因为赫敏不是我的女朋友。"

"噢！"韦斯莱夫人说,"不——我当然不相信！"

但她随后对赫敏表现得热情多了。

哈利、比尔和韦斯莱夫人在城堡里散步,消磨了一个下午,然后回礼堂用晚餐。卢多·巴格曼和康奈利·福吉坐到了教工桌子旁。巴格曼看上去很高兴,可是坐在马克西姆女士旁边的康奈利·福吉却绷着脸,一言不发。马克西姆女士埋头吃饭,哈利觉得她的眼眶好像有点红。桌子那头的海格老往她这边看。

晚餐比平时丰盛,但哈利没有吃下多少,因为他现在真的感到紧张了。当施了魔法的天花板由蓝色转为暗紫的暮色时,邓布利多在教工桌子旁站起身,众人安静下来。

"女士们,先生们,再过五分钟,我就要请大家去魁地奇球场,观

# CHAPTER THIRTY-ONE

## The Third Task

Triwizard Tournament. Will the champions please follow Mr. Bagman down to the stadium now.'

Harry got up. The Gryffindors all along the table were applauding him; the Weasleys and Hermione all wished him good luck, and he headed off out of the Great Hall, with Cedric, Fleur and Krum.

'Feeling all right, Harry?' Bagman asked, as they went down the stone steps into the grounds. 'Confident?'

'I'm OK,' said Harry. It was sort of true; he was nervous, but he kept running over all the hexes and spells he had been practising in his mind as they walked, and the knowledge that he could remember them all made him feel better.

They walked onto the Quidditch pitch, which was now completely unrecognisable. A twenty-foot-high hedge ran all the way around the edge of it. There was a gap right in front of them; the entrance to the vast maze. The passage beyond it looked dark and creepy.

Five minutes later, the stands had begun to fill; the air was full of excited voices and the rumbling of feet as the hundreds of students filed into their seats. The sky was a deep, clear blue now, and the first stars were starting to appear. Hagrid, Professor Moody, Professor McGonagall and Professor Flitwick came walking into the stadium and approached Bagman and the champions. They were wearing large, red, luminous stars on their hats, all except Hagrid, who had his on the back of his moleskin waistcoat.

'We are going to be patrolling the outside of the maze,' said Professor McGonagall to the champions. 'If you get into difficulty, and wish to be rescued, send red sparks into the air, and one of us will come and get you, do you understand?'

The champions nodded.

'Off you go, then!' said Bagman brightly to the four patrollers.

'Good luck, Harry,' Hagrid whispered, and the four of them walked away in different directions, to station themselves around the maze. Bagman now pointed his wand at his throat, muttered '*Sonorus*', and his magically magnified voice echoed into the stands.

'Ladies and gentlemen, the third and final task of the Triwizard Tournament is about to begin! Let me remind you how the points currently stand! Tied in first place, on eighty-five points each – Mr. Cedric Diggory and Mr. Harry Potter, both of Hogwarts School!' The cheers and applause sent birds from the

## 第31章 第三个项目

看三强争霸赛最后一个项目的比赛。现在请勇士们跟巴格曼先生到运动场上去。"

哈利站起身，格兰芬多的学生一齐为他鼓掌，韦斯莱一家和赫敏祝他好运。他和塞德里克、芙蓉、威克多尔一道走出礼堂。

"感觉还好吗，哈利？"他们沿石阶往下走到场地时巴格曼问道，"有信心吗？"

"挺好。"哈利说。这可以说是真话，哈利确实很紧张，但他一边走一边不断在脑子里温习练过的那些咒语，全都记得，这使他感觉好多了。

他们走进魁地奇球场，这里已经变得完全认不出来了。一道二十英尺高的树篱把场地边缘围住。在他们面前有一个缺口，那便是这个大迷宫的入口。里面的通道黑黢黢的，有点吓人。

五分钟后，看台上开始进人。数百名学生鱼贯入座，空气中充满了兴奋的话语声和杂沓的脚步声。天空现在是澄澈的深蓝色，星星一颗颗地出现了。海格、穆迪教授、麦格教授和弗立维教授走进运动场，向巴格曼和几位勇士走来。他们的帽子上都缀有闪光的大红星星，只有海格除外，他的红星是在鼹鼠皮背心的背后。

"我们将在迷宫外面巡逻，"麦格教授对勇士们说，"如果遇到困难，想得到救援，就朝天发射红色火花，我们会有人来帮你们，听明白了吗？"

勇士们一起点头。

"好，你们去吧！"巴格曼愉快地对四位巡逻队员说。

"祝你好运，哈利。"海格悄声说。四个人朝不同方向走开，分散到迷宫周围。这时巴格曼用魔杖指着自己的喉咙，念了句"声音洪亮"，于是他那经过魔法放大的声音便在看台上回响起来。

"女士们，先生们，三强争霸赛的最后一项比赛就要开始了！请允许我来报一下目前的比分！塞德里克·迪戈里和哈利·波特——85分，并列第一，霍格沃茨学校！"掌声和欢呼声把禁林里的鸟儿惊飞到渐渐暗下来的夜空中。"威克多尔·克鲁姆——80分，第二名，德姆斯特

## CHAPTER THIRTY-ONE — The Third Task

Forbidden Forest fluttering into the darkening sky. 'In second place, on eighty points – Mr. Viktor Krum, of Durmstrang Institute!' More applause. 'And in third place – Miss Fleur Delacour, of Beauxbatons Academy!'

Harry could just make out Mrs. Weasley, Bill, Ron and Hermione applauding Fleur politely, halfway up the stands. He waved up at them, and they waved back, beaming at him.

'So … on my whistle, Harry and Cedric!' said Bagman. 'Three – two – one –'

He gave a short blast on his whistle, and Harry and Cedric hurried forwards into the maze.

The towering hedges cast black shadows across the path, and, whether because they were so tall and thick, or because they had been enchanted, the sound of the surrounding crowd was silenced the moment they entered the maze. Harry felt almost as though he was underwater again. He pulled out his wand, muttered '*Lumos*', and heard Cedric do the same just behind him.

After about fifty yards, they reached a fork. They looked at each other.

'See you,' Harry said, and he took the left one, while Cedric took the right.

Harry heard Bagman's whistle for the second time. Krum had entered the maze. Harry sped up. His chosen path seemed completely deserted. He turned right, and hurried on, holding his wand high over his head, trying to see as far ahead as possible. Still, there was nothing in sight.

Bagman's whistle blew in the distance for the third time. All of the champions were now inside the maze.

Harry kept looking behind him. The old feeling that he was being watched was upon him. The maze was growing darker with every passing minute as the sky overhead deepened to navy. He reached a second fork.

'*Point me*,' he whispered to his wand, holding it flat in his palm.

The wand spun around once, and pointed towards his right, into solid hedge. That way was north, and he knew that he needed to go North-West for the centre of the maze. The best he could do was to take the left fork, and go right again as soon as possible.

The path ahead was empty, too, and when Harry reached a right turn and took it, he again found his way unblocked. Harry didn't know why, but the lack of obstacles was unnerving him. Surely he should have met something by now? It felt as though the maze was luring him into a false sense of security. Then he heard movement right behind him. He held out his wand,

朗学院！"又是一阵掌声。"芙蓉·德拉库尔——第三名，布斯巴顿学院！"

哈利能分辨出韦斯莱夫人、比尔、罗恩和赫敏在看台中排礼貌地为芙蓉鼓掌。他朝他们挥挥手，他们也笑着朝他挥手。

"现在……哈利和塞德里克，听我的哨声！"巴格曼说，"三——二——一——"

随着一声短促的哨音，哈利和塞德里克急忙奔进了迷宫。

高高的树篱在小径上投下乌黑的影子，不知是由于树篱又高又密呢，还是施了魔法的缘故，他们一进入迷宫，观众的声音就听不见了。哈利几乎感到自己又像到了水底。他抽出魔杖，念道："荧光闪烁。"他听见身后的塞德里克也这么做了。

走了约莫五十米之后，他们来到一个岔路口，两人对视了一下。

"再见。"哈利说完，走上了左边那条路，塞德里克走了右边那条。

哈利听到巴格曼的哨子又响了一声，克鲁姆进迷宫了。哈利加快脚步。他选的这条路上似乎什么也没有。他向右一拐，匆匆往前赶，一只手高高地将魔杖举过头顶，想尽量看得远一点儿，但还是什么也看不到。

远处传来巴格曼的第三声哨响，几名勇士全都在迷宫里了。

哈利不断朝身后看，又一次觉得仿佛有人在暗中注视着他。迷宫里每一分钟都在变暗，头上的天空变成了黛青色。他来到了第二个岔路口。

"给我指路。"他把魔杖平托在手掌上，轻声对它说。

魔杖旋转了一下，指定了他右边密实的树篱。那儿是北，他知道去迷宫中心要朝西北方向走。最好的办法是走左边那条路，然后尽快往右拐。

前面的路上也空荡荡的，到了一个右转弯，哈利拐了进去，依然没有任何障碍。哈利不知道为什么会这样，如此畅通无阻使他有些发慌。现在应该碰到一些什么了呀。这迷宫好像在用安全的假相诱惑他。突然，他听到身后有了动静，连忙挥出魔杖准备自卫，可是魔杖的光照出的

## CHAPTER THIRTY-ONE    The Third Task

ready to attack, but its beam fell only upon Cedric, who had just hurried out of a path on the right-hand side. Cedric looked severely shaken. The sleeve of his robes was smoking.

'Hagrid's Blast-Ended Skrewts!' he hissed. 'They're enormous – I only just got away!'

He shook his head, and dived out of sight, along another path. Keen to put plenty of distance between himself and the Skrewts, Harry hurried off again. Then, as he turned a corner, he saw –

A Dementor was gliding towards him. Twelve feet tall, its face hidden by its hood, its rotting, scabbed hands outstretched, it advanced, sensing its way blindly towards him. Harry could hear its rattling breath; he felt clammy coldness stealing over him, but knew what he had to do …

He summoned the happiest thought he could, concentrated with all his might on the thought of getting out of the maze and celebrating with Ron and Hermione, raised his wand and cried, '*Expecto Patronum!*'

A silver stag erupted from the end of Harry's wand and galloped towards the Dementor, which fell back, and tripped over the hem of its robes … Harry had never seen a Dementor stumble.

'Hang on!' he shouted, advancing in the wake of his silver Patronus, 'you're a Boggart! *Riddikulus!*'

There was a loud crack, and the shape-shifter exploded in a wisp of smoke. The silver stag faded from sight. Harry wished it could have stayed, he could have used some company … but he moved on as quickly and quietly as possible, listening hard, his wand held high once more.

Left … right … left again … twice he found himself facing dead ends. He did the Four-Point Spell again, and found that he was going too far east. He turned back, took a right turn, and saw an odd golden mist floating ahead of him.

Harry approached it cautiously, pointing the wand's beam at it. This looked like some kind of enchantment. He wondered whether he might be able to blast it out of the way.

'*Reducto!*' he said.

The spell shot straight through the mist, leaving it intact. He supposed he should have known better; the Reductor curse was for solid objects. What would happen if he walked through the mist? Was it worth chancing it, or should he double back?

## 第31章 第三个项目

却是急急忙忙从右面一条小路上跑出来的塞德里克。他神色仓皇，衣袖上冒着烟。

"海格的炸尾螺！"他嘶声叫道，"大极了——我好不容易才逃出来！"

塞德里克摇摇头，冲进了另一条路，从视野里消失了。哈利一心想把炸尾螺甩远一点，哈利又加快了脚步。一转弯，他看见了……

一个摄魂怪缓缓朝他滑来，十二英尺高，兜帽遮着面孔，腐烂结痂的双手直直地伸着。摄魂怪一步步逼近，凭着感觉朝哈利摸了过来。哈利能听到它喉咙里咯咯的喘息声。一种冰冷黏滑的感觉袭上他的全身，但他知道应该怎么做……

他竭力去想自己能想到的最愉快的事情，拼命集中精力想象着走出迷宫、同罗恩和赫敏一起庆祝的情景，一边举起魔杖喊道："呼神护卫！"

一头银色的牡鹿从哈利的魔杖顶端蹦出来，向摄魂怪奔去。摄魂怪倒退两步，被自己的长袍绊倒了……哈利还从没见过摄魂怪跌跤呢。

"不许动！"他跟着银色的守护神前进，喊道，"你是个博格特！滑稽滑稽！"

一声爆响，博格特炸成一缕青烟。银鹿消失不见了。哈利倒希望它能留下来，给他做个伴……他继续前进，尽可能走得又快又不发出声响，依旧是高举着魔杖，警惕地听着四下里的动静。

左拐……右拐……再左拐……他有两次发现自己走入了死胡同。他又念了一次定向咒，发现向东走得太远了。他折回来，往右一拐，看见前方飘浮着一团奇异的金色迷雾。

哈利小心地走上前，用魔杖指着迷雾。看样子是一种魔法。他不知道能不能把它炸开。

"粉身碎骨！"他喝道。

咒语径直穿过金雾，对它毫无影响。哈利心想他早该想到这一点的，粉碎咒是用来对付固体障碍物的。如果他从金雾中穿过去会怎么样？是上去碰碰运气，还是退回来？

## CHAPTER THIRTY-ONE  The Third Task

He was still hesitating, when a scream shattered the silence.

'Fleur?' Harry yelled.

There was silence. He stared all around him. What had happened to her? Her scream seemed to have come from somewhere ahead. He took a deep breath, and ran through the enchanted mist.

The world turned upside-down. Harry was hanging from the ground, with his hair on end, his glasses dangling off his nose, threatening to fall into the bottomless sky. He clutched them to the end of his nose and hung there, terrified. It felt as though his feet were glued to the grass, which had now become the ceiling. Below him the dark, star-spangled heavens stretched endlessly. He felt as though if he tried to move one of his feet, he would fall away from the earth completely.

*Think*, he told himself, as all the blood rushed to his head, *think* ...

But not one of the spells he had practised had been designed to combat a sudden reversal of ground and sky. Did he dare move his foot? He could hear the blood pounding in his ears. He had two choices – try and move, or send up red sparks, and get rescued and disqualified from the task.

He shut his eyes, so he wouldn't be able to see the view of endless space below him, and pulled his right foot as hard as he could, away from the grassy ceiling.

Immediately, the world righted itself. Harry fell forwards onto his knees on the wonderfully solid ground. He felt temporarily limp with shock. He took a deep, steadying breath, then got up again, and hurried forwards, looking back over his shoulder as he ran out of the golden mist, which twinkled innocently at him in the moonlight.

He paused at a junction of two paths and looked around for some sign of Fleur. He was sure it had been she who had screamed. What had she met? Was she all right? There was no sign of red sparks – did that mean she had got herself out of trouble, or was she in such trouble that she couldn't reach her wand? Harry took the right fork with a feeling of increasing unease ... but at the same time, he couldn't help thinking, *one champion down* ...

The Cup was somewhere close by, and it sounded as though Fleur was no longer in the running. He'd got this far, hadn't he? What if he actually managed to win? Fleetingly, and for the first time since he'd found himself champion, he saw again that image of himself, raising the Triwizard Cup in front of the rest of the school ...

## 第31章 第三个项目

他正在犹豫，猛然间一声尖叫划破了四周的沉寂。

"芙蓉？"哈利喊道。

一片寂静。他四下张望，芙蓉出了什么事？她的叫声好像是从前面传来的。哈利深吸一口气，冲进了被施了魔法的迷雾中。

世界颠倒了过来。哈利头朝下倒挂在那里，头发根根直立，眼镜脱离了鼻梁，随时都可能掉进无底的天空。他把它按在鼻尖上，恐惧地挂在那里。他的双脚好像粘在草地上似的，而草地现在成了天花板，在他下面是无边无际、星光灿烂的黑色夜空。他觉得只要一抬脚，就会立刻掉下去。

好好想一想，他对自己说，全身血液都涌到了头上，想一想……

可是他练过的所有咒语都不能用来对付天地的突然颠倒。他敢动一动脚吗？他听见自己的血液撞击着耳鼓。他有两个选择——要么鼓起勇气挪动脚步，要么发射红色火花求援，被淘汰出局。

他闭上眼睛，不去看下面无边无际的虚空，然后用尽全力把右脚从草地天花板上拔了出来。

世界立即恢复了原样，哈利跪倒在可爱的坚实大地上。受了刚才的惊吓，他全身有些发软。他深深吸了一口气，镇定一下，然后爬起来往前跑，一边跑一边回头看那团金雾，它在月光下貌似很无辜地朝他闪烁着光芒。

他在两条路的交叉处停下来，寻找芙蓉的踪迹。他敢肯定刚才是芙蓉发出的声音。她遇到了什么？现在怎么样了？没有看到红色火花——这是否表明她已经摆脱了麻烦，还是她遇到的麻烦实在太大，连魔杖都拿不出来了？哈利带着越来越强烈的不安走上了右边的岔路……但同时也禁不住想，一个勇士倒下去了……

奖杯就在附近某处，芙蓉似乎已经出局。哈利坚持到现在了，是不是？要是他真的赢了呢？一瞬间，他成为勇士后第一次又看见了那个幻想：自己在全校师生面前举起了三强杯……

## CHAPTER THIRTY-ONE   The Third Task

He met nothing for ten minutes, except dead ends. Twice he took the same wrong turning. Finally he found a new route, and started to jog along it, his wand-light waving, making his shadow flicker and distort on the hedge walls. Then he rounded another corner, and found himself facing a Blast-Ended Skrewt.

Cedric was right – it *was* enormous. Ten feet long, it looked more like a giant scorpion than anything. Its long sting was curled over its back. Its thick armour glinted in the light from Harry's wand, which he pointed at it.

'*Stupefy!*'

The spell hit the Skrewt's armour, and rebounded; Harry ducked just in time, but could smell burning hair; it had singed the top of his head. The Skrewt issued a blast of fire from its end, and flew forwards towards him.

'*Impedimenta!*' Harry yelled. The spell hit the Skrewt's armour again and ricocheted off; Harry staggered back a few paces and fell over. '*IMPEDIMENTA!*'

The Skrewt was inches from him when it froze – he had managed to hit it on its fleshy, shell-less underside. Panting, Harry pushed himself away from it and ran, hard, in the opposite direction – the Impediment Jinx was not permanent, the Skrewt would be regaining the use of its legs at any moment.

He took a left path, and hit a dead end, a right, and hit another: forcing himself to stop, heart hammering, he performed the Four-Point Spell again, backtracked, and chose a path that would take him north-west.

He had been hurrying along the new path for a few minutes, when he heard something in the path running parallel to his own which made him stop dead.

'What are you doing?' yelled Cedric's voice. 'What the hell d'you think you're doing?'

And then Harry heard Krum's voice.

'*Crucio!*'

The air was suddenly full of Cedric's yells. Horrified, Harry began sprinting up his path, trying to find a way into Cedric's. When none appeared, he tried the Reductor curse again. It wasn't very effective, but it burnt a small hole in the hedge, through which Harry forced his leg, kicking at the thick brambles and branches until they broke and made an opening; he struggled through it, tearing his robes and, looking to his right, saw Cedric jerking and twitching on the ground, Krum standing over him.

## 第31章 第三个项目

十分钟内他没有遇到任何东西，老是走进死胡同，有两次拐上了同一条错路。最后他到了一条新路，沿着它慢跑起来。魔杖的荧光摇曳着，他变形的影子在树篱上闪动。他又拐了一个弯，迎面撞见了炸尾螺。

塞德里克说的不假——炸尾螺大极了。有十英尺长，看上去好似一条巨蝎。长长的蜇针卷在背上，厚厚的坚甲在哈利魔杖的荧光下闪闪发亮，哈利用魔杖指着它。

"昏昏倒地！"

咒语碰到炸尾螺的坚甲，反弹了回来，幸亏哈利躲得快，但他闻到了头发的焦味，咒语燎着了他的头顶。炸尾螺从尾部喷出一股火焰，朝他飞扑过来。

"障碍重重！"哈利大喊。咒语又碰在炸尾螺的坚甲上弹飞了。哈利踉跄着后退几步，摔倒在地："**障碍重重！**"

炸尾螺在离他只有几英寸的地方停住不动了——咒语击中了它没有甲片保护的腹部。哈利喘着气爬起来，朝相反的方向拼命奔跑。障碍咒的效力不会很长，炸尾螺的腿脚随时都可能动起来。

他走了左边一条路，是个死胡同，走上右边一条路，又是死胡同。他只好停下来，心咚咚地跳着。他又用了一次定向咒，返回去选了一条往西北方向去的路。

在这条路上匆匆走了几分钟后，他突然停住脚步，旁边一条路上传来了声音。

"你要干什么？"塞德里克的声音说，"你到底想干什么？"

然后哈利听见了克鲁姆的声音。

"钻心剜骨！"

空气中顿时充满了塞德里克的尖叫。哈利惊恐万分，在路上狂跑起来，试图找个缺口钻过去，但没有找到，就又试着念了一次粉碎咒。并不十分有效，但总算在树篱上烧了一个小洞。哈利把腿插进洞里，使劲蹬踹着茂密的荆棘和树枝，终于，树枝断了，他踹开了一个豁口。哈利奋力钻过去，袍子都被撕破了。他朝右边一看，只见塞德里克倒在地上抽搐，克鲁姆正在俯视着他。

## CHAPTER THIRTY-ONE

## The Third Task

Harry pulled himself up and pointed his wand at Krum just as Krum looked up. Krum turned and began to run.

'*Stupefy!*' Harry yelled.

The spell hit Krum in the back; he stopped dead in his tracks, fell forwards and lay motionless, face down in the grass. Harry dashed over to Cedric, who had stopped twitching, and was lying there panting, his hands over his face.

'Are you all right?' Harry said roughly, grabbing Cedric's arm.

'Yeah,' panted Cedric. 'Yeah ... I don't believe it ... he crept up behind me ... I heard him, I turned round, and he had his wand on me ...'

Cedric got up. He was still shaking. He and Harry looked down at Krum.

'I can't believe this ... I thought he was all right,' Harry said, staring at Krum.

'So did I,' said Cedric.

'Did you hear Fleur scream earlier?' said Harry.

'Yeah,' said Cedric. 'You don't think Krum got her, too?'

'I don't know,' said Harry slowly.

'Should we leave him here?' Cedric muttered.

'No,' said Harry. 'I reckon we should send up red sparks. Someone'll come and collect him ... otherwise he'll probably be eaten by a Skrewt.'

'He'd deserve it,' Cedric muttered, but all the same, he raised his wand and shot a shower of red sparks into the air, which hovered high above Krum, marking the spot where he lay.

Harry and Cedric stood there in the darkness for a moment, looking around them. Then Cedric said, 'Well ... I s'pose we'd better go on ...'

'What?' said Harry. 'Oh ... yeah ... right ...'

It was an odd moment. He and Cedric had been briefly united against Krum – now the fact that they were opponents came back to them both. They proceeded up the dark path without speaking, then Harry turned left, and Cedric right. Cedric's footsteps soon died away.

Harry moved on, continuing to use the Four-Point Spell, making sure he was moving in the right direction. It was between him and Cedric now. His desire to reach the Cup first was now burning stronger than ever, but he could hardly believe what he'd just seen Krum do. The use of an Unforgivable Curse on a fellow human being meant a life term in Azkaban,

## 第31章 第三个项目

哈利爬起身来，用魔杖指着克鲁姆。克鲁姆抬头看见了，转身撒腿就跑。

"昏昏倒地！"哈利喊道。

咒语击中了克鲁姆的后背。他猝然停住，朝前一扑，脸朝下趴在草地上不动了。哈利冲到塞德里克身边。他已经停止了抽搐，躺在那儿喘气，两只手捂着脸。

"没事吧？"哈利抓住塞德里克的胳膊沙哑地问。

"没事，"塞德里克喘着气说，"没事……我不能相信……他偷偷走到我身后……我听见了，转身一看，他用魔杖指着我……"

塞德里克站了起来，身体还在发抖。他们看着地上的克鲁姆。

"真难以相信……我还以为他挺不错的呢。"哈利盯着克鲁姆说。

"我也是。"塞德里克说。

"你听到芙蓉的叫声了吗？"哈利问。

"听到了，"塞德里克说，"你认为克鲁姆也对她下手了吗？"

"我不知道。"哈利缓缓地说。

"把他留在这儿吗？"塞德里克小声问。

"不行，"哈利说，"我想我们应该发射红色火花，让人来把他弄走……不然他可能会被炸尾螺吃掉。"

"他活该。"塞德里克嘟哝道，但还是举起魔杖，向空中发射了一串红色火花。火花盘旋在克鲁姆上空，标出了他所在的位置。

哈利和塞德里克在黑暗中站了一会儿，环顾四周。然后，塞德里克说："噢……我想我们还是继续走吧……"

"啊？"哈利说，"噢……对……对……"

这真是很奇怪的一刻。刚才因为克鲁姆的缘故，他和塞德里克暂时团结了起来——而现在他们是对手这一事实又回到了他们的意识中。两人默默地走在黑暗的小路上，然后哈利拐向左边，塞德里克拐向右边。塞德里克的脚步声很快就消失了。

哈利继续向前走，不时用定向咒确定方向是否正确。现在是他和塞德里克两人的较量了。他夺取奖杯的愿望比以往任何时候都强烈，但他不能相信克鲁姆竟会做出那样的事情。穆迪告诉过他们，对人使

## CHAPTER THIRTY-ONE   The Third Task

that was what Moody had told them. Krum surely couldn't have wanted the Triwizard Cup that badly ... Harry sped up.

Every so often he hit more dead ends, but the increasing darkness made him feel sure he was getting near the heart of the maze. Then, as he strode down a long, straight path, he saw movement once again, and his beam of wand-light hit an extraordinary creature, one which he had only seen in picture form, in his *Monster Book of Monsters*.

It was a sphinx. It had the body of an overlarge lion; great clawed paws, and a long yellowish tail ending in a brown tuft. Its head, however, was that of a woman. She turned her long, almond-shaped eyes upon Harry as he approached. He raised his wand, hesitating. She was not crouching as if to spring, but pacing from side to side of the path, blocking his progress.

Then she spoke, in a deep, hoarse voice. 'You are very near your goal. The quickest way is past me.'

'So ... so will you move, please?' said Harry, knowing what the answer was going to be.

'No,' she said, continuing to pace. 'Not unless you can answer my riddle. Answer on your first guess – I let you pass. Answer wrongly – I attack. Remain silent – I will let you walk away from me, unscathed.'

Harry's stomach slipped several notches. It was Hermione who was good at this sort of thing, not him. He weighed his chances. If the riddle was too hard, he could keep silent, get away from her unharmed, and try and find an alternative route to the centre.

'OK,' he said. 'Can I hear the riddle?'

The sphinx sat down upon her hind legs, in the very centre of the path, and recited:

> *'First think of the person who lives in disguise,*
> *Who deals in secrets and tells naught but lies.*
> *Next, tell me what's always the last thing to mend,*
> *The middle of middle and end of the end?*
> *And finally give me the sound often heard*
> *During the search for a hard-to-find word.*

## 第31章 第三个项目

用不可饶恕咒,意味着要在阿兹卡班终身监禁。克鲁姆不可能那样不顾一切想得到三强杯的……哈利加快了脚步。

他发现自己总是走进死胡同,但越来越浓的黑暗使他确信他正在接近迷宫的中心。然后,当他走在一条又长又直的小路上时,又发现了动静,魔杖的光照在一个无比奇异的怪物身上,哈利只在《妖怪们的妖怪书》中见过它的图片。

是斯芬克斯。它的身体像一头大得吓人的狮子:巨大的脚爪、黄色的长尾,尾尖有一丛棕色的毛。但它却长着一个女人的脑袋。哈利走近时,它把长长的杏仁眼转向他。哈利举起魔杖,犹豫不决。它并没有蹲下身子准备扑上来,而只是走来走去挡住哈利的去路。

然后它说话了,声音低沉而嘶哑:"你已经很接近你的目标了。最快的办法就是从我这里过去。"

"那……那能不能请你让一下?"哈利说,他知道对方的回答会是什么。

"不行,"它说,继续走来走去,"除非你能答出我的谜语。一次猜中——我就让你过去。没猜中——我就会扑过来。不回答——我就让你走开,不伤害你。"

哈利的心沉了几沉。猜谜是赫敏的拿手好戏,但不是他的。他权衡了一下,如果谜语太难,他可以不回答,斯芬克斯不会伤害他,他可以另外再找一条通往迷宫中心的路。

"好吧,"他说,"我能听一下谜语吗?"

斯芬克斯坐到它的后腿上,挡在路中央,念道:

> 先想想什么人总戴着假面,
> 行动诡秘,谎话连篇。
> 再告诉我什么东西总是缝缝补补,
> 中间的中间,尾部的尾部?
> 最后告诉我想不出词的时候
> 哪个声音经常被脱口而出。

## CHAPTER THIRTY-ONE

### The Third Task

> *Now string them together, and answer me this,*
> *Which creature would you be unwilling to kiss?'*

Harry gaped at her.

'Could I have it again ... more slowly?' he asked tentatively.

She blinked at him, smiled, and repeated the poem.

'All the clues add up to a creature I wouldn't want to kiss?' Harry asked.

She merely smiled her mysterious smile. Harry took that for a 'yes'. Harry cast his mind around. There were plenty of animals he wouldn't want to kiss; his immediate thought was a Blast-Ended Skrewt, but something told him that wasn't the answer. He'd have to try and work out the clues ...

'A person in disguise,' Harry muttered, staring at her, 'who lies ... er ... that'd be a – an impostor. No, that's not my guess! A – a spy? I'll come back to that ... could you give me the next clue again, please?'

She repeated the next lines of the poem.

'The last thing to mend,' Harry repeated. 'Er ... no idea ... middle of middle ... could I have the last bit again?'

She gave him the last four lines.

'A sound often heard in the search for a hard-to-find word,' said Harry. 'Er ... that'd be ... er ... hang on – "er"! "Er"'s a sound!'

The sphinx smiled at him.

'Spy ... er ... spy ... er ...' said Harry, pacing up and down himself. 'A creature I wouldn't want to kiss ... *a spider!*'

The sphinx smiled more broadly. She got up, stretched her front legs, and then moved aside for him to pass.

'Thanks!' said Harry, and, amazed at his own brilliance, he dashed forwards.

He had to be close now, he had to be ... his wand was telling him he was bang on course; as long as he didn't meet anything too horrible, he might be in with a chance ...

He had a choice of paths up ahead. 'Point me!' he whispered again to his wand, and it spun around and pointed him to the right-hand one. He dashed up this one, and saw light ahead.

## 第31章 第三个项目

现在把它们连起来，回答我，
什么是你不愿亲吻的动物？

哈利张口结舌地望着斯芬克斯。
"你能再念一遍吗……念慢一点？"他试探地问道。
斯芬克斯对他眨眨眼，微微一笑，把那首诗又念了一遍。
"所有的线索加起来是一个我不愿亲吻的动物？"哈利问道。
斯芬克斯只是神秘地微微一笑，哈利认为这表示"是"。他在脑海里搜索。他不愿亲吻的动物有很多，首先想到的是炸尾螺，但是隐约感到这不是谜底。他必须努力解开线索……
"戴着假面，"他瞪着斯芬克斯自言自语，"总是说谎……呃……那是——imposter。不，这不是我的答案！是——spy？我过会儿再想这个……你能再说一下第二个线索吗？"
斯芬克斯把诗的下面两行又念了一遍。
"什么东西总是缝缝补补，"哈利重复道，"呃……想不出来……'middle 的中间'……能再念念最后几句吗？"
斯芬克斯把最后四句又念了一遍。
"'想不出词的时候脱口而出的声音'"哈利说，"呃……应该是……呃……等一等——'er'！'er'是一种声音！"
斯芬克斯朝他微笑着。
"spy……er……spy……er……"哈利踱着步说，"我不愿亲吻的动物……是 spider！蜘蛛！"
斯芬克斯笑得更亲切了。它站起来，伸直两条前腿，挪到一边给他让路。
"谢谢！"哈利为自己的聪明感到惊讶，赶紧冲了过去。
一定很近了，一定……魔杖告诉他方向完全正确，只要不遇到什么太可怕的事情，他也许有机会……
前面是个岔路口。"给我指路！"他又对魔杖说，魔杖转了一下，指向右边的一条路。他沿着这条路跑去，前面看到了亮光。

## CHAPTER THIRTY-ONE    The Third Task

The Triwizard Cup was gleaming on a plinth a hundred yards away. Harry had just broken into a run, when a dark figure hurtled out onto the path in front of him.

Cedric was going to get there first. Cedric was sprinting as fast as he could towards the Cup, and Harry knew he would never catch up, Cedric was much taller, had much longer legs –

Then Harry saw something immense over a hedge to his left, moving quickly along a path that intersected with his own; it was moving so fast Cedric was about to run into it, and Cedric, his eyes on the Cup, had not seen it –

'Cedric!' Harry bellowed. 'On your left!'

Cedric looked around just in time to hurl himself past the thing and avoid colliding with it but, in his haste, he tripped. Harry saw Cedric's wand fly out of his hand, as a gigantic spider stepped into the path, and began to bear down upon Cedric.

'*Stupefy!*' Harry yelled again; the spell hit the spider's gigantic, hairy black body but, for all the good it did, he might as well have thrown a stone at it; the spider jerked, scuttled around, and ran at Harry instead.

'*Stupefy! Impedimenta! Stupefy!*'

But it was no use – the spider was either so large, or so magical, that the spells were doing no more than aggravating it – Harry had one horrifying glimpse of eight shining black eyes, and razor-sharp pincers, before it was upon him.

He was lifted into the air in its front legs; struggling madly, he tried to kick it; his leg connected with the pincers and next moment he was in excruciating pain – he could hear Cedric yelling '*Stupefy!*' too, but his spell had no more effect than Harry's – Harry raised his wand as the spider opened its pincers once more, and shouted, '*Expelliarmus!*'

It worked – the Disarming spell made the spider drop him, but that meant that Harry fell twelve feet onto his already injured leg, which crumpled beneath him. Without pausing to think, he aimed high at the spider's underbelly, as he had done with the Skrewt, and shouted '*Stupefy!*' just as Cedric yelled the same thing.

The two spells combined did what one alone had not – the spider keeled over sideways, flattening a nearby hedge, and strewing the path with a tangle of hairy legs.

'Harry!' he heard Cedric shouting. 'You all right? Did it fall on you?'

## 第31章 第三个项目

一百米开外,三强杯在底座上闪烁着诱人的光芒。哈利撒腿跑了起来,突然,一个黑影冲到了他前面的路上。

塞德里克抢先了,他正在全速朝奖杯冲刺。哈利知道自己怎么也追不上了。塞德里克比他高得多,腿比他的长——

接着哈利看见左边树篱外有一个巨大的东西,正在另一条交叉的路上快速向这边移动,塞德里克眼看就要跟它撞上了,可塞德里克两眼只顾盯着奖杯,根本没看见——

"塞德里克!"哈利大喊,"当心左边!"

塞德里克扭头看见了,急忙一闪,避免了与那个东西撞在一起,但是动作太猛,他摔倒了。哈利看到塞德里克的魔杖飞了出去,一只硕大无比的蜘蛛爬过来,俯身向塞德里克压去。

"昏昏倒地!"哈利喊道,咒语击中了蜘蛛那庞大的、乌黑多毛的身体,但似乎只是朝它扔了一块石头。蜘蛛抽搐了一下,迅疾转身朝哈利冲来。

"昏昏倒地!障碍重重!昏昏倒地!"

没有用——可能是蜘蛛太大,或是它的魔力太强,咒语对它不起作用,反而更加激怒了它。哈利恐惧地看见了八只闪亮的黑眼睛和锋利的钳子,蜘蛛已经扑到他身上了。

蜘蛛用前腿把哈利举到空中,哈利拼命挣扎。他试图用脚踢它,腿碰到了它的钳子,立刻是一阵钻心的疼痛。他听见塞德里克也在喊"昏昏倒地!",但是他的咒语同样不起作用——蜘蛛又张开钳子,哈利举起魔杖高喊"除你武器!"

还算有效——这个缴械咒使蜘蛛放开了他,但这意味着哈利从三米高的高处摔了下来。已经受伤的腿吃不住身体的重量,他一下子瘫倒在地。他想都没想,就用魔杖对准蜘蛛的下腹部,像他对炸尾螺那样,大喊一声"昏昏倒地!";塞德里克也喊出了同样的咒语。

两个咒语合起来,产生了一个咒语起不到的作用:蜘蛛倒向一旁,压垮了一片树篱,毛乎乎的长腿横七竖八地摊在地上。

"哈利!"他听见塞德里克叫道,"你没事吧?它没倒在你身上吧?"

## CHAPTER THIRTY-ONE   The Third Task

'No,' Harry called back, panting. He looked down at his leg. It was bleeding badly. He could see some sort of thick, gluey secretion from the spider's pincers on his torn robes. He tried to get up, but his leg was shaking badly and did not want to support his weight. He leant against the hedge, gasping for breath, and looked around.

Cedric was standing feet from the Triwizard Cup, which was gleaming behind him.

'Take it, then,' Harry panted to Cedric. 'Go on, take it. You're there.'

But Cedric didn't move. He merely stood there, looking at Harry. Then he turned to stare at the Cup. Harry saw the longing expression on his face in its golden light. Cedric looked around at Harry again, who was now holding onto the hedge to support himself.

Cedric took a deep breath. 'You take it. You should win. That's twice you've saved my neck in here.'

'That's not how it's supposed to work,' Harry said. He felt angry; his leg was very painful, he was aching all over from trying to throw off the spider, and after all his efforts, Cedric had beaten him to it, just as he'd beaten Harry to ask Cho to the ball. 'The one who reaches the Cup first gets the points. That's you. I'm telling you, I'm not going to win any races on this leg.'

Cedric took a few paces nearer to the Stunned spider, away from the Cup, shaking his head.

'No,' he said.

'Stop being noble,' said Harry irritably. 'Just take it, then we can get out of here.'

Cedric watched Harry steadying himself, holding tight to the hedge.

'You told me about the dragons,' Cedric said. 'I would've gone down in the first task if you hadn't told me what was coming.'

'I had help on that, too,' Harry snapped, trying to mop up his bloody leg with his robes. 'You helped me with the egg – we're square.'

'I had help on the egg in the first place,' said Cedric.

'We're still square,' said Harry, testing his leg gingerly; it shook violently as he put weight on it; he had sprained his ankle when the spider had dropped him.

'You should've got more points on the second task,' said Cedric mulishly. 'You stayed behind to get all the hostages. I should've done that.'

'I was the only one who was thick enough to take that song seriously!' said

## 第31章 第三个项目

"没有。"哈利气喘吁吁地喊道。他低头看看自己的腿,血流不止。撕破的长袍上有一些黏稠的东西,是蜘蛛的钳子上分泌出来的。他试图站起来,可是腿抖得很厉害,支撑不住身体的重量。他靠在树篱上,大口地喘气,环顾四周。

塞德里克站在离三强杯只有几英尺的地方,奖杯在他身后闪烁。

"拿吧,"哈利喘着气对塞德里克说,"快拿啊,你已经到了。"

塞德里克没有动。他站在那里看着哈利,然后回头望着奖杯,在奖杯的金光映照下,哈利能看到塞德里克脸上渴望的表情。塞德里克又回头看看哈利,哈利正扶着树篱勉强站起来。

塞德里克深深吸了口气。"你拿吧,应该是你赢的。你两次救了我的命。"

"规则不是这样。"哈利说,他感到很恼火,他的腿疼得厉害,为了甩掉蜘蛛,弄得浑身都疼,在那么多努力之后,却又败给了塞德里克,就像那次请秋跳舞一样,"谁先到谁得分,是你先到。我说的是真的,我这条腿可没法赛跑。"

塞德里克朝昏倒的蜘蛛走了几步,离奖杯远了一些。他摇了摇头。

"不。"他说。

"别发扬风格了,"哈利不耐烦地说,"快拿吧,拿了我们好出去。"

塞德里克看见哈利紧紧抓住树篱,好让自己站稳。

"你告诉我有火龙,"塞德里克说,"要不是你事先提醒,我在第一个项目就被淘汰了。"

"是我先得到了帮助,"哈利急躁地说,一边试图用袍子擦去腿上的血,"后来你告诉了我金蛋的秘密——我们扯平了。"

"也是有人先帮助我的。"塞德里克说。

"我们还是扯平了。"哈利小心翼翼地试探着自己的伤腿,刚把重量压上去,腿就剧烈地颤抖起来,他被蜘蛛扔下来时扭伤了脚脖子。

"你第二个项目的得分应该更高一点儿,"塞德里克执拗地说,"你留在后面救出了所有的人质。我也应该那样做的。"

"只有我傻里傻气,把那首歌当真了!"哈利没好气地说,"快拿

## CHAPTER THIRTY-ONE  The Third Task

Harry bitterly. 'Just take the Cup!'

'No,' said Cedric.

He stepped over the spider's tangled legs to join Harry, who stared at him. Cedric was serious. He was walking away from the sort of glory Hufflepuff house hadn't had in centuries.

'Go on,' Cedric said. He looked as though this was costing him every ounce of resolution he had, but his face was set, his arms were folded, he seemed decided.

Harry looked from Cedric to the Cup. For one shining moment, he saw himself emerging from the maze, holding it. He saw himself holding the Triwizard Cup aloft, heard the roar of the crowd, saw Cho's face shining with admiration, more clearly than he had ever seen it before ... and then the picture faded, and he found himself staring at Cedric's shadowy, stubborn face.

'Both of us,' Harry said.

'What?'

'We'll take it at the same time. It's still a Hogwarts victory. We'll tie for it.'

Cedric stared at Harry. He unfolded his arms. 'You – you sure?'

'Yeah,' said Harry. 'Yeah ... we've helped each other out, haven't we? We both got here. Let's just take it together.'

For a moment, Cedric looked as though he couldn't believe his ears; then his face split in a grin.

'You're on,' he said. 'Come here.'

He grabbed Harry's arm below the shoulder, and helped Harry limp towards the plinth where the Cup stood. When they had reached it, they both held out a hand over one of the Cup's gleaming handles.

'On three, right?' said Harry. 'One – two – three –'

He and Cedric both grasped a handle.

Instantly, Harry felt a jerk somewhere behind his navel. His feet had left the ground. He could not unclench the hand holding the Triwizard Cup; it was pulling him onwards, in a howl of wind and swirling colour, Cedric at his side.

## 第31章 第三个项目

奖杯吧!"

"不。"塞德里克说。

他跨过纠结的蜘蛛腿走到哈利身边。哈利瞪着他。塞德里克是认真的。他是在放弃赫奇帕奇学院数百年来没曾得到过的荣誉。

"你去吧。"塞德里克说。看上去他是用了全部的毅力才说出这句话的。但他表情坚决,抱着双臂,看来是下定了决心。

哈利的目光移到奖杯上。在奖杯的光芒中,他一时思绪恍惚,仿佛看见自己捧着它走出迷宫。他高高地举起三强杯,耳边是人群的欢呼;他比以往更清晰地看见,秋的脸上洋溢着钦佩的光彩……然后幻觉消失了,他看到了昏暗中塞德里克固执的面孔。

"我们俩一起。"哈利说。

"什么?"

"两个人同时拿,仍然是霍格沃茨获胜。我们是并列冠军。"

塞德里克瞪着哈利,松开了抱着的手臂。"你——真想这样?"

"当然,"哈利说,"当然……我们互相帮助克服了困难,对不对?我们俩一起到了这里,让我们一起去拿吧。"

一时间塞德里克似乎不敢相信自己的耳朵,然后他绽开了笑容。

"听你的,"他说,"来吧。"

他抓住哈利的胳膊,扶着哈利一瘸一拐地朝奖杯走去。走到奖杯旁,两人分别把手举在一个闪光的把手上方。

"数到三,好吗?"哈利说,"一——二——三——"

他和塞德里克一人抓住了一个把手。

哈利顿时觉得肚脐后面好像被扯了一下。他的双脚离开了地面,但他无法松开攥着三强杯的手,这只手拖着他在呼啸的风声和旋转的色彩中向前飞去,塞德里克在他旁边。

# CHAPTER THIRTY-TWO

# Flesh, Blood and Bone

Harry felt his feet slam into the ground; his injured leg gave way and he fell forwards; his hand let go of the Triwizard Cup at last. He raised his head.

'Where are we?' he said.

Cedric shook his head. He got up, pulled Harry to his feet, and they looked around.

They had left the Hogwarts grounds completely; they had obviously travelled miles – perhaps hundreds of miles – for even the mountains surrounding the castle were gone. They were standing instead in a dark and overgrown graveyard; the black outline of a small church was visible beyond a large yew tree to their right. A hill rose above them to their left. Harry could just make out the outline of a fine old house on the hillside.

Cedric looked down at the Triwizard Cup and then up at Harry.

'Did anyone tell *you* the Cup was a Portkey?' he asked.

'Nope,' said Harry. He was looking around the graveyard. It was completely silent, and slightly eerie. 'Is this supposed to be part of the task?'

'I dunno,' said Cedric. He sounded slightly nervous. 'Wands out, d'you reckon?'

'Yeah,' said Harry, glad that Cedric had made the suggestion rather than him.

They pulled out their wands. Harry kept looking around him. He had, yet again, the strange feeling that they were being watched.

'Someone's coming,' he said suddenly.

Squinting tensely through the darkness, they watched the figure drawing nearer, walking steadily towards them between the graves. Harry couldn't make out a face; but from the way it was walking, and holding its arms, he could tell that it was carrying something. Whoever they were, they were

第 32 章

血，肉和骨头

哈利感到双脚撞到了地面上，他的伤腿一软，摔倒在地，手终于放开了三强杯。他抬起头来。

"我们在哪儿？"他问。

塞德里克摇了摇头。他站起身，把哈利拉了起来，两人打量着四周。

这儿已经完全出了霍格沃茨的地界，他们显然飞了好几英里——也许有好几百英里，因为连城堡周围的环山都不见了。他们站在一片黑暗的杂草丛生的墓地上，可以看到右边一棵高大的红豆杉后面一所小教堂的黑色轮廓。左边是一座山冈。哈利能辨认出山坡上有一所精致的老房子。

塞德里克低头看看三强杯，然后抬头看着哈利。

"有人对你说过这奖杯是个门钥匙吗？"他问。

"没有。"哈利说，他打量着这片墓地，周围阴森森的，一片寂静，"这也是比赛的一部分吗？"

"不知道。"塞德里克说，声音有点紧张，"拔出魔杖吧，你说呢？"

"好。"哈利很高兴塞德里克先提出来，而不是他自己。

他们抽出魔杖，哈利不住地扫视四周。他又有了那种异样的感觉，好像有人在监视他们。

"有人来了。"他突然说。

他们紧张地眯起眼睛望着黑暗中，一个人影在坟墓间一步步朝他们走来。哈利看不清那人的脸，但从步态和手臂的姿势看，那人好像抱着个什么东西。那不知是谁的人身材矮小，穿着一件带兜帽的斗篷，遮着面孔。再走近几步——他们之间的距离在不断缩小，哈利看出那

## CHAPTER THIRTY-TWO  Flesh, Blood and Bone

short, and wearing a hooded cloak pulled up over their head to obscure their face. And – several paces nearer, the space between them closing all the time – he saw that the thing in the person's arms looked like a baby ... or was it merely a bundle of robes?

Harry lowered his wand slightly, and glanced sideways at Cedric. Cedric shot him a quizzical look. They both turned back to watch the approaching figure.

It stopped beside a towering marble headstone, only six feet from them. For a second, Harry and Cedric and the short figure simply looked at each other.

And then, without warning, Harry's scar exploded with pain. It was agony such as he had never felt in all his life; his wand slipped from his fingers as he put his hands over his face; his knees buckled; he was on the ground and he could see nothing at all, his head was about to split open.

From far away, above his head, he heard a high, cold voice say, '*Kill the spare.*'

A swishing noise and a second voice, which screeched the words to the night: '*Avada Kedavra!*'

A blast of green light blazed through Harry's eyelids, and he heard something heavy fall to the ground beside him; the pain in his scar reached such a pitch that he retched, and then it diminished; terrified of what he was about to see, he opened his stinging eyes.

Cedric was lying spread-eagled on the ground beside him. He was dead.

For a second that contained an eternity, Harry stared into Cedric's face, at his open grey eyes, blank and expressionless as the windows of a deserted house, at his half-open mouth, which looked slightly surprised. And then, before Harry's mind had accepted what he was seeing, before he could feel anything but numb disbelief, he felt himself being pulled to his feet.

The short man in the cloak had put down his bundle, lit his wand, and was dragging Harry towards the marble headstone. Harry saw the name upon it flickering in the wand-light before he was forced around and slammed against it.

# TOM RIDDLE

The cloaked man was now conjuring tight cords around Harry, tying him from neck to ankles to the headstone. Harry could hear shallow, fast breathing from the depths of the hood; he struggled, and the man hit him – hit him with a hand that had a finger missing. And Harry realised who was

## 第32章 血，肉和骨头

人抱的东西像是一个婴儿……或者只是一包衣服？

哈利手中的魔杖放低了一些。他侧过头望望塞德里克，塞德里克也向他投来疑问的一瞥。两人又回过头盯着走近的人影。

那人在一块高耸的大理石墓碑前站住了，离他们只有六英尺。在那一瞬间，哈利和塞德里克与那个矮小的人影对视着。

接着，毫无征兆地，哈利的伤疤剧烈地疼痛起来。他有生以来从没感受过如此剧烈的疼痛。魔杖滑落到地上，他用双手捂住面孔，腿一弯倒在地上，眼前什么也看不见了，脑袋像要炸裂一般。

他听见远远的头顶上方有人高声而冷酷地说："干掉碍事的。"

一阵嗖嗖声，接着另一个人尖厉的高喊撕破了夜空。"阿瓦达索命！"

一片强烈的绿光刺透了哈利的眼皮，他听见什么东西在身旁沉重地倒下。伤疤疼到了极点，他恶心得想吐。然后疼痛减轻了，他恐惧地慢慢睁开刺痛的双眼。

塞德里克在他旁边四肢伸开躺在地上，他死了。

在永无尽头的一秒钟里，哈利呆呆地看着塞德里克的面孔，看着他睁着的、空洞无神的灰眼睛，像一座废弃的房屋的窗户，他的嘴巴半张着，显得有些吃惊。哈利的大脑无法接受眼前的景象，除了隐隐约约觉得难以置信外，他没有任何感觉。就在这时，他感到自己被拖了起来。

穿斗篷的矮个儿男人已经放下包袱，点亮了魔杖，正把哈利朝大理石墓碑拖去。在被一把推转过来、后背撞上墓碑之前，哈利在魔杖闪烁的光芒中看到了一个名字。

**汤姆·里德尔**

穿斗篷的男人用魔法变出绳子，把哈利紧紧地捆在墓碑上，从脖子到脚腕捆了一道又一道。哈利听见兜帽里面传出急促而轻微的呼吸声。他用力挣扎，男人打了他一下——打他的那只手上缺了一根手指。

## CHAPTER THIRTY-TWO    Flesh, Blood and Bone

under the hood. It was Wormtail.

'You!' he gasped.

But Wormtail, who had finished conjuring the ropes, did not reply; he was busy checking the tightness of the cords, his fingers trembling uncontrollably, fumbling over the knots. Once sure that Harry was bound so tightly to the headstone that he couldn't move an inch, Wormtail drew a length of some black material from the inside of his cloak and stuffed it roughly into Harry's mouth; then, without a word, he turned from Harry and hurried away. Harry couldn't make a sound, nor could he see where Wormtail had gone; he couldn't turn his head to see beyond the headstone; he could see only what was right in front of him.

Cedric's body was lying some twenty feet away. Some way beyond him, glinting in the starlight, lay the Triwizard Cup. Harry's wand was on the ground at his feet. The bundle of robes that Harry had thought was a baby was close by, at the foot of the grave. It seemed to be stirring fretfully. Harry watched it, and his scar seared with pain again ... and he suddenly knew that he didn't want to see what was in those robes ... he didn't want that bundle opened ...

He could hear noises at his feet. He looked down, and saw a gigantic snake slithering through the grass, circling the headstone where he was tied. Wormtail's fast, wheezy breathing was growing louder again. It sounded as though he was forcing something heavy across the ground. Then he came back within Harry's range of vision, and Harry saw him pushing a stone cauldron to the foot of the grave. It was full of what seemed to be water – Harry could hear it slopping around – and it was larger than any cauldron Harry had ever used; a great stone belly large enough for a full-grown man to sit in.

The thing inside the bundle of robes on the ground was stirring more persistently, as though it was trying to free itself. Now Wormtail was busying himself at the bottom of the cauldron with a wand. Suddenly there were crackling flames beneath it. The large snake slithered away into the darkness.

The liquid in the cauldron seemed to heat very fast. The surface began not only to bubble, but also to send out fiery sparks, as though it was on fire. Steam was thickening, blurring the outline of Wormtail tending the fire. The movements beneath the cloak became more agitated. And Harry heard the high, cold voice again.

'*Hurry!*'

The whole surface of the water was alight with sparks now. It might have been encrusted with diamonds.

'It is ready, master.'

## 第32章 血，肉和骨头

哈利知道兜帽里面是谁了。是虫尾巴。

"是你！"他惊叫道。

但虫尾巴没有回答。他已经捆完了绳子，正忙着检查捆得紧不紧。他的手指控制不住地颤抖着，摸索着一个个绳结。当确定哈利已被捆得结结实实、完全无法动弹之后，虫尾巴从斗篷里摸出一团黑色的东西，粗鲁地塞进哈利嘴里。然后，他一句话也没说，就匆匆走开了。哈利发不出声音，也看不见虫尾巴去了哪里。他不能扭头看墓碑后面，只能看见正前方的情景。

塞德里克的尸体躺在二十英尺开外的地方。再过去一点儿，三强杯在星光下闪闪发亮。哈利的魔杖丢在塞德里克的脚边。他猜想是婴儿的那个包袱就在附近，放在墓碑下面。它似乎躁动不安。哈利注视着它，伤疤又火辣辣地疼痛起来……他突然意识到自己不希望看到包袱里的东西……他不希望那个包袱被打开。

他听见脚边有声音，往下一看，只见一条大蛇在草上蜿蜒游动，围着他这块墓碑打转。虫尾巴呼哧呼哧的喘息声又响了起来，好像在推什么沉重的东西过来。然后他进入了哈利的视线，把一口石头坩埚推到了坟墓边。坩埚里似乎盛满了水——哈利听见了泼溅声——这口坩埚比哈利用过的所有坩埚都大，可容一个成人坐在里面。

地上包袱里的东西动得更起劲了，仿佛要挣脱出来。虫尾巴忙着用魔杖在坩埚底部点点画画。突然坩埚下蹿起了噼啪作响的火苗。大蛇向黑暗中游去。

坩埚里的液体似乎热得很快，表面不仅开始沸腾，而且迸射出火花，像烧着了一样。蒸气越来越浓，照看火苗的虫尾巴的身影都变得模糊起来。斗篷下的动作更急了。哈利又一次听到了那个尖厉冷酷的声音。

"快！"

现在整个水面都闪动着火花，好像缀满钻石一样。

"烧好了，主人。"

## CHAPTER THIRTY-TWO    Flesh, Blood and Bone

'Now ...' said the cold voice.

Wormtail pulled open the robes on the ground, revealing what was inside them, and Harry let out a yell that was strangled in the wad of material blocking his mouth.

It was as though Wormtail had flipped over a stone, and revealed something ugly, slimy and blind – but worse, a hundred times worse. The thing Wormtail had been carrying had the shape of a crouched human child, except that Harry had never seen anything less like a child. It was hairless and scaly-looking, a dark, raw, reddish black. Its arms and legs were thin and feeble, and its face – no child alive ever had a face like that – was flat and snake-like, with gleaming red eyes.

The thing seemed almost helpless; it raised its thin arms, put them around Wormtail's neck, and Wormtail lifted it. As he did so, his hood fell back, and Harry saw the look of revulsion on Wormtail's weak, pale face in the firelight as he carried the creature to the rim of the cauldron. For one moment, Harry saw the evil, flat face illuminated in the sparks dancing on the surface of the potion. And then Wormtail lowered the creature into the cauldron; there was a hiss, and it vanished below the surface; Harry heard its frail body hit the bottom with a soft thud.

Let it drown, Harry thought, his scar burning almost past endurance, please ... let it drown ...

Wormtail was speaking. His voice shook, he seemed frightened beyond his wits. He raised his wand, closed his eyes, and spoke to the night. *'Bone of the father, unknowingly given, you will renew your son!'*

The surface of the grave at Harry's feet cracked. Horrified, Harry watched as a fine trickle of dust rose into the air at Wormtail's command, and fell softly into the cauldron. The diamond surface of the water broke and hissed; it sent sparks in all directions, and turned a vivid, poisonous-looking blue.

And now Wormtail was whimpering. He pulled a long, thin, shining silver dagger from inside his robes. His voice broke into petri-fied sobs. *'Flesh – of the servant – w-willingly given – you will – revive – your master.'*

He stretched his right hand out in front of him – the hand with the missing finger. He gripped the dagger very tightly in his left hand, and swung it upwards.

Harry realised what Wormtail was about to do a second before it happened –

## 第32章 血，肉和骨头

"来吧……"那个冷酷的声音说。

虫尾巴扯开地上的包袱，露出里面的东西。哈利发出一声惊叫，但被嘴里塞的东西闷住了。

就好像虫尾巴猛地翻开一块石头，露出一个黏糊糊的、没有视觉的丑陋怪物——不，比这还要可怕，可怕一百倍。虫尾巴抱来的东西外形像一个蜷缩的婴儿，但哈利从没见过比它更不像婴儿的了。它没有毛发，身上仿佛长着鳞片，皮色暗暗的、红红的，像受了伤的嫩肉。胳膊和腿又细又软，它的脸——没有哪个活的孩子长着这样一张脸——是一张扁平的蛇脸，上面有一双闪闪发光的红眼睛。

那东西看上去完全没有自理能力，它举起细细的胳膊，搂住虫尾巴的脖子。虫尾巴把它抱在手中。这时虫尾巴的兜帽掉了下来，哈利看到火光中他那苍白虚弱的脸上带着厌恶的表情。虫尾巴把那东西抱到坩埚边，刹那间，哈利看见药水表面跳动的火花照亮了那张邪恶的扁脸。虫尾巴将那东西放进坩埚，随着一阵嘶嘶声，它沉了下去。哈利听见了它软绵绵的身体碰到坩埚底的轻响。

让它淹死，哈利想，他的伤疤灼痛得几乎无法忍受，拜托……让它淹死吧……

虫尾巴在说话，声音颤抖，好像吓得神经错乱了。他举起魔杖，闭上眼睛，对着夜空说道："父亲的骨，无意中捐出，可使你的儿子再生！"

哈利脚下的坟墓裂开了，哈利惊恐地看见一小缕灰尘应虫尾巴的召唤升到了空中，轻轻地落在坩埚里。钻石般的液面破裂了，嘶嘶作响，火花四溅，液体变成了鲜艳的蓝色，一看便知有毒。

虫尾巴在呜咽。他从斗篷里抽出一把又长又薄、银光闪闪的匕首。他的声音一下子变成了极度恐惧的抽泣："仆人……的肉……自—自愿捐出，可使……你的主人……重生。"

他伸出右手——就是少一根手指的那只手，然后用左手紧紧攥住匕首，朝右手挥去。

哈利在最后一秒钟才意识到虫尾巴要干什么，他紧紧闭上眼睛，

## CHAPTER THIRTY-TWO — Flesh, Blood and Bone

he closed his eyes as tightly as he could, but he could not block the scream that pierced the night, that went through Harry as though he had been stabbed with the dagger too. He heard something fall to the ground, heard Wormtail's anguished panting, then a sickening splash, as something was dropped into the cauldron. Harry couldn't bear to look ... but the potion had turned a burning red, the light of it shone through Harry's closed eyelids ...

Wormtail was gasping and moaning with agony. Not until Harry felt Wormtail's anguished breath on his face did he realise that Wormtail was right in front of him.

'B-blood of the enemy ... forcibly taken ... you will ... resurrect your foe.'

Harry could do nothing to prevent it, he was tied too tightly ... squinting down, struggling hopelessly at the ropes binding him, he saw the shining silver dagger shaking in Wormtail's remaining hand. He felt its point penetrate the crook of his right arm, and blood seeping down the sleeve of his torn robes. Wormtail, still panting with pain, fumbled in his pocket for a glass phial and held it to Harry's cut, so that a dribble of blood fell into it.

He staggered back to the cauldron with Harry's blood. He poured it inside. The liquid within turned, instantly, a blinding white. Wormtail, his job done, dropped to his knees beside the cauldron, then slumped sideways and lay on the ground, cradling the bleeding stump of his arm, gasping and sobbing.

The cauldron was simmering, sending its diamond sparks in all directions, so blindingly bright that it turned all else to velvety blackness. Nothing happened ...

Let it have drowned, Harry thought, let it have gone wrong ...

And then, suddenly, the sparks emanating from the cauldron were extinguished. A surge of white steam billowed thickly from the cauldron instead, obliterating everything in front of Harry, so that he couldn't see Wormtail or Cedric or anything but vapour hanging in the air ... it's gone wrong, he thought ... it's drowned ... please ... please let it be dead. ...

But then, through the mist in front of him, he saw, with an icy surge of terror, the dark outline of a man, tall and skeletally thin, rising slowly from inside the cauldron.

'Robe me,' said the high, cold voice from behind the steam, and Wormtail, sobbing and moaning, still cradling his mutilated arm, scrambled to pick up the black robes from the ground, got to his feet, reached up, and pulled them one-handed over his master's head.

## 第32章 血，肉和骨头

却阻挡不了那穿透夜空的惨叫直刺进自己体内，就好像他也被匕首刺中了一样。他听见了什么东西掉落地面的声音，听见了虫尾巴痛苦的喘息声，接着是令人恶心的扑通一声，有什么东西被扔进了坩埚。哈利不愿去看……但是药水变成了火红色，发出的强光射进哈利紧闭的眼帘……

虫尾巴在痛苦地喘息和呻吟。当那痛苦的呼吸喷到哈利脸上时，他才发觉虫尾巴已经来到他的面前。

"仇——仇敌的血……被迫献出……可使你的敌人……复活。"

哈利没办法阻止，他被捆得太紧了……他绝望地挣扎，想挣脱捆绑他的绳索，他从眼睛缝里看见银晃晃的匕首在虫尾巴那只独手中颤动。他感到匕首尖刺进了他的臂弯，鲜血顺着撕破的袍袖淌下。仍在痛苦喘息的虫尾巴哆嗦着从口袋里摸出一个小玻璃瓶，放在哈利的伤口旁，少量鲜血流到了瓶里。

虫尾巴拿着哈利的血摇摇晃晃地走向坩埚，把血倒了进去。坩埚中的液体立刻变成了炫目的白色。虫尾巴完成了任务，跪倒在坩埚旁，身子一歪，瘫在地上，捧着自己流血的断臂喘息、抽泣。

坩埚快要沸腾了，钻石般的火星向四外飞溅，如此明亮耀眼，周围的一切都变成了黑天鹅绒般的颜色。什么都没有发生……

但愿它已经淹死了，哈利想，但愿不会成功……

突然，坩埚上的火星熄灭了。一股浓浓的白色蒸气从坩埚里升腾起来，掩去了哈利面前的一切。他看不见虫尾巴和塞德里克，只见一片白茫茫的水汽……肯定不成功……它淹死了……拜托……拜托，让它死掉吧……

接着，透过眼前的白雾，他毛骨悚然地看到坩埚中缓缓升起一个男人的黑色身形，又高又瘦，像一具骷髅。

"给我穿上袍子。"那个冷酷尖厉的声音在蒸气后面说。虫尾巴抽泣着、呻吟着，仍护着他的残臂，慌忙从地上抓起裹包袱的黑色长袍，站起来，用一只手把它套到主人的头上。

## CHAPTER THIRTY-TWO — Flesh, Blood and Bone

The thin man stepped out of the cauldron, staring at Harry ... and Harry stared back into the face that had haunted his nightmares for three years. Whiter than a skull, with wide, livid scarlet eyes, and a nose that was as flat as a snake's, with slits for nostrils ...

Lord Voldemort had risen again.

## 第32章 血，肉和骨头

瘦男人跨出坩埚，眼睛盯着哈利……哈利看到了三年来经常在他噩梦中出现的面孔，比骷髅还要苍白，两只狂怒的大眼睛红通通的，鼻子像蛇鼻一样扁平，鼻孔是两条细缝……

伏地魔卷土重来了。

## CHAPTER THIRTY-THREE

# The Death Eaters

Voldemort looked away from Harry, and began examining his own body. His hands were like large, pale spiders; his long white fingers caressed his own chest, his arms, his face; the red eyes, whose pupils were slits, like a cat's, gleamed still more brightly through the darkness. He held up his hands, and flexed the fingers, his expression rapt and exultant. He took not the slightest notice of Wormtail, who lay twitching and bleeding on the ground, nor of the great snake, which had slithered back into sight, and was circling Harry again, hissing. Voldemort slipped one of those unnaturally long-fingered hands into a deep pocket, and drew out a wand. He caressed it gently, too; and then he raised it, and pointed it at Wormtail, who was lifted off the ground, and thrown against the headstone where Harry was tied; he fell to the foot of it and lay there, crumpled up and crying. Voldemort turned his scarlet eyes upon Harry, laughing a high, cold, mirthless laugh.

Wormtail's robes were shining with blood now; he had wrapped the stump of his arm in them. 'My Lord ...' he choked, 'my Lord ... you promised ... you did promise ...'

'Hold out your arm,' said Voldemort lazily.

'Oh, master ... thank you, master ...'

He extended the bleeding stump, but Voldemort laughed again. 'The other arm, Wormtail.'

'Master, please ... *please* ...'

Voldemort bent down, and pulled out Wormtail's left arm; he forced the sleeve of Wormtail's robes up past his elbow, and Harry saw something upon the skin there, something like a vivid red tattoo – a skull, with a snake protruding from its mouth – the same image that had appeared in the sky at the Quidditch World Cup: the Dark Mark. Voldemort examined it carefully, ignoring Wormtail's uncontrollable weeping.

# 第 33 章

# 食 死 徒

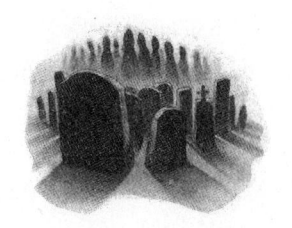

伏地魔将目光从哈利身上移开,开始检查自己的身体。他的手像苍白的大蜘蛛,细长苍白的手指抚摸着胸口、手臂、脸庞;那双红眼睛在黑暗中显得更亮,瞳仁是两条缝,如同猫眼。他举起双手,活动着手指,表情欣喜若狂,毫不理会倒在地上流血抽搐的虫尾巴,也不理会那条大蛇。大蛇不知何时又游了回来,咝咝地围着哈利打转。伏地魔把长得出奇的手指插进一个很深的口袋里,抽出一根魔杖。他把魔杖也轻轻抚摸了一遍,然后举起魔杖指着虫尾巴,把他从地面拎起,扔向哈利被绑的那块墓碑。虫尾巴跌落在墓碑旁,瘫在那里哭泣。伏地魔把鲜红的眼睛转向哈利,发出一声冷酷而尖厉的阴笑。

包裹着虫尾巴断臂的袍子已经被血浸透。"主人……"虫尾巴哽咽地说,"主人……您答应过……您答应过的……"

"伸出手臂。"伏地魔懒洋洋地说。

"哦,主人……谢谢您,主人……"

他伸出血淋淋的断臂,但伏地魔又冷笑一声:"不是这只,虫尾巴。"

"主人,求求您……求求您……"

伏地魔弯下身,拉起虫尾巴的左臂,把他的衣袖捋到胳膊肘上方。哈利看到那处皮肤上有个东西,好像是鲜红的文身图案———一个骷髅嘴里吐出一条蛇,是魁地奇世界杯赛上天空中出现过的那个图形:黑魔标记。伏地魔仔细地端详着它,全然不理会虫尾巴无法控制的抽泣。

## CHAPTER THIRTY-THREE  The Death Eaters

'It is back,' he said softly, 'they will all have noticed it ... and now, we shall see ... now we shall know ...'

He pressed his long, white forefinger to the brand on Wormtail's arm.

The scar on Harry's forehead seared with a sharp pain again, and Wormtail let out a fresh howl: Voldemort removed his fingers from Wormtail's Mark, and Harry saw that it had turned jet black.

A look of cruel satisfaction on his face, Voldemort straightened up, threw back his head, and stared around at the dark graveyard.

'How many will be brave enough to return when they feel it?' he whispered, his gleaming red eyes fixed upon the stars. 'And how many will be foolish enough to stay away?'

He began to pace up and down before Harry and Wormtail, eyes sweeping the graveyard all the while. After a minute or so, he looked down at Harry again, a cruel smile twisting his snake-like face.

'You stand, Harry Potter, upon the remains of my late father,' he hissed softly. 'A Muggle and a fool ... very like your dear mother. But they both had their uses, did they not? Your mother died to defend you as a child ... and I killed my father, and see how useful he has proved himself, in death ...'

Voldemort laughed again. Up and down he paced, looking all around him as he walked, and the snake continued to circle in the grass.

'You see that house upon the hillside, Potter? My father lived there. My mother, a witch who lived here in this village, fell in love with him. But he abandoned her when she told him what she was ... he didn't like magic, my father ...

'He left her and returned to his Muggle parents before I was even born, Potter, and she died giving birth to me, leaving me to be raised in a Muggle orphanage ... but I vowed to find him ... I revenged myself upon him, that fool who gave me his name ... *Tom Riddle* ...'

Still he paced, his red eyes darting from grave to grave.

'Listen to me, reliving family history ...' he said quietly. 'Why, I am growing quite sentimental ... But look, Harry! My *true* family returns ...'

The air was suddenly full of the swishing of cloaks. Between graves, behind the yew tree, in every shadowy space, wizards were Apparating. All of them were hooded and masked. And one by one they moved forwards ... slowly, cautiously, as though they could hardly believe their eyes. Voldemort stood in silence, waiting for them. Then one of the Death Eaters fell to his

## 第33章 食死徒

"它又出现了,"他轻声说,"他们都会注意到的……现在,我们会看到……我们会知道……"

他把长长的、苍白的食指按在虫尾巴胳膊的烙印上。

哈利前额的伤疤再一次剧痛起来,虫尾巴又发出一声哀号。伏地魔把手指从虫尾巴的印记上拿开,哈利看见印记变成了漆黑的颜色。

伏地魔脸上露出残酷的得意神情。他直起腰,把头一扬,扫视着黑暗的墓地。

"在感觉到它之后,有多少人有胆量回来?"他喃喃道,发光的红眼睛盯着天上的星星,"又有多少人会愚蠢地不来?"

他开始在哈利和虫尾巴面前来回踱步,一直扫视着墓地。大约一分钟后,他的视线又落到哈利身上,蛇脸扭曲起来,露出一丝残酷的微笑。

"哈利·波特,你正站在我父亲的尸骨上。"他轻轻地嘶声说,"他是一个麻瓜加笨蛋……就像你的亲妈一样。但他们都有用处,是不是?你小的时候,你妈妈为保护你而死……我杀死了我父亲,你看,他死后派上了多大用场……"

伏地魔又笑了起来。他一边来回踱步,一边扫视着四周,那条蛇还在草地上转悠。

"看到山坡上那座房子了吗,波特?我父亲在那儿住过。我母亲是个巫师,住在这个村子里,爱上了我父亲。可当她说出自己的身份之后,他抛弃了她……我父亲不喜欢魔法……

"他离开了我母亲,回到他的麻瓜父母身边,那时我还没有出生,波特。我母亲生我的时候难产死了,我在麻瓜孤儿院长大……但我发誓要找到我父亲……我向他报了仇,那个给了我跟他同样名字的傻瓜……汤姆·里德尔……"

他继续踱来踱去,红眼睛在坟墓间来回扫视。

"快听啊,我在这里回忆起家史来了……"他轻声说,"啊,我怎么变得这么多愁善感……可是看吧,哈利!我真正的家人回来了……"

空气中突然充满了斗篷窸窸窣窣的声音。在坟墓之间,在杉树后面,每一处阴暗的地方都有巫师在幻影显形,全都戴着兜帽,蒙着面孔。他们一个个走过来……走得很慢,小心翼翼,仿佛不敢相信自己的眼睛。

## CHAPTER THIRTY-THREE  The Death Eaters

knees, crawled towards Voldemort, and kissed the hem of his black robes.

'Master ... master ...' he murmured.

The Death Eaters behind him did the same; each of them approaching Voldemort on his knees, and kissing his robes, before backing away and standing up, forming a silent circle, which enclosed Tom Riddle's grave, Harry, Voldemort, and the sobbing and twitching heap that was Wormtail. Yet they left gaps in the circle, as though waiting for more people. Voldemort, however, did not seem to expect more. He looked around at the hooded faces, and though there was no wind, a rustling seemed to run around the circle, as though it had shivered.

'Welcome, Death Eaters,' said Voldemort quietly. 'Thirteen years ... thirteen years since last we met. Yet you answer my call as though it was yesterday ... we are still united under the Dark Mark, then! *Or are we?*'

He put back his terrible face and sniffed, his slit-like nostrils widening.

'I smell guilt,' he said. 'There is a stench of guilt upon the air.'

A second shiver ran around the circle, as though each member of it longed, but did not dare, to step back from him.

'I see you all, whole and healthy, with your powers intact – such prompt appearances! – and I ask myself ... why did this band of wizards never come to the aid of their master, to whom they swore eternal loyalty?'

No one spoke. No one moved except Wormtail, who was upon the ground, still sobbing over his bleeding arm.

'And I answer myself,' whispered Voldemort, 'they must have believed me broken, they thought I was gone. They slipped back among my enemies, and they pleaded innocence, and ignorance, and bewitchment ...

'And then I ask myself, but how could they have believed I would not rise again? They, who knew the steps I took, long ago, to guard myself against mortal death? They, who had seen proofs of the immensity of my power, in the times when I was mightier than any wizard living?

'And I answer myself, perhaps they believed a still-greater power could exist, one that could vanquish even Lord Voldemort ... perhaps they now pay allegiance to another ... perhaps that champion of commoners, of Mudbloods and Muggles, Albus Dumbledore?'

At the mention of Dumbledore's name, the members of the circle stirred, and some muttered and shook their heads.

## 第33章 食死徒

伏地魔沉默地站在那里等着。一个食死徒跪倒在地，爬到伏地魔跟前，亲吻他黑袍的下摆。

"主人……主人……"他低声唤道。

他身后的食死徒也是一样，每个人都跪着爬到伏地魔身边，亲吻他的长袍，然后退到一旁，站起身，默默地围成一个圈子，把汤姆·里德尔的坟墓、哈利、伏地魔和瘫在地上啜泣抽搐的虫尾巴围在中间。但圈子还留着一些间隔，好像等候其他人的加入。然而伏地魔似乎不再期待有人来了。他环视着一张张戴兜帽的面孔，尽管没有风，但圈子中似乎掠过一阵细微的沙沙声，似乎那圈子打了一个哆嗦。

"欢迎，食死徒们，"伏地魔平静地说，"十三年……从我们上次集会已经有十三年了。但你们还是像昔日一样响应我的召唤……就是说，我们仍然团结在黑魔标记之下！是吗？"

他抬起狰狞的面孔，张开两条细缝一样的鼻孔嗅了嗅。

"我闻到了愧疚，"他说，"空气中有一股愧疚的臭味。"

圈子又哆嗦了一下，似乎每个人都想向后退，却又不敢动。

"我看见你们，健康无恙，魔力一如从前——这样迅速地赶到！——我问我自己……为什么这帮巫师一直不来帮助他们的主人，帮助他们宣誓要永远效忠的人呢？"

没有人说话，没有人敢动。只有虫尾巴倒在地上，捧着流血的手臂啜泣。

"我回答自己，"伏地魔轻声说，"他们一定是相信我不行了，以为我完蛋了。他们溜回到我的敌人中间，说自己是无辜的，不知情，中了妖术……

"我又问自己，他们为什么就相信我不会东山再起呢？他们不是知道我很久以前就采取措施防止死亡吗？他们不是在我比任何巫师都更强大的时候，目睹过我无数次地证明自己法力无边吗？

"我回答自己，或许他们相信还存在更强大的力量，能够战胜伏地魔……或许他们现在已经效忠他人……说不定就是那个下里巴人的头目，那个泥巴种和麻瓜的保护人，阿不思·邓布利多？"

听到邓布利多的名字，圈子中的成员骚动起来，有人嘴里嘀咕着，不停地摇头。

## CHAPTER THIRTY-THREE    The Death Eaters

Voldemort ignored them. 'It is a disappointment to me ... I confess myself disappointed ...'

One of the men suddenly flung himself forwards, breaking the circle. Trembling from head to foot, he collapsed at Voldemort's feet.

'Master!' he shrieked. 'Master, forgive me! Forgive us all!'

Voldemort began to laugh. He raised his wand. '*Crucio!*'

The Death Eater on the ground writhed and shrieked; Harry was sure the sound must carry to the houses around ... let the police come, he thought desperately ... anyone ... anything ...

Voldemort raised his wand. The tortured Death Eater lay flat upon the ground, gasping.

'Get up, Avery,' said Voldemort softly. 'Stand up. You ask for forgiveness? I do not forgive. I do not forget. Thirteen long years ... I want thirteen years' repayment before I forgive you. Wormtail here has paid some of his debt already, have you not, Wormtail?'

He looked down at Wormtail, who continued to sob.

'You returned to me, not out of loyalty, but out of fear of your old friends. You deserve this pain, Wormtail. You know that, don't you?'

'Yes, master,' moaned Wormtail, 'please, master ... please ...'

'Yet you helped return me to my body,' said Voldemort coolly, watching Wormtail sob on the ground. 'Worthless and traitorous as you are, you helped me ... and Lord Voldemort rewards his helpers ...'

Voldemort raised his wand again and whirled it through the air. A streak of what looked like molten silver hung shining in the wand's wake. Momentarily shapeless, it writhed and then formed itself into a gleaming replica of a human hand, bright as moonlight, which soared downwards and fixed itself upon Wormtail's bleeding wrist.

Wormtail's sobbing stopped abruptly. His breathing harsh and ragged, he raised his head and stared in disbelief at the silver hand, now attached seamlessly to his arm, as though he were wearing a dazzling glove. He flexed the shining fingers, then, trembling, picked up a small twig on the ground, and crushed it into powder.

'My Lord,' he whispered. 'Master ... it is beautiful ... thank you ... *thank you* ...'

He scrambled forward on his knees and kissed the hem of Voldemort's robes.

'May your loyalty never waver again, Wormtail,' said Voldemort.

## 第33章 食死徒

伏地魔不予理睬。"这让我失望……我承认我感到失望……"

圈子中的一个人突然扑倒在地，他匍匐在伏地魔脚下，从头到脚都在发抖。

"主人！"他尖叫道，"主人，饶恕我！饶恕我们吧！"

伏地魔冷笑起来，举起了魔杖。"钻心剜骨！"

倒在地上的那个食死徒痛苦地扭动着、惨叫着。哈利相信这声音一定会传到周围的房子里……快叫警察来吧，他绝望地想……谁来都行……什么都行……

伏地魔抬起魔杖。受刑的食死徒平躺在地上，喘着粗气。

"起来吧，埃弗里，"伏地魔轻声说，"站起来。你求我饶恕？我不会饶恕。我不会忘记。漫长的十三年……我要你们还清十三年的债，然后才会饶恕你们。虫尾巴已经还了一些债，是不是，虫尾巴？"

他低头看着虫尾巴。虫尾巴还在那里抽泣。

"你回到我的身边，不是出于忠诚，而是因为害怕你的老朋友们。你活该忍受这种痛苦，虫尾巴。你知道这一点，是不是？"

"是，主人，"虫尾巴呻吟道，"求求您，主人……求求您……"

"可是你帮助我获得了肉身，"伏地魔看着虫尾巴在地上抽泣，冷漠地说，"尽管你是个没用的、卑鄙的叛徒，可是你帮助了我……伏地魔不会亏待帮助过他的人……"

伏地魔再次举起魔杖，在空中舞动，魔杖头上划出一道像熔化的白银般的光带，起先并没有形状，随后光带扭曲起来，变成了一只闪闪发光的人手，像月光一样明亮。它自己飞下来，安在虫尾巴流血的手腕上。

虫尾巴突然停止了抽泣，呼吸粗重而刺耳。他抬起头，不敢相信似的看着这只银色的手。它天衣无缝地接在他的手臂上，就好像戴了一只耀眼的手套。虫尾巴试着弯曲闪光的手指，又颤抖地从地上捡起一根树枝，把它捏成了粉末。

"我的主人，"他轻声说，"主人……太漂亮了……谢谢您……谢谢您……"

他跪着爬过去，亲吻着伏地魔的袍子。

"希望你的忠诚不要再动摇，虫尾巴。"伏地魔说。

## CHAPTER THIRTY-THREE  The Death Eaters

'No, my Lord ... never, my Lord ...'

Wormtail stood up and took his place in the circle, staring at his powerful new hand, his face still shining with tears. Voldemort now approached the man on Wormtail's right.

'Lucius, my slippery friend,' he whispered, halting before him. 'I am told that you have not renounced the old ways, though to the world you present a respectable face. You are still ready to take the lead in a spot of Muggle-torture, I believe? Yet you never tried to find me, Lucius ... your exploits at the Quidditch World Cup were fun, I daresay ... but might not your energies have been better directed towards finding and aiding your master?'

'My Lord, I was constantly on the alert,' came Lucius Malfoy's voice swiftly from beneath the hood. 'Had there been any sign from you, any whisper of your whereabouts, I would have been at your side immediately, nothing could have prevented me –'

'And yet you ran from my Mark, when a faithful Death Eater sent it into the sky last summer?' said Voldemort lazily, and Mr. Malfoy stopped talking abruptly. 'Yes, I know all about that, Lucius ... you have disappointed me ... I expect more faithful service in future.'

'Of course, my Lord, of course ... you are merciful, thank you ...'

Voldemort moved on, and stopped, staring at the space – large enough for two people – which separated Malfoy and the next man.

'The Lestranges should stand here,' said Voldemort quietly. 'But they are entombed in Azkaban. They were faithful. They went to Azkaban rather than renounce me ... when Azkaban is broken open, the Lestranges will be honoured beyond their dreams. The Dementors will join us ... they are our natural allies ... we will recall the banished giants ... I shall have all my devoted servants returned to me, and an army of creatures whom all fear ...'

He walked on. Some of the Death Eaters he passed in silence, but he paused before others, and spoke to them.

'Macnair ... destroying dangerous beasts for the Ministry of Magic now, Wormtail tells me? You shall have better victims than that soon, Macnair. Lord Voldemort will provide ...'

'Thank you, master ... thank you,' murmured Macnair.

'And here,' Voldemort moved on to the two largest hooded figures, 'we have Crabbe ... you will do better this time, will you not, Crabbe? And you, Goyle?'

## 第33章 食死徒

"不会的，我的主人……永远不会，我的主人……"

虫尾巴站起来，也加入到那个圈子中，脸上还带着泪光，反复端详着那只有力的新手。伏地魔朝虫尾巴右边的一个人走去。

"卢修斯，我狡猾的朋友，"他在那人面前停住，低声说道，"我听说你并没有放弃过去的行为，尽管你在世人面前装出一副道貌岸然的面孔。我相信你仍然愿意带头折磨麻瓜吧？可是你从来没有来寻找我，卢修斯……你在魁地奇世界杯赛上的举动倒是挺有趣……但如果你把精力花在寻找和帮助你的主人上，不是更好吗？"

"主人，我一直非常留心，"卢修斯·马尔福的声音迅速从兜帽下传来，"只要有您的任何信号，只要有关于您下落的任何传言，我立刻就会赶到您身边，什么也拦不住我——"

"可是去年夏天，一名忠实的食死徒把我的标记发射到空中后，你却逃走了。"伏地魔懒洋洋地说——马尔福先生突然闭了嘴，"是啊，我都知道，卢修斯……你令我失望……希望你以后更忠诚地为我效力。"

"当然，主人，当然……您宽宏大量，谢谢您……"

伏地魔走了两步，停下来，看着马尔福和旁边一人之间的空隙——这空隙够站两个人。

"莱斯特兰奇夫妇应该站在这里，"伏地魔轻声说，"可是他们被困在了阿兹卡班。他们是忠诚的。他们宁肯进阿兹卡班也不愿背弃我……当阿兹卡班被攻破之后，莱斯特兰奇夫妇将得到他们梦想不到的奖赏。摄魂怪将加入我们……他们是我们的天然同盟……我们将召回被驱逐的巨人……我将找回我所有忠诚的仆人，重新拥有一批人人畏惧的神奇动物……"

他继续走动，走过一些食死徒面前时没有作声，在另一些人面前停了下来，跟他们讲话。

"麦克尼尔……虫尾巴告诉我，你在为魔法部消灭危险野兽？不久就会有更好的东西让你去消灭的，麦克尼尔，伏地魔会提供的……"

"谢谢您，主人……谢谢您。"麦克尼尔喃喃道。

"啊——"伏地魔走到两个块头最大、戴着兜帽的人影面前，"克拉布……你这次会表现得好一点，是吗，克拉布？还有你，高尔？"

## CHAPTER THIRTY-THREE    The Death Eaters

They bowed clumsily, muttering dully.

'Yes, master ...'

'We will, master ...'

'The same goes for you, Nott,' said Voldemort quietly, as he walked past a stooped figure in Mr. Goyle's shadow.

'My Lord, I prostrate myself before you, I am your most faithful –'

'That will do,' said Voldemort.

He had reached the largest gap of all, and he stood surveying it with his blank, red eyes, as though he could see people standing there.

'And here we have six missing Death Eaters ... three dead in my service. One, too cowardly to return ... he will pay. One, who I believe has left me for ever ... he will be killed, of course ... and one, who remains my most faithful servant, and who has already re-entered my service.'

The Death Eaters stirred; Harry saw their eyes dart sideways at each other through their masks.

'He is at Hogwarts, that faithful servant, and it was through his efforts that our young friend arrived tonight ...

'Yes,' said Voldemort, a grin curling his lipless mouth, as the eyes of the circle flashed in Harry's direction. 'Harry Potter has kindly joined us for my rebirthing party. One might go so far as to call him my guest of honour.'

There was a silence. Then the Death Eater to the right of Wormtail stepped forward, and Lucius Malfoy's voice spoke from under the mask.

'Master, we crave to know ... we beg you to tell us ... how you have achieved this ... this miracle ... how you managed to return to us ...'

'Ah, what a story it is, Lucius,' said Voldemort. 'And it begins – and ends – with my young friend here.'

He walked lazily over to stand next to Harry, so that the eyes of the whole circle were upon the two of them. The snake continued to circle.

'You know, of course, that they have called this boy my downfall?' Voldemort said softly, his red eyes upon Harry, whose scar began to burn so fiercely that he almost screamed in agony. 'You all know that on the night I lost my powers and my body, I tried to kill him. His mother died in the attempt to save him – and unwittingly provided him with a protection I admit I had not foreseen ... I could not touch the boy.'

## 第33章 食死徒

两人笨拙地鞠了一躬，傻乎乎地嘟哝着。

"是，主人……"

"会的，主人……"

"你也一样，诺特。"伏地魔对笼罩在高尔先生阴影下的一个驼背人轻声说道。

"主人，我匍匐在您面前，我是您最忠诚——"

"够了。"伏地魔说。

他走到了最大的一个空隙跟前，用空洞的红眼睛打量着它，就好像有人站在那里似的。

"这里少了六个食死徒……有三个为我死了，有一个没胆子回来……他会付出代价。另一个，我想是永远离开我了……他当然会被处死……还有一个仍然是我最忠诚的仆人，已经重新为我服务了。"

食死徒出现了小小的骚动，哈利看见这些蒙面人偷偷交换着目光。

"他在霍格沃茨，我那个忠诚的仆人，靠了他的努力，我们的小朋友今晚才会来到这里……"

一圈人的目光齐刷刷地投向哈利。"不错，"伏地魔没有嘴唇的嘴巴扭曲出一个笑容，"哈利·波特大驾光临我的再生晚会。我们甚至不妨称他为我的特邀嘉宾。"

一片沉默。然后虫尾巴右边的食死徒向前走了一步，面具下传出卢修斯·马尔福的声音。

"主人，我们渴望知道……恳求您告诉我们……您是怎样完成了这个……这个奇迹……重新回到我们身边……"

"啊，说来话长，卢修斯，"伏地魔说，"这个故事的开头——还有结尾——都和我的这位小朋友有关。"

他懒洋洋地走到哈利身边，整个圈子的目光都落到他们两人身上。大蛇继续在那里转悠。

"你们当然知道，他们说这个男孩是我的克星，是吗？"伏地魔轻声说道，一双红眼睛盯着哈利，哈利的伤疤火辣辣地剧痛，使他差点儿尖叫起来，"你们都知道，在我失去法力和肉体的那个夜晚，我想要杀死他。他母亲为了救他而死——无意中使他获得了某种保护，我承认这是我没有料到的……我不能碰这个男孩。"

## CHAPTER THIRTY-THREE   The Death Eaters

Voldemort raised one of his long white fingers, and put it very close to Harry's cheek. 'His mother left upon him the traces of her sacrifice ... this is old magic, I should have remembered it, I was foolish to overlook it ... but no matter. I can touch him now.'

Harry felt the cold tip of the long white finger touch him, and thought his head would burst with the pain.

Voldemort laughed softly in his ear, then took the finger away, and continued addressing the Death Eaters. 'I miscalculated, my friends, I admit it. My curse was deflected by the woman's foolish sacrifice, and it rebounded upon me. Aaah ... pain beyond pain, my friends; nothing could have prepared me for it. I was ripped from my body, I was less than spirit, less than the meanest ghost ... but still, I was alive. What I was, even I do not know ... I, who have gone further than anybody along the path that leads to immortality. You know my goal – to conquer death. And now, I was tested, and it appeared that one or more of my experiments had worked ... for I had not been killed, though the curse should have done it. Nevertheless, I was as powerless as the weakest creature alive, and without the means to help myself ... for I had no body, and every spell which might have helped me required the use of a wand ...

'I remember only forcing myself, sleeplessly, endlessly, second by second, to exist ... I settled in a faraway place, in a forest, and I waited ... surely, one of my faithful Death Eaters would try and find me ... one of them would come and perform the magic I could not, to restore me to a body ... but I waited in vain ...'

The shiver ran once more around the circle of listening Death Eaters. Voldemort let the silence spiral horribly before continuing. 'Only one power remained to me. I could possess the bodies of others. But I dared not go where other humans were plentiful, for I knew that the Aurors were still abroad and searching for me. I sometimes inhabited animals – snakes, of course, being my preference – but I was little better off inside them than as pure spirit, for their bodies were ill-adapted to perform magic ... and my possession of them shortened their lives; none of them lasted long ...

'Then ... four years ago ... the means for my return seemed assured. A wizard – young, foolish and gullible – wandered across my path in the forest I had made my home. Oh, he seemed the very chance I had been dreaming of ... for he was a teacher at Dumbledore's school ... he was easy to bend to my will ... he brought me back to this country, and after a while, I took possession of his body, to supervise him closely as he carried out my orders. But my plan failed.

## 第33章 食死徒

伏地魔伸出一根细长苍白的手指，凑近哈利的面颊。"他母亲的牺牲在他身上留下了痕迹……这是一种古老的魔法。我应该记得的，但却愚蠢地忽略了……不过没关系，现在我可以碰他了。"

哈利感到那细长苍白的手指的冰凉指尖触到他的皮肤，他的头疼得仿佛要炸开了。

伏地魔在他耳边轻笑一声，移开手指，继续对食死徒们说话。"朋友们，我承认我失算了。我的咒语被那女人愚蠢的牺牲一挡，弹回到我自己身上。啊……痛得无以复加，朋友们，什么也抵挡不住。我被剥离了肉体，比幽灵还不如，比最卑微的游魂还不如……但我还活着。我是什么，到现在我都不知道……我，在永生的路上比谁走得都远。你们知道我的目标——征服死亡。现在经过检验，看来我的那些实验中至少有一两个起了作用……因为我没有死，尽管那个咒语是致命的。然而，我却像最弱小的生物一样无力，没有办法自助……我没有肉体，而能够帮助我的每个咒语都需要使用魔杖……

"我记得在那无法合眼的日日夜夜，我每分每秒只是反复强迫自己活下去……我躲到一处遥远的森林里，等待着……我的忠诚的食死徒们肯定会想办法找到我的……肯定会有一个人来用我自己无法施展的魔法，还我一个肉身……但我白等了……"

食死徒的圈子又打了一个寒战。伏地魔让恐怖在沉默中升级，然后继续说："我只剩下一个法力，我可以附在别人身上。但我不敢到人多的地方去，因为知道傲罗还在国外找我。我有时附在动物身上——蛇当然是我最喜欢用的——但在它们身上比当纯粹的幽灵好不了多少，因为蛇的身体不适合施魔法……而且我的附身还缩短了它们的寿命，它们都没活多久……

"后来……四年前……我的复活似乎有了指望。一个年轻愚蠢、容易上当的巫师走进了我落脚的那片森林，偏巧被我撞上了。哦，那似乎正是我梦寐以求的机会……因为他是邓布利多学校里的教师……他很容易受我摆布……他把我带回这个国家，后来我附在他身上，密切监视他，指导他执行我的命令。但是我的计划失败了，我没有偷到魔

## CHAPTER THIRTY-THREE    The Death Eaters

I did not manage to steal the Philosopher's Stone. I was not to be assured immortal life. I was thwarted ... thwarted, once again, by Harry Potter ...'

Silence once more; nothing was stirring, not even the leaves on the yew tree. The Death Eaters were quite motionless, the glittering eyes in their masks fixed upon Voldemort, and upon Harry.

'The servant died when I left his body, and I was left as weak as ever I had been,' Voldemort continued. 'I returned to my hiding place far away, and I will not pretend to you that I didn't then fear that I might never regain my powers ... yes, that was perhaps my darkest hour ... I could not hope that I would be sent another wizard to possess ... and I had given up hope, now, that any of my Death Eaters cared what had become of me ...'

One or two of the masked wizards in the circle moved uncomfortably, but Voldemort took no notice.

'And then, not even a year ago, when I had almost abandoned hope, it happened at last ... a servant returned to me: Wormtail here, who had faked his own death to escape justice, was driven out of hiding by those he had once counted friends, and decided to return to his master. He sought me in the country where it had long been rumoured I was hiding ... helped, of course, by the rats he met along the way. Wormtail has a curious affinity with rats, do you not, Wormtail? His filthy little friends told him there was a place, deep in an Albanian forest, that they avoided, where small animals like themselves had met their deaths by a dark shadow that possessed them ...

'But his journey back to me was not smooth, was it, Wormtail? For, hungry one night, on the edge of the very forest where he had hoped to find me, he foolishly stopped at an inn for some food ... and whom should he meet there, but one Bertha Jorkins, a witch from the Ministry of Magic?

'Now see the way that fate favours Lord Voldemort. This might have been the end of Wormtail, and of my last hope for regeneration. But Wormtail – displaying a presence of mind I would never have expected of him – convinced Bertha Jorkins to accompany him on a night-time stroll. He overpowered her ... he brought her to me. And Bertha Jorkins, who might have ruined all, proved instead to be a gift beyond my wildest dreams ... for – with a little persuasion – she became a veritable mine of information.

'She told me that the Triwizard Tournament would be played at Hogwarts this year. She told me that she knew of a faithful Death Eater who would be

## 第33章 食死徒

法石，不能保证长生不死。我被挫败了……又一次被哈利·波特挫败了……"

又一阵沉默，没有一丝动静，连红豆杉的树叶都静止了。食死徒们一动不动，面具后面闪闪发亮的眼睛盯着伏地魔，然后又盯着哈利。

"那个仆人在我离开他的身体后就死了，我又变得和以前一样虚弱。"伏地魔继续说道，"我回到那个遥远的藏身之地，我不想对你们夸口，说我当时并未担心自己再也不能恢复法力……是的，那可能是我最黑暗的时期……我不能指望再有一个巫师送上门来……而且我已不再幻想会有哪个食死徒关心我的状况……"

圈子中有一两个巫师不安地动了一下，但伏地魔没有理会。

"然后，不到一年前，就在我几乎放弃希望的时候，希望终于出现了……一个仆人找到了我。就是这位虫尾巴，他装死逃避了审判，被他以前看作朋友的人追赶得无处藏身，所以决定回到他的主人身边。他在长期以来人们传说是我藏身之地的国家寻找我……当然，一路上得到了老鼠的帮助。虫尾巴和老鼠有一种奇特的亲近关系，是不是，虫尾巴？他那些龌龊的小朋友们告诉他，在阿尔巴尼亚的密林深处有一个地方它们都不敢靠近，许多像它们那样的小动物都在那里被一个黑影附身，随后就死掉了……

"但他回到我身边的经过并不顺利，是不是，虫尾巴？一天夜里，他已走到那座森林边上，很快就要找到我了。他因为肚子饿，愚蠢地走进了一家酒馆……偏偏在那里遇见了伯莎·乔金斯——魔法部的一个女巫。

"现在看看命运是多么眷顾伏地魔吧。这次遭遇本来可能要了虫尾巴的命，也断送掉我复活的最后一丝希望。但虫尾巴表现出了出乎我意料的镇静，他说服伯莎·乔金斯和他一起在夜里散步。他制服了那女人……把她带到我面前。这个本来可能毁掉一切的伯莎·乔金斯，却成了我梦想不到的绝妙礼物……因为，我稍加说服，她就交代出了大量的情报。

"她告诉我今年霍格沃茨将举行三强争霸赛，还说她知道有一个忠诚的食死徒，只要我能和他取得联系，他就会心甘情愿地帮助我。她

## CHAPTER THIRTY-THREE — The Death Eaters

only too willing to help me, if I could only contact him. She told me many things ... but the means I used to break the Memory Charm upon her were powerful, and when I had extracted all useful information from her, her mind and body were both damaged beyond repair. She had now served her purpose. I could not possess her. I disposed of her.'

Voldemort smiled his terrible smile, his red eyes blank and pitiless.

'Wormtail's body, of course, was ill-adapted for possession, as all assumed him dead, and would attract far too much attention if seen. However, he was the able-bodied servant I needed, and, poor wizard though he is, Wormtail was able to follow the instructions I gave him, which would return me to a rudimentary, weak body of my own, a body I would be able to inhabit while awaiting the essential ingredients for true rebirth ... a spell or two of my own invention ... a little help from my dear Nagini' – Voldemort's red eyes fell upon the continually circling snake – 'a potion concocted from unicorn blood, and the snake venom Nagini provided ... I was soon returned to an almost human form, and strong enough to travel.

'There was no hope of stealing the Philosopher's Stone any more, for I knew that Dumbledore would have seen to it that it was destroyed. But I was willing to embrace mortal life again, before chasing immortal. I set my sights lower ... I would settle for my old body back again, and my old strength.

'I knew that to achieve this – it is an old piece of Dark Magic, the potion that revived me tonight – I would need three powerful ingredients. Well, one of them was already at hand, was it not, Wormtail? Flesh given by a servant ...

'My father's bone, naturally, meant that we would have to come here, where he was buried. But the blood of a foe ... Wormtail would have had me use any wizard, would you not, Wormtail? Any wizard who had hated me ... as so many of them still do. But I knew the one I must use, if I was to rise again, more powerful than I had been when I had fallen. I wanted Harry Potter's blood. I wanted the blood of the one who had stripped me of power thirteen years ago, for the lingering protection his mother once gave him, would then reside in my veins, too ...

'But how to get at Harry Potter? For he has been better protected than I think even he knows, protected in ways devised by Dumbledore long ago, when it fell to him to arrange the boy's future. Dumbledore invoked an ancient magic, to ensure the boy's protection as long as he is in his relations' care. Not even I can touch him there ... then, of course, there was the

## 第33章 食死徒

告诉了我很多事情……但我用来打破她身上遗忘咒的办法太厉害了。当我从她嘴里掏出所有有用的情报之后，她的精神和身体都已损伤得无法恢复。她已经派完了用场。我不能附在她身上，就把她处理掉了。"

伏地魔露出可怕的笑容，红眼睛变得空洞而冷漠无情。

"虫尾巴当然不适合附身，所有的人都以为他死了，如果他被人看到就太惹眼了。但是我需要他这样一个身体健壮的仆人，他虽是个蹩脚的巫师，却能够执行我的指示，使我初步获得一个软弱的肉身，我可以在这个身体里等待真正再生所需要的成分……靠着我自己发明的一两个咒语……还有我亲爱的纳吉尼给我的一点帮助，"——伏地魔的红眼睛望着不断转圈游动的大蛇——"用独角兽的血加上纳吉尼的毒液调制的药水……我很快就拥有了一个几乎像人一样的形体，并且有力气旅行了。

"偷魔法石是没希望了，我知道邓布利多一定会把它毁掉。但我愿意重新接受凡人的生命，然后再去追求长生不死。我把眼光放低了一些……只想恢复我原来的身体，我原来的力量。

"我知道要做到这点，需要三样强效的药引子，才能配成今天使我复活的魔药——这是一个古老的黑魔法。其中一样就在手头，是不是，虫尾巴？仆人的肉……

"我父亲的骨头，自然意味着我们要到这里来，这是埋葬他的地方。可是仇敌的血……虫尾巴建议我用任何巫师的血，是不是，虫尾巴？任何恨我的巫师……因为有那么多人仍然在恨我。但是我知道必须用谁……如果我想要复活，并且比失败前更加强大的话。我要哈利·波特的血。我要十三年前使我失去法力的那个人的血……因为他母亲留在他身上的保护也会存在于我的血液里……

"可是怎么把哈利·波特弄来呢？他被保护得那么好，我想这是连他自己都不知道的。很早以前，邓布利多在考虑安排这男孩的未来时，专门设计了一套保护方案。他用了一个古老的魔法，保证这男孩只要在亲人的照料下就会受到保护，连我都不能碰他……当然，后来是魁地奇世界杯赛……我想在那里他离开了亲人和邓布利多，所受的保护会弱一些。但我还没有力量从一大群魔法部的巫师中间把他劫走。然

## CHAPTER THIRTY-THREE — The Death Eaters

Quidditch World Cup ... I thought his protection might be weaker there, away from his relations and Dumbledore, but I was not yet strong enough to attempt kidnap in the midst of a horde of Ministry wizards. And then, the boy would return to Hogwarts, where he is under the crooked nose of that Muggle-loving fool from morning until night. So how could I take him?

'Why ... by using Bertha Jorkins's information, of course. Use my one faithful Death Eater, stationed at Hogwarts, to ensure that the boy's name was entered into the Goblet of Fire. Use my Death Eater to ensure that the boy won the Tournament — that he touched the Triwizard Cup first — the Cup which my Death Eater had turned into a Portkey, which would bring him here, beyond the reach of Dumbledore's help and protection, and into my waiting arms. And here he is ... the boy you all believed had been my downfall ...'

Voldemort moved slowly forward, and turned to face Harry. He raised his wand. '*Crucio!*'

It was pain beyond anything Harry had ever experienced; his very bones were on fire; his head was surely splitting along his scar; his eyes were rolling madly in his head; he wanted it to end ... to black out ... to die ...

And then it was gone. He was hanging limply in the ropes binding him to the headstone of Voldemort's father, looking up into those bright red eyes through a kind of mist. The night was ringing with the sound of the Death Eaters' laughter.

'You see, I think, how foolish it was to suppose that this boy could ever have been stronger than me,' said Voldemort. 'But I want there to be no mistake in anybody's mind. Harry Potter escaped me by a lucky chance. And I am now going to prove my power by killing him, here and now, in front of you all, when there is no Dumbledore to help him, and no mother to die for him. I will give him his chance. He will be allowed to fight, and you will be left in no doubt which of us is the stronger. Just a little longer, Nagini,' he whispered, and the snake glided away through the grass, to where the Death Eaters stood watching.

'Now untie him, Wormtail, and give him back his wand.'

## 第33章 食死徒

后这男孩回到了霍格沃茨,从早到晚都在那个喜欢麻瓜的蠢货的歪鼻子底下。我怎么才能把他弄来呢?

"啊……当然是靠了伯莎·乔金斯的情报。利用我那位潜伏在霍格沃茨的忠诚的食死徒,保证这男孩的名字被放进火焰杯。再利用我那位食死徒,确保男孩在比赛中获胜——保证他第一个接触三强杯——那杯子已经被我的食死徒换成了门钥匙,会把男孩带到这里,远离邓布利多的帮助和保护,落到我的手里。他就在这儿……你们都认为是我的克星的这个男孩……"

伏地魔慢慢走向前,转身对着哈利,举起了魔杖。"钻心剜骨!"

哈利从没经受过这样痛苦的折磨,全身的骨头都在燃烧,脑袋肯定是沿着伤疤裂开了,眼球在脑壳里疯狂地转动,他希望赶快停止……希望自己昏过去……死掉……

折磨突然结束了。他瘫软地挂在把他绑在伏地魔父亲墓碑上的绳索上,抬头透过一层雾气看着那双发光的红眼睛。夜空中回荡着食死徒的笑声。

"我想你们已经看到,认为这个男孩比我强的想法是多么愚蠢,"伏地魔说,"但我要彻底消除大家脑子里的误解。哈利·波特从我手里逃掉完全是侥幸。现在我就要杀死他,以证明我的力量,就在此时此地,当着你们的面,这儿没有邓布利多来保护他,也没有他妈妈为他做出牺牲。我会给他机会,他可以和我搏斗,这样你们就不会怀疑到底谁更加强大了。你稍等一会儿,纳吉尼。"他轻声说,大蛇在草地上游到了食死徒们站立的地方。

"把他放下来,虫尾巴,把他的魔杖还给他。"

## CHAPTER THIRTY-FOUR

# Priori Incantatem

Wormtail approached Harry, who scrambled to find his feet, to support his own weight before the ropes were untied. Wormtail raised his new silver hand, pulled out the wad of material gagging Harry and then, with one swipe, cut through the bonds tying Harry to the gravestone.

There was a split second, perhaps, when Harry might have considered running for it, but his injured leg shook under him as he stood on the overgrown grave, as the Death Eaters closed ranks, forming a tighter circle around him and Voldemort, so that the gaps where the missing Death Eaters should have stood were filled. Wormtail walked out of the circle to the place where Cedric's body lay, and returned with Harry's wand, which he thrust roughly into Harry's hand without looking at him. Then Wormtail resumed his place in the circle of watching Death Eaters.

'You have been taught how to duel, Harry Potter?' said Voldemort softly, his red eyes glinting through the darkness.

At these words Harry remembered, as though from a former life, the Duelling Club at Hogwarts he had attended briefly two years ago ... all he had learnt there was the Disarming spell, '*Expelliarmus*' ... and what use would it be, even if he could, to deprive Voldemort of his wand, when he was surrounded by Death Eaters, outnumbered by at least thirty to one? He had never learnt anything that could possibly fit him for this. He knew he was facing the thing against which Moody had always warned ... the unblockable Avada Kedavra curse – and Voldemort was right – his mother was not here to die for him this time ... he was quite unprotected ...

'We bow to each other, Harry,' said Voldemort, bending a little, but keeping his snake-like face upturned to Harry. 'Come, the niceties must be observed ... Dumbledore would like you to show manners ... bow to death, Harry ...'

# 第 34 章

# 闪 回 咒

虫尾巴走近哈利，哈利拼命用脚去够地面，想在绳索解开之前支撑住自己的身体。虫尾巴抬起新安上的银手，抽出哈利嘴里塞的破布，然后一挥手，割断了把哈利绑在墓碑上的绳索。

在一瞬间，哈利考虑过逃跑，可是他的伤腿直打战。他站在杂草丛生的墓地上，食死徒们靠拢上来，紧密地围在他和伏地魔周围，把那些没来的食死徒本应该站的空当都挤掉了。虫尾巴走到圈子外塞德里克的尸体旁，取来哈利的魔杖，粗鲁地塞到他手里，连看也没看他一眼，又径自回到食死徒的圈子里。

"你学过决斗是不是，哈利·波特？"伏地魔轻声问道，红眼睛在黑暗中闪着光。

听了这话，哈利想起两年前他曾参加过一个短期的决斗俱乐部，感觉好像是上辈子的事了……他在那里只学到了"除你武器"这样的缴械咒……可即使他能够夺走伏地魔的魔杖，又有什么用呢？周围都是食死徒，与他的比例至少是三十比一。他没有学过在这里用得上的东西。哈利知道他面临的是穆迪经常警告他们要防范的咒语……不可阻挡的阿瓦达索命咒。伏地魔说对了，这一次没有妈妈来拼死救他了……他完全没有保护。

"我们相互鞠躬吧，哈利，"伏地魔说着欠了欠身，但那张蛇脸始终望着哈利，"来吧，礼节是要遵守的……邓布利多一定希望你表现得很有风度……向死神鞠躬吧，哈利……"

## CHAPTER THIRTY-FOUR    Priori Incantatem

The Death Eaters were laughing again. Voldemort's lipless mouth was smiling. Harry did not bow. He was not going to let Voldemort play with him before killing him ... he was not going to give him that satisfaction ...

'I said, *bow*,' Voldemort said, raising his wand – and Harry felt his spine curve as though a huge, invisible hand was bending him ruthlessly forwards, and the Death Eaters laughed harder than ever.

'Very good,' said Voldemort softly, and as he raised his wand, the pressure bearing down upon Harry lifted too. 'And now you face me, like a man ... straight backed and proud, the way your father died ...

'And now – we duel.'

Voldemort raised his wand, and before Harry could do anything to defend himself, before he could even move, he had been hit again by the Cruciatus Curse. The pain was so intense, so all-consuming, that he no longer knew where he was ... white-hot knives were piercing every inch of his skin, his head was surely going to burst with pain; he was screaming more loudly than he'd ever screamed in his life –

And then it stopped. Harry rolled over and scrambled to his feet; he was shaking as uncontrollably as Wormtail had done when his hand had been cut off; he staggered sideways into the wall of watching Death Eaters, and they pushed him away, back towards Voldemort.

'A little break,' said Voldemort, the slit-like nostrils dilating with excitement, 'a little pause ... that hurt, didn't it, Harry? You don't want me to do that again, do you?'

Harry didn't answer. He was going to die like Cedric, those pitiless red eyes were telling him so ... he was going to die, and there was nothing he could do about it ... but he wasn't going to play along. He wasn't going to obey Voldemort ... he wasn't going to beg ...

'I asked you whether you want me to do that again?' said Voldemort softly. 'Answer me! *Imperio!*'

And Harry felt, for the third time in his life, the sensation that his mind had been wiped of all thought ... ah, it was bliss, not to think, it was as though he was floating, dreaming ... *just answer 'no' ... say 'no' ... just answer 'no' ...*

I will not, said a stronger voice, in the back of his head, I won't answer ...

*Just answer 'no' ...*

I won't do it, I won't say it ...

## 第34章 闪回咒

食死徒们又哄笑起来。伏地魔那没有嘴唇的嘴巴露出了微笑。哈利没有弯腰,他不会让伏地魔在杀他以前玩弄他……他不会让他得逞……

"我说了,鞠躬。"伏地魔举起魔杖——哈利感到脊梁骨一弯,好像有一只看不见的大手在无情地把他的后背往前按。食死徒们笑得更厉害了。

"很好。"伏地魔轻声说道,抬起了魔杖,哈利背上的压力也消失了,"现在你看着我,像男子汉一样……昂首挺胸,就像你父亲死时那样……

"现在——我们决斗。"

伏地魔举起魔杖,哈利还没来得及自卫,甚至连动都没来得及动一下,就再次被钻心咒击中了。剧烈的疼痛占据了一切,他不知道自己身在何处……白热的刀子扎着他的每一寸皮肤,头疼得肯定是要裂开了。他尖声惨叫,他有生以来从没有发出过这样凄厉的叫声——

然后这一切停止了,哈利翻身爬起,像虫尾巴被砍掉手后一样控制不住地颤抖。他跟跟跄跄地撞到食死徒组成的人墙上,他们把他推回到伏地魔跟前。

"暂停,"伏地魔说,两条细缝一样的鼻孔兴奋地张大了,"休息一会儿……很疼吧,哈利?你不希望我再来一次,是不是?"

哈利没有回答,他会像塞德里克一样死去。那双残忍的红眼睛正在告诉他这一点……他会被杀死的,而他对此毫无办法……但他不会屈服,他不会听伏地魔的摆布……他不会求饶……

"我问你要不要我再来一次,"伏地魔轻轻地说,"回答我!魂魄出窍!"

顿时,哈利感到脑子里没有了思想,这是他一生中第三次有这种感觉……多幸福啊,不用思考,他好像在飘浮,在做梦……说"不要"……说吧……说"不要"……

我不说,脑海深处有一个更有力的声音说道,我不回答……

说"不要"……

我不说,决不说……

## CHAPTER THIRTY-FOUR    Priori Incantatem

*Just answer 'no' ...*
'I WON'T!'

And these words burst from Harry's mouth; they echoed through the graveyard, and the dream state was lifted as suddenly as though cold water had been thrown over him – back rushed the aches that the Cruciatus Curse had left all over his body – back rushed the realisation of where he was, and what he was facing ...

'You won't?' said Voldemort quietly, and the Death Eaters were not laughing now. 'You won't say "no"? Harry, obedience is a virtue I need to teach you before you die ... perhaps another little dose of pain?'

Voldemort raised his wand, but this time Harry was ready; with the reflexes born of his Quidditch training, he flung himself sideways onto the ground; he rolled behind the marble headstone of Voldemort's father, and he heard it crack as the curse missed him.

'We are not playing hide-and-seek, Harry,' said Voldemort's soft, cold voice, drawing nearer, as the Death Eaters laughed. 'You cannot hide from me. Does this mean you are tired of our duel? Does this mean that you would prefer me to finish it now, Harry? Come out, Harry ... come out and play, then ... it will be quick ... it might even be painless ... I would not know ... I have never died ...'

Harry crouched behind the headstone, and knew the end had come. There was no hope ... no help to be had. and as he heard Voldemort draw nearer still, he knew one thing only, and it was beyond fear or reason – he was not going to die crouching here like a child playing hide-and-seek; he was not going to die kneeling at Voldemort's feet ... he was going to die upright like his father, and he was going to die trying to defend himself, even if no defence was possible ...

Before Voldemort could stick his snake-like face around the headstone, Harry had stood up ... he gripped his wand tightly in his hand, thrust it out in front of him, and threw himself around the headstone, facing Voldemort.

Voldemort was ready. As Harry shouted '*Expelliarmus!*', Voldemort cried, '*Avada Kedavra!*'

A jet of green light issued from Voldemort's wand just as a jet of red light blasted from Harry's – they met in mid-air – and suddenly, Harry's wand was vibrating as though an electric charge was surging through it; his hand

## 第34章 闪回咒

说"不要"……

**"我不说!"**

这几个字从哈利嘴里迸出来,在墓地上空回响,梦幻的状态突然消失了,就像被当头浇了一盆凉水似的——钻心咒在他浑身留下的疼痛又全部回来了——他重新意识到他在哪里,面前是什么……

"你不说?"伏地魔轻声说,食死徒们这时不笑了,"你不肯说'不要'?哈利,我需要在你死前教会你服从的美德……也许要再来一点疼痛?"

伏地魔举起魔杖,但这次哈利有所准备。他凭着在魁地奇比赛中练出的敏捷,朝旁边一扑,滚到大理石墓碑的背后,咒语没有击中他,但他听到了墓碑裂开的声音。

"我们可不是在捉迷藏,哈利,"伏地魔轻声说,那冷酷的声音在渐渐靠近,食死徒们在发笑,"你不能躲起来。这是否表示你已经对我们的决斗感到厌倦了?你是不是希望我现在就结束它,哈利?出来吧,哈利……出来决斗吧……很快的……甚至没有任何痛苦……我不知道……我没有死过……"

哈利蜷缩在墓碑后,知道一切都完了。没有希望……孤立无助。他听着伏地魔步步逼近,心里只有一个念头,这念头超越了恐惧和理智:他不能像捉迷藏的小孩一样,蜷缩在这里死去;他死时不能跪倒在伏地魔的脚下……他要像他父亲一样站着死去,要在自卫中死去,即使自卫是不可能的……

不等伏地魔的蛇脸转过墓碑,哈利站了起来……他握紧魔杖,举在身前,闪身冲了出去,正对着伏地魔。

伏地魔也有准备。在哈利喊出"除你武器!"的同时,伏地魔喊道:"阿瓦达索命!"

一道绿光从伏地魔的魔杖中射出,同时哈利的魔杖中射出一道红光——两道光在空中相遇——哈利的魔杖突然像通了电似的振动起来,他紧紧地攥住它,即使他想放手也放不下了——现在,一道细细的光

## CHAPTER THIRTY-FOUR   Priori Incantatem

had seized up around it; he couldn't have released it if he'd wanted to – and a narrow beam of light was now connecting the two wands, neither red nor green, but bright, deep gold – and Harry, following the beam with his astonished gaze, saw that Voldemort's long white fingers, too, were gripping a wand that was shaking and vibrating.

And then – nothing could have prepared Harry for this – he felt his feet lift from the ground. He and Voldemort were both being raised into the air, their wands still connected by that thread of shimmering golden light. They were gliding away from the tombstone of Voldemort's father, and then came to rest on a patch of ground that was clear and free of graves ... The Death Eaters were shouting, they were asking Voldemort for instructions; they were closing in, re-forming the circle around Harry and Voldemort, the snake slithering at their heels, some of them drawing their wands –

The golden thread connecting Harry and Voldemort splintered: though the wands remained connected, a thousand more offshoots arced high over Harry and Voldemort, criss-crossing all around them, until they were enclosed in a golden, dome-shaped web, a cage of light, beyond which the Death Eaters circled like jackals, their cries strangely muffled now ...

'Do nothing!' Voldemort shrieked to the Death Eaters, and Harry saw his red eyes wide with astonishment at what was happening, saw him fighting to break the thread of light still connecting his wand with Harry's; Harry held onto his wand more tightly, with both hands, and the golden thread remained unbroken. 'Do nothing unless I command you!' Voldemort shouted to the Death Eaters.

And then an unearthly and beautiful sound filled the air ... it was coming from every thread of the light-spun web vibrating around Harry and Voldemort. It was a sound Harry recognised, though he had heard it only once before in his life ... phoenix song ...

It was the sound of hope to Harry ... the most beautiful and welcome thing he had ever heard in his life ... he felt as though the song was inside him instead of just around him ... it was the sound he connected with Dumbledore, and it was almost as though a friend was speaking in his ear ...

*Don't break the connection.*

I know, Harry told the music, I know I mustn't ... but no sooner had he thought it, than the thing became much harder to do. His wand began to vibrate more powerfully than ever ... and now the beam between him and

## 第34章 闪回咒

束连接着两根魔杖,既不是红也不是绿,而是耀眼的深金色。哈利惊奇地顺着光束望去,只见伏地魔苍白细长的手指也握着一根颤动的魔杖。

然后完全猝不及防地,哈利感到自己的双脚离开了地面,他和伏地魔都升到了空中,两根魔杖仍然被那道闪烁的金线连在一起。他们从伏地魔父亲的墓碑前飞到一片没有坟头的空地上……食死徒们在喊叫,请求伏地魔的指示。他们跟了过来,重新把哈利和伏地魔围在中间。大蛇跟着他们游动,有几人抽出了魔杖——

连接哈利和伏地魔的那根金线突然散开了,但两根魔杖仍然紧紧相连,哈利和伏地魔的上方出现了上千道光弧。光弧在他们周围相互交织,最后形成了一张圆顶的金网,一个由光构成的笼子。食死徒们像野狗一样围在笼外,他们的叫声奇怪地减弱了……

"不要动!"伏地魔高声向食死徒们喊道,哈利看到他的红眼睛惊愕地张大了,看得出他对眼前的情景十分震惊,竭力想挣断连接两根魔杖的光丝。哈利用双手死死攥住魔杖,金线仍然连在一起。"没有我的命令不要动!"伏地魔朝食死徒们喊道。

突然一阵美妙的仙乐在空中响起……是从哈利和伏地魔周围振动的光网的每一根光丝上发出来的。哈利听出来了,尽管这音乐他以前只听过一次……这是凤凰的歌声……

对哈利来说,这声音代表着希望……是他一生中听过的最美妙、最令人愉快的声音……他感到这歌声像是在他内心而不是在他周围……这声音使他想到邓布利多,这声音几乎像是一个朋友在耳边说话……

不要断开连接!

我知道,哈利对音乐说,我知道不能断开……可是刚想到这里,维持连接的难度陡然增加了。他的魔杖更加猛烈地振动起来……连接他和伏地魔的金丝也发生了变化……仿佛有大颗的光珠沿着光丝滑来

## CHAPTER THIRTY-FOUR    Priori Incantatem

Voldemort changed, too ... it was as though large beads of light were sliding up and down the thread connecting the wands – Harry felt his wand give a shudder under his hand, as the light beads began to slide slowly and steadily his way ... the direction of the beam's movement was now towards him, from Voldemort, and he felt his wand shudder angrily ...

As the nearest bead of light moved nearer to Harry's wand tip, the wood beneath his fingers grew so hot he feared it would burst into flame. The closer that bead moved, the harder Harry's wand vibrated; he was sure his wand would not survive contact with it; it felt as though it was about to shatter under his fingers –

He concentrated every last particle of his mind upon forcing the bead backwards towards Voldemort, his ears full of phoenix song, his eyes furious, fixated ... and slowly, very slowly, the beads quivered to a halt, and then, just as slowly, they began to move the other way ... and it was Voldemort's wand that was vibrating extra hard now ... Voldemort who looked astonished, and almost fearful ...

One of the beads of light was quivering, inches from the tip of Voldemort's wand. Harry didn't understand why he was doing it, didn't know what it might achieve ... but he now concentrated as he had never done in his life, on forcing that bead of light right back into Voldemort's wand ... and slowly ... very slowly ... it moved along the golden thread ... it trembled for a moment ... and then it connected ...

At once, Voldemort's wand began to emit echoing screams of pain ... then – Voldemort's red eyes widened with shock – a dense, smoky hand flew out of the tip of it and vanished ... the ghost of the hand he had made Wormtail ... more shouts of pain ... and then something much larger began to blossom from Voldemort's wand tip, a great, greyish something that looked as though it was made of the solidest, densest smoke ... it was a head ... now a chest and arms ... the torso of Cedric Diggory.

If ever Harry might have released his wand from shock, it would have been then, but instinct kept him clutching his wand tightly, so that the thread of golden light remained unbroken, even though the thick grey ghost of Cedric Diggory (*was* it a ghost? It looked so solid) emerged in its entirety from the end of Voldemort's wand, as though it was squeezing itself out of a very narrow tunnel ... and this shade of Cedric stood up, and looked up and down the golden thread of light, and spoke.

## 第34章 闪回咒

滑去——哈利感到手中的魔杖抖动了一下,光珠开始缓缓地、稳稳地朝他这边滑来……光珠正离开伏地魔朝他这头移动,他的魔杖在剧烈地振动……

随着第一颗光珠接近哈利的杖尖,他手中的魔杖变得滚烫,他简直担心它会烧起来。光珠靠得越近,哈利的魔杖振动得越厉害。他确信魔杖肯定经不住光珠的一碰。他的魔杖仿佛马上就要在手中碎裂了——

他集中全部意念,努力将光珠逼向伏地魔那边。他耳中回响着凤凰的歌声,他目光坚定,喷射着怒火……慢慢地,慢慢地,光珠颤抖着停了下来,然后同样缓慢地开始朝另一头移动……现在是伏地魔的魔杖猛烈地振动起来……伏地魔看上去很震惊,几乎有些害怕……

一颗光珠颤抖着,离伏地魔的杖尖只有几英寸了。哈利不知道他为什么要这么做,也不知道这样做会有什么结果……但他一生从没有这样聚精会神,一心只想把光珠逼入伏地魔的杖尖……慢慢地……慢慢地……光珠顺着金线移动……颤抖了片刻……与杖尖相连了……

顿时,伏地魔的魔杖发出了一阵痛苦的尖叫,回响不绝……然后——伏地魔的红眼睛吃惊地瞪大了——一只由浓烟形成的人手飞出了杖尖,消失不见……是他为虫尾巴制造的那只断手的幽灵……又一阵痛苦的叫声……一个更大的物体从伏地魔的杖尖冒了出来,是一个灰色的大东西,仿佛是由最稠密的浓烟构成的……先出来一个头……然后是胸部和手臂……是塞德里克·迪戈里的身体。

如果哈利会因震惊而丢掉魔杖的话,那就是在此刻。但他本能地牢牢攥紧魔杖,使金色的光丝保持不断,尽管塞德里克·迪戈里灰色的幽灵(是幽灵吗?它看上去那么实在)整个从伏地魔的杖尖钻了出来,好像是从非常狭窄的管道中挤出一般……塞德里克的灵魂站起来,望望金色的光丝,说话了。

## CHAPTER THIRTY-FOUR    Priori Incantatem

'Hold on, Harry,' it said.

Its voice was distant and echoing. Harry looked at Voldemort ... his wide, red eyes were still shocked ... he had no more expected this than Harry had ... and, very dimly, Harry heard the frightened yells of the Death Eaters, prowling around the edges of the golden dome ...

More screams of pain from the wand ... and then something else emerged from its tip ... the dense shadow of a second head, quickly followed by arms and torso ... an old man Harry had once seen in a dream was now pushing himself out of the end of the wand just as Cedric had done ... and his ghost, or his shadow, or whatever it was, fell next to Cedric's, and surveyed Harry and Voldemort, and the golden web, and the connected wands, with mild surprise, leaning on his walking stick ...

'He was a real wizard, then?' the old man said, his eyes on Voldemort. 'Killed me, that one did ... you fight him, boy ...'

But already, yet another head was emerging ... and this head, grey as a smoky statue, was a woman's ... Harry, both arms shaking now, as he fought to keep his wand still, saw her drop to the ground and straighten up like the others, staring ...

The shadow of Bertha Jorkins surveyed the battle before her with wide eyes.

'Don't let go, now!' she cried, and her voice echoed like Cedric's, as though from very far away. 'Don't let him get you, Harry – don't let go!'

She and the other two shadowy figures began to pace around the inner walls of the golden web, while the Death Eaters flitted around the outside of it ... and Voldemort's dead victims whispered as they circled the duellers, whispered words of encouragement to Harry, and hissed words Harry couldn't hear to Voldemort.

And now another head was emerging from the tip of Voldemort's wand ... and Harry knew when he saw it who it would be ... he knew, as though he had expected it from the moment when Cedric had appeared from the wand ... knew, because the woman appearing was the one he'd thought of more than any other tonight ...

The smoky shadow of a young woman with long hair fell to the ground as Bertha had done, straightened up, and looked at him ... and Harry, his arms shaking madly now, looked back into the ghostly face of his mother.

## 第34章 闪回咒

"坚持住，哈利。"他说。

他的声音听来十分遥远，带着回声。哈利看着伏地魔……他的红眼睛仍然吃惊地瞪着……他对这一切和哈利一样感到意外……哈利还隐隐约约地听到了食死徒们惊恐的叫喊声，他们在金网的边缘转来转去……

魔杖里又发出一阵阵痛苦的尖叫……接着又一个东西从杖尖冒了出来……又是浓烟构成的一个人头，紧接着是手臂和身体……这是一个哈利只在梦中见过的老头，他像塞德里克刚才一样从魔杖里挤了出来……这个幽灵或鬼魂，或是别的什么，落到塞德里克旁边，拄着拐杖，略带吃惊地打量着哈利和伏地魔，打量着金网，还有连在一起的魔杖……

"这么说，他真的是个巫师？"老头说，眼睛望着伏地魔，"这家伙要了我的命……你跟他斗，孩子……"

可是又一个人头出现了……如同一个烟灰色的雕像，这是个女人……哈利拼命抓稳魔杖，双臂都在颤抖。他看到这女人落到地上，像其他人一样直起身子，张望着……

伯莎·乔金斯的幽灵瞪大眼睛望着眼前的这场搏斗。

"别撒手！"她喊道，喊声像塞德里克的一样带着回音，仿佛从很远的地方传来，"别让他害你，哈利，别撒手！"

她和另外两个幽灵开始沿着金网的内壁移动，食死徒们则在外面绕着金网乱跑……被伏地魔害死的幽灵一边绕着决斗者行走，一边小声地鼓励哈利，同时对伏地魔咬牙切齿地说着一些哈利听不见的话。

现在又一个人头从伏地魔的杖尖冒了出来……哈利一眼就看出了她是谁……仿佛他从塞德里克冒出来的那一刻起就期待着她出现似的……他一眼就认了出来，因为冒出来的是那个他今晚想得最多的人……

一个长头发的年轻女子的幽魂像伯莎那样落到地上，直起身子注视着他……哈利眼睛望着母亲的面孔，双臂剧烈地抖动着。

## CHAPTER THIRTY-FOUR   Priori Incantatem

'Your father's coming ...' she said quietly. 'He wants to see you ... it will be all right ... hold on ...'

And he came ... first his head, then his body ... tall and untidy-haired like Harry, the smoky, shadowy form of James Potter blossomed from the end of Voldemort's wand, fell to the ground, and straightened like his wife. He walked close to Harry, looking down at him, and he spoke in the same distant, echoing voice as the others, but quietly, so that Voldemort, his face now livid with fear as his victims prowled around him, could not hear ...

'When the connection is broken, we will linger for only moments ... but we will give you time ... you must get to the Portkey, it will return you to Hogwarts ... do you understand, Harry?'

'Yes,' Harry gasped; fighting now to keep a hold on his wand, which was slipping and sliding beneath his fingers.

'Harry ...' whispered the figure of Cedric, 'take my body back, will you? Take my body back to my parents ...'

'I will,' said Harry, his face screwed up with the effort of holding the wand.

'Do it now,' whispered his father's voice. 'Be ready to run ... do it now ...'

'NOW!' Harry yelled; he didn't think he could have held on for another moment anyway – he pulled his wand upwards with an almighty wrench, and the golden thread broke; the cage of light vanished, the phoenix song died – but the shadowy figures of Voldemort's victims did not disappear – they were closing in upon Voldemort, shielding Harry from his gaze –

And Harry ran as he had never run in his life, knocking two stunned Death Eaters aside as he passed; he zigzagged behind headstones, feeling their curses following him, hearing them hit the headstones – he was dodging curses and graves, pelting towards Cedric's body, no longer aware of the pain in his leg, his whole being concentrated on what he had to do –

'*Stun him!*' he heard Voldemort scream.

Ten feet from Cedric, Harry dived behind a marble angel to avoid the jets of red light and saw the tip of its wing shatter as the spells hit it. Gripping his wand more tightly, he dashed out from behind the angel –

'*Impedimenta!*' he bellowed, pointing his wand wildly over his shoulder at the Death Eaters running at him.

## 第34章 闪回咒

"你爸爸也来了……"她轻声说,"他想见你……会没事的……顶住……"

他果然出来了……先是脑袋,然后是身体——一个头发和哈利一样蓬乱的高个儿男子——詹姆·波特烟雾般的灵魂从伏地魔的杖尖升起,像他妻子一样落到地上,直起身子。他走近哈利,低头看着他,用同样遥远、带着回响的声音对他说话,但声音很低,伏地魔听不见——伏地魔看到被他杀害的人在他周围走来走去,吓得脸色铁青……

"连接断开后,我们只能待一小会儿……但我们会为你争取时间……你必须拿到门钥匙,它会把你带回霍格沃茨……明白吗,哈利?"

"明白。"哈利喘着气说,魔杖在他手里滑动,他拼命抓住它。

"哈利……"塞德里克的幽灵说,"把我的身体带回去,好吗?带给我的父母……"

"我会的。"哈利说。他竭尽全力握着魔杖,脸都拧歪了。

"撒吧,"他父亲小声说,"准备快跑……现在就撒……"

"好!"哈利高声喊道,觉得自己反正也坚持不下去了——他用力将魔杖向上一挑,金线断了,光网不见了,凤凰的歌声也消失了——但屈死在伏地魔手下的那些人的幽灵并没有消失——他们把伏地魔围了起来,不让他看见哈利——

哈利使出平生气力狂奔,把两名惊呆的食死徒撞到一边。他穿来穿去,用墓碑作掩护。他感觉到食死徒们的咒语在他身后嗖嗖追来,听到咒语打在墓碑上——他躲避着咒语和坟墓,朝塞德里克的尸体冲去。他忘记了腿上的疼痛,一心只想着他一定要做的事情——

"击昏他!"他听见伏地魔喊道。

在离塞德里克十英尺的地方,哈利急忙闪到一个大理石天使雕塑后面,避开了身后射来的红光,却见天使的翅膀尖被咒语打得粉碎。他攥紧魔杖,从天使后面冲了出来——

"障碍重重!"他将魔杖越过肩头,狂乱地指着身后追来的食死徒,高声吼道。

## CHAPTER THIRTY-FOUR    Priori Incantatem

From a muffled yell, he thought he had stopped at least one of them, but there was no time to turn and look; he jumped over the Cup and dived as he heard more wand blasts behind him; more jets of light flew over his head as he fell, stretching out his hand to grab Cedric's arm –

'Stand aside! I will kill him! He is mine!' shrieked Voldemort.

Harry's hand had closed on Cedric's wrist; one tombstone stood between him and Voldemort, but Cedric was too heavy to carry, and the Cup was out of reach –

Voldemort's red eyes flamed in the darkness. Harry saw his mouth curl into a smile, saw him raise his wand.

'*Accio!*' Harry yelled, pointing his wand at the Triwizard Cup.

It flew into the air, and soared towards him – Harry caught it by the handle –

He heard Voldemort's scream of fury at the same moment as he felt the jerk behind his navel that meant the Portkey had worked – it was speeding him away in a whirl of wind and colour, Cedric along with him ... they were going back ...

## 第34章 闪回咒

随着一声沉闷的叫喊,他知道自己至少拦住了一个,但没有时间停下来看了。他跳过奖杯,听见身后传来更多魔杖发射的声音,赶紧扑倒在地,伸手去抓塞德里克的胳膊,一阵光雨掠过他的头顶——

"闪开!我要杀死他!他是我的!"伏地魔尖叫道。

哈利和伏地魔之间只隔着一块墓碑。他抓住了塞德里克的手腕,可塞德里克太沉了,他搬不动,奖杯又够不着——

伏地魔的红眼睛在黑暗中闪着红光,哈利看到他嘴唇扭曲成一个狞笑,看见他举起了魔杖。

"奖杯飞来!"哈利用魔杖指着三强杯喊道。

奖杯腾空向他飞来。哈利一把抓住奖杯的把手——

他听见伏地魔在狂怒地叫喊,同时感到肚脐下被扯了一下,门钥匙起作用了——他被一阵五彩的旋风席卷而去,塞德里克在他身边……他们回去了。

## CHAPTER THIRTY-FIVE

## Veritaserum

Harry felt himself slam flat into the ground; his face was pressed into grass; the smell of it filled his nostrils. He had closed his eyes while the Portkey transported him, and he kept them closed now. He did not move. All the breath seemed to have been knocked out of him; his head was swimming so badly he felt as though the ground beneath him was swaying like the deck of a ship. To hold himself steady, he tightened his hold on the two things he was still clutching – the smooth, cold handle of the Triwizard Cup, and Cedric's body. He felt as though he would slide away into the blackness gathering at the edges of his brain if he let go of either of them. Shock and exhaustion kept him on the ground, breathing in the smell of the grass, waiting ... waiting for someone to do something ... something to happen ... and all the while, his scar burnt dully on his forehead ...

A torrent of sound deafened and confused him, there were voices everywhere, footsteps, screams ... he remained where he was, his face screwed up against the noise, as though it was a nightmare that would pass ...

Then a pair of hands seized him roughly and turned him over.

'Harry! *Harry!*'

He opened his eyes.

He was looking up at the starry sky, and Albus Dumbledore was crouched over him. The dark shadows of a crowd of people pressed in around them, pushing nearer; Harry felt the ground beneath his head reverberating with their footsteps.

He had come back to the edge of the maze. He could see the stands rising above him, the shapes of people moving in them, the stars above.

Harry let go of the Cup, but he clutched Cedric to him even more tightly. He raised his free hand and seized Dumbledore's wrist, while Dumbledore's

# 第35章

# 吐 真 剂

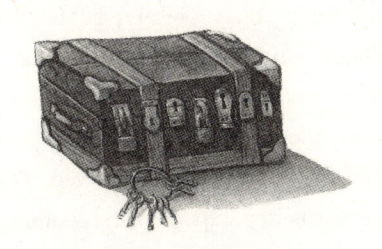

哈利感觉自己脸朝下摔到了地上，他的脸埋在草里，鼻子里全是青草的气味。在门钥匙带着他飞行时，他是闭着眼睛的，现在他还是紧闭双眼一动不动。所有的力气似乎都跑光了。他头晕得厉害，感觉身子下的地面像船甲板一样颠簸摇晃。为了稳住自己，他攥紧了仍在手里的两样东西：三强杯光滑、冰冷的把手和塞德里克的尸体。他感到好像只要放开其中一样，他就会滑入脑海边缘正在聚集的黑暗中。震惊和疲劳使他趴在地上，闻着青草的气味，等待着……等待着有人做些什么……等待着发生些什么……同时额头的伤疤一直在隐隐灼痛……

一阵声浪淹没了他，令他迷惑，到处都是声音，脚步声、叫嚷声……他原地不动，五官拧成一团，不想理会那些声音，仿佛这是一场噩梦，很快就会过去……

一双有力的大手抓住了他，把他翻了过来。

"哈利，哈利！"

他睁开眼睛。

眼前是繁星点点的夜空，阿不思·邓布利多蹲在他身前。周围是黑压压的人影，都向他拥过来。哈利能感到脑袋下的地面随着他们的脚步在微微震动。

他已回到了迷宫边缘，可以看到四周高高的看台，有人在上面走动，头顶上星光闪烁。

哈利放开奖杯，但把塞德里克抓得更紧了。他用腾出的手抓住邓

## CHAPTER THIRTY-FIVE    Veritaserum

face swam in and out of focus.

'He's back,' Harry whispered. 'He's back. Voldemort.'

'What's going on? What's happened?'

The face of Cornelius Fudge appeared upside-down over Harry; it looked white, appalled.

'My God – Diggory!' it whispered. 'Dumbledore – he's dead!'

The words were repeated, the shadowy figures pressing in on them gasped it to those around them ... and then others shouted it – screeched it – into the night – 'He's dead!' 'He's *dead*!' 'Cedric Diggory! *Dead!*'

'Harry, let go of him,' he heard Fudge's voice say, and he felt fingers trying to prise him from Cedric's limp body, but Harry wouldn't let him go.

Then Dumbledore's face, which was still blurred and misted, came closer. 'Harry, you can't help him now. It's over. Let go.'

'He wanted me to bring him back,' Harry muttered – it seemed important to explain this. 'He wanted me to bring him back to his parents ...'

'That's right, Harry ... just let go, now ...'

Dumbledore bent down and, with extraordinary strength for a man so old and thin, raised Harry from the ground, and set him on his feet. Harry swayed. His head was pounding. His injured leg would no longer support his weight. The crowd around them jostled, fighting to get closer, pressing darkly in on him – 'What's happened?' 'What's wrong with him?' '*Diggory's dead!*'

'He'll need to go to the hospital wing!' Fudge was saying loudly. 'He's ill, he's injured – Dumbledore, Diggory's parents, they're here, they're in the stands ...'

'I'll take Harry, Dumbledore, I'll take him –'

'No, I would prefer –'

'Dumbledore, Amos Diggory's running ... he's coming over ... don't you think you should tell him – before he sees –?'

'Harry, stay here –'

Girls were screaming, sobbing hysterically ... the scene flickered oddly before Harry's eyes ...

'It's all right, son, I've got you ... come on ... hospital wing ...'

'Dumbledore said stay,' said Harry thickly, the pounding in his scar making him feel as though he was about to throw up; his vision was blurring

## 第35章 吐真剂

布利多的手腕，邓布利多的脸时而清晰时而模糊。

"他回来了，"哈利小声说，"伏地魔他回来了。"

"怎么了？出了什么事？"

康奈利·福吉颠倒的脸出现在哈利面前，脸色苍白，神情惶恐。

"上帝啊……迪戈里！"他说，"邓布利多……他死了！"

这句话传了出去，正在往里挤的黑乎乎的人影惊骇地把它传给了周围的人……其他人喊了起来——尖叫声响彻夜空——"他死了！""他死了！""塞德里克·迪戈里！死了！"

"哈利，放开他吧。"他听见福吉的声音说，并感到有人在扳他的手指，想让他放开塞德里克软绵绵的尸体，但哈利死命抓住不放。

然后邓布利多的脸凑近了些，依旧模糊不清。"哈利，你帮不了他了，结束了。放开吧。"

"他要我把他带回来，"哈利低声说——说清这一点似乎很重要，"带给他的父母。"

"好的，哈利……放开吧……"

邓布利多俯下身，用对于一个瘦削老人来说超乎寻常的力气扶哈利站了起来。哈利摇摇晃晃，脑袋里像有锤子在敲，受伤的腿支撑不住他身体的重量。人群推推挤挤，使劲往前凑，黑压压地朝他逼近——"怎么回事？""他怎么了？""迪戈里死了！"

"他需要去校医院！"福吉大声说，"他病了，受了伤——邓布利多，迪戈里的父母在这儿。在看台上……"

"我带哈利去，邓布利多，我带他——"

"不，我想——"

"邓布利多，阿莫斯·迪戈里在跑……他过来了……你要不要先跟他说一下——在他看到之前——？"

"哈利，待在这儿——"

女生们在尖叫，在歇斯底里地哭泣……这幕情景在哈利眼前怪异地闪动着……

"没事，孩子，有我呢……走吧……去医院吧……"

"邓布利多说'待在这儿'。"哈利含混地说，伤疤的突突作痛使他

## CHAPTER THIRTY-FIVE    Veritaserum

worse than ever.

'You need to lie down ... come on, now ...'

Someone larger and stronger than Harry was, was half pulling, half carrying him through the frightened crowd; Harry heard them gasping, screaming and shouting as the man supporting him pushed a path through them, taking him back to the castle. Across the lawn, past the lake and the Durmstrang ship; Harry heard nothing but the heavy breathing of the man helping him walk.

'What happened, Harry?' the man asked at last, as he lifted Harry up the stone steps. *Clunk. Clunk. Clunk.* It was Mad-Eye Moody.

'Cup was a Portkey,' said Harry, as they crossed the Entrance Hall. 'Took me and Cedric to a graveyard ... and Voldemort was there ... Lord Voldemort ...'

*Clunk. Clunk. Clunk.* Up the marble stairs ...

'The Dark Lord was there? What happened then?'

'Killed Cedric ... they killed Cedric ...'

'And then?'

*Clunk. Clunk. Clunk.* Along the corridor ...

'Made a potion ... got his body back ...'

'The Dark Lord got his body back? He's returned?'

'And the Death Eaters came ... and then we duelled ...'

'You duelled with the Dark Lord?'

'Got away ... my wand ... did something funny ... I saw my mum and dad ... they came out of his wand ...'

'In here, Harry ... in here, and sit down ... you'll be all right now ... drink this ...'

Harry heard a key scrape in a lock, and felt a cup being pushed into his hands.

'Drink it ... you'll feel better ... come on now, Harry, I need to know exactly what happened ...'

Moody helped tip the stuff down Harry's throat; he coughed, a peppery taste burning his throat. Moody's office came into sharper focus, and so did Moody himself ... he looked as white as Fudge, and both eyes were fixed unblinkingly upon Harry's face.

'Voldemort's back, Harry? You're sure he's back? How did he do it?'

## 第35章 吐真剂

感到想吐，视线更加模糊了。

"你需要躺下来……走吧……"

一个比他魁梧强壮的人半拖半抱地带着他穿过惊恐的人群。哈利听见人们吸气、尖叫、高喊的声音。那人挟着他从人群中挤了出来，朝城堡走去。走过草坪、湖畔和德姆斯特朗的大船，哈利只听见那个男人沉重的喘息声。

"出了什么事，哈利？"扶哈利走上台阶时，那人开口问道。噔，噔，噔。是疯眼汉穆迪。

"奖杯是个门钥匙，"哈利说——他们穿过门厅，"把我和塞德里克带到了一片墓地上……伏地魔在那里……伏地魔……"

噔，噔，噔。走上了大理石楼梯……

"黑魔头在那儿？然后呢？"

"杀死了塞德里克……他们杀死了塞德里克……"

"后来呢？"

噔，噔，噔。穿过走廊……

"煎了一服药……恢复了他的肉身……"

"黑魔头恢复了肉身？他复活了？"

"然后食死徒来了……然后我们决斗……"

"你和黑魔头决斗了？"

"我逃了出来……我的魔杖……出了点奇怪的事……我见到了我的妈妈和爸爸……他们从他的魔杖里冒了出来……"

"进来，哈利……进来，坐下吧……你不会有事的……喝点儿药……"

哈利听到了钥匙插进锁眼的声音，一个杯子塞到了他手里。

"喝下去……你会好受点儿……喝吧，哈利，我需要了解确切情况。"

穆迪帮着把那杯东西倒进哈利嘴里，哈利呛得咳嗽起来，嗓子里像灌了胡椒一样火辣辣的。穆迪的办公室清晰起来了，穆迪也清晰起来了……他的脸色像福吉的一样苍白，两眼一眨不眨地盯着哈利的脸。

"哈利，伏地魔回来了？你确定吗？他是怎么做的？"

## CHAPTER THIRTY-FIVE   Veritaserum

'He took stuff from his father's grave, and from Wormtail, and me,' said Harry. His head felt clearer; his scar wasn't hurting so badly; he could now see Moody's face distinctly, even though the office was dark. He could still hear screaming and shouting from the distant Quidditch pitch.

'What did the Dark Lord take from you?' said Moody.

'Blood,' said Harry, raising his arm. His sleeve was ripped where Wormtail's dagger had torn it.

Moody let out his breath in a long, low hiss. 'And the Death Eaters? They returned?'

'Yes,' said Harry. 'Loads of them ...'

'How did he treat them?' Moody asked quietly. 'Did he forgive them?'

But Harry had suddenly remembered. He should have told Dumbledore, he should have said it straight away – 'There's a Death Eater at Hogwarts! There's a Death Eater here – they put my name in the Goblet of Fire, they made sure I got through to the end –'

Harry tried to get up, but Moody pushed him back down.

'I know who the Death Eater is,' he said quietly.

'Karkaroff?' said Harry wildly. 'Where is he? Have you got him? Is he locked up?'

'Karkaroff?' said Moody with an odd laugh. 'Karkaroff fled tonight, when he felt the Dark Mark burn upon his arm. He betrayed too many faithful supporters of the Dark Lord to wish to meet them ... but I doubt he will get far. The Dark Lord has ways of tracking his enemies.'

'Karkaroff's *gone*? He ran away? But then – he didn't put my name in the Cup?'

'No,' said Moody slowly. 'No, he didn't. It was I who did that.'

Harry heard, but didn't believe.

'No, you didn't,' he said. 'You didn't do that ... you can't have done ...'

'I assure you I did,' said Moody, and his magical eye swung around, and fixed upon the door, and Harry knew he was making sure that there was no one outside it. At the same time, Moody drew out his wand, and pointed it at Harry.

'He forgave them, then?' he said. 'The Death Eaters who went free? The ones who escaped Azkaban?'

'What?' said Harry.

## 第35章 吐真剂

"他从他爸爸的坟墓里,从虫尾巴和我身上各取了一点东西。"哈利说。他的脑子清楚了一些,伤疤疼得不那么厉害了。尽管办公室里光线昏暗,但现在他能清楚地看到穆迪的脸了,还能隐隐地听见远处魁地奇球场上人们的叫喊声。

"黑魔头从你身上取了点儿什么?"穆迪问。

"血。"哈利举起手臂。他的袖子被虫尾巴的匕首割破了。

穆迪长长地嘘了一声。"食死徒呢?他们回去了?"

"是的,"哈利说,"好多人呢……"

"他对他们怎么样?"穆迪轻声问道,"他原谅他们了吗?"

哈利突然想起来了。他应该告诉邓布利多,应该一回来就讲的——"霍格沃茨有一个食死徒!这儿有一个食死徒——食死徒把我的名字放进了火焰杯,故意让我最后获胜——"

哈利想站起来,但穆迪把他按住了。

"我知道那个食死徒是谁。"他平静地说。

"卡卡洛夫?"哈利急切地问,"他在哪儿?你抓到他了吗?把他关起来了吗?"

"卡卡洛夫?"穆迪古怪地笑了一下,"卡卡洛夫今晚逃走了,因为他感到自己胳膊上的黑魔标记烧灼起来了。他出卖了那么多黑魔头的忠实支持者,不敢去见他们……但我怀疑他不会走远,黑魔头有办法跟踪他的敌人。"

"卡卡洛夫不在了?他跑了?那——他没把我的名字放进火焰杯?"

"没有,"穆迪缓缓地说,"不是他。是我干的。"

哈利听见了,但是不能相信。

"不,"他说,"你没有……你不可能……"

"确实是我。"穆迪说,那只魔眼转到了后面盯着房门。哈利知道他是在看外面是不是有人。就在这时,穆迪抽出魔杖指着哈利。

"这么说他原谅了他们,是吗?原谅了那些逍遥在外、逃脱了阿兹卡班囚禁的食死徒?"

"什么?"哈利说。

## CHAPTER THIRTY-FIVE   Veritaserum

He was looking at the wand Moody was pointing at him. This was a bad joke, it had to be.

'I asked you,' said Moody quietly, 'whether he forgave the scum who never even went to look for him. Those treacherous cowards who wouldn't even brave Azkaban for him. The faithless, worthless bits of filth who were brave enough to cavort in masks at the Quidditch World Cup, but fled at the sight of the Dark Mark when I fired it into the sky.'

'*You* fired ... what are you talking about ...?'

'I told you, Harry ... I told you. If there's one thing I hate more than any other, it's a Death Eater who walked free. They turned their backs on my master, when he needed them most. I expected him to punish them. I expected him to torture them. Tell me he hurt them, Harry ...' Moody's face was suddenly lit with an insane smile. 'Tell me he told them that I, I alone remained faithful ... prepared to risk everything to deliver to him the one thing he wanted above all ... *you*.'

'You didn't ... it – it can't be you ...'

'Who put your name in the Goblet of Fire, under the name of a different school? I did. Who frightened off every person I thought might try to hurt you or prevent you winning the Tournament? I did. Who nudged Hagrid into showing you the dragons? I did. Who helped you see the only way you could beat the dragon? *I did.*'

Moody's magical eye had now left the door. It was fixed upon Harry. His lopsided mouth leered more widely than ever. 'It hasn't been easy, Harry, guiding you through these tasks without arousing suspicion. I have had to use every ounce of cunning I possess, so that my hand would not be detectable in your success. Dumbledore would have been very suspicious if you had managed everything too easily. As long as you got into that maze, preferably with a decent head start– then, I knew, I would have a chance of getting rid of the other champions, and leaving your way clear. But I also had to contend against your stupidity. The second task ... that was when I was most afraid we would fail. I was keeping watch on you, Potter. I knew you hadn't worked out the egg's clue, so I had to give you another hint –'

'You didn't,' Harry said hoarsely. 'Cedric gave me the clue –'

'Who told Cedric to open it underwater? I did. I trusted that he would pass the information on to you. Decent people are so easy to manipulate, Potter. I

## 第35章 吐真剂

他看着穆迪手里指向他的魔杖。这是个蹩脚的玩笑，一定是的。

"我问你，"穆迪平静地说，"他是不是原谅了那些从来没有寻找过他的渣滓？那些叛徒、胆小鬼，他们连为他进阿兹卡班都不敢。那些没有信义的下贱的东西。他们有胆子戴着面具在魁地奇世界杯赛上胡闹，但看到我发射的黑魔标记之后就一个个溜走了。"

"你发射的……你说什么呀……？"

"我告诉过你，哈利……我告诉过你。如果我对什么事情恨之入骨，那就是让食死徒逍遥在外。他们在我的主人最需要他们的时候背叛了他。我希望他惩罚他们，我希望他折磨他们。告诉我，他折磨了他们，哈利……"穆迪脸上突然露出神经质的笑容，"告诉我他对他们说只有我一直忠心耿耿……愿意冒一切风险帮他得到他最想要的——你！"

"你没有……不……不可能是你……"

"谁把你的名字作为另一个学校的学生放进了火焰杯？是我。谁吓走了可能伤害你或妨碍你获胜的每一个人？是我。谁怂恿海格让你看到火龙？是我。谁使你想到了打败火龙的唯一办法？还是我。"

穆迪的那只魔眼转回来盯着哈利。他的歪嘴咧得更大了。"不容易啊，哈利，帮助你通过这些项目，又不引起怀疑。我不得不使出我所有的心计，让人们看不出我插手的痕迹。如果你赢得太容易，邓布利多会起疑心的。只要你进了迷宫，而且最好先出发——这样，我就有机会除掉其他几名勇士，为你扫清道路。但我还得对付你的愚蠢。第二个项目中……我特别担心我们会失败。我一直盯着你，波特。我知道你没有发现金蛋的线索，所以我必须再给你一个提示——"

"你没有，"哈利嘶哑地说，"是塞德里克提醒了我——"

"是谁告诉塞德里克要在水下打开金蛋的？是我。我相信他会告诉你的。正派的人很容易被操纵，波特。我知道塞德里克想报答你上次

## CHAPTER THIRTY-FIVE  Veritaserum

was sure Cedric would want to repay you for telling him about the dragons, and so he did. But even then, Potter, even then you seemed likely to fail. I was watching all the time ... all those hours in the library. Didn't you realise that the book you needed was in your dormitory all along? I planted it there early on, I gave it to the Longbottom boy, don't you remember? *Magical Mediterranean Water-Plants and Their Properties*. It would have told you all you needed about Gillyweed. I expected you to ask everyone and anyone you could for help. Longbottom would have told you in an instant. But you did not ... you did not ... you have a streak of pride and independence that might have ruined all.'

'So what could I do? Feed you information from another innocent source. You told me at the Yule Ball a house-elf called Dobby had given you a Christmas present. I called the elf to the staff room to collect some robes for cleaning. I staged a loud conversation with Professor McGonagall about the hostages who had been taken, and whether Potter would think to use Gillyweed. And your little elf friend ran straight to Snape's store-cupboard and hurried to find you ...'

Moody's wand was still pointing directly at Harry's heart. Over his shoulder, foggy shapes were moving in the Foe-Glass on the wall. 'You were so long in that lake, Potter, I thought you had drowned. But luckily, Dumbledore took your idiocy for nobility, and marked you high for it. I breathed again.

'You had an easier time of it than you should have done in that maze tonight, of course,' said Moody. 'That was because I was patrolling around it, able to see through the outer hedges, able to curse many obstacles out of your way. I Stunned Fleur Delacour as she passed. I put the Imperius Curse on Krum, so that he would finish Diggory, and leave your path to the Cup clear.'

Harry stared at Moody. He just didn't see how this could be ... Dumbledore's friend, the famous Auror ... the one who had caught so many Death Eaters ... it made no sense ... no sense at all ...

The foggy shapes in the Foe-Glass were sharpening, had become more distinct. Harry could see the outlines of three people over Moody's shoulder, moving closer and closer. But Moody wasn't watching them. His magical eye was upon Harry.

'The Dark Lord didn't manage to kill you, Potter, and he *so* wanted to,' whispered Moody. 'Imagine how he will reward me, when he finds I have done it for him. I gave you to him – the thing he needed above all to

## 第35章 吐真剂

告诉他第一个项目是火龙的事，他确实这么做了。但即使这样，你似乎还有可能失败。我一直在盯着你……你在图书馆里的那些时间。难道你没发现你需要的那本书就在宿舍里吗？是我布置的，我把它给了那个叫隆巴顿的男孩，你记得吗？《地中海神奇水生植物及其特性》。它会告诉你关于鳃囊草的一切有用知识。我以为你会求助于周围每一个人。隆巴顿会马上告诉你。可你没有——你没有——你的骄傲和独立意识差点儿毁掉一切。

"我能有什么办法？再找一个天真的人去提醒你。你在圣诞节舞会上对我说有个叫多比的家养小精灵送了你一件圣诞礼物。我把那个小精灵叫到教工休息室去收集要洗的衣服。我大声和麦格教授谈论被扣的人质，猜测波特会不会想到使用鳃囊草。你的小精灵朋友马上跑到斯内普的储藏柜，又急急忙忙去找你……"

穆迪的魔杖依然指着哈利的心口，在他身后，墙上的照妖镜里有模糊的影子在晃动。"你在湖里待的时间太长了，波特。我以为你淹死了。还好，邓布利多把你的愚蠢当成了高尚，给你打了高分，我才松了口气。

"当然，你在今晚的迷宫里也得到了照顾。"穆迪说，"我在迷宫周围巡逻，能看透外层的树篱，并用咒语把许多障碍从你的路上赶走了。我击昏了芙蓉·德拉库尔，又对克鲁姆施了夺魂咒，让他去干掉迪戈里，为你扫清了夺杯的障碍。"

哈利瞪着穆迪，想不通这怎么可能……邓布利多的朋友，大名鼎鼎的傲罗……抓获了那么多食死徒……这不合情理……太不合情理了……

照妖镜里的影子变得清晰起来。哈利越过穆迪的肩膀看出是三个人的轮廓，他们越走越近。但穆迪没有看到，他那只魔眼正盯着哈利。

"黑魔王没能杀死你，波特。他是那么想杀你，"穆迪轻声说，"想想吧，要是我替他做到了，他会怎样奖赏我。我把你送给了他——你是他复活最需要的东西，然后又替他把你杀了。我会得到超过

## CHAPTER THIRTY-FIVE    Veritaserum

regenerate – and then I killed you for him. I will be honoured beyond all other Death Eaters. I will be his dearest, his closest supporter ... closer than a son ...'

Moody's normal eye was bulging, the magical eye fixed upon Harry. The door was barred, and Harry knew he would never reach his own wand in time ...

'The Dark Lord and I,' said Moody, and he looked completely insane now, towering over Harry, leering down at him, 'have much in common. Both of us, for instance, had very disappointing fathers ... very disappointing indeed. Both of us suffered the indignity, Harry, of being named after those fathers. And both of us had the pleasure ... the very great pleasure ... of killing our fathers, to ensure the continued rise of the Dark Order!'

'You're mad,' Harry said – he couldn't stop himself – 'you're mad!'

'Mad, am I?' said Moody, his voice rising uncontrollably. 'We'll see! We'll see who's mad, now that the Dark Lord has returned, with me at his side! He is back, Harry Potter, you did not conquer him – and now – I conquer you!'

Moody raised his wand, he opened his mouth, Harry plunged his own hand into his robes –

'*Stupefy!*' There was a blinding flash of red light, and with a great splintering and crashing, the door of Moody's office was blasted apart –

Moody was thrown backwards onto the office floor. Harry, still staring at the place where Moody's face had been, saw Albus Dumbledore, Professor Snape and Professor McGonagall looking back at him out of the Foe-Glass. He looked around, and saw the three of them standing in the doorway, Dumbledore in front, his wand outstretched.

At that moment, Harry fully understood for the first time why people said Dumbledore was the only wizard Voldemort had ever feared. The look upon Dumbledore's face as he stared down at the unconscious form of Mad-Eye Moody was more terrible than Harry could ever have imagined. There was no benign smile upon Dumbledore's face, no twinkle in the eyes behind the spectacles. There was cold fury in every line of the ancient face; a sense of power radiated from Dumbledore as though he was giving off burning heat.

He stepped into the office, placed a foot underneath Moody's unconscious body and kicked him over onto his back, so that his face was visible. Snape followed him, looking into the Foe-Glass, where his own face was still visible, glaring into the room.

Professor McGonagall went straight to Harry.

## 第35章 吐真剂

其他任何食死徒的荣誉,我将成为他最宠爱的亲信……比儿子还要亲……"

穆迪那只正常的眼睛凸了起来,那只魔眼紧盯着哈利。房门插着,哈利知道自己来不及掏出魔杖……

"黑魔王和我有很多共同之处,"穆迪现在看上去完全疯狂了,居高临下地朝哈利狞笑着,"比如,我们都有非常令人失望的父亲……极其令人失望。哈利,我们都耻辱地继承了父亲的名字,然后我们都愉快地……非常愉快地……杀死了自己的父亲,以确保黑魔势力的崛起!"

"你疯了,"哈利情不自禁地说,"你疯了!"

"我疯了?"穆迪失控地提高了嗓门,"我们走着瞧!看看是谁疯了。黑魔王已经回来了,由我辅佐他。他回来了,哈利·波特,你没有征服他——现在——我要征服你!"

穆迪举起魔杖,张开嘴巴。哈利把手插进长袍里——

"昏昏倒地!"一道耀眼的红光,伴随着木头断裂的巨响,穆迪办公室的房门被冲开了——

穆迪脸朝下直挺挺地倒了下去。哈利还盯着穆迪的脸刚才所在的地方,只见阿不思·邓布利多、斯内普教授和麦格教授从照妖镜里看着他。他扭过头,看到他们三个人站在门口,邓布利多在前面,手里举着魔杖。

在那一刻,哈利第一次完全理解了为什么人们说邓布利多是伏地魔唯一害怕的巫师。邓布利多向下看着昏迷的疯眼汉穆迪时,脸色是那样可怕,远超出了哈利的想象。邓布利多的脸上没有慈祥的微笑,镜片后的眼睛里也没有愉快的火花。那张苍老的脸上每一丝皱纹都带着冰冷的愤怒。邓布利多周身辐射出一种力量,就好像他在燃烧发热一样。

他走进房间,把一只脚插到昏迷的穆迪身下,将他翻了个身,露出脸部。斯内普跟了进来,看着墙上的照妖镜,他的脸还在镜中朝屋里望着。

麦格教授径直走向哈利。

## CHAPTER THIRTY-FIVE   Veritaserum

'Come along, Potter,' she whispered. The thin line of her mouth was twitching as though she was about to cry. 'Come along ... hospital wing ...'

'No,' said Dumbledore sharply.

'Dumbledore, he ought to – look at him – he's been through enough tonight –'

'He will stay, Minerva, because he needs to understand,' said Dumbledore curtly. 'Understanding is the first step to acceptance, and only with acceptance can there be recovery. He needs to know who has put him through the ordeal he has suffered tonight, and why.'

'Moody,' Harry said. He was still in a state of complete disbelief. 'How can it have been Moody?'

'This is not Alastor Moody,' said Dumbledore quietly. 'You have never known Alastor Moody. The real Moody would not have removed you from my sight after what happened tonight. The moment he took you, I knew – and I followed.'

Dumbledore bent down over Moody's limp form and put a hand inside his robes. He pulled out Moody's hip-flask, and a set of keys on a ring. Then he turned to Professor McGonagall and Snape.

'Severus, please fetch me the strongest Truth Potion you possess, and then go down to the kitchens, and bring up the house-elf called Winky. Minerva, kindly go down to Hagrid's house, where you will find a large black dog sitting in the pumpkin patch. Take the dog up to my office, tell him I will be with him shortly, then come back here.'

If either Snape or McGonagall found these instructions peculiar, they hid their confusion. Both turned at once, and left the office. Dumbledore walked over to the trunk with seven locks, fitted the first key in the lock, and opened it. It contained a mass of spellbooks. Dumbledore closed the trunk, placed a second key in the second lock, and opened the trunk again. The spellbooks had vanished; this time it contained an assortment of broken Sneakoscopes, some parchment and quills, and what looked like a silvery Invisibility Cloak. Harry watched, astounded, as Dumbledore placed the third, fourth, fifth and sixth keys in their respective locks, reopening the trunk, and each time revealing different contents. Then he placed the seventh key in the lock, threw open the lid, and Harry let out a cry of amazement.

He was looking down into a kind of pit, an underground room, and lying on the floor some ten feet below, apparently fast asleep, thin and starved in appearance, was the real Mad-Eye Moody. His wooden leg was gone, the socket which should have held the magical eye looked empty beneath its lid, and chunks of his grizzled

## 第35章　吐真剂

"走,波特,"她轻声说,薄薄的嘴唇颤抖着,好像要哭出来似的,"跟我走……去医院……"

"不。"邓布利多坚决地说。

"邓布利多,他必须去医院——你看看他——他今晚受够了——"

"他要留下来,米勒娃,因为他需要弄明白,"邓布利多简单地说,"理解是接受的第一步,只有接受后才能够康复。他需要知道是谁使他经历了今天晚上的磨难,以及为什么会这样。"

"穆迪,"哈利说,仍然完全不能相信,"怎么可能是穆迪?"

"那不是阿拉斯托·穆迪,"邓布利多平静地说,"你从未见到过阿拉斯托·穆迪。真正的穆迪不会在发生今晚的事情之后把你从我身边弄走。他一带走你,我就知道了——所以跟了过来。"

邓布利多弯下腰,从昏瘫的穆迪身上掏出了弧形酒瓶和一串钥匙。然后他转身看着麦格教授和斯内普。

"西弗勒斯,请你去拿你最强效的吐真剂,再到厨房把一个叫闪闪的家养小精灵找来。米勒娃,拜托你到海格家跑一趟,他的南瓜地里有一条大黑狗。你把那条狗带到我的办公室,说我一会儿就到,然后你再回到这儿来。"

斯内普和麦格或许觉得这些指示有些奇怪,但他们没有流露出来。两人立刻转身离去。邓布利多走到一只有七把锁的箱子跟前,将第一把钥匙插进锁眼,打开箱子,里面是一堆咒语书。邓布利多关上箱子,将第二把钥匙插进第二个锁里,再打开来,箱子里不再是咒语书,而是各种破损的窥镜、一些羊皮纸和羽毛笔,还有一件像是银色的隐形衣的东西。哈利惊奇地看着邓布利多将第三、第四、第五和第六把钥匙插进锁里,打开箱子,每次出现的东西都不一样。最后他将第七把钥匙插进锁里,掀开锁盖,哈利惊叫起来。

他看到箱子下面竟然是一个大坑,像一间地下室,约莫三米深的地板上躺着一个人,骨瘦如柴,仿佛睡着了。是真正的疯眼汉穆迪。他的木腿不见了,魔眼的眼皮下是空的,花白的头发少了好几

## CHAPTER THIRTY-FIVE    Veritaserum

hair were missing. Harry stared, thunderstruck, between the sleeping Moody in the trunk, and the unconscious Moody lying on the floor of the office.

Dumbledore climbed into the trunk, lowered himself and fell lightly onto the floor beside the sleeping Moody. He bent over him.

'Stunned – controlled by the Imperius Curse – very weak,' he said. 'Of course, they would have needed to keep him alive. Harry, throw down the impostor's cloak, Alastor is freezing. Madam Pomfrey will need to see him, but he seems in no immediate danger.'

Harry did as he was told; Dumbledore covered Moody in the cloak, tucked it around him, and clambered out of the trunk again. Then he picked up the hip-flask that stood upon the desk, unscrewed it, and turned it over. A thick glutinous liquid splattered onto the office floor.

'Polyjuice Potion, Harry,' said Dumbledore. 'You see the simplicity of it, and the brilliance. For Moody never *does* drink except from his hip-flask, he's well known for it. The impostor needed, of course, to keep the real Moody close by, so that he could continue making the Potion. You see his hair ...' Dumbledore looked down on the Moody in the trunk. 'The impostor has been cutting it off all year, see where it is uneven? But I think, in the excitement of tonight, our fake Moody might have forgotten to take it as frequently as he should have done ... on the hour ... every hour ... we shall see.'

Dumbledore pulled out the chair at the desk and sat down upon it, his eyes fixed upon the unconscious Moody on the floor. Harry stared at him, too. Minutes passed in silence ...

Then, before Harry's very eyes, the face of the man on the floor began to change. The scars were disappearing, the skin was becoming smooth; the mangled nose became whole, and started to shrink. The long mane of grizzled grey hair was withdrawing into the scalp, and turning the colour of straw. Suddenly, with a loud *clunk*, the wooden leg fell away as a normal leg regrew in its place; next moment, the magical eyeball had popped out of the man's face as a real eye replaced it; it rolled away across the floor and continued to swivel in every direction.

Harry saw a man lying before him, pale-skinned, slightly freckled, with a mop of fair hair. He knew who he was. He had seen him in Dumbledore's Pensieve, had watched him being led away from court by the Dementors, trying to convince Mr. Crouch that he was innocent ... but he was lined around the eyes now, and looked much older ...

## 第35章 吐真剂

撮。哈利望望箱底熟睡的穆迪，又望望办公室地上昏迷的穆迪，惊愕万分。

邓布利多爬进箱子里，弯下身子，轻轻落到熟睡的穆迪身旁，俯身看着他。

"被击昏了——中了夺魂咒——非常虚弱。"他说，"当然啦，他们需要让他一直活着。哈利，把假穆迪的斗篷扔下来——阿拉斯托冻坏了。需要把他交给庞弗雷女士，不过他看起来暂时还没有生命危险。"

哈利照办了。邓布利多把斗篷盖在穆迪身上，为他掖好，然后爬出箱子。他拿起放在桌上的弧形酒瓶，拧开盖子，把酒瓶倒过来，一股黏稠的液体洒在办公室的地板上。

"复方汤剂，哈利，"邓布利多说，"你看这多么简单，多么巧妙。穆迪向来只用他随身带的弧形酒瓶喝酒，这是出了名的。当然，冒充者需要把真穆迪留在身边，以便不断地配制汤剂。你看他的头发……"邓布利多望着箱子里的穆迪说，"被人剪了一年，看到参差不齐的地方了吗？但是我想，我们的假穆迪今晚也许兴奋过度，忘记按时喝药了……每小时喝一次……等着瞧吧。"

邓布利多拉出桌前的椅子，坐了下来，眼睛盯着地板上昏迷不醒的穆迪。哈利也盯着他。时间在沉默中一分一秒地过去。

看着看着，地上那个人的脸起了变化，伤疤渐渐消失，皮肤光滑起来，残缺的鼻子长全了，缩小了。长长的灰发在缩短，变成了稻草色。突然当啷一声，木腿掉到一旁，一条真腿长了出来。接着，那个带魔法的眼球从眼窝里跳了出来，一只真眼取代了它的位置。带魔法的眼球滚到地板上，还在滴溜溜地乱转。

哈利看到面前躺着一个男子，皮肤苍白，略有雀斑，一头浅黄的乱发。他认得这个人，在邓布利多的冥想盆里见过。哈利看到他被摄魂怪从法庭上带走时，还向克劳奇先生辩解说自己是清白的……但现在他的眼角已有皱纹，看上去老多了……

## CHAPTER THIRTY-FIVE    Veritaserum

There were hurried footsteps outside in the corridor. Snape had returned with Winky at his heels. Professor McGonagall was right behind them.

'Crouch!' Snape said, stopping dead in the doorway. 'Barty Crouch!'

'Good heavens,' said Professor McGonagall, stopping dead and staring down at the man on the floor.

Filthy, dishevelled, Winky peered around Snape's legs. Her mouth opened wide and she let out a piercing shriek. 'Master Barty, Master Barty, what is you doing here?'

She flung herself forwards onto the young man's chest. 'You is killed him! You is killed him! You is killed master's son!'

'He is simply Stunned, Winky,' said Dumbledore. 'Step aside, please. Severus, you have the Potion?'

Snape handed Dumbledore a small glass bottle of completely clear liquid; the Veritaserum with which he had threatened Harry in class. Dumbledore got up, bent over the man on the floor, and pulled him into a sitting position against the wall beneath the Foe-Glass, in which the reflections of Dumbledore, Snape and McGonagall were still glaring down upon them all. Winky remained on her knees, trembling, her hands over her face. Dumbledore forced the man's mouth open, and poured three drops inside it. Then he pointed his wand at the man's chest, and said, '*Rennervate.*'

Crouch's son opened his eyes. His face was slack, his gaze unfocused. Dumbledore knelt before him, so that their faces were level.

'Can you hear me?' Dumbledore asked quietly.

The man's eyelids flickered.

'Yes,' he muttered.

'I would like you to tell us,' said Dumbledore softly, 'how you come to be here. How did you escape from Azkaban?'

Crouch took a deep, shuddering breath, then began to speak in a flat, expressionless voice. 'My mother saved me. She knew she was dying. She persuaded my father to rescue me as a last favour to her. He loved her as he had never loved me. He agreed. They came to visit me. They gave me a draught of Polyjuice Potion, containing one of my mother's hairs. She took a draught of Polyjuice Potion, containing one of my hairs. We took on each other's appearance.'

Winky was shaking her head, trembling. 'Say no more, Master Barty, say

# 第35章 吐真剂

走廊上响起了急促的脚步声。斯内普带着闪闪回来了，麦格教授紧紧跟在后面。

"克劳奇！"斯内普呆立在门口，"小巴蒂·克劳奇！"

"天哪。"麦格教授呆立在那里，瞪视着地上的男子。

邋邋遢遢的闪闪从斯内普腿边探出头来。她张大了嘴巴，发出一声刺耳的尖叫。"巴蒂少爷，巴蒂少爷，你在这儿做什么？"

她扑到年轻男子的胸前。"你杀了他！你杀了他！你杀了主人的儿子！"

"他只是中了昏迷咒，闪闪。"邓布利多说，"请让开点。西弗勒斯，药水拿来了吗？"

斯内普递给邓布利多一小瓶澄清的液体，就是他在课堂上威胁哈利时提到过的吐真剂。邓布利多站起身，弯腰把地上的男子拖起来，使他靠墙坐在照妖镜下。照妖镜里，邓布利多、斯内普和麦格仍朝下在看着他们。闪闪依然跪在那里，双手捂着脸，浑身发抖。邓布利多扳开那人的嘴巴，倒了三滴药水，然后用魔杖指着那人的胸口说："快快复苏！"

克劳奇的儿子睁开了眼睛，他目光无神，面颊松弛。邓布利多蹲在他身前，和他脸对着脸。

"你听得见我说话吗？"邓布利多镇静地问。

那男子的眼皮颤动了几下。

"听得见。"他低声说。

"我希望你告诉我们，"邓布利多和缓地说，"你怎么会在这里？你是怎么从阿兹卡班逃出来的？"

小克劳奇颤抖着深深吸了口气，然后用一种不带感情的平板语调讲了起来。"我母亲救了我。她知道自己要死了，求父亲把我救出去，算是最后为她做一件事。父亲很爱母亲，尽管他从来不爱我。他同意了。他们一起来看我，给我喝了一服复方汤剂，里面有我母亲的头发。母亲喝了有我头发的复方汤剂。我们交换了容貌。"

闪闪摇着头，浑身发抖。"别说了，巴蒂少爷，别说了，你会给你

## CHAPTER THIRTY-FIVE    Veritaserum

no more, you is getting your father into trouble!'

But Crouch took another deep breath, and continued in the same flat voice. 'The Dementors are blind. They sensed one healthy, one dying person entering Azkaban. They sensed one healthy, one dying person leaving it. My father smuggled me out, disguised as my mother, in case any prisoners were watching through their doors.

'My mother died a short while afterwards in Azkaban. She was careful to drink Polyjuice Potion until the end. She was buried under my name, and bearing my appearance. Everyone believed her to be me.'

The man's eyelids flickered.

'And what did your father do with you, when he had got you home?' said Dumbledore quietly.

'Staged my mother's death. A quiet, private funeral. That grave is empty. The house-elf nursed me back to health. Then I had to be concealed. I had to be controlled. My father had to use a number of spells to subdue me. When I had recovered my strength, I thought only of finding my master ... of returning to his service.'

'How did your father subdue you?' said Dumbledore.

'The Imperius Curse,' Crouch said. 'I was under my father's control. I was forced to wear an Invisibility Cloak day and night. I was always with the house-elf. She was my keeper and carer. She pitied me. She persuaded my father to give me occasional treats. Rewards for my good behaviour.'

'Master Barty, Master Barty,' sobbed Winky through her hands. 'You isn't ought to tell them, we is getting in trouble ...'

'Did anybody ever discover that you were still alive?' said Dumbledore softly. 'Did anyone know except your father, and the house-elf?'

'Yes,' said Crouch, his eyelids flickering again. 'A witch in my father's office. Bertha Jorkins. She came to the house, with papers for my father's signature. He was not at home. Winky showed her inside and returned to the kitchen, to me. But Bertha Jorkins heard Winky talking to me. She came to investigate. She heard enough to guess who was hiding under the Invisibility Cloak. My father arrived home. She confronted him. He put a very powerful Memory Charm on her to make her forget what she'd found out. Too powerful. He said it damaged her memory permanently.'

'Why is she coming to nose in my master's private business?' sobbed

## 第35章 吐真剂

父亲惹麻烦的！"

但是小克劳奇又深吸了一口气，继续用平板的声音说了下去："摄魂怪是瞎子，它们嗅到一个健康人和一个将死的人走进阿兹卡班，又嗅到一个健康的人和一个将死的人离开阿兹卡班。父亲把我偷偷带了出去。我装成母亲的样子，以防有犯人从门缝里看见。

"我母亲在阿兹卡班没过多久就死了。她一直没忘了喝复方汤剂，死的时候还是我的模样，被当成我埋葬了。所有的人都以为那是我。"

那男子的眼皮颤动着。

"你父亲带你回家后，把你怎么办的呢？"邓布利多平静地问。

"假装我母亲去世。举行了一个低调而私人的葬礼，坟墓是空的，家养小精灵护理我恢复健康。父亲要把我藏起来，还要控制我，不得不用了好些咒语来制约我。我体力恢复之后，一心只想找到我的主人……重新为他效劳。"

"你父亲是怎么制约你的？"邓布利多问。

"夺魂咒，"小克劳奇说，"我被我父亲控制着，被迫从早到晚穿着隐形衣。我一直和家养小精灵待在一起。她是我的看守和护理。她同情我，说服我父亲有时给我一些优待，作为对我表现不错的奖赏。"

"巴蒂少爷，巴蒂少爷，"闪闪捂着脸抽泣道，"你不应该告诉他们，我们会倒霉的……"

"有没有人发现你还活着？"邓布利多轻声问，"除了你父亲和家养小精灵之外？"

"有，"小克劳奇说，眼皮又颤动起来，"我父亲办公室的一个女巫，伯莎·乔金斯。她拿着文件到我家来给我父亲签字。父亲不在家，闪闪把她领进屋，然后回到厨房来照料我。但是伯莎·乔金斯听见了闪闪和我说话，就过来查看，她从听到的话里猜出了藏在隐形衣下的是什么人。我父亲回来后，她当面问他。父亲对她施了一个非常强大的遗忘咒，使她忘掉了她发现的秘密。这个咒太厉害了，父亲说对她的记忆造成了永久的损害。"

"她干吗要来管我主人的私事？"闪闪抽泣道，"她为什么不放过

## CHAPTER THIRTY-FIVE    Veritaserum

Winky. 'Why isn't she leaving us be?'

'Tell me about the Quidditch World Cup,' said Dumbledore.

'Winky talked my father into it,' said Crouch, still in the same monotonous voice. 'She spent months persuading him. I had not left the house for years. I had loved Quidditch. Let him go, she said. He will be in his Invisibility Cloak. He can watch. Let him smell fresh air for once. She said my mother would have wanted it. She told my father that my mother had died to give me freedom. She had not saved me for a life of imprisonment. He agreed in the end.

'It was carefully planned. My father led myself and Winky up to the Top Box early in the day. Winky was to say that she was saving a seat for my father. I was to sit there, invisible. When everyone had left the box, we would emerge. Winky would appear to be alone. Nobody would ever know.

'But Winky didn't know that I was growing stronger. I was starting to fight my father's Imperius Curse. There were times when I was almost myself again. There were brief periods when I seemed outside his control. It happened, there, in the Top Box. It was like waking from a deep sleep. I found myself out in public, in the middle of the match, and I saw a wand sticking out of a boy's pocket in front of me. I had not been allowed a wand since before Azkaban. I stole it. Winky didn't know. Winky is frightened of heights. She had her face hidden.'

'Master Barty, you bad boy!' whispered Winky, tears trickling between her fingers.

'So you took the wand,' said Dumbledore, 'and what did you do with it?'

'We went back to the tent,' said Crouch. 'Then we heard them. We heard the Death Eaters. The ones who had never been to Azkaban. The ones who had never suffered for my master. They had turned their backs on him. They were not enslaved, as I was. They were free to seek him, but they did not. They were merely making sport of Muggles. The sound of their voices awoke me. My mind was clearer than it had been in years. I was angry. I had the wand. I wanted to attack them for their disloyalty to my master. My father had left the tent, he had gone to free the Muggles. Winky was afraid to see me so angry. She used her own brand of magic to bind me to her. She pulled me from the tent, pulled me into the forest, away from the Death Eaters. I tried to hold her back. I wanted to return to the campsite. I wanted to show those Death Eaters what loyalty to the Dark Lord meant, and to punish them for their lack of it. I used the stolen wand to cast the Dark Mark into the sky.

## 第35章 吐真剂

我们？"

"说说魁地奇世界杯赛吧。"邓布利多说。

"闪闪说服了我父亲,"小克劳奇依旧用那单调的声音说,"她劝了他好几个月。我有几年没出门了。我喜欢魁地奇。让他去吧,她说,他可以穿着隐形衣,他可以观看比赛。让他呼吸一下新鲜空气吧。闪闪说我母亲会希望我去的。她对我父亲说,母亲救我是想让我获得自由,而不是被终身软禁。父亲最终同意了。

"计划得很周密。我父亲一大早把我和闪闪带到顶层包厢,闪闪可以说她为我父亲留着座位。我坐在那里,谁也看不见我。等大家都离开后,我们再出来。看上去是闪闪一个人,谁也不会发现。

"但闪闪不知道我在强壮起来。我开始反抗父亲的夺魂咒。有时候我几乎恢复了本性。偶尔我似乎暂时摆脱了他的控制。在顶层包厢就发生了这种情况。就像大梦初醒一般,我发现自己坐在人群中,在观看比赛。在我的眼前有一根魔杖,插在一个男孩的衣服兜里。自打进了阿兹卡班之后我一直没机会碰魔杖。我把这根魔杖偷了过来,闪闪不知道。闪闪有恐高症,一直用手捂着脸。"

"巴蒂少爷,你这个坏孩子!"闪闪轻声说,眼泪顺着指缝往下流。

"你拿了魔杖,"邓布利多说,"用它做了什么呢?"

"我们回到帐篷里,"小克劳奇说,"然后我们听到了他们的声音。那些食死徒。那些没有进过阿兹卡班的家伙,从来没有为我的主人受过苦,他们背叛了他。他们不像我这样身不由己,可以自由地去寻找他,但他们没有。他们只会捉弄麻瓜。他们的声音唤醒了我。我的脑子几年来第一次这么清醒。我非常气愤,拿着魔杖,想去教训这帮对我的主人不忠诚的家伙。我父亲不在帐篷里,他去解救麻瓜了。闪闪看见我这样生气,非常害怕。她用自己的魔法把我拴在她身边。她把我拽出帐篷,拽到树林里远离了食死徒。我想阻止她,想回到营地去。我要让那些食死徒看看什么是对黑魔王的赤胆忠心,并要惩罚他们的不忠。我用偷来的魔杖把黑魔标记发射到了空中。

## CHAPTER THIRTY-FIVE  Veritaserum

'Ministry wizards arrived. They shot Stunning Spells everywhere. One of the Spells came through the trees where Winky and I stood. The bond connecting us was broken. We were both Stunned.

'When Winky was discovered, my father knew I must be nearby. He searched the bushes where she had been found, and felt me lying there. He waited until the other Ministry members had left the forest. He put me back under the Imperius Curse, and took me home. He dismissed Winky. She had failed him. She had let me acquire a wand. She had almost let me escape.'

Winky let out a wail of despair.

'Now it was just Father and I, alone in the house. And then … and then …' Crouch's head rolled on his neck, and an insane grin spread across his face. 'My master came for me.

'He arrived at our house late one night, in the arms of his servant Wormtail. My master had found out that I was still alive. He had captured Bertha Jorkins in Albania. He had tortured her. She told him a great deal. She told him about the Triwizard Tournament. She told him the old Auror, Moody, was going to teach at Hogwarts. He tortured her until he broke through the Memory Charm my father had placed upon her. She told him I had escaped from Azkaban. She told him my father kept me imprisoned to prevent me seeking my master. And so my master knew that I was still his faithful servant – perhaps the most faithful of all. My master conceived a plan, based upon the information Bertha had given him. He needed me. He arrived at our house near midnight. My father answered the door.'

The smile spread wider over Crouch's face, as though recalling the sweetest memory of his life. Winky's petrified brown eyes were visible through her fingers. She seemed too appalled to speak.

'It was very quick. My father was placed under the Imperius Curse by my master. Now my father was the one imprisoned, controlled. My master forced him to go about his business as usual, to act as though nothing was wrong. And I was released. I awoke. I was myself again, alive as I hadn't been in years.'

'And what did Lord Voldemort ask you to do?' said Dumbledore.

'He asked me whether I was ready to risk everything for him. I was ready. It was my dream, my greatest ambition, to serve him, to prove myself to him. He told me he needed to place a faithful servant at Hogwarts. A servant who would guide Harry Potter through the Triwizard Tournament without

## 第35章 吐真剂

"魔法部的巫师来了，到处施放昏迷咒。一个咒语射到闪闪和我站的树林里，打断了我们之间的纽带，我们俩都被击昏了。

"闪闪被发现后，我父亲知道我一定就在附近。他搜索了闪闪所在的灌木丛，也摸到了我躺在那儿。他等魔法部的其他人离开树林后，重新对我施了夺魂咒，把我带回了家。他撵走了闪闪，因为她没看好我，让我拿到了魔杖，差点儿让我跑掉。"

闪闪发出一声绝望的号叫。

"现在家里只有父亲和我两个人。后来……后来……"小克劳奇晃着脑袋，脸上露出了疯狂的笑容，"我的主人来找我了！

"一天夜里，他由仆人虫尾巴抱着来到我家。我主人得知我还活着。他在阿尔巴尼亚抓到了伯莎·乔金斯。他折磨伯莎，让她说出了很多情况。她对他讲了三强争霸赛的事，还告诉他们老傲罗穆迪要到霍格沃茨任教。主人继续折磨她，直到打破了我父亲给她施的遗忘咒。伯莎告诉他，我从阿兹卡班逃了出来，我父亲把我关在家里，不让我去找主人。因此，我的主人知道了我仍是他忠实的仆人——或许是最忠实的一个。根据伯莎提供的情报，我的主人想出了一个计划。他需要我，那天将近半夜时他上门来找我，是我父亲开的门。"

小克劳奇脸上的笑意更浓了，仿佛正在回忆他一生中最幸福的时光。闪闪的指缝间露出她那双惊恐的棕色眼睛。她似乎吓得说不出话来。

"神不知鬼不觉地，我父亲被我的主人施了夺魂咒。现在是他被软禁、被控制了。我主人迫使他像往常一样工作，好像什么都没发生似的。我被释放了，苏醒过来，重拾了自我，获得了多年没有过的活力。"

"伏地魔要你做什么？"邓布利多问。

"他问我是不是愿意为他冒一切风险。我愿意。能够为他效劳，向他证明我的忠诚，是我的梦想，是我最大的心愿。他告诉我，他需要在霍格沃茨安插一名亲信。此人要在三强争霸赛中指导哈利·波特，而且要做得不为人知。他要监视哈利·波特，保证他拿到三强杯；要

## CHAPTER THIRTY-FIVE   Veritaserum

appearing to do so. A servant who would watch over Harry Potter. Ensure he reached the Triwizard Cup. Turn the Cup into a Portkey, which would take the first person to touch it to my master. But first –'

'You needed Alastor Moody,' said Dumbledore. His blue eyes were blazing, though his voice remained calm.

'Wormtail and I did it. We had prepared the Polyjuice Potion beforehand. We journeyed to his house. Moody put up a struggle. There was a commotion. We managed to subdue him just in time. Forced him into a compartment of his own magical trunk. Took some of his hair and added it to the Potion. I drank it, I became Moody's double. I took his leg and his eye. I was ready to face Arthur Weasley when he arrived to sort out the Muggles who had heard a disturbance. I made the dustbins move around the yard. I told Arthur Weasley I had heard intruders in my yard, who had set the dustbins off. Then I packed up Moody's clothes and Dark detectors, put them in the trunk with Moody, and set off for Hogwarts. I kept him alive, under the Imperius Curse. I wanted to be able to question him. To find out about his past, learn his habits, so that I could fool even Dumbledore. I also needed his hair to make the Polyjuice Potion. The other ingredients were easy. I stole Boomslang skin from the dungeons. When the Potions master found me in his office, I said I was under orders to search it.'

'And what became of Wormtail after you attacked Moody?' said Dumbledore.

'Wormtail returned to care for my master, in my father's house, and to keep watch over my father.'

'But your father escaped,' said Dumbledore.

'Yes. After a while he began to fight the Imperius Curse just as I had done. There were periods where he knew what was happening. My master decided it was no longer safe for my father to leave the house. He forced him to send letters to the Ministry instead. He made him write and say he was ill. But Wormtail neglected his duty. He was not watchful enough. My father escaped. My master guessed that he was heading for Hogwarts. My father was going to tell Dumbledore everything, to confess. He was going to admit that he had smuggled me from Azkaban.

'My master sent me word of my father's escape. He told me to stop him at all costs. So I waited and watched. I used the map I had taken from Harry Potter. The map that had almost ruined everything.'

## 第35章 吐真剂

把奖杯偷换成门钥匙,以便将第一个抓到它的人带到我主人那里,但是首先——"

"你们需要阿拉斯托·穆迪。"邓布利多说。他的蓝眼睛喷射着怒火,尽管声音仍保持平静。

"是我和虫尾巴两个人干的。我们事先配好复方汤剂,一起去穆迪家,穆迪奋力反抗,响动很大。我们总算及时把他制服,推进了他自己魔箱的暗室里,拔了他几根头发,加到汤剂中。我喝了药,变成了穆迪,拿了他的木腿和那个带魔法的眼球。亚瑟·韦斯莱来查问听到响动的麻瓜时,我已经准备好了。我把垃圾箱弄得绕着院子转圈,我对亚瑟·韦斯莱说我听到有人闯进了院子,使垃圾箱转了起来。然后我打点起穆迪的衣物和黑魔法探测器,把它们和穆迪一起装在箱子里,动身去了霍格沃茨。我对穆迪施了夺魂咒,但是没弄死他,我需要问他问题,了解他的过去,他的习惯,这样就连邓布利多也不会识破了。我还需要用他的头发来配复方汤剂。其他材料都好弄,我从地下教室里偷了非洲树蛇皮,当魔药课教师发现我在他的办公室里时,我就说我是奉命来搜查的。"

"你们袭击穆迪之后,虫尾巴到哪里去了?"邓布利多问。

"他回到了我父亲的家里,照料我的主人,同时监视我父亲。"

"但你父亲逃出来了。"邓布利多说。

"是的。过了不久我父亲就开始像我那样反抗夺魂咒,有时候他心里明白发生了什么事。我的主人认为不能再让他出门了。他强迫我父亲与魔法部通信联系工作,让他说自己病了。虫尾巴疏忽大意,没有看住,让我父亲跑了。我主人猜想他是去了霍格沃茨。我父亲想把一切告诉邓布利多,想向他坦白,供认把我从阿兹卡班偷带出来的事。

"我的主人通知我说我父亲跑了。要我不惜一切代价截住他。我就留心等待着。我用了从哈利·波特手里收来的地图,那张几乎坏了大事的地图。"

## CHAPTER THIRTY-FIVE — Veritaserum

'Map?' said Dumbledore quickly. 'What map is this?'

'Potter's map of Hogwarts. Potter saw me on it. Potter saw me stealing more ingredients for the Polyjuice Potion from Snape's office one night. He thought I was my father as we have the same first name. I took the map from Potter that night. I told him my father hated Dark wizards. Potter believed my father was after Snape.

'For a week I waited for my father to arrive at Hogwarts. At last, one evening, the map showed my father entering the grounds. I pulled on my Invisibility Cloak, and went down to meet him. He was walking around the edge of the Forest. Then Potter came, and Krum. I waited. I could not hurt Potter, my master needed him. Potter ran to get Dumbledore. I Stunned Krum. I killed my father.'

'*Noooo!*' wailed Winky. 'Master Barty, Master Barty, what is you saying?'

'You killed *your* father,' Dumbledore said, in the same soft voice. 'What did you do with the body?'

'Carried it into the Forest. Covered it with the Invisibility Cloak. I had the map with me. I watched Potter run into the castle. He met Snape. Dumbledore joined them. I watched Potter bringing Dumbledore out of the castle. I walked back out of the Forest, doubled round behind them, went to meet them. I told Dumbledore Snape had told me where to come.

'Dumbledore told me to go and look for my father. I went back to my father's body. Watched the map. When everyone was gone, I transfigured my father's body. He became a bone ... I buried it, while wearing the Invisibility Cloak, in the freshly dug earth in front of Hagrid's cabin.'

There was complete silence now, except for Winky's continued sobs.

Then Dumbledore said, 'And tonight ...'

'I offered to carry the Triwizard Cup into the maze before dinner,' whispered Barty Crouch. 'Turned it into a Portkey. My master's plan worked. He is returned to power and I will be honoured by him beyond the dreams of wizards.'

The insane smile lit his features once more, and his head drooped onto his shoulder as Winky wailed and sobbed at his side.

## 第35章 吐真剂

"地图？"邓布利多马上问道，"什么地图？"

"波特的那张霍格沃茨地图。波特在地图上看见了我。有一天夜里他看到我到斯内普的办公室去偷复方汤剂的原料，但他把我当成了我父亲，因为我们的名字一样。那天夜里我收走了波特的地图。我告诉他，我父亲憎恨黑巫师。波特以为我父亲是去跟踪斯内普的。

"我等着父亲到达霍格沃茨，等了有一个星期。终于有一天晚上，地图显示我父亲进场地了。我披上隐形衣去迎他。他正走在禁林边上，这时波特和克鲁姆来了，我等了一会儿。我不能伤害波特，我的主人需要他。趁波特跑去找邓布利多时，我击昏了克鲁姆，杀死了我父亲。"

"不——！"闪闪哀号道，"巴蒂少爷，巴蒂少爷，你在说什么呀？"

"你杀死了你父亲，"邓布利多依旧用和缓的声音说，"尸体是怎么处理的？"

"背到禁林里，用隐形衣盖上。我拿着地图看到哈利跑进城堡，撞见了斯内普，邓布利多也出来了。我看到哈利带着邓布利多走出城堡，便从禁林里出来，绕到他们后面，上去和他们打招呼。我对邓布利多说，是斯内普告诉我要来这里的。

"邓布利多让我去找我父亲。我回到父亲的尸体那里，看着地图，等所有人都走了之后，我给尸体念了变形咒，把它变成了一块骨头……然后我穿着隐形衣，把尸骨埋进了海格小屋前新挖的泥土里。"

一片沉默，只有闪闪还在抽泣。

然后邓布利多说："今天夜里……"

"我在晚饭前主动提出把三强杯放进迷宫，"小巴蒂·克劳奇低声说，"把它变成了门钥匙。我主人的计划成功了。他恢复了力量，我会得到所有巫师做梦都想象不到的奖赏。"

他的脸上又现出疯狂的笑容，头垂了下去。闪闪在他身边哭泣。

## CHAPTER THIRTY-SIX

# The Parting of the Ways

Dumbledore stood up. He stared down at Barty Crouch for a moment with disgust on his face. Then he raised his wand once more and ropes flew out of it, ropes which twisted themselves around Barty Crouch, binding him tightly.

He turned to Professor McGonagall. 'Minerva, could I ask you to stand guard here while I take Harry upstairs?'

'Of course,' said Professor McGonagall. She looked slightly nauseous, as though she had just watched someone being sick. However, when she drew out her wand and pointed it at Barty Crouch, her hand was quite steady.

'Severus,' Dumbledore turned to Snape, 'please tell Madam Pomfrey to come down here. We need to get Alastor Moody into the hospital wing. Then go down into the grounds, find Cornelius Fudge, and bring him up to this office. He will undoubtedly want to question Crouch himself. Tell him I will be in the hospital wing in half an hour's time if he needs me.'

Snape nodded silently and swept out of the room.

'Harry?' Dumbledore said gently.

Harry got up and swayed again; the pain in his leg, which he had not noticed all the time he had listened to Crouch, now returned in full measure. He also realised that he was shaking. Dumbledore gripped his arm, and helped him out into the dark corridor.

'I want you to come up to my office first, Harry,' he said quietly, as they headed up the passageway. 'Sirius is waiting for us there.'

Harry nodded. A kind of numbness and a sense of complete unreality were upon him, but he did not care; he was even glad of it. He didn't want to have to think about anything that had happened since he had first touched

# 第 36 章

## 分道扬镳

邓布利多站起身。他低头望着小巴蒂·克劳奇,脸上露出厌恶的神情。然后他又一次举起魔杖,几根绳子嗖嗖地从魔杖里飞出来,缠住小巴蒂·克劳奇,把他结结实实地捆了起来。

邓布利多转身对麦格教授说:"米勒娃,你能不能守在这里,我送哈利上楼?"

"没问题。"麦格教授说。她显得有些恶心,就像她刚才望着的是一个呕吐的人。不过,当她抽出魔杖,指着小巴蒂·克劳奇时,她的手非常平稳。

"西弗勒斯,"邓布利多转向斯内普,"麻烦你去把庞弗雷女士叫来,我们需要把阿拉斯托·穆迪送进病房。然后你到场地上去,找到康奈利·福吉,把他带到这间办公室来。他肯定想亲自审问小克劳奇。你告诉他,如果他需要我,这半小时我在病房里。"

斯内普默默地点了点头,迅速离开了房间。

"哈利?"邓布利多温和地说。

哈利站起身,又摇晃起来;刚才他专心听小克劳奇说话,没有注意伤腿的疼痛,现在那疼痛变本加厉地回来了。他还意识到自己浑身发抖。邓布利多一把抓住他的胳膊,扶着他来到外面漆黑的走廊里。

"我希望你先到我的办公室去一下,哈利,"他们沿着走廊往前走,邓布利多轻声说,"小天狼星在那里等我们呢。"

哈利点了点头。他感觉麻木,仿佛置身于梦境中,眼前的一切似乎都不真实,但他并不在乎。他甚至为此感到高兴。这样,他就用不着去想他触摸三强杯后发生的一切了。他不想仔细研究那些记忆,尽

## CHAPTER THIRTY-SIX  The Parting of the Ways

the Triwizard Cup. He didn't want to have to examine the memories, fresh and sharp as photographs, which kept flashing across his mind. Mad-Eye Moody, inside the trunk. Wormtail, slumped on the ground, cradling his stump of an arm. Voldemort, rising from the steaming cauldron. Cedric ... dead ... Cedric, asking to be returned to his parents ...

'Professor,' Harry mumbled, 'where are Mr. and Mrs. Diggory?'

'They are with Professor Sprout,' said Dumbledore. His voice, which had been so calm throughout the interrogation of Barty Crouch, shook very slightly for the first time. 'She was Head of Cedric's house, and knew him best.'

They had reached the stone gargoyle. Dumbledore gave the password, it sprang aside, and he and Harry went up the moving spiral staircase to the oak door. Dumbledore pushed it open.

Sirius was standing there. His face was white and gaunt as it had been when he had escaped Azkaban. In one swift moment, he had crossed the room. 'Harry, are you all right? I knew it – I knew something like this – what happened?'

His hands shook as he helped Harry into a chair in front of the desk.

'What happened?' he asked, more urgently.

Dumbledore began to tell Sirius everything Barty Crouch had said. Harry was only half listening. So tired every bone in his body was aching, he wanted nothing more than to sit here, undisturbed, for hours and hours, until he fell asleep, and didn't have to think or feel any more.

There was a soft rush of wings. Fawkes the phoenix had left his perch, flown across the office, and landed on Harry's knee.

''Lo, Fawkes,' said Harry quietly. He stroked the phoenix's beautiful scarlet and gold plumage. Fawkes blinked peacefully up at him. There was something comforting about his warm weight.

Dumbledore had stopped talking. He sat down opposite Harry, behind his desk. He was looking at Harry, who avoided his eyes. Dumbledore was going to question him. He was going to make Harry relive everything.

'I need to know what happened after you touched the Portkey in the maze, Harry,' said Dumbledore.

'We can leave that 'til morning, can't we, Dumbledore?' said Sirius

## 第36章 分道扬镳

管那些记忆不断在他脑海里闪现,像照片一样清晰。疯眼汉穆迪被关在大箱子里。虫尾巴瘫倒在地,捂着他的断臂。伏地魔从冒着蒸气的坩埚里冉冉升起。塞德里克……停止了呼吸……塞德里克,请哈利把自己送到父母身边……

"教授,"哈利喃喃地说,"迪戈里先生和他夫人在哪里?"

"他们和斯普劳特教授在一起。"邓布利多说,他的声音在审问小巴蒂·克劳奇的过程中一直是那么平稳镇定,现在第一次有些发颤,"斯普劳特教授是塞德里克那个学院的院长,对他最了解。"

他们来到滴水嘴石兽跟前。邓布利多说了口令,怪兽左右分开,他和哈利走上活动的螺旋形楼梯,来到橡木大门前。邓布利多把门推开。

小天狼星就站在那里。他脸色苍白,面容消瘦,就像刚从阿兹卡班逃出来时那样。他一眨眼就从房间那头奔了过来。"哈利,你没事吧?我就知道——我就知道会出这样的事——发生了什么?"

他双手颤抖,扶着哈利坐到桌前的一把椅子上。

"怎么回事?"他更加急切地问。

邓布利多开始向小天狼星原原本本地讲述小巴蒂·克劳奇所说的一切。哈利心不在焉地听着。他太累了,身上的每根骨头都在隐隐作痛。他只想坐在这里,不被任何人打扰,就这样坐上好久好久,直到沉沉睡去,再也不要有任何思想、任何感觉。

一阵翅膀轻轻扑打的声音。凤凰福克斯离开了它栖息的枝头,从办公室那头飞过来,落在哈利的膝盖上。

"你好,福克斯。"哈利轻声说。他抚摸着凤凰金色和红色的美丽羽毛。福克斯平静地朝他眨了眨眼睛。凤凰栖在膝头暖烘烘、沉甸甸的,哈利觉得心头踏实了许多。

邓布利多停住了话头。他在哈利对面的办公桌后面坐了下来。他望着哈利,但哈利躲避着他的目光。邓布利多要向他发问了。邓布利多要强迫他回忆那所有的一切了。

"我需要知道,哈利,你在迷宫里触摸门钥匙后发生了什么?"邓布利多说。

"我们可以明天早上再谈,行不行,邓布利多?"小天狼星声音沙

## CHAPTER THIRTY-SIX    The Parting of the Ways

harshly. He had put a hand on Harry's shoulder. 'Let him have a sleep. Let him rest.'

Harry felt a rush of gratitude towards Sirius, but Dumbledore took no notice of Sirius' words. He leant forward towards Harry. Very unwillingly, Harry raised his head, and looked into those blue eyes.

'If I thought I could help you,' Dumbledore said gently, 'by putting you into an enchanted sleep, and allowing you to postpone the moment when you would have to think about what has happened tonight, I would do it. But I know better. Numbing the pain for a while will make it worse when you finally feel it. You have shown bravery beyond anything I could have expected of you. I ask you to demonstrate your courage one more time. I ask you to tell us what happened.'

The phoenix let out one soft, quavering note. It shivered in the air, and Harry felt as though a drop of hot liquid had slipped down his throat into his stomach, warming him, and strengthening him.

He took a deep breath, and began to tell them. As he spoke, visions of everything that had passed that night seemed to rise before his eyes; he saw the sparkling surface of the Potion which had revived Voldemort; he saw the Death Eaters Apparating between the graves around them; he saw Cedric's body, lying on the ground beside the Cup.

Once or twice, Sirius made a noise as though about to say something, his hand still tight on Harry's shoulder, but Dumbledore raised his hand to stop him, and Harry was glad of this, because it was easier to keep going now he had started. It was even a relief; he felt almost as though something poisonous was being extracted from him; it was costing him every bit of determination he had to keep talking, yet he sensed that once he had finished, he would feel better.

When Harry told of Wormtail piercing his arm with the dagger, however, Sirius let out a vehement exclamation; and Dumbledore stood up so quickly that Harry started. Dumbledore walked around the desk and told Harry to stretch out his arm. Harry showed them both the place where his robes were torn, and the cut beneath them.

'He said my blood would make him stronger than if he'd used someone else's,' Harry told Dumbledore. 'He said the protection my – my mother left in me – he'd have it, too. And he was right – he could touch me without

## 第36章 分道扬镳

哑地说,他把一只手放在哈利的肩膀上,"让他睡一觉吧。让他好好休息休息吧。"

哈利心头涌起对小天狼星的感激之情,但邓布利多仿佛没有听见小天狼星的话。他朝哈利探过身子。哈利很不情愿地抬起头,注视着那双蓝色的眼睛。

"如果我认为,"邓布利多温和地说,"用催眠的方法使你入睡,允许你暂时不去考虑今晚发生的一切,会对你有好处,我肯定这样做。但是我比你更清楚,暂时使疼痛变得麻木,只会使你最后感觉疼痛时疼得更厉害。你表现出的勇敢无畏,大大超出了我对你的期望。我要求你再一次表现出你的勇气。我要求你把所发生的一切告诉我们。"

凤凰发出一声轻柔而颤抖的鸣叫。那声音在空中微微发抖,哈利感到似乎一滴滚热的液体顺着喉咙滑进了胃里,他一下子觉得暖乎乎的,有了力量和勇气。

他深吸了一口气,开始向他们叙述。他说话时,那天晚上发生的一切都像放电影一样,在他眼前一幕幕闪现:他看见了那使伏地魔起死回生、表面冒着火星的魔药;他看见了幻影显形、突然出现在他们周围坟墓间的食死徒们;他看见了塞德里克的尸体,静静地躺在三强杯旁的地面上。

有一两次,小天狼星发出一点声音,似乎想说些什么,他的手仍然紧紧地抓住哈利的肩膀,但邓布利多举起一只手,阻止了他。这使哈利感到庆幸,因为万事开头难,现在既然打开了话匣子,再说下去就容易多了。他甚至有一种如释重负的感觉,似乎某种有毒的东西正从他体内被一点点地吸走。他以极大的毅力支撑着自己往下说,但他感觉到,一旦说完,他心头就会变得舒坦多了。

当哈利讲到虫尾巴用匕首刺中他的手臂时,小天狼星发出一声激动的喊叫,邓布利多猛地站起身,速度之快,把哈利吓了一跳。邓布利多绕过桌子,叫哈利伸出手臂。哈利给他们俩看了他被撕破的长袍和长袍下的伤口。

"他说,用我的血比用其他人的血更管用,会使他更加强壮。"哈利对邓布利多说,"他说那种保护力量——我母亲留在我身体里的那种力量——他也想拥有。他是对的——后来他再碰到我的时候,就不会

## CHAPTER THIRTY-SIX  The Parting of the Ways

hurting himself, he touched my face.'

For a fleeting instant, Harry thought he saw a gleam of something like triumph in Dumbledore's eyes. But next second, Harry was sure he had imagined it, for when Dumbledore had returned to his seat behind the desk, he looked as old and weary as Harry had ever seen him.

'Very well,' he said, sitting down again. 'Voldemort has overcome that particular barrier. Harry, continue, please.'

Harry went on; he explained how Voldemort had emerged from the cauldron, and told them all he could remember of Voldemort's speech to the Death Eaters. Then he told how Voldemort had untied him, returned his wand to him, and prepared to duel.

But when he reached the part where the golden beam of light had connected his and Voldemort's wands, he found his throat obstructed. He tried to keep talking, but the memories of what had come out of Voldemort's wand were flooding into his mind. He could see Cedric emerging, see the old man, Bertha Jorkins ... his mother ... his father ...

He was glad when Sirius broke the silence.

'The wands connected?' he said, looking from Harry to Dumbledore. 'Why?'

Harry looked up again at Dumbledore, on whose face there was an arrested look.

'Priori Incantatem,' he muttered.

His eyes gazed into Harry's and it was almost as though an invisible beam of understanding shot between them.

'The reverse spell effect?' said Sirius sharply.

'Exactly,' said Dumbledore. 'Harry's wand and Voldemort's wand share cores. Each of them contains a feather from the tail of the same phoenix. *This* phoenix, in fact,' he added, and he pointed at the scarlet and gold bird, perching peacefully on Harry's knee.

'My wand's feather came from Fawkes?' Harry said, amazed.

'Yes,' said Dumbledore. 'Mr. Ollivander wrote to tell me you had bought the second wand, the moment you left his shop four years ago.'

'So what happens when a wand meets its brother?' said Sirius.

'They will not work properly against each other,' said Dumbledore. 'If, however, the owners of the wands force the wands to do battle ... a very rare effect will take place.

受伤了。他碰了我的脸。"

在短短的一瞬间,哈利似乎看见邓布利多眼睛里闪过一丝胜利的喜悦。但哈利很快就认定自己准是看花了眼,因为邓布利多回到办公桌后的椅子上时,看上去又和哈利一向看见的那样苍老和疲倦了。

"很好,"邓布利多说着,又坐了下来,"伏地魔战胜了那个不同寻常的障碍。哈利,请你说下去吧。"

哈利继续往下说。他讲述伏地魔怎样从坩埚里浮现出来,并把他记得的伏地魔对食死徒们说的话告诉了他们。然后他告诉他们伏地魔怎样解开他身上的绳子,把他的魔杖还给他,准备与他决斗。

然而,当他讲到那道金光连接他的魔杖和伏地魔的魔杖时,他觉得嗓子哽咽了。他努力说下去,但伏地魔的魔杖里浮现出的那些东西,像潮水一样涌入他的脑海。他可以看见魔杖中冒出了塞德里克,还看见那个老人、伯莎·乔金斯……他的母亲……他的父亲……

就在这时,小天狼星打破了沉默,才使哈利松了口气。

"魔杖连接?"小天狼星问,望望哈利,又看看邓布利多,"为什么?"

哈利又抬头望着邓布利多,只见他脸上有一种被深深吸引的神情。

"闪回咒。"邓布利多喃喃低语。

他凝视着哈利的眼睛,两人之间闪过一道看不见的会意的目光。

"能获得重放咒的效果?"小天狼星机敏地问。

"非常正确,"邓布利多说,"哈利的魔杖和伏地魔的魔杖有着同样的杖芯。它们各自所含的那根羽毛是从同一只凤凰身上取得的。说实话,就是这只凤凰。"他说,指了指静静栖在哈利膝头的金红色大鸟。

"我魔杖里的羽毛是福克斯身上的?"哈利惊奇地问。

"是的,"邓布利多说,"四年前,你刚离开奥利凡德先生的店铺,他就写信告诉我说第二根魔杖被你买走了。"

"那么,如果一根魔杖遇见它的兄弟,会怎么样呢?"小天狼星问。

"它们不会正常地攻击对方,"邓布利多说,"不过,如果魔杖的主人硬要两根魔杖争斗……就会出现一种十分罕见的现象。

## CHAPTER THIRTY-SIX    The Parting of the Ways

'One of the wands will force the other to regurgitate spells it has performed – in reverse. The most recent first ... and then those which preceded it ...'

He looked interrogatively at Harry, and Harry nodded.

'Which means,' said Dumbledore slowly, his eyes upon Harry's face, 'that some form of Cedric must have reappeared.'

Harry nodded again.

'Diggory came back to life?' said Sirius sharply.

'No spell can reawaken the dead,' said Dumbledore heavily. 'All that would have happened is a kind of reverse echo. A shadow of the living Cedric would have emerged from the wand ... am I correct, Harry?'

'He spoke to me,' Harry said. He was suddenly shaking again. 'The ... the ghost Cedric, or whatever he was, spoke.'

'An echo,' said Dumbledore, 'which retained Cedric's appearance and character. I am guessing other such forms appeared ... less recent victims of Voldemort's wand ...'

'An old man,' Harry said, his throat still constricted. 'Bertha Jorkins. And ...'

'Your parents?' said Dumbledore quietly.

'Yes,' said Harry.

Sirius' grip on Harry's shoulder was now so tight it was painful.

'The last murders the wand performed,' said Dumbledore, nodding. 'In reverse order. More would have appeared, of course, had you maintained the connection. Very well, Harry, these echoes, these shadows ... what did they do?'

Harry described how the figures which had emerged from the wand had prowled the edges of the golden web, how Voldemort had seemed to fear them, how the shadow of Harry's father had told him what to do, how Cedric's had made its final request.

At this point, Harry found he could not continue. He looked around at Sirius, and saw that he had his face in his hands.

Harry suddenly became aware that Fawkes had left his knee. The phoenix had fluttered to the floor. It was resting its beautiful head against Harry's injured leg, and thick, pearly tears were falling from its eyes onto the wound left by the spider. The pain vanished. The skin mended. His leg was repaired.

'I will say it again,' said Dumbledore, as the phoenix rose into the air,

## 第36章 分道扬镳

一根魔杖会强迫另一根重复它施过的咒语——以倒序的方式。先是最近的咒语……然后是以前的……"

他询问地望着哈利，哈利点了点头。

"这就是说，"邓布利多慢慢地说，眼睛盯着哈利的脸，"塞德里克以某种形式重新出现了。"

哈利又点了点头。

"迪戈里又活过来了？"小天狼星反应很快地问。

"任何咒语都不可能把死者唤醒，"邓布利多语气沉重地说，"只会出现一种类似回音倒放的现象。魔杖里会冒出塞德里克活着时的一个影子……我说得对吗，哈利？"

"他对我说话了。"哈利说，他突然又禁不住颤抖起来，"那个……那个塞德里克的灵魂之类的东西，说话了。"

"是一个回音，"邓布利多说，"保留了塞德里克的相貌和性格。我猜想还出现了其他类似的形体……是以前伏地魔的魔杖下的牺牲品……"

"有一个老人，"哈利说，喉头仍然发紧，"伯莎·乔金斯，还有……"

"你的父母？"邓布利多轻声地问。

"是的。"哈利说。

小天狼星把哈利的肩膀抓得生疼。

"那根魔杖最近残害的人，"邓布利多点了点头，说道，"以倒序的形式闪现出来。当然啦，如果你让两根魔杖一直连接着，还会出现更多的幻象。很好，哈利，这些回音，这些幻影……它们做了什么？"

哈利叙述那些从魔杖里冒出来的身影怎样在金网边缘徘徊，伏地魔怎样感到恐惧，哈利父亲的影子怎样告诉他应该做什么，塞德里克的影子怎样提出它最后的请求。

说到这里，哈利觉得再也说不下去了。他转脸望望小天狼星，看见他用手捂住了脸。

哈利突然意识到福克斯已经飞离了他的膝头。凤凰扑棱棱地落到地上，美丽的头贴着哈利受伤的腿，大滴大滴透明的泪珠从它眼睛里涌出，落在蜘蛛留下的伤口上。疼痛消失，皮肤愈合。他的腿完好如初。

"我要再说一遍，"邓布利多说，这时凤凰飞到空中，重新落到门

## CHAPTER THIRTY-SIX   The Parting of the Ways

and resettled itself upon the perch beside the door. 'You have shown bravery beyond anything I could have expected of you tonight, Harry. You have shown bravery equal to those who died fighting Voldemort at the height of his powers. You have shouldered a grown wizard's burden and found yourself equal to it – and you have now given us all that we have a right to expect. You will come with me to the hospital wing. I do not want you returning to the dormitory tonight. A Sleeping Potion, and some peace ... Sirius, would you like to stay with him?'

Sirius nodded, and stood up. He transformed back into the great black dog, and walked with Harry and Dumbledore out of the office, accompanying them down a flight of stairs to the hospital wing.

When Dumbledore pushed open the door, Harry saw Mrs. Weasley, Bill, Ron and Hermione grouped around a harassed-looking Madam Pomfrey. They appeared to be demanding to know where Harry was and what had happened to him.

All of them whipped around as Harry, Dumbledore and the black dog entered, and Mrs. Weasley let out a kind of muffled scream. 'Harry! Oh, Harry!'

She started to hurry towards him, but Dumbledore moved between them.

'Molly,' he said, holding up a hand, 'please listen to me for a moment. Harry has been through a terrible ordeal tonight. He has just had to relive it for me. What he needs now is sleep, and peace, and quiet. If he would like you all to stay with him,' he added, looking around at Ron, Hermione and Bill, too, 'you may do so. But I do not want you questioning him until he is ready to answer, and certainly not this evening.'

Mrs. Weasley nodded. She was very white.

She rounded on Ron, Hermione and Bill as though they were being noisy, and hissed, 'Did you hear? He needs quiet!'

'Headmaster,' said Madam Pomfrey, staring at the great black dog that was Sirius, 'may I ask what –?'

'This dog will be remaining with Harry for a while,' said Dumbledore simply. 'I assure you, he is extremely well trained. Harry – I will wait while you get into bed.'

Harry felt an inexpressible sense of gratitude to Dumbledore for asking the others not to question him. It wasn't as though he didn't want them there; but the thought of explaining it all over again, the idea of reliving it one more time, was more than he could stand.

## 第36章 分道扬镳

边的栖枝上,"你今晚的表现十分勇敢,远远超出了我对你的期望,哈利。你所表现出的勇气,与那些在伏地魔鼎盛时期同他抗争至死的巫师们不相上下。你肩负起了一个成年巫师的重任,并发现自己完全挑得起这副担子——你让我们对你抱有更高的期望。你跟我一起到医院去吧。今晚我不想让你回宿舍了。服一些安眠药剂,好好地静下心来……小天狼星,你愿意陪着他吗?"

小天狼星点点头,站了起来。他重新变成一条黑色的大狗,跟着哈利和邓布利多走出了办公室,并陪着他们走下楼梯,向医院走去。

邓布利多推开门时,哈利看见韦斯莱夫人、比尔、罗恩和赫敏都围在显得焦头烂额的庞弗雷女士身边。他们似乎在追问哈利的情况和下落。

当哈利、邓布利多和黑狗进去时,他们都猛地转过身来,韦斯莱夫人发出一声压抑的惊呼:"哈利!哦,哈利!"

她拔脚向哈利奔来,但邓布利多走上前,挡在了他们俩之间。

"莫丽,"他举起一只手,说道,"请先听我说几句。哈利今晚经历了一场可怕的折磨。刚才又向我复述了一遍。他现在需要的是睡眠、清静和安宁。如果他愿意你们陪着他,"他又望望周围的罗恩、赫敏和比尔,补充道,"你们可以留下。但我不希望你们向他提任何问题,直到他做好回答的准备,不过今晚绝对不行。"

韦斯莱夫人点了点头。她脸色十分苍白。

她突然转向罗恩、赫敏和比尔,就好像他们在吵闹似的。她压低声音教训道:"你们听见了吗?他需要安静!"

"校长,"庞弗雷女士盯着小天狼星变成的黑狗,说道,"我可不可以问一句,这是什么——"

"这条狗陪哈利待一会儿,"邓布利多简单地说,"我向你保证,它受过十分良好的训练。哈利——我等你上了床再走。"

邓布利多不许别人向他提问,哈利心头涌起一股难以形容的感激之情。他并非不愿意他们待在这里,但一想到又要把事情原原本本地再说一遍,又要重新体验所有的一切,他就觉得无法忍受。

## CHAPTER THIRTY-SIX   The Parting of the Ways

'I will be back to see you as soon as I have met with Fudge, Harry,' said Dumbledore. 'I would like you to remain here tomorrow, until I have spoken to the school.' He left.

As Madam Pomfrey led Harry to a nearby bed, he caught sight of the real Moody lying motionless in a bed at the far end of the room. His wooden leg and magical eye were lying on the bedside table.

'Is he OK?' Harry asked.

'He'll be fine,' said Madam Pomfrey, giving Harry some pyjamas and pulling screens around him. He took off his robes, pulled on the pyjamas and got into bed. Ron, Hermione, Bill, Mrs. Weasley and the black dog came around the screen and settled themselves in chairs on either side of him. Ron and Hermione were looking at him almost cautiously, as though scared of him.

'I'm all right,' he told them. 'Just tired.'

Mrs. Weasley's eyes filled with tears as she smoothed his bedcovers unnecessarily.

Madam Pomfrey, who had bustled off to her office, returned holding a goblet and a small bottle of some purple potion.

'You'll need to drink all of this, Harry,' she said. 'It's a potion for dreamless sleep.'

Harry took the goblet and drank a few mouthfuls. He felt himself becoming drowsy at once. Everything around him became hazy; the lamps around the hospital wing seemed to be winking at him in a friendly way through the screen around his bed; his body felt as though it was sinking deeper into the warmth of the feather mattress. Before he could finish the Potion, before he could say another word, his exhaustion had carried him off to sleep.

Harry woke up, so warm, so very sleepy, that he didn't open his eyes, wanting to drop off again. The room was still dimly lit; he was sure it was still night-time, and had a feeling that he couldn't have been asleep very long.

Then he heard whispering around him.

'They'll wake him if they don't shut up!'

'What are they shouting about? Nothing else can have happened, can it?'

Harry opened his eyes blearily. Someone had removed his glasses. He

## 第36章 分道扬镳

"我去见过福吉之后，就马上赶回来看你，哈利。"邓布利多说，"我希望你明天也留在这里，等我向全校师生讲完话再说。"说完，他就走了。

庞弗雷女士领着哈利走向旁边的一张床，哈利瞥见真穆迪一动不动地躺在房间尽头的病床上。他的木头假腿和那个带魔法的眼球放在床头柜上。

"他没事吧？"哈利问道。

"他不会有事的。"庞弗雷女士说，一边递给哈利一套睡衣，并拉上他周围的帘子。哈利脱去长袍，换上睡衣，爬到了床上。罗恩、赫敏、比尔、韦斯莱夫人和那条黑狗都从帘子旁边绕了进来，分别坐在他两边的椅子上。罗恩和赫敏望着他，神情几乎是小心翼翼的，似乎有点儿怕他。

"我挺好的，"他告诉他们，"就是太累了。"

韦斯莱夫人不必要地抚摸着他的床单，眼睛里噙着泪花。

庞弗雷女士刚才匆匆去了一趟她的办公室，这时拿着一个小瓶子和一个高脚酒杯回来了，瓶子里装着一种紫色的药剂。

"你需要把它都喝了，哈利，"她说，"这种药可以使你无梦地酣睡一场。"

哈利接过酒杯，喝了几口。他一下子就觉得昏昏沉沉的。周围的一切都变得模糊了；病房的灯似乎正在隔着床边的帘子朝他友好地眨眼睛；他仿佛觉得自己的身体在温暖的羽毛床垫中越来越深地陷下去。没等他把药喝完，没等再说一句话，他就精疲力竭，沉入了无梦的睡眠。

哈利醒了过来，真暖和，真困啊，他没有睁开眼睛，只希望再沉沉睡去。房间里仍然光线昏暗；他想这一定还是夜晚，而且他觉得自己不可能睡了很长时间。

就在这时，他听见旁边有人小声说话。

"如果他们再不闭嘴，会把他吵醒的！"

"他们在嚷嚷什么？不会又发生了什么事吧？"

哈利费力地睁开惺忪的双眼。有人把他的眼镜摘掉了。他只能看

## CHAPTER THIRTY-SIX    The Parting of the Ways

could see the fuzzy outlines of Mrs. Weasley and Bill close by. Mrs. Weasley was on her feet.

'That's Fudge's voice,' she whispered. 'And that's Minerva McGonagall's, isn't it? But what are they arguing about?'

Now Harry could hear them, too: people shouting and running towards the hospital wing.

'Regrettable, but all the same, Minerva –' Cornelius Fudge was saying loudly.

'You should never have brought it inside the castle!' yelled Professor McGonagall. 'When Dumbledore finds out –'

Harry heard hospital doors burst open. Unnoticed by any of the people around his bed, all of whom were staring at the door as Bill pulled back the screens, Harry sat up, and put his glasses back on.

Fudge came striding up the ward. Professors McGonagall and Snape were at his heels.

'Where's Dumbledore?' Fudge demanded of Mrs. Weasley.

'He's not here,' said Mrs. Weasley angrily. 'This is a hospital wing, Minister, don't you think you'd do better to –'

But the door opened, and Dumbledore came sweeping up the ward.

'What has happened?' said Dumbledore sharply, looking from Fudge to Professor McGonagall. 'Why are you disturbing these people? Minerva, I'm surprised at you – I asked you to stand guard over Barty Crouch –'

'There is no need to stand guard over him any more, Dumbledore!' she shrieked. 'The Minister has seen to that!'

Harry had never seen Professor McGonagall lose control like this. There were angry blotches of colour in her cheeks, her hands were balled into fists; she was trembling with fury.

'When we told Mr. Fudge that we had caught the Death Eater responsible for tonight's events,' said Snape, in a low voice, 'he seemed to feel his personal safety was in question. He insisted on summoning a Dementor to accompany him into the castle. He brought it up to the office where Barty Crouch –'

'I told him you would not agree, Dumbledore!' stormed Professor McGonagall. 'I told him you would never allow Dementors to set foot inside the castle, but –'

'My dear woman!' roared Fudge, who likewise looked angrier than Harry had ever seen him. 'As Minister for Magic, it is my decision whether I wish to

## 第36章 分道扬镳

见近旁韦斯莱夫人和比尔的模糊身影。韦斯莱夫人已经站了起来。

"这是福吉的声音,"她小声说,"这是米勒娃·麦格的声音,是不是?可他们在争论什么呢?"

这时哈利也听见了:有人在大喊大叫,并朝病房这边跑来。

"真令人遗憾,不过也没有办法,米勒娃——"康奈利·福吉大声说道。

"你绝对不应该把它带进城堡!"麦格教授嚷道,"如果被邓布利多发现——"

哈利听见病房的门突然被撞开了。比尔拉开帘子,周围所有人的目光都盯着房门,没有注意到哈利坐起身,戴上了眼镜。

福吉大步走进病房。麦格教授和斯内普紧跟在后面。

"邓布利多呢?"福吉问韦斯莱夫人。

"他不在这儿,"韦斯莱夫人气愤地说,"部长,这里是病房,你是否认为你最好——"

可就在这时,门开了,邓布利多敏捷地走进了病房。

"出了什么事?"邓布利多严厉地问,看看福吉,又看看麦格教授,"你们为什么在这里打扰这些人?米勒娃,你真让我感到吃惊——我叫你看守小巴蒂·克劳奇的——"

"已经没必要看守他了,邓布利多!"麦格教授尖声嚷道,"部长确保了这一点!"

哈利从没见过麦格教授像现在这样冲动。她面颊上泛起愤怒的红晕,双手捏成了拳头。她气得浑身发抖。

"我们告诉福吉先生,我们抓住了制造今晚事件的食死徒,"斯内普低声说道,"他似乎感到他个人的安全也成了问题,一定要召来一个摄魂怪陪他进入城堡。他把摄魂怪带进了小巴蒂·克劳奇所在的那个办公室——"

"我告诉他你不会同意的,邓布利多!"麦格教授怒气冲冲地说,"我告诉他你不许摄魂怪再踏进城堡,可是——"

"我亲爱的女士!"福吉大声吼道,他此刻这副怒气冲天的样子也是哈利从没见过的,"我作为魔法部部长,有权决定自己是否愿意带保

## CHAPTER THIRTY-SIX    The Parting of the Ways

bring protection with me when interviewing a possibly dangerous –'

But Professor McGonagall's voice drowned Fudge's.

'The moment that – that thing entered the room,' she screamed, pointing at Fudge, trembling all over, 'it swooped down on Crouch and – and –'

Harry felt a chill in his stomach, as Professor McGonagall struggled to find words to describe what had happened. He did not need her to finish her sentence. He knew what the Dementor must have done. It had administered its fatal Kiss to Barty Crouch. It had sucked his soul out through his mouth. He was worse than dead.

'By all accounts, he is no loss!' blustered Fudge. 'It seems he has been responsible for several deaths!'

'But he cannot now give testimony, Cornelius,' said Dumbledore. He was staring hard at Fudge, as though seeing him plainly for the first time. 'He cannot give evidence about why he killed those people.'

'Why he killed them? Well, that's no mystery, is it?' blustered Fudge. 'He was a raving lunatic! From what Minerva and Severus have told me, he seems to have thought he was doing it all on You-Know-Who's instructions!'

'Lord Voldemort *was* giving him instructions, Cornelius,' Dumbledore said. 'Those people's deaths were mere by-products of a plan to restore Voldemort to full strength again. The plan succeeded. Voldemort has been restored to his body.'

Fudge looked as though someone had just swung a heavy weight into his face. Dazed and blinking, he stared back at Dumbledore as if he couldn't quite believe what he had just heard.

He began to splutter, still goggling at Dumbledore. 'You-Know-Who ... returned? Preposterous. Come now, Dumbledore ...'

'As Minerva and Severus have doubtless told you,' said Dumbledore, 'we heard Barty Crouch confess. Under the influence of Veritaserum, he told us how he was smuggled out of Azkaban, and how Voldemort – learning of his continued existence from Bertha Jorkins – went to free him from his father, and used him to capture Harry. The plan worked, I tell you. Crouch has helped Voldemort to return.'

'See here, Dumbledore,' said Fudge, and Harry was astonished to see a slight smile dawning on his face, 'you – you can't seriously believe that. You-Know-Who – back? Come now, come now ... certainly, Crouch may have

## 第36章 分道扬镳

镖,因为我要来见一位可能非常危险的——"

可是麦格教授的声音盖过了福吉的话。

"那家伙——那家伙一进办公室,"她指着福吉,全身颤抖,尖叫着说,"就朝克劳奇扑去,就——就——"

麦格教授拼命寻找字眼来描绘刚才发生的事,哈利感到肚子里生出一股寒气。他用不着听麦格教授把话说完。他知道摄魂怪做了什么。摄魂怪一定给了小巴蒂·克劳奇那个致命的吻,从小克劳奇的嘴里吸走了他的灵魂。小克劳奇现在已是生不如死。

"根据各种说法,这是他罪有应得!"福吉气势汹汹地说,"他似乎造成了好几个人的死亡!"

"可是他现在无法出来作证了,康奈利。"邓布利多说,他犀利地盯着福吉,似乎第一次清清楚楚地看透了他,"他不能提供证据,说明他为什么要杀死那些人了。"

"他为什么杀死他们?嘿,这不是明摆着的嘛!"福吉气急败坏地说,"他是个到处流浪的疯子!从米勒娃和西弗勒斯告诉我的情况看,他似乎以为自己所做的一切都是遵照了神秘人的旨意!"

"伏地魔以前确实对他发号施令,康奈利,"邓布利多说,"那些人的死,只是伏地魔施行卷土重来计划时附带产生的结果。那个计划成功了。伏地魔恢复了他的肉身。"

福吉大惊失色,就好像有人迎面给了他一记重击。他晕晕乎乎地眨巴着眼睛,呆呆地瞪着邓布利多,似乎不能完全相信刚才听见的话。

他结结巴巴地说话了,眼睛仍然瞪着邓布利多:"神秘人……回来了?胡说八道。别开玩笑了,邓布利多……"

"米勒娃和西弗勒斯无疑已经告诉过你,"邓布利多说,"我们听到了小巴蒂·克劳奇的坦白交代。在吐真剂的作用下,他告诉我们他怎样被偷偷带出阿兹卡班,伏地魔怎样——从伯莎·乔金斯那里得知他仍然在世——就从他父亲那里把他解救了出来,利用他去抓住哈利。告诉你吧,这个计划成功了。小克劳奇已经帮助伏地魔卷土重来了。"

"你听我说,邓布利多,"福吉说,哈利吃惊地看见他脸上居然闪现出一丝笑容,"你——你不可能真的相信这一切吧。神秘人——回来

## CHAPTER THIRTY-SIX    The Parting of the Ways

*believed* himself to be acting upon You-Know-Who's orders – but to take the word of a lunatic like that, Dumbledore ...'

'When Harry touched the Triwizard Cup tonight, he was transported straight to Voldemort,' said Dumbledore steadily. 'He witnessed Lord Voldemort's rebirth. I will explain it all to you if you will step up to my office.'

Dumbledore glanced around at Harry and saw that he was awake, but shook his head, and said, 'I am afraid I cannot permit you to question Harry tonight.'

Fudge's curious smile lingered.

He too glanced at Harry, then looked back at Dumbledore, and said, 'You are – er – prepared to take Harry's word on this, are you, Dumbledore?'

There was a moment's silence, which was broken by Sirius growling. His hackles were raised, and he was baring his teeth at Fudge.

'Certainly I believe Harry,' said Dumbledore. His eyes were blazing now. 'I heard Crouch's confession, and I heard Harry's account of what happened after he touched the Triwizard Cup; the two stories make sense, they explain everything that has happened since Bertha Jorkins disappeared last summer.'

Fudge still had that strange smile on his face. Once again, he glanced at Harry before answering. 'You are prepared to believe that Lord Voldemort has returned, on the word of a lunatic murderer, and a boy who ... well ...'

Fudge shot Harry another look, and Harry suddenly understood.

'You've been reading Rita Skeeter, Mr. Fudge,' he said quietly.

Ron, Hermione, Mrs. Weasley and Bill all jumped. None of them had realised that Harry was awake.

Fudge reddened slightly, but a defiant and obstinate look came over his face.

'And if I have?' he said, looking at Dumbledore. 'If I have discovered that you've been keeping certain facts about the boy very quiet? A Parselmouth, eh? And having funny turns all over the place –'

'I assume that you are referring to the pains Harry has been experiencing in his scar?' said Dumbledore coolly.

'You admit that he has been having these pains, then?' said Fudge quickly. 'Headaches? Nightmares? Possibly – hallucinations?'

## 第36章 分道扬镳

了？别开玩笑，别开玩笑了……不用说，小克劳奇也许以为自己是遵照神秘人的指令行事的——可是怎么能把这样一个疯子的话当真呢，邓布利多……"

"今晚，当哈利触摸到三强杯时，就被直接送到了伏地魔那里。"邓布利多坚定地说，"他亲眼目睹了伏地魔的起死回生。你不妨到我的办公室去，我会把一切都解释给你听。"

邓布利多把目光扫向哈利，看见哈利已经醒了，但他摇了摇头，说道："今晚我恐怕不能允许你向哈利提问。"

福吉脸上仍留着那古怪的微笑。

他也望了望哈利，然后又把目光转回到邓布利多身上，说道："你——呃——你准备对哈利的话照单全收，是吗，邓布利多？"

片刻的沉默，接着响起小天狼星的吠叫声。他竖起颈子上的毛，朝福吉露出了他的长牙。

"我当然相信哈利。"邓布利多说，此时他的眼睛灼灼发光，"我听了小克劳奇的坦白，也听了哈利讲述的他触摸三强杯后发生的一切；他们两人的话合情合理，把去年夏天伯莎·乔金斯失踪后出现的所有事情都解释清楚了。"

福吉脸上仍然带着那种奇怪的笑容。他又扫了哈利一眼，才回答道："你准备相信伏地魔已经回来了，听信一个精神失常的杀人犯和一个小孩的话，而这小孩……他……"

福吉又飞快地瞥了哈利一眼，哈利顿时明白了他的意思。

"你一定在读丽塔·斯基特的文章，福吉先生。"哈利轻声说道。

罗恩、赫敏、韦斯莱夫人和比尔都吓了一跳。他们谁也没有发现哈利已经醒了。

福吉微微红了红脸，但紧接着脸上露出一种顽抗和固执的神情。

"是又怎么样？"他望着邓布利多，说道，"我发现你一直把这小孩的某些情况隐瞒不报？蛇佬腔，对吗？举止行为处处都透着古怪——"

"我想，你是指哈利一直感觉到的伤疤疼痛吧？"邓布利多冷冷地说。

"这么说，你承认他一直感到这些疼痛喽？"福吉很快地说，"头疼？做噩梦？大概还有——幻觉吧？"

## CHAPTER THIRTY-SIX  The Parting of the Ways

'Listen to me, Cornelius,' said Dumbledore, taking a step towards Fudge, and once again he seemed to radiate that indefinable sense of power that Harry had felt after Dumbledore had Stunned young Crouch. 'Harry is as sane as you or I. That scar upon his forehead has not addled his brains. I believe it hurts him when Lord Voldemort is close by, or feeling particularly murderous.'

Fudge had taken half a step back from Dumbledore, but he looked no less stubborn. 'You'll forgive me, Dumbledore, but I've never heard of a curse scar acting as an alarm bell before …'

'Look, I saw Voldemort come back!' Harry shouted. He tried to get out of bed again, but Mrs. Weasley forced him back. 'I saw the Death Eaters! I can give you their names! Lucius Malfoy –'

Snape made a sudden movement, but as Harry looked at him, Snape's eyes flew back to Fudge.

'Malfoy was cleared!' said Fudge, visibly affronted. 'A very old family – donations to excellent causes –'

'Macnair!' Harry continued.

'Also cleared! Now working for the Ministry!'

'Avery – Nott – Crabbe – Goyle –'

'You are merely repeating the names of those who were acquitted of being Death Eaters thirteen years ago!' said Fudge angrily. 'You could have found those names in old reports of the trials! for heaven's sake, Dumbledore – the boy was full of some crackpot story at the end of last year, too – his tales are getting taller, and you're still swallowing them – the boy can talk to snakes, Dumbledore, and you still think he's trustworthy?'

'You fool!' Professor McGonagall cried. 'Cedric Diggory! Mr. Crouch! These deaths were not the random work of a lunatic!'

'I see no evidence to the contrary!' shouted Fudge, now matching her anger, his face purpling. 'It seems to me that you are all determined to start a panic that will destabilise everything we have worked for these last thirteen years!'

Harry couldn't believe what he was hearing. He had always thought of Fudge as a kindly figure, a little blustering, a little pompous, but essentially good-natured. But now a short, angry wizard stood before him, refusing, point-blank, to accept the prospect of disruption in his comfortable and

## 第36章 分道扬镳

"听我说，康奈利，"邓布利多说着，朝福吉跟前跨了一步，似乎又一次放射出那种难以言喻的力量——哈利在邓布利多击昏小克劳奇时就感觉到这种力量的存在，"哈利和你我一样清醒、理智。他额头上的伤疤并没有把他的脑子弄糊涂。我相信，只有当伏地魔潜伏在附近或特别想杀人时，哈利的伤疤才会疼。"

福吉从邓布利多面前后退了半步，但神情仍然那么固执。"请原谅，邓布利多，我以前从没听说魔咒伤疤会像警铃一样……"

"我亲眼看见伏地魔又回来了！"哈利大声喊道。他挣扎着想下床，但韦斯莱夫人把他挡了回去。"我亲眼看见了食死徒！我可以报出他们的名字！卢修斯·马尔福——"

斯内普突然动了一下，但当哈利望向他时，他的目光又转向了福吉。

"马尔福被宣告无罪了！"福吉显然觉得受了冒犯，说道，"一个非常古老的家庭——为美好的事业慷慨捐赠——"

"麦克尼尔！"哈利继续报出那些名字。

"也被宣告无罪了！目前在魔法部工作！"

"埃弗里——诺特——克拉布——高尔——"

"你只是在重复那些十三年前被判不是食死徒的人的名字！"福吉气呼呼地说，"你可以在过去的审判报告里找到那些名字！看在老天的分上，邓布利多——去年年底，这个男孩就满脑子胡编乱造的古怪故事——他的谎话越编越离奇了，你居然还全盘相信——这个男孩能够跟蛇对话，邓布利多，而你仍然认为他是值得信任的？"

"你这个傻瓜！"麦格教授喊道，"塞德里克·迪戈里！克劳奇先生！这些人的死绝不是一个疯子的随意行为！"

"我看不出为什么不是！"福吉也大声喊道，脸涨成了紫红色，火气不比麦格教授的小，"在我看来你们都决意要制造一种恐慌情绪，破坏我们这十三年来苦心营造的一切！"

哈利简直不敢相信自己的耳朵。他一向认为福吉是个和蔼可亲的人，尽管有些盛气凌人，有些自高自大，但本质上是很善良的。没想到此刻眼前站着的这个怒气冲冲的小个子巫师，竟断然拒绝相信他那井然有序、稳定舒适的世界有可能毁于一旦——拒绝相信伏地魔可能

## CHAPTER THIRTY-SIX    The Parting of the Ways

ordered world – to believe that Voldemort could have risen.

'Voldemort has returned,' Dumbledore repeated. 'If you accept that fact straight away, Fudge, and take the necessary measures, we may still be able to save the situation. The first and most essential step is to remove Azkaban from the control of the Dementors –'

'Preposterous!' shouted Fudge again. 'Remove the Dementors! I'd be kicked out of office for suggesting it! Half of us only feel safe in our beds at night because we know the Dementors are standing guard at Azkaban!'

'The rest of us sleep less soundly in our beds, Cornelius, knowing that you have put Lord Voldemort's most dangerous supporters in the care of creatures who will join him the instant he asks them!' said Dumbledore. 'They will not remain loyal to you, Fudge! Voldemort can offer them much more scope for their powers and their pleasures than you can! With the Dementors behind him, and his old supporters returned to him, you will be hard pressed to stop him regaining the sort of power he had thirteen years ago!'

Fudge was opening and closing his mouth as though no words could express his outrage.

'The second step you must take – and at once,' Dumbledore pressed on, 'is to send envoys to the giants.'

'Envoys to the giants?' Fudge shrieked, finding his tongue again. 'What madness is this?'

'Extend them the hand of friendship, now, before it is too late,' said Dumbledore, 'or Voldemort will persuade them, as he did before, that he alone among wizards will give them their rights and their freedom!'

'You – you cannot be serious!' Fudge gasped, shaking his head, and retreating further from Dumbledore. 'If the magical community got wind that I had approached the giants – people hate them, Dumbledore – end of my career –'

'You are blinded,' said Dumbledore, his voice rising now, the aura of power around him palpable, his eyes blazing once more, 'by the love of the office you hold, Cornelius! You place too much importance, and you always have done, on the so-called purity of blood! You fail to recognise that it matters not what someone is born, but what they grow to be! Your Dementor has just destroyed the last remaining member of a pure-blood family as old as any – and see what that man chose to make of his life! I tell you now –

## 第36章 分道扬镳

卷土重来。

"伏地魔回来了,"邓布利多又一次说道,"福吉,如果你立即接受这一事实,并采取必要的措施,我们还有可能挽回局面。首先最重要的一步就是让阿兹卡班摆脱摄魂怪的控制——"

"乱弹琴!"福吉又嚷道,"撤销摄魂怪?我只要一提出这个建议,准会被赶出办公室!我们半数的人就是因为知道有摄魂怪在阿兹卡班站岗,晚上才能睡个踏实觉的!"

"康奈利,如果知道伏地魔最危险的死党的看守是那些一声令下就会为他效劳的家伙,那么我们其他人就睡不踏实了!"邓布利多说,"那些家伙不可能对你忠心耿耿,福吉!伏地魔能够提供给它们的权力和乐趣,比你所能提供的多得多!伏地魔身后有摄魂怪的支持,加上那些昔日的死党回到他身边,到时候你就很难阻止他恢复十三年前的那种势力了!"

福吉的嘴巴张开又合上,似乎没有语言能表达他的愤怒。

"你必须采取的第二个措施——而且必须立即行动,"邓布利多进一步说道,"是派使者到巨人那去。"

"派使者到巨人那去?"福吉惊叫道,一下子又会说话了,"这又是什么疯话?"

"趁现在还不算太晚,向他们伸出友谊的手,"邓布利多说,"不然伏地魔就会把他们拉拢过去。他以前就做过这样的事,说是在所有的巫师中,只有他能向巨人提供权益和自由!"

"你——你一定是在开玩笑!"福吉吃惊得喘不过气来,一边摇头,一边又从邓布利多面前向后退缩,"如果魔法界得知我跟巨人有来往——人们对巨人恨之入骨啊,邓布利多——我的事业就完蛋了——"

"康奈利,你太迷恋你的官职了,这使你失去了应有的判断力。"邓布利多说,声音渐渐提高,人们可以感觉到他周身笼罩着的那个力量的光环,他的眼睛又一次灼灼发光,"你太看重所谓的血统纯正了!一向都是如此!你没有认识到,一个人的出身并不重要,重要的是他成长为什么样的人!你的摄魂怪刚才消灭了一个十分古老的纯血统家族的最后一位成员——你看看那个人所选择的人生道路吧!我现在告

## CHAPTER THIRTY-SIX  The Parting of the Ways

take the steps I have suggested, and you will be remembered, in office or out, as one of the bravest and greatest Ministers for Magic we have ever known. Fail to act – and history will remember you as the man who stepped aside, and allowed Voldemort a second chance to destroy the world we have tried to rebuild!'

'Insane,' whispered Fudge, still backing away. 'Mad ...'

And then there was silence. Madam Pomfrey was standing frozen at the foot of Harry's bed, her hands over her mouth. Mrs. Weasley was still standing over Harry, her hand on his shoulder to prevent him rising. Bill, Ron and Hermione were staring at Fudge.

'If your determination to shut your eyes will carry you as far as this, Cornelius,' said Dumbledore, 'we have reached a parting of the ways. You must act as you see fit. And I – I shall act as I see fit.'

Dumbledore's voice carried no hint of a threat; it sounded like a mere statement, but Fudge bristled as though Dumbledore was advancing upon him with a wand.

'Now, see here, Dumbledore,' he said, waving a threatening finger. 'I've given you free rein, always. I've had a lot of respect for you. I might not have agreed with some of your decisions, but I've kept quiet. There aren't many who'd have let you hire werewolves, or keep Hagrid, or decide what to teach your students, without reference to the Ministry. But if you're going to work against me –'

'The only one against whom I intend to work,' said Dumbledore, 'is Lord Voldemort. If you are against him, then we remain, Cornelius, on the same side.'

It seemed Fudge could think of no answer to this. He rocked backwards and forwards on his small feet for a moment, and spun his bowler hat in his hands.

Finally, he said, with a hint of a plea in his voice, 'He can't be back, Dumbledore, he just can't be ...'

Snape strode forwards, past Dumbledore, pulling up the left sleeve of his robes as he went. He stuck out his forearm, and showed it to Fudge, who recoiled.

'There,' said Snape harshly. 'There. The Dark Mark. It is not as clear as it was, an hour or so ago, when it burnt black, but you can still see it. Every Death Eater had the sign burnt into him by the Dark Lord. It was a means of distinguishing each other, and his means of summoning us to him. When

## 第36章 分道扬镳

诉你——只要听从我的建议，采取一些措施，那么无论你是否在位，人们都会把你看作有史以来最勇敢最伟大的魔法部部长。如果你不采取行动——历史也会牢牢记住：正是由于你的袖手旁观，让伏地魔第二次有机会摧毁我们辛辛苦苦重建的这个世界！"

"荒唐，"福吉小声说，继续一步步后退，"疯狂……"

接着是一阵沉默。庞弗雷女士呆呆地站在哈利的床边，用手捂着嘴。韦斯莱夫人仍然站在哈利面前，双手按住他的肩膀，不让他起身。比尔、罗恩和赫敏都吃惊地瞪着福吉。

"如果你这样执迷不悟，一意孤行，康奈利，"邓布利多说，"我们就只好分道扬镳了。你做你认为合适的事情。我——我则按我的意志行动。"

邓布利多的声音里没有丝毫威胁的成分，它听上去仅仅是一个声明，但是福吉气得暴跳如雷，仿佛邓布利多正举着一根魔杖朝他逼近。

"好啊，好啊，邓布利多，"他威胁地挥动着一根手指，说道，"我一直给你充分的自由。我一向对你尊敬有加。我也许并不赞成你的一些决定，但总是保持沉默。没有多少人会允许你聘用狼人，留用海格，或不请示魔法部就擅自决定给学生教什么东西。不过，如果你准备同我对着干——"

"我唯一想要对着干的，"邓布利多说，"是伏地魔。如果你也反对他，康奈利，那么我们还是同一阵营的。"

福吉似乎想不出该如何回答。他的两只小脚站立不稳，前后摇晃了片刻，用双手旋转着他那顶圆顶高帽。

最后，他说话了，声音里有一丝企求的成分，"他不会回来的，邓布利多，他不可能……"

斯内普大步走上前，越过邓布利多，他一边走，一边撩起长袍的左边袖子。他把胳膊伸过去给福吉看，福吉惊骇地向后退缩。

"看看吧，"斯内普声音嘶哑地说，"看看吧，黑魔标记。已经不像一小时前那么明显了，当时它被烧成了焦黑色，不过你仍然能看见。每个食死徒身上都有黑魔王打下的烙印。这是食死徒相互识别的一种方式，也是伏地魔召集我们回到他身边的暗号。当他触摸到某个食死

## CHAPTER THIRTY-SIX    The Parting of the Ways

he touched the Mark of any Death Eater, we were to Disapparate, and Apparate, instantly, at his side. This Mark has been growing clearer all year. Karkaroff's, too. Why do you think Karkaroff fled tonight? We both felt the Mark burn. We both knew he had returned. Karkaroff fears the Dark Lord's vengeance. He betrayed too many of his fellow Death Eaters to be sure of a welcome back into the fold.'

Fudge stepped back from Snape, too. He was shaking his head. He did not seem to have taken in a word Snape had said. He stared, apparently repelled, at the ugly mark on Snape's arm, then looked up at Dumbledore and whispered, 'I don't know what you and your staff are playing at, Dumbledore, but I have heard enough. I have no more to add. I will be in touch with you tomorrow, Dumbledore, to discuss the running of this school. I must return to the Ministry.'

He had almost reached the door when he paused. He turned around, strode back down the dormitory, and stopped at Harry's bed.

'Your winnings,' he said shortly, taking a large bag of gold out of his pocket, and dropping it onto Harry's bedside table. 'One thousand Galleons. There should have been a presentation ceremony, but in the circumstances ...'

He crammed his bowler hat onto his head, and walked out of the room, slamming the door behind him. The moment he had disappeared, Dumbledore turned to look at the group around Harry's bed.

'There is work to be done,' he said. 'Molly ... am I right in thinking that I can count on you and Arthur?'

'Of course you can,' said Mrs. Weasley. She was white to the lips, but she looked resolute. 'He knows what Fudge is. It's Arthur's fondness for Muggles that has held him back at the Ministry all these years. Fudge thinks he lacks proper wizarding pride.'

'Then I need to send a message to him,' said Dumbledore. 'All those that we can persuade of the truth must be notified immediately, and Arthur is well placed to contact those at the Ministry who are not as short-sighted as Cornelius.'

'I'll go to Dad,' said Bill, standing up. 'I'll go now.'

'Excellent,' said Dumbledore. 'Tell him what has happened. Tell him I will be in direct contact with him shortly. He will need to be discreet, however. If Fudge thinks I am interfering at the Ministry –'

'Leave it to me,' said Bill.

## 第36章 分道扬镳

徒的标记时，我们必须立即幻影移形，出现在他身边。一年来，这个标记越来越明显了。卡卡洛夫的也是这样。你说卡卡洛夫今晚为什么要逃跑？我们俩都感到标记在火辣辣地灼烧。我们都知道他回来了。卡卡洛夫害怕伏地魔会报复他。他背叛了他的许多食死徒同伴，肯定没有人欢迎他回到他们中间。"

福吉又从斯内普面前退了回去。他不停地摇着脑袋，似乎根本没有听清斯内普说的话。他瞪大眼睛，显然被斯内普胳膊上那丑陋的标记吓坏了，接着他抬头望着邓布利多，小声说道："我不知道你和你的人在玩什么把戏，邓布利多，但是我已经听够了。我不想再说什么。我明天再跟你联系，邓布利多，讨论这所学校的办学方式。我必须回魔法部去了。"

他走到门边又停住脚步，回过身来，大步走过房间，停在哈利床边。

"你赢得的奖金，"他简短地说，一边从口袋里掏出一大袋金币，扔在哈利的床头柜上，"一千个金加隆。本来应该有一个颁奖仪式的，但在目前这种情况下……"

他把圆顶高帽套在头上，走出了房间，把门在身后重重地关上了。他刚离开，邓布利多就转身望着哈利床边的一群人。

"有一些工作要做，"他说，"莫丽……如果我没有弄错的话，我是可以指望你和亚瑟的吧？"

"当然没问题。"韦斯莱夫人说，她脸色煞白，嘴唇也全无血色，但表情十分坚决，"他了解福吉是什么样的人。亚瑟就因为喜欢麻瓜，才阻碍了自己这些年在魔法部的发展。福吉认为亚瑟缺乏一个巫师应有的尊严。"

"好吧，我需要送一封信给亚瑟，"邓布利多说，"对所有那些能够在我们的说服下认清局势的人，我们都必须立即予以通知，亚瑟可以接触到魔法部那些不像康奈利这样目光短浅的人。"

"我去找爸爸，"比尔说着，站了起来，"现在就去。"

"太好了，"邓布利多说，"把发生的事情都告诉他，说我很快就会跟他直接联系。不过他必须谨慎行事。如果福吉认为我在插手魔法部——"

"没问题，交给我吧。"比尔说。

## CHAPTER THIRTY-SIX   The Parting of the Ways

He clapped a hand on Harry's shoulder, kissed his mother on the cheek, pulled on his cloak, and strode quickly from the room.

'Minerva,' said Dumbledore, turning to Professor McGonagall, 'I want to see Hagrid in my office as soon as possible. Also – if she will consent to come – Madame Maxime.'

Professor McGonagall nodded, and left without a word.

'Poppy,' Dumbledore said to Madam Pomfrey, 'would you be very kind, and go down to Professor Moody's office, where I think you will find a house-elf called Winky in considerable distress? Do what you can for her, and take her back to the kitchens. I think Dobby will look after her for us.'

'Very – very well,' said Madam Pomfrey, looking startled, and she too left.

Dumbledore made sure that the door was closed, and that Madam Pomfrey's footsteps had died away, before he spoke again.

'And now,' he said, 'it is time for two of our number to recognise each other for what they are. Sirius ... if you could resume your usual form.'

The great black dog looked up at Dumbledore, then, in an instant, turned back into a man.

Mrs. Weasley screamed and leapt back from the bed.

'Sirius Black!' she shrieked, pointing at him.

'Mum, shut up!' Ron yelled. 'It's OK!'

Snape had not yelled or jumped backwards, but the look on his face was one of mingled fury and horror.

'Him!' he snarled, staring at Sirius, whose face showed equal dislike. 'What is he doing here?'

'He is here at my invitation,' said Dumbledore, looking between them, 'as are you, Severus. I trust you both. It is time for you to lay aside your old differences, and trust each other.'

Harry thought Dumbledore was asking for a near miracle. Sirius and Snape were eyeing each other with the utmost loathing.

'I will settle, in the short term,' said Dumbledore, with a bite of impatience in his voice, 'for a lack of open hostility. You will shake hands. You are on the same side now. Time is short, and unless the few of us who know the truth stand united, there is no hope for any of us.'

Very slowly – but still glaring at each other as though each wished the other nothing but ill – Sirius and Snape moved towards each other, and

## 第36章 分道扬镳

他伸手拍拍哈利的肩膀，又吻了吻母亲的面颊，然后穿上斗篷，大步流星地走出了房间。

"米勒娃，"邓布利多转向麦格教授，说，"我想尽快在我的办公室见到海格。还有——马克西姆女士——如果她也愿意来的话。"

麦格教授点点头，一言不发地离去了。

"波比，"邓布利多对庞弗雷女士说，"劳驾，你能不能到穆迪教授的办公室去一趟？你在那里会找到一位痛不欲生、名叫闪闪的家养小精灵。你尽量安慰安慰她，然后把她带到下面的厨房里。我认为多比会替我们照顾她的。"

"好——好吧。"庞弗雷女士显得有些吃惊，随即也离去了。

邓布利多确信门已经关好，庞弗雷女士的脚步声已经远去，才又开口说话。

"现在，"他说，"我们中间的两个人可以互相认识彼此的真面目了。小天狼星……你能不能变回你平常的样子？"

大黑狗抬头看了看邓布利多，然后摇身一变，成了一个男人。

韦斯莱夫人惊叫一声，从床边直往后退。

"小天狼星布莱克！"她指着他，尖声叫道。

"妈妈，闭嘴！"罗恩喊道，"这没什么！"

斯内普没有惊叫，也没有退缩，但脸上的表情混杂着愤怒和恐惧。

"他！"他瞪着小天狼星，气冲冲地咆哮道——小天狼星的脸上也露出同样厌恶的表情，"他在这里做什么？"

"我邀请他的，"邓布利多轮番望着他俩，说道，"你也一样，西弗勒斯。你们两个我都很信任。现在你们应该抛弃昔日的分歧,互相信任。"

哈利认为邓布利多简直是在请求奇迹发生。小天狼星和斯内普恶狠狠地盯着对方，脸上都是仇恨到极点的表情。

"在短时期内，"邓布利多说，语气里透着一丝不耐烦，"只要你们不公开敌视对方，我就满意了。你们不妨握握手。现在你们属于同一阵营了。时间紧张，我们少数几个知道真相的人必须团结一致，否则大家都毫无希望。"

小天狼星和斯内普很慢很慢地走上前，握了握手，但仍然恶狠狠

## CHAPTER THIRTY-SIX    The Parting of the Ways

shook hands. They let go extremely quickly.

'That will do to be going on with,' said Dumbledore, stepping between them once more. 'Now I have work for each of you. Fudge's attitude, though not unexpected, changes everything. Sirius, I need you to set off at once. You are to alert Remus Lupin, Arabella Figg, Mundungus Fletcher – the old crowd. Lie low at Lupin's for a while, I will contact you there.'

'But –' said Harry.

He wanted Sirius to stay. He did not want to say goodbye again so quickly.

'You'll see me very soon, Harry,' said Sirius, turning to him. 'I promise you. But I must do what I can, you understand, don't you?'

'Yeah,' said Harry. 'Yeah ... of course I do.'

Sirius grasped his hand briefly, nodded to Dumbledore, transformed again into the black dog, and ran the length of the room to the door, whose handle he turned with a paw. Then he was gone.

'Severus,' said Dumbledore, turning to Snape, 'you know what I must ask you to do. If you are ready ... if you are prepared ...'

'I am,' said Snape.

He looked slightly paler than usual, and his cold, black eyes glittered strangely.

'Then, good luck,' said Dumbledore, and he watched, with a trace of apprehension on his face, as Snape swept wordlessly after Sirius.

It was several minutes before Dumbledore spoke again.

'I must go downstairs,' he said finally. 'I must see the Diggorys. Harry – take the rest of your potion. I will see all of you later.'

Harry slumped back against his pillows as Dumbledore disappeared. Hermione, Ron and Mrs. Weasley were all looking at him. None of them spoke for a very long time.

'You've got to take the rest of your potion, Harry,' Mrs. Weasley said at last. Her hand nudged the sack of gold on his bedside cabinet as she reached for the bottle and the goblet. 'You have a good long sleep. Try and think about something else for a while ... think about what you're going to buy with your winnings!'

'I don't want that gold,' said Harry in an expressionless voice. 'You have it. Anyone can have it. I shouldn't have won it. It should've been Cedric's.'

The thing against which he had been fighting on and off ever since he

## 第36章 分道扬镳

地互相瞪着，似乎都希望对方遭到厄运。他们很快就把手松开了。

"这样还差不多。"邓布利多说着，又一次挡在他们俩之间，"现在你们俩都有任务。福吉的态度尽管我们也有所预料，但改变了整个事态。小天狼星，我需要你立即出发。你去通知莱姆斯·卢平、阿拉贝拉·费格、蒙顿格斯·弗莱奇——那几个老朋友。你暂时隐蔽在卢平那里，我会到那里跟你联系。"

"可是——"哈利说。

他真希望小天狼星能留下来。他不想这么快就跟他告别。

"你很快就会见到我的，哈利，"小天狼星转过头，对他说道，"我向你保证。但我必须尽我的一点儿力量，你明白的，是吗？"

"是，"哈利说，"是的……我当然明白。"

小天狼星很快地握了握他的手，朝邓布利多点点头，然后又变成了黑狗，跑到门边，用一只爪子拧开门把手，转眼就不见了。

"西弗勒斯，"邓布利多转向斯内普，说，"你知道我要吩咐你做什么。如果你没意见……如果你准备好了……"

"没问题。"斯内普说。

他的脸色显得比往常更苍白了，冷冰冰的黑眼睛闪烁着怪异的光。

"那么，祝你好运。"邓布利多说，脸上带着一丝担忧，望着斯内普一言不发地尾随小天狼星而去。

又过了几分钟，邓布利多才开口说话。

"我必须到楼下去，"他最后说道，"我必须见见迪戈里夫妇。哈利——把剩下的药水都喝了。我过一会儿再来看望你们大家。"

邓布利多离去了，哈利无力地倒在枕头上。赫敏、罗恩和韦斯莱夫人都望着他，良久没有人说话。

"你必须把剩下的药水都喝下去，哈利。"最后韦斯莱夫人说道。她伸手取药瓶和高脚杯时，轻轻推了推床头柜上的那袋金币。"踏踏实实地睡一觉。暂时想点儿别的事情……想想你准备用奖金买些什么！"

"我不要这些金币，"哈利淡淡地说，声音里毫无热情，"你拿去吧。谁都可以拿去。我不应该赢得它们。它应该属于塞德里克。"

这时，他离开迷宫后一直拼命压抑、拼命克制的情感，一下子全

## CHAPTER THIRTY-SIX    The Parting of the Ways

had come out of the maze was threatening to overpower him. He could feel a burning, prickling feeling in the inner corners of his eyes. He blinked and stared up at the ceiling.

'It wasn't your fault, Harry,' Mrs. Weasley whispered.

'I told him to take the Cup with me,' said Harry.

Now the burning feeling was in his throat, too. He wished Ron would look away.

Mrs. Weasley set the potion down on the bedside cabinet, bent down, and put her arms around Harry. He had no memory of ever being hugged like this, as though by a mother. The full weight of everything he had seen that night seemed to fall in upon him as Mrs. Weasley held him to her. His mother's face, his father's voice, the sight of Cedric, dead on the ground, all started spinning in his head until he could hardly bear it, until he was screwing up his face against the howl of misery fighting to get out of him.

There was a loud slamming noise, and Mrs. Weasley and Harry broke apart. Hermione was standing by the window. She was holding something tight in her hand.

'Sorry,' she whispered.

'Your potion, Harry,' said Mrs. Weasley quickly, wiping her eyes on the back of her hand.

Harry drank it in one. The effect was instantaneous. Heavy, irresistible waves of dreamless sleep broke over him, he fell back onto his pillows, and thought no more.

部袭上心头,使他快要不能自已。他感到内眼角一阵火辣辣的刺痛。他使劲眨眨眼皮,瞪着上面的天花板。

"这不是你的错,哈利。"韦斯莱夫人轻声说。

"是我叫他和我一起去拿奖杯的。"哈利说。

现在那种火辣辣的感觉又跑到了他的喉咙里。他真希望罗恩把目光移开。

韦斯莱夫人把药水放在床头柜上,弯下腰,伸手搂住哈利。哈利从不记得有谁这样搂抱过自己,就像母亲一样。当韦斯莱夫人把他拥在怀中时,他那天晚上目睹的一切似乎全都沉沉地压在了他的心头。母亲的面庞,父亲的声音,塞德里克倒地死去的身影,似乎都开始在他的脑海里飞舞旋转。最后他简直受不了了,拼命拧着面孔,把那竭力冲破喉咙爆发出来的痛苦吼叫强压下去。

突然,传来了很响的拍打声,韦斯莱夫人和哈利赶忙分开了。赫敏站在窗户边,手里紧紧握着什么东西。

"对不起。"她低声说。

"你的药,哈利。"韦斯莱夫人赶紧说道,一边用手背擦了擦眼睛。

哈利一口把药水喝光了。效果立竿见影。沉重的、不可抗拒的无梦的酣睡立刻把他笼罩;他跌回到枕头上,什么也不想了。

## CHAPTER THIRTY-SEVEN

# The Beginning

When he looked back, even a month later, Harry found he had few memories of the following days. It was as though he had been through too much to take in any more. The recollections he did have were very painful. The worst, perhaps, was the meeting with the Diggorys that took place the following morning.

They did not blame him for what had happened; on the contrary, both thanked him for returning Cedric's body to them. Mr. Diggory sobbed through most of the interview. Mrs. Diggory's grief seemed to be beyond tears.

'He suffered very little, then,' she said, when Harry had told her how Cedric had died. 'And after all, Amos ... he died just when he'd won the Tournament. He must have been happy.'

When they had got to their feet, she looked down at Harry and said, 'You look after yourself, now.'

Harry seized the sack of gold on the bedside table.

'You take this,' he muttered to her. 'It should've been Cedric's, he got there first, you take it —'

But she backed away from him. 'Oh, no, it's yours, dear, we couldn't ... you keep it.'

\* \* \*

Harry returned to Gryffindor Tower the following evening. From what Hermione and Ron told him, Dumbledore had spoken to the school that morning at breakfast. He had merely requested that they leave Harry alone, that nobody ask him questions or badger him to tell the story of what had happened in the maze. Most people, he noticed, were skirting him in the corridors, avoiding his eyes. Some whispered behind their hands as he passed.

## 第 37 章

## 开　始

**即**使一个月后回想起来，哈利对后来几天的记忆也只是零散的片段。就好像他经历的事情太多，把脑子都塞满了，再也记不住任何事情。他零星记得的那些片段十分惨痛。最令人心痛的莫过于他第二天上午与迪戈里夫妇的见面。

他们没有因为所发生的事情而责怪哈利；相反，他们都感谢哈利把塞德里克的遗体带给了他们。在见面中，迪戈里先生大部分时间都在无声地哭泣，而迪戈里夫人已经伤心得欲哭无泪了。

"那么，他并没有受多少痛苦。"迪戈里夫人听哈利讲了塞德里克的死亡经过，说道，"不管怎么说，阿莫斯……他死的时候刚赢得三强杯。他一定是很高兴的。"

当他们起身准备离开时，迪戈里夫人低头望着哈利，说："你也好好保重吧。"

哈利抓起床头柜上的那袋金币。

"你们拿去吧，"他喃喃地对她说，"这应该属于塞德里克，是他先到达的，你们拿去吧——"

但是迪戈里夫人后退着闪开了。"哦，不行，亲爱的，我不能……你留着吧。"

第二天晚上，哈利回到了格兰芬多塔楼。据赫敏和罗恩说，邓布利多那天早上吃早饭时对全校师生讲了几句话。他只是要求大家别去打扰哈利，不许任何人问他问题，或缠着他讲述那天在迷宫里发生的事情。哈利注意到，大多数人在走廊里都绕着他走，避开他的目光。

## CHAPTER THIRTY-SEVEN  The Beginning

He guessed that many of them had believed Rita Skeeter's article about how disturbed and possibly dangerous he was. Perhaps they were formulating their own theories about how Cedric had died. He found he didn't care very much. He liked it best when he was with Ron and Hermione, and they were talking about other things, or else letting him sit in silence while they played chess. He felt as though all three of them had reached an understanding they didn't need to put into words; that each was waiting for some sign, some word, of what was going on outside Hogwarts – and that it was useless to speculate about what might be coming until they knew anything for certain. The only time they touched upon the subject was when Ron told Harry about a meeting Mrs. Weasley had had with Dumbledore before going home.

'She went to ask him if you could come straight to us this summer,' he said. 'But he wants you to go back to the Dursleys, at least at first.'

'Why?' said Harry.

'She said Dumbledore's got his reasons,' said Ron, shaking his head darkly. 'I suppose we've got to trust him, haven't we?'

The only person apart from Ron and Hermione that Harry felt able to talk to was Hagrid. As there was no longer a Defence Against the Dark Arts teacher, they had those lessons free. They used the one on Thursday afternoon to go down and visit him in his cabin. It was a bright and sunny day; Fang bounded out of the open door as they approached, barking and wagging his tail madly.

'Who's that?' called Hagrid, coming to the door. *'Harry!'*

He strode out to meet them, pulled Harry into a one-armed hug, ruffled his hair and said, 'Good ter see yeh, mate. Good ter see yeh.'

They saw two bucket-sized cups and saucers on the wooden table in front of the fireplace when they entered Hagrid's cabin.

'Bin havin' a cuppa with Olympe,' Hagrid said, 'she's jus' left.'

'Who?' said Ron, curiously.

'Madame Maxime, o' course!' said Hagrid.

'You two made it up, have you?' said Ron.

'Dunno what yeh're talkin' about,' said Hagrid airily, fetching more cups from the dresser. When he had made tea, and offered round a plate of doughy biscuits, he leant back in his chair and surveyed Harry closely through his beetle-black eyes.

## 第37章 开　始

有些人在他走过时用手捂着嘴，互相窃窃私语。他猜想，他们许多人都相信了丽塔·斯基特的文章，认为他心理不正常，很可能是个危险人物。也许，对于塞德里克是怎么死的，他们都有自己的想法。但哈利发现他并不怎么在乎。他最喜欢跟罗恩和赫敏在一起，谈论其他话题，或者罗恩和赫敏自己下棋，让他一个人静静坐着。他觉得他们三个似乎已达到一种默契，已不需要用语言来表达；每个人都在等待某种信号或只言片语，告诉他们霍格沃茨外面发生的事情——在没有得到确切消息之前，对未来作种种推测都毫无用处。他们只有一次触及这个话题，那是罗恩对哈利讲述韦斯莱夫人回家前与邓布利多见面的经过。

"妈妈去问邓布利多，你今年夏天能不能直接到我们家去，"罗恩说，"但邓布利多还是希望你回德思礼家，至少是先回他们那里。"

"为什么？"哈利问。

"妈妈说邓布利多有他自己的道理，"罗恩说着，愁闷地摇了摇头，"我想我们必须得相信他，对吗？"

除了罗恩和赫敏，哈利觉得还能与之交谈的就是海格了。现在黑魔法防御术课没有了，他们可以自由处置那些课时。于是，他们就利用星期四下午的一节课，到下面海格的小屋去拜访他。那是一个明媚的艳阳天，他们刚一走近，牙牙就从敞开的门里跳了出来，激动地叫着，摇晃着尾巴。

"谁呀？"海格一边问，一边走到门口，"哈利！"

他大步赶过来迎接他们，用一只粗胳膊把哈利使劲搂了一下，又胡噜胡噜哈利的头发，说道："见到你真高兴，伙计。见到你真高兴。"

他们走进海格的小屋，看见火炉前的木桌子上放着两套水桶大小的茶杯和茶托。

"和奥利姆喝了杯茶，"海格说，"她刚走。"

"谁？"罗恩好奇地问。

"马克西姆女士呀，那还用说！"海格说。

"哦，你们俩和好了？"罗恩说。

"不明白你在说什么。"海格快活地说，一边又从碗柜里拿出几个杯子。他沏好茶，端来一盘岩皮饼分给大家，然后靠在椅子上，用黑溜溜的眼睛仔细打量着哈利。

## CHAPTER THIRTY-SEVEN    The Beginning

'You all righ'?' he said gruffly.

'Yeah,' said Harry.

'No, yeh're not,' said Hagrid. ''Course yeh're not. But yeh will be.'

Harry said nothing.

'Knew he was goin' ter come back,' said Hagrid, and Harry, Ron and Hermione looked up at him, shocked. 'Known it fer years, Harry. Knew he was out there, bidin' his time. It had ter happen. Well, now it has, an' we'll jus' have ter get on with it. We'll fight. Migh' be able ter stop him before he gets a good hold. That's Dumbledore's plan, anyway. Great man, Dumbledore. S'long as we've got him, I'm not too worried.'

Hagrid raised his bushy eyebrows at the disbelieving expressions on their faces.

'No good sittin' worryin' abou' it,' he said. 'What's comin' will come, an' we'll meet it when it does. Dumbledore told me wha' you did, Harry.'

Hagrid's chest swelled as he looked at Harry. 'Yeh did as much as yer father would've done, an' I can' give yeh no higher praise than that.'

Harry smiled back at him. It was the first time he'd smiled in days.

'What's Dumbledore asked you to do, Hagrid?' he asked. 'He sent Professor McGonagall to ask you and Madame Maxime to meet him ... that night.'

'Got a little job fer me over the summer,' said Hagrid. 'Secret, though. I'm not s'posed ter talk abou' it, not even ter you lot. Olympe – Madame Maxime ter you – might be comin' with me. I think she will. Think I got her persuaded.'

'Is it to do with Voldemort?'

Hagrid flinched at the sound of the name.

'Migh' be,' he said evasively. 'Now ... who'd like ter come an' visit the las' Skrewt with me? I was jokin' – jokin'!' he added hastily, seeing the looks on their faces.

It was with a heavy heart that Harry packed his trunk up in the dormitory, on the night before his return to Privet Drive. He was dreading the Leaving Feast, which was usually a cause for celebration, when the winner of the Inter-House Championship would be announced. He had avoided being in the Great Hall when it was full ever since he had left the hospital wing,

## 第37章 开 始

"你挺好吧?"他粗声粗气地问。

"挺好。"哈利说。

"不对,你不好,"海格说,"你肯定不好。不过你会好的。"

哈利什么也没说。

"我就知道他会回来的,"海格说,哈利、罗恩和赫敏都吃惊地抬头望着他,"这么些年我一直知道,哈利。我知道他在那里,等待时机。这件事肯定是要发生的。好了,现在它发生了,我们必须承认现实。我们要战斗。我们可以阻止他获得权力、称霸天下。那是邓布利多的计划。邓布利多,他真是个了不起的人啊。只要有他在,我就不怎么担心。"

看到他们三个人脸上怀疑的表情,海格扬起乱蓬蓬的眉毛。

"坐着干着急是没有用的,"他说,"该来的总归会来,一旦来了,我们就接受。哈利,邓布利多把你做的事情都告诉我了。"

海格望着哈利,胸膛剧烈地起伏着。"你父亲如果还活着,他也会这么做的,这就是我对你的最高赞扬。"

哈利也对海格报以微笑。这是他这些日子来脸上第一次露出笑容。

"邓布利多叫你做什么,海格?"他问,"那天晚上,他派麦格教授来请你和马克西姆女士去见他。"

"给我这个夏天找点儿活干,"海格说,"不过,是保密的。我不能说,即使对你们也不能说。奥利姆——就是你们说的马克西姆女士——可能会和我一起干。我想她会的,看样子我已经把她说服了。"

"与伏地魔有关吗?"

海格听到这个名字,畏惧地向后缩了一下。

"大概吧,"他含糊其词地说,"好了……谁愿意跟我去看看最后一条炸尾螺?我在开玩笑——开玩笑!"看到他们脸上的神情,他又急忙加了一句。

在返回女贞路的前一天夜里,哈利在宿舍里收拾箱子时,心情十分沉重。他害怕离校宴会,这通常被搞成一种庆祝活动,将宣布学院杯冠军的得主。自从他离开病房后,就一直避免在人多的时候进入礼堂。他情愿在别人几乎都走光时再进去吃饭,就是为了躲避同学们凝视的

## CHAPTER THIRTY-SEVEN    The Beginning

preferring to eat when it was nearly empty, to avoid the stares of his fellow students.

When he, Ron and Hermione entered the Hall, they saw at once that the usual decorations were missing. The Great Hall was normally decorated with the winning house's colours for the Leaving Feast. Tonight, however, there were black drapes on the wall behind the teachers' table. Harry knew instantly that they were there as a mark of respect for Cedric.

The real Mad-Eye Moody was at the staff table, his wooden leg and his magical eye back in place. He was extremely twitchy, jumping every time someone spoke to him. Harry couldn't blame him; Moody's fear of attack was bound to have been increased by his ten-month imprisonment in his own trunk. Professor Karkaroff's chair was empty. Harry wondered, as he sat down with the other Gryffindors, where Karkaroff was now; whether Voldemort had caught up with him.

Madame Maxime was still there. She was sitting next to Hagrid. They were talking quietly together. Further along the table, sitting next to Professor McGonagall, was Snape. His eyes lingered on Harry for a moment as Harry looked at him. His expression was difficult to read. He looked as sour and unpleasant as ever. Harry continued to watch him, long after Snape had looked away.

What was it that Snape had done on Dumbledore's orders, the night that Voldemort had returned? And why ... *why* ... was Dumbledore so convinced that Snape was truly on their side? He had been their spy, Dumbledore had said so in the Pensieve. Snape had turned spy against Voldemort, 'at great personal risk'. Was that the job he had taken up again? Had he made contact with the Death Eaters, perhaps? Pretended that he had never really gone over to Dumbledore, that he had been, like Voldemort himself, biding his time?

Harry's musings were ended by Professor Dumbledore, who stood up at the staff table. The Great Hall, which in any case had been less noisy than it usually was at the Leaving Feast, became very quiet.

'The end,' said Dumbledore, looking around at them all, 'of another year.'

He paused, and his eyes fell upon the Hufflepuff table. Theirs had been the most subdued table before he had got to his feet, and theirs were still the saddest and palest faces in the Hall.

'There is much that I would like to say to you all tonight,' said

## 第37章 开 始

目光。

当他和罗恩、赫敏走进礼堂时,一眼就发现平常的那些装饰物都不见了。往常的离校宴会上,礼堂都用获胜学院的色彩装饰一新。然而今晚,教工桌子后面的墙壁上悬挂着黑色的帷幕。哈利立刻就明白了,这是对塞德里克表示敬意。

真正的疯眼汉穆迪现在坐在教工桌子旁,他的木腿和那个带魔法的眼球都回到了原来的位置。他显得特别紧张不安,每当有人跟他说话,他就惊跳起来。哈利知道这不能怪他。穆迪在自己的箱子里关了十个月,这肯定加重了他担心遭人袭击的恐惧。卡卡洛夫的座位空着。哈利一边和其他格兰芬多同学一起坐下,一边暗想不知卡卡洛夫此刻在哪里,不知伏地魔有没有抓住他。

马克西姆女士还在,就坐在海格旁边。他们正悄声谈论着什么。在桌子那边,坐在麦格教授身边的是斯内普。当哈利望着他时,他的目光在哈利身上停留了片刻。他的表情很难捉摸。看上去还像以前一样阴沉、讨厌。哈利在斯内普移开目光后,仍然注视了他很长时间。

在伏地魔回来的那天夜里,斯内普遵照邓布利多的命令做了什么?还有,为什么……为什么……邓布利多这样确信斯内普真的与他们站在一边?他曾经是他们这边的密探,邓布利多在冥想盆里曾经这么说过。斯内普变成了专门对付伏地魔的密探,"冒着极大的生命危险"。难道他重操旧业,又干起了这份工作?他也许与食死徒们联系上了?假装自己从来没有真正投靠过邓布利多,而是像伏地魔本人那样一直潜伏着,等待时机?

哈利正想得出神,邓布利多教授突然从教工桌子旁站了起来,打断了他的思路。礼堂里本来就比平常的离校宴会安静许多,这时更是鸦雀无声。

"又是一年,"邓布利多望着大家说道,"结束了。"

他停下话头,目光落在赫奇帕奇的桌子上。在邓布利多站起来之前,这张桌子上的情绪就一直最压抑,桌旁的那一张张面孔也是整个礼堂里最悲哀最苍白的。

"今晚,我有许多话要对你们大家说,"邓布利多说,"但我首先必

## CHAPTER THIRTY-SEVEN    The Beginning

Dumbledore, 'but I must first acknowledge the loss of a very fine person, who should be sitting here' – he gestured towards the Hufflepuffs – 'enjoying our Feast with us. I would like you all, please, to stand, and raise your glasses, to Cedric Diggory.'

They did it, all of them; the benches scraped as everyone in the Hall stood, and raised their goblets, and echoed, in one loud, low, rumbling voice, 'Cedric Diggory.'

Harry caught a glimpse of Cho through the crowd. There were tears pouring silently down her face. He looked down at the table as they all sat down again.

'Cedric was a person who exemplified many of the qualities which distinguish Hufflepuff house,' Dumbledore continued. 'He was a good and loyal friend, a hard worker, he valued fair play. His death has affected you all, whether you knew him well or not. I think that you have the right, therefore, to know exactly how it came about.'

Harry raised his head, and stared at Dumbledore.

'Cedric Diggory was murdered by Lord Voldemort.'

A panicked whisper swept the Great Hall. People were staring at Dumbledore in disbelief, in horror. He looked perfectly calm as he watched them mutter themselves into silence.

'The Ministry of Magic,' Dumbledore continued, 'does not wish me to tell you this. It is possible that some of your parents will be horrified that I have done so – either because they will not believe that Lord Voldemort has returned, or because they think I should not tell you so, young as you are. It is my belief, however, that the truth is generally preferable to lies, and that any attempt to pretend that Cedric died as the result of an accident, or some sort of blunder of his own, is an insult to his memory.'

Stunned and frightened, every face in the Hall was turned towards Dumbledore now ... or almost every face. Over at the Slytherin table, Harry saw Draco Malfoy muttering something to Crabbe and Goyle. Harry felt a hot, sick swoop of anger in his stomach. He forced himself to look back at Dumbledore.

'There is somebody else who must be mentioned in connection with Cedric's death,' Dumbledore went on. 'I am talking, of course, about Harry Potter.'

A kind of ripple crossed the Great Hall, as a few heads turned in Harry's

## 第 37 章 开 始

须沉痛地宣告，我们失去了一位很好的人，他本来应该坐在这里，"他指了指赫奇帕奇的同学们，"和我们一起享受这顿晚宴。我希望大家都站起来，举杯向塞德里克·迪戈里致敬。"

大家都这样做了，所有的人。大家纷纷起立，礼堂里响起一片凳子移动的声音。他们都举起高脚酒杯，用低沉浑厚的嗓音齐声说："塞德里克·迪戈里。"

哈利透过人群瞥见了秋·张。泪珠无声地顺着她的面颊滚落。大家重新坐下来时，哈利也沉痛地低头望着桌子。

"塞德里克充分体现了赫奇帕奇学院特有的品质，"邓布利多继续说道，"他是一位善良、忠诚的朋友，一位勤奋刻苦的学生，他崇尚公平竞争。他的死使你们大家受到震撼，不管你们是否认识他。因此，我认为你们有权了解究竟是怎么回事。"

哈利抬起头，望着邓布利多。

"塞德里克·迪戈里是被伏地魔杀死的。"

礼堂里响起一片惊慌的低语。大家都惊恐地、不敢相信地盯着邓布利多。邓布利多则显得十分平静，望着他们的嘀咕声渐渐归于沉默。

"魔法部不希望我告诉你们这些。"邓布利多继续说，"有些同学的家长可能会对我的做法感到震惊——这或者是因为他们不能相信伏地魔真的回来了，或者是因为他们认为我不应该把这件事告诉你们，毕竟你们年纪还小。然而我相信，说真话永远比撒谎要好，如果我们试图把塞德里克的死说成是一场意外事故，或归咎于他自己的粗心大意，那都是对他形象的一种侮辱。"

这时，礼堂里的每一张脸都朝着邓布利多，每一张脸上都写着震惊与恐惧……噢，并不是每一张脸。哈利看见在斯莱特林的桌子上，德拉科·马尔福正在跟克拉布和高尔窃窃私语些什么。哈利感到内心突然涌起一股火辣辣的怒气。他强迫自己把目光转回到邓布利多身上。

"在谈到塞德里克的死时，还必须提及另外一个人，"邓布利多继续往下说，"当然，我说的是哈利·波特。"

礼堂里起了一阵波动，有几个人把头转向哈利，随即又赶紧转回去，

## CHAPTER THIRTY-SEVEN    The Beginning

direction before flicking back to face Dumbledore.

'Harry Potter managed to escape Lord Voldemort,' said Dumbledore. 'He risked his own life to return Cedric's body to Hogwarts. He showed, in every respect, the sort of bravery that few wizards have ever shown in facing Lord Voldemort, and for this, I honour him.'

Dumbledore turned gravely to Harry, and raised his goblet once more. Nearly everyone in the Great Hall followed suit. They murmured his name, as they had murmured Cedric's, and drank to him. But, through a gap in the standing figures, Harry saw that Malfoy, Crabbe, Goyle and many of the other Slytherins had remained defiantly in their seats, their goblets untouched. Dumbledore, who after all possessed no magical eye, did not see them.

When everyone had once again resumed their seats, Dumbledore continued, 'The Triwizard Tournament's aim was to further and promote magical understanding. In the light of what has happened – of Lord Voldemort's return – such ties are more important than ever before.'

Dumbledore looked from Madame Maxime and Hagrid, to Fleur Delacour and her fellow Beauxbatons students, to Viktor Krum and the Durmstrangs at the Slytherin table. Krum, Harry saw, looked wary, almost frightened, as though he expected Dumbledore to say something harsh.

'Every guest in this Hall,' said Dumbledore, and his eyes lingered upon the Durmstrang students, 'will be welcomed back here, at any time, should they wish to come. I say to you all, once again – in the light of Lord Voldemort's return, we are only as strong as we are united, as weak as we are divided.

'Lord Voldemort's gift for spreading discord and enmity is very great. We can fight it only by showing an equally strong bond of friendship and trust. Differences of habit and language are nothing at all if our aims are identical and our hearts are open.

'It is my belief – and never have I so hoped that I am mistaken – that we are all facing dark and difficult times. Some of you, in this Hall, have already suffered directly at the hands of Lord Voldemort. Many of your families have been torn asunder. A week ago, a student was taken from our midst.

'Remember Cedric. Remember, if the time should come when you have to make a choice between what is right, and what is easy, remember what happened to a boy who was good, and kind, and brave, because he strayed

## 第37章 开 始

望着邓布利多。

"哈利·波特逃脱了伏地魔的魔爪,"邓布利多说,"他冒着生命危险,把塞德里克的遗体带回了霍格沃茨。他在各方面都表现出了大无畏的精神,很少有巫师在面对伏地魔的淫威时能表现出这种精神,为此,我向他表示敬意。"

邓布利多严肃地转向哈利,又一次举起了他的高脚酒杯。礼堂里的人几乎都这么做了。他们像刚才念叨塞德里克的名字一样,低声说着哈利的名字,为他敬酒。但是,哈利透过纷纷起立的人群的缝隙,看见马尔福、克拉布和高尔,以及斯莱特林的许多人都固执地坐着没动,碰也没碰他们的酒杯。邓布利多毕竟没有魔眼,没有看见他们的举动。

大家再次落座后,邓布利多又说道:"三强争霸赛的目的是增强和促进魔法界的相互了解。鉴于目前所发生的事——伏地魔又回来了——这种联系比以往任何时候都更重要。"

邓布利多看看马克西姆女士和海格,看看芙蓉·德拉库尔和她那些布斯巴顿的校友,又看看斯莱特林桌子旁的威克多尔·克鲁姆和德姆斯特朗的同学。哈利看到,克鲁姆显得很紧张,甚至有些害怕,似乎以为邓布利多会说出一些严厉的话来。

"这个礼堂里的每一位客人,"邓布利多说,把目光停留在德姆斯特朗的同学们身上,"只要愿意回来,任何时候都会受到欢迎。我再对你们大家说一遍——鉴于伏地魔又回来了,我们只有团结才会强大;如果分裂,便不堪一击。

"伏地魔制造冲突和敌意的手段十分高明。我们只有表现出同样牢不可破的友谊和信任,才能与之抗争到底。只要我们目标一致,敞开心胸,习惯和语言的差异都不会成为障碍。

"我相信——我真希望我是弄错了——我相信我们都将面临黑暗和艰难的时期。在这个礼堂里,你们中间的有些人已经直接受到伏地魔毒手的残害。你们许多家庭被弄得四分五裂。一星期前,我们中间的一位同学被夺去了生命。

"请记住塞德里克。当你们不得不在正道和捷径之间做出选择时,请不要忘记一个正直、善良、勇敢的男孩,就因为与伏地魔的不期而遇,

## CHAPTER THIRTY-SEVEN   The Beginning

across the path of Lord Voldemort. Remember Cedric Diggory.'

Harry's trunk was packed; Hedwig was back in her cage on top of it. He, Ron and Hermione were waiting in the crowded Entrance Hall with the rest of the fourth-years for the carriages that would take them back to Hogsmeade station. It was another beautiful summer's day. He supposed that Privet Drive would be hot and leafy, its flowerbeds a riot of colour, when he arrived there that evening. The thought gave him no pleasure at all.

"'Arry!'

He looked around. Fleur Delacour was hurrying up the stone steps into the castle. Beyond her, far across the grounds, Harry could see Hagrid helping Madame Maxime to back two of the giant horses into their harness. The Beauxbatons carriage was about to take off.

'We will see each uzzer again, I 'ope,' said Fleur, as she reached him, holding out her hand. 'I am 'oping to get a job 'ere, to improve my Eenglish.'

'It's very good already,' said Ron, in a strangled sort of voice. Fleur smiled at him; Hermione scowled.

'Goodbye, 'Arry,' said Fleur, turning to go. 'It 'az been a pleasure meeting you!'

Harry's spirits couldn't help but lift slightly, as he watched Fleur hurry back across the lawns to Madame Maxime, her silvery hair rippling in the sunlight.

'Wonder how the Durmstrang students are getting back?' said Ron. 'D'you reckon they can steer that ship without Karkaroff?'

'Karkaroff did not steer,' said a gruff voice. 'He stayed in his cabin and let us do the vork.' Krum had come to say goodbye to Hermione. 'Could I have a vord?' he asked her.

'Oh ... yes ... all right,' said Hermione, looking slightly flustered, and following Krum through the crowd and out of sight.

'You'd better hurry up!' Ron called loudly after her. 'The carriages'll be here in a minute!'

He let Harry keep a watch for the carriages, however, and spent the next few minutes craning his neck over the crowd to try and see what Krum and Hermione might be up to. They returned quite soon. Ron stared at Hermione, but her face was impassive.

## 第37章 开 始

就遭到了这样悲惨的厄运。请永远记住塞德里克·迪戈里。"

哈利的箱子已经收拾好了；海德薇也回到了箱子上面它的笼子里。哈利、罗恩、赫敏和四年级的其他同学一起，在拥挤的门厅里等待马车把他们送往霍格莫德车站。这又是一个美丽宜人的夏日。哈利猜想，晚上到达女贞路时，那里肯定很热，院子里枝繁叶茂，花圃里姹紫嫣红的鲜花竞相开放。想到这些，他并没有感到丝毫喜悦。

"哈利！"

他扭头望去。芙蓉·德拉库尔匆匆登上石阶，进入城堡。在她后面的场地那头，哈利可以看见海格正帮着马克西姆女士给两匹巨马套上挽具。布斯巴顿的马车就要出发了。

"希望我们后会有期，"芙蓉走到哈利身边，伸出一只手，说道，"希望我在这里找到一份工作，提高一下我的英语。"

"你的英语已经很棒了。"罗恩声音有些窒息地说。芙蓉朝他微笑着。赫敏在一旁皱起了眉头。

"再见，哈利，"芙蓉说着，转身离开，"这次见到你们十分愉快。"

哈利目送芙蓉匆匆穿过草坪朝马克西姆女士奔去，银亮的头发在阳光下像波浪一般荡漾，他的情绪不由自主地愉快了些。

"不知道德姆斯特朗的同学怎么回去，"罗恩说，"你说，没有了卡卡洛夫，他们还能驾驶那艘船吗？"

"卡卡洛夫并不掌舵，"一个沙哑沉闷的声音说，"他待在舱房里，活儿都由我们来干。"克鲁姆来跟赫敏道别了。"我可以跟你说几句话吗？"他问赫敏。

"噢……可以……好吧。"赫敏说，看起来有点慌乱，跟着克鲁姆穿过人群，不见了。

"你最好快点儿！"罗恩冲着她的背影大声喊道，"马车很快就要来了！"

在接下来的几分钟里，罗恩让哈利留意马车，自己一个劲儿地伸长脖子，想看清克鲁姆和赫敏在做什么。那两人很快就回来了。罗恩盯着赫敏，但赫敏脸上没有什么表情。

## CHAPTER THIRTY-SEVEN  The Beginning

'I liked Diggory,' said Krum abruptly, to Harry. 'He vos alvays polite to me. Alvays. Even though I vos from Durmstrang – with Karkaroff,' he added, scowling.

'Have you got a new Headmaster yet?' said Harry.

Krum shrugged. He held out his hand as Fleur had done, shook Harry's hand and then Ron's.

Ron looked as though he was suffering some sort of painful internal struggle. Krum had already started walking away when Ron burst out, 'Can I have your autograph?'

Hermione turned away, smiling at the horseless carriages which were now trundling towards them up the drive, as Krum, looking surprised, but gratified, signed a fragment of parchment for Ron.

The weather could not have been more different on the journey back to King's Cross than it had been on their way to Hogwarts the previous September. There wasn't a single cloud in the sky. Harry, Ron and Hermione had managed to get a compartment to themselves. Pigwidgeon was once again hidden under Ron's dress robes to stop him hooting continually; Hedwig was dozing, her head under her wing, and Crookshanks was curled up in a spare seat like a large, furry ginger cushion. Harry, Ron and Hermione talked more fully and freely than they had done all week, as the train sped them southwards. Harry felt as though Dumbledore's speech at the Leaving Feast had unblocked him, somehow. It was less painful to discuss what had happened now. They broke off their conversation about what action Dumbledore might be taking even now to stop Voldemort, only when the lunch trolley arrived.

When Hermione returned from the trolley and put her money back into her schoolbag, she dislodged a copy of the *Daily Prophet* which she had been carrying in there.

Harry looked at it, unsure whether he really wanted to know what it might say, but Hermione, seeing him looking at it, said calmly, 'There's nothing in there. You can look for yourself, but there's nothing at all. I've been checking every day. Just a small piece the day after the third task, saying you won the Tournament. They didn't even mention Cedric. Nothing about any of it. If you ask me, Fudge is forcing them to keep quiet.'

## 第37章 开 始

"我一直很喜欢迪戈里,"克鲁姆很唐突地对哈利说,"他总是对我很有礼貌。总是这样。尽管我来自德姆斯特朗——和卡卡洛夫一起。"他皱着眉头补充道。

"你们找到新校长了吗?"哈利问。

克鲁姆耸了耸肩膀。他像芙蓉那样伸出手,与哈利和罗恩分别握了握。

从罗恩的表情看,他的内心似乎正在忍受某种痛苦的挣扎。克鲁姆已经准备走开了,罗恩突然说道:"你能给我签个名吗?"

赫敏转过脸,望着那些没有马拉的马车顺着车道朝他们缓缓驶来,脸上浮现出微笑:克鲁姆显得既惊讶又欣慰,为罗恩在一片羊皮纸上签了名。

在他们返回国王十字车站的路上,天气和他们去年九月来霍格沃茨时完全不同。天空万里无云。哈利、罗恩和赫敏费了半天劲儿,总算找到一个空的包厢,坐了进去。小猪又被罗恩的礼服长袍遮住了,因为它不停地尖声大叫,海德薇脑袋缩在翅膀下打瞌睡,克鲁克山蜷缩在一个空座位上,活像一个大大的、毛茸茸的姜黄色靠垫。火车载着他们向南驶去,哈利、罗恩和赫敏摆脱了一星期来的沉默,畅快淋漓地交谈着。哈利觉得,邓布利多在离校宴会上的讲话,似乎涤荡了他心中的烦忧。此刻再谈论所发生的事情,他不感到那么痛苦了。他们热烈地谈论着邓布利多现在会采取什么措施阻止伏地魔卷土重来,直到送午饭的小推车过来,才停住话头。

赫敏到小推车那里买完饭回来,把钱放回书包,掏出了一份她一直装在书包里的《预言家日报》。

哈利望了望,拿不准自己是否真想知道报纸上说了什么。赫敏见哈利望着报纸,便平静地说:"报上没说什么。你自己可以看看,确实没有什么。我每天都要检查一下。只在第三个项目后的第二天发了一条短消息,说你赢得了三强杯。他们甚至提都没提塞德里克。对这件事只字未报。如果你问我的意见,我认为是福吉强迫他们保持沉默的。"

## CHAPTER THIRTY-SEVEN    The Beginning

'He'll never keep Rita quiet,' said Harry. 'Not on a story like this.'

'Oh, Rita hasn't written anything at all since the third task,' said Hermione, in an oddly constrained voice. 'As a matter of fact,' she added, her voice now trembling slightly, 'Rita Skeeter isn't going to be writing anything at all for a while. Not unless she wants me to spill the beans on her.'

'What are you talking about?' said Ron.

'I found out how she was listening in on private conversations when she wasn't supposed to be coming into the grounds,' said Hermione in a rush.

Harry had the impression that Hermione had been dying to tell them this for days, but that she had restrained herself in the light of everything else that had happened.

'How was she doing it?' said Harry at once.

'How did you find out?' said Ron, staring at her.

'Well, it was you, really, who gave me the idea, Harry,' she said.

'Did I?' said Harry, perplexed. 'How?'

'*Bugging*,' said Hermione happily.

'But you said they didn't work –'

'Oh, not *electronic* bugs,' said Hermione. 'No, you see ... Rita Skeeter' – Hermione's voice trembled with quiet triumph – 'is an unregistered Animagus. She can turn –'

Hermione pulled a small sealed glass jar out of her bag.

'– into a beetle.'

'You're kidding,' said Ron. 'You haven't ... she's not ...'

'Oh, yes she is,' said Hermione happily, brandishing the jar at them.

Inside were a few twigs and leaves, and one large, fat beetle.

'That's never – you're kidding –' Ron whispered, lifting the jar to his eyes.

'No, I'm not,' said Hermione, beaming. 'I caught her on the windowsill in the hospital wing. Look very closely, and you'll notice the markings around her antennae are exactly like those foul glasses she wears.'

Harry looked, and saw that she was quite right. He also remembered something. 'There was a beetle on the statue the night we heard Hagrid

## 第37章 开 始

"他无法使丽塔保持沉默，"哈利说，"丽塔不会放过这样一篇精彩故事的。"

"噢，自从第三个项目之后，丽塔就什么也不写了。"赫敏说，她似乎在拼命克制着什么，语气有些奇怪，"不瞒你们说，"她又说道，声音有些发颤了，"丽塔·斯基特暂时不会再写任何东西了。除非她想让我泄露她的秘密。"

"你在说些什么呀？"罗恩说。

"我终于弄清，她在不应该进入场地时，是怎么偷听到别人的秘密谈话的。"赫敏一口气说道。

哈利有一种感觉，似乎赫敏这些日子来一直渴望把这件事告诉他们，但看到所发生的那么多状况，她只好忍着没说。

"她是怎么做的？"哈利赶忙问道。

"你是怎么弄清的？"罗恩盯着赫敏问。

"咳，其实说起来，还是你给了我灵感呢，哈利。"赫敏说。

"我？"哈利一头雾水，"怎么会呢？"

"窃听。"赫敏快活地说。

"可是你说窃听器不管用——"

"哦，不是电子窃听器，"赫敏说，"是这样……丽塔·斯基特——"赫敏压抑着得意的情绪，声音微微颤抖，"——她是一个没有注册的阿尼马格斯。她能变成——"

赫敏从书包里掏出一只密封的小玻璃罐。

"——变成一只甲虫。"

"你在开玩笑吧，"罗恩说，"你没有……她不会……"

"哦，没错，正是这样。"赫敏高兴地说，一边朝他们挥舞着玻璃罐。玻璃罐里有几根树枝和几片树叶，还有一只胖墩墩的大甲虫。

"那不可能——你在开玩笑——"罗恩把瓶子举到眼前，低声说。

"没有，我没开玩笑，"赫敏满脸喜色地说，"我在病房的窗台上抓住了她。你仔细看看，就会注意到这只甲虫触角周围的记号和她戴的那副难看的眼镜一模一样。"

哈利一看，发现赫敏说得完全正确。他也想起了一些事情。"那天晚上，我们听见海格对马克西姆女士谈起他妈妈时，就有一只甲虫贴

## CHAPTER THIRTY-SEVEN    The Beginning

telling Madame Maxime about his mum!'

'Exactly,' said Hermione. 'And Viktor pulled a beetle out of my hair after we'd had our conversation by the lake. And unless I'm very much mistaken, Rita was perched on the window-sill of the Divination class the day your scar hurt. She's been buzzing around for stories all year.'

'When we saw Malfoy under that tree ...' said Ron slowly.

'He was talking to her, in his hand,' said Hermione. 'He knew, of course. That's how she's been getting all those nice little interviews with the Slytherins. They wouldn't care that she was doing something illegal, as long as they were giving her horrible stuff about us and Hagrid.'

Hermione took the glass jar back from Ron and smiled at the beetle, which buzzed angrily against the glass.

'I've told her I'll let her out when we get back to London,' said Hermione. 'I've put an Unbreakable Charm on the jar, you see, so she can't transform. And I've told her she's to keep her quill to herself for a whole year. See if she can't break the habit of writing horrible lies about people.'

Smiling serenely, Hermione placed the beetle back inside her schoolbag.

The door of the compartment slid open.

'Very clever, granger,' said Draco Malfoy.

Crabbe and Goyle were standing behind him. All three of them looked more pleased with themselves, more arrogant and more menacing, than Harry had ever seen them.

'So,' said Malfoy slowly, advancing slightly into the compartment, and looking around at them, a smirk quivering on his lips. 'You caught some pathetic reporter, and Potter's Dumbledore's favourite boy again. Big deal.'

His smirk widened. Crabbe and Goyle leered.

'Trying not to think about it, are we?' said Malfoy softly, looking around at all three of them. 'Trying to pretend it hasn't happened?'

'Get out,' said Harry.

He had not been near Malfoy since he had watched him muttering to Crabbe and Goyle during Dumbledore's speech about Cedric. He could feel a kind of ringing in his ears. His hand gripped his wand under his robes.

## 第37章 开始

在雕像上。"

"正是这样,"赫敏说,"我们在湖边谈话之后,威克多尔从我的头发里捉出了一只甲虫。除非是我弄错了,但我敢说在你伤疤疼的那天,丽塔一定躲在占卜课教室的窗台上偷听来着。她一年到头四处飞来飞去,寻找可以大做文章的材料。"

"那天我们看见马尔福在那棵树下……"罗恩慢慢地说。

"他在跟丽塔说话,丽塔就在他手上,"赫敏说,"当然啦,马尔福知道这个秘密。丽塔就是这样对斯莱特林们进行那些精彩的小采访的。他们才不在乎她做的事情是不是合法呢,只要他们能在她面前胡乱造谣,诽谤我们和海格就行。"

赫敏从罗恩手里拿回玻璃罐,笑嘻嘻地望着甲虫,甲虫气愤地隔着玻璃嗡嗡直叫。

"我告诉过她,我们一回到伦敦,我就放她出来。"赫敏说,"我给罐子念了一个牢固咒,这样她就没法变形了。我叫她一年之内不得动笔写东西,看能不能改掉诽谤和侮辱别人的恶习。"

赫敏平静地笑着,把甲虫放回了她的书包里。

包厢的门被人拉开了。

"干得很聪明,格兰杰。"德拉科·马尔福说。

克拉布和高尔站在他身后。哈利还从没见过他们三个这样得意,这样傲慢,这样气势汹汹呢。

"这么说,"马尔福朝包厢里跨进一步,缓缓地打量着他们,嘴角颤抖着露出一丝讥笑,慢慢地说,"你抓住了某个可怜的记者,波特又成了邓布利多最喜欢的男孩。真了不起。"

他脸上阴险的笑容更明显了。克拉布和高尔发出阵阵怪笑。

"尽量不去想它,是吗?"马尔福望着他们三个,轻声轻气地说,"尽量假装什么也没发生?"

"滚出去。"哈利说。

邓布利多致辞哀悼塞德里克时,哈利看见马尔福跟克拉布和高尔窃窃私语,从那以后,哈利还一直没有和马尔福挨得这么近过。他感到耳朵里嗡嗡直响。他的手不由自主地抓住了长袍下的魔杖。

## CHAPTER THIRTY-SEVEN  The Beginning

'You've picked the losing side, Potter! I warned you! I told you you ought to choose your company more carefully, remember? When we met on the train, first day at Hogwarts? I told you not to hang around with riff-raff like this!' He jerked his head at Ron and Hermione. 'Too late now, Potter! They'll be the first to go, now the Dark Lord's back! Mudbloods and Muggle-lovers first! Well – second – Diggory was the f–'

It was as though someone had exploded a box of fireworks within the compartment. Blinded by the blaze of the spells that had blasted from every direction, deafened by a series of bangs, Harry blinked, and looked down at the floor.

Malfoy, Crabbe and Goyle were all lying unconscious in the doorway. He, Ron and Hermione were on their feet, all three of them having used a different hex. Nor were they the only ones to have done so.

'Thought we'd see what those three were up to,' said Fred matter-of-factly, stepping onto Goyle, and into the compartment. He had his wand out, and so did George, who was careful to tread on Malfoy as he followed Fred inside.

'Interesting effect,' said George, looking down at Crabbe. 'Who used the Furnunculus curse?'

'Me,' said Harry.

'Odd,' said George lightly. 'I used Jelly-Legs. Looks as though those two shouldn't be mixed. He seems to have sprouted little tentacles all over his face. Well, let's not leave them here, they don't add much to the decor.'

Ron, Harry and George kicked, rolled and pushed the unconscious Malfoy, Crabbe and Goyle – each of whom looked distinctly the worse for the jumble of jinxes with which they had been hit – out into the corridor, then came back into the compartment and rolled the door shut.

'Exploding Snap, anyone?' said Fred, pulling out a pack of cards.

They were halfway through their fifth game when Harry decided to ask them.

'You going to tell us, then?' he said to George. 'Who you were blackmailing?'

'Oh,' said George darkly. '*That.*'

'It doesn't matter,' said Fred, shaking his head impatiently. 'It wasn't anything important. Not now, anyway.'

'We've given up,' said George, shrugging.

But Harry, Ron and Hermione kept on asking, and finally Fred said, 'All right, all right, if you really want to know … it was Ludo Bagman.'

## 第37章 开 始

"你从一开始就输定了,波特!我警告过你!我告诉过你选择伙伴要谨慎,记得吗?那是去霍格沃茨的第一天,我们在火车上相遇时?我告诉过你不要跟这些下三烂的人泡在一起!"他冲罗恩和赫敏摆了摆脑袋,"现在已经来不及了,波特!黑魔王回来了,最先完蛋的就是他们!泥巴种和喜欢麻瓜的家伙!嗯——不是最先——迪戈里才是——"

说时迟那时快,就好像有人在包厢里点爆了一箱烟火。从不同方向发出的咒语放射出耀眼的强光,刺得哈利睁不开眼睛,一连串噼噼啪啪的巨响几乎震聋了他的耳朵。他眨眨眼睛,低头望着地板。

马尔福、克拉布和高尔都不省人事地躺在门口。哈利、罗恩和赫敏都站着,刚才他们三个使用了不同的恶咒,而且这么做的还不止他们。

"我们想看看他们三个到底想干什么。"弗雷德一本正经地说,踏着高尔的身体走进了包厢。他的魔杖拿在手里,乔治也是这样。乔治跟着弗雷德进入包厢时,故意踩在了马尔福身上。

"多么有趣的效果,"乔治低头看着克拉布,说道,"谁用了火烤咒?"

"我。"哈利说。

"真巧,"乔治开心地说,"我用了软腿咒。看来这两种咒语不能混合使用。他好像满脸都冒出了小触角。好吧,我们别把他们撂在这儿,他们可不是什么漂亮的装饰品。"

罗恩、哈利和乔治又踢又推又拉,把昏迷不醒的马尔福、克拉布和高尔(他们每个人受到几种咒语的混合袭击,模样更加难看了)弄到了外面的走廊里,然后回到包厢,把门重新拉上。

"谁玩噼啪爆炸?"弗雷德说着,掏出一副牌来。

刚玩到第五局,哈利拿定主意,决定向他们问个明白。

"那么,你们可以告诉我们了吧?"他对乔治说,"你们在敲诈谁?"

"噢,"乔治闷闷不乐地说,"不提也罢。"

"没什么,"弗雷德说着,不耐烦地摇了摇头,"没什么大不了的。至少现在已经不重要了。"

"我们已经放弃了。"乔治耸了耸肩膀,说道。

可是哈利、罗恩和赫敏不依不饶地追问,最后,弗雷德说:"好吧,好吧,既然你们真的想知道……是卢多·巴格曼。"

## CHAPTER THIRTY-SEVEN  The Beginning

'Bagman?' said Harry sharply. 'Are you saying he was involved in –'

'Nah,' said George gloomily. 'Nothing like that. Stupid git. He wouldn't have the brains.'

'Well, what, then?' said Ron.

Fred hesitated, then said, 'You remember that bet we had with him, at the Quidditch World Cup? About how Ireland would win, but Krum would get the Snitch?'

'Yeah,' said Harry and Ron slowly.

'Well, the git paid us in leprechaun gold he'd caught from the Irish mascots.'

'So?'

'So,' said Fred impatiently, 'it vanished, didn't it? By next morning, it had gone!'

'But – it must've been an accident, mustn't it?' said Hermione.

George laughed very bitterly. 'Yeah, that's what we thought, at first. We thought if we just wrote to him, and told him he'd made a mistake, he'd cough up. But nothing doing. Ignored our letter. We kept trying to talk to him about it at Hogwarts, but he was always making some excuse to get away from us.'

'In the end, he turned pretty nasty,' said Fred. 'Told us we were too young to gamble, and he wasn't giving us anything.'

'So we asked for our money back,' said George, glowering.

'He didn't refuse!' gasped Hermione.

'Right in one,' said Fred.

'But that was all your savings!' said Ron.

'Tell me about it,' said George. "Course, we found out what was going on in the end. Lee Jordan's dad had had a bit of trouble getting money off Bagman as well. Turns out he's in big trouble with the goblins. Borrowed loads of gold off them. A gang of them cornered him in the woods after the World Cup and took all the gold he had, and it still wasn't enough to cover all his debts. They followed him all the way to Hogwarts to keep an eye on him. He's lost everything gambling. Hasn't got two Galleons to rub together. And you know how the idiot tried to pay the goblins back?'

'How?' said Harry.

## 第37章 开 始

"巴格曼?"哈利敏锐地说,"你是说他也卷进——"

"不是,"乔治愁眉苦脸地说,"不是这码子事儿。他傻瓜蛋一个,还没有这样的脑子。"

"哦,那是怎么回事?"罗恩问。

弗雷德迟疑了一下,说道:"你们还记得我们在魁地奇世界杯赛上跟他打赌的事吗?就是我们赌爱尔兰赢,但克鲁姆会抓住金色飞贼?"

"记得呀。"哈利和罗恩慢慢地说。

"咳,那傻瓜付给我们的是小矮妖的金币,是他从爱尔兰的吉祥物那里捡到的。"

"那又怎么样呢?"

"那还用说,"弗雷德不耐烦地说,"金子消失了,不是吗?到了第二天早上,连影子都没了!"

"可是——那一定是不小心弄错的,是不是?"赫敏说。

乔治很尖刻地笑了起来。"是啊,我们一开始也这样想。我们以为,只要写封信给他,告诉他弄错了,他就会把钱还给我们。没想到满不是那么回事。他对我们的信根本不理睬。我们在霍格沃茨三番五次想跟他谈谈,可他总是找各种借口摆脱我们。"

"到了最后,他态度变得非常恶劣,"弗雷德说,"对我们说,我们年龄太小,不能赌博,他一分钱也不会给我们。"

"然后,我们想要回本钱。"乔治怒气冲冲地说。

"他不会拒绝了吧!"赫敏屏住呼吸说。

"让你说着了。"弗雷德说。

"可那是你们的全部积蓄呀!"罗恩说。

"这还用你说。"乔治说,"当然啦,后来我们总算弄清了是怎么回事。李·乔丹的爸爸向巴格曼讨债时也碰了钉子。后来才知道,原来巴格曼在妖精那里惹了大麻烦。他向他们借了一大堆金子。世界杯赛后,他们把他堵在树林里,抢走了他身上所有的金币,还不够还清他的债务。妖精们一直跟着他来到霍格沃茨,密切监视着他。他赌博输光了一切,身上连两个金币也没有了。你知道那个傻瓜打算怎么向妖精还债吗?"

"怎么还?"哈利说。

## CHAPTER THIRTY-SEVEN  The Beginning

'He put a bet on you, mate,' said Fred. 'Put a big bet on you to win the Tournament. Bet against the goblins.'

'So *that's* why he kept trying to help me win!' said Harry. 'Well – I did win, didn't I? So he can pay you your gold!'

'Nope,' said George, shaking his head. 'The goblins play as dirty as him. They say you drew with Diggory, and Bagman was betting you'd win outright. So Bagman had to run for it. He made a run for it right after the third task.'

George sighed deeply, and started dealing out the cards again.

The rest of the journey passed pleasantly enough; Harry wished it could have gone on all summer, in fact, and that he would never arrive at King's Cross ... but as he had learnt the hard way that year, time will not slow down when something unpleasant lies ahead, and all too soon the Hogwarts Express was slowing down at platform nine and three-quarters. The usual confusion and noise filled the corridors as the students began to disembark. Ron and Hermione struggled out past Malfoy, Crabbe and Goyle, carrying their trunks.

Harry, however, stayed put. 'Fred – George – wait a moment.'

The twins turned. Harry pulled open his trunk, and drew out his Triwizard winnings.

'Take it,' he said, and he thrust the sack into George's hands.

'What?' said Fred, looking flabbergasted.

'Take it,' Harry repeated firmly. 'I don't want it.'

'You're mental,' said George, trying to push it back at Harry.

'No, I'm not,' said Harry. 'You take it, and get inventing. It's for the joke-shop.'

'He is mental,' Fred said, in an almost awed voice.

'Listen,' said Harry firmly. 'If you don't take it, I'm throwing it down the drain. I don't want it and I don't need it. But I could do with a few laughs. We could all do with a few laughs. I've got a feeling we're going to need them more than usual before long.'

'Harry,' said George weakly, weighing the money bag in his hands, 'there's got to be a thousand Galleons in here.'

'Yeah,' said Harry, grinning. 'Think how many Canary Creams that is.'

The twins stared at him.

## 第37章 开 始

"他把宝押在你身上了,伙计,"弗雷德说,"押了一大笔钱,赌你会赢得争霸赛。是跟妖精们赌的。"

"噢,怪不得他总想帮助我赢呢!"哈利说,"好了——我确实赢了,不是吗?他可以把你们的金币还给你们了吧?"

"才不呢!"乔治摇了摇头说,"妖精的表现和他一样恶劣。他们说你和迪戈里并列第一,而巴格曼赌的是你大获全胜。所以巴格曼只好匆忙逃命了。第三个项目一结束,他就逃跑了。"

乔治沉重地叹了口气,又开始发牌。

旅途剩下来的时光过得非常愉快;实际上,哈利真希望火车就这样一直开下去,开整整一个夏天,他永远不会到达国王十字车站……但他这一年经过重重困难已经懂得:当某件不愉快的事等在前面时,时间是不会放慢脚步的。仅一眨眼的工夫,霍格沃茨特快列车就停靠在 $9\frac{3}{4}$ 站台了。同学们纷纷开始下车,过道里又是一片混乱和嘈杂。罗恩和赫敏提着箱子,走出了包厢,艰难地跨过马尔福、克拉布和高尔的身体。

但哈利没有动弹。"弗雷德——乔治——等一等。"

双胞胎转过来。哈利打开箱子,取出他在争霸赛中赢得的奖金。

"拿着吧。"他说,把袋子塞进乔治手里。

"什么?"弗雷德说,惊得目瞪口呆。

"拿着。"哈利坚决地重复道,"这钱我不想要。"

"你发神经了。"乔治说,一边拼命把袋子推还给哈利。

"不,我没有。"哈利说,"你们拿去吧,继续搞发明创造。这是给笑话店的。"

"他确实发神经了。"弗雷德用几乎敬畏的声音说。

"听着,"哈利很坚决地说,"如果你们不收,我就把它扔到阴沟里。我不想要它,也不需要它。但是我需要一些欢笑。我们可能都需要一些欢笑。我有一种感觉,很快我们就会需要比往常更多的欢笑。"

"哈利,"乔治微弱地说,掂量着手里的那袋金币,"里面有一千个金加隆呢。"

"是啊,"哈利笑着说,"想想吧,值多少个金丝雀饼干啊。"

双胞胎兄弟呆呆地望着他。

## CHAPTER THIRTY-SEVEN   The Beginning

'Just don't tell your mum where you got it ... although she might not be so keen for you to join the Ministry any more, come to think of it ...'

'Harry,' Fred began, but Harry pulled out his wand.

'Look,' he said flatly, 'take it, or I'll hex you. I know some good ones now. Just do me one favour, OK? Buy Ron some different dress robes, and say they're from you.'

He left the compartment before they could say another word, stepping over Malfoy, Crabbe and Goyle, who were still lying on the floor, covered in hex marks.

Uncle Vernon was waiting beyond the barrier. Mrs. Weasley was close by him. She hugged Harry very tightly when she saw him, and whispered in his ear, 'I think Dumbledore will let you come to us later in the summer. Keep in touch, Harry.'

'See you, Harry,' said Ron, clapping him on the back.

'Bye, Harry!' said Hermione, and she did something she had never done before, and kissed him on the cheek.

'Harry – thanks,' George muttered, while Fred nodded fervently at his side.

Harry winked at them, turned to Uncle Vernon, and followed him silently from the station. There was no point worrying yet, he told himself, as he got into the back of the Dursleys' car.

As Hagrid had said, what would come, would come ... and he would have to meet it when it did.

## 第37章 开 始

"千万别告诉你们的妈妈这钱是哪儿来的……尽管她现在不那么热心要你们进魔法部了,现在想来……"

"哈利……"弗雷德还要说什么,但哈利拔出了魔杖。

"听着,"他板着脸说,"快收下,不然我就给你念个恶咒。我现在知道几个很厉害的恶咒呢。你们就算帮我一个忙吧,好吗?给罗恩另外买几件礼服长袍,就说是你们送给他的。"

不等双胞胎再说一个字,哈利就离开了包厢,跨过马尔福、克拉布和高尔走了。马尔福他们仍然躺在地板上,身上带着恶咒留下的痕迹。

弗农姨父在隔墙外面等着他。韦斯莱夫人就站在他近旁。她一看见哈利,就过来一把搂住他,并贴着哈利的耳朵低声说:"我想邓布利多会让你夏末到我们家来的。保持联系,哈利。"

"再会,哈利。"罗恩说,拍了一下他的后背。

"再见,哈利!"赫敏说,然后她做了一件以前从没做过的事情:她吻了吻哈利的面颊。

"哈利——谢谢。"乔治喃喃地说,弗雷德在他旁边拼命点头。

哈利朝他们眨眨眼睛,然后转向弗农姨父,默默地跟着他离开了车站。现在还没有什么可担心的,他一边钻进德思礼家的汽车后座,一边这样想道。

正如海格说的,该来的总归会来……一旦来了,他就必须接受。